TOIL OF THE BRAVE

Books by INGLIS FLETCHER

THE WHITE LEOPARD
  (A Tale of the African Bush)

RED JASMINE
  (A Novel of Africa)

Carolina Series

RALEIGH'S EDEN

MEN OF ALBEMARLE

LUSTY WIND FOR CAROLINA

TOIL *of* THE BRAVE

By INGLIS FLETCHER

B_M

THE BOBBS-MERRILL COMPANY

PUBLISHERS

INDIANAPOLIS · NEW YORK

First Edition

The long Toil of the Brave
  Is not lost in darkness,
Neither hath counting the cost
  Fretted away the zeal of their hopes.
Over the fruitful Earth
  And athwart the seas
Hath passed the light of noble deeds
  Unquenchable forever.

—PINDAR, *Isthmian Odes*
Translation by Sir John Sandys

Acknowledgement

AT EDENTON, North Carolina (the Queen Anne's Town of colonial times), the past walks arm in arm with the present.

A hundred years before the American Revolution, in the country bordering on Albemarle Sound, colonists came to take up land along the great rivers and the beautiful creeks of the coastal plain.

They had their land from eight Peers of the Realm, the Lords Proprietors, who in turn held a grant to the fabulous empire of the Carolinas through the careless generosity of King Charles II of England. The Proprietors made their endeavour to colonize the bounteous land in order to enrich their own pockets.

By the time of Queen Anne, there were plantations of large acreage and some small hamlets and villages in the Albemarle.

The planters lived by the bounty of the great rivers, the never-ending forests and the fertile earth. These men and women made history, which is part of the lives of the people who live in the towns and villages and countryside today. They are not ghosts of the past, but living people. They are spoken of in terms of such familiarity and intimacy that strangers often mistake them for people of today, and are astonished to find they are listening to gossip of men and women who lived a hundred and fifty or two hundred years ago.

The wide stone steps of the Courthouse on the Green are worn deep by the footsteps of men who have for a hundred and eighty years come seeking King's justice before the bar or in the council chamber. After the Revolution, until this day, they still cross the same worn threshold into the courtroom, where great jurists have sat in the same high carved chair expounding the common law, our inheritance from Great Britain.

The small village on Queen Anne's Creek was the home of many leaders of the Whig party in the time of the Revolution. It gave to its country a signer of the Declaration of Independence, a signer of the Federal Constitution, an Associate Justice of the Supreme Court appointed by George Washington, a chairman of the first Committee on Naval Affairs, with authority tantamount to that of the present-day Secretary of the Navy. A second signer of the Declaration of Independence sought sanctuary in the village and there lived out his last years in peace.

Twenty miles distant, across Albemarle Sound, in Bertie County, another signer of the Federal Constitution was born.

Royal Governors lived and fought their duels, died and were buried in their private burial grounds on their plantations, in the counties bordering on Albemarle Sound.

Nearly two centuries from the time the first colonists, sent by Sir Walter Raleigh, landed on Roanoke Island, the struggling village on Queen Anne's Creek gave abundantly in able men to help guide the cause of liberty.

It gave more than leadership in the Revolution.

The countryside was settled by yeomen from England, men who loved their land, their farms, their crops. They were freeholders. They held their land by grant from John, Lord Granville, the Lord Proprietor who would not sell his land to the Crown. They paid their yearly rental "of some twenty shillings, threepence, for every hundred acres, at or upon the Feast of the Annunciation of the Blessed Virgin Mary, and the Feast of Saint Michael the Archangel, in every year by equal and even portions, to be paid at the Courthouse of Chowan, to the said Earl's Deputy."

These yeomen of the countryside gave aid, in corn and grain, hogs and cattle. From their forests they cut masts for ships, and sent tar, pitch and turpentine for naval stores. They stood solidly behind the Whig leaders of the Revolution, in the same way that their forbears had stood, firm as a rock, behind the Barons at Runnymede, on that day when they wrested from a tyrant king new rights for the people, in what is called, to this day, the Magna Charta.

To the town on Queen Anne's Creek I am indebted for its records, filed in its ancient Courthouse, in the Cupola House and in the Vestry of St. Paul's Church.

I am indebted to the little colonial houses that peep out amongst the modern buildings and give fleeting glimpses of the past, to street names: King, Queen, Eden Alley, Cheapside, Granville, Oakum, the Plumb Line Walk and the Rope Walk.

I am indebted to the many descendants of those early Carolinians for stories and anecdotes, for glimpses of colonial silver and furniture and portraits.

The names of the old plantations remain as a link to the past: Eden House, Balgray, Scots Hall, Mount Galland, Black Rock, Buncombe Hall, Hayes, Montpelier, Athol, Mulberry Hill, Strawberry Hill, Sandy Point, Greenfield, Drummond's Point. These are the Sound Plantations. On the Chowan River are Wingfield, Martinique and Bandon.

Some of the plantation houses have disappeared. *But the fertile land has survived*, to feed other armies, in other years.

I wish to acknowledge my indebtedness to Mrs. Lyman Cotten, of the Library of the University of North Carolina, for her enthusiastic and diligent search to unearth bits of information concerning Cosmo de' Medici, who espoused the cause of liberty in the American Revolution.

I am indebted to the Hayes Collection for introducing to me the letters of Penelope Dawson, that sprightly and intelligent daughter of a Royal Governor, who took the part of the colonies with energy and enthusiasm.

I am indebted to Ruth and Charles Cannon for the historical records of the Piedmont, the country of General Nathanael Greene's great retreat from Lord Cornwallis' invading armies.

I wish to acknowledge also my gratitude for the following reference material used in this book:

The North Carolina Historical Commission for the John Collet map of 1770.

The North Carolina Historical Commission for *The Papers of John Steele*, edited by Henry M. Wagstaff.

The North Carolina Historical Commission for *Records of the Moravians in North Carolina*, edited by Adelaide L. Fries.

The Dietz Press, Inc., Richmond, Virginia, for *Sports of Colonial Williamsburg*, by William C. Ewing.

Harvard University Press for *The Odes of Pindar*, translated by Sir John Sandys (Loeb Classical Library).

Dauber & Pine Bookshops, Inc., New York, for *King's Mountain and Its Heroes*, by Lyman Copeland Draper.

Williamsburg Restoration, Inc., Department of Research.

Most deeply am I indebted to Edenton (the village on Queen Anne's Creek) for being what it is—in the past and in the present.

INGLIS FLETCHER

Contents

TOIL OF THE BRAVE

CHAPTER

1

RIVER PLANTATION

THE sun rose with an upward push of colour toward the zenith. A mocking-bird swinging in a myrtle tree lifted its full-throated nightingale song, a lingering farewell to darkness. The early morning breeze off the river carried with it the fragrance of wild jasmine, which grew along the hedges dividing the old cotton patch from the deep woods.

A line of field slaves moved lazily down the lane of the quarters line toward the open fields. Spring ploughing had begun. Slow-moving oxen trudged through the sandy soil, dragging the ploughs, guided by the skilful hands of field slaves. The time for preparing the land for the season's planting had come. The buds of sycamore were pushing off the old dried balls, and the brown weathered leaves of the oak were giving way to the steady pressure of rising sap. Spring was having its way in the pasture where the young mares frisked about, nibbling at the first green grass showing its colour.

An old Negro with a hand seeder followed behind the plough, dropping corn in the rows. He wore a white shirt of duck and breeches cut off short; his legs and feet were bare. He sang as he moved his arms rhythmically:

> "Heigho, heigho!
> One for the worms,
> And one for the crow,
> And one for the master—
> Heigho! heigho!"

The lot was alive with the activities of early morning. Cows mooed, anxious to relieve full udders of their load of rich, warm milk. Mules and oxen pushed their way to the watering trough. Feeders, slaves too old for heavy work, carried golden-eared corn to the mangers, eight ears to the horse. Harness jingled, high-wheeled carts rumbled

17

off. Stable-boys saddled riding horses. Voices shouted and cursed sharply. In the shelter of the barns it was shady and cool. The fields were open to the warm sun of spring. Another ancient Negro, bent with years, lifted his great bellowing voice to call the hogs hidden in the young pine groves. Little pickaninnies ran about the lot, picking up stray bits of rope, rusty nails, iron parts from discarded ploughs. Senator Ferrier came home late last night from his journey to Hillsborough, where he went to make the laws. . . . If he cotch you idling around, when there's work to be done, he'd be mighty full of wrath. He lak the barn pretty; yes, sar, everything in its place. . . . Negro stable-boys ran to ready up the tack room, and sweep the passageway. . . . He didn't want the senator to turn a cold eye on him, no, sar, he didn't.

"Senator he look jes' lak one of they eagles, mighty fierce, if he have wrath in him," the oldest feeder went on to say to a groom who was busy rubbing down Black Bess. "He bound to call for he horse, first thing, and ride from one end of the field to the other." He chewed on a twist of tobacco.

"Wish he would stay down and make they laws," the stable-boy grumbled. "Madam she make no trouble at all. She jes' look about and smile real pretty and say, 'Everything going well, Zeke?' "

A dozen yards from the rambling plantation house was the kitchen. Tulli, the old cook, sat on a three-legged stool in front of the great fireplace, giving orders to half a dozen house slaves, and returning the banter of several field-hands seated at a long table, eating their breakfast of hominy grits and strips of bacon.

From her point of vantage, Tulli could warm her rheumatic bones (spring mornings on the Chowan River are cool) and keep an eye on the milkhouse, where one of the maids was skimming the rich cream from a crock of last night's milk. She could see also the long gallery that led from the kitchen to the main house. In her mind's eye she could look through "they wall" into the serving pantry.

In half an hour, at the most, Senator Alexander Ferrier would walk into the dining-room for the morning meal. When that happened the activity of kitchen, milkhouse and serving pantry would rise to fever heat. The senator was no man to be kept waiting.

It would be an extra good meal, for the first strawberries Jake had raised in the glass-house would start it. The rich cream Julie was now skimming would be in a silver bowl, so the senator could dip out the right amount to please his fancy. The eggs, which had been snatched from the nests of scolding hens not five minutes past, lay in a rush basket. A small hour-glass of sand was at Cook's elbow, to remind her just how long they should lie in the pan of boiling water. A brightly shining copper kettle held the hominy grits on an iron hearth-trivet—hominy fresh ground from the mill on Brownrigg Creek. That was a proper good mill, though no Negro would pass by at night on account of the wraithlike figure of the miller's dead wife, said to walk along the mill-pond at night, her transparent draperies floating behind. Wrapped in her wedding sheet they had found her, one morning, near the mill-race.

Two young Negro girls were occupied setting up breakfast trays to be carried upstairs to the ladies—Madam, the senator's Spanish wife, and her daughter, Miss Angela. They ate lightly of fruit and chocolate and a small bit of corn bread cooked to a crisp brown.

Tulli glanced over her shoulder to see that nothing was missing. "Promisy, go pick some roses. You know how Madam she lak fine rose on her breakfas' salver."

"They ain't in bloom. I looked this mawnin' when I come."

"You do lak I say. White Cherokees is a-bloomin' in Jake's glasshouse. Julie, you set dose silver straight and don't you pick up knife by the blade. Haven't I tol' you every day for a fortnight: Lift knife and fork by he handles?"

"Yes'm. Yes'm."

"Promisy, move you' shanks or you'll feel my hand on dose buttocks you lak to wave around so prominent."

The men at the long table guffawed. Promisy, a tall girl with a high head and flat back from carrying burdens on her head, switched out of the kitchen, muttering to herself. No one would dare sass back to Miss Tulli.

"You Julie, whop up six eggs for Master's waffles, and don't set youself up jest 'cause Eph he kiss you last night under dat big holly tree."

The girl looked up, startled, while the other Negroes shouted with laughter.

"No good to laugh at she," Tulli said, her eyes encompassing them, sliding about the room, resting a brief instant on each man and girl. "Spicey, I see you and dat no-good fella from upriver fishery huggin' an' scufflin' by de honeysuckle hedge, not so many nights past. Better you watch youself, less'n you carry a bush-baby, afore leaves droppin' from de trees."

The laugh was louder. Spicey hung her head and busied herself with her mistress' tray. Tall, gangling Jake caught her arm. "Told you to have done with dat Niggra, Spicey. He jes' messin' round. He got a stiddy gal up Virginie line."

Spicey jerked her arm away. "Leave be," she said. "Don't lay a hand on me."

Tulli nodded her old turbaned head. "Plenty boys on dis plantation, wi'out steppin' ovah from our own people," she said. "And that's for you, too, Jubel. Let Wingfield folk mate with Wingfield folk; let river folk make our own babies, so's de Master will have the children heself. We needs more folk than we got, when de new house gets built."

Promisy came back with a bunch of white Cherokee roses in her hand. Selecting the most perfect, she put it in a little silver cup on Madam's tray.

The second-best was left for Promisy to carry to the young mistress. Promisy did for Angela, the senator's stepdaughter, and the two young children, Philip and little Bella, who had been born after the senator had brought the foreign lady home from Brunswick Town and made her his wife.

There was the sound of children's voices, a girl's "No, no! I won't let you put my dress on. I want Tulli to dress me. I won't!"

With a rush of running feet, a dark-eyed girl between four and five and a boy of about seven burst into the kitchen. The girl was dressed in an underbodice and flowered petticoat to her ankles. She was clutching a rust-brown dress in her arms. The boy Philip was at her heels, holding onto the skirt.

"You can't wear that dress today. It's a Sunday dress, Bella. This isn't Sunday, is it, Jake?"

Jake looked up from his breakfast, his knife raised halfway to his mouth. "No, Marse Philip. 'Tain't nowise of a Sunday. Dat's purely a fac'."

"Keep you hush, Jake," Tulli shouted, sheltering the girl child in her arms. "She'll wear jes' what she please. 'Tain't none of yours, Mas' Philip, what this child wear."

Her prominent black eyes glared at the boy. He backed off. "She's always wanting to wear her Sunday dress," he muttered.

"Tha's all right. She wear what she please. Come here, little pigeon, let Tulli slip it over you' pretty curls." She glanced at Philip. "Seem lak you dress mighty fine youself, in you' apple-green breeks and coat and you' shammyskin weskit. Lawks, and you' fine buckle shoes, too!"

Philip drew himself up grandly. "I'm going to have breakfast with my father this morning."

A wail from little Bella: "I want to have my breakfast with my father."

Tulli's soothing voice broke in, "Miss Bella she going to sit right here by her old Tulli. That she is. She going to sit on that little stool and help turn the waffles and she goin' have she little table, right in front of she, by the fire."

Bella sat down quite happily on the three-legged stool. The tearful face gave way to a sunny smile. Philip, at a gesture from the wise old Tulli, retreated from the kitchen. The field-hands, with broad smiles on their black faces, filed out of the kitchen. They considered Tulli a wise one, almost as wise as blind old Lungu, who made *Mankwala* on the plantation people if they brought him a present. If the moon hung right in the heavens, he would mutter potent words over the crops at seeding time, or at the harvest festival.

Promisy took two roses and tucked them under the riband that bound Bella's dark curls. The child craned her neck, trying to see her reflection in the polished copper of a big cooking pot.

"Looks mighty pretty, Miss Bella, mighty pretty."

When the senator came downstairs, Philip was waiting in the dining-room, standing by his chair. Alexander Ferrier was a Scot, from Edinburgh, who had come to the colony twenty years earlier and espoused the cause of the colonies in revolt. With vigour and in no minced words, he spoke against the Stamp Act and the Boston Port Bill. He served the newly made state of North Carolina in the Senate and sat on the Governor's Council. A tall heavy-framed man, with a strong face and commanding eyes, stern-spoken, he had a kinder heart than appearances would indicate.

He smiled at Philip and patted the boy's shoulder, as he said good morning. "Let us be seated, son. Your mother says she and Angela are going to Queen Anne's Town this morning. Has Tack made the boat ready?"

"Yes, sir. She's tied up at the landing." He smiled broadly. "I've been down already. She's ship-shape, sir, and there is a stiff breeze from the north."

"Good! Good! We'll inspect the sloop before I start off. I'm sorry

I can't go to Queen Anne's Town with your mother and your sister Angela. I must ride directly to New Bern to see the Governor."

Philip said wistfully, "I wish I could go with my mother to the village."

"Not this time, my son. I don't like for you to break off in your studies."

Philip looked gloomy. "I don't like the new master from Williamsburg. I learn more when Parson Earle teaches us himself. He doesn't try to be so . . . so classical."

The senator smiled. "Be an obedient boy and get good marks and you shall have a present on your birthday."

The breakfast came in, and the senator ate while he read his accumulated mail. He had been in Hillsborough for a week, at a meeting of the Committee of Correspondence.

"Run down to the boat, son. I want to look her over. Tell Jake to order my horse. I will join you as soon as I say good-bye to your mother."

The boy walked sedately from the room. Once outside he snatched up his little three-cornered hat and rushed to the landing, where the Ferrier sloop lay tied to the dock.

In her room Madam Ferrier was speaking to her daughter.

"Angela," she said severely, "I will not have you talk to your father in the way you did last night."

Angela, a tall dark girl as Castilian in appearance as her mother, stood beside her mother's bed. Her oval ivory-tinted face was expressionless, but her large black eyes were stormy.

"You shall apologize to him. I can't think what came over you to be so rude."

"He took a letter from me and read it. Besides, he isn't my real father. A stepfather hasn't a right——"

Her mother interrupted. "He has every right. Neither of us thinks it suitable you should carry on a correspondence with a British officer while we are at war."

"Spain is not at war with England. I haven't forgotten that I am Spanish, even if you have."

"Angela!"

"It is true, Mother. You act as if you were a colonial."

"I've married one, my dear."

"I don't care. I won't have Mr. Ferrier interfering with my affairs. I will write to Captain Anthony Allison if I please. I don't care what he says."

Francisca Ferrier looked at her rebellious daughter. Madam was sitting up in bed, her breakfast tray on her knees. Her little white lace cap half concealed her black hair, Spanish-black, long and heavy. She had the same great oval eyes as her daughter, almost Moorish in their mystic depths. But Angela's were angry eyes; they were not deep wells of wisdom, nor did they carry, as Francisca's did, the quiet acceptance of fate that came from some distant Moorish ancestor.

"He thinks he will control me, tell me whom I must marry. I will not have it. My father was Miguel Gonsalvo, not Alexander Ferrier, and I will not apologize."

"Angela, leave the room! I do not care to look at you when your face is distorted in anger."

The girl wavered a moment, then walked out, her long maroon wool wrapper trailing behind her.

Madam sighed as she sipped her chocolate. Angela was so difficult. So was Alexander. They were constantly putting each other on edge. Francisca would not acknowledge even to herself that they were both jealous of her affection. But it was true. From the very beginning it had been that way. Lately Angela was getting out of hand. At eighteen she was strong-willed and difficult.

She had chosen last night to assert her will, to defy the senator on a matter of a letter from one Anthony Allison, a British officer with whom she fancied herself in love.

She had taken a poor time to defy her stepfather, snatch the letter from his hand and say harsh, impudent things to him. Alexander was tired from the long journey on horseback from the Hillsborough meeting. He was discouraged with the progress of the war, the indifference, the political wrangling.

Angela had always resented Alexander from the time Francisca married him, eight years before. Angela was a possessive person, ridiculously loyal to her own father, Miguel Gonsalvo, dead these ten years.

Francisca's thoughts were interrupted by a knock on the door. In answer to her "Come in," Alexander entered, booted and spurred, his heavy riding cape over his arm.

He leaned over to kiss her, a fond, affectionate kiss that had in it something of the lover. "I am sorry to have to make this journey, my darling, but the Governor's request is couched in terms that make it a command."

"What do you think it is?" his wife asked.

"Something to do with the militia, I suppose. It's almost time for the ninety-day men to have completed their term and they will be streaming home from the North." He sighed. "I have a feeling, Francisca, I'd like to stay home and look to spring seeding. It is so tranquil here, so far from war and thoughts of war. Yet, we've been at war with England for four years. It's the same in Queen Anne's Town. They give no thought to what is happening. They have already forgotten Valley Forge, where fifty of our North Carolina men died, and two hundred were sick unto death from privation. They've forgotten how Colonel Shepherd's North Carolina regiment spent the desperately cold winter in an inadequate detention camp in Maryland, at Georgetown. It was a terrible winter for our people, but we've forgotten." He stared into her eyes but he didn't see her.

"We've got to have salt and pork and shoes and warm clothes for the armies in the field, but most of all we want arms and ammunition. My God, how can we fight a war without money—and the British pouring troops into America, trained troops with great generals?"

Francisca did not speak. She knew he was relieving his mind of some of the worrying thoughts.

"We have to get hold of one hundred and forty hogsheads of tobacco to pay for the twenty-three pieces of heavy cannon that came into Queen Anne's Town in the *Holy Heart of Jesus*. I saw Captain Biddle. He's been working with Joe Hewes in Philadelphia. They've sent out the *Eclipse*, the *Rainbow* and the *Fanny*, all fourteen guns, on a privateering cruise. They may get badly needed salt, if they capture prizes from the West Indies."

He kissed Francisca a second time, holding her close against him for a moment. "Perhaps I was too harsh with Angela last night," he said reflectively. "I would have overlooked her stubbornness if she had not been so persistent about holding onto friendship with that British officer. By God, Francisca, we've broken with Britain! Let the cut be clean. This is the spring of 1779, not the beginning of the war. But some of the freeholders in North Carolina are still clinging to the hope that the war will be over tomorrow, before we have fought the battles! I don't want Angela consorting with any damn enemy officer."

Francisca said, "She was rude and I will punish her, but Angela does not consider herself an American. She considers herself Spanish. Therefore this Captain Allison is not an enemy to her as he is to you, Alexander *mío*."

"Stuff and nonsense!" He looked at her sharply. "You don't still consider yourself Spanish, do you?"

"Whither thou goest . . . Thy people shall be my people," she quoted, looking up into his eyes. She added, "I wish you and Angela could find a common ground somewhere. I am weary of this incessant argument."

Ferrier did not answer for a moment, then he said, "I think we should marry Angela to some personable young man. She is a well-developed girl. She needs marriage." He looked at his wife warily, as though marshalling all his arguments to combat her disapproval of his words.

To his surprise, she agreed. "I think you are right. We Latins develop young. We need the release that marriage gives, and the restraint also. Yes—but where is the personable young man? All those of marriageable age have left the village and gone to war. There is no one left."

"That is true, but I'll have this in mind." He pressed her hand. "I'll be in the village in time to come home with you at the end of the week. I hope you will have a pleasant visit to Strawberry Hill. My respects to Parson Earle and his good wife Charity."

He went away then. Francisca heard his spurs strike the steps as he went downstairs.

The door opened and Angela put her head inside. "Is he gone?" she asked.

Francisca nodded. She was annoyed with her daughter, annoyed because of her rudeness, angered at the silly display of jealousy.

Angela hesitated. "I was going to apologize, but it is too late."

"Yes, it *is* too late, Angela. I am hurt in my heart that a child of mine, my first-born, should behave in so unseemly a manner."

At her mother's words the girl's lips quivered. "I'll tear after him. I'll apologize. I'll get down on my knees."

"No, you are not sorry for your rudeness, Angela. You are sorry because you have hurt me. Go into your room and meditate for two hours. When your spirit is humble, you may come to me."

Angela left the room quietly, without words. She knew from her mother's calm, dispassionate voice that she was very angry with her. Tears were streaming down her cheeks when she reached her room.

She shut the door and locked it, and took up the little breviary her mother had given her on her tenth birthday. But she could not read. She sat looking out the window at the wide Chowan River, flowing so quietly and evenly between the cypress-lined banks. Quiet now, but deep. The river was not always quiet. Sometimes its breast was lashed into whitecaps by the fury of the gales from Hatteras that whipped up the Sound. Then the trees bent and gave way, and small craft were driven onto the narrow beaches.

She took up the book and sat down before the fire.

A maid took the tray from Francisca's bed and mended the fire. Then she went out, closing the door quietly. Francisca slid deeper into the feathers and stretched her body into a more comfortable position. It was the custom of the household not to disturb her during the hour after breakfast, the time set aside for her devotions.

She felt so alone, with no one to turn to for guidance! Her first thought was for Alexander. He had been so good, so kind, ever since the day her husband's ship was wrecked. She remembered him then so clearly. It was the first time she had seen any of the passengers. Miguel had not allowed either her or Angela to leave the cabin of his ship from the time they left Martinique until they were off the Carolina Banks. A great merchant ship appeared out of the fog, well laden. It was north-bound. There was excitement on deck; sailors ran about; officers shouted orders at the top of their lungs. Miguel had changed then. He came to the door of their cabin. She did not know him; even his face was altered. There was no gay laughter, no braggadocio left. He backed against the door, his hands behind him on the knob.

"You may as well know now, Francisca, this ship of mine is no simple merchantman sailing from Spain to the Indies. It's prizes I'm after, English, Dutch or Portuguese—I care nothing save that they're rich."

"Miguel!"

"Don't stare at me with frightened eyes! Where do you think I got the money that has supplied you with jewels and satin and velvet all these ten years? You poor simpleton! No captain of a merchant-man could make all that money in a lifetime. You wanted to come for a voyage with me. You insisted. You may as well know."

She smelled the wine fumes as he turned his head. "I was a silly, convent-bred girl who knew nothing of the world, Miguel."

"I sink ships. I kill men. As for women—" he gave a laugh—"I solace the women if they be handsome and have wide hips."

Francisca glanced toward the berth where little Angela lay asleep. "Miguel, the child. Lower your voice."

"Acting as though you didn't care about the women I've solaced. By God, I gave them some happy moments before they went into the water."

"Miguel, you're drunk."

"That I'm not. Must a man be drunk to fight? We're bearing down on a ship with all her sails spread, but we'll overhaul her."

"But the storm! You told me it would blow to a gale before morning."

"So it will, but we'll have her sunk by then." He came near her, caught her in his arms. She leaned back from his sour fetid wine breath. "There'll be time for love-making then, and trinkets for you, my pretty one. She's Spanish, from Cadiz, blown northward by the winds of the past week. Spanish, for Cuba, with a rich cargo . . . Deus! I'll rake her decks, strip her and sink her."

Francisca gasped. "You would fire on a Spanish ship, Miguel! That would be treason to our country." She released herself from his arms.

He scarcely noticed. He was a madman in pursuit of prey; a savage unrestrained. "What do I care what country? She has gold, and trade goods."

She trembled in revulsion. Was this Miguel, the lover for whom she had given up family and home?

The ship was plunging. Little Angela cried out in her sleep.

"Shut the brat's mouth!" Miguel cried, suddenly angered. He strode across the room, but Francisca was ahead of him.

"No!" she cried. "No! Keep away! Keep away!" Her voice rose.

Miguel pushed her aside, reached for the child. "A girl!" he shouted with scorn. "What use is a girl? Nothing but to be the plaything of some man. It's sons I want. I'm a man to beget strong sons. But you give me no sons." Once more he reached for the child.

"Miguel!" she screamed. "Miguel! Don't! Don't!"

The door opened slowly. A man stood at the entrance, a big, broad-shouldered, strong-featured man who seemed to fill the door. He did not enter, but stood at the threshold looking at Miguel, who had turned to face him.

"Get out!" Miguel spat the words. "Get out!"

Calm grey eyes turned to Francisca. "Is the man annoying you, madam?"

"He is my husband," she whispered, in broken English.

"I asked if he were annoying you, whoever he is?"

Miguel crossed the room. He had his hand at his belt, on the handle of a knife. "I am the captain of this ship. Get out, I say."

"Ah! That explains why it is such a filthy ship."

Before Miguel could draw his knife, the mate came running across the deck, his queued hair standing out behind him.

"Captain! Captain! To the bridge! The ship has turned. 'Tis no merchantman. 'Tis a frigate, a Britisher, well mounted! They have run up the Union Jack."

Gonsalvo leaped through the door and ran forward.

Francisca saw that the man at the door was well, even richly dressed, in subdued colours. His hair was powdered, his storm cape was lined with fur.

"I am sorry if I intruded, madam," he said. He turned and walked away.

Francisca Gonsalvo stood at the cabin door and watched the activities on deck with anxious eyes. The waves were mountainous. The sails rattled and snapped in the strong wind as the seamen strove to reef canvas. One poor soul lost footing. He fell to the deck, where he lay sprawled in a queer, crumpled mass. She put her hands over her face for a moment. She heard the mate shouting, "The fog has lifted. We're off Hatteras." *Hatteras!* That dread cape! The ship had put about and was standing south. The child cried sharply in her sleep and thrust her arms above her head, as though she were clutching at something. Francisca hurried to her side and pulled the cover over her.

"The ship will sink!" Francisca said the words aloud. "The ship will sink!" She saw it sinking, with a flash of clear vision that she had experienced at times ever since she was a small child. She stood stiffly, her eyes staring blankly. She saw, as though from above, the figures of herself and Angela. They were lying flat on some object, a door or a plank raft. She saw the ropes that held them. She was wrapped in the stranger's fur-lined cape. Angela was rolled in a blanket, by her side. The waves were carrying them closer and closer to a long, barren, sandy beach.

Only for a moment she saw this, as one would glance at a picture and glance away. It was a portent. The ship would be sunk. She must hurry. She put her little store of jewels in a skin bag about her neck. Then, dressing in a dark, warm dress, she woke Angela and told her to put on a warm frock. The child, at seven, was quick and intelligent. There was no need of explanation.

Outside there were an explosion and wild shouts. "She's firing on us! Let her have it! The deck guns! Deus, what fools!" Her husband's voice came from the bridge. "Santa María, have you no brains? I'll have you lashed! The fourteen-pounders! Fire!" A great reverberation followed, which shook the ship. Then a crash. Francisca saw the foremast topple. It fell, a mass of sail and rigging.

So great was the swell of waves that the sea at times seemed to cover the ship. Men were shouting, "The rudder's gone. . . ." Miguel's voice . . . She glimpsed her husband by the poop rail, shouting orders between his cupped hands: "Over the side with bags of oakum! Place them on both sides of the rudder, to prevent its striking the ship."

The bowsprit was gone now. "Lash the tiller!" shouted Miguel. "Let the ship lay to!" The wind was blowing hard from northeast, driving the disabled ship southward toward the mouth of the Cape Fear River.

A seaman, who was overside, reported the shank of the rudder was wrenched and split.

"Steer the ship by the cable and a spar," shouted one of the Martinique passengers. The seaman struggled to get a chain through two rings on a bolt below the split rudder, but he was swept into the water. He sank before her eyes, but no one looked his way or threw a line to aid him. Another seaman went over the side with a strong rope, which he fastened to a ring. He passed the end of it over the quarter, but the bolt, under stress, broke and drew out, leaving them worse off than before. When the wind was at its height, a shot took a second mast.

"The boats! The boats!" There was a rush to the boats, but some of them had been shot away; others were under the tangle of sail and line and mast.

"We run a great risk of perishing in the ocean." The voice came to Francisca's ears. The tall man was standing at the door. "Are you ready to abandon ship, madam?"

Miguel staggered across the deck, blood dripping from a wound in his head. Francisca ran to him, leaving the terrified child clinging to the stranger's hand. "Miguel, my dear, you are wounded."

He looked at her dazedly. "The boats! The boats! Get into the boats!" He turned and ran back to the poop deck. A moment later he was shouting to the gunners: "Close in and broadside!"

The steersman was helpless; the ship swung with the wind and the irresistible pull of the current.

Francisca ran a few steps after her husband, but a loose end of canvas caught her as the wind whipped it from the broken mast. She fell to the deck. There was pain, and then a deep well of darkness.

Even now, she could not think of that time without terror overcoming her. In her comfortable bed, under covers, she shivered as if in an ague.

Nothing more she knew, until she wakened in the little house of Gil Roi, a Frenchman who made shingles in Green Swamp. There were no survivors, according to him, only herself, lashed to a small raft, her arm around her little daughter. He told her how he had gone out, when morning came after the great storm, to look for wreckage and found her.

It was days before she took interest in anything about her. In the interim she was taken to Brunswick and lay in the house of a fisherman, cared for by his good wife. Day after day she lay looking through the window to the broad mouth of the Cape Fear River. Even the efforts of little Angela to rouse her from her apathy were without avail.

It was here the stranger had found her again. Only a seaman or two had survived, he said, but the passengers had been picked up by fishing boats, he among them. Both ships were gone. It had been a duel of ships. She was in North Carolina, his own country. He was kind to her, the stranger; Ferrier was his name. He lived near Queen Anne's Town, two hundred miles north, near the Virginia line. He would come again. She listened but did not speak. She had no desire for life. She turned her face and buried it in the pillows. "Miguel! Miguel!" In her heart she knew she was not calling to the captain who went down with his ship, but to the lost Miguel, the gay young lost Miguel, whom she had loved so ardently.

The sound of children's voices brought Francisca out of the past.

Philip was shouting, "Angela! Angela! Get your horse! Let us go down the River Road. The dragoons are riding by. They are camping by the great tree, near the mill-pond. Jake told me."

Angela burst into the room. She was habited in dark blue with a crimson scarf on her little hat. "May we, Mother? Philip can ride postilion behind me."

"Take a groom with you, and don't go too close to the camp, dear. Soldiers are not always trustworthy."

"But they fight for us!" Philip cried.

Francisca was rebuked. "Of course they fight for us. And we are grateful," she said. But she cast a warning glance at Angela.

Angela mounted her skittish mare from the block. The groom hoisted Philip up behind her. They went by the path that led through the deep woods to the turn of the River Road, near the mill-pond. When they reached the road they saw that one platoon had dismounted and were making camp. A fire had been started and a provision waggon drawn up. A pretty young girl, with flaxen hair, was coming from the cowshed, carrying a pail of milk. Angela saw her. It was the little Walker girl, not quite right in her head. She stood watching the men, her blue eyes staring, her mouth half open.

A young officer went up to her. Angela, from her position obscured by a growth of young pines, watched them. The man said something. The girl shook her head in denial. The man took a coin from his pocket and held it up, but the girl still shook her head. She set the milk pail on the ground and stared at him, running her finger up and down the brass buttons on his blue and buff coat. The man laughed, caught the girl around the middle, planted a kiss on her mouth. He laid his hand for a moment on the low bodice of her dress. Then he caught up the milk pail and went back to camp.

Angela wheeled her horse and started home, in spite of Philip's shrill protest. She was outraged.

"The fool!" she said aloud. "Anyone could have seen the girl was daft."

She rode home at a gallop, paying no heed to the little branches of pine and gum that whipped against her face. She was angered, fiercely indignant, that an officer would take advantage of a daft girl. If it had been a common soldier . . . but an *officer!* "It is a riffraff army!" she cried. Anthony would never stoop to such an act. But Anthony was a gentleman.

CHAPTER

2

A COMPANY OF DRAGOONS

A COMPANY of dragoons clattered down Broad Street in Queen Anne's Town to the accompaniment of rattling bridle chains and dangling sabres and the excited shouts of small boys. Market-day crowds followed close and stared silently at the splendid buff and blue uniforms, the fine mounts and well-polished boots of the dragoons. Such a sight was unusual in the Albemarle. The soldiers who marched through the streets of the village on Queen Anne's Creek were for the most part the Home Defenders of the North Carolina militia. They wore faded, ragged uniforms or homemade jerkins of crudely tanned deer hide, without insignia. The blue coats, the yellow facings of the dragoons were as fresh as though they had never seen a battle or stormy weather.

Forty men, forty beautiful horses, three officers—a captain, a lieutenant and an ensign—with long blue capes faced in red! No wonder the children ran after them shouting with delight, and the women stood at street corners and in windows to watch the spectacle. This was an aspect of war that they had not before encountered. They waved handkerchiefs and scarves. One young boy, more thoughtful than the others, ran to his home and came out again waving a small flag as the troopers rode past. The colour sergeant dipped his colours, to the delight of the crowds.

Market day gave the riders a greater audience than they would have had on a more sedate and quiet midweek day. The hitching racks were crowded with mules and high-wheeled carts, and field and saddle horses lined the rails along the shore and the Green.

There were drovers and husbandmen, yeomen from Chowan River as far away as Bennett's Creek. Planters from Tyrrell and Bertie had come across the ferries or sailed their own craft across the river and Sound to attend the animal auctions, or bring their own produce to the larger market at Queen Anne's Town. And their wives and daughters came to trade at Hewes and Smith's Goods Store at the corner of Broad and King Streets.

In the bay lay three schooners—one from Baltimore, an oyster boat; one from far northern Boston; and the third the *Holy Heart of Jesus*, carrying twenty-three cannon for the defense of the village and the Sound. This ship was anchored near the Dram Tree, within plain view of Hayes, the plantation of the great Whig leader, Samuel Johnston.

The dragoons turned into King Street and came to a halt at the head of the Green, in front of the Courthouse. The trumpet sounded, the ranks separated; half the company rode down the west side of the Green and the other took the east. They met at the water side, close to the wharf, joined ranks and rode along the shore.

The small manoeuvre was carried out with precision and soldierly ease. By this time half the town was following, silent for the most part. Eyes were fixed on the young captain. He had a thin face and aquiline nose, and dark flashing eyes under straight black brows. His long cape concealed his body but there was no concealing his graceful easy carriage. His tricorn, laced in gold, sat slightly aslant, jauntily, over his smoothly clubbed hair. A small shadow of a moustache lined his upper lip, and his straight even teeth showed white in his dark face as he gave his sharp, staccato orders. The people watched him, openly curious. Cosmo de' Medici was as mediaeval in appearance as the paintings of the great Cosmo of his name and he resembled him in visage and grace.

Behind the captain rode two other officers. One, a captain also, wore the uniform of a staff officer of the Continental Line. He was a heavier man in figure, sandy in colouring, with a strong bony face and a long firm jaw—homely almost, in contrast with De' Medici. He might pass unnoticed in a crowd of men; yet he had the essence of quiet strength that was not without interest to a subtle observer. The third officer, Ben Mills, an ensign, was young, the down on his lip little more than a fuzz. Blond and red-cheeked, he kept his round blue eyes straight ahead while his captain's sharp glances missed nothing in their swift scrutiny of the crowds that lined their roadway.

"Observe, Peter," murmured De' Medici as he fell in beside the staff officer, Peter Huntley. "See the beautiful maidens at the landing. Are they not enchanting? Our stay in this village may not be dull, eh?"

Peter Huntley glanced toward the wharf. A middle-aged woman, stout but regal in appearance, was descending the narrow plank from the deck of a small sloop. She managed, in spite of her weight, her voluminous skirts and the slippery boards, to maintain an air of serene dignity. Two young girls followed, and a Negro serving-woman. Peter did not have time to see the faces of the girls clearly as he passed, but he noticed that one was tall and had a mass of dark hair held in place by a comb.

"She has the look of Spain, that one," said De' Medici with a quick sidewise glance. "I think I shall make it my pleasure to become acquainted with the *señora*; then the *señorita*." He smiled slyly. Peter did not like the smile on De' Medici's lips. It recalled too many things, presaged too many love encounters, too many stolen caresses! The Scottish Huntley did not have the facile way with woman that was so natural to the Latin De' Medici.

"We will give them a show, eh?" De' Medici's voice rang out a command. The riders wheeled, closed ranks and jingled their gay and noisy way to the rim of the village where the Rope Walk bisected the meadow. Here Queen Anne's Creek found Albemarle Sound after meandering through dark cypress and juniper-lined banks from the deep woods and the pocosin beyond Yeopim Road. The villagers followed the soldiers to watch them dismount to make camp. This they did with the casual ease of men long accustomed to tasks of march and bivouac and battlefield. Men of the North Carolina Line, they were better drilled, better uniformed than the Home Guard. They held their heads high, their backs straight, and they sat tall in their saddles.

A countryman dressed in homespun, his broad hat set on the back of his head, gazed at them with suspicion in his eyes. "Might ye have seen a battle?" he asked a dragoon who was slipping a girth and pulling the saddle back over his horse's rump.

"Might," the dragoon answered, intent on folding his saddle blanket sweaty side inward so that the felt would dry soft.

The countryman nodded his head approvingly as the soldier rubbed down his horse. "Where be they fought?" he asked.

"White Plains and——"

"Monmouth?"

The dragoon looked up at the question. He saw a lean brown face, skin drawn tight over cheek and jawbone. A long scar ran from the man's ear to the base of his neck. "Why Monmouth, countryman?"

"I was there at Monmouth." The countryman turned away.

The soldier watched him disappear into the constantly increasing crowd. He spoke to the corporal: "Yon man has been a soldier. Like to know why he is here, out of uniform."

"One of them bounty-payers. Served his enlistment and come home to plant a crop, like a thousand others." The corporal spat contemptuously. "When you're in a war you're in a war and I've got my disgust of these ninety-day and six-month men, fretting about families at home, running off to plant a crop. All the crop they are planting is begetting a squawking baby. Then they come sneaking back for army pay when harvest's over."

"Pay did you say, Corp'l? Pay! Why, I haven't seen a pay warrant for so long that——"

"Damn your hide, you fool! Keep your mouth shut! Don't you know what you're here for?"

Tim Reeder scratched his head. "The captain said we'd be recruiting after we left Halifax, didn't he?"

"That he did and that he means to do. What help will you be, yapping about no pay? I've a notion to report you."

A worried look came over the broad face of the youth. "You wouldn't do that, Corp'l. I'll curry your horse for a week."

"Two weeks!" The corporal's answer was brisk and sharp. "Curry and feed my mount for two weeks."

"Aye, then, two weeks," the dragoon agreed, well pleased to have passed a crisis. He had been taken from the guard-house at Williamsburg for this recruiting detail on the promise of exemplary behaviour, with no liquor or card games or chasing after camp-followers. He stood watching the corporal swagger away. A long sigh that ended in a whistle escaped him. A fool he was with his loose tongue and scatterbrain. Here he was only ninety-odd miles from New Bern, and bliss, with Belinda Yessop waiting to wed with him. He tapped the bosom of his tunic absently, where a letter from her crackled against his heart, labouriously written but legible. She wrote:

> I've been lonesome, my lad. Waitin is a terrible task, so I've took a bit of work as dairymaid at the Palace. It's not too bad and the shillins I make and save will help buy the bit of land we want, when the war is over.

His Excellency pays me well, a shillin a week. The great man doesn't know I'm livin, but his lady comes to the buttery sometimes, lifting her fine silk skirts with her little white hands.

"My good girl," she says to me one day, "I don't think it's proper to set the butter in a mould with the King's Arms on it and we in rebellion. Do you now?"

"No, my lady," says I, "but I have no other to mould with, by your leave." And with that she goes out, her skirts rustling and I'm still mouldin butter with the King's Crown on it—and still takin the King's shillin when I can get one, and we in strong rebellion. Tim my lad, hasten to New Bern and perhaps we can get you work as a hostler or a farrier to the Governor. Don't forget I am waitin, Reeder, and keep yourself clean and fresh for your Belinda, and I'll do the same for you!

Tim went about currying the corporal's horse. "I'll give her a coat of satin sheen." He whistled happily as he worked and paid no heed to the crowd who stood beyond the tents and the campfire, for, as the corporal said, "It's recruiting we're on and we must look happy and well-content so the bumkins will envy our life of gay adventure and hard fighting and join us to take the General's shilling."

The corporal came back as Tim was finshing off. "Wouldn't put too much polish on the mare, dragoon, or the captain will be wanting you for *his* orderly." With a grin on his face he walked away. Reeder put the currycomb and brush in the saddle-bags and made his way toward the campfire. The odours of cooking told him it had been a long spell since he had breakfasted on the road near Middle Swamp. As he reached the campfire Captain de' Medici and the staff officer of the Continental Line passed him.

"I have the lists," he heard the captain say. "There are a dozen big plantations hereabouts, some on the Sound, others up the Roanoke and the Chowan Rivers. We should have no trouble . . ." They passed out of Reeder's hearing. He stood looking after the retreating figures. What did the captain mean, talking about "have no trouble"? Reeder hoped there would be another skirmish before they reached New Bern. It had been dull with not a shot fired since they left Virginia two weeks ago. How could there be? They had outflanked Dunmore's men near Petersburg, and the British Southern Army, having taken possession of Savannah, in Georgia, designed to possess themselves of Port Royal and, if possible, Charles Town—everyone knew that. Tim gave it up. He got his tin pannikin and joined the crowd about the cook fire. He would make no mind about these things. Let the officers do the thinking. Enough for a dragoon to keep his horse and himself fit, and be handy with his horse pistols when the time came.

Captain de' Medici and Peter Huntley rode back to the village to take up their quarters at Horniblow's Tavern at the head of the Green, next to the Courthouse. Peter noticed that De' Medici's lean, swarthy face wore a serious look. He did not wonder. Recruiting dragoons where men were scarce or indifferent to the needs of the army, trying to squeeze horses from planters who had been called to furnish mounts for the army for four long years, wasn't an agreeable job. More than that, he knew that De' Medici had had no pay for himself or his men for four months. Every day he was obliged to placate the disgruntled men who wanted their lean pay to send home to their families. Dispatch after dispatch had been sent to his Excellency the Governor at New Bern. Caswell was adept with the pen and wrote suave but evasive letters in reply, telling the captain that armies had always lived off the land, and the ingenuity and resourcefulness of the officer was the basis of contented, well-fed, well-equipped troops.

"Damn it all, Huntley!" De' Medici broke out. "A man can stand just about so much. Every day I swear like a bandit at my men to keep from bursting into tears at their plight. They beg for their pay; they tell me pitiful stories of starving wives and children. I close my eyes when they desert, and report them left behind ill, hoping they will come back to join us after they've visited their homes and seen their families."

"I'm sure you will get money when we get to New Bern and you can talk to Governor Caswell."

De' Medici shook his head. "His Excellency knows more ways of saying no than anyone in the Province. I've been told that by a hundred officers."

"Perhaps he hasn't anything in the treasury. You remember how short we were last winter at Valley Forge, but somehow the General got money to pay off before the whole army deserted. Perhaps Governor Caswell will do something soon."

De' Medici shook his head again. "I ask for money. He sends me a list of the Albemarle planters from whom I am supposed to wring money and horses. The country is already dried up from the draft for South Carolina. Every man North Carolina can spare has been sent south. They are in straits there, since Savannah fell. I am desolate, desperate. Alas, sir, your language is not a fit one to portray my despair."

Peter grinned. "You know you can talk the bird from the hawthorn bush, Captain. I'll wager you get your allotment of horses here, and the country boys will fall over one another's feet to sign papers and ride with De' Medici's dragoons."

The captain shook his head. "No. My doom approaches. I have left my good fortune behind me. See, I make a sign with my fingers to hold off the evil eye which is upon me. . . . Once all went to my satisfaction. My friend General LaFayette says to me: 'Cosimo, you are magnificent. You raise the cavalry. You train your men to ride like demons. I have a wager you will meet Tarleton and you will defeat him!' So, instead, what does he do to me? Lends me to North Carolina to recruit! God is looking away from Cosimo."

The malicious March wind blew a gust from the Sound. It blew and whirled the long full skirts of a group of women and girls who were crossing the Green from the wharf. It caught a bright scarf from the throat of the raven-haired girl they had noticed at the wharf and sent it flying through the air, billowing like a sunset cloud of crimson.

Peter saw it first. He stood up in his stirrups and his arm lifted to snatch it from the air, but a contrary wind propelled its gossamer fold through his gauntleted fingers. His skittish mare pranced and cavorted and reared back, almost unseating him. Bit in strong teeth, she plunged toward the ballast-stone kerb. The women, like a covey of frightened quail, separated in the middle of the street, some scurrying one way, some another.

The horse, truly alarmed, was growing unmanageable. Women screamed, De' Medici shouted, pulling in his mount. The mischievous wind tossed the silk against the mare's face. The scarf slipped down and became entangled in her prancing hoofs. A moment later the crimson scarf was ground deep into the mud of the street.

A girl's clear voice came to Peter's ears. "Barbarian! Barbarian! Do you have to ruin my scarf?" He looked down into the enormous black eyes, angry and scornful. He dismounted quickly and recovered the bright silk from the slime and mud.

"I am sorry," he apologized, "frightfully sorry." The girl turned at the sight of the length of silk, stained and rumpled, and presented a stiff, angry back to the embarrassed Peter.

De' Medici dismounted, came up beside her, his cocked hat under his arm, his slim elegant body bent forward, his smooth voice very, very solicitous. "Madam, our apologies! We are desolate. Please accept."

Peter, disgruntled by his own awkward slowness, stood with reddening face, his outstretched hand holding the limp silk. The girl did not glance at him again or listen to his words. She had ears only for De' Medici. Well, let De' Medici do the apologizing. The other women took refuge on the Courthouse steps to be out of the way of his pawing horse.

He mounted quickly and rode down the street in the direction of the wharf. Let De' Medici smooth the ruffled plumage! He was adept at such things. Did the girl think he had purposely allowed his horse to trample her silken scarf? He was conscious of smiling faces of white men and women and grinning blacks. He became aware that he still held the offending scarf clutched in his hand. He thrust it under the cantle of his saddle and turned his mare down the street that bordered the water, out into the open country. He would punish the blasted animal for making him seem such an uncouth boor. He ran the mare until she was covered with white lather and the mischief was out of her. Gad, the girl was beautiful! He liked a girl who had spirit.

It was almost an hour later when he turned and rode back to Horniblow's where he and De' Medici had engaged rooms for their stay in the village on Queen Anne's Creek.

The Suffolk coach had just arrived and was discharging its passengers when Peter rode into the tavern yard. He found his orderly waiting to take his mount back to the encampment. He would go directly to his room without stopping for a posset or to speak to any of the men gathered in the public room. All he could think of was a bath and a change of linen.

Ten or twelve men were in the great room. Some were passengers from the coach who were stopping for the night; others from near-by villages had come in for trading, or selling their farm animals; still others waited for the coach for Hertford and the eastern villages along the Sound. It was a pleasant room with a great fire burning in the farther end; benches and settles and small tables where men sat talking, mugs of ale and other drinks on the tables. A door led to the dining-room where serving-maids were busy setting up tables, carrying in trays of cutlery and glasses, preparing for supper. A smaller room opened off the public room, a small parlour, where half a dozen men sat talking before a fireplace, smoking their churchwarden pipes, while they watched two men at a small table playing chess. Peter had heard of Horniblow's. Following the custom of the Old Country, the prominent Whigs of Queen Anne's Town and the surrounding counties of the Albemarle made it their daily meeting place.

Peter followed the half-grown boy up the stairs to the second floor. The boy paused before a door at the end of the hall and pushed it open with the toe of his heavy boot. "The captain said to unpack you' box and hang you' clothes in the press. I hopes you is satisfied, sar." He rubbed an imaginary speck of dust from Peter's box which had been placed on a wooden chair under the window. Peter tossed a coin which the boy caught handily. "Want I should have the washerwoman clean the lady's scarf?" he asked, suppressing a grin. "Mandy can surely make it fresh as new."

Peter pulled his shirt over his head and tossed it into the corner. The scarf, the offender, lay on the bed, a wilted and bedraggled object, quite out of place among a soldier's belongings. A slow flush came over his cheeks. Even the tavern boy had seen the humiliating incident. Doubtless he had laughed with the rest of the village. Peter glanced sharply at the boy. No smiles, but his look of innocence was belied by bright twinkling eyes.

Peter was for the moment inclined toward anger, then his habitual good nature was restored. He laughed and produced a second, larger coin. "Bring the rag back in ten minutes and you shall have this. But mind you, no waving it around in the public room."

"No, sar! No, sar!" The grin was wide and unabashed at sight of the shilling. "Fifteen minutes, sar. Give me fifteen and I'll bring it back good as new. Mandy is a master hand with the press iron."

"Very well, fifteen minutes, but not a second longer." Peter picked up his fat round watch. "It's twenty until three. Now run, my lad." The boy started for the door. Peter called: "Wait, do you know the young lady?"

"Yes, sar. 'Twas Mistress Angela Ferrier you 'most spattered with mud. She live up the Chowan River nigh to fifteen miles from the village. Her mama and her, dey was all walkin' up the Green from the landing when you——"

"That will do!" Peter said shortly. "Get out of here!" The boy shot out of the room, the door banging behind him.

CHAPTER

3

PENELOPE BARKER'S FOR TEA

THE three young women rushed to the window to peer at the strange officers as they crossed the Green and entered Horniblow's hospitable door.

Madam Penelope Dawson, of Eden House, in Bertie County, was seated in Lawyer Thomas Barker's red leather chair. She placed her slender satin-shod feet on a cricket set before the fire, and arranged her voluminous skirts in elegant folds so that she presented a picture of ease and grace. Her clear, cultured voice, her fashionable intonation fell on the room and dampened the girls' eagerness, smothering their gay chatter.

"If you must peep, young ladies, peep with discretion and dignity. Never allow a man to assume that you have the slightest curiosity about him." She spoke from the wisdom gathered from a deserved reputation of a beauty famous in the Carolinas. She had been a widow for several years. She had more poise and dignity than the average woman of twenty-six. Her family boasted two Royal Governors of wealth and culture. Her mother was the stepdaughter of Governor Eden, and her father, Gabriel Johnston, was another Royal Governor. She had earned the right to make pronouncements on all matters of social and political conduct.

She spoke to the three but her grey eyes rested on Angela Ferrier. The younger woman met her eyes with a cool level glance. Cecily Armitage and Sarah Blount blushed and moved away from the window. Angela pushed the curtain aside and looked out boldly, unmoved by Madam's words.

"I am sure your father, the senator, would be annoyed at such boldness, Angela," Madam continued, speaking to Angela's straight back, "and your mother——"

Angela watched the officers go up the steps, cross the long gallery and enter the wide door of the tavern; let the curtain fall into place.

41

She moved slowly back to the fireplace, opposite Madam's chair. A slow smile crossed her full red lips.

"The captain is as dark as a Moor and as handsome as a god," she said as if she had not heard Madam's words. "The other is sandy with a face hewn from a boulder."

A little predatory gleam came into Madam's eyes. "A dark captain," she repeated. "Young?"

"Young and moves with elegance." Angela's eyes had a secret smile as they rested on Madam. After all, Penelope Dawson was very little older than she was.

"I thought the blond one had a kind, strong face," Cecily said timidly.

"Grim," Angela said, remembering her encounter. "Uncouth. He moves awkwardly."

"Not so." Sarah spoke up. "Didn't you see how he gentled that vicious horse? I think he is wonderful."

"You may have him, Sarah," Angela said casually. "I choose the dark captain."

Madam laughed. "Will he choose you, Angela? Dark men to blonde women. That is an old saying."

"Not with us Spaniards. My father was as dark as a Moor, and handsome. And you know my mother's complexion. They were lovers like Abélard and Héloïse; like Paolo and Francesca."

"It would not be wise to speak such words before your stepfather, the senator."

Angela's dark eyes met Madam's without expression. The two girls, seated on the little love seat, glanced at each other with round eyes. Angela was so indiscreet. She would annoy Madam Dawson. Everyone knew she didn't like silly young girls; they bored her. She despised pretence. And she was so gracious in her own home. Everyone loved to go to Eden House.

"I think them both personable young officers," Sarah said crisply. "We have so few men at home since the war, it is good to see a new face."

Their hostess, Madam Penelope Barker, returned to the drawing-room at the moment, leaving the door open for her plump serving-woman, Midget, who carried a silver tray with the best Chelsea tea-set. The maid put the tray on a Queen Anne table and drew it close to the fire. Madam Barker sat down in the Chippendale chair that Mr. Barker had purchased at Francis Corbin's auction, when the Cupola

House was sold to Dr. Armitage, Cecily's father. Cecily had recently returned from Charles Town, where she had been attending the Madam's School.

"I feel as though I should apologize every time I serve this wretched yapon tea," Madam Barker said, her plump little hands fluttering among the delicate cups. She looked up at Madam Dawson, her head on one side. "Sugar, Penelope? It is really stupid of me but I can never remember."

"Sugar, and don't skimp. I don't have to watch my figure."

Penelope Barker laughed easily. "I know I should but I don't. Thomas is so comforting. He says he cannot abide a scrawny woman." She spoke smilingly, without annoyance. Penelope Barker had had rare beauty too, when she was as young as Penelope Dawson. She had had her quota of husbands. Penelope Barker favoured lawyers; she had garnered three of them, all brilliant men, each in his own way. She was now in her middle years. She had grown a little plump but she moved with the quick easy step of youth. Her face was smooth save for a few radiating lines at the corners of her eyes and mouth, "laughing lines" her husband Thomas Barker called them.

Cecily and Sarah exchanged fleeting glances as they rose to assist their hostess; Cecily suppressed a giggle by closing her lips firmly. The rivalry between the two Penelopes persisted with increasing and diminishing tempo. The two women never quite gave up friendship but it was stretched to a thin edge at times. One of the Penelopes had a tongue that could bite, the other spoke with a smooth humour, a sweetness that sometimes carried a sharp sting. But their intimacy had a resilience that buffeted the storms.

Penelope Dawson set her teacup on the table with a little clatter. "I should think you would apologize. This tea is really disagreeable. Hyperion is superior."

Angela broke the silence that followed. "I see my mother coming down the street. Pray excuse me." She went into the hall to open the door. Madam Ferrier dismissed her serving-woman, who went across the garden to the kitchen. She smiled at Angela.

"Ah, there you are, my child. Am I late for tea? I found such enchanting taffetas at Mr. Smith's store. A French ship, you know, and as for the laces for a trousseau——" Angela pulled straight the ribands on her mother's little bonnet and patted her cheek lightly.

"Am I too, too dishevelled, *cara?* It is fatiguing, very, this shopping."

"You are lovely, *Mamacita*. Wait. Let me tuck this lock into place. Now you are sleek and beautiful." She opened the door. Madam Ferrier walked in. She moved slowly with the same easy grace that so became her daughter; although she had gained some pounds in the years that she had been bearing the senator's children, she still moved easily, almost majestically.

Angela glanced around the room. Three women of beauty, each in her own way: the two Penelopes and her Spanish mother. But Francisca Ferrier had something the other women lacked: that subtle femininity as old as Eve, moulded and refined by centuries of European culture. She was not a talkative woman. She was more often silent as others talked, her fine olive-skinned hands busy with some needlework, listening, but always a part of the group about her. Her participation was not through words but through a quality of attentiveness which shone in her mobile face and large dark eyes.

She walked into Penelope's drawing-room and became at once its center. She kissed Penelope Barker lightly on the cheek, extended her hand to the other Penelope, sat down in the elbow chair on the opposite side of the fierplace from Penelope Dawson, spreading her wide skirts about her, making herself comfortable as a feline makes itself comfortable by the fire, taking always the choicest spot. The young girls left the window and surrounded her, leaning forward to be kissed, or sinking down at her feet on little hassocks and fireside benches.

"Madam, allow me to fetch you tea." "Madam, will you have a crumpet?" "A bit of spice-cake, Madam?" The clear young voices surrounded, caressed, in their anxiety to serve their favourite. She thanked each one by a glance, warm and intimate.

Madam Dawson sipped her tea, watching the charming little tableau with a smile. She wondered, as she had wondered many times before, just what quality Francisca possessed that was absent in other women of her acquaintance. Perhaps she had more tolerance, and looked on life more dispassionately.

Sarah Blount said, "Did you see the dragoons riding through the streets, Madam?"

"Didn't they make a brave show?" Cecily Armitage touched the silken skirt. A shy girl, not yet developed to the point where one could say she was pretty or plain, she adored Madam Ferrier. In secret she thought of herself as like her though her brown hair and light brown eyes bore no resemblance to the Spanish woman. "So well uniformed, so brave-looking," she added.

"So you did look, Cecily?" Angela said, laughing. "Even if it was unmaidenly." Blood rose painfully in Cecily's throat.

"Angela!" her mother said. "You shall not tease my little Cecily."

"The blond one, the ensign. He looked little more than a young boy. I've never seen such blue eyes in my life—and his lashes!" Sarah spoke quickly, words tumbling from her red lips. "He rode so well, sitting his horse so firmly."

"Ah, she noticed his lashes." Madam laughed quietly.

Sarah laughed too. "Yes, I did, but it was the dark captain who enchanted me. He is wonderful, like a mediaeval knight. He had such a firm strong voice when he gave orders; so soft when he spoke to us."

Angela was silent. She too had noticed the beautiful caressing voice.

"And none of you noticed the bonny sandy Scot?" Madam Ferrier's eyes teased. "All looking for beauty and none of you thinking of strength in a man's face?"

Laughter rippled and filled the room. The girls all spoke at once. "Angela! Ask Angela. She noticed the sandy Scot."

Madam's eyes sought those of her daughter. "Ah?"

"Tell her. Tell her about your scarf, Angela."

Angela shrugged, trying to look indifferent. "I do not think him strong. He is a boor; *gauche* and unmannerly." She got up, set her cup on the table and went back to the window.

Madam Barker offered a second cup of tea. Madam Dawson refused. She was tired of this senseless chatter of young girls. They were being given too much importance. Aimless talk bored her. "I cannot abide this yapon tea, my dear. Sometimes I think I'll convert myself into a Tory. I would if I thought it would bring me some decent India tea and a little more variety in our food."

"Oh, Madam Dawson!" the girls' voices rose. "You could never."

Penelope Barker put the cup back on the tea table. She was frowning slightly. "Penelope, you can't mean that. You know——"

Madam Dawson looked at her hostess' troubled face and laughed. "Now, Penelope, don't give us a lecture on tea-drinking, just because you presided that day at Elizabeth King's tea-party, when we all signed that paper never to drink tea again. You don't have to be the public custodian of our political views."

"I certainly don't, but at the same time, when the fortunes of war are going so strongly against our cause, I think it very small to complain because you have to deny yourself a little tea, and give part of your abundance for our soldiers."

"Yes. Yes. I know our North Carolina soldiers are out fighting Greene's and Washington's battles in the North and General Lincoln's in South Carolina. I remember my duty, and I thank God for hams in the smokehouse and fowl in the runs. At the same time, I like tea and I miss it."

There was a little silence. The tea-kettle sang. The wood in the fire-place snapped and sent out a flash of fine iridescent sparks.

Madam Ferrier worked placidly, her eyes on the long scarf she was knitting. The maidens were silent. They were embarrassed and uneasy, not from the spoken word but from the undercurrent of antagonism that showed itself for a brief moment. Not for a moment did they think Madam Penelope Dawson was a Tory like the Pollocks, but people did talk secretly, saying that she sometimes embarrassed her near relative Samuel Johnston, the Whig leader in the Albemarle.

Angela, at the window, said: "Three officers are turning in the gate with Mr. Barker."

"It is Captain de' Medici and his officers," Madam Ferrier said. "I asked them to come in for a dish of tea, Penelope." She smiled at Madam Barker. "I told them you would be so happy to welcome them to Queen Anne's Town."

Madam Barker rose hastily. "Certainly. Certainly. I will call Midget to bring fresh tea and some of Mr. Barker's Madeira."

"Let me go to call Midget, Madam Barker." Angela left the room and went out into the hall. The girls rose from the hassocks, patted their curls, straightened laces and ruffles, then sat down sedately in chairs arranged stiffly along the walls.

Penelope Dawson was not above settling her skirts into more graceful lines. The folds of her fichu showed her round swelling breasts, her smooth throat. She drew herself up, her slim figure and fine head outlined against the dark crimson of the Queen Anne chair.

Only Madam Francisca Ferrier was undisturbed. The swift clicking of her needles made the only sound in the quiet room. She glanced about her. She was aware of the expectancy, the almost feverish expectancy of the young girls, the mature, seasoned interest of the older women, Angela's undisguised antagonism. The room seemed to fade and she had a fleeting glimpse of time extended beyond the limits of her normal knowledge. Something that disturbed the balance, some portent of unhappiness. She seemed to see her daughter standing before her, tears streaming from her eyes. These moods had come to her before—not often, but they always foretold some danger. No sign of her uneasiness showed in her face. The rhythm of her knitting remained unbroken.

Angela lingered in the dining-room after she had delivered Madam Barker's message to Midget. She lingered because she did not wish to meet the dark captain in Penelope Barker's small drawing-room under the eyes of a dozen people. She wanted to meet him some other way, in some circumstance that had the full flavour of romance, or of danger. To hear her mother's placid voice saying, "Captain de' Medici, this is my young daughter, Angela," would be anathema to her. She wanted to speak to him first on the banks of the Sound with the moon spreading a rippling silver carpet at their feet, or on some shaded footpath that followed the black waters of Queen Anne's Creek, with the cool dark mystery of the cypress that grew thickly along the edge of the water. Not before a crowd of women: Cecily's nervous giggle; Sarah's observant eyes; Penelope Dawson's calm grey eyes measuring her in hostile rivalry.

Angela caught up her cloak and threw it over her shoulders. She opened the door into the little hall and started for the front door. Her way was blocked by the bulky figure of a man. He turned as she closed the door. It was the sandy-haired Scot's cool hazel eyes that met hers. His expression did not change. He has only one, Angela thought angrily; one expression and it is no more changeable than a stone block.

He bowed slightly and took a step forward. Drawing the offending scarf from his tunic, he extended it toward her.

"Pardon me, may I return your scarf? I am sorry . . ." he began.

Angela lifted her head, her eyes fixed somewhere behind him. "I have no desire to speak to you, sir."

"But your scarf, your lovely scarf . . ." His voice was not stony. It was low and had a warmth, but Angela's ear was not attuned to its persuasive quality.

"Will you please stand aside, sir? You are blocking my way."

The officer's face reddened; he moved aside and stood at the drawing-room door. "But your scarf? What will I do with it?"

"Whatever you please. Trample it under your horse's hoofs if you like. I certainly would not wear a damaged scarf." She turned the brass doorknob and jerked the door open.

The officer started to say it was no longer damaged, it had been washed and was as fresh and clean as if it had never once seen the mud at the Courthouse door; but there was no time. The door was shut. He heard the sharp click of her buckled shoes as she crossed the gallery and went down the steps. He swore softly. He would like to throttle the girl. He heard voices in the drawing-room. He thrust the scarf back into the breast of his tunic and buttoned the brass button firmly. He threw his cape on the wooden bench, opened the door of the drawing-room and went in.

The bright glow of the fire, the candles on the tea-table, the soft warm voices of welcome beat against the anger in him. Under the spell of eager eyes, of flashing laughter, Peter Huntley forgot the arrogance of the raven-haired girl, whose coolness and hauteur belied her passionate mouth and the slumbering depth of her dark eyes. Unawakened, he thought to himself. Through the window he saw her hurrying figure move through the garden that gave on the Courthouse Green. But she had spirit; that he acknowledged.

"Indeed, yes, madam," he found himself answering Madam Dawson's question. "I have been recently in Philadelphia. I saw Mr. Hewes your representative in Congress. It was he who told me to come to Queen Anne's Town to call on Mr. Samuel Johnston."

"Sam is my cousin," Madam Dawson said. "At the moment he is at Bertie Courthouse but he will be with me at Eden House tomorrow night."

Peter bowed. "So Mr. Barker told me."

"You ride with Captain de' Medici, but I see from your uniform that you are a staff officer of the Continental Line."

"Madam is observing," Peter said, smiling slightly. "I find very few women who notice the difference in uniform between State Guard or State Line and the Continental Line officers."

Madam Dawson shrugged her shoulders. "Most women are stupid, Captain. Don't you find them so?"

"I know little about women, madam. I confess they defeat me."

She allowed her glance to move slowly from his face to his stalwart, soldierly figure; then swiftly to the graceful De' Medici. The Italian was conversing with Penelope Barker and Madam Ferrier, while the two young women sat gazing at his dark animated face.

"I was thinking you put it the wrong way, my dear Captain. If women defeat you it is because you are indifferent to them, is it not so?"

Peter laughed. When he laughed, solemnity melted. His expression became unexpectedly boyish. "If you had said I was terrified of them, it would be closer to the truth, Madam Dawson."

"Nonsense! I am sure I have had enough experience reading character to know. Besides, are we not both Scots? And a Scot cannot fool another Scot."

Peter pulled the fireside stool closer to Madam Dawson's silken skirts, and sat down. "I should have known. My dear mother always told me that a Scotswoman could see direct to the heart of a man."

"You are from Edinburgh?"

"I had my schooling there and in England. My father came from the Isle of Mull, but I was born near the Western Moutains, at Inveraray on Loch Awe."

"Ah, yes. I should have known. You are a dour lot, you island men. You have the sea in your blood, but your hearts are tender."

"Aye. And the mountains, too." A veiled look came over Peter's eyes, candid as a child's a moment before. "War hardens, madam. It seals off emotion and scars, scars that are deep."

There was movement across the tea-table. Madam Penelope Dawson rose to her feet and dropped her voice. "My plantation is across Albemarle Sound in Bertie County. I will send my galley for you tomorrow at three. Samuel Johnston will be with me over Sunday. You can visit with him there at Eden House, quietly, without interruption."

"Thank you, madam. I would not want to cause you trouble."

Her beautiful smile flashed. "My dear Captain, we live on a plantation. One guest or twenty—it is all the same to us. I think you have not encountered our Albemarle before. If you had, you would know its hospitality."

"Thank you, Madam Dawson. I shall take pleasure."

"Three o'clock at Hewes's Wharf." She rose to her feet and extended her hand, which Peter raised to his lips. She walked across the room to make her adieus to Penelope Barker.

Peter watched her. A knowledgeable woman, he thought. How the devil did she know that the papers he was carrying to Samuel Johnston were marked "Secret and Confidential"?

Thomas Barker walked to the door with the two officers. They stood, hats under their arms, on the steps, while he finished a long

story about the situation in Queen Anne's Town, which he had begun in the drawing-room. It had to do with supplies for the army,
warehoused in the village this twelvemonth past; wanted supplies—
coats and blankets and army shoes in quantity, cobbled by the
Quakers in Pasquotank and Perquimans. All held, he told them in his
thin, tired voice, because there were no wagons to move them north,
when General Nash sent for them. "That was some time since,
gentlemen, before the heroic death of the general at Germantown.
But talk to Mr. Smith, of Hewes and Smith's. He knows more about
the supplies than I do."

"They are calling for supplies for the Southern Army?" De' Medici
said, asking a question.

"Yes. Judge Iredell is lately returned from court at New Bern. He
says the report is that the British are landing men, and the situation in Georgia is progressively worse. But I am keeping you standing unhatted in this mist. Go through the garden." He indicated a
small wicket-gate beside the house. "It will bring you out at the
Green, a step from Horniblow's. Good night, gentlemen. I will see
you tomorrow."

"A very fine gentleman," remarked De' Medici as they made their
way across the damp earth of the garden path.

"A fine gentleman," repeated Peter, "but I wouldn't want to have
him as my opponent in court."

"That will not happen, Captain. You are far too canny to have
any case of yours come to court." De' Medici opened the gate that
gave on the Green. A few steps more and they were at Horniblow's.
A coach was drawn up ready to depart. A stout woman was climbing
sidewise up the steps set against the door. She moved slowly like a
land crab, trying to keep her skirts down to cover her limbs decently.
The stable-boy who held the steps tittered as the wind whisked
around the corner, lifted the drab skirt to show a gay red garter
knitted of red wool.

"Move up. Move up," the driver called. "We're late starting. We
won't reach the ferry before dark. Move up, woman! I'm bound to
get to Bertie Courthouse before nightfall."

"Hist, mon. I'll move as I see fit." The exasperated woman stood
on the top step, struggling to get herself and her basket through the
door. "You'll make Dishon's easy enough, less'n ye don't know how
to handle your lead horses. I'd make it myself if I had the reins between my fingers."

The passengers inside the coach laughed. The driver grumbled un-intelligibly and climbed up on the box.

De' Medici laughed at the little scene. " 'Tis the same the world over. Better to let women take their own way, in their own time." Peter said nothing. He stood looking after the coach as it rattled down King Street. He had had a glimpse of a familiar face half concealed in the semi-darkness of the coach.

It took a few moments to set the man in the place where he had seen him before. He remembered vividly the scene. It was in Paris one afternoon when he had accompanied the Commissioner to a reception given by the Foreign Minister, Vergennes. He had stepped out of the crush, to walk for a moment in the garden. A summer-house . . . three men seated at an iron garden table, their heads close together: Silas Deane, of the Commissioner's staff; a British naval officer he had known slightly in London—Gordon Rutherford—the scion of a Carolina family, who had stayed loyal to the King; the third, an officer he had never seen before. An unusual face, thin, lean and intense, with well-marked features: the uniform of what Peter afterward learned was Ferguson's Legion. Peter remembered his amazement that Deane should be talking with the two British officers. There was something secretive about it, almost furtive. Peter stepped behind a flowering shrub so that he was out of the range of Deane's vision. That was before the trouble between Commissioner Franklin and the three agents: the Lees, Arthur and Charles, and Izard. It happened before Deane came back to Philadelphia with his complaints and his intrigues.

Peter felt he could not be mistaken in the man in the coach. He was too well trained to forget the features of the British officer he had seen in such unusual circumstances. But what could he be doing here, in this small village in the Albemarle? It might be chance resemblance, but he doubted it. The incident made him uneasy. He liked things to fit neatly into place. This was outside the pattern. Cosmo, with his hand on the doorknob, was calling to him to make haste. Peter removed his eyes from the retreating coach and followed De' Medici into the pleasant warmth of the inn.

Lawyer Barker went back into the drawing-room and stood with his back to the fire, his hands under the tails of his plum-coloured coat. He waited until Midget had carried off the tea dishes and the decanters, before he answered Penelope's unspoken question. They were in accord, these two, in spite of difference in ages. He knew well enough that his lively little spouse was burning to question him about the two young officers. The moment the door was closed she pulled his chair to the fire. But she had her own devious little ways of gaining her information—never a direct line between two points. Her methods amused him. He never crowded her. He let her take her own course.

"Sit down, my dear," she said. "Wait, let me get your plaid to wrap around your knees."

"It's a cold wind that is blowing. An east wind brings the ocean," Thomas said. He sat down in his comfortable chair, placed so no draught would reach him, and stretched his feet to the blaze. He reached down and unfastened his knee-buckles. "This one needs a stitch, my dear. I don't want to lose the buckles Sir Richard gave me."

"I'll mend it tonight," Penelope said, seating herself on the fire bench. She ran her hand over his thin shanks. "Are your stockings wet, Thomas?" she asked, solicitously. He leaned back in his chair, comfortable and relaxed. He liked Penelope's ministrations. How easily she makes things comfortable, he thought as he watched her. Having been married to three solicitors, she must know the minds of lawyers by now. She knows we want our comfort after a day of bickering and fighting in court.

"How did the case go?" she asked. He knew she wanted to talk about the officers, but she was too adroit a woman—be solicitous first about his well-being and comfort; then show interest in his affairs. Never too much interest. Just sufficient to flatter him and give him the opportunity to talk, to boast a little over his small triumphs in a small court. It salved his hurts and made the wound less, for Thomas Barker might have played a bigger part on a larger stage. He had the mind and the legal knowledge, but he was no longer the man he had been when he was Provincial Agent. He watched the man he had trained, Samuel Johnston, rising to heights he could not reach; and he did not envy Sam his success, not for an instant; but sometimes it irked him when he had to plead insignificant cases about insignificant people, with Jemmy Iredell on the bench. Why, Jemmy was but a youth who had read his Blackstone under the eye of Sam Johnston, whom he, Barker, had led through the winding and devious paths of the common law. Now Jemmy sat on the bench as a justice. That was

Caswell's doing. No doubt he knew enough law, but he was young. Thomas Barker did not say, even to himself, that it should have been he who sat in the tall chair in the Chowan Courthouse, not these younger men. The law had disintegrated under the Rebellion. Often he quoted the Latin: *Silent leges inter arma*. It had always been true down the ages, *The laws are silent in times of war*.

He sighed and rubbed his warming thighs with a hand on which the blue veins stood out like cords. Not the hand that Sir Joshua Reynolds had painted, he thought, as he held it up to the blaze. Nor was his face the face that Reynolds had seen. Ah, well, the years, the passing years! His eyes met the inquiring gaze of his wife.

"De' Medici is here to recruit a company of dragoons," he said, thinking she had withheld her curiosity long enough. "He's been recruiting in Hillsborough and Halifax. Now he is in Queen Anne's Town for three weeks before he goes to New Bern. He wants horses from the Sound plantations."

A questioning look passed over Penelope's face. "No," her husband said, "no, I'll not sell your mare or the stallion. I have already sent them to the Bear Swamp plantation. They are well secreted there."

Relief replaced interrogation in Penelope's eyes. "I am glad. We have given enough to this Rebellion; quite enough. I'm sure Pene Dawson won't give up her horses. She always manages somehow to keep what she has."

"Eden House and Black Rock, Scots Hall and Mount Galland Plantations, you mean?"

"Yes, I do."

He saw the shadow of discontent fade from her face under his direct gaze. Thomas always disconcerted her. He seemed to draw out her deepest, most secret thoughts.

"No. I'm not envious," she hastened to say.

"Methinks the lady doth protest too much." His voice was light but sarcasm gave it a slight edge. "It is hard to rise above the Royal Governors, isn't it, my dear?"

"No, no. After all Charles Eden was half pirate; everybody says so. I suppose her father, Gabriel Johnston, was all right. One of our *good* Governors, wasn't he?"

"So they say. But that did not keep him from making good use of Eden House, Black Rock and Mount Galland, his wife's dower."

"Was he so very learned?" she asked as though she hoped her husband would deny Governor Gabriel Johnston's culture.

"Yes. He was learned, and a sound man. Yes, sound, and he loved Penelope, his daughter and your very present rival."

A blush covered her round cheek. "How can you jest? How can we be rivals? She is twenty-six, younger than I am by some years. Do I have to acknowledge how many? No, my dear, no."

He tipped her chin with his index finger. "My dear, you are not her rival, you are her superior."

His wife smiled with pleasure at the compliment from her often caustic mate.

"After all, Penelope Dawson may have a background of two Royal Governors. She was born to her high heritage. But you, my dear, of your own charm and will have secured three barristers by marriage. First-rate barristers, all of them, and one of them the brother of a belted Earl, and that, Penelope, is no inconsiderable feat."

CHAPTER

4

THE STRANGER

Angela walked briskly down the street, a prey to indignation and annoyance. The man was impudent and impertinent. How dare he attempt to force her to take the wretched scarf! Even while these thoughts raced through her mind she knew Captain Huntley had done no such thing. Nor had he been impudent. But she had taken a dislike to him. She preferred to accuse him of impudence in order to justify her own behaviour.

"I don't like him," she said aloud, then glanced over her shoulder to see if anyone were near by. The Green was quite deserted. The activity was at the wharf, where a number of galleys and canoes and little sail-boats were preparing to put off. The planters and yeomen and their wives from across the Sound and up the Chowan River were going home. The vessels which had brought fowl, eggs, hogs and juniper shingles in the morning were departing laden with goods from Hewes and Smith's purchased by the women and plantation necessities which the men had traded for the products of their thrift.

Angela was not interested in the boats. She did not even glance at the *Two Sisters*, which had run the British blockade of the West Indies, not without danger, to bring in French taffetas and other goods. The girl ran up the Pollocks' steps, hoping that Ann had not gone up to Balgray for over the Sabbath. She wanted to talk with Ann. She wanted someone who would listen to her encounter with Captain Huntley and be sympathetic with her in her indignation. Angela had other reasons. Ann Pollock knew Anthony Allison. She alone knew their hopeless love for each other. It was through Ann she had first met Anthony, on the ship coming home after her two-year visit to her mother's people in Malaga. Her Aunt Josefa and Uncle Tomás had taken her in charge as far as Lisbon, to meet the ship on which Cullen and Ann Pollock were sailing, after a visit to England. She remembered with what poignancy of despair she had said farewell to her dear ones. They were going back to her beloved Spain. She would get aboard a foul sailing vessel and for three long months be buffeted by the winds and waves of the Western Ocean. She had not seen Anthony until they reached the Azores. From there to Nassau she had seen him and talked with him every day. Gordon Rutherford was with him. Gordie, now in the navy, was on leave to visit his father on the Cape Fear River. Gordie was a handsome fellow. If she had not first seen Anthony and been enamoured of him, she might have fallen in love with Gordie. But she hadn't.

Cullen Pollock had been seasick from the moment he set foot on the ship at Plymouth until they got off at Nassau. But Ann had thrived on sea air. Angela sometimes thought Ann quite forgot that she had a husband mooning down in the cabin. There were so many young naval officers, going out to join the West Indian Fleet; so many that she asked Gordie if there were ships enough to go around. He assured her that the West Indian Fleet was stronger than it had ever been, under Sir Peter Parker, its finest commander.

He himself would join it at Jamaica, after he had visited his father on the Cape Fear River.

"But why do you have so many ships?" Angela had persisted.

Gordie laid a finger on his lips. "Sh! Pretty little girls must not ask grown-up questions."

Angela thought of that incident again, as she had many times since the war began. It was easy to understand now why they wanted a great fleet in waters close to the rebelling colonies.

She hammered with the knocker. She thought she heard voices within and a stealthy footstep. But the door remained closed. She let the brass knocker fall again. This time the door opened. Ann herself answered it. The look of uneasiness faded from her face when she saw Angela.

"Angela, my dear! I did not know you were in town today." She stood aside. "Do come in." She shut the door. Without turning Angela thought she heard the bolt slide into place. She walked into the little sitting-room which looked on the Sound—a pleasant room that was much like Ann herself, with a little confusion but not to the extent of being untidy. Gay-flowered chintzes, brightly burning fire, mantelpiece, tables, and little glass cabinets filled with choice bits of china, pewter, bisque and Staffordshire figurines, snuff-boxes and fans picked up in one country and another in her travels.

"Sit down. Sit down." Ann drew a chair to the fire. "It is growing chilly since the wind came up." She sat down facing Angela. A plain woman of distinction, someone had said of Ann Pollock. Very natural, very warm, she had many friends in spite of her husband's known leaning on the Tory side.

These things passed through Angela's mind as she sat waiting for the opportunity to talk about her affairs. Ann was excessively talkative, asking about each member of the Ferrier family, even the children's governess.

"Is your mother spending the night with Penelope Barker?"

"No, she is going to the Charles Johnsons'. Parson Earle is visiting his daughter at Strawberry Hill. He is ill with a slight cold and he delights in my mother's company."

"Has the senator gone to attend the Assembly at New Bern?"

"Yes, but he will be home by the end of the week."

Ann was silent for a moment. She kept glancing toward the door. Angela said hurriedly, "Are you expecting someone? Do you want me to leave?"

"No, no. I was just going to ask you to stay with me. Cullen has gone over to Bertie, to open Balgray. I am going up in a day or two." She looked at Angela. "You will stay, won't you?"

"I don't know. The man has carried my satchel out to Strawberry Hill. I really should go. Mother is still at Madam Barker's. She expects me to come back. I . . ."

Ann got to her feet. "I'll send a slave over at once to tell her you are staying with me." She gave Angela no time to protest again, but left the room, closing the door behind her. Angela leaned back in her chair, her eyes half closed. The interruption in thought had caused anger to die down. She would not speak of Huntley. Why should she give the incident any importance? She heard Ann speaking outside the door. Angela did not understand what she was saying. A man's voice answered.

"I know she is here. I saw her cross the Green."

Ann's voice rose a little. "Do you think it is wise, Anthony?"

Anthony! Angela sat motionless, her heart pounding. Anthony! Her hands grasped the arms of the chair.

"Damn wisdom!" The door opened and Anthony Allison came into the room. Behind his tall figure she saw Ann's white face, her eyes frightened. He came across the room, moving swiftly. Without words he leaned forward; catching her hands in his, he raised Angela to her feet. They stood facing each other.

"I must know," he said. "I must know."

"Nothing can change me," she answered, knowing what he wanted to hear. "And you, Anthony?"

"You know there could never be anyone but you, my sweet." His hands went up her arms slowly, until they reached her shoulders. He stood looking down at her as though he could never take his eyes from her. Angela's lips moved; she thought she spoke aloud, but perhaps it was only that unheard voice which had repeated his name a thousand times in the long solitude of the nights.

"My name, so sweet on your lips." His hands dropped from her shoulders. She moved into his arms, to the long pressure of his lips on her mouth.

Ann came into the room and closed the door. She spoke quietly but Angela felt alarm and fear in her voice: "Now you have discovered yourself to Angela, what must we do?"

"Do?" Anthony slowly turned, as he released Angela from his embrace, but his arm kept her at his side. "Do?"

"Yes. What shall we do?"

Anthony looked at Angela, smiling. His lips still turned upward at the corners, she thought. She had not, in the surprise of the moment, realized the significance of Ann's question, "What shall we do?" It came over her like a great onrushing wave. She noticed for the first time that he did not wear uniform. He was soberly dressed, as a travelling merchant would dress, or a barrister or a doctor.

"Anthony," she cried in alarm, "you are in danger. Every moment in danger."

He lifted her hand to his cheek, brushing it against his eyes, then to his lips. "You must not be worried, Angela. You must remember one thing: I am not your Anthony. I am Jeremiah Morse of Boston. I am travelling south to buy food for the Grand Army. I am——"

She pulled herself away, her hand across her lips, her eyes questioning. "You are——" He stopped her words with his lips.

"Do not speak a word that we do not want to hear. Spoken words go on the air, they disintegrate, they move from one mind to another. We will not think the word, my sweet angel."

Ann said, "I hope you are not taking too great a chance."

"What chance could I be taking? No one in this part of America has ever seen or heard of me, no one but two women, both loyal——"

Angela's eyes flashed. "But I am not a Tory."

Anthony paid no attention to her words. "—loyal to me," he finished.

"Since you have allowed Angela to know you are here," Ann said, "she may as well know a little more. Anthony is going on the stage to Bertie Courthouse. Cullen will meet him there tomorrow. I go up from here the following day. From there he will continue on his journey. Where and when I do not know and do not want to know," she finished decisively. "It is a secret that we must keep inviolate, Angela darling." She looked anxiously at the now frightened girl.

"Inviolate." Angela's voice trembled. "I know."

The gentle pressure of Anthony's arm about her waist was comforting.

He led her to a chair and sat down beside her, holding her hands; there was assurance in the firm clasp and in his blue eyes that looked into hers. His face was very serious. She could not remember ever having seen the lines that were etched from nose to mouth, deep lines, or his eyes so tired. He has suffered, she thought.

"I do not ask anything of you, my Angela, only don't give up loving me. This cannot go on for long, this fighting. The sooner it comes to an end the better it will be for England and for you in the Provinces. It is unnatural and horrible. Civil war is always tragic. It causes a man to do things that he does not choose to do, but must, in honour. Do you understand, sweet Angela?"

She nodded her head without speaking. Two tears forced their way from her eyes and rolled down her cheeks. She did not know why she shed tears. They clouded her eyes, causing his image to be misty and dim. Now that he was before her she wanted to see him clearly, to impress his features into her mind and heart. She brushed her hand across her face.

"Don't weep. Let me take another image away with me—your smile, which has always held me captive." Her heart pounded in her breast. It was as always. How often before had they thought the same things, one speaking the words the other thought.

The little French clock on the mantel gave forth a small tinkling chime. Five o'clock.

Ann went to the window and stood looking across the Green toward the Courthouse. "The coach has just come in from Hertford. They change horses, then go on to Bertie. It will not take longer than fifteen minutes."

Anthony got to his feet. Angela stood up, her dark eyes enormous in her white face. "I cannot let you go. I cannot endure the long weary days without your love."

"Forget your anxiety. You have all my love, always remember that," he said in a low voice.

"Go with God," she whispered brokenly.

Ann Pollock interrupted: "You must go, Anthony." She opened the door, caught up his cloak from the hall seat, thrust it into his hand. "Do not cross the Green. Go through the garden gate to the side entrance of O'Malley's ordinary. You will meet fewer people that way."

Anthony did not kiss Angela again. He stood for a moment looking at her face, his firm hands holding hers closely. Then he dropped her hands and turned quickly. A moment later the door closed.

Angela and Ann Pollock looked at each other. Ann spoke first. "I cannot conceive why he is so foolhardy. Do you suppose he has come all the way from Howe's headquarters? Such danger! Such adventure! Through the American lines around Philadelphia!" Ann spoke dramatically. Angela with her vivid imagination could see Anthony moving stealthily by night, or boldly.

"Where is he going? Why does he do these hazardous things?"

"To get to Ferguson's Legion. To gain information. I begged him not to go through New Bern or Wilmington. If he can reach Cross Creek he has a better chance."

"A spy . . ."

"Angela, don't. Didn't he tell you not to say the word aloud?"

Angela's gaze travelled over the Sound. Daylight was fading. The familiar forms of cypress trees on the shore, the boats in the little bay, the piled-up naval stores on the wharf, became a mass of shadow that accentuated the last glimmer of afterglow on the waters of the Sound. The Tyrrell shore was heavy with night shadows, the uneven line of turpentine pines lost in the gloom.

"I am not English. I am of Spanish blood," Angela said suddenly. "I am not concerned with the right or wrong of a war of brothers against brothers. I think it is horrible, but to be a spy is horrible. It is degrading to deceive, to pretend to be something one is not."

"You speak like a child. There are always spies, or secret agents, on both sides. Some people have another word. They say hero when you say spy. I can't think what ails you." Ann spoke sharply.

Angela did not heed. "But I love him. I love him," she said brokenly. "Oh, Ann, I love him."

Ann put her arms around the girl. "There, there, my dear, I knew he was wrong to see you. I implored him not to."

Angela pulled away. Her eyes flashed. "How dare you? You say you are my friend. The only one who has been my confidante."

Ann spoke patiently. "I am Anthony's friend also. It is he, not you, who faces danger. The fewer who know the secret the better."

"You think I am not fit to share his secret, his danger?" Angela moved to the door. "I am going," she said. "You are abominable."

"No! You are not going. Sit down and concern yourself with reality for once. The question is as to your discretion. But we don't discuss that. We can only pray that he gets through to the British lines."

Her plain speech made Angela wince. "Oh, Ann, forgive me. I am tortured by his danger. They hang . . ."

"Be quiet! I told you this is not your concern. It is Anthony's. Let him carry the burden. He has met danger before." Her tone was contemptuous. "Anthony is no weakling. Have done with nonsense. There is nothing you can do about it. If I were in your place, I'd go down on my knees and thank God that I had a strong man to love me."

Angela's eyes filled with tears which she brushed away angrily. "You are right, Ann. I am the weak one. I am not worthy of his love."

"And don't begin to feel sorry for yourself, either. I don't understand you Spaniards, up to the mountain-tops one moment, down to the depths of the ocean the next."

"We are born so, Ann; we can't be different."

"When you have had to bear real sorrow you will know the difference."

Ann's words bore in on Angela. She didn't understand but she knew Ann had some hidden grief that the world didn't know, nor would know from her.

"Come, let's go for a walk along the creek. I love to walk beside the water in the twilight."

Angela followed her into the hall. Ann threw a red cape about her shoulders and held out Angela's cloak. She called to a houseman to follow them with a lanthorn. "We will stop at Bauhman's and see if they have any salads. Their garden is always two weeks ahead of ours. I would like some greens for supper; would you?"

Angela choked. Ann could think of eating salad greens! As for herself, she felt that she could never eat again, not until the horrible weight was lifted from her heart.

A watchman was walking up and down the wharf where the hogsheads of pork were stored waiting for the little schooners to take the cargo to the Islands, or run the blockade of the Chesapeake. They walked slowly. The breeze was soft and inviting and bore the promise of spring. As they neared Queen Anne's Creek they saw the lights of the campfires beyond the Rope Walk and heard the shouts and laughter of the soldiers.

Two horsemen were silhouetted against the water, leisurely trotting toward them. They drew up. A man's voice called out gaily, "Good evening, ladies. Are you not timid in the dark, or are you looking for company?"

Ann spoke. "We are not timid, nor do we wish company."

The second man spoke sharply. "Have done, Mills. Can't you see these ladies do not want to speak with soldiers?" To Ann he said, "You will pardon my companion. He is a rough uncouth soldier."

Ann laughed. "Captain de' Medici, I know your voice. I heard you giving orders to your men when you marched around the Green. I am Mrs. Pollock, and this is my friend Miss Ferrier." The horsemen dismounted and came closer.

"I am sorry," the young ensign said. "I thought . . ."

"Only ladies from the lower wharf would walk out alone? We are not alone; we have Primus there to protect us. I do assure you he carries a long knife which he uses expertly." There was laughter in her voice. Young Mills stumbled an apology.

"Don't be disturbed," Ann said kindly. "On second thought, we *are* timid and we *would* like company. If you care to walk back to my house on the Green, we will be delighted."

They walked along through the soft twilight. Cosmo fell in step with Angela. "We missed seeing you at Madam Barker's. The *señora*, your mother, told us you would be in presently. We were desolated when you did not return."

"I wanted to visit Ann, Mrs. Pollock," she said.

"The gods are very good to me now," he went on. "I have said to myself, 'Surely Miss Ferrier will hold no ill feeling because of an unfortunate——' "

Angela interrupted. She did not want any discussion of the episode. "Indeed not. Please do not mention it."

Cosmo's voice lowered to a confidential key. "My friend Peter is the best fellow in the world. But where women are concerned—ah——" His tone indicated that Peter Huntley thought little of the feminine sex.

"Ah, Captain Huntley is a woman-hater?" Angela felt her face burning.

"Well, I would not go so far, but his mind is on other things. If you care to know——"

"I am not interested in Captain Huntley," Angela replied.

"Permit me." Cosmo put his hand under her elbow to assist her across a puddle. "Let us not waste a moment on Peter," he said. Angela thought there was laughter in his voice, but she could not be sure.

They had reached the gate. Cosmo said, "Mills, my good boy, please lead my horse to Horniblow's, will you? I think if Madam Pollock will permit me, I will make a little call on these charming ladies."

"Pray do come in," Ann said.

They went into the little sitting-room. The candles had been lighted, the fire burned cheerily, a tray with decanter and glasses was on a small table.

"Please sit down," Ann said. "I will be back in a moment, then we will have a glass of Madeira." She left the room. Cosmo looked at Angela across the table. He leaned forward, his dark eyes regarding her.

"We must be friendly," he said at once. "I like you. I feel *simpatico*, just as with the *señora*, your mother. With her I am a friend almost before speaking together. Yes, we are *simpatici*."

"My mother speaks Italian," Angela said, a little pride in her voice.

"Do I not know? Already she calls me Cosimo." He laughed engagingly, showing very white teeth. "But we would be *simpatici* even without language."

"I understand a little Italian," she suggested.

"Ah, that is good, very good. How often do I say to my friend Peter, 'English is no language for making love.' "

A little glow went over Angela. How charming he was, this dark captain. One would not believe in him too much but . . .

Ann came into the room followed by a Negro carrying another decanter. She found De' Medici and Angela laughing.

"It is my Italian. The captain finds it very amusing," Angela explained.

"Amusing? No, no. Delicious." Cosmo hastened to Ann. He took the glass decanter from her. "This is too heavy for such small, lovely hands," he said. He poured the wine into the clear glasses. He lifted his glass to Ann, then to Angela. Bowing with easy grace, he said, "To friendship, the most fine of all the arts, and the most seldom experienced!"

In return they raised their glasses, smiled at his delightful accent and his irresistible friendliness.

Ann said, "I am sure you have many friends, Captain de' Medici."

Cosmo shook his head sadly. "No, no. Only a few have the grace to be a friend. It takes loyalty and understanding and, most important, it is unpossessive. You smile," he said to Angela. "It is because I express myself so badly in your language."

"No, Captain. I am not smiling at you. If I smiled it was because I agree with you so thoroughly."

"Ah! That is better. We are *simpatici*." He turned to Ann. "She must be so. She is so like the *señora*." He lifted his glass again. "I would like to drink a toast to that fine lady, the Señora Ferrier, your mother."

"You are sweet," Angela said impulsively.

Ann looked at her, smiling a little. Something in her glance made Angela remember Anthony. Only a short time ago she had had nothing in her heart but heaviness. Now she was laughing, not remembering Anthony and the danger that surrounded him. She must be a light person. But Ann had herself said to think of something else. Well, so she would. She turned a smiling face to De' Medici. "I thank you for that thought of my mother, Captain. She is wonderful, so wonderful that I sometimes ask myself how I can be her child." She added, "Perhaps I am more like my father."

"I have not had the good pleasure to meet Senator Ferrier, although I possess a letter to him from Mr. Wylie Jones."

"Mr. Ferrier is my stepfather," Angela said. De' Medici's expressive eyes turned from one to the other. "My name is Angela Gonsalvo." The words sounded abrupt, even harsh to her own ears, but she could not bring herself to say more.

Ann bridged the gap. "Sometime you must ask Madam to tell you about the shipwreck, when she and little Angela were cast up on the Outer Banks, but not now, for I want to talk with you about your camp and the enlistments. I read the notice on the Courthouse door that you want enlistments."

Angela settled back, grateful to Ann. Somehow she couldn't bear to think of the shipwreck. Even after all these years, she still wakened in the night with the weight of the heavy moving waves forcing her down into the cold sea.

"You read the notice?" Cosmo spoke with surprise in his voice, his mobile face alight. "Now that is splendid. When the constable, he say, 'Put the notice on the Courthouse door,' I doubted that anybody would read it."

Ann smiled. "We always read notices that are posted on the Courthouse door. We are a tiny village, and it is a part of our excitement. New Bern has a printed paper of its own, where one can read war news and obituaries and births and marriages." She leaned forward, her eyes twinkling. "Do you know how we announce deaths in Queen Anne's Town?"

Cosmo shook his head, but he was interested.

"My man Primus, whom you saw tonight guarding two venturesome females taking their evening stroll, puts on a black coat and black breeks and buckled shoes. He has a full-bottomed wig which belonged to my husband's father, Squire Thomas Pollock, and a black cocked hat. He walks from door to door, knocks and holds out a silver tray, on which is a scroll with the announcement of death, penned in heavy black ink. The person at the door reads the death notice and Primus goes on to the next house, until every home in the village is visited."

De' Medici gave Ann the closest attention, nodding his head from time to time.

"Are we not quaint?" she asked when she had completed the story.

De' Medici did not smile. "I think it is a very touching and sweet custom, madam," he said. "Very personal, almost as though the person who was so late in death had made a call on a friend. But why, may I ask, is your servant Primus the one to be called to so dignified and important a task?"

Ann did not know. He had always, in her time, been the one who announced the passing of a resident of the village. "Perhaps it is because he is old and dignified."

"Not too old to carry a sharp knife," De' Medici said quickly.

Ann laughed. "I think it is because he is the only Negro who has a full-bottomed wig."

De' Medici put his glass on the tray. "This has been delightful."
He raised Ann's hand to his lips. "Thank you for the little story.
These things reveal much of a people. Such a kind way. There is
something Biblical, yes?"

"What do you mean?" Ann questioned.

" 'The messenger of death came.' I do not make a quotation correctly."

Ann was thoughtful. "It is one of those old customs which we
accept without question, but I cannot think of anything more appropriate. Primus is a godly man, deeply religious. I must tell him what
you have said. It will fill him with happiness."

De' Medici said to Angela, "I will do myself the honour to call on
Senator Ferrier, as soon as he returns."

"We expect him the end of the week," she answered. "Then we
will go up the river to the plantation."

With a bow the captain left them.

Ann said, "A delightful gentleman, my dear. Such distinction."

Angela thought the room had lost some of its brightness, but she
did not put her thought into words.

A bell rang. "Good heavens! The dressing-bell. Come, let us make
haste. I'll lend you my apricot. It's getting tight about my waist, but
it will fit you." Ann put her arm around Angela as they walked up
the stair to make ready for supper.

CHAPTER

5

EDEN HOUSE

THE galley landed at Eden House pier, a wooden structure which extended out from a high bank into the placid river.

After the boat left the Sound and entered the river the wind died down and the oarsmen took their places. The Chowan River flowed broad and deep between swamps, lined with cypress trees tangled with vines of grape and trumpet, honeysuckle and a waxy green bamboo. On the opposite shore the bank rose to a height of twenty feet or more, with heavy dark forest of pine and hardwoods.

Peter Huntley was the only passenger when he boarded Madam Dawson's boat at Hewes's Wharf, promptly at three o'clock. The steersman was a black man dressed in tunic and breeks of dull red woollen. He touched his forehead when Peter stepped aboard. The rowers sat with oars aloft, waiting. They saluted smartly and the oars rattled into place. The man at the tiller gave an order and two rowers hoisted a square sail. After they had cleared the small bay and made into the Sound, a lively breeze filled the canvas and the helmsman set his course for Avoca Point on the opposite shore.

At this season Albemarle Sound was tawny from the inrush of freshet waters of the Roanoke. The south bank was heavily wooded, primitive, filled with solitude. The scene filled the eyes with its rare beauty and the soul with its peace. Yet the forest held danger and the stealthy savagery of wild animals. The wilder savages, the Indians, had receded, and the forest gave way before the sharp biting blade of broad-axe and the persistent edge of the heavy cross-cut saw.

Peter's eyes followed these encroachments into the forest, the outline of fields, the smoke rising from unseen chimneys. The Negro pointed: Duckenfield, where Madam Pearson lived, the mother of Sir Nat; Balgray, the Pollock family baronial holdings; then from the point back along Salmon Creek, Rutledge Riding.

The familiar name caught Peter's attention. "Mr. Adam Rutledge?"

"Yes, *sar*. Mr. Adam. Yes, sar."

"Is he at his plantation?"

"No, sar. Mr. Adam he is fightin' a wah for those folks up North."

Peter smiled. He had met Major Rutledge at headquarters camp at Valley Forge. That was shortly after he had returned from Paris the first time. He remembered Adam Rutledge with pleasure, a fine upstanding soldierly officer. So this was his place!

"Can you see the house from the water?"

"Yes, sar. No, sar. That is, yo' could befo' they had the fah."

"Ah. So there was a fire."

"Yes, sar." He swung the boat out of the path of a floating log. "We done had a fah too, at Eden House. Ours was a bigger fah. One whole wing was burned." After a moment he added, "That was a long time ago, when the old Governor died, and Mis' Penelope was a small girl. Yes, sar, mighty big fah, bigger than Mr. Rutledge's fah."

Peter smiled at the old man's loyalties; even a fire at Eden House was bigger than the neighbor's. "When will we see Eden House?" he asked after a time.

"Presently, after we come in the Chowan, sar."

Half a dozen slaves were lounging about the small landing. They all ran forward with willing hands, boys stumbling over one another in their eagerness to catch the lines and free-board, to pull the galley alongside the dock. The sun still lay in full strength on the river but the landing was in shadow, the quiet still river reflecting the green of the vines and bushes that covered the high bank. The blossoms of the dogwood trees made waxen stars in the dense green of trailing vines and evergreen behind bare limbs of the bushes. In the distance the sound of voices and laughter came pleasingly to his ears. A fish broke the water, leaped high, dropped in an arc of shining beauty back into the quiet water.

"Shad frog, he croak las' night," Peter's informant told him. "Croak lak he bound to bust he throat."

Peter looked perplexed.

"Shad frog holler. Shad fish come along mighty short time, sar. That's way we know. Then after shad, the herring he run. River full, so full you can see them jus' below water." He extended his arm, pointing across the river. "Look yonder. See men, dey set the net stakes over there. Herring bound to come dis way soon."

Shad and herring! Peter was a fisherman. He had the fisherman's itch to "wet a line" in the river. He wondered whether shad would rise to line bait, now when the smaller fish lay in the river.

He stepped ashore. A Negro boy dressed in neat house livery, wearing a sober dark-blue coat with crested brass buttons and tan breeks, picked up Peter's saddle-bags. "This way, sar. Madam Dawson she say come right into her sitting-room where she having her tea."

Peter climbed the steps. The hand-rail made of saplings was rickety and tumbling down. The steps cut into the earth, with sapling treads, were easy and in good order.

Eden House was a rambling low house with dormers and a gambrel roof, a long central block and one wing. The fire had evidently consumed the west wing years since and it had never been rebuilt. An attractive house with heavy wide chimneys, laid in Flemish bond with narrow Dutch brick. Vines covered one corner; an ivy of some sort and two rose vines with young green leaves framed the front stoop. On either side to the rear were the farm buildings in little groups, smoke-house, milkhouse and stables.

Peter thought the place had more of an air of comfort than elegance. This thought persisted as he entered the house. A wide hall had a fireplace directly in front of the door. The wide boards of the floor had a mellow worn look. The side-tables were covered with hats and gloves. A pair of freshly varnished riding boots were against the stair rail. A brace of hunting dogs lay in front of the fire. They rose lazily as Peter entered, and walked toward him, nosing his hands in friendly welcome. The boy disappeared upstairs with his bag.

"Come in here, Captain Huntley."

Peter followed his hostess' voice, went into a small room off the hall. This room too had a crackling fire. Madam Dawson sat at a round tea-table pouring a cup of tea for one of her four guests. She passed the cup to a tall serious-looking man who was standing near the table, and extended her hand. Peter raised it to his lips and bowed to each of them as Madam Dawson mentioned their names: Mr. and Madam Pearson, of Duckenfield, a near-by plantation, and Judge Charlton and his wife. The Charltons' place, Canahoe, was on the Roanoke River.

"Bring up a chair, Captain Huntley," Madam said, handing him his cup. "Today, in honour of your first visit to Eden House, I have drawn on my reserve of China tea." She smiled at him. Peter felt at once important and welcome. He replied appropriately.

Madam Pearson, a stout, florid person, said: "Madam Dawson has been telling us that you are from Scotland. My first husband, Mr. Duckenfield, was a Scot. My son, Sir Nathaniel, is in the Queen's Seventh Regiment of Dragoons, or was before this Rebellion. He was stationed at Edinburgh. He resigned at once. Nat could never take up arms against the Carolinians, whom he loves."

Mr. Pearson said nothing. He was a sombre man with a pinched look about his mouth and nose. He looked dyspeptic. Peter wondered if his wife's loquaciousness had anything to do with it. She dominated the conversation, rambling on about her darling son.

"Nat has so many friends here; Jemmy Iredell was his intimate. It was really too bad when Hannah chose Jemmy instead of Nat. I felt it at the time. I really felt it. I told Hannah it would have been much better for her to accept a title and the wealth and prestige that goes with it than to take Jemmy Iredell who everyone knows is as poor as poverty. Even if Jemmy's relative is Earl Macartney, he'll never inherit that title, never."

"We don't hold with titles, you know, Madam Pearson," Penelope Dawson's voice cut in. "We're all very equal and free now. Isn't that what this Rebellion is about, Judge?"

The judge's bushy eyebrows did not conceal the twinkle that was in his dark eyes. "Presumably, madam. Presumably," he said.

Madam Pearson interrupted: "Nonsense, Penelope! Everyone who has any sense knows that titles will never lose their attraction. Why, Joseph Hewes told me himself that everyone in Philadelphia speaks of the General's wife as Lady Washington. If we win this war, they will make George Washington a king." She paused and looked from one face to another. "Why, how can we live and be governed properly without a king?"

Lawyer Pearson uttered his first words. "I think it is time to be leaving. I want to get home before nightfall; the paths are miry."

"Must you?" murmured Madam Dawson.

Madam Pearson got up obediently. "I am afraid we must. Do bring your charming young guest over to Duckenfield, my dear. I do so want to hear the latest news from Scotland."

Peter bent over her hand.

"But I hear from Nat," she told him as she buttoned her riding apron over her skirt. "He sends letters from Ireland or by some French ship captains whom he knows. He goes so often to Paris. Have you ever been in Paris, Captain?"

"Yes, madam."

"How nice! It does give a young man an air to have had a Grand Tour. We sent Nat to Europe for the Grand Tour." She was still talking about Nat when they reached the carriage block. She mounted her horse with ease. "Please straighten my spatter apron, Captain. That is it, that little button near the bottom. Thank you so much. Do come to Duckenfield Hall. Mr. Pearson and I love to have guests." She leaned down. "It is a pleasure to meet someone who has lived abroad. I do miss London."

"Come, my dear. Good day, sir." The patient Mr. Pearson put heel to his horse and trotted down the drive, his wife following. To Peter's surprise she sat easily in the saddle. A whistle escaped him.

"Quite a conversationalist!" Judge Charlton had followed them out and stood near the mounting-block. "A good woman. None better, and so kind. Her whole life is bound up in her son, as you see."

"And Sir Nat?" Peter's eyes twinkled.

"A fine fellow. 'Pon my word, he is. He dashed off to England when Miss Hannah Johnston, Sam's sister, chose my friend Judge Iredell, and the war caught him. I've no doubt he would really like to be on this side of the water."

They walked back into the house. Madam Charlton was standing, taking leave of Penelope. "We are going to New Bern next week. Spring court, you know. I do hope the river goes down. It has been really impassable this week. Bell's ferry had to leave off running."

Penelope said, "I hope all the rivers aren't out of banks. I'm expecting Samuel tonight. Have you heard, Judge?"

"I think the Cashie is passable. Tell Sam I want to see him. How long will he be here?"

"Over Sunday, I hope. But you know how he is. Impatient to be home at Hayes."

"I thought his family was at the Hermitage for a month."

"So they are. But Samuel has meetings the first of the week. Dr. Williamson is in Queen Anne's Town from the Dismal Swamp camp, and Will Hooper is expected next week."

"Ah, politics!"

"Ah, yes. War and politics go hand in hand. Sometimes I wish Samuel were a soldier instead."

Peter stood by the fire after the guests had made their adieus. Madam Dawson walked to the hall with them. Peter heard her say:

"He has introductions to Samuel. I really know nothing, but I liked him at once. Better in fact than the spectacular Captain de' Medici, though I must say *he* has extraordinary charm."

Peter smiled to himself. The words were agreeable enough to his ears. It wasn't often that a charming woman compared him with the dashing Cosmo to his advantage. He was still smiling when Penelope Dawson came into the room. She laughed.

"You listened! It would have served you right if you had heard something disagreeable instead of——"

"Something very heart-warming and pleasant." He bowed gallantly, with just enough exaggeration to suggest Cosmo.

She said, "Well, it's true enough, Scot speaking to Scot." She pulled a bell cord. When the slave came she told him to show Captain Huntley to his room. "You have an hour to rest and change. We sup early in the country." She spoke again as he neared the door. "Tonight I shall expect you to tell me everything about yourself, your family and all your exciting life."

Huntley grinned. "Not so exciting, madam. Dull, I'm afraid."

"Nonsense. I count on you to make it entertaining, whether it is or not." She added brightly, "And perhaps before we finish supper we will have Samuel here with us."

"And then I'll have to repeat the story."

"No. Not the one you tell me, my dear boy. Samuel will want the real story, annotated and with references."

Peter said, "I'll try to make yours as enlightening as though it were written for the *Gentleman's Magazine*."

Penelope made a small *moue* with her red lips. "Not the *Gentleman's* style, I pray. More like *Tristram Shandy* or *Sir Charles Grandison*."

Peter walked up the steep stairs followed by the boy. She is delightful, he thought. I shall really enjoy this visit.

The Negro showed him into a bedroom gay with bright chintzes and frilled curtains. The ample dormers faced the same way as the front of the house, to the sweep of the Chowan, its banks now in shadow, its slow-moving channel centering the long, slanting sun rays. Small birds were twittering in the bare branches of a gum tree outside his window. A fire burned in the little corner grate. The tester bed was plump and high with its feathers, under the shiny chintz counterpane. He longed to test its soft inviting warmth but he knew that would be fatal. He would never awaken in time for supper. The Negro boy put a log on the fire. He threw open the door of a walnut press. "I done rubbed you' coat with the press iron, and you' cravat. Mis' Pene she lak to dress mighty fine for she supper. I bring the hot water. Want I shave you, sar? And roll you' hair? I always roll Master Johnston's hair when he come."

"Right, you may shave me and roll my hair."

"Yes, sar. Sit right there by the window, sar. Mayhap you see the herons flying and fish breakin'."

Peter sank into the comfortable chair. Six weeks travelling with the dragoons made him appreciate this luxury.

"Scipio my name, sar."

"Well, Scipio, give me a close shave and two rolls over my ears and fasten the club tight. I can't abide hair that strays out of the case."

"Yes, sar. I do dat."

Peter nodded in the chair. Scipio applied hot towels, scrubbed and scraped and pomaded. It was so easy to sleep. He woke to Scipio's softly spoken words: "If you please to wake up, I will give you good bathing, sar."

Peter sat up and rubbed his eyes. While he dozed, the Negro had brought a tub into the room, filled with warm water. A tall pewter ewer with steam arising stood on the floor beside the tub which had been placed on a white shag rug.

"Bath, sar? Present you' back while I scrub with fine brush."

Peter hesitated a moment only. Such luxury! A man to bathe and shave him and dress his hair. He noticed a decanter on the candle stand. Scipio followed his glance. "Yes, sar. Madam say gentlemans take they drink when they bathe. Yes, sar, soon as I scrub good, I bring drink."

Peter laughed. It reminded him of his childhood, his nurse saying if he were a good boy and didn't splash the floor, he could have a nice cup of chocolate. When Scipio handed him the glass he almost choked. Tears came to his eyes as the fiery liquid trickled down.

"Mostly it does that if gentleman don't know the way. We drink so." He tilted the empty glass, his head back, swallowed quickly. "Lak that. Quick so he don't touch much tongue on the way. Next time you know how, sar."

Peter, still breathless, nodded. He had never swallowed such raw stuff in all his days. He made a mental resolution that if he did have to drink it, he would toss it far back and swallow quickly, if he wanted to save his tongue.

He heard voices, and horses neighing. Scipio looked out the window. "Here come Master Samuel and another gentleman. Excuse me if I leave, sar. I must shave and roll him and Master Sam. He lak powder, too." He left the room in haste. Peter heard him shouting in the hall: "Zango, you, get in Captain's room and carry away that wash-water. Jump you now. Master Sam will want he bath. Scrub out dat tub good, you."

Zango jumped. He all but fell into the room. A tall, gangling, half-grown boy, he splashed water and banged tub and ewer and made a great clatter. "Dressing-bell, he ring one-half the hour before supper-bell." He came back to say, "Scipio say first come dressing-bell. When supper-bell ring, Madam she wait in hall, by fah." He fell over himself getting out, shut the door with a bang, opened it, closed it very quietly and went away.

Peter sat down in the chair by the window and laughed.

The dressing-bell had rung some time since; Peter, his thoughts busy with the coming meeting with Samuel Johnston, did not notice the passing time until he heard the second gong.

He stuck a twist of paper into the blaze and lighted two candles that flanked the tilted shaving glass on the chest. He touched the rolls of hair over his ears, straightened his shoulders so that the coat of his uniform sat squarely. He was glad that he had followed De' Medici's advice and had brought a second coat. It looked well, the blue with buff facings. He had discarded his boots for buckled shoes and silk stockings. The soft leather of his breeches fitted snugly over his strong thighs. The finish was as soft as chamois skin and almost the colour. Peter was not a vain man or a popinjay. He knew that he had none of the masculine beauty of De' Medici or of Gordon Rutherford. As Rutherford came to his mind, he thought instantly of the muffled face of the man in the coach. Had he, the stranger, seen and recognized him? He wondered. Peter was not unknown. For three years he had been with the Minister, both in London before the war, when he was Provincial Agent, in Paris later. Men's voices and steps passing his door brought him sharply back to the present. He opened his door, then went back to snuff the candles. He was disappointed that there was another guest, but he counted on an opportunity to speak with Mr. Johnston alone.

Two men stood in the hall in front of the fire when Peter came down the stairs. He had a moment before they were aware of his presence. One tall, one of medium height with his back turned. The first was in profile—a strong face, serious. He wore a dark-blue coat, the waistcoat was a variegated brocade, and the cravat and sleeve had ruffles of fine Mechlin. He turned as Peter approached, and smiled. Peter thought, He is a calm man but not cold. He extended a welcoming hand. It was Samuel Johnston.

"Ah, Captain Huntley. It is good of you to come up the river." His handshake was firm, friendly. Peter replied that it was a pleasure to make the journey to Eden House.

"Allow me to present you to my dear friend William Hooper." Johnston turned to the other man.

Peter's candid face broke into a smile. "Mr. Hooper. This is an unexpected pleasure. I missed seeing you at Hillsborough, but had hopes of finding you at New Bern."

William Hooper smiled slightly and bowed. Peter hastened to explain: "I have a letter, sir, from Mr. Wylie Jones of Halifax, as well as one from Mr. Joseph Hewes."

The smile deepened about Hooper's rather full lips and his dark fine eyes lighted. "No better introduction could be asked," he said. His voice was deep and resonant but it did not have the smooth pleasant quality that marked Samuel Johnston's speech. William Hooper, the Signer, although a representative of North Carolina at the draughting of the Declaration of Independence, was Northern-born, schooled at Harvard University.

Johnston indicated a chair and sat down. The others followed. He said, "My cousin tells me that you have letters for me also."

"I have, sir," Peter answered. "Shall I fetch them now?"

Johnston waved his hand. "No. No. There is plenty of time after supper." Peter did not say from whom his introductions were. He did not want to announce even before so well established a man as William Hooper that the letter to Johnston was from the Secret Committee of Foreign Affairs. That would at once place him.

Instead he said to Hooper, "Mr. Hewes's letter, which unfortunately I left in my case at Horniblow's, will tell you that I am checking on the lottery tickets for Colonel Pierce."

That was the story the committee and the minister had decided Peter was to tell. It would give him a legitimate reason to be travelling from the North to the South, consulting with various leaders of the Whig party, without arousing too much speculation. As an officer of the Continental Line, on detached or special assignment, he was in a position to investigate without being conspicuous.

"Hewes and Smith are agents for the tickets here, are they not?" Johnston asked.

"Yes, sir. I have already spoken to Mr. Smith. The sale is going very well here, very well indeed."

Hooper said thoughtfully, "It seems a pity that the army is forced to put on a general lottery to raise funds. What does General Washington say?"

Peter hesitated. Johnston answered for him. "The General has to shut his eyes to a great many things, no doubt."

Madam Dawson came into the room. She was beautifully dressed in blue, turned over a dark red petticoat, her chestnut hair piled high and powdered.

She greeted William Hooper with warmth. He kissed her cheek lightly and stood holding both her hands.

"I do declare you grow lovelier each day, Pene. I believe Queen Anne's Town women are the loveliest, the most charming women in the Province."

Penelope tossed her head. "Please do not place me in Queen Anne's Town, Mr. Hooper. We Bertie County women think we are just as alluring as the village women."

Sam Johnston laughed. "You said the wrong thing there, Will. You know the county people are proud. They hold themselves superior to us poor villagers."

Penelope put her hand lightly on Hooper's arm. "I'll forgive you this once, Will." She moved off toward the dining-room. Johnston and Huntley followed.

Johnston lowered his voice. "I had a letter from Mr. Lovell, of the Foreign Affairs Committee. He told me you would be here shortly after his letter. It is wise for you to be concerned with the lottery affairs. It is a legitimate excuse to arrange meeting the men you need to see."

"Did Mr. Lovell give you details?" Peter asked.

"No. He said you would supplement his information. By the way," he added, "if you like you can speak freely before Hooper. He is quite cognizant of the minister's wishes in the matter."

"Splendid," Peter said with satisfaction. "Whenever you can spare the time."

They entered the dining-room. Penelope indicated seats: Will Hooper on one side, Peter on the other, her cousin opposite. "You will play host, Samuel." She turned to Peter. "Sam is a famous host.

His household at Hayes is more than generous in its hospitality. His wife and his charming sisters are rare hostesses, I do assure you."

"I agree," Hooper said. "Many a fine ball we have attended, dancing with your sisters and their friends. By the way, has Madam Iredell quite recovered from her illness?"

"Yes, quite. The sisters are, at the moment, all at the Hermitage. A little change and rest for them."

Penelope said to Peter: "Do you have a recruiting mission with Captain de' Medici?"

"No, madam. I joined the Captain at Hillsborough, when he said he was riding this way. I met him at a ball—very merry it was."

Johnston said: "No doubt. Our good people of Hillsborough have a real love of entertaining. In the old days when it was the summer capital of the Royal Governors it was indeed gay, very gay."

"It is not far behind when our Assembly or the Provincial Council meets there now, or when there is a wedding." Will Hooper smiled at some remembrance.

Madam Dawson leaned back. The house servants moved about, serving the well-cooked plantation food. The crackling fire on the hearth gave warmth. The wine was excellent. Peter felt the strangeness of an outsider melt away. It seemed as if he must have been on this spot before, a part of the pleasant easy life of the early day of which they were talking. But Penelope had not completed her interrogation. She turned her large eyes on him. He saw in their depths a curious intensity and insistence.

"You are only passing through? You are not staying on in the village?"

"For a short time only, madam."

"Captain Huntley is concerned with the lottery. He represents the Paymaster-General, Colonel Pierce," Sam Johnston answered.

"Oh! How very interesting! When will they have the drawing?" Penelope asked. "It is really such a tremendous prize."

Peter laughed. "I'm afraid you will think me a dullard, Madam Dawson. I can't answer your questions. I only check lottery tickets sold, and tickets left on hand."

Her curiosity died instantly. "Ah," she said, giving him an inscrutable smile, "an accountant."

The men sat at table drinking their port after Madam Dawson left the dining-room with the admonition not to linger too long. The talk was of the conduct of the war and the prospect of peace.

Hooper, who had lately come from the North, felt the prospects of an early peace were menacing, because of the opposition to the commander-in-chief through the Conway and Lee factions.

Johnston smoked his pipe, asking a question now and then. Peter sat quietly, listening. As the two men talked, the situation in the Southern colonies became clearer to him. He was glad to know something of the Whig leaders because the opening of the Southern campaign would change the whole complexion of the war. The settled axiom of the Revolution, in the South, was that the government was instituted for the good of the people, and that when it no longer answered this end and they were in danger of slavery or a great oppression, they had a right to change it. Hooper said, "That was part of Iredell's charge to the Grand Jury at the spring court at New Bern. He maintained that such must ever be the government of this country, to keep the hearty support of the people."

Johnston quoted Iredell again—the first principles of liberty which are the common right of all mankind, and the sacred ties of honour, which even the worst people cannot violate without infamy; we must guard our liberties with care. The trial by jury must be deemed one of the principal.

Hooper nodded his head in affirmation. "Iredell took some time making up his mind to come over to the American side, but I think he has gone farther than most of us now. I agree with him about the depreciation of the currency of the state. This is a very serious and alarming evil. Our prices are getting out of control."

"Yes. The price of corn is five pounds a barrel and flour has gone to three pounds a hundred. Our people cannot afford to pay or be in competition with our government, buying for the army." Johnston rose and walked to the fireplace and knocked the dottle out of his pipe into the coals. Peter noticed his height and strength of body as compared with Hooper's less firm flesh and shorter frame.

Hooper, his mind still on Iredell, said: "I understand Caswell is going to appoint him Attorney-General. By that, I am sure all feeling that there was some Tory left in him has disappeared."

Johnston laughed. "They accuse us all of Toryism, from time to time. If a man happens to have been born with some little advantage of class, there are many to sneer and accuse: Jemmy because of his relationship to McCullough and Earl Macartney; me because my uncle Gabriel Johnston was a Royal Governor."

Hooper said wryly, "But neither you nor Iredell has been called the greatest Tory in the Convention by the great Thomas Jefferson."

Johnston raised his heavy brows. "Jefferson still casting aspersions?"

"Yes. Openly. He seems to have a peevish feeling for us Carolinians, ever since the Mecklenburg Declaration."

Johnston said, "A guilty conscience, perhaps?"

"I don't know, Sam. He goes out of his way to be disagreeable to me. Tory indeed!"

Johnston turned to Peter apologetically. "I am afraid we have dropped into the usual habit of friends who see each other infrequently. We spend our time talking about affairs of no interest to our guest. I hope we have not bored you too much, Captain. I am sure you could tell us things that would interest us greatly."

Peter knew Johnston had made an opening for him. But he did not have time to follow the lead. A slave came into the room.

"Madam she say tell you, 'Mr. Ferrier boat is at landing.' Captain Somebody with a funny name just came to the do'. He say Mr. Ferrier and Miss Ang'l' coming. Please to step to the drawing-room."

The advent of the unexpected guests made the quiet talk with Johnston impossible. Peter was not sorry. Although he had no doubt in his mind about Hooper's intense loyalty to the cause of the Revolution, he felt constraint about speaking to Johnston with anyone else present.

When they entered the drawing-room, the guests had not come up from the landing. Madam Penelope had gone out to the gallery. Cosmo de' Medici was with her. They stood looking toward the landing. Johnston and Hooper walked down the path.

The landing was lighted with lanthorns and, along the steps that ascended the bank, lightwood flares burned brightly, showing the way. Sounds rose from the water, clear and distinct—the soft-toned voices of Negroes, the grating of a boat against the wharf, the splash of oars, a girl's clear voice speaking; there was the acrid smell of burning lightwood.

Twilight had faded into black night and the stars in numbers pierced the curtain of the sky and shone almost as bright as stars in midsummer. The heavens were close, only a little removed from the tawny spires of pine and cypress, so it seemed to Peter. The air was soft and caressing against his face. Madam Dawson and Cosmo did not notice that he had come out, and was standing at the rail, looking past the dark garden toward the moving lights on the landing.

"How beautiful the night is!" Penelope's voice was as soft and

velvety as the night. "How tranquil! That is why I love it here at
Eden House."

"We have serene nights like this in Italy," Cosmo said. "Nights
that are made for romance, when a man may seek his mistress and
walk with her in a quiet garden." He hummed a sad little melody in
a minor key. Even without words it spoke of love.

"I suspect you are a great lover." Penelope's voice had something
in it, something that carried a hint of anticipated pleasures.

"We Latins are always lovers," he answered. "We love, we kiss, we
love again."

"Unfaithful men!"

"Ah, no. Each love teaches a little more. By the time we are old
we have, what do you say, the fervour and essence of love so deeply
embedded that we are lovers until we die."

Penelope said nothing. Peter could hear the swift intake of her
breath. She moved away from him a little, closer to De' Medici in
the darkness. Peter knew without seeing that Cosmo had lifted
her hand to his lips. After a moment he heard Cosmo speaking
softly.

"Is it not better to love, if only for a little, to let the emotions flow
naturally, than to be like Peter here, so reserved, so wrapped in dignity that he does not feel? Mother of God, what stone the Scots
are!"

"Not all Scots are made of stone." The richness of her voice stirred
Peter, standing so close to her. They seemed to be still unaware that
he was near them in the darkness.

"There can be no life without love." What more Cosmo would
have added remained unsaid. The torches moved into the garden,
the guests came within earshot. Penelope stepped to the gallery
rail.

"Good evening, Senator. Good evening, Angela. This is delightful.
Come in, come in, my dears." She kissed Angela lightly on the cheek
and extended her hand to Ferrier. They all went into the house.
Peter lingered outside. Cosmo moved nearer. It was typical of Cosmo
that he did not greet Peter, but launched at once into his own
affairs.

"It is a surprising night," he said. "How stupid of the others to
break up our little tête-à-tête! I might in time have made a little
progress with the charming widow."

The light from the drawing-room window fell directly on his face as he leaned negligently against a white pillar. He was smiling slightly, a pleased smile.

"You seemed to be making very good progress," Peter said shortly.

"Little you know, my dear Peter. That lady is of wide understanding. She is not one to carry a heart on a sleeve. She can look through one and see what goes on behind the spoken word. She would not believe words that I would say and she would smile at my little effort at love-making."

Peter said, "You are incorrigible."

"No, no, my serious Peter. You must learn to take life lightly. Hold it in your hands as a plaything or—" he shrugged—"it will take you by the throat."

"Suppose you really fell in love," Peter began.

"I do not understand this 'fall in love' you English speak of. I only know I feel love, then *pouf*, it is gone."

"Shall we go into the drawing-room?" Peter asked. He was weary of the discussion. He was amazed that the arrival of Angela Ferrier had disturbed him so much. But what was the use of thinking about her? She would have eyes only for Cosmo. Hadn't they told him she was Spanish? Spanish, Italian—it was all the same. She would not have any eyes for Peter Huntley.

"You must stay with us, Senator. You can't think of going up the river tonight," Penelope was saying when Peter and Cosmo came in. She stopped long enough to introduce Peter to the senator, who shook hands cordially.

The senator protested. "We thought we would stop at Balgray but the ferryman, Dishon, told me that Will Hooper and Sam were here, so we proceeded on upstream."

"I'll not take 'No,' Senator," Penelope said, her engaging smile showing her even white teeth. "There is plenty of room and why double back to Balgray? You may leave as early as you like in the morning.

Take the senator's boxes to the north bedroom," she told the Negro; "Captain de' Medici's bags to Captain Huntley's room. Miss Angela will be with me."

The senator looked at Angela. She said nothing. Peter thought the hand that was holding her cape trembled a little; certainly a look of disappointment came over her face when the senator said, "Thank you, Penelope. You are gracious as always. Then in the morning I will be a few miles closer to the plantation."

"Did Madam go up yesterday?" Penelope asked.

"No, she is staying with Parson Earle at Strawberry Hill for a few days. Angela will make a little visit with the Pollocks. Perhaps you will send her over in the morning, by canoe or horseback."

"Certainly. I shall be glad to furnish a horse, but do not press her to leave Eden House so soon. It has been months since she has stayed with me. She can help me entertain my charming guests."

Angela spoke quietly. "I promised Ann . . ." A look from her stepfather silenced her. "Thank you so much, Madam Dawson." Her voice was flat, the bright buoyant personality was gone. She could not conceal her disappointment. Penelope Dawson did not appear to notice.

Will Hooper engaged Ferrier in conversation. They stood on one side of the room near the windows. Johnston joined them as the servant passed the drinks.

Ferrier was a stern man. The lines of his face were cut deeply with no lines of laughter, nor had his eyes any sparkle. There was a tenseness or rigidity that might have come from some early Covenanter ancestor, or it might have been a religious intolerant who, with other followers of Knox, sent beautiful gay Mary to her doom. Intelligence he had aplenty. When he talked of the conditions the colonies would have to face before the war ended, and the era that would follow the war, he said: "Even if we win, it will take a decade to establish ourselves as a nation."

Peter saw that the other men, more brilliant perhaps, with more flexible minds, lacked the fundamental solid foundation of knowledge. A reader of Adam Smith's pamphlets, Ferrier believed that the land must be held as the basis of wealth. If they were to succeed as a nation, in unity, there must be some meeting ground of common interest. This constant struggle in the Congress for power, the Northern group against the Southern members, the Adamses and Lees against Washington as the commander-in-chief; the constant bickering, the belittling of the General, the undermining of Franklin and Hamilton—all had a bad effect on the common soldier who had left his home to fight for thirty or sixty days. The men in the ranks were bewildered by the dilatory methods of the leaders. No wonder they threw down their arms and deserted by the hundreds. The winter of Valley Forge with its tragic hardships and privations was one to promote disunity and desperation in the hearts of men who scarcely knew what they were fighting for or what it would gain them in the end.

"We must have unity if we hope to become a nation." Every voice was silent as Ferrier finished. His words beat against them as cold, as merciless, as a driving storm of sleet and snow.

Peter, who had been quiet during the discussion, felt impelled to speak. "Sir, do you not think we have passed the deepest of our suffering? Surely the man who has led us out of the horror of Valley Forge is strong enough to lead us to victory."

"Washington has the strength. But have the people the sense to follow him? Will they not be turned by the bitter criticism, the villifying to which he is even now subjected? I have no confidence in the commonalty. They are not accustomed to thinking, only to being led. If they choose the right leader . . ." He let his hand fall to the table. A vase of flowers turned over, spilling its contents. No one noticed, so disturbed they were by Ferrier's words.

Penelope Dawson said, "If we could only be sure which leader to believe! Our people in this province are so divided." She turned to Peter. "Captain Huntley, tell us. You have seen much, from many points of vantage. We see only what is here before us. Do you think General Gates will be able to cope with Clinton and Cornwallis, if they come?"

Peter hesitated. He did not want to assume the position of one who spoke with authority, yet he felt that he must dispel the gloom that Ferrier's words had cast on these people. It was all the more difficult because there was so much truth in what had been said. Truth, yes, but without faith. He replied briefly, "General Gates defeated Burgoyne."

Will Hooper interjected, "Burgoyne was ripe for the licking he got. You can't give Gates the full credit. He had good officers. Gentleman Johnny was wrong in so many of his guesses it made things easier for Gates." Hooper turned his chair to face Peter. "You don't think Gates a first-rate general, now, do you?"

"No, sir. I don't."

"Who do you think is better equipped to lead the Southern campaign?"

Peter hesitated a moment.

"We have a general in our army who is not yet very well known in the South," he said. "His name is Nathanael Greene."

CHAPTER
6

WHIG LEADERS

PETER listened to the talk of leaders who stood high in the political life of the Province. These were men who had contributed much to the progress of the war and who, as he knew, would soon be called on for more sacrifice of goods and body in aid of a cause that for the moment seemed almost in its death gasp.

People in this part of the country knew nothing of the horror of war. They had been mercifully spared. They had not heard the shouts of the wounded or the death-rattle of the dying. Since the beginning of the revolt when the North Carolinians had defeated the Scotch Tories under MacDonald at Widow Moore's bridge and driven the Royal Governor to take refuge in His Majesty's ship *Cruizer*, at the mouth of Cape Fear River, the red-coated soldiers had been fighting battles far from the Province's boundaries. The men of North Carolina had gone out to war by the thousands—in Washington's army and the army of Gates in the South. On the western border were poised Indian fighters ready to fly to the call to arms. Strong men of the western counties and beyond had formed bands of from a hundred to two hundred men, under the leadership of Colonels Charles McDowell, Sevier and Shelby, ready to fight the Indians and avert any uprising there. The British were known to have sent their spies and scouts among the Cherokees and the tribes across the mountains to cause disturbances. The Tories were very strong in the West. From the border to the South Carolina line neighbour mistrusted neighbour. Even families were split, brother against brother, father against son. But no battles were fought; no bright blood soaked the soil from the coastal plains to the mountains that towered to the smoky skies along the western border.

But war was coming closer, day by day. Dark clouds were rising over the Carolinas; from the South the danger hung heavy and enveloping.

Since he entered, Alexander Ferrier had dominated the room. He had just come home from New Bern where he had attended a meeting of the Council, at the Governor's Palace. The talk was war and nothing but war, he told the company. Domestic problems were set aside. The Governor had not minced words; the danger was very present. When objections rose to sending troops to South Carolina, the men of wisdom and knowledge dissented. Others, making political talk for their folk at home, made the objections.

"Let South Carolina look to her own borders," Allen Jones had argued. "Let her stand on her own feet." Ferrier's grey eyes had the tired look of a man discouraged when he told of the wrangling, the heated words in the Provincial Council meeting.

"I spoke up then. I couldn't withhold my words. I asked them to recollect that South Carolina had come gallantly to our aid in 1710, when the Tuscaroras were warring. Suppose we do have some companies in South Carolina now. Are they there only to help that Province and not also to defend our own? For years we have kept the enemy away from our shores and our borders. Now the danger is even greater than at the beginning of the war. We need to send troops to South Carolina. At all costs we must keep the British army from advancing. If Charleston falls, so falls our Southern border." Ferrier sat back. "I'm afraid I lost my temper," he said, shamefacedly. "But the Governor thanked me for my efforts. The vote was overwhelmingly to send troops south."

Peter thought there was a degree of similarity between Johnston and Ferrier, but where Johnston was calm, Ferrier was grim; nor did he have the touch of humour that gave warmth to Johnston. "Austere" was the word to use with reference to Ferrier. But a solid fundamental honesty of character was common to both men.

"Where the men are to come from, or the money to equip them, God knows," Hooper said, after a moment's thought. "We have almost reached the bottom of the barrel."

De' Medici, who had been seated on a stool near Penelope Dawson, got up and walked to the side of the room where the men were gathered. "The Governor has sent me here to recruit for my dragoons," he said, when Hooper stopped speaking. "I lack forty men and twice that number of horses. I intend to call at every plantation on the Sound and on the two rivers, to fill my quota of both men and horses."

Johnston glanced at Ferrier. After a moment's pause he said: "No need for all that effort, Captain de' Medici. On Tuesday we are having a district meeting at the Courthouse on another matter which concerns the war. If you like, you can meet and speak to the various planters at that time, without leaving Queen Anne's Town."

De' Medici was delighted. He had the Latin's easy indolence. "An excellent idea, Mr. Johnston. I will make my endeavour on Tuesday."

Penelope said, "We have had enough politics for the evening. I am sure these gentlemen will be bored with us. Will someone pull the bell? I think we all need posset to cheer us after such depressing news."

Peter got up and went to the fireplace. A strip of crewel-work concealed the bell cord, which hung from the ceiling to the level of the mantelboard. Angela rose at the same time. For an instant their hands touched. "Beg pardon," he murmured. She drew back quickly, and seated herself on the fire bench. Her nearness was disturbing. The softness of her hand, the delicate fragrance of orris and verbena, the quick intake of breath—everything about her appealed to the senses. He hoped he showed nothing of his feeling. De' Medici was such a clever devil. His quick dark eyes missed little. When Peter turned around again Angela was talking to Cosmo, determinedly ignoring his presence. He resented her. Why couldn't she be civil? She had, ever since they came into the room, avoided looking at him. He smiled a little. Perhaps it was better that way. He had had a very good opportunity to watch her as he listened to the talk of the Albemarle men. She was even lovelier by candlelight. She had the clear ivory skin of the South, a clear skin that had a glow of colour under the surface. The languor of her dark eyes was contradicted by the broad, rather humorous, mouth and a firm chin.

Penelope got up to supervise the making of the posset, the ingredients of which a slave had brought in and placed on a Pembroke table near the fire. Sam Johnston and Alexander Ferrier sat down at a table which had been set up for a game of draughts. Will Hooper drew up a chair to watch. The game was one of a series which had gone on for years.

"Must you stare?"

Peter, surprised that Angela would trouble to address him, stood looking at her without replying. After a moment he said, "I could fight better if I knew what we are fighting about, Miss Angela."

"Are we fighting?"

Peter raised his brows, then grinned. "I don't know what you may call it. Is feud the customary word?"

"This is trivial!" Angela said, impatient that he took the matter so lightly.

"Indeed it is not trivial to me. It borders on the tragic."

"You are talking like one of Mr. Garrick's plays, twisting my words about, making them sound ridiculous." Her foot tapped the fender, impatient. "I don't like it."

"My dear Miss Ferrier, I cannot think how I have offended. I am flying a flag of truce, hoping to settle a sanguinary battle."

"Oh," she said angrily, and her cheeks reddened, "you are impossible!" She walked away and joined the group around the posset bowl.

Peter watched her go, bewildered by her unconcealed animosity. Oh, devil take it! It would have been pleasant if she had shown a little interest. But no matter. He had no time for women and their vagaries, now.

The little glass-encased clock struck ten. No one noticed it but him. They were drinking their second round of possets. The drink had an enlivening warmth that was very pleasant.

Penelope left the room and returned a little later with a guitar under her arm, which she laid on Angela's lap. "Angela has promised to sing for us." To Peter she said, "Angela has a lovely voice. Her mother has taught her many old songs of Spain. Not like our English ballads. Haunting, deep songs that make you dream; but I would not think of spoiling your pleasure by trying to describe them to you."

Angela moved over on the little seat, spread her skirts and placed the guitar into position, slinging the bright scarlet riband over her shoulder. The light from the candles in the wall sconces laid soft shadows over her, softened her clearly marked features. She ran her long fingers over the strings, tuned an ivory key or two, her dark head bent to catch the tone. Lovely and graceful she was, but remote as the Moorish country she remembered.

> "Granada, thy towers touch the sky.
> Granada, o'erhead the falcons fly . . ."

The song died away, the last mournful note trembled on the strings. Penelope sat looking into the fire, her thoughts far away. Perhaps she remembered some half-forgotten love words or some secret dreams. Cosmo spoke low words of praise which Peter did not hear. He did not move. The passionate longing in Angela's voice touched a chord in him that made him sad, with the nostalgic sadness of the Moorish lover whose words she had sung.

He stood up and walked to the window that overlooked the water. The moon was high, and a rippling silver sheen marked the course of the broad river. He saw the shadow of a boat heading for the landing, saw the flash as the dripping water fell from the oars. Three people sat in the long canoe. Penelope joined him.

"What are you looking at so intently?" she asked, standing close beside him. She cupped her hands beside her face to look out through the small window-pane.

"I was watching the canoe on the river. I think you are about to have visitors," Peter answered. The canoe slid along the landing. A man jumped out and secured the boat. A second man and a woman got out.

Penelope said, "Scipio, send someone with torches. There is a boat at the landing."

De' Medici strolled to the window and stood beside Peter. "It is quite wonderful, this America. Here we are thousands of miles from the capitals of the world and what do we find? Lovely women and hospitality as extensive as anything one could find in Europe. Guests arriving and departing. I find it all so delightful. Pleasant, is it not, my brave Scot?"

"Pleasant enough," Peter muttered. He had thought the same thing but he resented Cosmo putting his thoughts into words.

Cosmo dropped his voice to a confidential tone. "That Angela, she gives you looks that are very grim, Pietro. Does she still mourn for her riband? I advise you to be lavish. Promise her a dozen Roman scarves, as lovely as rainbows. Be desolated, humble yourself."

Peter stiffened. "I'll be damned if I will humble myself for any woman."

Cosmo shrugged, lifted his eyebrows, made a hopeless gesture with his hand. "Oh, you Northern men! I swear by the saints you are incomprehensible. You must be, oh, so serious. You think always of your pride, your masculine honour. Do you not know that love—" he pronounced it "loff"—"is a game to play delicately, ver', ver' lightly?"

Peter grinned. "Love wasn't mentioned."

Cosmo caught his arm. "These Anglo-Saxon men! Very fine they are, very high in ideals, but they are all serious. Me, I think war and love are one and the same. You play it with the rapier, not with the broad-axe. But look, the guests arrive."

Voices were recognizable as the visitors came up the gallery. "It is Ann Pollock and Cullen," Penelope said to Johnston. She left the room to greet the newcomers. Cosmo and Angela sat down near the fire. Samuel Johnston left the draughts table and joined Peter at the window. They were across the room from the others.

Johnston said, "I regret there has been no opportunity to talk with you. Now it will be impossible." He hesitated a moment as though considering something, lowered his voice and said, "Some of the Whig leaders have grave doubts about Cullen Pollock. It took him some time to give up his loyalty to the Crown, longer than most of us. I myself do not doubt him. I like Cullen and I like Ann, his wife."

Peter nodded. He understood. He would not in any case have spoken of political matters or been led into political discussion. He appreciated Johnston's thoughtfulness. He realized that it was difficult for him to say anything derogatory about a man who was his friend. He must have considered it important. Peter had been warned that there were many Tories in North Carolina, but he was told that they lived in the western part of the Province near the mountains and the southern border. Cross Creek, where the Scots had settled after Culloden, was the hotbed of Toryism. Johnston's warning made him aware that the coastal plain had its Loyalists.

Penelope was in the hall talking to her guests. Her voice was audible in the drawing-room. "I did not know you were at the plantation, Ann. Good evening, Cullen. I do hope you are yourself again after that long siege of fever."

There was a moment's pause, then a woman's voice. "Penelope, may I present our guest, Mr. Jeremiah Morse, of Boston?"

A swift discordant sound broke the momentary silence. Angela's hand had fallen across the strings of the guitar. Her face, which had been turned toward Cosmo, became chalk-white. The smile froze on her lips, she looked stricken. With a visible effort she pulled herself together, but she did not turn her head toward the door or look at the newcomers. Peter gazed at her curiously, then moved so that he could see the guests.

A dark-haired woman, built on Junoesque lines, stood at the doorway, her figure shrouded in a long red cape. As she advanced into the room, her eyes turned to her companions. Both were men. One was thin almost to emaciation, with a pale, deeply lined face and the tired eyes of a disillusioned man. The second moved into the light. He paused and looked about the room quickly, as a man accustomed to measuring for friend or enemy. His eyes rested on Angela Ferrier. For a moment he hesitated; the expression on his face was one of surprise, even apprehension.

The change was so swift that Peter was uncertain whether he had imagined it or whether it was the shadow cast by the flickering of the firelight. One thing was certain: the man at the door was the same man he had seen in the coach in front of Horniblow's.

CHAPTER
7

THE GOVERNOR'S DAUGHTER

THE small Negro boy came in early to make the fire. Peter was already awake. Cosmo's black curly head was buried deep beneath the bolster, which he had neglected to take from the bed the night before. Peter wondered how he breathed, with a feather quilt over him and a mass of pillows about him, but he slept peacefully, not hearing the poker clang against the firedogs. Peter looked at his watch. It was a quarter past seven. Madam Dawson had told him the night before that breakfast was served from nine on. The air that came in through the small-paned window was soft. Birds were singing. He saw a cardinal swaying on the limb of a tree. Dozens of small brown birds with flashes of yellow in wing and tail were eating the blue berries of the juniper. He got out of bed and looked from the window. Below, the plantation was alive with activity. There were Negroes in the fields driving sleek dark mules before the plough, making rows.

He pulled on his breeches and boots. The boy had set a jug of steaming water on the trivet on the hearth. Peter felt wonderful, in spite of the series of toddy toasts he had drunk the night before.

He thought of the events of the preceding evening after the ladies had retired. Cosmo had got a little drunk and boasted of Italian horsemanship. Peter remained cold sober. He knew he had to keep his head clear. He must watch this man Morse. He was not positive it was the same man he had seen in Paris with Ensign Rutherford. There had not been a glimmer of recognition in Jeremiah Morse's eyes when he looked at Peter last night. Whether he was adept at play-acting, or whether he had not seen Peter in Paris, Peter could not determine. Peter was certain his own countenance had not betrayed him. When Morse had made some aimless conversation, Peter had answered frankly. He felt sure that if there had been any suspicions, they had been put to rest. Even if Morse had placed Peter as having belonged to Dr. Franklin's staff, in Paris, he would not connect him with Silas Deane.

The Pollocks and their guest had stayed only a short time. Cullen Pollock complained of a chill. He had not whipped the fever after all. Morse had seemed to be impressed by Angela. He seated himself near her when the drinks were passed, and they spoke together in low tones, under the cover of the general conversation. Peter, remembering Angela's expression when she saw Morse enter the room, felt positive that they had met before, although Mrs. Pollock had included Angela when she made the general introduction of her guest.

As he shaved he went over all the possibilities. Silas Deane had been known to keep up correspondence with certain Englishmen. Presumably these men belonged to the group in opposition to the government and were particularly violent against Lord North and Lord Germain. Dr. Franklin himself had corresponded with Hartley, hoping against hope that there would be some method of making peace.

There was Thornton, Arthur Lee's secretary, whom Peter had always suspected. More than one Frenchman had warned him that Thornton was in the pay of Lord North. Then there was Hezekiah Ford; he had seen a copy of a letter from Governor Henry of Virginia to the delegates of the state, among the memos the committee had given him before he left the North. He remembered the contents as vividly as though he had the page before him: "Within these last few days I have received information by a paper sent by Honorable Arthur Lee, Esq., at Paris, that Hezekiah Ford is secretary to Mr. Lee. Every member of the Privy Council, as well as myself, is exceedingly alarmed at the circumstance; having the most perfect conviction that Mr. Ford is altogether unfit to be near the person of the American Commissioner. This Hezekiah Ford has passed for a member of the Church of England and was for some time chaplain to a Carolina regiment. He was suspected of writing a seditious paper, exhorting men to resist, by force, a draft ordered by law for the militia to fill the Virginia regiments in Continental service. . . . He went, at great hazard to himself, on board a British ship of war, the St. Alban, lying off Hampton Roads. He remained there a considerable time before proceeding to New York, continuing with the enemy until he chose to go to England . . . besides this there seems to be good ground to suspect this same Mr. Ford of being concerned in counterfeiting our paper money."

Congress took action and the Committee on Foreign Affairs communicated with Arthur Lee, to make him acquainted with the character of Mr. Ford. Even after that Lee wrote to Congress: ". . . this letter will be delivered to you by Mr. Hezekiah Ford, who has served me faithfully for eight months as secretary. He will give you the best information in his power of the state of affairs here."

Then there was Lee's letter to Mr. Jefferson, saying that he had not the smallest reason to suspect Ford; and the third letter in the file on Ford was from Whipple, the New Hampshire member of Congress. "What can have become of Ford? Ford is supposed to have had dispatches for Congress, but nothing further has been heard from him."

Here was a possibility—Ford or Thornton. He went over the other spy suspects: Stephen Sayre, Thomas and George Diggs. The committee had given Peter little information on the other men save that they were "American-born, lived in England since the Revolution, but George had visited the United States in 1778. It has fallen to our knowledge that Mr. Thomas Diggs of Maryland has exerted himself with great assiduity and address in gaining intelligence and doing other services for England."

Then there was the man whom the Committee of Foreign Affairs had sent him to find, John Folger. What connection, if any, was there between Deane's missing report and these suspected men?

Peter swore. He had nicked himself on the jaw. He determined to put his problem aside for the moment; all he could do here was have an eye and an ear open. Pollock—what was it he had heard about Cullen Pollock? Some disagreeable circumstance. He gave up trying to remember. A man can't think on an empty stomach. He glanced at De' Medici. He had moved, turned on his back. His closed eyes, long dark lashes on his olive cheeks, gave him a boyish look. Peter slipped on his coat and went downstairs.

The dining-room was empty. He went to the board and lifted some of the covered dishes and helped himself to meal gruel and strips of lean bacon. A slave came into the room carrying a tray that held a pot of hot chocolate.

"Morn', sar. What yo' like fo' you' eggs?"

"Boiled soft," Peter said, sitting down at the table. "I'm early. I don't suppose anyone is up yet."

"Yes, sar, Miss Pene. She's been out at the lot dis long time ago." Peter looked surprised.

"Yes, sar. Ever' mornin' Miss Pene she am gone yonder ridin' she hoss."

Peter thought he should have been out on "he hoss" too.

"She be comin' in presently." The servant went to the door and raised his voice to a shout. "Bring in hot bread, Milly; run with you' laigs; quick now less'n I fotch you a belt with the flat o' ma hand."

The young Negro girl came running from a building set in a kitchen garden. Peter took it to be the kitchen. The man-servant took the dish from her hand as she came to the door. He passed the hot scones to Peter and placed a dish of red preserves beside his plate. The food was delicious. Peter ate and praised and took a second rasher of bacon when the eggs appeared. Before he had finished Penelope Dawson came in. She wore a cloth habit, and had a white silk kerchief tied over her hair, knotted under her chin. Her cheeks were red, her eyes sparkling. Peter placed a chair for her.

"You look as fair as the morning," he said admiringly. "One need not ask whether you enjoyed your ride."

She filled a cup with chocolate. "You should have been with me, Captain. I rode to Mount Galland—one of my plantations, upriver from here," she explained.

"So early?" murmured Peter.

Penelope smiled. "I'm a planter," she said. "They are ploughing in the fields. I wanted to see how they are getting on." She helped herself to a scone and told the servant to order two eggs for Mr. Johnston. "The run of the glass," she said. "Tell Cook who they are for. She will know just how to cook them."

"My cousin is a great favourite here," she told Peter. "He comes frequently, but not frequently enough. I'm afraid I lean on Sam too much, carrying all my plantation problems to him to be solved. He is much too busy these days to have to plan for me. I know that with my mind, but my heart turns to him whenever I have difficulties."

"I am sure Mr. Johnston must have many responsibilities of state," Peter said.

"Yes, he has, and then I add mine—where to send my children to school . . ."

"Children?"

She smiled. "Didn't you know? My daughter Penelope is at Williamsburg and my son Billie at Annapolis, attending King William's

School." She sipped her chocolate slowly, enjoying it. She has a gift of savouring everything, Peter thought. She is very young, much younger than I thought when I first saw her.

"I wanted little Pene to go to Williamsburg. I had my schooling there, at Mr. Dinwoodie's. It was a lovely experience." She sighed. "I am afraid my daughter will not have the delightful memories I have of my schooldays. I stayed at the Palace with Governor Din-widdie's family. My father and the Governor of Virginia had been close friends. My mother died when I was young. My father wanted me to have suitable surroundings. Williamsburg was London, to us in the Province."

She paused and smiled a little smile of happy remembrance. "One time I went with Elizabeth and Rebecca, the Governor's daughters, to Nomini Hall to visit with the Carter children. I quite lost my heart, I was so enchanted with their young tutor. The Carter girls—there was such a flock of them. The older ones, I recollect, were all in love with the tutor. And the dancing master came to the Palace to teach us our steps—an old Frenchman who always said, 'Young laz'ees! Young laz'ees!' when we were remiss with our deportment. Dancing and deportment and music lessons. That was before I met John Dawson, whose father was the president of William and Mary College.

"Dear Father wanted me to be educated in a neat and fashionable manner. What I should have been learning was how to conserve the forest or manure the land to get good crops. But youth is delightful, isn't it, Captain Huntley?"

Peter hesitated, thinking of his young days in island loneliness. "Yes, I suppose so," he said, after a moment.

"Were you always a silent child?" she asked with penetrating insight.

"Yes, and always reading," he answered, "or riding my ponies up the glen, tramping the hills with the gillies or watching the fishermen with their nets. Sometimes going out through the Minch into the North Atlantic in the fishing boats."

"Did your mother allow that?"

"I cannot even remember my mother," he answered. "My father and a brother ten years older made up our family. My brother was killed on the Continent; only my father and I were left, and our old nurse, with her husband, to do for us."

"Were you and your father companionable?"

Peter replied, "I don't know, really. We sat together in the evening, not talking, each of us with his book. I suppose that is a sort of companionship. My father was somewhat of a recluse. For a time he was a political exile in Holland; they let him come home finally, but he took no part in public life. Perhaps he took an oath, like the one required after Culloden. I don't know, really."

"Were you in Holland with him?"

"For a time, yes."

She looked at Peter thoughtfully. "Do not think me inquisitive, but have you never been in love?"

Peter smiled at her, an engaging smile that changed the solemn expression of his face unbelievably. "I really don't know, Madam Dawson. I've thought I was in love half a dozen times, when I was at the university at Edinburgh, and in Paris."

"You want awakening," she said frankly. "I would say you were virginal."

Peter laughed aloud. "I'm not so green. Remember I've had some years in France."

She nodded. "Yes, I remember, but I do not count these little excursions and adventures. I mean something quite different."

A quizzical look came into his greenish eyes and his lips twitched in a half-smile. "One can always hope," he murmured.

Penelope was on the point of retreat when she heard footsteps in the hall. She glanced over her shoulder. "Here comes Sam," she said. "He will be monstrous hungry. He has been up as long as I have been, and ridden to Mount Galland, also."

Johnston came into the room. He greeted Peter cordially and at once made his way to the sideboard and came back to the table with a heaping plate. The servant hovered over him, filling his water goblet, his chocolate cup, passing hot scones. "You' eggs will be served at once, sar. Cook say he is fresh just off the nest."

"Splendid!" Johnston said, then turned to Penelope. "I must say your meat is better cured than mine was this year. It was too warm a day when we killed and I lost some of my hams."

"That is a small tragedy, Sam, especially this year when feed is so scarce."

"I hope you saved out enough corn to carry you through until the pasture is heavier."

She nodded. "I think so. I have had the feeling all along that I must sell all my corn to the army. Now I think I had rather they would take the pork than the corn. There are the mules and horses to think about."

Johnston raised his heavy eyebrows. "De' Medici is hot after horses, Pene. Are you going to sell him any?"

"I think so, two or three at least. Some of the Black Rock Plantation stock."

Johnston nodded. "I trust you are not keeping too many of your hunters here at Eden House."

"No. I moved the best mares to Mount Galland—all that are going to drop colts this spring."

They talked about plantation affairs. Peter was amazed at the woman's knowledge. Pene caught the expression of wonder in his eyes. Smiling, she said, "You are astonished that a woman should be interested in such mundane things as hogs and stock and the yield of corn to the acre."

"Frankly I am, Madam Dawson. You have me bewildered."

Johnston said, "My cousin has been handling her affairs since she was eighteen. She knows more about planting than I do."

"Nonsense, Sam. All I have done is to try to follow my father's wishes, except experimenting with silkworms in my mulberry trees. I did try, as you know, Sam." They laughed together over some unsuccessful experiment.

A female slave came into the room, a young girl with satiny black skin. "Cook says will you step out to the kitchen please, Mistress? She like to know what about dat sugar you said you was goin' to deal out."

Madam Dawson rose. "Will you pardon me if I turn domestic for a short time?"

When the door closed after her departure, Johnston said to Peter, "There was no opportunity to talk with you last night. I had thought of coming up to your room, until I found that Captain de' Medici was in with you. Perhaps it is as well. The walls sometimes have ears. We will take the opportunity when we go into town, unless an opening should arise here that is not too obvious."

Peter momentarily considered speaking to him of Morse and his suspicions, then thought better of it. "I don't like to take your time, sir, but there are a few things the committee thought you should know. Our dispatches have not been coming through to their satisfaction lately. Several times the riders have been shot at. One was killed between here and Suffolk, on the Sand Hill Road. Sometimes they have been waylaid along the Great Dismal, and their pouches taken. New methods have had to be devised." He paused, hearing a step in the hall.

"We will speak of this later," Johnston said in a lowered voice. When the door opened he was speaking of spring planting. "We are trying to convince our people to double-plant this year. Beans and corn in the same hill. We were very short-cropped last season, so we plan to plant more heavily this year. We must have food for the army." He looked up. "Ah, Ferrier, good morning. Come and sit here beside me." He shouted for the servant.

The slave came quickly. "Yes, sar." And without further orders, he brought a full plate and placed it on the table in front of the senator. Peter got up and went to the end of the table, to pour a cup of chocolate for him.

"Thank you, Captain Huntley."

"I hope you rested well," Johnston said, lighting a pipe.

"Very well. Very well indeed." The senator turned to Peter after he had taken a few bites. "I went to the university with a Peter Huntley. He was from the Isle of Mull, if I remember correctly. A very tall, powerful man he was, but he was more interested in books than in the games we indulged in. Was he by any chance a relative of yours?"

"My father, sir. He is the only other Peter Huntley."

The senator smiled broadly. "That is a coincidence, isn't it, Sam? When I saw you last night I thought there was a slight resemblance, but you are not so tall."

"My father had three inches the better of me, and a length of arm that made it impossible for me to get the better of him with the foils."

"Yes, yes, I remember. Peter was our very strong fencer." The senator picked up a strip of bacon in his fingers. "Johnston will tell you that you are among good Scots here—not so many as settled at Cross Creek, but we have the advantage: we didn't take oath after Culloden."

"My uncle was killed on that field, and my father had to flee into exile." Peter's face hardened. "We never took oath to be loyal to the King of England but we took another oath." He stopped short. "No matter," he said in a changed tone.

Ferrier said, "Aye, lad, I know. 'Tis easy and natural for some of us to join with the rebels here; old grudges die hard." Peter nodded.

Johnston spoke of something else, for he saw that Peter was deeply moved. Huntley sat back from the table, listening. His work with the mission in France and his work with the Committee of Foreign Affairs had trained him in observation.

Cosmo came down, yawning sleepily. He poured himself a cup of chocolate. To the servant he said, "Yes. Eggs, boiled soft, and a rasher of bacon."

The door opened and Angela walked in. She had her arms full of garden flowers, lilacs and a spray of white blossoms. Scipio took them from her, to carry to the piazza where the two mulatto girls were arranging flowers for the house.

The men rose, and Johnston held a chair for her. Cosmo went to the sideboard, plate in hand. She smiled at him, spoke to Johnston, nodded to Peter.

Ferrier moved near Peter and engaged him in conversation about Mull and affairs of the university, recalling his own days there; reminiscences about Peter's father, his prowess in fencing, his skill as a horseman, his studious bent. He drew Angela into the conversation from time to time, but she answered in monosyllables and soon found excuses for turning from the two men.

She was gay and natural with De' Medici, who sat beside her. They spoke in Spanish. Peter gave no indication that he understood what they were saying. Once De' Medici asked her, "Why are you so studiously cold to my friend?"

"Am I?"

"The snow on the Pyrenees could be no colder, nor a northern wind on the Vega."

"Perhaps I do not like your friend."

"That is ridiculous, everyone likes him. You are in love with him, yes?"

Angela's cheeks grew fiery red, her eyes flashed. "That is nonsense. I do not like you when you talk nonsense."

De' Medici smiled broadly. "My little child, you give yourself away. Do you not know that unreasoned hate is akin to love? I think that you are still very, very young."

"Let us talk of something else." Angela's cheeks were still flushed, her voice trembled.

"Let us indeed. Let us talk of Cosmo, a subject much nearer to my heart."

Angela's expression changed. A smile came to her lips. "And to me also, Captain."

Peter sat without stirring. "Eavesdroppers never hear any good of themselves," was so true that it hurt. Cosmo was a silly fellow where women were concerned. He said daring and slightly impudent things to them, but they all seemed to like it. He, Peter, was a dolt. Cosmo was right when he said that Peter did not have the light touch with women. Certainly he didn't with Angela Ferrier. He found her difficult to talk to at all times. With Penelope Dawson he had no such trouble. His words with her were light enough, for she laughed often at his quips. But Penelope was warm and understanding and experienced. He believed Cosmo was right—Angela was very, very young. He believed more experienced women were more interesting. But to the devil with women, he had other things to think of now. He turned his mind to the problem of Mr. Morse of Boston, travelling through the South to buy food for the Northern army. He tried to fit him in with Thornton, whom he had never seen. There was that other possibility, the young man, the special messenger sent from Paris. This aspect of his own mission he had not revealed to Mr. Johnston, nor had he spoken of the missing million. Then there was the matter of John Folger, who had supposedly brought urgent and important dispatches to Congress and had disappeared after leaving the French ship at New Bern.

Ferrier broke into the little tête-à-tête Cosmo and Angela were carrying on in Spanish. "Have you been in the Province before, Captain de' Medici?" he asked.

"Indeed, yes, sir. I came here to Queen Anne's Town to register some land I had bought. The land lay in the Granville Grant, so I was obliged to come to Lord Granville's agent, Mr. Francis Corbin." Cosmo gave him all his attention.

"So you own land in Granville County?"

"A thousand acres I bought. Some say it is sorry soil, but I am hopeful."

Johnston asked, "If you do not consider it an impertinent question, how did you happen to buy land in Carolina?"

De' Medici's face became grave. "Indeed, no, I do not think your question impertinent, Mr. Johnston, but friendly. That is what I so much like in your people. You are friendly, as natural as children. You ask questions with a simple directness that confuses us Latins. We have little knowledge of direct inquiry. We must go about gaining our knowledge in some devious way." He laughed at himself. "You see? Even now I make a long unnecessary explanation, instead of answering your question with the same simple directness that it is asked."

"Perhaps we are too direct. Perhaps we should be a little less obvious," Sam Johnston observed.

Penelope returned while De' Medici was talking. She had her keys with her, and a small woven basket. "We are certainly naïve," Penelope said, seating herself at the head of the table and reaching for the chocolate pot. "Take your Francisca, for example. She gives the feeling of simplicity, but she is very complex. One thinks of her as having concealed strength and wisdom. Is that not so, Senator?"

The senator nodded. The smile that came on his lips had a little bitterness, or was it chagrin? "I find all women complex," he said slowly, "subtle and complex. But let us return to the original question." He looked at De' Medici.

"I was sojourning in France," Cosmo continued the interrupted explanation. "At my home I was—well, let us say involved in a political discussion. It was better for me to go on a tour, my father said. The Medici have ever been averse to dark places and they have no love for dungeons, so I went to France. There I found many young men as hot as Tybalt, for a new liberty that was being talked of wherever young men got together."

He let his dark eyes move from one to the other in the group—a serious De' Medici quite different from the gay, almost superficial De' Medici.

"You, here in America, have little knowledge of the thing you are doing. This revolt, this civil war or revolution, which you Englishmen are fighting in a new country, has had a tremendous impact on other countries. France, Italy, Holland and Spain, I visited them all. Young men the world over look to you . . ." He broke off, embarrassed to find himself so serious. He shrugged his shoulders, made a characteristic gesture with his slender hands.

"I say to myself I, Cosmo de' Medici, will have a part in this. I have some money, so I buy myself some land. To have land, to plant, that is the custom of Italy. So now I have one thousand acres in Granville. I am—what do you say?—now I am a planter."

BALGRAY

"I MISTRUST that man Morse," Penelope told Peter. "I mistrust him without reason. I fancy myself as a dispassionate person who can stand off and judge people without emotion. Then I find myself taking an unwarranted dislike." She smiled ruefully.

Peter quoted. " 'I do not love thee, Dr. Fell.' "

"Exactly. With as little reason. Mr. Morse is a very pleasant person. His voice is cultured, his manners are without flaw, but . . ."

Peter wanted her to continue, but he did not want to put himself in the position of being eager. But she fell silent and he was forced to wait.

They were riding through the deep woods, in the direction of Balgray—a narrow path, deep-cut. Peter thought that the Indians must have used it for long years before the white men came, in moving from one fishing ground to another. Penelope had told him that the old Indian Town of the Chowanoc was a few miles above them on the opposite side of the river.

"My father took me to the site of Indian Town where the marl beds are. He let me dig for Indian arrows. He was a learned man, my father. He was a professor at St. Andrews, an Orientalist; a writer on political subjects, when the King sent him to Carolina as Royal Governor. He wanted me to grow up with some wisdom, based on a background of history. I remember that day so vividly. It was autumn and the river-banks were rich in yellow and scarlet. The sycamores were molten gold. We landed in a small cove and climbed the high bank. I walked in the woods, chasing a rabbit, getting tangled in wild grape and creeping trumpet vines, falling and scratching my face against sharp spikes of holly trees, filling my skirts with chinquapins and hickory nuts. He sat by the river looking out over the water, dreaming some dream. He was often like that, silent, solitary, drawing on some deep-seated knowledge that was his.

"He said, 'The Elizabethans were the greatest of all Englishmen. They were bolder and had more courage, selfless. The unknown taunted them, urging them to follow some uncharted sea. No one ever sailed wider or farther into the unknown, save the Portuguese.'

"I sat down by his side, taking time to pull sand spurs from my garments while he talked.

"'Do you know, little Pene, that a great Elizabethan captain was here on this river?' I must have looked up, startled, some expression of wonder in my round childish eyes.

"'Sir Walter?' I asked. 'Did he go away and leave Queen Elizabeth?' My father smiled and shook his head.

"'Nay, my little one. Sir Walter never sailed to these beautiful shores. He was tied by a woman's apron strings.'

"'Did Queen Elizabeth wear aprons?' I questioned. A new thought entered my head. 'Father, was Queen Elizabeth a real person? Did she wear aprons when she was a little girl?'

"He laughed aloud at that. 'I don't know, sweeting, but if it were fashionable when she lived, I'm sure she did wear aprons.'

"I pondered the thought for some time. She was a real little girl, not always grown up like the picture with a frill of lace and a crown and a fine frock of brocade. He was not listening, so after a little I too fell silent."

"You must have been a charming child," Peter said.

"A child full of curiosity, annoying everyone with many questions, so my stepmother often told me. . . . But to go back to my father and the autumn day at the Indian Town. After a time he spoke to me of Sir Walter Raleigh's cousin, Sir Richard Grenville. 'The greatest captain of all the Elizabethans, to my way of thinking. He was the very essence of the Elizabethans. He may have sat here, in the very spot you are in, for all I know, eating his dinner off golden plates, while his musicians played sweet music for his delight. Sweeting, you must learn to read Spanish so you will know about these things—how Grenville came to the Outer Banks to plant a colony; how he sailed up our river. Yes, I must have you taught Spanish.' I snuggled against his side, listening to the sound of his voice until I grew drowsy.

"When I woke up, the sun was setting over our Bertie forests. My father was looking down at me. 'You slept, my little child. So easily, so sweetly.' His voice was very tender and lovely."

Peter glanced at the speaker. The tears stood in her eyes. After a moment she spoke again, a little sadly, "People will tell you that Gabriel Johnston was one of the 'good' Governors of this Province. We had had enough of the others before he came, but to me he was a great man, the kindest, the gentlest father a child ever had." Tears overflowed her eyes and lay on her cheek. She did not trouble to brush them away.

Peter remained silent, as though he were thinking of something else, for Penelope was speaking, not to him, but from an overflowing heart lost in memories of an adored father.

"I married John Dawson, whom I had met in Williamsburg," she said after a long silence. "He was a lawyer, one of the executives of my father's estate. He passed away. Then my mother died, and I was left alone, a widow with two children."

They rode slowly. The path was wide enough to ride two abreast. She looked at Peter. Her eyes seemed to him strangely unknown and disquieting.

"You have never thought of marrying again?" he asked, then hastened to add, "I am sorry. I shouldn't have asked so intimate a question, but the words came."

She smiled sadly, a sort of lonely anguish. She was a woman secret, and enigmatic. Peter thought of her at the moment as symbolic, ageless.

"There has been no one who could hold my thought for more than a short time. Emotion, yes, but short, too short to count. A flame that rose for an instant, then died."

Peter kept his glance averted, as though the passing panorama of woods held his attention—dark pines and the tender young green of hardwoods, the vibrating pink of redbud, the ivory whiteness of dogwood. Birds were winging across their path—the flashing cardinal, the yellow breast of a wild canary. He heard a crow's raucous cry. The dead brown leaves rustled, invaded by some small animal that scampered across the floor of the forest. Yellow jasmine hung suspended in the shadows like the stars in a night sky.

Penelope touched his arm for an instant. "I cannot think why I have talked to you this way. It has been years since I have spoken of my father to anyone save Sam and my friend Mary Warden."

Mary Warden. Peter had heard the name before, but he could not remember the circumstance.

Penelope continued, "Mary is my very dear friend. The only one approaching a confidante. A charming, lovely woman."

"Why have I not met this Mary Warden?" Peter asked, not because of interest but to give Penelope another train of thought.

"She has been away, at New Bern, at Charlotte Town, or Hillsborough. She goes always with her husband, William Warden. William is a member of the Provincial Council."

Peter remembered then. Warden, a lawyer, was on his secret list with a question mark following.

"I love Mary as though she were my sister. She is a wonderful character. She has what so few women have—integrity."

Penelope touched her mount with her spur.

They had come now to an intersection—a broader road which stretched straight as a bee-line through the forest. "The Governor's Road, we call it," Penelope volunteered. "Tradition has it that it was built by one of my grandmother's husbands, Governor Charles Eden. It terminates at Bath, on the Pamtico. Our inhabitants of Queen Anne's Town will tell you that Charles Eden had dark dealings with the pirates who preyed off the Banks, the notorious Blackbeard in particular, dividing spoils of the pirates' raids—sugar and rum for the Indies, gold and jewels for the Plate route."

"How very interesting!" Peter murmured. "It reminds me of the smugglers' castle in Mull, with a tunnel that ended on the lonely beach."

Penelope laughed. "I too have a tunnel under my house which ends on the Chowan River. The same Governor Eden was responsible for its building, so his pirate friends could sail up the river and visit him in secret." She smiled. "I am afraid my grandmother's husband was considered by most people to be one of the 'bad' Governors, although he did many good things to protect the people from the criminal indifference of the Lords Proprietors' government."

They came to another path that angled left from the Governor's Road.

"We have only a short distance to go. In truth we have been on Balgray land for some time."

"Tell me something about the Pollocks we are about to visit." Peter tried to make the request casual, but, ever since their visit the night before, he had been curious.

She gave him a swift, searching look and, womanlike, did not answer his question directly. Instead, she said, "You may fool some people with your story of travelling through the South in the interest of the army lottery, but not me. I know you are here for some other reason. It is probably some secret mission that you cannot reveal. But I warn you, I am not fooled. I knew from the start that story was a trumped-up affair."

Peter laughed. "Am I so transparent?"

"No, no, indeed. Sam will tell you that I have known many secrets concerning the conduct of the war. Many secret meetings have been held at Eden House. Governor Henry and Governor Caswell met there to make plans, when the danger of a slave rebellion was great."

"Slave rebellion?"

She looked at Peter in surprise. "Did you not know? Always there is that danger to us here."

"Not now, surely."

"Now more than any time for months. We must be very watchful, very. We have emergency plans. Eden House is one stronghold. I have arms for the neighbourhood hidden. In every district we have one house designated. In case of a black rebellion, all of the neighbours would gather at this house. Mulberry Hill, on the Sound, is another. Wingfield on the Chowan is the centre for the upper end of that county."

Peter was silent. This information was valuable. It might have bearing on some of the things that puzzled him.

Almost in answer to his thought Penelope spoke. "We watch every black runaway, every white man who talks with the Negroes. We have men to watch on market days and fairs, even at church."

"I had no idea."

"It is the same in the West, only there it is the Indians that the British are trying to incite to rebellion against our people. In Virginia, so close to us, Lord Dunmore, the last Royal Governor, stirred up an abortive slave rebellion. Our own Royal Governor Martin, who is on His Majesty's Ship *Cruizer*, off the entrance to the Cape Fear, is trying to rouse the Scots, the Negroes and the Indians."

Peter repeated his own words: "I had no idea."

She drew rein. Ahead of them was a wide opening in the forest through which could be seen a large rambling house, broad, with side wings. Many small buildings were clustered about it. The group was larger and more impressive than any place he had seen since he arrived.

"Nice, is it not?" Pene said, reading his thoughts. Then she spoke deliberately. "Sometime you will trust me."

"I trust you now," he cried impulsively. "Indeed, yes, I do, but it is not *my* secret that is involved. From that you can draw conclusions."

"Say no more. I quite understand."

"I need your help, yet I cannot tell you why I need it. Will you trust me?"

Her eyes shone and a little dimple appeared at the corner of her lips. "Have I not already proved that when I told you I have concealed arms?"

"Yes. And in other ways. But I asked you a question that remains unanswered."

"The Pollocks? Cullen has only recently signed Parson Earle's Test. He was in the beginning quite outspoken against the Whigs." She pulled up. An old Negro shuffled out of the gatehouse to open the white-washed plank gate. Penelope's mare was close to his mount. She said in a low voice, "I would never have thought of telling their guest, Mr. Jeremiah Morse, that I have arms concealed in my house."

Not a muscle of Peter's face changed. "If I were a woman," he said, "I would always trust my intuition."

A Negro opened the gate, with a smiling answer to Madam Dawson's greeting. As they trotted up the long, tree-lined drive, Penelope talked of old Squire Pollock, the grandfather of Cullen, and his great holdings. "Fifty thousand acres of land, or more, he left to his children—land in Bertie and Tyrrell and the southern counties. He was a shrewd old gentleman, they all say, a confirmed Tory, a prototype of the old fox-hunter in the *Spectator*."

"Are his sons following in his footsteps, like father like son?"

Penelope averted her eyes. "I do not want to suggest that Toryism is inherited, else I stand accused, and Sam Johnston with Iredell also. We all have strong ties in England at this moment."

They came in sight of a lovely stream of water that cut through the forest, wide enough to admit a sailing vessel of considerable tonnage. The house rested on the bank of Salmon Creek with a view of the river from the side windows—an impressive setting, with the dark forest for background. Several saddle-horses were pawing at the rack, and one handsome travelling carriage, with a matched pair of greys.

"It looks like Dr. Cathcart's chaise, but I don't believe it is," Penelope said as they dismounted. She unhooked her dust skirt and tucked it in the saddle-bag. She unknotted the kerchief she had tied over her hair and put on a little riding hat, which she had extracted from the saddle-bag. Peter watched her, an amused expression in his green eyes.

"You disdain these vanities," she said with a toss of her head.

"You are quite wrong, Madam Dawson. On the contrary, I was thinking that part of a woman's attractiveness is in her small coquetries. They are so feminine, so dainty, they are like a delicate perfume."

"Peter! You have been learning tricks from De' Medici. He could easily have said that."

Peter simulated disappointment. "But not I?"

Her laughter was ready. "You pretend dourness and disdain of women. I believe you are a romantic at heart."

Peter put his finger to his lips. "Hist, woman! Dinna ye be tellin'."

She tucked her hand under his arm. "Come, Peter. We will see who rode to Balgray on those two strange saddle-horses. They are so muddy and splashed they must have come through one of the Tyrrell pocosins. Hurry, I'm quite curious."

They walked up the steps to the piazza and Peter lifted the knocker. An old Negro, white-haired and bent, opened the wide spirit door; a smile came over his face when he saw Madam Dawson. "Step in. Step in, ma'am. Master will be proud, very proud."

"Thank you, Cush. Are they in the drawing-room?"

"No, ma'am, they be still sitting at table. But step in."

They heard voices as they proceeded down the hall, followed by silence when Cush announced Madam Dawson.

Peter had the impression that some secret subject had been under discussion. Now they were uneasy lest their voices had carried beyond the room.

At the table were Cullen and Ann, his wife. Mr. Jeremiah Morse, of Boston, sat beside Angela Ferrier. Beyond were two men Peter had not seen before. Peter thought the Pollocks showed a slight degree of embarrassment.

Madam Dawson's acknowledgement of the introductions was very casual, even cool.

"Mr. Nielson I have already met. I have heard Mr. Hamilton's name mentioned." Hamilton, a man of rounded, well-fed figure and red face, laughed heartily.

"Nothing to my credit, I'll be bound," he answered good-humouredly. "I may say that many times I have heard of Madam Penelope Dawson, always in praise."

"Thank you, sir." Penelope's voice was cool.

Archibald Nielson was a tall, aristocratic man. He stood easily by his chair. His eyes rested for a moment on Peter in appraisal, then moved away, unsatisfied.

Ann Pollock said "Do sit down, Pene. Primus, bring chairs."

"Thank you, no. We are on our way to Duckenfield. I brought a message to Angela. Her father said he would be down from River Plantation in the morning and would take her in to Queen Anne's Town with him."

Angela said, "Thank you, Pene. I was sorry not to see you this morning before I came over to Ann's. I borrowed a horse, but your groom took it back with him."

"I saw you ride off." Penelope's glance was direct. "I was riding down the lane."

For some reason, Angela's face reddened. She looked down at her clasped hands.

Penelope said, "Come, Captain, we must be off." Ann protested a little. Peter withheld his surprise; there had been no word of riding to Duckenfield.

"Don't come to the door, Cullen," Penelope said. "The morning air is very damp. Dangerous when one has been so ill."

Cullen sank back in his chair. In the morning light he looked very white and drawn.

Ann walked to the door, her hand through Penelope's arm. "I was hard-pressed to get my household together, let alone take care of extra guests. None of my linen is unpacked or the blankets out." She paused and bit her lip.

Peter thought, These men have been here overnight but why are their horses at the rack showing signs of hard riding? Penelope put his thought into words as they rode through the gate and turned toward Duckenfield at the confluence of the two great rivers. "Those horses had been through the pocosin a short time ago. Why do you suppose—?" she said thoughtfully.

"Who are Mr. Neilson and Mr. Hamilton?"

"Two of our leading Tories. Mr. Hamilton was a merchant of Halifax, a good-humoured man and a high liver. Archibald Nielson was Governor Tryon's secretary. Formerly he was a friend of my cousin Sam and James Iredell. The war separated them." The path was narrow. They rode in silence; neither spoke until they were about to dismount at Duckenfield.

"A Tory meeting, if I ever saw one. Did you notice their discomfiture when we stepped into the room? But what is Angela doing there? She doesn't belong. Her father would be furious with her. I believe it has something to do with Jeremiah Morse." Pene turned to look at Peter. His own worry about that very thing was plain on his face.

Penelope spoke sharply: "Peter Huntley, I believe you are in love with that girl." Peter's face grew a painful red. "You are. I know you are."

He tried to deny but his attempt was feeble. "I don't think so," he stammered. "Anyway she despises me and shows it."

Penelope stamped her slender foot. "You are foolish to look to Angela for favour. It annoys me to see a man like you afraid of a silly girl. Look at your face."

"I am sorry," he said contritely. "Please don't punish me."

Penelope was obliged to laugh. "It's true I am annoyed with you. You are worth a dozen Angela Ferriers." She ran up the steps.

Madam Pearson came out on the piazza. "Oh, Penelope, you dear girl! You did bring that charming captain over!"

"Why shouldn't I bring Captain Huntley to Duckenfield?"

"No reason of course, but if you had been I, or I had been you— whatever am I saying? I mean that I shouldn't have wondered at all if you had wanted to keep him for yourself."

Penelope smiled at Peter. "You see how you are regarded in some quarters?"

Peter said, "I don't know how to handle the situation, I vow. This is something for Cosmo."

Penelope disappeared into the house without answering. Madam Pearson said brightly, "So impulsive, don't you think? So beautiful, but just a wee bit spoiled. Not that I condemn her. Who wouldn't be spoiled, a beautiful, wealthy young widow with dozens of men courting her?"

Peter said, "You have a beautiful view from here, Madam." She turned to explain the beauty of the scene that stretched before their eyes.

"The Meeting of the Waters is what the Indians named it. The Chowan on one side, two miles wide, and the Roanoke on the other; together they form the great Albemarle Sound. See, we stand now in Bertie County." She waved her hand. "On that side is the Tyrrell shore, on the other Chowan County. Queen Anne's Town is just in that little bay, and directly ahead is the Atlantic Ocean."

Peter followed the sweep of her hand. "The Atlantic?"

Madam Pearson leaned closer. "My husband says I must not say that. The ocean is sixty miles or more down the Sound. He says I cannot possibly see it because of the Banks. You know about our Banks? Pirates and dreadful people who wreck ships?"

Peter did not heed. The view that filled his eyes was superb. The deep forest on either shore, the great stretch of water.

"We must step inside. Mary Warden is here. Have you met Mary, Captain Huntley?"

"I haven't had the pleasure."

"A dear, dear girl. Too sad that she is married to such an old man. She lives over there below the village. Her plantation is Queen's Gift."

"What a very unusual name!"

"Yes, isn't it? Something about King Charles or Queen Anne, or something." Madam Pearson was vague.

They found Penelope and Mary Warden standing in the drawing-room, their hands clasped together in a gesture of warmth and deep affection.

Peter had a moment, while Madam Pearson spoke to a servant, to look at the two women. Mary Warden was not so tall as Penelope Dawson, but she carried herself well with her head high. She had dark hair and the largest brown eyes Peter had ever seen, fringed by the longest black lashes.

There were vitality and warmth and a suggestion of sadness in her face that arrested him. She raised her eyes and met his frankly intent glance. She dropped her hands to her side and moved back a step or two. Penelope turned. "This is Captain Huntley, our guest, Mary," she said. "Peter, I was speaking to you of Madam Warden this morning. I did not know we would find her so soon." She turned back to Mary. "Oh, Mary, I have really missed you this time. When did you get home? Where is William?"

"On Tuesday. William remained in Charlotte Town. I stopped a few days at Salisbury and came home." She said to Peter, "I couldn't be away when spring is so lovely here."

Her voice complemented her looks. It was low and had a quality of resonance that was very unusual.

"Where is Mr. Pearson?" Penelope asked.

"He is down on the shore. They are preparing to haul up the long net."

"Perhaps you would be interested, Captain." Penelope said. "They have a famous fishing ground here. Why don't you step down to the shore?"

"Oh, yes, why don't you, Captain? Mr. Pearson loves to have visitors. You see, he works forty or fifty men, just the nets and boats."

"You will like it," Penelope added. Peter thought she wanted to talk privately with her friends.

Madam Pearson said, "I'll walk as far as the garden hedge with you, Captain. I can't go all the way down. The path is so steep and my knee is quite useless."

She pointed out plantations as they walked to the point. "You can't see the houses. Rutledge Riding is up there between Eden House and here. Mr. Charleton lives over there where you see the lightning-struck pine. Scots Hall is beyond. It belongs to Penelope. She had it from her mother, you know. I can't think who is living there at the moment. Bring my husband back with you for tea." She stood on the bank watching Peter descend, calling out directions to him.

The fishing was immediately below, he saw when he made the turn in the path below the summer-house. A group of men stood on the beach; four or five long canoes with eight to ten men, at different stations for a matter of a mile, were manoeuvring a net inshore. Peter found Lawyer Pearson, who greeted him warmly. Away from his wife he was quite talkative.

"You now see a lawyer turned fisherman." He smiled. "I assure you it pays better than the law." He pointed toward the net which was now being hauled into shallow water. The slithering silver fish gleamed in the sunlight—the larger bodies of shad among the thousands of herring.

"An excellent haul! An excellent haul!" Pearson said, rubbing his hands together delightedly. With a word of apology he moved off to the beach where his overlooker was directing the Negroes onshore. The black men had waded out, and stood waist-deep in the cold water. It reminded Peter of other fishing days, in far different circumstances. He watched awhile, then went back up to the house.

When he went into the drawing-room he found Sam Johnston and Cosmo. Johnston greeted him. "Will Hooper left his farewells. He had an opportunity to drive on to New Bern with Wylie Jones, who stopped at Charleton's; so he went on."

Cosmo was sitting between Penelope and Mary Warden on a yellow satin sofa. The women were both laughing at some remark he had made. Peter thought his friend must have been successful on his visit to the near-by plantations, seeking mounts for his dragoons, for he was in high spirits. Either that or the presence of two lovely women had changed his early-morning mood of gloom over the prospect of mounts or men in "this, oh, so desolate world!"

His own good feeling had deteriorated rapidly after seeing Angela seated close to Mr. Jeremiah Morse. Madam Dawson's accusation that he was in love with Angela disturbed him even more. Was he in love or had his interest been aroused by her attitude toward him? Peter was not a man to spend many minutes thinking of himself, or examining his sensations. He was more inclined toward immediate action, yet here he was spending time thinking of a provocative girl instead of putting his mind to the duties at hand. He sat watching Madam Pearson fussing among the tea-things, stirring the tea-grounds, covering the pot with a monstrous cosy, so that it could steep a few minutes longer.

Everything seemed to be in abeyance. His order on leaving the North had been to wait at Queen Anne's Town for dispatches. He knew his destination was New Bern ultimately; the delay here might mean that the suspected person or persons were in the vicinity. He felt as though he had come to an impasse in his search for secret agents of the enemy or traitors among the Whigs. Perhaps dispatches would be at Horniblow's by the time he returned. The General had promised him that when this task was finished he could return to the army and active fighting. He wanted that. He didn't like a game played in drawing-rooms or council chambers. He preferred to fight with a sword in his hand. Now he was engaged in a task that made everyone he came in contact with a potential subtle traitor, or at least a suspect.

Madam Pearson spoke his name twice before he was aware. "Captain, Captain, a tuppence for your thoughts."

"They are not worth a ha'penny," he hastened to say. He rose from his chair and took the cup she was holding.

"This is for Madam Warden, without sugar, a good thing, for my Damara is running low. Pene likes a little jam in her tea, very Russian, you know. I think she learned the trick from that new Dr. Young, who visited Sam. Did you meet him? Very distinguished. They say he was physician to the Empress of Russia, just fancy!"

Mary Warden took the cup, smiling up at Peter. "Pene has been telling me that you were in Paris with Mr. Franklin. Do draw up a chair and tell me something about him." Peter drew up a chair and sat down beside her. "I met his daughter, Madam Bache, in London. That was during the time he was agent there. I met Mr. Franklin once. He was drinking tea at Madam Emsley's when I dropped in one afternoon. He was delightful."

Peter said, "I found him so, and more."

Mary Warden continued, "It was the day that he lost the secret code after he had come from a levee at St. James's. He was very perturbed."

Peter laughed. "I was there at the same time. Believe me, it was a period of deepest anxiety, everyone in the office scurrying around looking under furniture and rugs."

"Did he ever find it?"

Peter said, "Yes, Lord George Germain's office sent it over by hand, with a very polite note saying that it had been found on the parade ground of the Horse Guard. A very subtle hint that Mr. Franklin and his secret code had been trespassing." Peter smiled a little in retrospect. "It is the only time I ever heard Mr. Franklin profane. He covered the ground thoroughly. He despised Germain, anyway."

Some thought deepened the sadness in Mary Warden's eyes. "London was delightful in those days. It saddens me to think they will never come again."

Madam Pearson's voice recalled them. "My husband had a letter from Adam Rutledge this morning. He is with General Washington now."

A subtle change came over the woman beside him. Without moving, she seemed to withdraw into herself.

Pene said, "Oh, do read it to us. I haven't heard a word from Adam for a year, not a word."

Madam Pearson got up and went to the escritoire at the end of the room, rummaging among the confusion of papers on the desk and in the pigeon-holes. "Ah, here it is. I'm surprised I found it so soon. I tell Mr. Pearson that his desk is beyond hope, but he doesn't heed me."

Pene held out her slim hand. "Let me see it. May I read it aloud, or is it confidential?"

"Oh, no. Not at all. Just a nice friendly little letter, inquiring about everybody. He spoke of you, Pene, and asked about Mary. It is from Philadelphia. I wish he would write more news, but men are like that."

Penelope unfolded the letter and read:

"Dear Pearson:

"Yours of 21st January at hand. We are having the devil's own time about money to pay the troops. We are desperate. A warrant for paying the Fourth Connecticut Regiment for November and December, made out to Lieut. Chas. Fanning, was lost by him and never found, but his Excellency made out another. I want to inform you, since some villain may present it to you for payment. Now I have on my desk several advances against the Virginia and North Carolina Lines, for which the paymaster has ordered stoppage. The poor devils are in despair. We have no surplus of clothing or cash. Ineffective work here caused the General to send me to Philadelphia to see if I can straighten accounts. Pay-rolls are mislaid, or worse. Now Mr. Pierce, the Paymaster-General, requests the sum of five hundred thousand dollars to complete the payment of the First Army.

"I enclose a letter from Reading Blount, Deputy Paymaster-General for North Carolina. He is out of cash. Benjamin Harrison, in the same position in Virginia, informs me that his chest is also empty. I paid James Legar, of First North Carolina Regiment, one hundred ninety-five dollars out of my own pocket. This constituted his pay and subsistence since 1st. Mar. 1779.

"I am ordered to write to the treasurers of North Carolina and Virginia advising that warrants are being sent, and requesting them to give immediate attention.

"I have been told that nine hundred thousand dollars have been issued by Congress to be transmitted by Jos. Clay, for General Lincoln for use of military chest in that department. Draw your own conclusions from this item.

"This is desolate work. I sit at a desk and look at these figures of sums of money due, nay, long overdue, to our suffering soldiers; trying to spread a little here, a little there. Spreading thin. The pay of colonels raised to seventy-five dollars a month works hardship on us here.

"I have made several excursions to visit field paymasters. Everywhere I find the greatest want of money. The rate of desertion is appalling. The Maryland regiments marching South have charges against them for which settlement should be made.

These things you should know, and again draw conclusions. I am to be relieved of this work soon, thank God; then I go back to my regiment.

"I understand that a very good man, Captain Peter Huntley, will be soon in our part of the world. Do what you can for him. He will be in touch with Hewes and Smith's, as disposers of lottery tickets. As to that scheme, the General looks the other way. However, I have been informed that the two-hundred-thousand-dollar fund, of which I spoke in my last to you, should be mentioned to no one. It will not answer in any measure toward payment of troops.

"All our Continental troops are now joined. The Jerseys and West Point are to be defended by militia. They are proceeding toward New York and will probably make an attack, as it is but thinly garrisoned, since British troops have sailed to New England *and elsewhere.*

"We shall want more money. The army is so large now, and the *importance of the coming campaign* requires that the General should be supplied with money for exigencies or perhaps operations may cease.

"General Arnold has a large garrison of militia at West Point. On the approach of the French toward New York, we shall undoubtedly have a very large army.

"Show this to Johnston or Hooper. Hewes already has this information. For the love of God, get some money in North Carolina.

"ADAM RUTLEDGE.

"Secret & Confidential"

Peter, hearing a noise, glanced up. Angela and Jeremiah Morse were on the piazza outside the open window. How long they had been there he did not know. He was conscious of Penelope saying:

"I think this must be the wrong letter, Madam Pearson." Her voice was serious.

"Oh, perhaps it is, but does it matter? It is all so very dull." No one spoke. Peter thought of the sentences that were emphasized. The army planned to move south. There was no question of that now. New York was probably a feint. This was important.

Mary Warden made an exclamation. She turned to Peter, a look of consternation on her face. "I'm afraid those people on the piazza heard the last part of the letter."

Peter said, "I'm afraid so."

Penelope leaned across Mary Warden's knees to speak to Peter. "I am sorry I continued to read. I did not realize."

Peter said, "Don't worry. They probably didn't hear you. They are very much engrossed in each other." His voice had an edge.

"I pray God they were," was the answer.

Cosmo had made few comments on Adam Rutledge's letter, but the comments were significant. "I thought I was the only one who had troubles about money, but I see that is not so. The great General himself is in the same ship with me. Therefore I endeavour the more, so all will work successfully for the great man."

Peter had no way to know what Morse or Angela had heard. Morse was amiable and polite. He had sought out Peter. He talked of the beautiful country—so much timber, he said, and naval stores sufficient to provide John Paul Jones and Captain Hopkins with everything they needed. Said he, "If it were not for this unnecessary war, my firm would be interested in tar, pitch and turpentine. We could, with the potential of these forests, even compete with Sweden in naval stores." He spread his hands, a gesture of negation. "But no, we must submerge our natural commercial instincts to the necessities of war."

Peter listened, assuming an interest that he did not feel. "Have you been successful in making your purchase in Queen Anne's Town?" he asked politely.

"Beyond my hope. The Perquimans Quakers have been manufacturing shoes. They are stored in quantity at Hewes and Smith's warehouse. But I must wait . . . wait for waggons to move them to Philadelphia. It is too bad the articles can't be shipped by boat, isn't it? But no, the British blockade of the Chesapeake and the Banks prevents." He smiled amiably. "Again this war interferes with trade. If the war were not to be fought, and General Washington had his way, there would be a long canal dug through the Great Dismal Swamp. Then boats could operate without sailing in the open sea."

Peter raised his heavy brows. "I hadn't heard of that project."

"Nor had I until a short time ago when I stopped at Colonel Gregory's camp at the edge of the Dismal. I met a man there, an extraordinary fellow named Williamson, a medical man."

Peter looked expectant. He knew well enough who Dr. Hugh Williamson was.

"He told me about his idea of swamp drainage to keep the soldiers from having fevers. An interesting idea. Have you run across this doctor?"

"No, I have not had that pleasure, but I understand that he lives in Queen Anne's Town."

"So I have been told. Quite a village for extraordinary men, don't you think? Mr. Johnston and Mr. Hewes and Mr. Iredell, a trio to consider seriously. Yes, very seriously. Then there are the Harveys at the Point, and Judge Charleton, and Archibald Corrie, of Tyrrell."

Peter thought Morse had assembled his list of leaders quite well, almost as if it had been long prepared. To appear interested he said, "You neglect Mr. Will Hooper; he is in Queen Anne's so frequently, he almost belongs."

"That is quite true. A Signer, was he not, along with Joseph Hewes?"

"I believe so."

The others were grouped near the table. Peter could see Angela beyond Mary Warden's slight figure. She was talking animatedly, her eyes sparkling, her colour high. He brought himself back to Morse with reluctance.

"And Horniblow. Is he not a character? I declare he delights me. I drank a posset with him a few days ago. He told me that he was a great friend of General Benedict Arnold. By the way, Arnold is commanding militia at West Point. He is not too pleased to take over thirty and ninety-day men."

Peter stared at Morse unthinkingly. Was it a concidence that Morse had mentioned the same circumstance about which Adam Rutledge had written to Lawyer Pearson?

He noticed Morse hesitate a second. His words came more swiftly, as though he wished to cover an indiscretion. "I stopped overnight at West Point on my way south. I met the General for the first time. An able man, I would say."

"Undoubtedly," Peter answered.

Penelope called out, "Captain, I think it is time to be starting for Eden House, if we want to get home before nightfall." Peter excused himself. He felt Morse's eyes on his back as he crossed the room to make his devoirs to his hostess.

Madam Pearson patted his arm. "Come to us again soon. Mr. Pearson loves to have young people about. We miss Nat so much." Tears

showed in her eyes. Peter felt sudden sympathy. It was hard for her,
with her beloved son in an enemy country. He felt ashamed that he
had laughed to himself at her loquacity. Mother love was strong in her
heart and her soul. He lifted her hand to his lips. "The war cannot
last forever," he said.

"That is what my husband says, but it seems an eternity to me."

They left then. Aside from a cool nod when she came in, Angela
had said not one word to him.

Mary Warden rode home with them for a few days' visit at Eden
House. Peter followed them, along a short cut through the pocosin.
The sun was low and darkness not far off. Peter was not sorry to ride
far back; he had plenty to think about. The information contained in
Adam Rutledge's letter was not all new to him. He had heard the
plan discussed in officers' meetings and in meetings of the Secret
Committee, but the fact that the commander was about to put it into
operation was news. It made it all the more necessary for him to clear
the way before the army moved south. He made up his mind to
go into Queen Anne's Town Sunday evening instead of Monday
morning.

They were passing through the deep swamp. Under the entwined
canopy of boughs the light was dimmed. Frogs' hoarse croaking came
from the black water, among the thick growths of cypress. Fumes of
rotting vegetation, slime and stagnant water sent off a putrid odour.
A thin mist hung low among the trees, concealing, making more mysterious the grotesque growth. They rode along a narrow strip of black
earth, with the dark water on either side. The path was hard-beaten,
as though many feet had passed that way.

Penelope called over her shoulder, "It is an old Indian path through
the swamp. They say it is used now by runaway slaves, though I've
never seen one myself."

Peter urged his horse forward until he was close behind. "I shouldn't
care to ride through this stretch at night," he remarked.

"Nor I. Nor anyone about here. The Negroes are terrified of the
place, or pretend to be." She spoke thoughtfully. "One never knows
what the black man thinks—it is possible they may want to keep
everyone away."

A ray of bright sunlight slanted down through the heavy crown of
trees and made a reflection in the black water. The path broadened
and made a little island of land, guarded by water and a reef of cypress
knees. He looked down. At one side were the charred remains of a

small campfire. Peter thought it had been alight not long before. Penelope went by without noticing. They overtook Mary, who had reined her horse. She was looking about her curiously.

"We are on Rutledge Riding land, aren't we?" she asked Penelope.

"I think so. I'm not sure where Balgray leaves off and Adam's timber begins."

Mary looked into the deep aisles of the forest with searching eyes. "I must be. I think it was about here that he stood off those runaway slaves. Don't you remember?"

Penelope looked more closely. "I imagine it was. What a frightful experience that was, Mary! For a long time afterward I was terrified to stay alone at night. I bolted every window and door and made Scipio sleep on a mat outside my door."

Madam Warden turned to Peter. "Several slaves Mr. Rutledge bought ran away and hid in the pocosin. They lived there for months, going out only at night to raid fowl runs and smokehouses. They succeeded in inveigling a number of his old slaves to join them. One night a house slave was carried off, a woman." She spoke quietly, her usually vibrant voice flat, without inflection. "Mr. Rutledge went after the blacks alone. He went into the swamp. He was obliged to kill two of the most desperate. The ringleader he subdued!" Her voice trembled a little. "He is very courageous."

Penelope took up the tale. "What followed will interest you, Captain. The ringleader was a native Zulu, straight from Africa, a tremendous, powerful fellow. The overlooker put him in irons in the slave dungeon. Adam had broken his arm, I think, in a fight. Another planter or slave-owner would have killed the fellow. But Adam recognized the black had courage and something unconquerable. He had the gyves struck off. He talked with him and found he was a chieftain. He put the slave on honour."

Peter saw that Mary Warden was giving Penelope the closest attention. There was something more to this than interest in a tale. "What happened? Was he successful?"

"Entirely. Adam made the fellow—Herk is his name—his bodyservant. He gave him the run of the house and the plantation. We were all against it. We were afraid the great Zulu would kill Adam some night while he slept. In truth the village was making wagers, but Adam took the right course. The man is his slave, in truth, not from ownership, but from loyalty."

"I like this Adam Rutledge," Peter said impulsively. "I admire that degree of understanding in a man. He must be very fine." He glanced at Mary. She turned her head aside, but not before he saw her lips were trembling.

"Adam is all of that." Penelope spoke with emphasis. "One of our very finest planters. I always feel proud that we are friends."

Mary touched her horse with her heel and led off. Penelope lingered a moment. "That is the tragedy of Mary Warden," she murmured. Peter remembered then what she had told him earlier, "married to a man twenty years older." It was evident to him now that she was deeply in love with Adam.

"It is hopeless," Penelope continued, as they rode side by side through the trees. "Adam has an invalid wife, who adores him and clings to him like a limpet. Sometimes I could weep my eyes out for them."

"I met Major Rutledge in Philadelphia," Peter observed. "I thought him an extraordinarily fine officer."

"And now you know his story."

They moved out of the deep swamp into a more open stretch of land where the pines grew stately and tall, with no underbrush or tangled vines. "This is Adam's turpentine woods. He makes tar over yonder, and sends it to the Indies and England. Or he did before the war. Sometimes they manage to get his ships to the French Islands and from there to Portugal, if the captains are lucky and the British blockade is not drawn too tight."

At supper that night Peter watched Mary Warden with more interest. He thought, She is strong in spite of her feminine ways and her gentle manner. He read things in her face; he thought she would have great moral courage, integrity.

Samuel Johnston joined them as they were finishing supper. He had come back from a trip to Mount Galland. He sat down beside Penelope and they fell into plantation talk. Mary was engaged with Cosmo.

"You must come to Queen's Gift, and bring Captain Huntley. I am sure my steward will find a horse or two for you. I would give you a definite answer now, but I have been away from home so much of late that I do not know what stock is available."

Cosmo thanked her. "You are all so kind, so generous," he said.

"We want to win a war," she said simply.

After the ladies and Cosmo had gone into the drawing-room for music, Johnston pulled an old leather easy chair in front of the fire and motioned to Peter Huntley to sit down.

"Even in April, sometimes May, the warmth of a fire is good. My father used to say he could think more clearly looking into flames. The fire burned up extraneous matter, leaving only the real metal. . . . Interesting, wasn't it, Ferrier knowing your people? A small link of the past to the present forges a strong future."

Peter said, "Thank you, sir. I devotedly hope it may prove strong enough to stand the strain of war."

Johnston took his clay churchwarden pipe from a rack. "Now let us have the story," he said.

Peter hesitated a moment. He wanted to put the story into clear, concise words, and he did not want to overlook any important point. After a moment's thought he said:

"It begins back a few years in Paris and has to do with the misunderstanding in the position and rank of the Commissioners—the two Lees, Mr. Izard, Silas Deane and Mr. Adams. They were all jealous of Mr. Franklin. There were jealousy and intrigue among the Lees and Silas Deane. I was acting as a sort of aide to Mr. Franklin; actually I had no title. I had been engaged because I spoke French and Dutch and Spanish, having spent in my youth a number of years on the Continent, during my father's exile. I am not capable of deciding who was right and who was wrong. My loyalty was to Mr. Franklin, whom I admire extravagantly. Nor do I feel any doubts of the loyalty of the Lees, Mr. Adams or Mr. Izard. They were all patriotic men. Mr. Deane—" Peter stopped to tamp the pipe Mr. Johnston handed to him—" Mr. Deane is another matter. I am not so sure of Mr. Deane. However, I will keep to the known facts. I am sure from records I have seen that Mr. Arthur Lee was misled by falsehoods, and that for a time Congress and our military authority were misled by false information of British plans."

"You know this to be true?"

"Yes, I suspect Thornton, Mr. Lee's secretary. It might have been some other agent, but Thornton was the most logical, since he was later known to be in Lord North's pay. To test him, you have only to go through Mr. Lee's letters of the spring of '76. The real object of the British attack was the cities of New York and Charles Town. Lee's report, 'confidentially obtained,' was that the British northern attack was to be through Quebec and Albany, and the southern attack through Virginia.

"I won't go into all the details but you will remember that Sir Peter Parker's attempt at Charles Town was halted. The Americans

successfully defended Sullivan's Island, which controlled the approach
to Charles Town. That was in June of '76."

"I remember that well enough. We were alarmed here in North
Carolina," Johnston replied.

Peter stopped talking while he watched his host poke the fire into
a blaze. "New York fared much worse. It was against that city that
the main body of the British forces were hurled."

Johnston sat down again.

"It was before this overwhelming force that Washington was com-
pelled to retreat, and New York was lost. You can see how Arthur
Lee's confidentially obtained advices were erroneous. The plan he
announced for 1776 was adopted by the British for their campaign of
1777. This we know now. At the time, we did not see where Lee's
erroneous reports were leading us."

"Bungler!" Johnston said.

"Then take Lee's letters of 1777. It was in February, I think, that
he announced that Howe would act against New England. Carleton
would make his way over the Lakes to keep the middle colonies in
awe, while Burgoyne, with armament from England of ten thousand,
would invade the South, probably Virginia and Maryland."

Peter got up and took his place, back to the fire. "I hope I am not
boring you, Mr. Johnston. I was told to give you a summary of the
events so you could see how these matters fit together."

"Please continue."

"This intelligence, which was entirely erroneous, was probably sent
to France with the single view of creating a false impression there as
to the real plans of the British campaign. The intelligence found its
way to Thornton.

"The real plan was not for Howe to invade New England, but to
move on Philadelphia; for Burgoyne to attack not Virginia but New
York, via Canada. He was to be met on the Hudson River by Clinton
and thus encircle New England. Carleton to 'make his way over the
Lakes to keep the middle colonies in awe,' was not in the British plans
at all, and Lee's statement of February of 1777, that Boston would
certainly be attacked in the spring, was as false as the other."

"The wretch!" Johnston exploded. "The wretch!"

Peter hastened to complete what he intended to say. "Mr. Franklin
never felt that Lee was disloyal. He was truly patriotic. But he was
no judge of men. He had managed to surround himself with a set
of spies, all unbeknownst to him."

Johnston shook his head vigorously. "A man of so little judgement should have been removed at once, and brought home."

"That is not all, Mr. Johnston. In the summer of 1778, Lee wrote he had it on exceedingly good information that the plan of operation in America was as follows: 'General Howe is to evacuate Philadelphia, sending five thousand of his troops and ten of his ships of war to Quebec. The rest of the troops with the fleet will return to Halifax.'

"Well, as you know, Philadelphia was evacuated as a matter of necessity. The British army was melting away by desertion and the river liable at any minute to be blockaded by the French. The plan of the plotters was to lead General Washington into believing that Howe, instead of marching across New Jersey, would go by sea. So they would draw off Washington to allow Howe to retreat in safety to New York.

"Fortunately Arthur Lee's letter did not reach America in time to take effect. And the General, seeing the only available retreat for Howe was to march through New Jersey, gave them battle at Monmouth."

"Our North Carolina men were there," Johnston said with satisfaction.

"There are other things that Thornton did that all but ruined our chances on the sea."

"John Paul has some of his roots in our soil," Johnston said. "For some time he visited our good friend Wylie Jones at Halifax. It was there he took the name of Jones, in tribute to his benefactor, in loving tribute. Joseph Hewes is his friend also. He was instrumental in getting ships when Jones wanted them most."

"I did not know that. I have had much correspondence with the commander, particularly over his detention in Dutch waters by the Dutch authorities." He took a turn about the room, while Johnston lighted fresh candles. "That is the background. I am coming now to the reason for my being here. It has to do with Mr. Franklin and the lost million and an unknown messenger sent from Paris by Silas Deane—and his disappearance in Carolina, on the way from New Bern to Suffolk."

CHAPTER

9

QUARTERS LINE

LATE Saturday evening Madam Pearson sent a messenger to say that Parson Earle would hold services at Duckenfield on Sunday morning, and would they all come over? From Eden House Mary Warden, Samuel Johnston and Peter attended. At the last moment Penelope said she could not go with them. Her steward had come to her about some matter of the plantation that called for immediate attention. Cosmo slept.

Penelope stood on the piazza to wave them good-bye. "Be sure and bring the Parson back for dinner, Sam," she called, as her cousin was mounting his horse from the block. Peter thought she looked worried, but it might have been the bright sunlight which caused her to squint her eyes. He watched her turn and walk toward the little office, at the end of the garden, where the steward was pacing up and down impatiently.

"You will enjoy the Parson," Mary Warden told him as they trotted along the drive that led to the Governor's Road. "He is a cultured man, very human and full of life."

"And a great rider. He had rather follow the hounds than preach, I've been told," Peter said.

"Ride and fish. It was he who taught our people how to fish herring commercially. He understands handling the long nets, as they do in his native Ireland. He taught the yeomen upriver to plant flax, to spin and weave."

"You are fortunate to have a satisfactory rector," Peter observed.

Samuel agreed. "We are indeed. All classes of people interest him. He would as lief ride twenty miles to visit a yeoman and his family or a fisherman, as he would go to the call of a wealthy planter. He lives up the Chowan. His place adjoins Ferrier's plantation. He has a fishery on the river at the junction of Brownrigg Creek. We must take you up to see it some day soon. I want you to visit Wingfield, also, Mr. Brownrigg's seat just above. In fact I should like you to see something of our plantation life, Captain. We think the Albemarle rather superior in that respect."

"If Eden House is an indication, I can quite agree without seeing any more."

"I don't wonder you feel that way," Mary said quietly. "Penelope is something very special. But there are other lovely places." She smiled at Sam. "Hayes, of course."

"Not a show place, certainly," Samuel said. "It will be more attractive when I get the new house built," he explained to Peter. "I had started to build, but the war came along." He smiled ruefully. "I found soon enough that during war is no time to build."

Mary continued, "Then there are Montpelier and Belvidere; Mulberry Hill, where the Blounts live; and Sandy Point, which belonged to Lovyck, a contemporary of Governor Eden whom the Governor made his heir."

"Don't forget Greenfield and Drummond's Point," Sam added. "I think that the Yeopim district is one of the most attractive of all the Sound shore."

Peter smiled. "I will have to stay here a long time to visit all the plantations you mention."

Mary said, "You must promise to come to Queen's Gift. Sam, don't you think he should visit Rutledge Riding?"

"Perhaps we can ride home that way. Is the house open?"

"No, Sara is in New York with her father, having a beautiful time with the British officers, she writes. And Lavinia is in Charles Town."

"A bad place to be right now," Samuel Johnston observed. "You had best have William send word for her to come home, before the British march up from Georgia."

Mary's mobile face expressed anxiety. "Do you think we will have a real invasion?"

"Without a doubt. Peter here will tell you the same."

Mary said, "I had planned to go down to Mulberry Broughton for a visit."

"Stay at Queen's Gift, my dear Mary. You are safe here. We live in security in this little Eden of ours."

"Pray God you always will!" Peter said, fervently.

Parson Earle was a powerful, rugged figure, with a jovial expression, and the manner of a man who is earnestly interested in each person with whom he talks, exclusive of all others. He held service in the large dining-room, where a small altar had been arranged on a side-table. He read the service in a short, staccato way, and preached briefly on the value of tolerance. Then he led the hymn, in a voice powerful rather than musical. He had already held service for the slaves earlier in the morning and baptized two Negro children. He read the marriage lines for a Negro couple who had been living together for twenty years and had seven children. "At least I have made them honest in the eyes of God and Holy Church," he said to Johnston with a keen relish. "The woman, Phyllis, told me she expected another and she wanted this one 'born honest.'"

Peter sat behind Angela Ferrier and Mrs. Pollock. He saw nothing of the Boston gentleman or Cullen Pollock, but he heard Ann telling Mary that their Northern guest was still with them. "He and Cullen rode off to look at some timber early this morning. I told them the Sabbath was no day to go over to Tyrrell to look at turpentine trees, but they went just the same."

While the two women were talking, Peter spoke to Angela. She greeted him a shade more cordially than usual. She was radiant, her eyes bright, a soft colour tinting her usually pale face.

She looks like a woman in love, Peter thought. Depression seemed to descend on him. To detain her a moment he inquired about Mr. Ferrier.

"He will come down from the River Plantation on Monday," she said so indifferently that Peter felt chilled and rebuffed. But the pleasure of being near her was great, and he endeavoured by talking to give himself the doubtful pleasure of being near her a little longer. She turned away and spoke to Mary.

"Please tell Penelope that I will be over this evening. I expect my father to be here in the morning in the canoe. I will go with him to the village. Do you think Madam Dawson has a place for me?"

"Of course. You may share my room. I have the east room with two great tester beds."

Mr. Pearson spoke to Peter. "I wish you had stayed last evening. We had a wonderful haul. I think I have never seen so many herring since I've been in this country."

"What will you do with them, since there are no ships coming from the North now?"

"I have already sold them to Cullen for Mr. Morse. He will have them put into hogsheads and salted. Later he will have them sent by waggon to the army."

Peter thought, Perhaps my suspicions are wrong. Perhaps Morse is really a merchant, buying for the army. Then an idea came to him. "Where is he sending them?" he asked.

Pearson answered readily, "South, to Charles Town."

The answer did not help Peter. The herring might be for the Continental army; on the other hand Morse might be preparing a cache of food for the British, if they should succeed in taking Charles Town.

Madam Warden came across the room. "We are starting for Eden House in a few moments," she told Peter. "The rector will ride over with Dr. Cathcart in his travelling carriage."

A succession of visitors called all day Sunday—a custom that had its origin from the earliest days, when the Sabbath was a day for rest and visiting. The men roamed about the grounds and sat on the piazza. The women for the most part stayed within or walked in Penelope's flower garden which extended to the river-bank. Some came because Parson Earle was there, others to accept the Eden House hospitality: Lockharts and young Lowther from along the Chowan, the Bests from Devil's Elbow, the Bonners from their place in Tyrrell on the Roanoke and the Dickinsons from Salmon Creek. They came on horseback or chaise. Some who lived within a mile or two walked, for the day was mild, almost warm.

Cosmo de' Medici was delighted. After young Lowther's offer of a horse, almost every planter there followed his lead. "If this keeps up, I will not have to call on the Sound-side planters," he told Peter jubilantly. "Imagine, instead of having to plead, beg, threaten or call on men to do patriotic duty, these men offer." He consulted his notebook. "Ten in all, Peter, just fancy. Perhaps we will get all the mounts we need without calling on other communities. Those who didn't give horses have offered hay and corn," he continued. "Was there ever a place like this?"

He ran up the piazza steps. A moment later Peter heard laughter from the drawing-room. Cosmo had done his work, and would now follow his endeavour with the ladies.

Peter talked with Lawyer Pearson. He liked the quiet man. Since hearing Rutledge's letter, he had respect for him, knowing that the task of raising money for the army was beset with difficulties and worry. Pearson was looking at Parson Earle. He was the centre of a group of planters. His pleasant face was beaming, his smile broad and inclusive. He looked as if he had a heart that was filled with warmth and affection. He remembered the names of children, of bed-ridden old people. He spoke to one planter of an ailing slave whom he had baptized a few months ago.

"St. Paul's is fortunate to have such a man as rector," Pearson remarked. They were strolling along the boxwood-bordered path that led to a small garden-house on the bank of the river. "A fortunate parish indeed. We have not always been so happy in our clergy."

Peter commented, "He seems a man of parts. One would not expect that in a small community."

"That is true. Earle was an officer in the Irish Guards, before he took orders. Some people in the village say he is still more a guardsman than a clergyman, with his fox-hunting and his fishing. But I will say he is both. He may lose a few narrow parishioners, but still and all he holds his people in line. 'Tis said he lived in a great castle in Ireland, at a village called Bandon. That I don't know, but as you say, Parson Daniel Earle is a man of parts."

They had reached the summer-house and sat down to enjoy the view of the water. A moment later a slave followed them with a decanter and glasses on a tray which he set on a small iron table. "Mistress say you must have a drink of wine she have got from Indies."

"Thank you," Pearson said. The Negro bowed and went away.

Peter poured the wine and handed a glass to the lawyer. "To our hostess!" he said. Lifting his glass, he bowed in the direction of the house.

Pearson smiled. "A rare woman," he said as he lifted his glass, "a rare woman, and there is another." He nodded his head in the direction of Mary Warden, standing with several women.

"I think this occasion calls for a second toast, to Madam Warden." Peter filled Pearson's glass, and, when it was down, said, "And we must not forget Madam Pearson, your charming lady."

"Thank you, Captain Huntley. I can drink that toast with fervour. A better woman never lived. I assure you she has a bosom full of mother love." He stood up and drank. "Sad, sad indeed for her to be so far from her beloved son." There was a moment's silence—voices came dimly·from the garden, a boat grated against the wharf. "A mother is a creature beyond our ken, Captain. When she bears her sorrow with fortitude she is great."

Peter held his glass. A sunbeam fell across the ruby liquid. He

lifted it. "To Madam! May the end of war bring home her son!"
Pearson drank in silence.

The guests were all in the garden now. The bright dresses of the
women made the garden bloom. Light laughter of women, the deeper
voices of men came to their ears. Pearson glanced at the sun-dial, set
in a bed of pinks. "A quarter before four," he said. "Did someone
say the Parson was going to hold sunset service?"

Peter shook his head. "I have not heard of it."

They walked slowly through the garden to join the group on the
bank of the river. They stood in a semicircle, facing the water. A
great oak tree spread its green crown above their heads. From their
quarters the Negroes were coming in little groups of two or three.
They stood aside at a respectful distance. The moment the last long
rays of sun lay on the river, the Parson came out of the house and
took his place under the tree. In a resonant voice he read the Gospel
for the day. When he came to the words, "Let us pray," the people
knelt on the young green grass. Peter bowed his head. He felt moved
by the solemnity of the words, the earnest appeal for divine help to a
discouraged, suffering army. Praying for strength and praying for
victory.

He thought of Cromwell praying thus for divine guidance, in an
English garden, before the Battle of Naseby.

A voice rose, an old hymn, ageless:

> "I have a sin of fear, that when I've spun
>   My last thread, I shall perish on the shore:
> But swear by thyself, that at my death thy Son
>   Shall shine as He shines now, and heretofore;
> And, having done that, Thou hast done,
>   I fear no more."

Peter opened his eyes. A long ray of sunlight came through the
pines that stood back of the house, and fell on the cross suspended on
the speaker's breast. A woman near by caught her breath. "An omen,"
she whispered to the man beside her. "God has sent an omen." Others
were singing now. Peter joined the chorus, "I fear no more." He
noticed Cosmo. He was kneeling, a reverent expression on his face.
His lips were moving.

When the people rose to their feet, he saw Angela and Jeremiah
Morse on the far side of the semicircle. He remembered the sound
of a boat against the dock when he was talking with Pearson. The

guests were moving toward the house, for the most part silently. The air was hushed, the river without a breeze to ruffle its smooth surface. A frog croaked, followed by a chorus. From the forest, a bat flew on sable, silent wings, uttering its shrill cry. A chill went down his spine; he shivered.

"The night falls swiftly," he heard Johnston say to Mary Warden. "Shall I get a wrap for you?"

"Thank you, no. Penelope wants us in the dining-room for supper."

"Where is Penelope?" he asked.

Mary replied, "She's been down to the quarters line. There she is, talking with Dr. Cathcart."

"I hope none of the slaves is ailing."

"I fancy not. Probably a new baby," Mary answered lightly. "Come, let us start, the others will follow."

Peter lingered outside. Penelope had walked a few steps with the doctor.

"Don't come, Penelope." Dr. Cathcart's voice carried to where Peter stood. "Go in to your guests. Your steward will conduct me to the cabin."

"Very well, Doctor. But if you need me, have him send one of the boys. I have medicines of all varieties in the dispensary."

The doctor went down the lane to the slave quarters. Penelope turned toward the house. She looked worried. When she saw Peter she waved her hand.

"Come, let us go in," she said, when she came up to him.

Peter walked beside her. At the door he said, "Can I be of any help?"

She looked up quickly. "Thank you, Peter. It is nothing—I hope it is nothing. Two of the Negroes are ill, a man and his wife. . . . I went down to see them this afternoon. They both have fever, a burning fever. The man is delirious."

"It is fortunate that Dr. Cathcart came in."

"Isn't it? He doesn't really practise now, but I trust him."

"What would you have done if he hadn't been here?"

"I would have had to send to the village for Dr. Armitage, or Dr. Dickinson. Come, let us forget worry. 'A full stomach is a panacea for worries,' my father used to say."

In the hall she moved close to him. "I still think there is something amiss with Morse. Doesn't he appear to you to have more of the cut of a military man than a merchant?"

Peter nodded. "He is here for no good."

She said, "I don't want Angela to get involved in some political——"

"Ferrier's daughter couldn't be anything but a staunch Whig." Peter tried to be reassuring.

"Remember, Peter, she is not Ferrier's daughter. She fancies herself Spanish to the core, and therefore has no part in this revolt."

Peter said, "If I can predict a little, Spain will soon be in this. Not to assist us, but because she is longing for an opportunity to sting England."

"I don't want to say Angela would be actually disloyal. But she is young and without experience. A handsome man making love to her might, if he were so inclined, win her confidence and pick up information."

Peter said, "I hope from my heart that you are wrong."

"You do love her." Penelope stood very close; the perfume of her hair was in his nostrils. She looked at him earnestly.

"I don't know. I certainly have no reason."

"Love is never reasonable. Come, let us go into the dining-room. The guests will think me a very poor hostess."

Peter lifted her hand to his lips. "There is one guest who will always think of you as a perfect hostess."

The hunt board groaned with good plantation food—ham and a fresh roast of pork; platters of fried chicken; half a dozen dishes of pickles and preserves; scones and corn bread. Plates were heaping, glasses filled. Hearty trencher-men these Carolinians, thought Peter as he went to the side-table. His plate was heaped as high as any and he enjoyed the food quite as much.

Cullen Pollock spoke to him. "I hope you are enjoying our river, Captain. We are childishly proud of our water-ways and our forests."

"With good reason," Huntley answered. "Do you plant many acres?"

"Around two thousand at Balgray, and in Beaufort and Craven Counties. My brother has a place on the Cape Fear, but Balgray my grandfather seated before 1700."

"You must like the land," Peter ventured.

The thin, emaciated face lighted up. "I love it. I can think of nothing more beautiful than a fresh-turned field, unless it is the same field at the harvest."

"Have you been with the army?" Peter asked the question deliberately. A change came over Pollock's face. The life went out of it.

"No. I may as well tell you what the whole village will tell you, that I opposed this Revolution. People call me a Tory. I am not quite sure of the meaning of the word. If it means I am for British domination and taxation, I am not a Tory. If it means I am opposed to any war that will devastate our fine land, then Tory is what I am. I see no reason for war. No, I'm not a Quaker, but perhaps I have a little Quaker blood."

Peter felt a reluctant respect for Pollock. He fancied he spoke honestly. War devastated the beautiful land, laid it waste and unyielding.

"Will Hooper said in a speech he made at our Courthouse, 'Every soldier made is a farmer lost.' Those are my sentiments exactly. I am a planter, not a fighting man. But my neighbours have another word for me." He spoke bitterly, as a man who carries a deep-seated anger. Peter was glad when someone spoke to Cullen and the conversation was cut off.

A man in that state of mind might easily fall victim to a persuasive agent. Rancour against his traducers had eaten into him. Peter turned about, searching for the Bostonian. Morse was across the room, looking directly at him. When Peter turned he dropped his eyes to the plate he held in his hand and began to eat.

A certain exhilaration came over Peter. Morse was puzzled by him, Peter's presence disturbed him. After a little Morse crossed the room to Peter.

"Pardon me for staring at you, Captain Huntley, but your face is familiar. I seem to have seen you before, but I can't quite place you."

"London or Paris?" Peter asked helpfully. He knew Morse had made this gesture to cover.

"Paris—by Gad, I have it! Paris and Dr. Franklin." He turned to Ann Pollock. "You know I told you I had seen Captain Huntley before. He has given me the cue. It was at some affair the French gave for Dr. Franklin. You were in his party."

"It could be," Peter answered with the same apparent frankness Morse had displayed. "I have been present at a number of affairs for the minister."

Ann Pollock said, "Oh, Captain Huntley, how interesting to be so close to that great man. How did it happen? Were you a Commissioner? You must know a thousand secrets."

Peter laughed. "Indeed no, Madam Pollock. It was something between a clerk and an office boy, without the prestige of either position."

"Didn't you know secrets?"

"No one trusted me with secrets. I sat at a desk adding figures all day, or checking cargoes going to America. I was too lowly to know about important matters, nor did I care. I was young and Paris is . . ." He paused, sighing, and he raised his brows to Morse. Peter hoped he had managed to create the impression with Morse that he was a gay dog, and Paris an exciting mistress. He felt sure he had been successful, when Morse's face cleared.

"Ah, Paris!" he cried. "Oh, to be young and in Paris!"

People were leaving the room, saying their farewells to Penelope. Slaves were at the horse rack with lighted lanthorns. Those who rode carried lanthorns, to guide them along the road. The moon came up late that night, and the river and forest roads were dark. Peter noticed that many of the men had a rifle boot slung to their saddles. Others had pistols in their belts. One or two of the older men who rode in gigs had swords beside them on the seat. One woman sat down on the cold steel and rose hastily, calling, "That horrible sword! It's always in the wrong place," and wondered why the men guffawed at her words.

The Pollocks were among the last to make their adieus. Angela walked the length of the piazza with them. Peter thought Morse held her hand to his lips a prodigiously long time. The guests had driven away. Parson Earle came out, his little satchel in his hand. "Where's Cathcart? He hasn't driven off and left me behind?"

Penelope looked startled as if in the excitement of leave-taking, she had forgotten. "Where is he?" she said to Peter. "Hasn't he returned?"

"Shall I go and look for him?" Peter asked.

"Please do." To the rector she said, "Come inside, Parson Earle. The doctor went to look at one of the slaves who is sick."

Peter went down past the office to the lane lined with cone-shaped juniper and holly trees. Slaves were seated in doorways and on steps in front of the little cabins. Evil-smelling smudge fires burned before each house, for early-spring merrylegs were thick in the air. At the last cabin a bright fire burned, about which half a dozen black figures moved grotesquely. They were chanting some weird melody in their slow movements about the fire. On the low porch in front of the cabin, two women crouched, their knees to the rough planks, their arms crossed, hiding their faces. They moaned softly. A drum, the drummer hidden by bushes, beat out a slow, solemn rhythm.

"Let the drum beat!" a sing-song voice cried, "Let the drum beat!" followed by some native words Peter did not understand. They were obviously exorcising the evil spirits.

He stepped up on the low porch. No one paid any attention to his coming. The room was poorly lighted by a fire on the hearth and the flickering light of one candle stuck in a stone jug. Cathcart, his coat off, was bending over a bed made from plank, in one corner of the room. Two slaves sat by another bed opposite, whether men or women Peter could not discern. The man on the bed over which the doctor leaned was thrashing about, his arms and legs jerking. Every so often he shouted a word, "*Mungulu, Mungulu*," in his native tongue. Two men were trying to keep him quiet by sitting on his legs.

"I think we will have to strap him or he will throw himself out on the floor." The doctor straightened up and saw Peter.

"Madam Dawson sent me to tell you that Parson Earle was ready to leave."

"He may be ready, but he won't leave," Cathcart said shortly. He began to turn down his ruffled sleeves which had been rolled above his elbows. "I've got a very sick man here and I won't leave until I find out what ails him." He turned to the man who stood by the fire.

"You seem to know how to care for sick people. I want the cover kept over him. I'll show you how to tie him in, and have the women give him hot drinks until you get him into a sweat. Do you understand?"

"Yes, sar. Mingo, he understand."

"Good. Where is that boy with the straps?" A young boy came in carrying a pair of harness reins. Cathcart showed Mingo how to adjust the straps about the sick man's torso and legs. "Not too tight, we don't want them to cut his flesh. Let the buckles come under the bed, so." The man struggled, tried to sit up, screaming.

The drum beat steadily, the chant rose as the dancers around the fire increased their tempo.

"Damn *Mankwala!*" Cathcart muttered, struggling into his coat, and straightening his wig. "They make medicine outside and I try inside. Between the two of us we should get the fever down." He moved to the other bed, on which Peter could now see the man's wife lying. The doctor held the candle over her for a moment. The two watchers looked up at him solemnly, the whites of their eyeballs glistening. The woman lay still, her hands crossed over her breast, her eyes closed. The doctor bent closer. The light showed beads of perspiration on the black forehead. "Keep her warm. She will sleep. But do not leave her. Do you understand?" Both women nodded.

"Come on, Huntley. Let's get out." They were on the porch when the man gave an unearthly scream. They turned and saw that he had pulled the straps apart. He sat bolt upright in bed, shouting loudly. The doctor muttered an imprecation and went back into the room. Peter followed. He caught the black man as he was about to leap to the floor, and threw him back on the bed. Cathcart tossed the quilt over him and the Negroes held it taut, holding the sick man flat on his back.

"A strait-jacket is the only thing," Cathcart said. "Get me another quilt and a blanket." A black figure detached itself from the gloom and went out the door, silhouetted a moment by the light of the fire, a gigantic figure of a man with broad, powerful shoulders. "Wait," called Cathcart. "Aren't you Mr. Rutledge's man Herk?"

"Yes, sar, I——"

"Come back. Let someone else go for the bedding. I want you to help me here." They held the sick man's wrists and worked him into an easy position, the quilt across his loins. He tried to bite, but Herk jerked his hand aside so that the man's teeth clamped into his own flesh. He screamed like a wild animal.

Peter's blood chilled. The African jungle was close, very close. Cathcart gave directions to Herk without raising his voice. When they had the man quieted he said, "Why are you here? Is Mr. Rutledge home?"

"No, sar. I come ahead. I stop here to see Mingo. They tell me man sick, come quick."

"And you came to make *Mankwala?*" Cathcart inquired.

"No, sar. That is for men who know little. This sickness I myself have seen."

"That so? Where?" the doctor asked.

"The army, sar. Men sick this way in the army. Many, many sick."

Cathcart's voice showed that he was worried. "You are to say nothing about army sickness to these people, Herk. You understand?"

"Sar. Herk's tongue is silent."

Cathcart was satisfied. He went once again to the woman, holding the candle down close, shaking his head as though he were not satisfied with what he saw.

"Is the woman worse?" Peter inquired as they walked toward the house.

"No worse, but no improvement. I think she will be dead by morning. She has complications. It isn't that. I was trying to see if she had erupted."

"Erupted?"

"Yes. Did Herk's words have no meaning for you? These Negroes have the pox."

CHAPTER

10

THE SCOURGE

CATHCART made his announcement at breakfast. It fell heavily on the pleasant happy group. Only Penelope presented a calm face. "I feared as much," she said.

Dr. Cathcart was very grave. "Penelope, you have been exposed, and the Parson, who went to the cabin yesterday. Peter here held the man in his arms last night, when he was struggling, and breathed the sick man's fetid breath. I am afraid you will all have to stay here a few days until we see what develops."

The Parson said, "By Gad, sir, I can't do that. My Vestry is meeting tonight. Important meeting concerning a bastard child of Iredell's patron McCulloh. There are other meetings. I must think of my congregation."

"It is your congregation that I am thinking about," the doctor said dryly. "It is quite possible that you would expose them." He looked down at his plate. There was silence around the table. "We don't know how smallpox spreads. Some doctors contend that it is during the period of high fever, some say it is when the pustules scab off. . . . I wish to God Williamson were here."

"Where is he? Can we send for Dr. Williamson?" Penelope half rose from her chair, then sank back. "I am terrified of a spread of this horrible disease among our people."

"I sent a message into Queen Anne's Town early this morning. If it reaches him he will surely come. In the meantime we must await developments. It would mean *all* the Negroes of all the plantations, for they have been coming in droves to visit the sick man."

"I am glad you didn't go near the quarters, Sam." Penelope addressed Johnston.

"So am I. We have that meeting on Tuesday for representatives of all the eastern counties. The Governor cancelled the Committee of Correspondence and the ball at the Palace, because smallpox is running wild in New Bern."

The Parson said nothing. Angela sat slumped in her chair. Her face is white; she is terrified, thought Peter. He felt sorry for her. Pox was a tragedy for a woman.

"I understand good results have come from inoculation," he said.

"So Williamson contends. He has made a number of experiments in Colonel Gregory's camp, but there are no materials nearer than Norfolk, if there are any there." He applied himself to his bacon and eggs. No one else touched food. After a time, he looked up.

"You may as well eat, all of you. Resistance to the scourge is half the battle. It may amount to nothing. I've seen men nurse a dozen cases and go free themselves. But I'm not going to chance it. All of you who have been exposed directly must stay here. I've sent word to my own family." He turned to Penelope. "You will have to put up with us—Parson Earle, the captain and me—a little longer, Sam, you and De' Medici, Mary and Angela may leave whenever you have a mind to."

Mary said gently, "I made the sick round with Penelope."

Angela rose from the table. She was even whiter than she had been a moment before when Peter had glanced at her. She was trembling violently. She caught the table edge for support.

"I have been exposed," she said, looking at Cathcart. "I have been exposed."

"Angela, don't be idiotic. You can't have been," Penelope cried. "You are hysterical. Sit down and eat your breakfast."

Angela repeated the same words. "Yesterday I went to the cabin. The woman was calling for water. I gave her a drink, and lifted her head from the pillow."

Cathcart spoke gruffly. "What the devil do you mean, giving water to a fever patient?"

Penelope spoke sharply. "What were you doing in the quarters?"

"I went with Mr. Morse. He wanted to see the Negroes and talk with them."

There was a long silence, broken by the girl's flat voice continuing her explanation. "Mr. Morse . . ." She hesitated a moment. "He is studying the Negroes in the South. He will write a piece about them for a paper. He visited the slave quarters at Balgray and Duckenfield too—I went with him. You know how they are. They won't talk to strangers, so I . . ." She paused and sank into the chair, her eyes fixed on Cathcart. "Does it mark terribly?" she asked in a voice that quavered.

Peter looked at Penelope meaningly. She nodded imperceptibly. Both were thinking the same thing: Why was Jeremiah Morse interviewing Negroes, unless it had to do with a slave rebellion? Peter paid no heed to Cathcart's ambiguous reply to Angela's question.

Penelope said, "We must send a messenger to Balgray and ask Mr. Morse to come over."

"Let me write the note," Angela said hurriedly.

"No, I'll do it myself." Penelope got up and left the room.

Cathcart spoke to Johnston. "If Williamson isn't in the village, I'm sure he will be in Gregory's camp near the Dismal. Send someone up. My messenger may not find him."

"I'll go, myself." De' Medici's face was sober. "That is, if I cannot be of service here."

Cathcart said, "Splendid! If you will go to Williamson, you will be doing a great favour to us, to the whole community. We must stop this scourge right here."

A mournful wail broke the silence that followed his words, and then shrieks and moaning. A drum began to beat—A series of short swift notes, a silence, then a heavier drum sound, slow and dirge-like.

Cathcart rose. The lines in his face deepened. "A death," he said.

A moment later Scipio's frightened face appeared at the door. "Mr. Doctor, Herk is waiting. He say they die. Both of they, and one man be sick."

"Dammit to hell!" the doctor muttered, and left the room hurriedly.

Through the window Peter saw him approach Adam Rutledge's body-servant. They walked quickly away, the giant Zulu a few steps behind the doctor. The sound of wailing became louder.

The Parson said, "There is comfort in that pagan habit of wailing. A release of some kind, when the spirit is desolate."

Peter said, "The Arabs have a saying that 'among friends Death is but a festival.' "

"Curious." The Parson had recovered his poise, accepted the situation with grace.

Mary Warden moved to the chair beside Angela and spoke to her, quieting the girl's fears. "I wouldn't worry, Angela. You are strong and healthy, and have every chance."

De' Medici walked into the hall with Peter. "I will send over a change of linen," he volunteered.

"Please, and my small cases. You will do me a favour if you meet the post-rider and send me any letter that may come."

"I shall constitute myself your messenger. Peter, this is something to cause worry. I hope there is no outbreak in the village. Do you think I should move my men?"

"Where?" asked Peter. "The pox is raging in New Bern and other towns as well. Better wait, or perhaps it would be well if you spoke to this medical man, Williamson. I've been told he is keeping Gregory's army in splendid condition."

"Thank you, Peter. It is an idea. Holy Virgin! It would be intolerable to add a plague to our other worries."

They went up to the room they shared together. Cosmo called for Scipio to pack for him. He turned to Peter. "Before I leave I want you to help me compose a letter to the Governor. Your language, it defeats me. It is very bad to talk—but to write . . . !"

Peter waited until Cosmo had rummaged through a mass of papers in his box. He crumpled some, sent others sailing across the room. Scipio paused in his packing to watch Cosmo.

"The captain is like the wind," he observed, "the strong wind that brings the hurricane." He bent his aged back and picked up a few papers, laying them in precise order on the mahogany table.

"No!" Cosmo shouted. "No, don't bother. Burn them. They are nothing. Nothing."

Peter watched, a smile on his lips.

"Ah, here it is. Now, my Pietro, do not smile that way, as though you were superior. I am in a worry, I assure you, and that is the bad of it. This must be a letter to wring money from that stone, Señor Caswell. I have spent half the night writing, while you sleep as a man without worry on your soul. It is not equal. You have no worry, I have all. You have only to count a few tickets to a gaming lottery, snap a band on those not sold and count a few dollars."

"Three thousand six hundred dollars and twenty cents, some of it in golden half-joes," Peter murmured. "Hoarded for years, no doubt."

"I care not. Let him send money in dollars, cents, centavos, reals, or this funny paper money, but write me a letter, my Pietro, write!" He pushed a quill and ink across the table. "See, I wait upon you, me, a—what you call—descent of the great Cosmo. I place a chair for you, thus. I have cut a new quill."

He laid the paper on the table in front of Peter. Peter had trouble reading it. It was lined and interlined and scratched. When he had finished, he said, "No, this will not do. You must not make demands on the Governor."

"I have tried everything. This time I make my demand."

"No. Wait. Let me think." Peter sat holding his head in his hands. It was a problem. He knew Caswell had no money for the troops. He knew that De' Medici, so eager to help, to serve, had drawn on his own diminishing funds to pay his men, to buy forage. For all his gay light spirit, underneath the man had profound yearning to make men free.

He took up a blank sheet of paper, dipped the quill into the inkpot and began to write, while Cosmo gloomily paced the room.

Edenton
2nd April 1779

Sir:
By the bearer, Lt. Ben Mills of the Light Dragoons, I take the liberty to trouble your Excellency concerning the recruiting money, as I was ordered on the account, and have a number of horses and no men to mount them. It would answer no purpose for me to return to New Bern in this situation. I believe men are to be had, had we the money to recruit them.

Capt. Ashe was at Halifax waiting for that purpose when I left that place a few days since.

Our troops of horse are augmented to forty, so that Capt. Ashe's troop and my own are wanting thirty-two troopers. These at the usual bounty of thirty dollars will take nine hundred and sixty.

I should be extremely happy if your Excellency will point out some way to come by the above sum.

There may be some public moneys in Edenton, if the gentlemen will part with it. I am to meet Mr. Barker, the lawyer, Messrs. Johnston and Iredell Tuesday. They are the Whig leaders here, as you know. 'Tis said that the South Carolinians are going to ask for North Carolina troops, and General Howe is forming an expedition against Augusta.

When Cosmo read the page, gloom gave way to delight. "It is of a splendour, this writing." He threw his arms about Peter and kissed first one cheek then the other, after the fashion of the Latins. He sat down in the chair Peter had vacated and wrote busily, for a moment, his brow furrowing, his tongue working with each word he set down. "I must, to save conscience, put some words of my own on this paper. Examine it please. There must be some of Cosmo in it, yes?"

Peter read:

> We have nothing new at this place, having so recently come. We had an elegant ball the night before we left Halifax. All were exceedingly merry.
>
> I have the honour to be, with all due respect, your Excellency's most Ob. and most Humbl. Servt.
>
> Cosmo de' Medici
>
> To his Excellency
> Governor Richard Caswell
> At the Palace, New Bern.

"There. Finis, my friend, finis. If these words do not bring assistance, I will go walk onto a ship and sail home. That I do not want to do, until this freedom is accomplished."

"Do you think our armies will be victorious?" Peter asked, curious to learn De' Medici's answer. Cosmo turned from the mirror where he was engaged in slipping into his buff and blue coat, with the assistance of Scipio. His dark face expressed his astonishment at Peter's question. He answered quietly, without his usual emphatic mannerisms. For once he was without emotion, which made the deep honesty of his words so convincing.

"We cannot fail, for we have selfless purpose on our side."

A knock at the door interrupted. Johnston stood in the hallway, dressed in travelling clothes. "If you are ready, Captain, we will be starting. Ferrier is at the wharf. Cathcart asked him not to come up."

De' Medici put his tricorn hat on at a rakish angle over his clubbed hair. "I am at your service, sir." To Peter he said, "I will execute all your commissions." Johnston walked on ahead to the stairs. Cosmo leaned close to Peter. "If you cannot win the maid now, you are a dullert."

Peter grinned. "I am a 'dullert,' " he agreed.

"If you take the pox, I will come over to nurse you, dragoons or no dragoons. Mind you, I am meaning that, from my heart."

Peter was suddenly grave. "I believe you, Cosmo. I believe you would."

It was a sober group that stood at the head of the steps going down to the wharf. Cathcart had told them that both Negroes were indeed dead, the woman quietly in the night, the man violently in the early morning.

Johnston said, "This is bad. I am glad you are here, Cathcart. Your presence will quiet the Negroes. We will get Williamson here if it is humanly possible."

"I'll feel happier if you do, Sam. It's a responsibility for an old man who hasn't kept up with his medicine. There are many changes these days, brought on by the necessities of war."

"Where is Angela?" Johnston asked.

"I've ordered her to take a draught and go to bed. Her father wanted to send her up to the River Plantation, but I put my foot down. No good exposing all that family until we see what develops."

"She is dreadfully frightened," Mary said.

Dr. Cathcart observed, "The child will make herself sick with her fears."

Penelope Dawson said, "I got the impression that she was worried, very worried, but not about the pox." She moved away. No one understood her but Peter. No one spoke for a moment.

Johnston laid his hand on Cathcart's arm. "I dislike leaving. I would not go, only that you are here to look after them."

Cathcart nodded. "They pass into my keeping." He glanced at Penelope standing straight and slim at the edge of the bank, her wide skirts billowing, her beautiful eyes watching the people on the wharf.

"She is our charge, Sam. I've felt that strongly ever since her father left us her guardians and her consultants. Never a week passed that I have not looked in on her. Somehow I feel that Gabriel wanted it so, when he named us in his will." The two men moved away. Peter heard no more. Voices rose from the water and the splash of oars made a dim accompaniment to the rhythm of drums, which had been sounding constantly since morning.

Parson Earle and Peter walked down to the quarters. "I must do what I can," the rector told him. After the first outburst he had accepted the situation with good humour. "My wife tells me I need a rest, but what with a fishery to oversee and a parish that extends over several counties, I have little time for rest." He laughed jovially. "Not that I need rest. That is Charity's idea."

Cathcart overtook them. "We must get these people buried, before the drums drive everyone mad."

The Parson nodded. "Madam Dawson spoke to me about that. She will get out her father's chapel silver, so I can hold a regular service in the chapel in the woods."

The doctor pursed up his lips and looked dubious. "If it is possible, I want to keep them from congregating."

Daniel Earle pointed in the direction of the quarters. "What do you call that?"

A great crowd of Negroes clustered in front of the white-washed cabin where the bodies lay. The doctor cursed, then apologized to the Parson.

"Go right ahead. Go right ahead." Earle laughed. "I know a few strong oaths myself, left over from my soldiering days. I've found them quite useful, during the fishing season . . . and at other times, I confess."

As they came closer, they saw a circle of men and women sitting on the ground. They were swaying back and forth, chanting in a weird, minor key. The women were casting ashes over their heads. The ashes drifted down over their faces and necks, making grey streaks that stood out startlingly on their dark, glistening skins. A rooster with its head cut off was flopping about in the centre of the circle, flinging blood on the chanters. A man's powerful voice sang:

> "*Let the big drum roll!*"

A chorus answered:

> "*Let the big drum roll, let the big drum roll!*
>
> "The little bird has come out of the deep river
>   from the great river of God."
> "*Let the big drum roll, let the big drum roll!*"
>
> "At the river of beads and pearls
>   I have found fowls which pound,
>   Using mortars hewn from blood trees."
> "*Let the big drum roll, let the big drum roll!*"
>
> "Their beaks are white, bringing pearls
>   From the Land-where-I-wash-my-wrongs!
>   It is far from here where you have brought me,
>   Who have no feet."

"Let the big drum roll, let the big drum roll!"
"Let us cover it with ashes. . . ."

There was a movement among the singers. Instead of showering ashes on their heads, they flung them at the fowl which, with dying contortions, flapped its wings wildly.

The Parson shut his eyes. "Heavenly Father, what pagan ritual are we witnessing?"

Herk moved from the crowd at the outer rim of the circle and stood beside Dr. Cathcart. He heard the Parson's words. He spoke, addressing no one, looking off toward the forest. "It is the way of Bantu people. They mean no harm, sars. It tells of the soul, having no feet. The River of God, the deep river, washes clean. The birds with beaks of white are the white young souls, who cry aloud by the deep river against the spilling of blood."

Daniel Earle opened his eyes and stared at the speaker. "Bless my soul! Bless my soul!"

"They sing of another life, sar. Life where Death passes."

"Pagan, straight from the darkest jungles," the rector muttered, but he made no effort to stay the pagan chant. Instead, he took his shovel hat from his head, and stared down at the buttons of his long gaiters. The breeze stirred his coat-tails and ruffled his carelessly clubbed hair.

Cathcart walked away, and entered the cabin. The squatting mourners, who crammed the little porch, moved aside, looking up at him with blank, expressionless features as he passed. The chant died away as the rooster fluttered its last. Someone picked the fowl from the earth and carried it away.

The rector spoke in bewilderment. "Only yesterday, I baptized three of them! Let's go back to the house. Somehow I feel quite nauseated."

Peter said nothing. The rector kept muttering, "Pagan as the jungle! Bless my soul, I wonder if *all* my teaching has been for naught. . . . Young man, I wonder if all our Christian teaching is as useless."

"But Herk said they believed in a hereafter, in a God who would wash away sins in a deep river," Peter sought to remind the discouraged man.

"Baptism, a hereafter—so he did . . . well, perhaps it is not so pagan after all, just a different way to express the same truth."

Peter thought the method of expression was vastly different but he did not venture to put his thoughts into words.

After dinner Penelope asked Peter and Parson Earle into the library to get the chapel plate out of the secret place. They had decided to hold the burial service at sundown in the small chapel Governor Gabriel Johnston had built in the woods beside a small stream.

The Parson sat down wearily in the broad-seated Russia leather chair by the fire. He had had little to say since the morning episode. Something disturbed him. He seemed dispirited, not his usual jovial self. Sometimes his lips moved. Penelope glanced at him several times but did not question him. Peter stood by the window, looking into the garden. Early-blooming shrubs were covered with a white mass of small flowers, touching the window where he stood.

Penelope went to the fire-place, opened a panel near the broad chimney-breast, and took out the chapel plate—two handsome silver flagons, one silver cup and two silver salvers. Peter turned at the Parson's exclamation of pleasure as he lifted the silver cup lovingly in his hands and examined it closely.

"My father sent to London to have it made," Penelope said. "I was a very small child when it came, but I remember my father unpacking the case and putting it piece by piece upon the mantel there. I sat in a little chair by the fire, watching him. I remember very well his pleasure and delight. Other pieces of plate came at the same time."

Then she lifted a silver tea-kettle and lamp out of the secret place, and two tankards. "I must keep these out," she said. "My father liked to have toasts drunk from them every night." She put the tea-kettle on the low table. Peter saw the closet was filled with plate. Coffee and teapots, a second silver kettle and lamp, elaborately chased in the French fashion. There were sets of tableware, canisters for tea, castors and salt-cellars. A tall muffineer, a rack on which hung long-handled narrow spoons, tongs, two very large punch ladles, stacks of plates, boxes which he presumed held knives and forks and spoons.

"We had everything in duplicate," Penelope said, "double china sets and glasses. My father loved guests in Eden House, many guests. He had furniture for nine bedrooms." She smiled at Peter. "Nine bedrooms is a cottage in England, but here it was ample to house a family and guests."

Parson Earle put the chapel plate on the mantel, where it shone softly against the white panels. He said, "I can well understand your father's love of guests. We country folk are all like that. There is an excitement when a chaise or a travelling carriage draws up to the block or horsemen come up the drive. We are perhaps more gregarious than village or city folk, because we have long periods of solitude."

"Solitude is good for the soul," Penelope said. She took a bit of chamois from the cupboard and began to polish the silver cup.

Earle got up and went to the bookshelves. "The library of a scholar," he said, "one of broad reading. See, we have Smith's *Moral Sentiments*, besides *War on Beasts*, and Howell's *State of England*. Jolliamond, on *Discourses between an Indian Philosopher and a French Missionary; Gulliver's Travels* leaning against *Christian Faith*. Voltaire, *Peregrine Pickle* and *Roderick Random* beside a dozen Latin and Greek grammars and Joubert's French and Latin. Ah, and Nelson's *Justice*, side by side with *Antidote against Papacy*. This is delightful. One day I must browse, really browse."

Penelope lifted the brightened cup to the mantel and began on the flagons. "The library is small. Most of my father's books went to Dr. Cathcart and Sam Johnston. My stepmother took forty volumes. Why I can't imagine, for she never read a book in her life."

Peter admired two hawthorn jars on the overdoor shelf.

"They belonged to Governor Eden," she told him. "We have several pieces that belonged to him, which came to me through my mother."

The Parson was deep in a book, sitting on the little library steps. Penelope finished polishing the silver and set the pieces on the table.

Peter glanced out the window. He saw a Negro boy leading two saddle-horses to the stables. A moment later the old Negro butler, who bore the name "Governorcharleseden," after his former owner, announced "Madam Pollock and a strange gen'l'm'n" were in the drawing-room. Penelope glanced significantly at Peter as she left the room. The Parson looked up from the book which had engrossed him, Churchill's *Works*.

"I really envy Madam Dawson these volumes. I tried to buy the set at James Milnor's sale at Halifax, but some fellow outbid me. Fletcher of Saltoun's *Works* were up too, but I was outbid. Being a poor parson has its drawbacks. I did get Shaftesbury's *Characteristics*, but I paid a guinea for the book. My wife brought me to task for that extravagance, particularly when she sent me to get a drop-leaf table of walnut, which I let slip by. I remember I bought two pairs of spectacles in a shagreen case, which I couldn't see through, and a surtout, very much worn." He laughed silently, his whole body shaking, his white wig, already slightly askew, tipping farther over his eyes. "I really should never be allowed to go to an auction. That is God's truth. I lose all sense of proportion, but I like it, I swear I do. Somehow I can always justify myself for my little auction extravagances." He looked at Peter, peering over his spectacles. "Did you ever attend an auction?"

"No, sir. Except at Boothby's or Tattersall's."

"No, no, I don't mean that variety of auction. I mean a country auction, where household and personal goods go under the hammer. If you want humour, nature in the raw, my son, you'll find it at an auction.

"Why, right in Queen Anne's Town, when Francis Corbin's effects went on sale at Cupola House—Corbin was Lord Granville's agent who was almost tarred and feathered by some village roughs, but he talked his way out—that was about the same time they had trouble with the Regulators, in the Western counties—during Tryon's day. Well, sir, that was a day. I remember . . ."

Peter did not discover what it was that the Parson remembered, for Penelope came in, followed by Ann Pollock and Morse. He thought Morse looked worried but his manner showed no change.

Ann greeted Peter and the Parson warmly, and Morse bowed pleasantly.

"We had the note, Penelope," Ann said. "Do tell me what is happening. We heard a lot of confusion and wailing in the quarters as we rode up. Anyone dead?"

Penelope pulled the bell cord. "It is Dr. Cathcart who wants to see you. I'll send for him to come here." Governorcharleseden answered the bell. "Please go to Dr. Cathcart's room and ask him please to step here."

Governor said, "Yes'm," and went out.

The Parson put the book back in its place on the shelf and dusted his fingers. "I think I'll go to my room and catch a little nap before the service, with your permission, Penelope." Peter glanced at Penelope as the Parson left the room. She shook her head, imperceptibly. Morse strolled to the bookshelves.

Ann said, "This is all so mysterious, Pene."

Dr. Cathcart came in, in time to hear her words. "Nothing mysterious, but a little worrying. We had two deaths from smallpox among the slaves, last night, and another suspect."

Ann raised her eyebrows. "We haven't any sickness at Balgray, other than the usual run of ague. I had all the house slaves come to the dispensary yesterday."

Cathcart turned to Morse, whose back was to the room. Peter, who was still near the window, viewed him in profile, but no muscle of his face moved when the doctor was speaking.

"It was Mr. Morse I wanted to see," Cathcart said gently. "I am afraid, sir, I shall have to keep you under observation for a few days."

Morse wheeled. His hand went to the sword hilt that wasn't there. The veins on his forehead stood out. He caught Peter's fixed glance. His hand dropped, and colour crept slowly from his neckcloth to his forehead.

"Observation!" he said abruptly, a rasping note in his voice.

Dr. Cathcart did not notice the small signs that told so much to Peter. "Yes. We have smallpox here. I must keep everyone who was directly exposed under my eye until I am sure there is no danger."

"But, sir, you cannot include me. I . . ."

The doctor interrupted. "Angela has already told me that you were in the cabin with the sick couple yesterday."

Morse, rigid, sank back against the support of the shelves. "Yes, that is true. Miss Ferrier wanted to show the quarters to me. You see, sir, I am writing——"

Cathcart's dry voice stopped him before he could complete his excuse. "So she told us. You have visited other Negro huts, also. I only hope that you will not spread the plague."

"What must I do?" he asked the doctor, recovering his poise. "I want to conform in every way possible."

"I have asked the others who have been exposed to stay at Eden House for a few days, until we see what develops. We do not know why the scourge spreads. Williamson contends for 'immunization and isolation.' "

Morse's face lost its mobility. "But I can't do that. My business is important. I must continue my journey south."

Cathcart said, "These other gentlemen have affairs important to them also, but I have persuaded them they must consider the health of others."

Ann Pollock looked from one to another, apprehension in her eyes. "Do you mean I have to stay here? With Cullen in such wretched health?"

"No, Ann. You were not directly exposed, as the gentleman was.

Angela has told us that they held the sick woman while they gave her a cup of water."

Morse's face was dark. He spoke angrily, grasping Cathcart's arm. "I tell you I can't stay!"

"I am afraid you must." There was no mistaking the doctor's intention.

Ann laughed shrilly. "They may put you into the slaves' dungeon and feed you through a slit in the wall."

Penelope looked at Ann. "You know we have no slave dungeon at Eden House."

"Well, you have a tunnel—a tunnel that leads to the river. It will do as well. I can't think what has come over you, to detain a man. You exceed your authority, Doctor."

Cathcart did not trouble to look at Ann or answer. To Morse he said, "Madam Dawson has been so kind as to offer you the hospitality of her home. If you will come with me, I will show you to your room." Morse gave Ann a warning look as he followed Cathcart. At the door the doctor turned. "You had better go home, Madam Pollock. We have enough on our hands without the trouble of a hysterical woman."

Ann sank back in the chair. "Where is Angela? Why did she have to tell that they had been to the quarters? The girl is a fool. She had no right to talk." She paused when she caught Peter's questioning gaze fixed on her. She made an effort, forcing a smile to her lips, but her eyes were wary.

"Angela is in bed. She is not well. The doctor gave her a sleeping draught," Penelope said. She, too, was watching Ann closely.

"I hope to God she won't get it." Ann was concerned. "What happened? How do you know you have the scourge?"

"Fever. Delirium."

"Delirium!" Ann grew pale, the blood drained from her face.

Penelope caught her arm. "She hasn't it yet. Her fever may be just the usual swamp fever."

"Fever!"

Peter said, "Do not be so alarmed, Madam Pollock. There is only a small chance Miss Ferrier may have become infected. At least that is the way the doctor feels about it. Dr. Williamson, when he comes, may want to inoculate everybody. . . ."

"Oh, how horrible! I knew a child who had to have his arm removed after inoculation."

"Well, we knew a thousand in the army who took inoculation and did not lose an arm, so please do not take it so hard."

Ann refused to be comforted. Peter thought, Her anxiety is not for Angela Ferrier but for Jeremiah Morse. Her question confirmed that in his mind:

"What is he going to do with Mr. Morse?"

"Nothing but give him a bitter draught," Peter assured her, "very bitter."

Penelope laughed, and, with a touch of sarcasm, added, "We all lived through it, Ann, so do not think you need to be distressed for Mr. Morse. He looks a stout fellow. I think he can bear up under it, if I did."

Penelope's words brought Ann up quickly. She closed her lips firmly and rose. "Do you think the doctor will allow me to speak to my guest before I leave?"

Peter said, "I fancy your guest will not want to speak to you, if Dr. Cathcart's medicine is effective. I think it contains nux vomica."

"Then I will write a message, if you will give me a quill and some paper."

"Certainly." Penelope went to the mahogany escritoire. She took paper from the pigeon-hole, and placed the inkpot and quill and sand-box in a convenient place.

Ann pulled the Wellford chair in front of the desk. She sat looking down on the dark red Turkey carpet for a moment before she began to write.

Penelope walked to the table and stood beside Peter. " 'There is something more than meets the eye,' " she quoted, her voice very low.

He nodded. "I must talk with you later," he said.

Ann finished writing. She picked up a stick of red sealing-wax. She went to the fire-place and held it to the flame for an instant. She walked back to the desk, folded and sealed the letter, stamping the wax with a ring she wore on her finger.

"Please ring for Governor, Penelope. I want to send this up to Mr. Morse."

Penelope's face was expressionless. She pulled the cord. When Governor entered, Ann placed the letter in his hand. "Please take this to Mr. Morse," she said. "Give it into his hands yourself. You know who Mr. Morse is?"

Governor's black face cracked in a grin. "Yes, ma'am. I knows he. I jus' been hold he head over the basin. Yes'm."

The little chapel in the woods was crowded with the house servants. The field slaves stood at the door and under the open windows. Dr. Cathcart at first demurred at holding a special service but the Parson overrode him.

"We have enough pagan ritual around here," he said emphatically. "This will be a Christian burial."

So in vestments, with the Gabriel Johnston chalice and urns gleaming on the altar massed with dogwood blossoms, the rector of Saint Paul's met the cypress-wood coffins of the slaves. "I am the Resurrection and the Life." The words flowed evenly and in full volume over the dusky audience.

If they did not understand the words Parson Earle uttered, they understood the majesty of the service and it gave them comfort. It gave comfort, also, to see the little group of white men and women, who came to pay their solemn respects to the dead—Madam Dawson, with Mary Warden at her side, flanked by Dr. Cathcart and Peter. Jeremiah Morse was next to Peter.

Angela was not at the chapel. Dr. Cathcart told Peter she was indisposed with a slight fever, nothing to cause alarm—no more than the usual fever so prevalent in this swampy country.

No untoward incident occurred, save that when the rector met the bodies carried by the house slaves and spoke the words, "I am the Resurrection and the Life," then the dull, dirgelike boom of a drum rolled out. Its beat came evenly and with profound solemnity at regular intervals, as a great bell might toll.

For a moment the rector hesitated, only a moment, then went on with the service for the dead. The drum sounded throughout the service, and continued as the procession walked the short distance through the tall pines to the slaves' burial-ground, close to the enclosed plot that held the bodies of the earlier plantation-owners, including a Royal Governor.

Peter thought of the song he had heard, "Let the great drum roll." Once they were outside the simple white-washed chapel, the sound rolled through the trees. It seemed to come from the earth, from the skies, from the depths of the swamp beyond.

The Negroes were silent until the last clod of earth was shovelled into place. Then a great cry went up, voices crying in anguish, "*Mungulu, Mungulu, Mungulu.*"

The drum sound increased with each cry, growing wilder and wilder, until the ears were full, body and flesh quivered under the wild rhythm.

Suddenly it ceased. The air was still, no cries, not even a bird note. The black people seemed to vanish into the deep forest.

The rector's hushed voice broke the silence of the little group, released them from their rigid immobility. "Pagan," he breathed, "absolute paganism." His face was red, his wig slightly askew. He began muttering a Latin prayer and made the Sign of the Cross above the little group. Silently he turned and walked toward the house, followed by the others. No one spoke, as they moved through the pine trees, down the lane. Only when they reached the garden that surrounded Eden House was there a word uttered.

Cathcart rubbed his hands together. "The Parson won't get over this for a long time. Now he'll believe what I've already told him, the jungle is at our own doors."

No one answered. Penelope and Mary went into the house. Peter and Cathcart lingered on the piazza. Peter turned to Jeremiah Morse, who still was pale and a little shaky from the doctor's drastic treatment of nux vomica and a powerful purge.

"There is something for your writings, Morse."

Morse looked up startled as a man awakened from a trance. "Yes. Yes, of course. . . . Did you ever hear anything like that drum? God's truth, I thought I was in a jungle country. I was ready to join in some wild savage dance!"

The doctor looked at him quickly. "The drums affect some people that way; the steady, incessant beat is a stimulant that can put a man into a frenzy."

Morse drew himself together at the doctor's matter-of-fact words. He became self-conscious, his face flushed. Muttering something about weakness because of the dosage he had had, he went quickly into the house.

"The man is nervy," the doctor observed, "mighty nervy. I'm going for a walk, Huntley. I want some clean air in my lungs. Will you come?"

"No, thank you, Dr. Cathcart. I've some writing to do, in case a messenger comes this afternoon."

The doctor looked at him keenly. "Best way to keep yourself in health is to take a good purge and long walks." He went indoors. Peter stood for a moment, looking at the river. The sun had gone under a cloud, the river was grey and chill.

There was nothing on the surface to show that the six people supping at Eden House were other than invited guests, chosen with care by a skilful hostess, with an eye for a successful house-party. Angela did not appear. She was sleeping, Mary Warden told Penelope, when they all sat down for a late supper.

By common consent no mention was made of the pox or the burial of the two Negroes who had died of its scourge.

The doctor and the rector of St. Paul's exchanged tales of early days of the Albemarle, the rector's herring fishery, the struggle to induce yeomen in the upper end of the county to plant flax, that their wives might spin and weave fine linen. Cathcart spoke of the grand days, Thomas Pollock's fifty thousand acres, his thousand slaves; the long-drawn-out squabble of Governor Eden and Edward Moseley, the duels on the Courthouse Green between Burrington, the Governor, and some forgotten enemy. Of Sir Richard Everard, the next Governor, and his brawling. Even the clergy drank and brawled, remarked Parson Earle. "Come in some afternoon and take a look at the Vestry Records. Drunkenness, disposal of bastard children, took up a great deal of the time of our early Vestries. One power the church had—if a vestryman did not attend meetings or refused to serve, he was liable to a fine." The rector laughed jovially. "I rather wish that ruling were in effect now. We had the fees from Weights and Measures Office too. I don't know that it brought many shillings."

Cathcart said, "Wasn't it Edward Moseley who had the money from the Crown to buy silver for the altar, and refused to order it? I seem to remember something that sounded like a shady transaction."

The Parson pushed his plate aside and leaned forward. "I'm glad you spoke of that affair, Cathcart. I ran onto the true story of that the other day while I was looking over some records and letters. The money for the silver was in the hands of Henderson Walker, the Deputy-Governor. He died without ordering the silver or accounting for the funds. Moseley married Walker's widow—Ann Lillington, I think her name was—so he inherited the church-silver debt along with others. He was too much of a gentleman to put the blame where it belonged, so he weathered the criticism until such time as he accumulated enough cash to buy the silver."

Penelope said, "That is very interesting. I'd heard the other story. Everyone in Queen Anne's Town has, I presume, though it happened in the early years of the century."

Parson Earle asked Morse a question about Breed's Hill which he answered, but volunteered nothing more. Some battles were spoken of—Saratoga, Burgoyne and his spectacular career, his play-writing, his great defeat, the American and British losses.

Peter listened, but offered nothing. Instead he repeated what Cosmo had told him. "De' Medici was at the Battle of Germantown. Our loss did not exceed seven hundred killed, wounded and taken prisoner. Colonel Caswell, the Governor's relative, received a short wound in the hand." Peter turned to Cathcart. "General Nash was killed in the battle. Your Albemarle man, Colonel Buncombe, and Lieutenant Colonel Erwin, were both taken prisoner at the same time. General Nash, before he fell, had taken possession of sixteen pieces of the enemy's cannon."

Cathcart's face clouded. "We lost a great man in Nash—I have heard, unnecessarily."

Peter went on, telling Cosmo's story. "By some unlucky mistake, in a thick fog, a party commanded by General Washington in person met General Greene's division. Each took the other for fresh troops of the enemy, and retreated. General Nash and his party were obliged to give way, and in the retreat he fell."

No one spoke for a moment. Penelope asked a question of Peter concerning Dr. Franklin, "always one of my heroes."

Peter repeated one anecdote, social not political, but into the story he brought the names of Silas Deane, Vergennes and Beaumarchais. He did this with great deliberation. Cathcart helped him unwittingly by saying, "I cannot make up my mind about Silas Deane, whether he is a scoundrel and a traitor, or a much-maligned man, as he claims in his Memorial to Congress."

Peter listened for some word from Morse, but he sat silent, his body stiff, his eyes on the table in front of him. His face was expressionless. Peter's arrow had missed its mark. Cathcart was looking at him, expecting an answer.

Peter said, "Dr. Franklin liked him, but he likes most people. Some of the other Commissioners suspected Deane; at least some of his companions were under suspicion. . . ." He paused and glanced casually about the table until he was looking at Morse. He thought he detected a slight flicker in the man's eyelids. He went on:

"You know how those things go, Doctor, in politics and diplomacy; men wary and suspicious of one another. As for myself, my position was too lowly to give me any first-hand information."

Morse lost some of his rigidity at Peter's words. His eyes lost their watchful look. He entered the conversation easily and naturally. "Boston has it that Mr. Adams did not trust the people who accused Mr. Deane."

"That may be. Mr. Adams came to Paris either after Mr. Deane left or a short time before." He waited a moment, then added, "One thing I do know, Mr. Adams and his friends certainly made things difficult for Dr. Franklin and for our General."

Penelope faced Morse. "Being a New Englander, Mr. Morse, you would, I am sure, side with Mr. Adams?"

But Morse was not to be trapped even by the most innocent question. He said, "Not in all his views, madam. I have the greatest admiration for General Washington. Certainly I would not criticize him, especially now, when everything is going against him."

Although it was not mentioned, the Conway affair was in the minds of everyone at the table.

Mary Warden said little. She kept looking at Morse as though he puzzled her. After a time, Penelope gave the signal and the two women left the men to their port and their toasts.

It was late before Peter had an opportunity to speak with Penelope alone, but he knew she had seen Morse's hand go to his side in the instinctive gesture of a man who depended on his sword. Certainly not the first thought of a quiet merchant of Boston.

It was well past eleven when the last bedroom candle was lighted, and the last foot ascended the stairs. All the guests had said their good nights, save Peter, who lingered in the library. Penelope had whispered to him to remain. She wanted to talk with him after the rest had gone to bed.

Governorcharleseden had mended the fire and changed the candles, while Scipio closed doors and windows, for the wind was rising. "'Bout to blow him up a wind," Governor muttered. "Seem lak always he blow up a wind when a body is laid in the ground."

Scipio stood listening, his head nodding like a Chinese mandarin. "Yes'm, it sho' does. Las' time dat boy he drown in Salmon Creek, de wind he roar lak a lion."

"Now let's have no more such talk, Governorcharleseden, and don't you go down to the quarters, frightening my people."

"Dey is already skeered, Mistress. Dat man he say time is coming for Nicodemus to show heself, and when he come, all the black folks goin' to rise right up."

Peter leaned forward. The look on the old man's face was one of innocence . . . or was it guile? He did not understand the Negroes. Penelope said nothing for a moment. She had her back turned, as she placed a silver candlestick on the mantel-board. After a moment she said, "Nicodemus may have prophesied a number of things, but he didn't say that the black folk should rise up. Some stranger said that." She turned around to look at the butler. "Don't let me ever hear that you've been listening to some stranger's silly talk."

Scipio dropped the heavy curtain to cover the window and came forward. "Dees men he don' talk to Governorcharleseden or to Scipio. Dey know better. Dey talk to ign'rant folkses, in the quarters. Dey say, 'Slaves will rise and go after de white folks wid de guns.'"

Not a muscle changed in Penelope's face. She took the second lighted candle from Governor and placed it on the mantel, standing off to see that they were exactly at the same distance from the portrait of Governor Gabriel Johnston which hung over the mantel.

"Silly talk," she observed, as though the matter were of no moment, "a lot of big, silly talk."

Governor spoke quickly. "Dat what I tell Scipio, big talk by big-mouth fella. Black man he come from Ferginnie, he talk an' talk."

"Where is he going to get the guns?" Penelope moved across the room and straightened a book on the table. Peter was filled with admiration at her way of extracting information.

Scipio answered quickly, eager to show his knowledge. "Dey got 'em hid in de swamp . . . den dey goin' take folkses' muskets from dey houses, when Nicodemus come."

"Nicodemus? I seem to remember the name."

"It's Bible name, Mistress."

"Yes, I know, but didn't my father have a man by that name?"

Both Negroes were silent. After a time Governor said, "Yes'm, dat he did. He had boy name Nicodemus. Dat boy was whopped with kiboka, a great whop of skin, till he died."

Penelope's voice rose. "My father didn't allow his people to be whipped."

"No, ma'am. Dat's God's truth, he say no whoppin' at Eden House. But he had a overlooker, a mean man, who whopped."

Scipio crossed the room and stood near Governorcharleseden.

"Nicodemus he buried deep in swamp, twix' here and Mr. Rutledge place. In the deep swamp. All the people say he goin' rise right up one of dese days, jes' lak our Lord Jesus, and black men he be free." His eyes rolled, the white reflecting the glow of the fire.

So that was the way they worked: hanging a plot of rebellion and insurrection on some old superstition, coupled with a Biblical story.

"Well, our people know better than to believe such fancy tales." Penelope spoke with decision. "Only silly people would believe any strange man talking that way."

"He gone, now, that Ferginnie man, he go over to Balgray. He left mighty sudden when dose two died of pox." Governorcharleseden chuckled. "His fine coat-tails they stan' out mighty straight, when he goes flyin'."

Scipio shook his head from side to side. "Left hyah in a big hurry, dat Ferginnie fella did."

"You may go now," Penelope said, sitting down in a chair near a table. "Don't forget to tell Cato I want a saddle-horse tomorrow morning by seven at the latest. Good night."

The two slaves left the room. Penelope turned to Peter.

"Well. There it is. A Virginia Negro has been here, filling our people with a story about Nicodemus coming out of his grave and calling for the black men to rebel against their white masters."

"A dastardly, contemptible plot," Peter said angrily. "I can't see how any white man could conceive such a thing."

"Well, it's been attempted before, with the Indians as well as black men. The thing to worry about is how to stop it before it really happens." She sat looking at the fire, her brow furrowed, her index finger pressed against her chin. "I wish Sam were here," she said.

"If we could catch up with the instigator . . ." Peter said.

Penelope looked up. "Of course, that is it. We must find this black man, and have him sent back to Virginia. No, that won't do. We must not have him sent. Our Negroes must drive him away. That will be very much better."

She stood up and started for the door.

Peter asked, "Where are you going?"

"To put on a habit, so we can ride over to Duckenfield, you and I."

"What, now? Tonight?"

"Yes, at once. Lawyer Pearson must be warned." Peter reminded her that Scipio had said the Negro had gone to Balgray.

"I know," she said impatiently. "But we can't talk to Cullen and

Ann. If the villain goes to Balgray, his next stop will be Duckenfield, and so on until all the plantations have been visited." She stopped suddenly, looking at Peter with widened eyes, and came back to the fire-place. "Morse," she whispered. "Do you think? Remember Angela said they had visited Negroes here and——"

Peter said, "It was on the tip of my tongue to suggest that perhaps the quarry was closer home."

"He seems so nice, so well mannered." He saw she was reluctant to believe ill of a man of good appearance, a man of her own social class.

"Did you notice how he started to draw his sword?"

"Yes. I noticed."

"The man is a soldier. He shows it in a dozen ways."

"What can we do?" she asked. She leaned forward. The glow of the fire was warm on her face and her neck. The rose taffeta she wore seemed to settle about her in a roseate cloud. She looked very young, very troubled.

"Should you speak to the doctor, or the Parson?" he asked.

She shook her head; a long curl slipped across her shoulder and touched her round bosom. "No. The fewer people who know of this, the better. Not that I distrust either, but they would be watching for some slip on Morse's part, and put him more on his guard. If he is what we think he is, he is a very clever man, not readily caught napping. Let me think."

She lifted her slim hand to cover her eyes, her elbow resting on the arm of the chair. Peter got up and walked across the room. Naturally a restrained man, he was opposed to violent or startling action. Rather he would put himself in the place of such a man, and try to reason what he would do.

He was too absorbed in this trend of thought to notice that Penelope had risen to her feet, until she spoke. "How long will it take you to get ready?"

He hesitated a moment only. "Long enough to draw on my boots."

She looked at him keenly. "You don't want to go?"

"I hesitate to go and leave Morse here. Which is his room?"

"The last one down the hall, two doors beyond your own. Surely you can't go there without his suspecting he is being watched?"

Peter knew she was right about that.

She smiled a little. "I think the last dose Dr. Cathcart gave our friend will keep him from travelling very far tonight. We will be home before anyone wakens in the morning." She paused, catching a little of his anxiety. "If there were anyone else to go with me——"

Peter walked to the door. "No. I will go. As you say, we will be back before anyone knows we are gone."

When Peter came down the stairs, Penelope was waiting for him in the hall. She had changed to a dark habit, and her hair was bound up in a black net. "I looked in on Angela. She is very restless, but I have my maid Lucy sitting with her and Mary is in the adjoining room."

They went to the back of the house by the light of a solitary candle. On the back gallery they found a lantern, which Peter lighted with his flint. He had taken the precaution to buckle a pistol holster under his shoulder. It snuggled against his side, a hard core of comfort, as it had been on numerous other occasions. He had thought of his sword but discarded the idea.

The wind was blowing steadily from the southeast. It whipped around the corner of the house and struck them full strength as they crossed between the garden and the stables. Madam Dawson walked close to Peter for protection, but she made her way steadily, without comment, as though her mind were on other things.

They paused to knock at the overlooker's door. There was no answer. The door swung open. Peter lifted the lanthorn; the room was empty.

Penelope said sharply, "I suppose he's still in a drunken state, lying up with some black wench. I'd have sent him off the plantation long ago, only he swears each time never to get out of control again. He has a nice wife in the village and two little children, but he has a taste for dark meat." She spoke with vexation, rather than indignation, as one speaks of an old situation that should be changed but never was.

"Can you saddle your horse?" she asked as they drew near the stables.

Peter laughed. "I've been riding with Cosmo's dragoons for a month. It would be disgraceful not to throw a saddle or tie a belly-strap. Wait, I'll go in first. Just tell me which stalls." He stepped back quickly as a tall figure rose from a pile of hay. The lanthorn light fell on a huge black man. Peter, not knowing the Eden House people, thought it might be the "Ferginnie" man until he spoke.

"Mistress, it is Herk. I catch my sleep here, by the horses."

Penelope said, "Good. Will you saddle two horses?" The man

went into the cavernous depths of the stable, without lanthorn or
light.

"They see in the dark," Penelope said. "It is Adam Rutledge's
man. You may place all confidence in him." She walked outside and
stood near the door. The sky was dark, the stars overclouded. The
animals were restless, moving back and forth in their stalls, as they
will in a strong wind. The wind brought the effluvia of manure and
rotted matter, which stung the nostrils.

Presently Herk came out of the gloom leading three horses, bridled
and saddled. Penelope mounted, her slim booted foot for an instant
in Peter's clasped hands. He put foot in the stirrup and threw his
leg over the horse's rump, catching the other stirrup as the horse
turned. Penelope led the way, Herk following. At the last, Penelope
decided against taking a lanthorn. "The horses know the way well
enough," she told Peter.

They trotted down the lane that led from the plantation to the
Governor's Road. Penelope shouted something to him. Peter could
understand nothing she said. Her voice disintegrated in the wind.
Herk rode forward to answer. Evidently his hearing was keener. He
rode up beside Peter. "Madam she say we save time ride through
swamp. Not good, Master."

Peter called out, "Should we not stick to the road? We may get off
the path in the dark."

Penelope's answer floated back. "Herk knows the way. Herk will
guide us safely."

11

ORDEAL BY POISON

THEY came to Duckenfield and wakened a sleepy Negro at the gate-house. He ran ahead of them to the house and opened the door for them after lighting candles in the hall. Penelope went into the drawing-room. The room, lighted by one candle, became mysterious. The Holland-covered chairs were ghostly against the shadows. The candle illuminated the portrait of Sir Nat over the mantel; the flickering light cast a moving shadow on his wide mouth and gave the illusion of laughter. Penelope stood looking up at the painting.

"He was always so gay," Penelope said. "Laughter came easily to Nat. I miss him. Wherever he went there was gaiety. So handsome, with the fine elegance of a gentleman of the world . . . Sometimes I wonder how Hannah Johnston could have passed him by for Jemmy Iredell."

Peter didn't speak. Penelope didn't expect an answer. "Not that I don't admire Jemmy. He has intelligence and industry and ambition, three graces for a man seeking the high places."

She was interrupted by a step on the stair. Through the open doorway they saw Lawyer Pearson descending. He had a bed candle in his hand and had a dark robe over his sleeping shirt. His feet had been thrust hastily into black list slippers. His head, wigless, was covered with a stocking cap, a tassel of which fell over one shoulder. On his thin, intelligent face was an expression of surprise, even consternation. He glanced at the clock. It was midnight.

Without preamble or introduction Penelope Dawson told him the story. The lawyer's face was grave as he listened. Peter took no part in the discussion that followed. He had no previous experience that would be of any value in dealing with Negroes, nor did he understand them as these people did. He observed that neither blamed their people, only the outsider who had come among a happy contented folk to disturb them and lead them into trouble. That must be prevented at all costs.

As they were in the hall, ready to depart, Pearson asked an opinion from Peter.

"About the Negroes, I can't venture to advise. If you suspect that the plan is one that originates with the enemy, would it not be a matter for your Provincial Council? I hesitate to make even this small suggestion, since I am not familiar with the workings of your Council or your Committee of Correspondence."

If Pearson had purposely given Peter an occasion to show his hand, he was disappointed. The matter of Jeremiah Morse he proposed to keep to himself. He hoped Madam Dawson would be discreet. She was. She did not speak of her suspicions. They were well beyond the gatehouse before she spoke.

"I said nothing about Morse. I thought that was your province. Since you said nothing about him, I, too, was still."

"Thank you, Madam Dawson. I knew I could rely on your discretion. It is a delicate matter even to think of a man as a spy, with only intuition as the accuser. He might turn out to be a patriot—then where would you be?"

"I don't imagine you ever allow yourself to be placed in such a position, Peter Huntley. I fancy you always look several steps ahead before you put your foot down."

"The Scots have a saying, ' 'Tis better to step an inch ahead than to jump a foot, then be jumping back.' That's the way I feel about Morse. I want to see a long way ahead. Besides, this isn't really my affair. I don't think he has anything to do with lottery tickets."

"Still trying to make me think that is your only reason for being in Queen Anne's Town?"

"My dear Madam Dawson, I would never even try to deceive you. Your eyes are too keen; your imagination too active."

"Madam Dawson, Madam Dawson—why not Penelope? We are surely on the same side of the cane-field. I am not so old that you must be so constantly respectful." She pulled her horse so that they were riding side by side. Herk had gone on ahead. It was very dark but through the trees stars could be seen, shining brightly. The wind had died down.

Penelope laid her hand for a moment on Peter's arm, a light touch, friendly and affectionate. "Somehow I trust you, I believe in you."

"Why? I might be the villain in the piece, not Morse, or some unknown person."

"I trust you. My heart tells me that you have strength and honesty and that you never deviate from what you believe to be right."

"Thank you . . . Penelope."

She laughed a little. "Don't make such a mouthful of it. It isn't so bad."

"A beautiful name. If I remember, it well became a beautiful, faithful woman."

"Only this Penelope has no Ulysses. Don't think me forward, talking about myself, but I value friendship. I am a woman who can be friends with a man without allowing emotion to enter. I have found it pays. Friendship outlasts the ordinary love of man and woman. . . . Extraordinary love . . . well, that is something I have never experienced."

Peter's answer was never spoken. Herk came up to them on foot. "It is better to go through swamp without horses. Wait here, in quiet. I will take them to safe hiding."

Penelope dismounted with Peter's aid. For a moment her lithe body was pressed against his as she slipped to the ground. There was a fragrance about her, clear and clean and invigorating. He released her with regret. It would have been pleasant to hold her, press his lips against hers, but the moment passed.

"What is the reason?" he asked, after a brief silence.

"I do not know. Herk has some reason which I do not question."

They stood close in the darkness. They were at the edge of the pocosin. Frogs were croaking, a few bird sounds broke the silence at intervals. Without a noise to give warning of his approach, Herk was standing at their side.

He started off into the swamp. "It is well to keep close, Mistress, and walk in silence. Bad boys are about. Mistress would want to return Ducken'?"

"No, no, Let us go on." Penelope walked between the two men, on the heels of Herk. Peter came close behind. She reached her hand to guide him, a pressure now and then, to warn him of a log or a hole in the path, or a turning. Frogs croaked loudly, stopping as they passed, a giveaway of their presence had anyone been aware. They proceeded slowly, but without interruption. Penelope moved easily, as one accustomed to walking without effort. The night was warm and fragrant with the perfume of some unseen flowers.

Peter felt a strangeness. Something like nostalgia swept over him for his homeland, and the smell of the gorse and the heather. Years of cities had set it far back, but it was still there, deep within him, a love of the earth and the spring. Fresh-turned earth lying open to the sun and the dews of night . . . the feel of earth, vibrant under his feet, the soughing wind in the pine trees, the fragrance of needles crushed under his feet, reflected against him, drawing out old dreams, old emotions so long buried. This land was his also, because he had fought for it; and by God above, it was worth the fight!

Penelope stopped. A long pressure of her hand cautioned him. He looked beyond her, beyond the bulky shadow that placed Herk. Through the trees, shining dimly, was a flickering light. He stood without breathing, watching, but the light did not advance. It remained stationary. He pressed close to Penelope, his lips close to her ear. "Runaway slaves?"

"I don't know. It may be."

Herk said, "Wait," and moved away in the shadows.

Penelope was motionless. She neither stirred nor spoke. Peter had the feeling that she was listening, intensely, apprehensively. He, too, felt the pressure of some unknown force; whether it was danger or not he could not determine. They moved cautiously, for the swamp water was on either side of them, and only the path was solid under their feet.

After some time Herk came back. This time they advanced inch by inch, a pause to listen, then forward. After a time they came to the edge of a clearing, a little island hemmed in by interlaced vines. The cypress trees grew tall here, their grotesque roots deep in the water. The firelight, brighter now, cast moving shadows on the black water and the tangle of cypress knees that rose from it.

Peter felt a shiver go through Penelope's body, pressed close against him, but she did not speak. From the cover of tangled grape and evergreen vines, they watched, forced to silence by their wonder, and the scene of jungle savagery.

In the centre of a circle near the fire sat seven Negro men. One or two of them were old, very old. Opposite them, within this circle of forty or fifty men squatted on the ground, stood two Negroes.

Peter at once took in the significance. It was a trial of some sort, according to a tribal custom, he conjectured. An elder was speaking from his seat on a log. His voice was clear and resonant; he might be a judge expounding the law or a lawyer presenting a case.

Herk came to Peter's side. "It is the Ferginnie boys. Our people speak to them. They say, 'It is not good to kill white people, not good or kind!' Because the Ferginnie boys have kill one or two of our people, they must die. They say they do not kill. White men kill. Our people say, 'Very well. You will take the Ordeal.'" He paused significantly.

Penelope said in a hushed voice, "Ordeal by poison."

"It is so, Mistress. They pound poison now." Two men near the fire were pounding something in a stone mortar, while the circle watched. After a time they transferred the powder from the stone mortar into a pannikin; over this they poured boiling water, to make a potion.

In a whisper, Herk said, "Better now to go."

Penelope said, "No, we will stay." A Negro in the circle moved his body. Then they saw Governorcharleseden seated on one side of the old man, Scipio on the other side.

"The Ancient speaks now," Herk whispered. One man stepped forward heavily without a word, as though he were without speech, and accepted the cup. He hesitated a moment, then came a sharp order from the Ancient.

"If he is guilty, death comes." Herk's voice was dispassionate. The Negro lifted the cup and drank.

A vibrating silence followed the act, an interval in which time seemed to stand still. The ebon figures were stone. The swamp gave forth no sound. Then the Negro staggered past the edge of the circle, retching and puking, his groans audible.

"The boy is without guilt," Herk said. The circle and the Elders turned their eyes from the first to the second. He was long reaching for the proffered cup. He stood with bowed head, his long arms hanging motionless at his side. The Ancient spoke one word sharply, like the crack of a whip. The man lifted his hand, drawing his body back until he stood against the solid wall of the circle made by the men who had risen from their crouching position.

"The smell of guilt," Herk said. Some intuition must have told him, for the poison took effect almost as soon as it was swallowed. With a horrible scream the man fell, his body writhing in convulsions. Every back was turned now. Penelope covered her face with her hands. Peter put his arm about her shaking body.

"We will go," Herk said. "We will not wait to see the lashes laid on the back of the near-guilty." He led them silently through the dark as they made their way back to the spot where Herk had hidden the horses. They were in the open country now, between fields where the starlight was bright. A brisk wind blowing from off the water seemed to cleanse the air, making it fresh and clean.

Penelope spoke no word as they rode homeward. Not until they reached the gates of Eden House did she break the silence. "I think we will hear no more of slave rebellion."

Herk answered, "The day comes without danger, Mistress."

"Thank you, Herk," Penelope said, as she and Peter went toward the house.

She paused a moment at the foot of the stairs. "I need not warn you Peter, that 'silence is golden.' "

"You will not speak of this, even to Mr. Johnston?"

"No. Least of all to Sam. He has a stern sense of justice. White man's justice. He might feel that punishment should be meted out."

"And you?" Peter pressed the point.

"Justice has been served," she said. "Good night, Peter, and thank you a thousand times."

He raised her hand to his lips. "My manners, to a lovely woman, and a wise one."

She smiled as she lifted her candle, which Peter had lighted. "Thank you, Peter, for what you are, a strong rock to lean upon."

Peter lingered to drink a glass of water before going to his room. Everything was quiet, the household deep in slumber, he thought, but as he turned to enter his room, he saw the door of the chamber Morse occupied close quietly. Evidently not all the people in the house slept.

Three days passed without word from Dr. Williamson, in fact without any communication from the world beyond the limits of the plantation. Angela remained in bed. A mild fever, Dr. Cathcart told them at breakfast, too early to be sure just what it foretold. Earle spent most of his time in the library, or riding one or another of Penelope's hunters. He seemed to have forgotten completely his earlier impatience, and he rather rejoiced in his enforced rest. "I may as well savour it to the full," he told Peter as they rode along the lanes toward Mount Galland. "I'm becoming fatalistic, the older I grow. It may not be according to church doctrine but a comforting belief. Hey! What's this?" he exclaimed, pointing with his crop in the direction of the Negro burial plot.

Peter looked in the direction he pointed. The newly made graves had been completely surrounded by a fence, made of sections of cane stripped of leaves. The hollow stalks stood at least six feet high, and they were placed so close that each rested against the other.

"Some custom or other," Peter said. "It's all beyond me. You people live in close quarters to the Negro; you must have made a study of their native beliefs and their African customs."

The Parson smiled ruefully. "You have us by the short hair, Captain. We don't take the trouble, we are the most indolent people. Many a time I've thought about investigating the blacks' beliefs, if only to ascertain how far my own teaching of the Christian faith has sunk in. Since the occurrence here the other day, I've seriously doubted. I'm afraid our religious teaching is purely extraneous. They simply add it to their pagan customs, without discarding any of the latter."

Peter agreed. "You live very close to a strange and unknown people," he commented. "You take much for granted." He was thinking of the Ordeal. In fact he thought of it every time his eyes fell on Governor or Scipio, wondering what thoughts went on behind the blank stare, the impenetrable expression.

The afternoon of the third day, while he and Mary Warden walked in the garden, they saw a long canoe with eight men at the oars approaching the landing. Two men sat in the stern, conversing earnestly. Mary uttered an exclamation, and one hand went to her throat. Noting his scrutiny, she recovered herself.

"It is Dr. Williamson," she cried.

"And the other?" Peter questioned.

"I can't see his face clearly. Adam Rutledge?" She tried to keep the tremor from her voice and the look of pleasure from her face, but she was not wholly successful. Her eyes shone, the colour came.

"So it is," Peter said, turning his eyes toward the canoe.

"I must tell Pene and the doctor." She turned and walked quickly to the house, where she vanished indoors. Peter walked to the edge of the bank that overlooked the wharf. He had an opportunity to view the famous Dr. Williamson, as he mounted the flight of steps that led from the landing to the garden. He was a tall, broad-shouldered man, with heavy unpowdered hair tied in a club with a black riband. He moved quickly and lightly as though eager to go forward, propelled by an immense energy. He glanced upward. Peter saw his face with its rugged, strongly cut nose and wide mouth.

A hawk or an eagle. More truly an eagle, with large, deep-set, brown eyes heavily hooded—a dreamer's eyes, yet in their darkness were penetration and awareness that went beyond the dreamer into the realm of action. But it was his hands that caught Peter's attention, long fingers, but capable and strong. A man of energy and strong and bold originality.

Adam Rutledge caught Peter's hand in a close grasp. "This is very pleasant, meeting you again," he said. "Dr. Williamson, here is Captain Peter Huntley."

Williamson's glance swept Peter's face. A steady, level glance, which penetrated beyond externals. "Good, very good," the doctor said. "We have talked of you, Huntley. Adam has told me something of your work in Paris . . . we must talk about it later. How are things here?"

"Dr. Cathcart will give you details, Dr. Williamson. To the layman everything seems about the same as when he sent word to you."

"Certainly it would be so. The period of incubation has not passed yet. But I will go in." He moved swiftly toward the front door. Adam Rutledge lingered. Peter thought, His face has deeper lines than I remembered, he looks more serious. But even lines could not alter the strength and beauty of Rutledge's features. His hair was as yellow as corn, and his eyes level and steadfast.

In answer to Peter's question he said, "We are in a state of turmoil. Even the General is showing the weight of the past years, the worries and discouragement. You have heard about New York and the group of critical men in Congress and in the army, who are hacking at him with axe and broadsword, trying to destroy the tree at the roots? It is a dastardly crime. What he has had to go through—no money to pay the troops, desertions and mutiny—a man of less strength than General Washington would have been swept away before now. But let us talk of something else. We brought your saddle-bags. De' Medici said there were letters . . ."

He did not complete the sentence. Peter followed his eyes. Mary Warden had come out of the house and was walking toward them. The eyes of the two men met, and held. For a moment Adam did not stir, but his deep-drawn breath gave Peter an indication of the feeling of the man beside him. Peter turned away and walked toward the stables. Adam and Mary did not notice. They were two people unaware of anything but each other, but Peter did not soon forget the strong feeling that swept over Adam's face. For a moment he seemed to see the man's naked soul, looking out of his eyes. He felt embarrassed to have seen such emotion, yet strangely elated to think that there were two people in the world so deeply moved at the sight of each other. It made him feel lonely and a little sad. He glanced upward at the windows of the room where Angela lay. The shutters were closed, as they had been all day.

He thought again of the incident of the night before, after he and Penelope had returned. He had not been able to go to sleep for some time. After turning on his pillow a dozen times, he got up and went to the window. He noticed a small ray of light in the room Morse occupied. Shortly afterward he thought he heard a stealthy footfall. He went to the door and listened. A creaking board told him that someone had crossed the space at the head of the stair. He opened the door a crack and glanced out. A shadow, heavier than the darkness of the hall, was against the door that led to Angela's room. He stood watching. He thought he heard the faint lifting of a latch. He closed the door silently. He could not bring himself to spy in such fashion. He could not understand the dead feeling that came over him. His past experience with women had not prepared him for this, this despondency, this discouragement. Angela Ferrier had given him nothing, ever, that might cause him to hope that her attitude toward him meant more than the vagary of a petulant child, but she was not a child. He remembered how close she had been sitting to Morse at table the day they had walked into the dining-room at Balgray. Her thigh must have touched Morse's leg from knee to hip. The thought brought a hot flash of anger. He had no idea what their relations might be. Innocence or worldliness might be hers. Her Spanish blood might make her vulnerable at the hands of an unscrupulous man. The thought angered him the more. He found himself walking swiftly, his hands clenched at his side.

He came in sight of the stables. He stopped abruptly. Morse was dismounting from a mud-splashed bay mare. He tossed the reins to a stable-boy and started up the brick path to the side entrance of the house. His boots were as mud-stained as his mount's flanks. Black swamp mud. Morse looked up and found Peter staring at him. The scowl left his handsome face, and he became at once the suave merchant.

"Beastly roads," he murmured. "I've been riding over the plantation."

Peter said nothing. His own boots had looked the same when he came in from the swamp. He thought Morse was nervous but he made an effort to appear natural.

"I wonder how long we are to be imprisoned here," Morse said, avoiding Peter's steady gaze. "Gad, man, I can't stay here forever just because a yokel doctor says I must, I . . ."

"Dr. Williamson arrived a few minutes ago," Peter said. He found it difficult to be civil to the fellow. He continued to look at him, from his boots to his face.

"By Gad, Huntley you are an uncivil fellow! Every time I look up you are staring at me!" Morse moved a step nearer. "I find you very annoying."

"With that I agree," Peter said.

Morse's hand went to the sword that wasn't there. He reddened and looked away. "Pardon me, Huntley," he said with an attempt at a careless laugh. "It's this enforced detention. I swear it is getting on my nerves."

Peter held himself in check. What he would have liked to do was to slap the fellow's handsome face.

Morse, murmuring something about changing, turned on his heel and went toward the house. Peter watched him go. He did not know how long he stood motionless after Morse disappeared through the door. He was recalled to himself by Herk. The Negro had come out of the stable leading a big bay hunter, saddled and ready. Herk, too, was watching Morse. He came over to Peter, touching his cap with his fingers. "He mighty angry. He ride into swamp and get heself covered with swamp mud, looking for he man."

Peter stared blankly at Herk.

"He Ferginnie black man. He find him, maybe lying in the black water, stone-dead."

"Ah," Peter said slowly. "Thank you, Herk."

Herk touched his cap again and walked away leading the hunter.

They had gathered in the drawing-room after dinner, waiting for Dr. Williamson and Dr. Cathcart to come in. Mary Warden and Adam Rutledge sat watching Penelope and Parson Earle, who were engaged in a game of draughts. Morse sat by a small table reading an old copy of the *Gentleman's Magazine*. From time to time he looked toward the door impatiently. Peter sat near the window. The night was warm and sultry, the air depressing. He watched Governorcharleseden and Scipio, as they moved about, arranging the posset table, bringing new candles to replace those that had burned to a nubbin. He could not, in his mind, reconcile these quiet, well-trained servants with the primitive men he had seen in the pocosin, dealing out pagan justice a few nights before. He remembered Penelope Dawson's wise observation, "We take these people as they are on the surface. My father always told us, my brother and me, not to attempt to delve into the mysteries of the pagan mind." He had seen the wisdom of what she had said—better to accept the thing that appeared on the surface, too much knowledge . . .

He got up and left the room, remembering that he had not looked at the case De' Medici had sent him. He stopped at the foot of the stair to get a candle. Scipio came out of the drawing-room and lighted it for him, with a splinter he brought from the dining-room. He thanked the black man and went upstairs.

In his bedroom he sat down at the desk and took out the key to his case. He noticed then that the lock was broken. On top of the papers was a note from De' Medici.

I found your case broken open, and the papers disturbed. I hope nothing is missing. I gave Horniblow the devil for letting anyone go into your room. He swears *no* one entered, but how can he know? I found Williamson. By now he is probably with you, scratching your arm with his infernal pick. My arm is sore and swollen. But he says I won't get the pox. This village is in alarm—talk of pox, slave rebellion, Washington in retreat, Charles Town in alarm. I supped with Sam Johnston last night. Mr. Iredell was there, a knowledgeable man but gloomy over our situation. He and Johnston have much to lose if the British get here, since their people hold high places at home. Several Tories have been run out of the village, put under the pump, or the ducking stool. One man sat in the stocks for a day. A smith by the name of Clem Hull is the leader. He swears to run every Tory into the Sound. My men have had several fights at the Red Lion. I arranged a short-time loan with Hewes and Smith Company, so I have paid my men something. Little enough. Gad, this is no way to fight a war! Your desolate and discouraged

Cosmo

P.S. No post has arrived since you left. The dispatch rider was killed near Middle Swamp, between here and Suffolk. The second in two months.

Queen Anne's Town.

Horniblow Tavern.

Peter leafed through his papers. As far as he could tell, there was nothing missing. He grinned to himself. The searcher, whoever he was, would find nothing but figures and records of the lottery. But it gave him pause that his belongings had been searched at all. Another thought came to him. Morse had nothing to do with this. There must be someone else who suspected Peter of carrying dispatches, or perhaps they were looking for currency collected from the lottery, which he might be carrying.

He put the papers into the case and shoved it under the bed. Someone had unpacked his saddle-bags. His fresh linen lay on the bed, and folded neatly on the pillow was Angela's bright crimson scarf. He caught it up and thrust it into the saddle-bags. As he crossed the hall to go back downstairs, the two doctors came out of Angela's room. They were absorbed in talk and did not look in his direction. He heard Williamson say, "Her fever is higher than I like. No eruption on her chest, but it is too early for that."

Cathcart said, "Two cases in the quarters have been segregated." They moved on downstairs. Peter waited until they had opened the door and entered the drawing-room. Then he went across the hall. Angela's door was ajar. He pushed it open. A candle stood on a bedside table. An old Negro woman sat near the bed, her hands folded in her lap. She looked up as Peter entered but made no protest as he approached the bed. Angela lay very quiet. Her eyes were closed. She was breathing heavily like one who has had a sleeping potion. Her hands were folded across her breast. It made him think of death. He leaned over and took her hand in his. The skin was hot and dry. He held it closely a moment, then laid it at her side. The Negro woman spoke his thought, "She fold them so, lak she was daid. Do you think she die, Doctor?"

Peter gazed at her flushed cheeks, her red mouth and her pointed chin. She looked so young, so young. He leaned over and laid his cheek against her breast. The rapid beating of her heart seemed to penetrate him, set his own heart to a quickened rhythm. Anguish-contracted lips set his jaw to a harsh line of determination.

"No," he said quite clearly. "No. She will not die."

His words seemed to penetrate the girl's consciousness. Her lips moved. "Not die . . . not die . . ." she repeated. Her eyelids did not flutter, only her cracked lips moved. "Not die . . . not die . . ." A thin whisper.

The Negro woman stroked her hand. "Not die," she said, "not die."

Peter turned and left the room. He was deeply shaken. He had spoken without thought, from something deep within him. She would not die. He would not let her. All uncertainty of his feeling for her died away. He loved her with all the strength that was in him.

When he went down to the drawing-room a little later, he found Williamson in the centre of the room, bending over a pewter basin of hot water, placed on a candle-stand. On a near-by table, quills and small bottles and lancets lay on a white cloth. Dr. Cathcart stood there. His sleeves were rolled to his elbows, and he was dipping a quill into a pomade jar.

Mary Warden stood beside the two doctors, her ruffled sleeve turned back. Morse and Earle were coatless; they too were rolling back their linen shirt-sleeves.

Penelope was sitting in an elbow chair. As Peter came into the room she said, "I stole a march. Dr. Williamson has already scratched me with his devilish little lancet and spread his poison." She lifted her foot from a cricket, allowing the silken skirt to slip aside, showing a laced satin shoe and a trim ankle. "I've chosen a limb instead of an arm," she announced. "Mary is much too modest to expose herself."

"Nonsense," said Mary. "This won't take on me. I've tried inoculation three times before and nothing ever happens."

"Don't be too sure, miss," Williamson said. "For that I'm going to give you double dosage."

Peter slipped his coat from his shoulder and prepared his arm. Morse said grumpily, "I've had it before, too. I don't see the sense of repeating."

Williamson looked at him over his spectacles. "You don't? Well, sir, many a man has refused inoculation, to his sorrow."

When it came to Morse, he said quickly, "Not my sword arm, please."

Williamson muttered something and lifted Morse's left arm. He cut; his lancet moved swiftly, cutting a cross. Dr. Cathcart handed him two quills which he had dipped into the pomade jar on Williamson's directions. The doctor dug the quills deeply into the cuts which were bleeding. "Bind it up with a bit of cotton over the wound," he said gruffly. "We'll see if this one takes or not."

He looked at Peter's arm and motioned him to roll down his sleeve. "Good enough scar you have there, Huntley. We'll chance it." Peter buttoned the cuff of his linen shirt and put on his coat.

"I think it's time for a rum," Dr. Williamson said. He dipped his hands into the hot-water basin and dried them on a huck towel Mary handed him. "Soon over," he said. "Not like the army when I do hundreds at a sitting." Dr. Cathcart asked a question. The two were deep in medical discussion. Mary and Penelope walked toward the door, their arms about each other's waists. Mary's blue dress complemented the wine taffeta Penelope wore.

"Where are you going?" Dr. Williamson asked, turning from the posset table, silver cup in his hand.

Penelope said, "I thought we would look in on Angela for a minute."

"I don't want her disturbed. I've given her a sleeping draught," Williamson said. "I'll look in on her myself. If you want to go to bed, we will excuse you," he added. Penelope swept a fine curtsy.

Dr. Cathcart said, "Curtsy your best, my dear. I doubt if you will be able to dip so gracefully when the inoculation takes effect."

Penelope made a grimace. "You won't forgive me for not offering my arm to the experiment instead of . . ."

Mary tugged at her arm. "Come, my dear, let us leave the gentlemen to their toasts."

"I hope you don't feel the necessity of drinking to every woman you can think of," Penelope added, laughing.

The toasts were many and drunk with gusto. Dr. Williamson had a few days away from the army work. Adam Rutledge was home for a week before going on to New Bern and an unmentioned destination. Peter kept his head by confining himself to very small drinks. Morse was drinking cautiously. After a time he said good night and started upstairs. Peter followed shortly after. Before he left the room, Adam Rutledge said, "I would like to have you come over to Rutledge Riding with me in the morning, Huntley."

"Tut, tut," Cathcart interrupted. "Captain Huntley has been exposed. I'm keeping him here."

"Let him go," Williamson said. "That inoculation scar of his is as good a guarantee as we need."

"Thank you very much," Peter said quickly.

"Just a minute. Have you been near pox patients since you've been inoculated?"

"Several times."

"Then I think we need not detain him, Cathcart."

Cathcart shrugged. "All right, since you say so, Williamson. Only over to Rutledge's plantation. You won't come in contact with any crowd of people."

"Very well, directly after breakfast, Huntley. Good night." The others said good night and Peter left, closing the door after him.

Something awakened Peter from a sound sleep. He opened his eyes without moving his head on the pillow. The door was opening cautiously. The moon, low in the heavens, gave a dim luminous light that made the objects in the room seem veiled and ethereal. Through his half-closed eyes he watched, keeping himself rigid, unmoving. As the door swung wider he saw it was a woman's figure clad in some white garment that took on the luminous quality of the moonlight. She held a candlestick in her hand, shielding the light, casting a flickering glow upon her face. Peter saw that it was Angela. Her eyes were closed. She walked slowly, uncertainly. A sudden flow of wind lifted the curtains. The light flickered and went out.

He knew she was asleep, unaware. His heart was pounding as she made her way toward the bed. Bending over, she reached down her hand and touched his cheek. She leaned down and put her face against his. "Anthony, Anthony, don't leave me!" she whispered. "Don't leave me! Don't leave me!" The candlestick fell to the rug with a soft thud. She wrapped her arms about his neck, her lips seeking his. "Anthony," she repeated, "don't leave me! Without you I shall die." She began to cry softly; tears fell on his cheeks.

Peter did not speak. For a moment his arms held her close. Then he loosened her arms gently. She made no protest. Before he could sit up she turned and glided away, crossing the patch of light that lay on the floor. For a moment she seemed as fragile, as ethereal, as the moonlight. Then the lock clicked and the door swung shut.

Peter got out of bed. His blood was racing, his hands trembled. He cursed softly at his awkwardness in finding his clothes. Before he was half-dressed, he heard a terrified shriek, Lucy's voice crying, "Mistress, Mistress, she's gone, she's gone!"

Peter flung the door wide. The hall was empty. In a moment doors opened, and candlelights appeared, shadowy startled people. Cathcart was first to reach Lucy's side. "Master Doctor, Master Doctor, I close my eyes only one, one little minute, and she is gone." The Negress put her hand in front of her eyes. Swaying from side to side she began to moan.

Penelope, her dark hair flowing down her back, a yellow robe over her nightclothes, caught the woman by the shoulder. "Be quiet! Stop that howling! Tell me where she went."

"I saw her come from there." She pointed down the hall toward the bedchamber where Peter slept.

Williamson, rubbing his eyes, opened the door of his room. "What's this hullabaloo?"

"Angela has disappeared," Cathcart said.

"Disappeared? Nonsense. Where could she go? Not down the stairs surely. Let me into her room."

Peter, at his words, left the shadow of the doorway where he stood and went quietly down the stairs and into the garden. Something had occurred to him. What was it that awakened him? Not Angela, coming into his room, but something before that. It came to him like a flash—he had been dreaming of Morse closing his door, walking down the hall toward the stairs. In his dream the man was in travelling garb, his saddle-bags flung over one arm. The closing door, the footsteps had been real.

The hall door, opening to the garden, was open. He went swiftly into the gloom of the garden. The trees and bushes made fantastic shadows against the patches of moonshine. Peter saw a moving shadow, not white, but dark, against the heaving background of a box hedge. Peter followed the path that led to the stable, so keen on pursuing the fleeing shadow that he did not pause to think that he might be quite visible himself as he crossed the open space.

He heard pawing against the floor of the stable and a horse whinnied. He went into the dark stable, his hands stretched out to find the door of the first stall. Instead he came in contact with a man's body. He heard a muttered curse. A blow descended, hard and swift. Peter reeled under the excruciating pain, and fell forward on the straw-covered floor. A moment later a man led a horse through the doorway. He mounted hastily and rode across the lot into the open field that bordered the deep woods.

When Peter regained consciousness, some hours later, he found he was in his bed, a wet towel on his forehead and the pungent odour of smelling salts in his nostrils. Penelope was sitting by the bed.

"Angela?" he whispered. "Did he take her away?"

Penelope changed the cloth on his head, before she answered. "No, Morse didn't take her away. Dr. Cathcart found her on the grass near the sun-dial."

Peter didn't speak for a time. "Was she hurt? Is she . . . ?"

"You are not to talk," Penelope said.

He moved impatiently. The effort caused pain to shoot through his head. . . . He closed his eyes. The water from the cloth she had laid on his forehead trickled down over his face. He tried to speak.

Penelope laid her finger on his lips. "Be quiet, Peter. I will tell you about Angela. She has the pox."

He tried to sit up, then fell back against the bolster with a groan.

"Dr. Williamson says it is mild, very mild. We have a linen mask on her face, so she will not scratch. He doesn't think she will be marked."

Peter said nothing. Penelope continued, "Dr. Cathcart found her. She had fainted from the exertion. He said it was delirium that made her wander away. She was shaking with a chill. Lying in her night-rail in the dew like that was enough to kill her. They carried her in, wrapped her in blankets and gave her a hot posset. That caused the eruptions to come out. Dr. Williamson says it is a good thing to have pox break out. What we want to know is what happened to you. Was it Morse? Don't talk, just press my hand." Peter squeezed her fingers.

"Ah, I thought so. When we got around to thinking about him, we realized he had fled. Adam sent Herk down the Governor's Road, to try to overtake him, but we were too late. . . . With Angela raving and calling for 'Anthony,' and you lying here as white and still as the dead, we've had a hectic twenty-four hours." She turned the cloth so that the cool side was against his forehead. "I might add that Morse took all his clothes and one of my fleetest mares when he left."

Peter cursed softly. He tried to push the cloth away from his eyes but the effort was too great.

"The doctor says you are not to move," Penelope ordered. "Here comes Mary. We are going to bathe your poor head in vinegar. You have a fearful bump as big as a hen's egg." Peter groaned aloud. He heard Cathcart's voice.

"You got a wicked blow, Huntley. The butt of a pistol, I think. Now don't move. I may hurt you."

Peter felt the doctor's fingers press against the back of his neck, torture, then darkness.

CHAPTER

12

PETER MAKES A VOW

INSTEAD of Peter visiting at Rutledge Riding, Adam came to Eden House the afternoon before he left for New Bern. For a week Peter had, as Scipio expressed it, "laid he on he baid." He was quite willing to obey Dr. Cathcart's orders to be absolutely quiet. Whenever he moved, he remembered Morse, and not pleasantly.

Adam came into Peter's chamber and drew a chair to the bedside, in line with his vision, so he did not have to move his aching head.

"I browbeat the doctor into letting me come in," he said. "Cathcart is a stickler but I persuaded him that I would not excite you unduly."

Peter laughed. "With a conscientious medical man and two beautiful nurses, no sane man should complain, but——"

"I know you want to be about your work. That is the reason I came. The fact is that I am, in a sense, doing the same kind of work, only mine is to the West. After I visit the Governor in New Bern, I am going over to the mountain country." Rutledge opened a bundle of letters he held, selected one and laid the others on the counterpane, within reach of Peter's hand.

"I've a letter from the Committee. Some instructions for me, but a paragraph will be of interest to you. I'll read it: 'We want you to be on the lookout for Captain Peter Huntley. He will be at Queen Anne's Town or New Bern. Say to him that we have sent dispatches for him in care of Governor Caswell. One part of his work will be lightened. We have discovered that a certain Anthony Allison was put ashore somewhere on the Carolina Banks by H.M.S. *Viper* with orders to get information about barracks, installations, forts, etc., number of troops, Continental and State, in the Southern Province.

"'Captain Allison is an officer in Ferguson's Corps, which will be a part of Clinton's Southern Army. Our Intelligence has no description of Captain Allison other than that he is a clever, efficient officer.

180

He has maps of the Neuse and Cape Fear and South Carolina districts, furnished by Gordon Rutherford, H.M.N., a member of a prominent Cape Fear family. Captain Huntley is to seek out this man, discover where he is operating, but if possible not to discover himself to Allison in any capacity other than that of inspection of lottery tickets.' "

Peter listened, his face showing his discouragement. Adam folded the letter and, having unbuttoned the coat of his uniform, placed it in the breast pocket.

"I have a confession on my own score, Huntley. After your——" he smiled—'little accident, I wrote the committee full particulars regarding Morse, or Allison, as far as I know them. I told about his attack on you, which was told me by my man Herk, who found you and brought you to the house. I have also sent a dispatch to New Bern, to the proper people, asking them to be on the lookout.

"Whether Morse will return to the Banks for a rendezvous with the gunboat, or proceed to Charles Town by land, we have no way of knowing. My own guess is that he will go to Cross Creek, to Farquhar or some other Tory, and from there down the Cape Fear by boat.

"The Royal Governor Martin is on H.M.S. *Cruizer*, somewhere in the mouth of the Cape Fear. If Morse can reach any of the blockading ships, he will proceed to Savannah by water."

"You are very kind, Major Rutledge. You have no idea how I have worried, lying here, not able to do one thing, knowing that damn villain was roaming about the country," Peter said gratefully.

Adam smiled. "We're all in the same war. One other matter. The situation in the western districts is serious. From Virginia to South Carolina in the foothills and mountain valleys are little nests of acknowledged Tories. Our Intelligence reports that the British have men there, who are instructed to go into the Cherokee Indian country, to stir the Indians to massacre and rapine, as they have endeavoured to light the fires of rebellion in Virginia, among the slaves."

Peter said, "I believe that was part of Morse's assignment here."

Adam nodded. "Penelope told me. I have written a full account of that abortive attempt and the part you played. I sent it to the committee."

Peter flushed. "Really you are too kind. I did nothing. It was Madam Dawson and your man Herk—I was extra luggage." But nevertheless he was pleased. The days spent here had not been entirely wasted.

Adam said, "Dr. Williamson has gone back to the Dismal, and the Parson to his parish. Angela Ferrier is progressing, a very mild attack, Dr. Cathcart tells me." He rose preparatory to leaving. "The letters Sam Johnston sent over. He thought you would be interested in reading them. Something to take up your time and keep you in touch with what is going on elsewhere." He stood looking down at Peter.

"I have often thought this country, this Albemarle of ours, a little haven, a little of Eden in a world of tumult. So quiet, so peaceful. The land gives so bountifully: its woods, its fertile fields, its bounteous streams. The drawn sword of war is far away, yet its cutting edge is felt, in a slave rebellion, an enemy intruder, a divided citizenry."

His eyes strayed to the window. He stood for some moments looking out on the fields beyond the garden and the stables. There was sadness in his face and a nostalgic longing.

He turned back. An unconscious sigh escaped him. "I miss my land, more than any time, in the spring." He squared his shoulders as though to throw off the mood, and shook hands with Peter.

"I will see you in New Bern before the Assembly is over; if not then, in the West." A smile spread over his clear-cut features. "The Tories are really strong in the West," he said, and left it at that, rousing Peter's curiosity. Rutledge, lately at headquarters, knew the plan of things to come, the pattern of campaign. He was giving him a small suggestion, a starting place to let his imagination roam.

Peter lay for a time looking at the waving pines outside his window. The wind came soughing, speaking to him of spring. He was despondent when he should have felt gay. Sap running, the warm earth in its fertile abundance, the young tender green in the long rows of ploughed land, the promise, if he only knew what lay ahead. The weight of the bitter years was heavy upon him. He could not, like Adam Rutledge, see ahead through the weight of a losing war, to clearer skies of victory and peace. The battles fought by heart-weary men, dropping to the icy ground in fatigue, sodden masses of discouraged men sleeping in rain and snow. Valley Forge had set its imprint deep into his soul. He could not bring his tired mind to think of troops fresh, eager for battle, marching briskly to fife and drum and streaming banner. Only men inert on the frozen earth, their feet close to the embers of dying fires. Angela Ferrier—a few steps from him, as far away as the stars!

He reached for the letters. The first one was from Madam Blair, in Queen Anne's Town, a connection of Penelope Dawson's. It described the exodus from Queen Anne's Town when Admiral Sir George Collier with his fleet entered Hampton Roads. The country was terrified. Aided by General Matthews, who commanded land forces, the fleet had attacked Fort Nelson. The garrison had at once abandoned the fort and retreated to the Great Dismal Swamp.

Portsmouth, Norfolk and Suffolk fell to Sir George. Booty was seized, valuable property destroyed, Suffolk was burned, Norfolk gutted.

Alarm in Queen Anne's Town grew with each passing hour. The enemy was less than fifty miles away. Any day the fleet might enter Albemarle Sound. Wise observers maintained the inlets were too shallow for a sizable warship to pass through, but the state of alarm grew rapidly.

There were no troops to guard the village or repel a sudden invasion. Its wealth would be bait to tempt the enemy. The war was growing in relentless fury. Atrocious crimes were committed by wretches who hovered like vultures at the rear of the enemy forces. No house was secure, no gentleman safe; females were raped, even children suffered wanton cruelty.

We have recovered all our things safe, I believe with little damage. After moving furniture out of the town we move it back. Alarming accounts come in continually. No one minds now except a few weak people. Yet some people who brought goods in yesterday are sending them back today. Mrs. Barker and Mrs. Nash packed up everything, even to pictures and looking-glasses that were screwed to the wall.

"They say" the British will be here tomorrow, by Wednesday, by Thursday, certainly by next week. Where they have their intelligence, I don't know.

Mr. Hewes and others were carried out last night. The Dismal Swamp has been on fire for days, the reeds burn and pop like muskets. That foolish fellow W—— came to town last night, said there were large fires kindled, and many guns fired out there. I think it is only his own fear. I refuse to be frightened again without more certain account of danger being near. Mr. Hewes's warehouse was broken into last night. There have been people taken up this morning. A Negro of Mr. Rayner's, it is said, will be hanged. Two sailors were taken sleeping at the foot of Sam's garden; they were about the house all night.

Peter laid the pages on the bed and took up another letter. It was from Will Hooper, the Signer, to Judge Iredell. Sam Johnston had scribbled a line across the top, "Dear Huntley: You can get a pretty fair insight into conditions from Will Hooper's letter. My brother-in-law, Iredell, sent it to me. It supplements some of the affairs we have discussed. I think the letter worthy of preserving. S.J."

Finian, 1779.

Dear Iredell:

I am by no means apprehensive of America. The present conduct of Great Britain proves its despair; these burnings and ravagings are the convulsive agonies of expiring power, and as, in a natural body, such agonies are more violent in proportion to the former strength of the corporeal system, so we have reason to expect that the most important kingdom upon earth will not be dismembered without giving a most violent shock to the limb which is to be severed from it. Strange infatuation, is it not, thus to alienate us forever from any connection with themselves and wantonly to give away what alone remains within their reach, a common share of our trade with the most of mankind?

I drop this painful subject; it is painful to observe the dissolution of our friends, but inexpressibly so to find them surviving their reputation.

Remember what you and Mr. Johnston have always said when I expressed my fears about Wilmington, *Cui bono?* What could the enemy get by it? To rob the pine trees, bear away the sandhills . . . ?

I have been very uneasy since I learned that the landing of the British troops had suggested the removal of the women and children from Queen Anne's Town. It evinces the incapacity of the Virginians to make a stand against a very inferior foe. How miserably we have been deceived in our own internal resources! Return to the Continent the troops which the French have drawn from it to the West Indies by their naval operation there, and our Independence would be of short duration.

Fourteen hundred troops shake the Dominion to the very centre—the Dominion that boasted it could singly maintain the contest with Great Britain.

I begin to think that the South Carolinians have more stuff in them than old General Armstrong was willing to give them. They discover as yet no want of personal prowess; like the animal

spirits of a warm climate, I hope however that their heat will not
exhaust their strength, and leave victory to be gathered by those
who fit exertions to the occasion, and husband themselves for a
distant day.

W.H.

Peter folded the page carefully and laid it aside. The letter confirmed what he had heard before, that William Hooper was one of
the forward-thinking men of the Revolution. A pity, he thought, that
he and Thomas Jefferson should be at loggerheads. Fights and bick-
erings and quarrels among the leaders! Peter, having a soldier's outlook, had little patience with the politicians. They did not possess
what the men at Valley Forge had gained, the selfless devotion to
the country's needs.

Perhaps there were some leaders who gave freely of themselves
and their ability, but they were balked by the lesser, selfish men, the
disturbers.

He turned to the letters. On one Penelope had scribbled a line:
"Cosmo to Penelope."

Lovely Chatelaine of Eden House:
    It was regretful that I must leave your presence in such haste as
to present almost the appearance of running away. But with
your divine understanding, I feel that my ancient and family
tradition of offering always a bold front to the enemy remains
intact.
    My little troop of horse I remove from Queen Anne's Town to
the Capital City. Before I leave, Mr. Smith was so good as to
honour Cosmo's note for a sum of moneys, not entirely sufficient,
but adequate to pay for food for my voracious men. Horses we
have now, and almost a full complement of men. We drill well
and presented quite a dash when we made a little drill on the
parade ground in front of the Governor's Palace this morning.
    New Bern turned out to see us, and comments were excellent
for the foreign Captain de' Medici. The French are here in numbers. I would say that the "Nobility of France" is sadly less in
Paris, so many wait here. They come to offer their swords to the
great cause of Liberty. They arrive by ship up the river and at
Wilmington also. French ships come loaded with trade goods
and some munitions; among the human cargo ducs, comtes and
many of the lesser nobility. Some soldiers come, some adven-

turers, drawn by the promise of one Silas Deane of Dr. Franklin's staff. Our friend Peter will tell you of that.

His Excellency is embarrassed by these many French volunteers. He have no way to care for them; no money to outfit regiments they offer to recruit, but where?

The Governor he is a man diplomatic. He writes each one a very fine letter to Congress and to General Washington at headquarters. The French officers will thus pass out of North Carolina in excellent spirits. Some will stop in Queen Anne's Town, visiting Mr. Iredell and M. Stephen Cabarrus, they tell me.

The Governor gives a ball for the French, but the pox interferes. 'Tis said here that the Governor's lady did not want to execute a ball, because of the small furnishings in the Palace. One never knows about these small gossips.

Will you remember Cosimo to your household? I trust the beautiful Miss Ferrier is recovered, and that my little Pietro pursues his suit with more vigour than I have seen him display in the past.

My Kind Hostess, to you my deepest and sincerest Felicitations.

Cosmo de' Medici

New Bern.

The days went by slowly enough. Then one day Dr. Cathcart looked in on him. "You may get up today." His round, apple-red cheeks, his smiling mouth, the cheery expression of his face showed that he no longer had any worries.

"My other patient has been released, with no hurt more than a mark that she can cover with a beauty patch." He sat down and offered his tortoise-shell snuff-box.

"I think so well of your condition that I will allow you one good sneeze." Peter refused politely. Cathcart placed a pinch of snuff on the back of his hand, inhaled, and in a few seconds sneezed violently into a great silk kerchief. "No idea how it clears the head, Huntley. I recommend it highly."

He chatted a few minutes, then got to his feet, pausing to adjust a knee-buckle on his breeks, which had come loose. Peter reached for his wallet under his pillow.

"Tut, tut. None of that. I'm not a practising physician any longer." Peter protested but Cathcart would have none of it.

"I'll send Scipio to help you dress. I would suggest a walk in the garden. As a matter of fact you could have been up several days ago. Williamson said to let you up on Monday, but I'd rather err on the side of too long in bed." He went away, his buckled shoes tapping the bare boards. Even his footsteps sounded cheerful.

Scipio came into the room, his black face shining. He was smiling broadly. He carried Peter's uniform freshly pressed, and an ewer from which steam arose. "The doctor say I'se to bathe and shave and dress you, Mr. Captain, so you can walk in the gyarden."

Peter was surprised to find that he felt stronger than he expected, after a week "on the bed." He hummed a little song as Scipio dressed his hair and clubbed his queue.

"Madam she go to Rutledge Riding on she horse, she an' Miss Mary. They ride away some time ago, a-talkin' aba't spring plantin' and crops, jes' lak always."

Peter thought of questioning Scipio about the ordeal by poison, but thought better of it. Let sleeping dogs lie, he said to himself. I'll never understand these black people. I'd only make a mess of it by any enquiry.

"I give you my arm to walk the stairs," Scipio said, after Peter had taken a few turns about the room. "Look, Mr. Captain, I fotched Master Gabriel's gol'-head cane for you, 'case you wan't strong in you' legs." He held out a walking-stick of ebony, with a gold knob atop.

Peter laughed. "It isn't my legs, it's my head. . . . Thank you, Scipio."

"Heads can cause a lot of hurt," Scipio observed. He gathered up his shaving implements and brushed a blob of lather off his red coat. "A lot of hurt," he repeated.

Peter walked in the garden to view the sunset reflected on the waters of the Chowan. A soft gentle wind blew from the Sound, bringing the odour of pines and cedar and fresh-burned tar—the acrid heavy smell that made him think of great warehouses of naval stores he had visited at Brest, and the decks of ships fresh caulked, with thin ribands of black tar. A far-off memory of childhood in Holland came into his mind, when once he went to the docks with his father, and strayed into a warehouse of naval stores. He had picked up a little blob of tar; boylike, he had put it in his pocket. The day grew hotter, the tar melted. He remembered very vividly the housekeeper's anger. "I'll cut the wee pocket out of the breeks and ye canna hae anither, till ye've enough of sense not to be pickin' up filth frae the street."

Peter was smiling at the memory when he stepped inside the summer-house. Not until he was within did he see Angela. The yellow light of the late sun, shining through the cross-slatted side walls, cast a diapered pattern on the floor and on her white muslin skirt. She was seated in a canvas garden-chair, her body relaxed, her eyes closed. Her extraordinarily long lashes lay on her ivory-tinted cheeks. He stood still, looking his fill of her, his eyes unguarded, his desire for her showing clear. He saw her in gentleness, in her sweet beauty, without the hard animosity that looked from her eyes when they would open and discover him standing above.

The incident of the scarf and his awkwardness—surely she was carrying a simple matter too far. He looked in unconscious ecstasy at her. He wanted to know her thoughts, share her feelings, her griefs, her joys. He wanted with all the strength of his mind to have her confidence and her trust. His thought of her was tender, protecting.

She opened her eyes. Seeing Peter standing in the doorway, she rose to her feet slowly, with infinite grace. For a long moment sleep lingered in her eyes, making them soft and warm; then they changed, reflecting nothing, neither anger nor pleasure. They were dispassionate, viewing him from the great distance of her inner thought.

"I am sorry. I did not know you were here." He felt angry, as the words escaped him. Was he to be continually apologizing to the woman? By Gad, no! He felt resentment toward her as though she had assailed his masculine strength. A change came over her. She gathered up her book and little sewing-basket from the bench, a studied deliberateness in her movements. She stood for a moment looking directly at him.

"Allow me to pass, sir." Her words were cool and calculated. He did not move. Some perverse sense of his masculine superiority came over him. He did not budge from his position in the doorway, nor did his grey-green eyes waver as he looked down at her.

Angela said, "To scream for a servant would be undignified." He smiled coolly, made master of himself by her words, meant to insult.

"If you must scream for help, let it be for a reason," he said. He took a step forward, encircled her with his arms. She tried to push him away, her two hands clenched into fists. With her in his arms, her long slim body against his, Peter felt his pulse leap. For once, he would be master. For once. He pressed his lips against her warm, passionate mouth, the long hard kiss of a lover long denied. She grew rigid in his arms without struggling. He released her at once, and stood back against the door, looking at her with unreadable eyes.

She pushed her hair into place with her slender fingers. Her eyes were hard as his own. She motioned him away.

"Not so quickly, my dear," he said, looking at her without moving. She found herself trembling before this masterful figure, trembling at her own helplessness. He knew she would not scream.

"Not so quickly." He moved a step closer. She shrank back until her hands touched the boards. He did not heed the sudden look of fright in her dark eyes, for desire was strong in him. His arm closed about her, his face close to hers.

"One day I will marry you, I vow I will," he said. Then he kissed her deliberately, slowly, savouring the perfume of her lips, the lithe strength of her slim body held so closely against him. He kissed her softly, then with swift, cruel hardness. She did not fight back. She was passive in his arms.

When he released her, she gathered up her belongings and left the summer-house slowly, without speaking or looking at him. Peter watched her move along the garden path with lazy undulating grace. He had no regret for his violence. He was glad, glad that he had held her body against his own. Within his loneliness, there were warmth and the strength of the romantic. There was tenderness too, and warm devotion.

The girl wanted a master and he, at the moment, had made up his mind to be that master of her will and her body. But not yet.

The sudden exultation died. Peter found himself looking at the water from which the afterglow of the sunset had gone, leaving only the cold grey shadows of the quiet river.

CHAPTER

13

INTERLUDE

CLEM HULL, the smith, walked from his house on the water-front to the Red Lion, near the northern gate. Not a long stroll for a man of heavy frame and tough sinews, even with the handicap of a lame leg, but time enough to consider what he was going to say, when he met his fellow artisans over a tankard of ale.

The Red Lion was the artisans' club. After the day's work they gathered to drink their ale, to talk of their work, to hear the latest news from the travellers who stopped for the night. To throw darts, or sit on an upturned keg, over a game of draughts, afforded them the same pleasure that their betters enjoyed at Horniblow's.

Many a criticism of the ways of the gentry had its inception at the Red Lion. When men had drunk their fill, tongues loosened, old grudges, old envies, came to the surface and took voice.

Clem Hull was such a one. He was as bold as he was brawny, and his tongue could lash out; or he could wheedle a man to do his will. Vulcan he was, with a heavy, powerful torso, and great strong arms and thighs, where the muscles rose and fell with rippling strength when his hammer struck the hot metal laid on his anvil. His lameness in one foot would have been a handicap to most men, but to him it was the goad, the spur, to keep alive the hatred of men who belonged to a class above him. The bitterness of the child had grown into hatred in the man. He tricked and spoke scandal of men who paid him the King's shilling for work loosely done. A shoe that pinched and lamed, a plough that split, a singletree that broke when a chaise was in midstream—it was all the same to him. Knowing there was but one other farrier in the village, he waited. Let them come to him, the great gentlemen on their fine horses, with their fine gigs. His father was a bondman of old Squire Pollock. He had grown up at Balgray.

190

Squire Tom had treated him fairly. He expected a full day's work and got it, or his overlooker laid on with the lash. But he favoured Clem Hull. There was something about the bold, surly face of the young boy that interested the Squire. He took him from the stables and set him at coopering and blacksmithing.

"At the end of your bond you'll have a trade and be fit to care for yourself." So he trained him and gave him more freedom than other children of bondmen, and in the end gave him a year on his apprentice time. Clem was as grateful as it was possible for him to be. If he ever had a spark of affection it was for the Squire. But it was the Pollocks who had caused his lameness.

An accident it was, the carelessness of an overlooker at Balgray, slinging work-tools about. A mowing-hook carelessly thrown down on the earthen floor of the smithy, and a severed tendon. The Squire had taken the wounded child to Queen Anne's Town. Dr. Armitage did what he could, and he had skill beyond other surgeons in the Albemarle, or even Norfolk, but he could not prevent the drawn tendon and the resulting lameness.

That was some years past, thirty at least. The Pollocks of this generation had forgotten the accident. Certainly Cullen never realized it was because of an accident which happened on his grandfather's plantation that the smith walked heavily, with a sidewise twist. He frequently stopped at the smithy, near Joseph Hewes's shipyard, to have his horses shod or plantation tools mended, and paid no mind to the surly silence of the farrier.

Clem had married a village girl who bore her mother's name. It was said she was sired by a fine Tory gentleman who now lived in England. It didn't matter to Clem; she was a good wench who did his bidding, cooked his meals, and bore his drunken abuse meekly and in silence. Her name was Martha, which Clem shortened to Martie. When she went to the Sound to get water for her tubs, she carried two buckets on a yoke swung over her shoulder. As she walked along the path, and bent to dip the water, many a waterfront lounger's eyes followed the turn of her ankle, her strong thighs and full bosom, with the avid gaze of envy.

Clem was a rare lucky lad, one sailor said to his mate as they walked along the path by Hewes's shipyard. "If he ben't such a brawny fellow and quick with the fists, I'd beat him to his bed one night."

"Best not try that," said the first. "Last winter he well nigh killed a fellow off a coast boat as made invitation to her. He be strange that way, and nae willin' to share the lass. Best keep to the girls down the water-front, sailor, if you want to go out with yon ship of yours."

The seaman shrugged. "No matter. We sail at sunrise for New Bern Town. I've a good girl there who keeps an outlook for my ship and me, but a fellow gets lonesome for a woman's soft breast to lean against; but I've no mind to get me a broken jaw, by the smith's fist."

All this Clem knew. There was little that did not come to his ears, which were hairy like Pan's. His keen grey eyes under his heavy brows observed shrewdly and he remembered what he heard and saw.

His strength, his quick tongue, made men afraid, yet there was admiration also, for a man who could speak boldly and look back into any man's eyes, gentleman or yeoman or husbandman. The making of a leader was in Clem Hull, and the revolt gave him his chance.

He had no wish to shoulder a musket, but he made muskets. Instead of a farrier, he became an armourer, a gunsmith. He remade, he repaired, he moulded. Men were beholden to him. He was necessary; his work became important to soldier and seaman. In his dark soul he took satisfaction. He almost forgot hatred and small revenge in the importance of the work. To make a flint-box, to repair a lock, to rifle a musket barrel, these were things of necessity. When the *Holy Heart of Jesus* came into the bay and anchored near the Dram Tree, Clem was first on the Green to watch the sailors unload, for who but Clem Hull could assemble the cannon, set them on stout oak carriages, make them ready to turn on the enemy?

Now he walked to the Red Lion. When he stepped over the threshold men turned their heads, craned their necks, and welcomed him with shouts. Had he not worked for their defence? Made their guns? Clem was their friend. He was different from the old sullen fellow.

He greeted the men at a table near the door and sat down on a bench, his back against the wall where he could survey the room. Each night he sat in the same place. No one presumed to usurp his throne—not even Southey Wren, the yeoman from Rockahock Landing, who had drilled the Edenton Light Horse. Wren had been a soldier who took the King's shilling in his youth and he had not forgotten what they had taught in camp or the things he had learned for himself on the battle-fields of Europe.

There was an unspoken rivalry then, between the two. Sometimes

ey sat at draughts the whole of an evening. At darts Clem was
aster, but at the quieter, thoughtful game Wren took precedence.
'Tis a game like a battle-field," he would tell the onlookers. "It
kes a world of thought, to lay the traps. Once the trap is laid, pouf,
e game is over! Three moves, four or five, perhaps even six, yet
e game is won when the trap is completed."

This superiority worried Clem. In his slower, heavier way, he re-
ected Wren's quicker wit. "Naetheless," he said when Wren
mped the board to the King row, "naetheless, ye cannot down me
ith darts, nor the musket either. I can load and fire faster, and that's
e trick to soldiering, not thinkin' out traps to beguile a man into the
rong spot."

Tonight Clem and Wren had their usual game of draughts. Clem
on three straight. At the end of the third he placed his great hands
n the table, staring at Wren. "What's wrong, man? Any time you
t me win three games, I know ye've not got your mind set to it."

"You're right, Clem. My mind is running round and round, thinkin'
bout muskets and shootin'."

Clem's big laugh rang out. The men at the tables and at the
ounter turned their heads. A laugh, a great hearty laugh from Clem
Iull, and what's the world a-comin' to and all?

"Laugh," Southey Wren said. "Laugh. But this is a different
nought." He leaned over to speak confidentially. The onlookers
rifted away. " 'Tis like this, Clem. More than once I thought I'd
e telling you about a rifle that shoots four times hand running"

Clem spat. "There never was such a piece, man, in the world."

"Yes, there is. No—wait: I'll be telling you a little story, then I'll
ake you a little drawin' with my chalk here." He laid a flat stick of
halk, such as a carpenter uses, on the table and began. "I've never
een one to talk my own affairs."

"That you haven't," Clem acknowledged.

Southey went on, paying no heed to the interruption. "I've been
laces in the army. It was in 1759 I joined up with the Royal North
British Dragoons, and a month later we was in Germany. We fought
t Minden and that's where Germain, whom they've got in high places
ow, showed the white feather. . . . Three battles we fought, chased
he French through Warburg, across the river, defeated a French
arty at Zierenberg and took the town and three hundred prisoners."

"Never heard of those names," Clem muttered, looking at Wren
ith more respect.

"We had an officer, a cornet named Patrick Ferguson. Aye, h
was a rare fine lad, always lookin' after his men. Every spare minut
he was on the rifle range, practisin'. I pulled target for him many
morning at daybreak. He taught me all I know about arms."

Wren paused, pulled an old pipe from the pocket of his blu
smock and lighted it with a coal a waiter boy brought him. His hanc
were horny from the plough and he picked up the coal with his fi
gers, without using tongs.

"I liked the lad, so when he bought a commission in the Seve
tieth Regiment of Foot, I went with him. We went to the Caribbe
Islands in the West Indies. We put down an insurrection of thos
heathen Caribs, on St. Vincent's Island. There we stayed until '7
There we parted. Captain Ferguson went to Halifax, in Nova Scoti
a bitter cold place. I had no stomach for cold, for the tropics was i
me. I served out my enlistment and got on a ship coming to Americ
We landed on the Cape Fear River. I looked it over, but I heard c
the Chowan River, where English yeomen had taken up land. I wa
born on a farm and the land was in me, so I set out for the Chowa
and there I settled, near Augustine Dishon's place, on Rockahoc
Creek. You know me as a yeoman and a miller, but it's a lot of so
dierin' I did. Don't forget that, Clem Hull."

Clem looked at Wren with respect. "A real fighting man," he sai
"and I didn't know. I thought you were one of those drillmaste
that never got farther than the barracks."

Wren did not listen. His mind was on his story. "What I'm getti
at is this: Captain Ferguson, all the time target-practising as I told y
was workin' on a new invention, a rifle that fired four times, lik
this." He took up the chalk and began to make a crude drawing o
the bare boards of the table.

Clem leaned over, his heavy features twisted in his effort to cor
centrate.

Wren finished the drawing, dusted the chalk off his fingers. "Wel
keep that before your eyes while I tell you somethin' more. This rif
he had fixed up could be loaded at the breech, without using a ram
rod. You can see how fast it can fire."

Clem nodded.

"Captain Ferguson tried it out before some experts at Woo
wich. . . . Generals and all were there, a great array. It was raini
and a high wind, but he fired during four or five minutes at the rat
of four shots a minute, at a two-hundred-yard target."

"Mother of God!" Clem muttered.

"Not all. He walked forward at the rate of four miles an hour, firin' four times a minute. Then he poured a bottle of water into the pan and barrel of the rifle, when loaded, so as to wet every grain of powder, and in less than half a minute, by crummy, he fired it off, without extractin' the ball. Then the big thing—he laid himself on his back and fired, and with the high wind, rain and all, he missed the target only three times."

"Holy Michael!" Clem ejaculated.

"It was a big thing, a big thing. I forgot to tell ye that fat King George was watchin' all the time, sittin' under a striped canvas coverin'."

"Holy Michael!" Clem repeated.

"That's not the great of it, all that target-hittin'. I've seen him ridin' his horse, let the reins fall on its neck, draw his pistol, toss it in the air and catch it as it fell, aim and shoot the head off a bird sitting on the limb of a tree."

"Never! Never in this worl'!" Clem spoke loudly. "Never such a marksman!"

"You don't have to believe," Southey said indifferently. "I've seen, with these two eyes."

After a silence Clem said, "Where's this man now? Is he on our side?"

Southey Wren shook his head. "No. He's a soldier, he is. Some of our boys who went out north with Washington's army heard of him. They said he was at the Brandywine with a company of picked riflemen. He was at Chad's Ford with General Knyphausen. My friend told me he saw him. They tell the tale that Ferguson had his rifle on General Washington, who was inspecting with only a French hussar as an escort."

Wren called the pot-boy. "Bring us two tankards of your best," he said. He turned again to Clem. "If Ferguson had his aim on the General, the only reason he isn't dead today is because Ferguson withheld his fire." He put another line on the drawing. The pot-boy came with the ale. Wren said, "Between us we might make such a rifle."

"Aye," Clem said. "That is what I've been a-thinkin'."

Two tankards were lifted silently. Two men drank deep. After they finished, Wren leaned over the table and wiped away the chalk lines with the tail of his smock.

Clem laughed scornfully. "Think any of they can read your lines and make a musket liken to it?"

Wren didn't smile. He glanced about the low, smoky room with searching eyes. "A military man learns to be secret," he said. "There be plenty of King's men left in this country, though they walk up and write their names to the Parson's Test."

Clem's face darkened, a fanatical light gleamed in his eyes. "Aye, you speak right, but we have ways of ridding the country of the damn scum. Jist you wait, Southey, jist you wait."

Anthony Allison left Farquhar Campbell's house at midnight. It was the dark of the moon, an excellent time to make the downriver trip to Brunswick. The canoe, with four loyal Highlanders at the oars, moved slowly down the dark river. Anthony had plenty of time to think of the events of the past fortnight, too much time, in truth. He had lain up at Campbell's house, near Cross Creek, invisible even to the house servants during the day. In the evening he crept out of the attic where he slept, and joined his host. Campbell sent his wife early to bed these nights. "Our womenfolk are loyal, but sometimes a shrewd question may trap them. Better that they know nothing." That suited Anthony. Too many people knew his identity as it was. He could have kicked himself a hundred times for his folly in Queen Anne's Town. His heart had led him to do what his mind had told him was more than unwise. Ann Pollock had warned him. But he was obdurate; he must have his own way where the girl was concerned. Well, he had had his way. He cursed softly.

One of the oarsmen turned, a dark shadow against the moving shadows of the river. "You spoke?" the voice came softly.

"No," Allison answered. "No." His mind returned to the meeting with Angela Ferrier at Ann Pollock's, the subsequent meetings at Balgray, at Eden House. It was folly, sheer folly. Women! They dragged a man to danger. Suppose it had come to a climax, his mission been jeopardized. Huntley, with his cold, keen eyes—he was sorry to have had to knock him cold with his pistol butt. But, by Gad, the man would have had him in a moment! He hoped he hadn't killed him. He didn't mind shooting an enemy, but this underhand sneaking spy business was not to his liking . . . black men lying in the swamp water, stiff in death, backs riddled from the lash. What had happened to those men? His stomach turned over at the thought of a black rebellion. Thank God, that wasn't his kettle of fish any longer!

Huntley was after him—why? How the fellow knew what he was up to defeated him. Or perhaps he didn't know. Just one of those flukes.

He was jumpy, nervy. He must get over that or he would be suspected by everyone. Slip into the skin of Jeremiah Morse, Anthony my son, he said to himself. *Be* Jeremiah, think Jeremiah, live Jeremiah, a merchant, a close, shrewd buyer, a Boston man. God condemn them for Lexington and Breed's Hill . . . a colony was a colony, a province a province. Let well enough alone. Did they have to rebel? There were plenty of men in England who despised the Hanoverian King and his ministers. Pitt and Fox, Wilkes and Barré were friendly to the Americans. Yes, even General Cornwallis had lifted his voice in Parliament in defence of the Colonies. God's truth, it was a heavy world!

He slipped deeper into the bottom of the long canoe, his legs stretched out. He hoped he wouldn't get Jeremiah Morse's coat dirty. He wanted to be neat when he presented himself to Governor Martin, aboard H.M.S. *Cruizer*, which Campbell assured him was in the mouth of the Cape Fear River.

He shifted his position cautiously, let his head rest against the gunwale, and looked at the stars. How tranquil the stars! That constellation showing brightly in the great arc of the heavens, Casseopeia, a constellation guiding his course. The Pleiades, the little sister who was missing, red Mars on the horizon. Venus would rise as a morning star, Venus and love . . . Mars and Venus, war and love . . . That was it: war and love. Angela's mouth so warm, her passionate body so inviting . . . he closed his eyes better to savour the memory of her voice, her arms around his body drawing him close. A girl to love. There had been others, since the time he had first met her on the ship coming from the Azores. He remembered a slim blonde girl in Antigua, who came to stay with him when he went ashore. She had given him pleasant hours, and expected nothing beyond those pleasant hours. Angela was different: she was demanding. She wanted him wholly, she would not be satisfied with half-loves. He breathed deeply, evenly. After a little time he slept.

When he woke, the morning star shone in a pale, brightening sky. The elder man at the oars, MacKenzie, said, " 'Tis best to lie up for the day. The farm yonder is Loyalist. Meester Campbell he sent word."

They were met at a small wharf by an aging, toothless man, who beckoned them to follow him. He took a path that led through the timber, over a rough ploughed field to a small cottage half hidden in the trees. The man was deaf. He offered tea made of herbs, and a piece of corn-meal cake. After a few trials at conversation Anthony gave up. He lay down on a plank bed with rawhide lacings, pulled a tattered plaid over him and went to sleep. It was dark when Mac-Kenzie wakened him.

"'Tis slow, paddling only by night," MacKenzie said when they were again in the canoe. "Verra slow. But we'd best be cautious."

The best part of a week was spent, sometimes dodging into small creeks as boats went by, dragging rafted logs. Anthony went ashore once only, at Park's store, to get supplies. He met two men looking for Colonel Waddell's place. He got away from them after some questioning, and determined not to leave the boat again near any habitation. He loathed this work he had undertaken under pressure. He longed to be with his company once more. He did not care what Major André had told him, that "to spy with honour is to be a hero." He hoped he would see André again. He had been told he was in Charles Town, gaining information for Clinton's officers.

Off Eagles' Island, near Wilmington, MacKenzie noticed they were being overtaken by a boat. "Best you sit low, Mr. Morse, and be busy with trolling, until we see who we've got comin' upon us."

Anthony leaned over the side and set about drawing in the troll lines. The boat, a cutter manned by a dozen men in the uniform of state militia, came close. An officer stood up, a beardless young lieutenant. "Any luck?" he called. MacKenzie held up two shad they had caught the evening before, and kept on hand for just such a purpose.

"Where you from?" the officer called.

"Up-river a stretch. Goin' down-stream to visit my daughter; fishin' along the way."

"Where does your daughter live?"

"Near Old Town. Jethro Welch's her husband."

One of the soldiers said, "I know Welch. He fishes off Old Town Creek."

"Aye, lad, that he does."

The officer gave an order and the boat made a sweeping circle, coming up on the starboard side of the canoe. At the moment they turned Anthony pulled up the troll line; a shad, a four-pounder, was well hooked. He was so taken up with the excitement of landing the fish that he forgot the cutter and the officer. He stood up in the

canoe, balancing himself with legs wide-spread. He called to Mac-
Kenzie, "Land him, lad! Hit him!"

MacKenzie, leaning forward, caught the fish in mid-air. Swiftly
he unhooked the shad and flung it into the patrol boat. It landed
square in the centre of the boat. "With MacKenzie's compliments,"
he called out. The boat pulled away, men calling their thanks.

"A nice bit of play-acting, sir," the old man told him. "You paid
them no mind, like a proper fisherman."

"It wasn't play-acting. When I saw that fish, I forgot the cutter
completely. I was afraid I wasn't going to land that fellow, without
a scoop."

MacKenzie nodded. "Well, it was all right. They dinna suspect. But
we're getting warm in this river. There's too many patriots to my liking. Mr. Campbell, he told me to put you ashore off Old Town
Creek. After that you'll have to make yer way by yer lone."

Anthony nodded. Campbell had discussed the plan with him. The
night before he left, they had sat long, with a map before them. He
had it all in his head: paths through the turpentine woods, at Old
Town Creek; the road through the swamp, the narrow path that led
to old St. Phillips, to Brunswick. The Loyalist homes had been designated.

He paid off the men, shook hands warmly with MacKenzie. The
old man walked across the narrow beach to spot a path that led up
the twenty-foot bank. "I dinna know, laddie, I dinna know. If I
hadn't taken the oath after Culloden never to bear arms against the
King, I might hae taken the other side in this war."

Anthony stared at him. The old Scot looked back at him with
steely gaze. "It's wise to remember that there's always one side . . .
then there's another. This is a guid country, laddie, a fair fine country. Guid fortune, laddie!" He turned and walked back to the canoe,
where his men were waiting.

Anthony watched the canoe pull away. Then he sat down on a
driftwood log to watch the sun rise over the flat sandy shore on the
opposite side of the river. A great red ball of fire broke through the
heavy cloud bank, which hung low, marking, he supposed, the line
of the ocean beach, some miles distant. He took a hunk of corn
bread from the poke MacKenzie had given him, and ate it dry. Not
a palatable way to breakfast.

Two cardinal birds flew past his vision, and lighted in a bush that
overhung Old Town Creek. He caught the flash of a mocker's white

and grey striped tail. Its song was short and quick, like a catbird's call or a blue jay's; not in full throat, as when it resembled a nightingale. A hare scudded across the thin strip of beach. A deer broke from the heavy woods above the bank and made its way down to the water. It stood looking at him with large mournful eyes. Anthony did not stir, scarcely breathed, as the animal drank its fill of creek water. The deer moved slowly up the creek, breaking through the brush that spilled over with bright yellow stars of jasmine. On the bank the dogwood bloomed in profusion, great clusters of white against the skeleton limbs. A log floated downriver, a living log, a great crocodile. Then the flashing tail churned the placid river as it snapped at a black cormorant flying low. The grotesque fowl, its obscene head doubling and extending, gave a shrill screech, flapping its wide-spread wings. Anthony noticed that now only one leg dangled under the slick, boat-shaped body. He shivered. It was a lonely, cruelly lonely spot.

In early days, three times heroic men had attempted settling on this creek, but naught remained but the undefiled forest, the limpid stream, the sluggish flow of the river.

He finished his corn bread and drank, dipping his cupped hands deep in the sweet water. He must fix his position before he started southward toward the mouth of the river.

He looked for a secluded spot where he would be concealed from the river and from the bank above. He saw a little cove where a few bushes grew, where the overhanging bank would hide him. He sat down on the sand and unfastened his belt. The large silver buckle was a safe hiding place for a map traced on thin paper. He drew it out and laid it on the sand. Two small pieces of driftwood worn smooth by the river held the paper flat. He studied it closely for some time, then broke off a small twig from a bush and, without looking at the map, traced its outline in the sand, placing each stream, each stretch of forest, each lake in its proper place. He gave close attention to the location of houses. The large plantations that bordered the river he must avoid. Therefore he could not follow the easier way close to the river, for the planters were, for the most part, revolters. He memorized the names of the plantation-owners from the map. Moray was above Old Town Creek; three Davis plantations below. Up the creek lived Hazel and Allen; Moore, below. Brunswick must be avoided. He could not learn whether Fort Johnston was now in the hands of the rebels or not. A star marked Loyalist men, where he could hide if necessary. A charcoal burner's hut, a small house in a clearing. Damn these planters! What came over these men of many acres, to join rebels? Why not stay loyal to the King and save those fertile acres?

After several sand drawings, Anthony had the map clear in his mind. He destroyed the original by chewing the thin paper to a pulp and pounding it to bits on a log of wood. A voice broke the silence, a strong rough voice, with the trace of a bur.

"It's a good thing, me lad, that 'tis a loyal man, not a rebel, that observes ye drawing maps of this region."

Anthony whirled about, drawing his pistol. A man stood by the stream. He had come so silently that he made no sound or broke no twig in his descent from the high bank. A short thick-set man, wearing leather breeks and a hunter's green tunic, he had a thick cudgel in his hand.

"Ye can't prime and load, my lad. I'd have had my dogs on ye long since, had I been wanting." He nodded toward the sand. Anthony obliterated the map with the toe of his boot, anger deep in him.

"I've been watching ye for some time," the man continued.

"Who are you?" Anthony demanded. "Why are you watching me?"

"Tut! Such high words from a man caught red-handed making drawings of the countryside." He whistled a low call. Two great mastiffs bounded down the path, slipping and sliding. Seeing a stranger, they froze, growling.

"Being polite and not high, I'll answer. I'm steward for Mr. David Moray. Yon's his plantation." The man nodded to indicate the far side of the creek. "Above are his turpentine woods. I strolled over to see how tree-boxing was coming on and the men told me a boat had put in early, at sunrise, leaving one man ashore."

Anthony cursed. The Scot grinned. "My master, Mr. Moray, is old and bedridden. He takes no part in this conflict, but he has a strong feeling in him for the old country. Past ninety, he is."

Anthony remembered Campbell's words, "David Moray is old. He is no rebel, neither has he been actively loyal. Best avoid his place. He has never housed our people."

Anthony said, "And you—are you a King's man?" He had to ask. The fact that the man had not taken him gave him hope.

"That I am not, but my Culloden oath keeps me from shouldering a musket. Neither will I give over a man."

Anthony drew a long breath. The Scot spoke sternly. "Make your way out of here before others find you; before I forget. . . ." Anthony moved cautiously toward the path that led to the forest, avoiding the dogs.

"There's plenty of men about, not neutral as I be, young sir. The dogs won't follow 'less I speak."

Anthony scrambled up to the floor of the forest. Tall pines, without litter or underbrush, lay before him. He must avoid beaten paths. They would lead to the turpentine workers. He took his compass from his pocket, set a course southwest, remembering on his map the location of Lockwood's Folly. The swamps lay ahead of him, but he knew there were ways through them. If only he were lucky enough to find a little clearing, beyond Brunswick Town, where dwelt a man named Gil Roi, who was loyal to the King! Gil Roi would have information about the *Cruizer*, or some other British ship which might be lying in the river or along the coast, but he must have a care. Campbell had told him that it would not be difficult. Martin Howard and his family had gone to Jamaica, the Hamiltons to the West Indies Islands and from there to Georgia. Some escaped through New Bern, others the Cape Fear. Ocracock was out of the question, for the rebels' river galley *Caswell* controlled the inlets in that vicinity.

That day he walked through the woods, avoiding paths, fording streams, his clothes riddled. Bramble-scratched, he plodded on, skirting swamps as well as he could, always keeping away from open fields. Ten miles the map made it but he must have walked fifteen before nightfall.

He rested then, at the rim of a great swamp. Afraid to lie on the ground because of vipers, he climbed into a tree that had branches near the ground. He could not sleep for fear of falling. The night sounds of the forest were constant—croaking frogs, the heavy bellow of crocodiles. The screech of a hoot owl filled him with alarm until his mind placed the sound.

At daylight he plunged boldly into the swamp. There was dry land somewhere. He followed a path, having no other recourse. He came onto a body of water, whether a lake or an arm of the river he did not know. Half hidden under a bush he discovered a bateau, a homemade boat. He untied the rope and pushed off, poling it with short, jerky plunges in the mud bottom of the shallow water.

A girl stood on the bank and watched Anthony make an awkward landing. She was partly concealed by the heavy reeds on the bank.

She was motionless, looking at him with heavy-lidded eyes. He caught the glint of the barrel of the musket she held over her arm. He smiled and called a greeting to her, but there was no answering smile, nor did she smile when he jumped from the bateau and lighted in the water, short of the bank, splashing his already sodden clothes. As he walked toward her he saw that she was handsome, not more than eighteen or twenty, with a fine lithe figure. Her swelling bosom showed beneath her white fichu and her trim waist was small, laced tight, a dark velours bodice covering a gown of mustard-coloured cotton. Her skin was dark and smooth. Her large oval eyes were as black as swamp water. A broad forehead and heavy brows almost met over a thin, high-bridged nose. Her small mouth was full-lipped, above a slightly receding chin.

As he neared her and she stepped out from the reeds, he saw that her slim brown legs were bare and that she wore *sabots*.

"It is not permitted to land," she said, shifting the musket. "What you want, m'sieu?"

Anthony said, "I want to dry my clothes. I want something to eat, but most of all I want to sleep." He thought he saw a flicker of interest in the blank stare.

"You are runaway?" she asked.

"I am runaway," he replied.

"I will take the pistol." Anthony took the pistol from his belt and handed it to her. "Proceed," she said shortly, and motioned him to walk ahead of her. He glanced around and saw a well-beaten path through the reeds. He walked in silence for some time, always conscious of the musket aimed at the small of his back. This was intolerable! The long journey to end as captive of a woman! Presently they came to open ground. Giant oaks took the place of cypress and pine and juniper, through which he had been travelling. Then he saw a small cottage, as grey as the moss that hung from the heavily crowned oaks. It was built of shakes, roughly cut. It fitted under the trees as though it had grown from the earth. Fowl runs were on one side. Half a dozen dogs rushed forward, mongrels. They retreated at a sharp word from the girl behind him. A carding-wheel stood on the crude porch, a rush-bottomed chair beside it, and an osier basket of fleece.

Opposite the house he saw a long pile of lumber and several bundles of shingles such as sheathed the house. A circle of huge pines beyond the oaks cut them off from the world.

As they came up to the steps, a white crane hobbled out from the house. Making queer clucking noises, it reached out its long bill toward the girl and touched her arm.

She spoke to the bird in French, her voice low and caressing.

Anthony spoke to her in the same language. "There is no need for you to hold that heavy gun. I won't run away. I'm too dog-weary. Put it down and hold my pistol, if you must. It won't fire, unless you have dry powder."

The girl laughed. She put the musket on a bench. "My father he tells me to watch, so I watch. Did I not do it well?"

"Too well!" said Anthony. "I don't like being disarmed by a woman."

She laughed again. "That is natural, so natural. I think I like you." She laid the pistol beside the gun. "You are sorry to look at, sir, very sorry." She became solicitous. "I will get breeches that are dry," she said, going into the house. She returned almost immediately with a pair of skin breeches over her arm, and a skirt such as woodsmen wear and a pair of *sabots*.

"Slip inside, sir." Anthony entered the low-ceilinged room. It was broad and long with a small fire burning in a wide fire-place. Spotlessly clean, the room had a pleasant feeling of comfort and hominess. Shag rugs were scattered over the broad floor, and there were a simple table and benches. In the corners, fitted against the chimney-breast, were two beds, built of plank, polished and shining. Anthony had seen such bright chimney beds in Holland and France. They were seats by day; by night woven curtains hanging above them gave privacy. They were covered by woven counterpanes, of geometrical design of maroon and white.

Anthony looked about for a place to change. The girl said, "I will close the door so you may strip. Yonder is a basin and ewer." She went out to the kitchen, closing the door behind her firmly. He heard her stirring about and the rattle of dishes. He stripped to the skin and washed. After drying himself on a rough towel, he put on the dry clothes, intended for a large man with heavier calves. He set the knee-buckles over and managed to make himself presentable, combing his hair before a small oval reflecting-glass. He stood for a moment looking at a carved figure over the fire-place, a woman's head and shoulders, the straying hair painted black, cheeks and lips reddened—obviously part of a ship's prow. It had been cunningly set into the wall, until it seemed part of the room. The girl knocked and entered, carrying a tray in her hand. She noticed that he was absorbed in the fragment of the figurehead.

"My father found it on the shore. It washed up after the great storm, when he found the lady and the little girl."

"A lady and a little girl?"

"Yes, they were lashed to a door. They came in on a great wave."

Anthony said nothing. He thought of Angela and the story he had heard in Queen Anne's Town.

"My father told me that he saw the ships fighting off the shore. One blew up in fire and went down. The other sailed away, southward. For a long time things washed onto the shore, dead men too, and a seaman's chest with rolls and rolls of silk, picked out in gold and silver."

"What became of the silk?" Anthony asked. He was seated at the table, eating eggs made into a savoury omelet, drinking fresh milk.

"I have the silk. When I make marriage I will use."

"When will your father be home?" Anthony asked.

"Nex' week. He goes into the woods to cut shingles."

Anthony said, "Then I must go on."

The girl turned quickly. "*Non. Non.* You stay. My father tells me always make welcome for a man who runs away. . . ." Anthony waited for her to continue. "That is what all our people do: they run away into this big swamp, so the Spaniards do not catch them and carry them away in their great high ships."

"Your father fled from the Spanish?"

"Maybe my father. Certainly my grandfather, and all the others who live on the other side of the swamp. They have been here long time now, many years, long before I was born. Maybe before my father he was born."

Anthony looked more closely. Now that he had been fed, his powers of observation quickened. Certainly the girl had strong French characteristics, the full oval eyes, the high nose, the curved lips.

"What is your name?" she asked, looking at him from her place by the fire.

"Morse. Jeremiah Morse."

She made a small *moue*. "How very ugly name for such a pretty man!" Anthony flushed. "Do not be angry. It is well to be beautiful. When I take my bath in the creek, I know I am beautiful. When I splash the water over my naked body I laugh aloud, to see the little drops race down my limbs. It is so pretty."

Anthony thought, Is this girl all innocence, or is she all-knowing? She got up and removed the dishes from the table, humming to herself, her voice throaty and seductive. He sat close to the fire. As the day waned a cool breeze blew in the open door. The girl closed the door and drew the gay little curtains. "No one sees in through the paper," she remarked, "but the colours are cheerful, no?"

Anthony fought sleep. He got up and went to the door and walked about. The young half-moon shone over the treetops. He must sleep tonight. Tomorrow he would go on to the coast, to Lockwood's Folly.

He went back into the room. The girl was busy folding the woven coverlet she had taken off the bed in the far corner by the chimney. She plumped up the pillow and folded back the covers. There were sheets on the bed.

"You wish to sleep. Your eyes they tell me . . ."

Anthony said, "I am dead for sleep."

"Come get into bed. See what a fine soft mattress I make from moss that grows on our trees."

He sat on the edge of the bed, ready to drop back clothed as he was.

The girl protested. "You must take away the rough clothes. You will sleep good tonight and rest. Tomorrow I will guide you to the coast." She went out of the room.

Anthony undressed in the semi-darkness of the room, lighted only by the firelight. He laid the clothes on a chair. He took his pistol from the mantel, put it under his pillow and crawled in. The sheets were smooth. He was asleep almost as his head touched the pillow.

How long he slept he did not know. He opened his eyes slowly. It took moments for him to orient himself. A candle was burning on the table, burned almost to the end. The girl was moving about softly. She had removed the white fichu and the laced bodice. As he watched her, she stepped free of her skirts and stood in her short white shift. She lifted the candle and blew it out. The embers gave off a slow glow.

Anthony saw her coming toward him. He closed his eyes. She stood for a moment hesitating, then turned the cover back and got in beside him. She was warm and fragrant against him. The great need of a woman's body swept over him.

In the morning, before cock-crow, the girl woke him. "It is time," she said. He sat up, rubbing the sleep from his eyes. She was dressed as she had been the day before, excepting that she had a cloth cape, with a hood, swinging from her shoulders. On the chair his own clothes lay, decent and in order. He dressed, ate his eggs and drank milk from an earthen mug. She did not speak of the night. She spoke only of the day ahead of them. It was a slow journey through the swamps to the sand hills. It would take time and they must be cautious. There were men who would watch for travellers and take them to the authorities. She had not asked him why he was fleeing or from whom. Better not to know, she said, with extraordinary sagacity. She put some corn-cakes into a little flat reed basket and slung it from her shoulder like a rucksack.

The white crane stalked after them as far as the thin rope fastened to his leg would allow, then set up a queer squawking protest as the girl moved away. Anthony stepped into the bateau while the girl stood on the bank and spoke to the dogs. The animals, unwilling but obedient, went back to the house at her command.

Motioning to him to be seated, the girl took the pole. Skilfully she manoeuvred the boat through lily pads and water plants, across the little lake. When they came to the opposite bank, she lifted a tangle of vines and creepers that made a curtain over the entrance to a small stream. There, between the heavy growth of osiers, she poled the boat. Cypress trees grew heavy here, feathered with tender green, the new growth of the spring. They came to an open larger lake. As they entered, white cranes in hundreds rose from the banks, flying low across the water.

A smile came across the girl's face, a tender warm smile. "My beauties!" she said softly. "Fly back to your nests. We will not harm you."

She did not speak again until they were across the lake. Then she poled the boat to solid ground on the shore. "From here we walk. We will walk until the sun is there." She pointed skyward, with her well-shaped hand. "Then we will rest for a time, until the sun is there." She again pointed to the sky. Anthony nodded. They would walk until midday and rest until four.

Late that night, they came to the sand hills. She made a small fire of driftwood, scooping out a little hole in the hill, then cooked a fish she took in her osier basket, and they ate it with corn-cake, washed down with a sweet wine she poured from a flask. It was dark and the salt tang of the ocean was against his nostrils and on his lips. He leaned back against a hill of sand, watching the girl crouched by the

fire. How skilful she was in her small preparations for the meal! She
got up and walked about, testing the wind with her raised hand; the
wind ballooned her cape and whipped her long dark hair which had escaped its confining braids. Then she gathered a pile of driftwood.
After that was done she leaned over and scraped a spot in the sand
close to the fire, well in the shelter of the hill. She lay down in the
little hollow, arranging her cape over her. She lay for a moment looking at Anthony. The firelight glowed on her face. Her eyes were very
bright and deep. Then she held out her arms. He slept deeply that
night, the heavy pounding of the surf in his ears.

In the morning when he awoke, he was alone. He stood up searching among the sand hills for trace of her. There was no sign of life,
no sound but the shrill whistle of sandpipers running up and down
the beach, and the lonely cry of the curlew.

When the sun was at its height, he saw a ship. It came close to the
shoals and anchored. A boat put out. He got up and went down to
the beach. It was all as she had told him in the night—the morning
would bring a ship.

He must stand on the beach and make the signal. The ship would
take him away. He must not forget her, she told him, her lips against
his cheek. A man must remember, sometimes, the comfort that a
woman gave.

When the boat came near, he gave the signal—and a signal came
from the boat. As the silent men rowed across the shoals, he remembered he had not even asked her name

CHAPTER

14

GARDEN-PARTY

PENELOPE BARKER sat before her mirror, while her maid Josie, a good-looking mulatto girl, arranged her reddish-brown hair in two drooping curls that fell softly over her firm white shoulder. She was wearing a sprigged muslin with a bodice and panniers of plain blue of heavy cotton material, which her mantuamaker called nankeen, and was very like silk in its effect.

She moved her head from side to side, a little French gilt mirror in her hand to catch each angle. When one is young, she thought with a degree of bitterness, one can have a straggling lock or two, but as one advances, no. Everything must be in order. Josie stood off to view the result, with the satisfaction of an artist.

"I am sure, Mistress, that the barber, Mr. Aly, couldn't do no better, though he do set some fine curls in Mr. Barker's wig. And this evenin' I see Mr. Iredell a-comin' from the shop with his head all white, lookin' mighty fine."

"Yes, of course, certainly," Madam Barker said absently. Turning this way and that, she posed before the long mirror which her second husband, Craven, had given her. She sighed. The faded gilt glass had once reflected a younger and lovelier Penelope. She remembered what a handsome couple they had made, standing together. He was a dashing figure, the brother of a belted Earl, a fact which he never forgot even in those early days when their stipend was slow in coming. She remembered how she had pleaded with him to take the deed to the little house Hodgson had willed to her; how he had willed it back to her when he died. She remembered the very words of his last testament: "I, James Craven, late of Draughton near Skipton, in Craven, in the County of York, in Great Britain, now of Queen Anne's Town. In the Province of North Carolina . . . my loving wife" . . . She had been that . . . she had loved all her husbands, each

209

for some reason concerning their characters . . . "Land . . . tenements and hereditaments with appurtenances which I purchased of her before our intermarriage . . . in the year of Our Lord 1752 and executed by her by the name of Penelope Hodgson . . ." The very house where she now lived with Barker!

Black cattle and sheep, his plantation at the Brick House . . . the old plantation called Paget's, and the range called the Great Marsh. He had willed her back the house and the old plantation. Strange: he was a man who must *own* his land. He was good, too, about leaving her children money as a token of affection; he was so thoughtful. To his godson, Will Badham, he left silver and money. That was all so long ago, almost twenty-five years, a quarter of a century. Arthur Dobbs was Governor then, before Tryon and all the grandeur of his administration, his Palace at New Bern, the Regulators' uprising. Her cousin Sarah Blount had witnessed James Craven's will, she remembered. Francis Corbin, Lord Granville's agent, Wyriot Ormond and William Heritage, as well as John Watson, of Suffolk, Virginia, his good friends, he had named as executors, along with herself. Yes, she had loved Jimmie. She was as young as Penelope Dawson was now.

She turned around slowly, so that the full sweep of her skirts came under her scrutiny. Nankeen . . . she wished the overdress had been a luscious satin. But the war, the war. Take what you can get. She thrust her blue-silk-shod foot forward. Josie stooped to tie the lacing ribands. So good of Joe Hewes to send her a dozen pairs of shoes from Philadelphia! One felt better, well shod.

"My white chip bonnet with the blue trimming," she said to Josie, "and my parasol. We are sure to stroll in the gardens at Pembroke."

"Yes, ma'am." The maid left the room.

Penelope Barker sat down in a stiff-backed chair. She would wait in her chamber until Cecily Armitage and Sarah Blount came for her. They would ride out in the Blount chaise. She did not have proper horses now, so that she could use Lord Craven's coach. Thomas was adamant about that. "No display in war-time, madam," he had said to her that very morning, when she had broached the matter of borrowing a pair of fine carriage horses from Hayes. "You will do nothing of the kind. If you can't have your own horses, you won't borrow."

"Are we so poor, Thomas?" she had said pathetically.

"No, but lawyers have hard scratching in time of war. People don't bother to go to court; they settle. And lawyers don't collect. 'Laws are silent in time of war.' That's a Latin proverb, but it might read: 'Lawyers are payless.' "

"I'm sorry, Thomas," she said, suddenly contrite. "I'll write a note to Cecily. She and Sarah Blount will be delighted to carry me out to Pembroke."

"Mind you tell the ferryman to have a care when he takes your horses on. Sometimes he's damn careless." He rose and took his three-cornered hat and lifted his gold-headed cane from the rack.

"It does seem a pity for Lord Craven's coach to be sitting idle in Jemmy Iredell's stable."

"It is a travelling carriage, not a coach, my dear Penelope, and I have my doubts as to whether it ever belonged to Lord Craven."

"James said it did. Or perhaps he told me that the Earl sent the money to have it built in Philadelphia. I forget which."

Thomas kissed his wife's upturned cheek, a little twinkle in his sharp eyes. "You were born too late, my dear. You should have lived in Queen Anne's time, and had your painted sedan chair and liveried lackeys, to carry you down our muddy Broad Street."

Penelope sighed. "I always longed to ride in a sedan chair."

"You would have graced it, my dear," said Thomas.

He walked to a small desk and took out a legal document, stamped with the seal of the state in red wax. He laid the paper in Penelope's lap.

She looked up quickly. "What is this?" she asked, a little apprehension in her face.

Barker smiled, a thin smile with some bitterness behind it. "Nothing to trouble you, my dearest Penelope. This paper, signed, sealed and delivered, tells you that your husband, Thomas Barker, Esquire, of Queen Anne's Town, in the County of Chowan, is a free citizen of the newly made State of North Carolina."

Her face lightened. "Oh, Thomas! The Assembly did act on your petition!"

"Yes, some weeks ago, on the twenty-third of January, to be exact, but I had the papers only yesterday."

She sat very quietly, holding the stiff papers against her bosom, her eyes shining through a film of tears. He took the papers from her hands.

"Oh, Thomas, Thomas!" She got to her feet, throwing herself into his arms. "I'm so glad! I'm so glad!" She began to sob.

"There, there, my dear. It wasn't so important. I knew I was a good citizen. A paper from the Commons cannot make me any more loyal than I was already."

"I know. I do think they were so *mean*, so very mean. Joe Hewes and Sam Johnston could have fixed it without so much talk—or Bennett, though I wouldn't have expected him to do for you what your friends hadn't seen fit to do."

Thomas patted her back. "The processes of the law are slow, my dear, damnably slow, when it is your own case."

"Mean," she repeated, "when you did so much for everyone while you were Provincial Agent in London. How could they forget that you and Emsley got the Board of Trade to exempt North Carolina from taxation the other colonies had to pay?"

He unclasped her hands from his neck and pushed her gently into her chair. "I'm afraid Tryon had a lot to do with that, my dear, and it wasn't utopian. If New York and North Carolina could have been won over, it would have split the unity of the dissenting colonies. Then, my dear, there are some honest men who resent the fact that we did not present the fiery memorial they sent to us to present to the Board of Trade; but rewrote it into a more conciliating form. They haven't forgiven or forgotten."

Penelope spoke indignantly. "How can they be such fools! Why, your memorial got the Act of Parliament passed in our favour. People are so stupid. You are always so right, Thomas."

Thomas said, "I'm not sure, now, that Emsley and I were right. Appeasement has a way of striking back. I don't know." He stood for a moment looking at the fire, his face serious.

"Read me what it says." Penelope's eager voice broke in on his reverie.

He opened the document, mumbled a few lines. ". . . name of the State of North Carolina, etc. Mr. Jones, for the joint committee of both houses appointed to receive and consider Petitions of all such persons as shall pray to be admitted as Citizens of this State, report as follows: . . . Petition of Thomas Barker, Esqre., a native of America, a former citizen of this State . . . find that facts mentioned in this petition are true . . . who, for his known zeal and assiduity in representing our affairs at the several Public Boards in England, as our Agent at that critical time referred to in the Petition, and from his firm attachment to the Cause of America, during her late struggles, to this time, claims our particular regard.

"We therefore unanimously recommend him to be received again into the Bosom of his Country, by admitting him a Citizen thereof, and restoring to him his property."

Thomas finished reading. Penelope regarded him with shining eyes, this time without tears. "How nice!" she whispered. "How very nice!"

He bowed elaborately over her hand. "Welcome to your new country, Citizeness Barker!"

She laughed aloud. "Ah, Thomas, you are so very amusing. *Citizeness* Barker."

"And, madam, I swear I was in excellent company. The Assembly took in Thomas Hogg, of Wilmington, and John Burgwin, Esq., of Wilmington (you remember he was in Bath, taking the waters, on account of a fractured leg, when war was declared), and William Hooper got in because he hastened from England to Paris, when we revolted, and, on the recommendation of Mr. Franklin, renews his citizenship, and Sam Marshall and John London. So you see we are all in good company, we new citizens. I declare we should all celebrate together."

"Perhaps we can," said Penelope, who loved a celebration. "Perhaps in New Bern, at the Palace."

"Who knows?" said Thomas. "Who knows?"

"I don't care. I intend to tell Joe Hewes what I think of him, and Tom Benbury, too. Isn't he speaker of the Commons? And particularly Sam Johnston. Why, you taught him everything he knows. Everything. You *made* Sam Johnston."

Thomas' face took on a look of sternness. "No, my dear. Never say that again. The good God made Sam and equipped him for greatness. I had the good fortune to guide him for a while." He kissed her hand before he bowed himself out of the room.

Penelope laughed. Thomas was delightful; one was never bored with Thomas, even though at times he turned to sarcasm. Never to her. She smoothed her skirts away from her trim waist as she thought of the little breakfast-table chat. Dear Thomas! She put the little white chip bonnet over her high head-dress—a coquettish slant over one eye gave it zest—took her fan, her reticule, her parasol of ruffled Spanish lace, which Gordie Rutherford had sent her from Malaga, just before the war. What a nice young man he was, so thoughtful to elders! She wished he had not become a Tory and stayed in the Royal Navy. It must have hurt his father, who was such a patriot.

A match between him and Sarah Blount would have pleased Sarah's father. As it was, that was out of the question.

The knocker resounded through the house. She heard young girls' laughter. Cecily Armitage had been taken with Gordie when he had visited at Eden House. Cecily was such a quiet little person men were likely to overlook her, especially handsome young men like Gordie, whom all the women chased, young and old. She put a little powder on her nose with a bit of swan's down and slipped a few crushed verbena leaves into her bodice. She must look her best, for she had heard that several strange French gentlemen would be at the Cabarrus garden-party. Rutherford made her think of Penelope Dawson. Pene was really angry when her stepmother married John Rutherford. She didn't even have a decent period of mourning, and Gabriel Johnston a Royal Governor! Frances Rutherford, she thought, was an upstanding woman, but grasping. She wondered if she had ever relinquished the gold snuff-box willed to Penelope by her father. He *should* have willed it to her. He had it from her mother, Penelope Eden. But people were strange. Frances had succeeded in carrying away several things from Eden House that were not willed to her.

She walked slowly from her chamber to the small panelled drawing-room, anticipating the young girls' enthusiastic admiration of her new costume.

Cecily and Sarah sat decorously beside Madam Barker in Dr. Armitage's carriage. It was about two miles to Pembroke Creek, where Mr. Stephen Cabarrus and his good wife lived. A man of liberal sentiments, Cabarrus had joined the American cause at the beginning. Reared in France, of Spanish ancestry, he had the inherited hatred for England which belonged to the French background.

The fat black horses jogged along the dusty road, out past Boadley's estate to the banks of the creek. There the ladies got down from the carriage and, having descended to the Pembroke canoe, were rowed across the creek by four blacks belonging to the Cabarrus household.

"All Queen Anne's Town and all the county folk will be at Pembroke today," Madam remarked. She sat stiff and straight in the stern of the long canoe, her skirts wrapped completely in one of Dr. Armitage's carriage robes.

Cecily sat facing Madam. She was full of youthful excitement about the visitors. "I caught a glimpse of the Frenchmen. They looked so splendid. Their uniforms had colour and they were so well tailored, and their hair was perfection. The little side rolls lay so close and firm against their heads—and their ruffles were so crisp."

Sarah said dolefully, "That's the trouble of living way out at Mulberry Hill; we never see anyone but fishermen in the Sound or the Negroes at work in the fields. Cecily can sit right at her own chamber window and see everything that happens in Broad Street."

"In Cheapside also," Cecily said. "And sometimes those happenings are not so nice. Sometimes the men drew their swords and fought, right in the street. My father threatens to put a lattice fence on Broad Street and on King Street too, as far as Mr. Nat Allen's."

Sarah said, "Oh, he wouldn't do that really! Especially on King Street. It is so nice to see your garden and Mr. Allen's as one walks by; and Mr. Hewes sitting out on Mr. Allen's veranda. Poor man, he looks so thin and ill!"

"So he is." Madam joined the conversation. "He works too hard. My Thomas says the man will kill himself from overwork at the Philadelphia Congress."

Cecily rolled her big blue eyes. "I think he is dying of love. He has mourned so for Miss Isabelle. Every day he goes across the creek to Hayes to stand at her grave. Nellie Blair told me so."

"Nellie is full of imagination," Madam said.

"I don't care. I think it is the most romantic love story in the world. He grieves and grieves and sighs."

"And sells merchandise and leases ships to Robert Morris and his committee, for a round figure. Don't forget he has time for that, miss."

Cecily pouted. "I will have him romantic. I think it would be wonderful to die of a broken heart."

"Better to live with a mended one, my dear," Madam said sensibly. "Where do you get these notions, Cecily?"

"My mother was awfully romantic. I've heard my father say so many times."

Madam looked at the young girl who had assumed a drooping, languid attitude in keeping with her words. She, Penelope Barker, could have told Cecily a few things. What she would have said was that Amanda Armitage was a silly fool, who preferred a harum-scarum, no-account young Virginian to Armitage. The doctor was always a sound man, but he didn't make eyes at the ladies or sing sad songs. But she held her tongue. The woman was dead—by her own hand, some folk said. She had run away with Holbrook and left young Cecily behind, with only an old black nurse to look after the child. Armitage had never spoken her name, as far as Madam Barker knew. Cecily was making this romantic stuff out of whole cloth. She must have a talk with the girl. She wished Mary Warden would take her out to Queen's Gift. To sit in her chamber window, watching men rampaging up and down Cheapside, was not a pleasant occupation for a young girl.

"Do you think Angela will be at Pembroke today?" Sarah asked Cecily.

"I think so. She is quite well now. Angela was at Eden House for weeks. Such a romantic thing to happen to a girl!"

"I can't conceive smallpox being romantic. The disease has a horrible stench, and such horrible markings. But Angela was lucky. She only has one little mark."

"I don't mean the pox, Madam Barker. But to be isolated with two young men. The dark captain! He is like some wonderful tale by Smollett."

"Smollett! Cecily! You are never reading Smollett! I must tell your father. You are much too young."

Cecily implored, "Please, please don't tell my father. I didn't know when I started reading."

"But you went right on?" Madam asked severely.

"Yes, Madam, I did," Cecily answered, smiling a little. "The library wasn't locked, and it was so very interesting. Is sin always so romantic?"

"Bless my soul!" ejaculated Penelope Barker. "Bless my soul!"

The canoe grated against the landing. The rowers stepped out, holding the canoe in place so the ladies could step out readily. They saw Stephen Cabarrus hurrying down the path, a welcoming smile on his lips.

"Do not step until I come to assist, Madam. Have patience! I will be on the landing in a small moment."

The visitors from France were the cynosure of all eyes, the men as well as the ladies. Stephen Cabarrus took them from one to another of the ladies, for introduction. This surprised the good village folk, who were quite content with a roof introduction, considering the old custom that all guests under a roof have been made known to one another when they entered the door.

Stephen did his graceful best, but he was long occupied, as only a few spoke French, and only one of the Frenchmen, Normont de la Neuville, spoke English. He struggled valiantly, as did his wife, to keep the company from occupying opposite sides of the room and staring at one another. He breathed a sigh of relief when Jemmy and Hannah Iredell came in accompanied by Penelope Dawson. Both Penelope and Jemmy spoke fluent French. At once Penelope became the centre.

Monsieur Pucheu led her to a sofa, La Tour brought her a glass of punch, but La Neuville, being the brother of the Chevalier de la Neuville and thus taking precedence, sat down beside her and straightway engaged her in conversation.

The other young Frenchmen stood about, casting sheep's eyes at the maidens, until Madame Cabarrus announced supper. Stephen had already given the guests the names of their partners for supper.

Cecily Armitage drew Monsieur Pucheu. She cast a surreptitious glance at Sarah, to complete her triumph. Monsieur de la Neuville may have had more rank, but Monsieur Pucheu was divinely handsome in his gay hussar uniform. He bent his body so elegantly before her, with his elbow crooked.

She rose, swept a deep curtsy, and laid her hand as light as thistledown upon his arm. She almost giggled aloud, for into her mind came the days of practice at the Madam's School, when the young girls had curtsies tested—their ability to curtsy, move into an easy gliding walk, after they had touched, only touched, the arm of their escort. Only at school other girls took the part of the gallants. Now, for the first time, Cecily walked beside a real gallant. She hoped she was not too awkward, that her shoe latchet would not become untied. She wished she had worn her pale yellow dimity instead of the pink. Pink made her face so red. Madam Dawson had all white with a wide hat with black velvet ribands. She was distinguished. Cecily was afraid she was provincial; she struggled with her embarrassment. She felt so very awkward walking all the way into the garden where the tables were set, without saying a word. Then the thought came to her that perhaps Monsieur Pucheu was as embarrassed as she was. Forgetting herself, she turned to him and smiled up at him. Waving her hand toward Madame Cabarrus' garden beds, she said in her schoolgirl French, "The flowers are excellent."

Pucheu smiled back, laughed at her accent, and spoke the sentence in proper French. Cecily repeated it after him several times until he was satisfied.

Then she undertook a lesson in English. "The flowers are beautiful." Pucheu attempted English. Then it was Cecily's turn to laugh. She was pleased. They were getting along famously.

They walked down the path to where the garden touched the water. Here, on a wide bricked terrace, little tables had been set up. A long table, with food, was across one end. House servants stood waving green branches to keep off flies and other insects so prevalent in the summer. The Frenchman was adept in procuring the best food and drink. He found a little table pleasantly located at the very brink of the water. Sarah Blount and young Benbury joined them and they had a merry little party. Cecily, enjoying herself, forgot to languish.

Suddenly Monsieur Pucheu stopped talking. He sat staring over Cecily's shoulder. She and Sarah both turned, attracted by his concentration. Angela Ferrier and the Wardens, William and Mary, were coming down the path from the house, Angela walking with Normont de la Neuville. He was talking animatedly. Admiration shone in his dark eyes.

Pucheu turned to Cecily. Her heart sank. "Who is she?"

"Angela Ferrier," she answered. He repeated the name, only he said "Angèle," caressingly. It was always like that, Cecily thought despondently. The men's eyes turned to Angela. She looked beautiful. She had a new gown, white with flounces, and she wore a large leghorn hat loaded with red roses, and little streamers of black velvet fell down to her waist. She carried a little parasol, hung over her wrist, made of many ruffles of white lace. She walked slowly, giving close attention to the French officer.

"Very beautiful!" murmured Pucheu. "Very, very beautiful!" The newcomers walked by the table. Angela nodded carelessly. Pucheu rose, bowed, his hand over his heart. He stood in the path so that La Neuville was obliged to pause while introductions were made.

Cecily said, "Angela, you look so well. Weren't you marked at all? Anywhere?"

Angela smiled and touched the patch under her left eye. "Haven't I concealed my deficiencies with skill?"

La Neuville said, "Sometimes a little deficiency emphasizes perfection."

Pucheu murmured, "Allah alone is perfect."

Angela smiled, showing her brilliant white teeth. "Monsieur is indeed gallant." She moved away to the table beyond them and sat down.

Her escort bowed and followed. He placed his chair in such a way that Pucheu was cut off from a clear view of Angela.

Cecily lapsed into silence. Sarah and Tommy Benbury took on the burden of conversation. Pucheu edged his chair sidewise until he could look at Angela over his brother officer's broad shoulder. He made no pretence of being interested in the group at the table where he was seated. Sarah nudged Cecily, but Cecily, with downcast eyes, went on eating without knowing what touched her lips. After a time she murmured some excuse. She got up and walked to the house.

Some time later, Madam Barker found her sitting on a sofa in Madame Cabarrus' little retiring-room, weeping. "Cecily, whatever is wrong?" she asked.

Cecily buried her face on the arm of the sofa, her tears staining the brocade. "It's Angela!" she cried, her shoulders shaking. "She always spoils everything."

"What do you mean?" Madam spoke impatiently. "What has Angela done to you?"

"Nothing but look so beautiful."

"Nonsense!" Penelope Barker said. "Angela Ferrier isn't beautiful. She is showy. Men are taken in by showy women." She softened her words by laying her hand on Cecily's shoulder. "Don't be silly. I suppose one of those popinjay Frenchmen has looked away from you toward Angela."

"Yes, Madam. How did you guess?"

A slight smile came over Penelope Barker's generous mouth. "Men always do, especially foreigners. They pay court to the handsome, bold females, but they marry charming little sillies like Cecily Armitage."

The girl sat up quickly, dabbing at her eyes with a little cambric handkerchief. "Oh, Madam!"

"Yes, 'Oh, Madam!' Now go to the basin and bathe your eyes, so you don't look a fright, and we'll go outside. Mr. Iredell has brought some fine, upstanding officers from Halifax with him, young Montfort and young Cameron from Hillsborough, and there's a Collins boy from across the Sound, who is looking for you."

"Oh, Madam!" Cecily jumped up from the sofa and ran to the wash-stand and began to dabble water on her eyes.

Madam reached into her reticule and took out a square of cambric.

Opening it, she extracted a bit of swan's down which she dipped into a diminutive box of powder. She dabbed the down on Cecily's nose and eyelids, rubbing it in with her fingers. "Remember," she said, "never to let men see you cry. Men can't abide a sniffling woman. Now, you look presentable."

They walked out through the hall, onto the long gallery. Some of the guests were strolling about the garden, some still seated at table. A little knot of men stood close by, talking. Madam beckoned. A tall boy with reddish-brown hair and quick, intelligent eyes came quickly across the grass.

"This is Cecily Armitage, Cameron," she said. "Why don't you take her punting, down on the creek?"

The young lad looked at Cecily, a pleasant smile on his lips. "Will you?" he asked.

"I'd adore punting," Cecily said, lifting her big pansy eyes. "It's lovely down where the lilies grow."

Madam watched them walking across the lawn to the water's edge, where some small boats were tied up. Other young couples were already in boats, their gay, happy voices coming back over the water. She was smiling when Stephen Cabarrus came up to tell her that she was wanted in the card-room.

"Youth is as changeable as an April day," she observed, as she walked back into the house with her host, "as changeable and as fleeting."

Stephen glanced at her, a questioning look in her eyes. He tapped her arm lightly with his fingers. "You are much too young to begin match-making, Madam. Leave that to the elders."

Madam Barker smiled. "You always know the right thing to say, Stephen."

"You flatter me. I wish that youth were not quite so fleeting, that these fine young men could look ahead to laughter and love, not to battles." His eyes swept the gay company. "A year—what happens? Where will these bright, happy creatures be? Some of them with earth laid over them." He added passionately, "If we elders could only spare them, save them these frightful experiences!"

Penelope Barker shook her head. "Everyone, man or woman, must live his own life. We can't live for anyone else. Pray only that they will meet life boldly."

Cabarrus nodded his head once or twice. "Yes, boldly and with courage. But I tell you, Madam, that we of the Council, we take a great responsibility when we send these young men to war."

"I know. But do not let it weigh you down, Stephen. They must meet life as best they can."

He opened the door into the drawing-room. A dozen voices were lifted to greet them. "We want one more at this table," Jemmy said. "Hannah and I will engage you and Sam Johnston in a rubber of whist."

Penelope Dawson was seated at a table with La Tour, Mary Warden and Thomas Barker. She glanced up and smiled at Madam Barker and turned back to her cards, which she shuffled expertly. For a few moments all was quiet in the room. Stephen stood in the doorway watching them settle down to the grave and solemn business of cards. Through the window he saw the young people strolling about. Laughter, snatches of song from the river . . . The genial smile of the host faded from his lips. He left the room and closed the door. In the hall he met his wife. Her usually smiling face bore a troubled expression.

"There is a dispatch-rider wanting to see you. He said he came from the Governor. I've had some food sent into the library." She touched his cheek lightly with her plump fingers. "He is very young and he looks so weary."

She went through the hall toward the garden. Stephen knew she was thinking of their son, who was in the mountains with McDowell's scouting party. He went into the library, and closed the door behind him.

Stephen Cabarrus left the exhausted lad sleeping on a sofa, while he went among his guests to assemble those who were affected by the Governor's communication, which the messenger had brought.

He summoned Samuel Johnston first, then Alexander Ferrier, taking them from the whist tables. Robert Smith and Thomas Benbury, Jasper Charlton, of Bertie; George Wynn, of Hertford; Montfort, of Halifax. Thomas Relf was not at Pembroke, having written that he was ill. William Boyd he called in from a boat. Benjamin Spruill, of Tyrrell, came in just as they were assembling in the library. All were members of either the Senate or House of Commons.

Johnston took the paper marked with the seal of the state and read the message:

"Gentlemen:

"The raging of the smallpox in Town of New Bern having prevented your assembly here in time appointed by Law for the annual meeting of the General Assembly, and being myself of the opinion that our public affairs require as speedy a meeting of the Legislature as might be possible, but not having the power to call same at any other place, than that to which the same stood adjourned, I was induced to request your attendance at this place (Smithfield), not only for the purpose of making your Election of public officers of the State, who are directed by constitution to be annually chosen, but also to take under consideration sundry weighty matters for your deliberation, such as:

1. The state of your . . .
2. " Pay of our Militia which have been and now are in actual service.
3. " Sending of further aid to assistance of the Southern States and
4. Providing our Militia with arms and accoutrements.

To show the necessity of your entering immediately upon consideration of these matters, I lay before you sundry papers containing information respecting same.

"Also letters from Governor Patrick Henry, of Virginia.

"I shall also direct the public accounts will be laid before you, by which you will be acquainted with the exhausted state of the Treasury. You will also receive General Bryan's resignation, whose place you will please supply by appoint of such person as you think proper.

"R. Caswell.

"Smithfield, N.C."

When the reading of the Governor's message was finished, Ferrier said, "I shall be obliged to leave at once, Cabarrus. I must go up to River Plantation and make arrangements to leave for Smithfield in the morning."

Henry Montfort left with him. He was staying at Strawberry Hill with Parson Earle, and his plans would be changed, since the assembly would not meet at New Bern.

Johnston and Charlton lingered after the others left. Johnston said, "I think this Assembly will act on some serious questions."

Charlton raised his heavy grey brows. "You mean electing a Governor?"

"No. That is a foregone conclusion. Caswell will be re-elected. Didn't you notice he mentioned letters from the Governors of Virginia and South Carolina, to be acted upon? What can that be other than that the war situation is worsening? I'm afraid, Jasper, that our noble state will not enjoy its immunity from the heel of the invader for very many months. We are woefully unprepared. We have talked and talked, without any action." He nodded his head toward the garden. "Those young Frenchmen, and a dozen like them, who have offered their swords, wanting to recruit regiments. There is De' Medici cooling his heels at New Bern, drawing on his own funds. We have done nothing. We know the situation at Charles Town is grave. We will do nothing. I tell you the sand is running low. We must act, or we will be caught between two great invading armies, one from the North, one from the South. Wait a moment. I want you to read a letter Iredell had from Will Hooper. I don't concur with every word, but there is truth in it."

He took the folded sheets from his pocket and handed them to Charlton, who went to the window for better light.

My dear Sir: Masonborough.

Are we to ascribe it to a dearth of guns or restraint upon the press, that no pen appears to lash the private and public vices of this licentious state? I never heard of a revolution brought about with such a succession of blunders in Council, errors in the field, as have marked the progress of America to Independency.

They are not follies of individuals or separate states . . . the whole continent seems to have run stark-staring mad, and to have a full and equal representation in the Continental Congress of this assumed character.

When General Clinton made a capital movement from New York, could the merest driveller in public affairs be for a moment in suspense, as to the true destination of the armament which he embarked? Yes, the Continental Congress were, or affected to be. They sagaciously concluded that General Clinton, to gratify personal pique, to convince the world of his own prowess, to wipe away the stain which the British arms had suffered in the former attempt on Charles Town, was going pell-mell to run his head against the walls of Fort Moultrie and possess himself of the all-important capital that led to—*Cui bono?*—to pilfer a parcel of Jew merchants, burn their shops, and then, with his army, starve upon rice gruel, or perish with a putrid fever, for the honour of Great Britain. And that this truly farcical idea might not rest merely in speculation, this harassed broken-hearted country must be called in to play a part in this ridiculous expedition.

Our troops go to the southward never to return; *a soldier made is a farmer lost*. The South Carolinians will requite us as heretofore. They will take advantage of the necessities of our men when they get them amongst them; by supplying wants which they can very *humanely* excite, they will entrap all our countrymen into their own regiments. Unless the councils of our country fall on wiser men, the day of our perdition is not a great way off.

I hope to God that the next Assembly will redeem us from our present dangerous situation, or make some capital approaches to it.

Yours truly and affectionately,

Will Hooper.

P.S. A vessel arrived from Cadiz. Her cargo sold to Webb, Littlejohn & Co. at the rate of 800 percent. The purchasers were also to allow 400 percent for insurance; invoices made out in Spanish Reales of Plate.

Penelope Dawson raised her curved brows, as Samuel Johnston slipped into the seat vacated by La Tour and picked up the cards. He shook his head slightly, said, "Later," and made his lead. The game continued only a short time; the Ferriers' departure caused a flurry of leave-takings. Johnston said to Penelope, "Send your boat around to the wharf and I will drive you to Hayes." She agreed. They ferried across Pembroke Creek, and took the road to Queen Anne's Town, Johnston driving, his coachman behind in the boot.

"It was a messenger from the Governor. Because of the smallpox the Assembly is to meet in Smithfield."

Penelope said, "We were fortunate that Cathcart got it stopped. There haven't been any cases in Queen Anne's Town?"

Johnston smiled. "Williamson's equipment for inoculation did yeoman service. We have escaped so far."

When they arrived at Hayes the sun had set, but the sky behind the rim of pines along the Tyrrell shore was blood-red. They got out of the chaise and stood for a moment looking at the reflection in the waters of Albemarle Sound.

"I think nowhere in the world could there be a finer prospect to please the eye," Johnston said.

Penelope looked at the serious face of her cousin. "You love your home, Sam. It is sad that you must be away so often for such long periods."

"That is what my wife says." They went into the quiet house.

He held open the door to his library. "It is unbearably quiet since Fanny and the children went to Hermitage. Especially in the evening. Sometimes I row across the creek and spend an evening playing backgammon at Horniblow's or drop in on Hannah and Jemmie . . . or Thomas Barker."

"It must have been a horrid experience for Mr. Barker to have to re-establish himself as a citizen," Penelope observed. "He is a proud man, one who would loathe to ask favours."

"Especially from a group of men, many of whom he holds contemptible."

Penelope took off her hat and tossed it on a sofa. Johnston rang the bell. When the houseman came he ordered rum and lemons.

"By the way, Pene, I've a barrel of good, light Jamaica for you. We had some come in last week. Captain Barrits brought excellent Madeira from Spain, when he brought the cannon. I ordered some put in my warehouse for you."

"Thank you, Sam. You think of everything." They were silent while the man mixed a punch and poured it into the silver cups.

"What is coming up at the Assembly?" Penelope asked as she sipped her drink.

"A number of things: the permission for Edenton to hold fairs; Bryan Crosby, of Hillsborough, wants permission to return to England."

"The fool!" Penelope drained her cup. "He won't like it there; he will be always suspect."

"I told him that. There is a matter of the new militia draft, which will have rough going." He filled her cup, and one for himself, then stood beside the mantel, his elbow resting on the board. "There is some talk of appointing Jemmy Attorney-General. Hooper has proposed it to Governor Caswell, through Judge Ashe, in case Mr. McGuyre declined. I doubt the prudence of Jemmy's accepting an employment when the pay depends on a capricious Assembly, which has, on other occasions, exhibited such signal proofs of ingratitude to public merit."

"I think Jemmy should accept, if it is offered to him," Penelope said. "Ever since he resigned the judgeship, he has been as restless as a homeless spaniel. Jemmy needs the spur of an office. He needs the fees."

"I know. But to encumber himself with a burdensome office—that is folly. Iredell is a capital addition to our courts. Ashe thinks there is absolute necessity for a good attorney at Salisbury, to prosecute those cases left over from the insurrection. I agree we must keep a close eye on the Tories of the West."

Penelope held out her cup. "Three is my real limit," she said as Johnston filled it. She leaned back in her chair, looking up at him, a thoughtful expression on her mobile features. "Adam Rutledge told me that he was going west as soon as he saw Caswell. That means that the Government in Philadelphia, or General Washington, fears trouble in that section."

Johnston nodded. "At the last meeting of the Committee of Safety we decided to send word to the western leaders to be alert for trouble along the mountain barrier, from the South Carolina and Georgia lines to the high mountains. A plan is made. In case of Tory uprising, Indian trouble or an invasion from the South, the leaders of the back country will be prepared."

"What do you mean by 'leaders of the back country'?"

Johnston lighted his clay pipe before he answered, and took a chair against the side of the little table. "There has been a great deal of alarm over the Indian situation in the mountains. They propose to use the old organization planned for Indian warfare. Half a dozen men, the McDowells, Colonel Sevier, Campbell and Cleveland—each has at his command from a hundred to two hundred trained men who live in the back country. At a signal they will all leave their farms in the backwoods and mountains, and rally for defence. We have not had to call them yet, but if the British do succeed in arousing the Indians to assist the western Tories in a formidable invasion, we will be prepared to resist. Or—what to me is a more present danger—if the British army succeeds in advancing to Charles Town, and swarms over the fertile country behind the coastal plains, then we will have an organized group ready to defend our Southern border. We cannot depend on our ill-trained militia. The bungling of the Assembly in the drafts has made nothing but confusion."

He got up and paced the floor. Penelope did not speak either, for a time; she was, with her quick imaginative mind, seeing the danger that lay ahead of them. "We are stupid fools," she burst out, "silly, stupid fools in this state! We have had no conception of what war means. It has been so far away. This flurry of alarm from Virginia has really meant nothing to us. The danger to Charles Town has meant less than nothing. Today I heard two men talking; one said, 'Let

Charles Town take care of herself, it's nothing to us, less than nothing!' "

Johnston turned about. There was more anger in his voice than she had ever heard. "If Charles Town falls, then we are undone." He resumed his pacing. After a time he said more quietly, "It is an old military axiom: 'Fight your battles as far from your border as can be.' We North Carolinians must fight our battles for our own defence at Savannah and Charles Town, or we will be obliged to fight a strong enemy on our own sacred ground."

Penelope left soon afterward. A boy rowed her across Queen Anne's Creek. At the wharf she found her boat tied up, awaiting her orders. She would go back to Eden House in the early morning.

She made her way along the rough boards of the long dock, holding her skirts high to avoid tarred ropes and salt dripping from the barrels of pork, waiting for boats. Sailing through the inlets into the open sea made for dangerous voyaging, with British ships lying off Hatteras and the Virginia Capes. At the landing she saw James Iredell waiting. He had seen the boat coming across the creek and was on hand to welcome her; they walked up the path to the Courthouse Green.

In front of the Courthouse a crowd had gathered, listening to Clem Hull, who was standing on the Courthouse steps, shouting and gesticulating. "What good is a draft?" they heard him cry. "What good, when a rich man can pay a substitute to go to war? Let every man shoulder his musket and march. Let every man go, rich planter, and yeoman, artisan and slave."

"What about *your* musket?" said a voice from the edge of the crowd.

"For shame!" called another voice.

Clem Hull turned quickly, his bold eyes flashing. "I *make* muskets," he cried angrily. "I make muskets. Without me you would have no defence. Be you Tory?" he continued, glaring on the outskirts of the crowd, now almost lost in the dusk of evening.

"We hae plenty of Tories in Queen Anne's Town but we will send them out."

"That we will!" shouted a drunken voice. "Down with all Tories and traitors!"

James Iredell was silent as he piloted Penelope. Skirting the crowd on the Green they crossed in front of Horniblow's. The lights in the inn were many. They sent cheerful splashings of light on the long gallery. Men moved in and out of the doors. Saddle-horses, tied to the long racks, stamped impatiently. A belated stage swayed out of Broad Street into King and stopped in front of Horniblow's with a great rattling of harness and shouts of driver and boot-boy.

Passengers disembarked, for the most part drovers, who had piloted their herds into Virginia, to be sent north on ships—a swearing, rough lot, who belonged at the Red Lion, rather than Horniblow's.

Iredell made that comment as they turned the corner into Broad Street. They made their way to the Iredell home, which stood on Church Street, not far from St. Paul's.

Candles were lighted in the houses. On Penelope Barker's steps were a group of young people, their gay voices calling out in the dusk. They heard Thomas Barker say, "Step in. Step in. My wife is waiting for you." A voice answered in French.

"Penelope Barker has wasted no time in entertaining the officers of France," Jemmy Iredell commented.

"She is always hospitable to young people," Penelope Dawson said. They walked up the steps and entered the house where Hannah Iredell was waiting, a delicate, fragile Hannah, whose smile had in it both sweetness and tragedy.

CHAPTER

15

THE ASSEMBLY

PETER HUNTLEY sat on the gallery of the Governor's temporary home in Smithfield and waited for the secretary to call him to his interview with Richard Caswell. The rush chair on which he was seated was near a window which made him an uninvited listener to all the conversation that went on inside the room. There was little doubt that it was the secretary's office. There were comings and goings of legislators and opening and closing of doors. A voice said, "He is edgy this morning. Half the men he has seen are talking money."

"And our cupboard is bare?"

"Bare, and scraped to the bone."

"Why not print more?"

"Why not indeed? Already what we have printed is little better than useless."

"Were you in New Bern when they burned up all the old Provincial Notes?"

"Yes, and when the new ones were made and they were giving them away as souvenirs. I declare, I'm like the countryfolk. I want my pay in hard money; shillings or guineas or golden joes suit me the best. *Sh-h*, someone is coming."

A door opened. A heavy voice said, "I'm sorry, your Excellency. My orders are to have cash in hand before the ship is unloaded."

Peter did not hear the Governor's reply. He watched the little crowds of people walking by, staring curiously, hoping for a glimpse of the Governor, or some great political figure who had come to the meeting of the Assembly. A woodsman, dressed in hunter's buckskins, carrying a rifle, opened the wicket and came up the path. He walked lithely, his moccasined feet making no noise, a man used to quiet movement among the tall trees and the dense undergrowth of the forest.

His keen pale blue eyes focussed on Peter. He hesitated a moment, then addressed him. "It's Mr. Rutledge I'm a-seeking."

Peter said, "Adam Rutledge? Is he in Smithfield? I haven't seen him."

"I been told he was; making talk with the Governor."

Peter replied, "If you step inside, the Governor's secretary will doubtless know when Major Rutledge is expected."

The man walked into the house. He came out a moment later and sat down on the edge of the gallery floor, his feet dangling. He laid his long rifle on the floor boards and extracted a pipe of tobacco from a leathern pouch which was hooked to his belt. Noting Peter's eyes on him, he hesitated a moment, then proffered a bit of rolled leaf. "Have a chaw?" he asked.

Peter declined. "I've just smoked a pipe," he said.

The woodsman nipped a piece off the roll, popped it into his mouth. He put the remainder into the pouch and pulled the string. "Never smoked," he volunteered after a time. "A woodsman has no business smoking. Could start a fire if the woods was dry, or betray your location to some skulking Indian."

Peter asked, "Are you an Indian fighter?"

"Maybe so. Leastways I had one of the varmints creep up on me." He lifted his brown hand and swept a stocking cap from his head. His pate was hairless, with a great red scar circling the skull. He grinned at Peter's horrified expression, and put the cap in place. "Most people are like to have their stummick turned at a scalped man. Me, it doesn't bother any more. Did when I was young. Made up my mind that nary a female would look at a scalped fella. After that, I felt better and quit courtin'." He grinned again, his eyes twinkling brightly.

Peter laughed. "Are you a friend of Major Rutledge's?"

The merry twinkle died; the pale eyes became wary. "Be you?"

Peter said, "I hope so. I haven't known him long."

The man seemed to close up. After a time he said, "You be a furriner." Peter was saved an explanation by Cosmo de' Medici coming out of the door. He had a downcast look, but when he saw Peter he brightened.

"I had the misfortune to follow a dozen men who all wanted money, money, money. His Excellency was in a bad humour. He gives me nothing." He spread his hand. "Nothing. He tells me to come again. That is the same as always. Come again, come again."

He discovered the woodsman. He stood surveying him gloomily. "I trust, my fellow, that you do not come to beg for money."

"Money!" The woodsman laughed. "What would Enos Dye do with money? I have my rifle, the woods are full of animals and the fish are in the streams. Why should I ask for money?"

Cosmo cast his eyes upward. "Merciful heavens, behold a philosopher!"

"*They* send for me to come. They need me. I need no money." The man spoke simply, no boasting.

"My Pietro, I believe this man. He needs nobody. If only I could attain such independence."

The secretary came to the doorway, and spoke to Peter. "His Excellency will see you now, Captain Huntley." Peter followed him into the room where the Governor was sitting at a table piled high with books and papers.

"Captain Huntley."

The Governor looked up when the secretary spoke. "Come in, Captain," he said, without rising or extending his hand. Peter bowed. He took his credentials from his breast pocket and gave them to the secretary, who in turn handed them to the Governor.

It took Mr. Caswell several minutes to read through the papers. "You may go, Welburn," he said to the secretary. The young man left the room, casting a look of curiosity toward Peter as he went. He would have liked very much to know the contents of the papers, Peter thought.

As soon as the door closed, the Governor turned to Peter. "Well, Captain Huntley, have you had any success since you came to North Carolina?" Peter thought there was a degree of rancour in the voice.

"None," Peter said, omitting the affair of Jeremiah Morse. "Nothing. Not one trace of Folger, in New Bern or Wilmington."

His Excellency tapped the palm of one hand with an ivory paper-cutter. "I met the man at an inn. He had credentials—" his keen eyes bored into Peter—"as good as these you have presented. Folger said he had come from France, by ship in the Pamtico. He carried dispatches for the committee and Congress. He had had some trouble on the ship—he was very vague as to details—something which caused him to become suspicious that he had been followed from France. There could be only one reason—the dispatches he carried. Folger told me he was so alarmed that he went to the captain of the ship and asked him to put the dispatch case in his safe. The captain did so, sealing it so that he would not run into any difficulties later as to the contents of the case.

"Folger took it from the captain when he left the ship. The seal was unbroken. I asked him why he came to me. He said he was told in Paris that there was a packet for me in the case, and he wanted to open it in my presence.

"The whole tale seemed to have a taint, although I had no reason to doubt the fellow.

"We opened the box. One of my secretaries was present. There was no letter for me. Suddenly the fellow cried out. A packet labelled for Congress was unsealed at one end; a bundle of papers slipped out. We all stooped to pick them up from the floor where they had fallen. They were blank. Thirty-two pages of blank paper."

Peter said, "Invisible ink?"

"No. We tried them against a flame, and with chemicals."

"What do you make of it, sir?"

Governor Caswell shook his head. "I don't know. I have wondered if the fellow planned the little scene himself."

"Why?" came to Peter's lips. "Why?"

"I asked myself that question, later when the idea came to me. Perhaps because he wanted me to write a letter to the Committee on Foreign Affairs and tell them just what I have told you."

"Did your Excellency write that letter?"

"I did, at Folger's earnest request. Afterward, I began to doubt my judgement. Perhaps he himself extracted the papers and used me to cast the blame somewhere else. The papers may have been taken before the packet left Paris. At least the blank sheets bore a French water-mark." He laid the cutter on the table and leaned back, folding his hands on top of the table. "I have one of those sheets which my secretary found after Folger had left. It was on the floor, under my desk."

"I'd like to see that paper, sir."

"Unfortunately it is in my home at King's Town." He paused, looking down at his hands. Suddenly he looked up and met Peter's eyes. "Do you make anything of it, Captain?"

Peter said, "If I could see the paper, perhaps I could tell one thing. There are several types used at our office; different departments have different papers. The water-mark might help."

"Of course. You shall have the paper as soon as this Assembly is over."

"What became of Folger?" Peter asked.

"That is the real mystery. He sent the dispatches by one of my couriers who was on his way to Congress, with a letter telling what I have just told you, but he disappeared. From the time he gave the box to the courier up to now he has never been glimpsed, although we had a careful search made."

"Perhaps he went back on the same ship," Peter ventured.

"That may be. At any rate I've been obliged to write a dozen letters to Congress concerning Folger and his thirty-two pages of blank paper. I confess I am weary of the affair." He leaned forward. "Now they send you. Captain Huntley, can you tell me why it is really so important?"

Peter replied, "Your Excellency, I don't know. All I was told to do was to speak with you, and try to trace Folger."

The Governor touched a small bell that called his secretary. "I'll be obliged to you, Captain, if you will stay here during this meeting, and return to New Bern when I go. You might get some information from the Customs—passengers returning to France at that time. I'd have to consult my files for the date. Good day, Captain." The Governor rose and shook hands, with seeming cordiality. "After this Assembly, I will have more time. Now . . ." He lifted his shoulders wearily, as though the burden resting upon them were heavy.

Peter went out into the sunlight. For a moment, after the darkened room, he was almost blinded. He stood quite still, opening and closing his eyes to make sure that it was Angela Ferrier he saw, walking slowly down the street, between her father and Adam Rutledge.

Adam saw Peter and nodded, smiling. They all looked up.

"This is extraordinary," Peter said, half aloud.

The long, lean figure of the woodsman rose from the gallery and stood at the foot of the steps. Rutledge quickened his pace and grasped the hand of Enos Dye, led him aside, spoke in low tones. The others walked up the steps. Peter was glad he had on his best coat and breeks, and that he wore silk stockings, with buckled shoes. He put his hat under his arm and bowed. Ferrier grasped his hand, obviously pleased. Angela made a slight bow, but Peter reached for her hand and bent over it, brushed it with his lips. It was the first time he had seen her since the little scene in the summer-house.

"This is delightful," he said, looking straight at Angela. She turned her face.

Ferrier slipped his hand under Peter's arm. "We are about to pay our manners to his Excellency. Come in with us. The Governor will be pleased."

"I have just quitted the Governor," Peter said.

Ferrier was disappointed. "I would have liked to present you, and tell the Governor about my acquaintance with your father. No matter. I shall tell him anyway. Come, Angela." Angela, with a murmured word of apology, passed in front of Peter. Ferrier paused at the door. "Where are you domiciled, Captain?"

"At Madam Brady's, sir."

"Splendid! Splendid! That is where we are staying. Sam Johnston and Rutledge are there and two senators from the West. We shall see you at supper, then." Angela had disappeared into the darkened hall. Ferrier followed.

At the gate, Peter met Adam and Dye. "I was told you were here, Huntley. Let me present a very old and valued friend, Enos Dye."

The woodsman grasped Peter's hand with a clasp he felt for some time afterward. "We've talked," Dye said briefly.

"Good!" Adam spoke absently, as though he had something on his mind. He took his fob from the pocket of his waistcoat. "It's time for our appointment now. I believe we follow Ferrier. Pardon us, will you, Captain? The Governor has asked Dye to give him some information."

Peter sat in his tiny hall bedroom at Madam Brady's, waiting for the supper gong. He had come in, napped, bathed, straightened his hair, and for half an hour made his restless way from chair to window and back again. His room was on the front of the house. Instead of a window, a door opened onto the upper gallery. Although he had watched assiduously, he had not seen Angela return to the boarding-house. Perhaps she had not come. Perhaps they had stayed on, to sup with the Governor.

He sat down at his table and took out a note-book. He put down the conversation he had had with Caswell. There must be some answer to the disappearance of Folger. If he was innocent, and if the enemy had got hold of the original papers, there would be no object in doing away with him. If he had sold the papers to some enemy agent, there would still be no reason to have him killed.

No, the man had gone away of his own accord. Since they had made a thorough search of New Bern and the vicinity, he must have gone back to the ship. In a few days Peter would return to New

Bern. The ship's list might prove helpful. He was depressed. He did not relish failure. He would take opportunity to talk with Adam Rutledge. He was *wise*. His counsel would be worth having.

"What luck! What extraordinary luck!" He was not thinking of Adam Rutledge as he said the words aloud. His mind had gone back to Angela Ferrier. One thing: he was determined not to step back into his old, rather humble role. He had held her in his arms. He had kissed her. He was in love with her. What the next step would be, he must leave to fate, but he was determined to marry her.

The supper gong sounded, breaking in on his thoughts.

The landlady, plump, red-faced and smiling, showed him to his place at the long table. He sat down beside Adam Rutledge, who introduced him to Robert Irwin, of Mecklenburg, and John Hogan, of Orange. Peter watched the door anxiously.

The vacant seats were soon filled. Sam Johnston and Jasper Charlton sat at the far end of the table. Robert Smith, as member from Queen Anne's Town, came in late and took a chair opposite. Only two places remained vacant. After grace had been said by Sam Johnston, the door opened and Angela and Senator Ferrier came into the room. With an apology for being late, Ferrier took the seat beside Peter, Angela beyond.

Talk was general and concerned only the bills and affairs of the Assembly. Peter listened to talk of the sale of the armed brigantine *Pennsylvania Farmer*; the necessity of repacking pork and beef, flour, pease and rice now held in Hewes and Smith's warehouse in Queen Anne's Town; the advisability of getting arms from Virginia and South Carolina; James Iredell's resignation as judge last session.

Samuel Johnston said, "I am opposed to wasting the Assembly's precious time in wrangling over whether the members be paid ten or thirteen dollars a day; whether they will get an extra allowance for a day's travel wasted in going to New Bern; or over raising the Governor's salary."

Hogan spoke up. "It's well enough for you to talk, Sam. You have plenty of this world's goods, but some of us aren't so fortunate. With this great depression in our currency and the exorbitant rise in every necessity of life, what are people to do? Already they are saying that the eight hundred and fifty thousand dollars we ordered printed are not adequate."

Irwin broke in. "The Governor has applied to Congress for two million or more, to carry on military operations in this state."

"He must think we are going to have a war."

No one answered. Smith changed the subject. "We've found a lot of canvas and Ozanburg stored in warehouses to make all the tents we need. The trouble is, with this department buying, and that department duplicating, state and government bidding against each other, we've sent prices skyward and we haven't a notion where we stand."

Ferrier turned to Peter. "You must think us very incompetent down here."

"No, sir. It is the same, I hear, everywhere. It is all so new to us, this business of carrying on in unity."

"Disunity would be a better word," was Ferrier's comment. Angela said not a word. Peter could see only her profile. Once or twice he tried to make conversation, but the talk became general again: Salisbury insurrection . . . the necessity of having more troops in the western part of the state . . . moving troops to Halifax . . . to the West . . . General Rutherford.

Peter was glad when Johnston rose. There was a quick scraping of chairs, and the men went out on the gallery to smoke their long pipes. The May evening was warm and pleasant. The smell of lilacs and jasmine came from the little garden behind the paling fence.

Peter went over to Angela, who stood talking to Adam and her father. "Will you go for a walk through the village, Angela?" he enquired.

She turned slowly at the sound of her name. Peter thought, She would not answer me, only that her father is here. After a moment she said, "Thank you, Captain Huntley, but I must be getting dressed for the ball. Captain de' Medici is going to escort me."

Mr. Ferrier said, "Why don't you go with them, Peter? Most of the young folk are going to the lodge room to step a measure. I know they will be delighted to have you go with them."

Peter declined. "I have some letters to write, sir."

Ferrier said, "Nonsense! Letters can always wait." •

"Not these, sir. Mr. Johnston just told me that a dispatch-rider would be leaving early in the morning. I must send in some reports by him."

Angela excused herself. She must dress so she would be ready when Madam Jones called for her.

Peter held the door open for her. She said, "You are insufferable, Mr. Peter Huntley."

"Thank you. Thank you so much," he replied, and bowed with exaggerated courtesy.

She tossed her head and swept by him into the hall.

When he rejoined the gentlemen, Ferrier said, "You are quite too serious, Peter. I remember your father was the same. Play a little, my lad. I realize now that I didn't enjoy myself so much as I should have when I was young. A little frolicking is good for one."

Peter smiled slightly. "I really must get these letters off my mind tonight."

"Come to my room when you have finished," Adam Rutledge suggested. "I have a little matter to take up with you."

"Thank you, I will."

"A fine lad," he heard Ferrier say, as he left them. "A very fine lad. I don't know when I have met anyone who has impressed me as he has. A young gentleman of parts."

"I like him," Adam said. "He knows his way about."

Peter ran up the stairs, quite pleased with what he had just heard. Mr. Ferrier liked him. A notion had come into his head that made him feel gay. A bold stroke indeed, but he might succeed. He would ask the senator for his daughter's hand in marriage. Why not? Why not? As he opened the door to his room, he found himself singing a gay Highland tune.

> "I leughed at their tales, till last week i' the gloamin'
> I daundered alane down the hazelwood green.
> Alas! I was reckless, and rue sair my roaming.
> I met a young witch wi' twa bonnie black een."

Three hours later he knocked at the door of Adam Rutledge's room. He found Adam coatless, seated at a small table littered with papers, a quill in his hand, a page half covered with writing spread before him. He pushed the horn inkstand aside and tossed the pen on the table. "I'm glad you came, Peter. I'm about to exhaust myself writing these reports."

"Perhaps I came too early." Peter hesitated in the doorway.

"No, indeed. Come in! I'm glad of the excuse to push these aside." He rose and went to a chest, and poured two glasses of rum, squeezing a little lemon, adding water from a ewer from the wash-stand. "To Miss Angela!" he said, raising his glass.

"To Miss Angela!" Peter repeated after him.

"A beautiful girl. She will grow into a lovely woman," Adam remarked, as he finished his drink. "A spirited young girl, but haughty."

"I find her so," said Peter ruefully. "She . . ."

"Pay no heed to her whimsies. These girls are all alike; they 'adore' to make a man feel humble."

Peter said, "I don't feel humble. Somehow I feel that a good chastening would be suitable."

Adam laughed. "One thing in your favour, Peter: her father is all on your side."

Peter reddened. "Do I show my feelings so plainly?"

"When a young man can't take his eyes from a girl, it is usually an indication. You haven't a wife tucked away somewhere?"

"Heaven forbid!"

Adam put his glass down. "I'd forget the girl and present my case to the father." He seated himself once more at the table and leafed through some papers. He found what he was looking for, and trimmed the candle for a better light. "I've been talking with the Governor. He asked me to give you what assistance I could, in the Folger matter. I have nothing to offer, other than a communication from the committee to say that the matter might be dropped for the present, since other and more pressing affairs are on the calendar. I suppose you will receive your orders in due course, but this dispatch says that, if you think advisable, you are to go with me to the western part of the state, to Salisbury, where there is some difficulty with the Tories." He put the paper in Peter's hand. "Read it at your leisure. What I would like now is a summary of what you have done in the Jeremiah Morse affair. They seem to think, in Philadelphia, that Jeremiah is of prime importance."

Peter took a chair near the window and launched into the story of his movements from the time he left Eden House. He told of his further search at New Bern, his journey to Cross Creek and Campbell Town, where he had better success.

"The Tories in Cumberland County are frightened," he said. "They do not know what this disarming ordered by the Commons presages. I found a man there who had rowed a stranger, a Boston merchant, down the Cape Fear River—a countryman, with no loyalties that gold would not change. He said a man named MacKenzie was in charge. I saw MacKenzie, but he wouldn't talk—a good Scot who keeps his man's word and his spoken oath. But I am a Scot also, and after a time he said, 'Laddie, I don't be saying yea nor will I say

nay, to your question,' when I asked him outright if he took Jeremiah
Morse from Campbell Town to Brunswick. 'It's a fair impudent
question,' he said, 'but the Scots were ever nosey, and I'm not remembering any names.'

"From the way he said this I was sure I was on the right track. I
went down the Cape Fear, pausing the night at Mr. David Moray's
plantation—an old man, but very bright in his mind. Knowing his
loyalties were to this government, I asked questions and found that
his steward had seen such a man as I described Morse, at Old Town
Creek, drawing maps in the sand. Through a grape-vine the slaves
have, he found that Morse had gone to a swamp, where live a little
colony of Frenchmen, descendants of refugees who made their escape
from the Spanish in Florida, some years back."

Adam nodded. "Yes, I know of these people. They made the
shingles for my house."

Peter paused to light his pipe. He saw that Adam was deeply
interested. "I visited the swamp and discovered that a man named
Gil Roi, a renegade from the group, lived with his daughter on a little
island in the swamp, away from the others. Just why, I didn't ascertain, or ask. They evidently have some sort of justice of their own,
and had sent this man Roi to Coventry." He laughed, "I don't want
to make this as long as a story in the *Gentleman's Magazine*."

"Go on. You have my deepest attention."

"This is a queer thing. This Gil Roi is the man who rescued
Madam Ferrier and her daughter, when they were washed up on the
shore, near Lockwood's Folly, after their ship had been wrecked.
Roi told me, with great detail, of the great storm, the two ships engaged in a sea battle . . . the beautiful woman and the young child he
had saved." Peter's pipe had gone out. He put it on the table. The
soft breeze blew the curtains. Voices rose from the street, laughter.
He heard Cosmo's voice, and a girl's sweet, clear laughter.

He faced Rutledge. "It was a strange story, stranger still that I
should be seated in the little cottage in the deep swamp, learning of
the rescue of the girl I love."

"The destiny of man is unpredictable."

Peter scarcely heard the words.

"The man talked and talked. He sat there, living again an act of
heroism that gave him some secret, inner satisfaction. The girl—
well, I couldn't make out the girl. She was handsome but silent,
almost surly. She would say nothing; answered my questions and her

father's in monosyllables. Roi swears he never saw anyone answering the description I gave of Morse. But he had been in the woods, making shingles, he told me. . . ." Peter got up and moved about the room. "I cannot rid myself of the feeling that the girl knew something. But she would not speak. I went away quite positive that Morse had been there and had got away in some ship. Roi as much as acknowledged that ships put in close to shore, unnamed ships."

"There's always smuggling along the Banks, since the earliest days. It was a pirate rendezvous for Blackbeard and others equally infamous," Rutledge told him.

"Well, that is my endeavour—which ended nowhere, or on the shores of the Western Ocean."

"If so, your man is in Charles Town by now."

"That's what I think. Anyway, I left the swamp, dissatisfied." He smiled a little, a whimsical smile that changed the whole expression of his face. "I gave Roi some gold. I am afraid I was a little extravagant, considering his information was valueless to me."

"I wonder," said Adam. Peter flushed. Rutledge knew the reward was not for information about a Boston merchant, but for a rescue from the sea.

They were interrupted by a soft knock. Cosmo put his head in the doorway. "Ah, this is fortunate! You still escape sleep." He came in, closing the door behind him.

"I have come to seek advice, Major Rutledge." He waved the bundle of papers he was holding. "I am confused, very confused."

Rutledge said, "Sit down, while I fix you a drink."

"Thank you, sir." Cosmo sat down, after he had laid the papers on the table. He, too, had removed his coat and wrist ruffles, and turned back the sleeves of his linen shirt. His dark hair was rumpled as though he had been running his quick restless fingers through the side curls.

"These things I do not comprehend," he began, after a drink to fortify his flagging spirits. "The Governor sends me these papers, all about I do not know what. It say I am not attached; the Government say I am attached to the State; the State say I am detached. It say they pay for uniforms—but no. I get no money, and *all these* . . ." He tapped the papers with his index finger. "This happened, not now, but last year. . . . But you read, Major Rutledge, read him aloud, so Pietro may hear." He smiled at Peter. "I have no secrets from Pietro."

Adam straddled a hard-bottom chair, the ladder-back supporting his arms, as he held the papers near the candle.

"BOARD OF WAR.

"Nov. 2, 1778.

"Agreed to Rept. to Congress.

"That Capt. de' Medici, of N. C. Dragoons, having applied to the Board of Directors for his Future Govt., the Board beg leave to state the case of said Troops.

"That they have found it impracticable to provide for them, they having been unemployed in the field, excepting forty who were lately completely fitted out and sent to General McIntosh, under Capt. Ashe, under an exception that the men whose terms were nearly expiring would agree to stay for two months beyond their engagements. But soon after their arrival at Ft. Pitt, their terms having expired all but 14 quit the service and went home. That Capt. de' Medici having been sent to Carolina to purchase horses 18 months ago and sent in a few, just before the departure of Congress for Yorktown, the Board, uneasy for his delay for so immoderate a Length of Time, wrote to him and directed him to come to Philadelphia to settle his accounts. On his arrival we were informed that he had by order of Col. Bland, who met with him at Halifax, in N.C., recruited upward of thirty men for a term of three years or during the war and gave them furloughs with orders to meet at Halifax at the beginning of this month. He has also 11 men in Philadelphia.

"That the whole of said men are unprovided with clothes and accoutrements except some men have been provided in Halifax by order of Capt. de' Medici, though horses are few.

"That from them not being annexed to any Corps, they cannot in the opinion of the Board be of much utility to the States unless they can be employed to the Southward under General Lincoln; and then much expense will accrue in fitting them out for the field. Wherefore the Board begs leave to report that the case of these troops be referred to the Committee appointed for the direction of the Southern expedition.

"by order Richard Peters."

"You see? It is of old date, 1778. They allow me to recruit by order of Colonel Bland. I have my horses; I have my men. We are well drilled. Now they say, 'No, we do not want you.' I think it is very unfair. The same thing they do with a dozen French officers who

come here to America and they are at New Bern, very, very angry at
such treatment. 'They are insult', they say. 'In Paris they tell us to
go to America; we are needed to fight for liberty for all. So we give
up our places, our homes, we cross the Western Ocean at great cost
and much discomfort—for what?' "

He put his clenched fist on the table. "For some person, some com-
moner who is not even an officer in the Army, to write such a letter.
It is an insult. What must I do? Where do I go? To whom do I and
my dragoons belong?"

Peter thought the letter stupid and confused. He glanced at Adam.
His blond head was bent over the letter, reading it the second time.
He paused, put his finger on a sentence in the middle of the page.

Cosmo read it aloud: . . . "unless they can be employed to the
Southward under General Lincoln." He turned his dark, enquiring
eyes to Adam. Suddenly he sprang to his feet. "Ah! I see. I take
these as orders. I go south to Charles Town. That is good, very good
indeed." His expression changed. "But the moneys, the funds?"

Adam turned the letter over. On the back was a short notation:

To be paid up to Jan. 1st—after discussion a motion made and
passed to also provide clothing for said troops. Ordered referred
to Board of War.
NB. Supply them with such clothing as due them.
Endorsed.

Cosmo waited expectantly, his brown eyes never moving from
Adam's face, his fingers opening and closing nervously.

Adam said, "I would present this paper to the officer in command
of the Supply Department, in New Bern, and to the paymaster.
Draw uniforms and back pay and proceed to General Lincoln."

"I will. I will do that instantly. Thank you. Thank you, Major
Rutledge. You have solved all Cosmo's troubles." He turned and
embraced Peter. "Did I not say Major Rutledge is wise?"

Adam laughed, "Mind you, this is not official, De' Medici. I have
no authority in this matter, but that is what I would do in like case."

"Before the sun is up, I will be riding my horse in the direction of
New Bern. My men will be very happy. They want to engage, to hear
gunfire again; not this sitting on backsides, waiting."

After he had left the room, Adam said, "We have done very wrong
to invite these young men to offer their swords for our cause, then

make no place for them. The Governor told me this morning that at least a dozen Frenchmen had arrived within the fortnight. He had no place for them, nor the authority to allow them to recruit regiments in the state."

Peter said, "Again it falls back to Silas Deane. He promised everything imaginable to young officers—gold, advantages, fame—if they would come to America. And so they came. Adventurers, some of them mercenary, but many of them like Cosmo, inflamed with the nobility and justice of our cause. The Governor sends them on to headquarters. They are flattered by the letters he writes to General Washington about them. Then he washes his hands of the whole thing."

Rutledge made no further comment but Peter got the impression that he did not agree with Mr. Caswell's treatment of the ardent young patriots.

Peter rose to go. It was well past midnight. Rutledge said, "I expect to be able to leave here by Saturday or Sunday, for the West. Enos Dye will go with us. We will need him in the mountain country. A fine woodsman, none better. I had him with me the year I went to the Illinois country, for Governor Henry."

Peter said, "I will be pleased to go with you, but I dislike very much being defeated as I have been by Morse and Folger."

Adam laid his hand on Peter's shoulder. "I know. It is a matter of pride with you. But the committee says that the Folger case is of no immediate importance. Something that can be picked up later. Morse—well, that's a different tale. If he goes to the Charles Town area, we have competent men there, who will take up where you left off."

"I wrote my report and gave it to the Governor's secretary to go off by courier in the morning."

"Good. That is a slate wiped clean. I hope you have a good horse, for it will be a long journey to the West, and difficult."

Peter thought his horse was strong and sturdy. Rutledge lighted a candle nub for him to carry down the dark hall. Just before he opened the door Rutledge said, "Did you ever see Major André?"

Peter turned quickly. "No. Never. Of course I knew about him . . . the Mischianza and other activities in Philadelphia. Why do you ask?"

"I was wondering if Morse—but no . . . I suppose the two things don't fit together." Peter waited for Rutledge to continue. "I had word that André had been seen in Charles Town, disguised as a countryman. It might be . . ." Adam did not finish the sentence.

Peter said good night and went down the hall to his room, shielding the flickering candle flame with his hand.

The hall was long and dark, with many doors. He wondered in which room Angela slept, so near him, yet as far away as the stars.

He undressed in the dark, and slipped into bed. For a moment his thoughts were filled with the dark girl, her slim loveliness, her grace; even the scornful glance she gave him had a certain flavour. . . . He was young and healthy and his active mind could not dwell sadly on a provocative girl more than a few moments. Another prospect was opening to him: the western border and Enos Dye's great mountains that rose majestically, a barrier that reached upward, blue and misty, until it dissolved into the blue sky.

Peter came across Alexander Ferrier outside the hall where the Assembly met and, at the senator's invitation, started to Madam Brady's with him. It was late afternoon and the sky overcast. The air was warm and heavy. "A weather-breeder," Ferrier remarked. "I don't like the look of that cloud bank." He waved his hand toward the southeast. "We get our strong winds from that direction, Cape Hatteras."

At the senator's suggestion, they strolled along a path that led beyond the village, to a little grove of trees, where the people of the village held picnics. Here they sat down on a bench near a small stream. Ferrier talked of the session. It had been hopelessly dull, with nothing accomplished; wrangling whether to draft or not. At the end of the day salary increases had been voted, a measure which he had opposed. Peter sat listening, his eyes following the flight of a mocker, which ended in a pine tree on the opposite bank of the stream. The late sun sent pale streams of light into the dense wood. The bird sat on a branch and began to try its voice, in a small succession of trills. The tranquillity of the forest was all about them, the war and battles were far away. Suddenly Peter knew this was the time to speak to Angela's father.

CHAPTER

16

THE VILLAGE

ANGELA ran up the steps of the Pollock house on the Green like a whirlwind, and banged the brass knocker sharply, then turned the knob. The door was unlocked and she walked in, calling "Ann!" twice, in a high, clear voice. No one answered, so she walked through the little sitting-room to the gallery that overlooked the garden and Albemarle Sound. There she saw Ann kneeling on a pad spread on the ground, transferring some small plants from one bed to another. A Negro gardener stood by giving advice. "Madam! The rows are mighty crockit. How you think dose little flowers will look, growin' crockit like dat?" Ann laughed, and straightened a row by removing a plant.

When Angela called her name, Ann rose, dusted her hands together and walked toward the house, unpinning her overskirt as she crossed the lawn to the gallery. She kissed Angela. "When did you come back from the Assembly?" she asked. Taking a chair that faced the water, she pointed to a second chair. "Sit down. Tell me all about Smithfield. Was it gay? Was Mrs. Hooper there, and Mrs. Wylie Jones? Was there a ball?"

Angela said, "It was frightfully dull. No one there at all interesting, only one ball—and we stayed at a horrid boarding-house. . . . I was sorry I went."

Ann said, "It's been dull here too—absolutely nothing going on since the garden-party at Pembroke."

"I didn't want to go to Smithfield. If it had been New Bern and a ball at the Palace, it would have been glorious. Where are the Frenchmen?"

"They're gone—to New Bern, I believe. They say they are coming back and will give a ball in the Panel Room at the Courthouse. Perhaps it's talk only. You know the French."

Angela agreed. She leaned back in her chair listlessly. Ann called a house servant to bring glasses and a chilled shrub.

Angela sipped the pleasant drink and set the glass on the tray which the slave had put on a small table. Ann glanced at her. The girl looked pale and had dark smudges under her eyes.

"What's wrong, Angela?" she asked. To her dismay Angela began to cry. She put her hands before her face, her shoulders shaking. "My dear child! What *is* wrong?"

Angela took her hands away from her face and dabbed at her eyes with her handkerchief. "I've had a horrid fight with my stepfather. I was awfully angry and said a lot of things I shouldn't have said. My mother will be angry with me, too, and that makes me very sad. But I declare I won't marry that man. Mr. Ferrier can lock me in my room and put me on bread and water, but I declare I won't marry him."

Ann said, "Marry whom? Do behave like a grown-up person and quit crying."

The tears continued to overflow Angela's dark eyes, but she made an effort to speak more distinctly. "Captain Huntley. I detest him."

Ann looked at her speculatively. "Captain Huntley? Well, I *am* surprised."

Angela turned her head quickly, to face Ann. "Why are you so surprised?" she asked.

"I didn't know that you knew him very well, and besides that I shouldn't think you would be the kind of a woman he would *want* to marry."

"I think you're horrid, Ann. You are the only friend I have. I come to you for comfort, and you say such things to me. I believe you like Peter Huntley."

"I scarcely know Captain Huntley, but he appeared to me as rather an unusually fine young man, with some degree of common sense. I think you should feel flattered."

"Well, I'm not!" Angela said petulantly. "You know I'm in love with Anthony. Surely you couldn't mention him in the same breath with Anthony."

Ann picked up some wool from a basket and began to knit on a sock. "I'm not sure that a comparison would be favourable to Anthony. I'm not sure that I would give Mr. Anthony Allison my whole-hearted admiration."

"What do you mean, Ann? Do you know something that I do not

know? What is wrong?" Angela leaned forward, her hands clutching the arms of the chair. "You must tell me, Ann. It isn't fair that I be kept in ignorance. Where is he? What happened at Eden House, that he went away? Was he engaged in something dishonourable? You don't know how I've suffered, not hearing a word from him. Not a line."

Ann did not meet her eyes. She was occupied counting stitches. After a moment she said gravely, "I wouldn't ruin my whole life for a man I knew as little about as Anthony. And when it comes to marriage, it is wise to be guided by your parents. An immature girl, such as you are, with no knowledge of the world, could make a very serious mistake. Does your father approve of Captain Huntley?"

"He told me he liked him. He said he would speak to my mother. It seems that Captain Huntley is a 'match.' He has money and a family that my stepfather knows, in Scotland." She spoke scornfully.

There was no sound but the clicking of Ann's needles. The garden was quiet. A few bumble-bees buzzed around the honeysuckle vine that shaded the gallery. "It is better to be guided by your parents," Ann repeated. "Many a girl has found that out when it was too late."

Angela rose and picked up her broad-brimmed hat from the chair. "I can't think what's come over you, Ann," she said. "You're the last person I would think of as moralizing."

Ann didn't answer. She laid her knitting down and walked through the house with her guest. At the door, she detained Angela a moment. "I hope, my dear, you will be wise enough to be guided by your father and mother. If I were you, I would endeavour to put Anthony Allison completely out of my mind."

Angela said, "I shall not try to put Anthony out of my mind. I love him."

Ann stood in the door and watched the young girl's fluttering skirts disappear through Elizabeth King's rose-harboured gateway. Ann knew that all the women of the village were meeting there, to sew and make little flags. The following week the freeholders of the county and along the river would rally on the Courthouse Green, to receive the great flag Joseph Hewes had sent down from Philadelphia—a beautiful silk flag to belong to the village, and to be used on great occasions. The women at Elizabeth King's were seated in the same room where they had signed the paper not to drink tea as long as the British Government taxed it. Now they were sewing little replicas of Joe Hewes's flag, to carry at the rally. All the women of the town and near-by plantations, everyone, had been asked—except Ann Pollock.

She closed the door slowly and went upstairs to her room. For a long time she stood at the window, her eyes fixed on the wharf at the end of Broad Street. She did not notice the unwonted activity; nor did the brigantine *Pennsylvania Farmer* engage her attention. Only when the ship came slowly about to anchor near the Dram Tree did she notice the flapping sails and the scurry of small boats making their way from the dock to the incoming vessel. She was sick at heart. She loved Cullen, her husband, but every night on her knees she prayed to God that he would give way, forget old loyalty to the Hanoverian King and espouse the cause which would make men free of tyranny.

Angela heard the buzzing sound of many women's voices before she set foot on the gallery. Like a great swarm of bumble-bees, the voices rose and fell. She stood for a moment, hesitating. She wished she had not promised to make flags. She was disturbed in her mind by the things Ann Pollock had said. From Ann she had expected sympathy and understanding; instead Ann had been cold, almost as though she had pushed her aside and closed the door. The warning which Ann had implied against Anthony troubled her more than her encounter with her stepfather. But before she could turn and retreat, Cecily Armitage saw her and called.

Madam King came bustling toward her. "You are late, Angela. We have a great lot of crosses for you to cut out." She thrust some material into her hand, with a pattern made of parchment. "See, you do it this way; fold it so that you cut a number at once. The girls will appliqué them to the blue background and we will set the piece into the red and white strips."

Angela took the material and went into the bedroom where the young girls were working: Cecily and the Blounts, Mary Creecy and Mary Bonner. Someone handed her a pair of shears. Cecily said, "Sit down by the bed and I'll give you this lapboard. You can work more easily with the board to cut on."

Fingers were flying, tongues in unison. Questions flew all about her ears, bombarding her. Did she go to the ball in Smithfield, and were there many people there, and who was her escort and what did the people wear? And would there be an Inaugural Ball at the Palace?

Sarah Blount said, "Look at Cecily. She is extremely jealous because Angela went to the ball with Captain de' Medici."

Mary Creecy said, "Not so. It's the Frenchman, Pucheu, she's enamoured of. She told me so."

Susanna Vaile said, "What's come over Cecily? She loses her head over every young fellow who wears breeks."

Cecily threw the shears with which she was cutting crosses onto the counterpane, her colour high and blue eyes flashing. "I think you are *mean, mean, mean!* You know I don't like anyone but Jaspie Charlton."

Angela said, "Why can't you leave her alone? What's wrong with you?"

"It's so easy to tease Cecily. But it's such fun to see her get excited," Mary Creecy said.

Madam Barker appeared at the door. She began gathering up the blue squares on which the girls had appliquéed red and white crosses. "We are going to stop now," she said. "Madam King has had a present of a pound of Bahia tea from Sam Johnston. She's going to serve off the tea-party table and use the same Chelsea china we used when we made our resolves in '74."

"How wonderful!" Cecily exclaimed. "I've always wanted to see the famous tea-set."

"It's been ages since I've had a drop of real tea," Angela said. She followed the others into the drawing-room and took a seat between Mary Warden and Madam Tom Jones. They were discussing the Flag Ceremony.

Mary said, "We've had the flag all this time, and haven't done anything about it. I think it ought to be made very impressive—a public ceremony on the Green, and something special for our militia boys who are leaving."

Madam Jones interrupted: "My husband thinks the same thing, Mary. He believes it is a time to reaffirm Parson Earle's Test. You know we have quite a number of people here who are very shaky in their loyalty. With the enemy victorious in the North, we will find the Tories creeping out from under logs and compost beds, the vermin!" She leaned across Angela, lowering her voice. "Tom says he heard in Commons, the other day, that there had been a British spy right in our village—a young man who pretended to be a merchant. I can't remember his silly name, but he was in reality an officer in the King's army."

Angela turned cold. She felt a horrible sensation, as though she had received a blow in the pit of her stomach. She wanted to elbow the woman aside and get out, but she didn't move. She heard the woman's voice as from a long distance. She could not take in the meaning of what she was saying. Only a few words stood out clear, above the rumble of talk in the room: "followed him . . . Campbell Town . . . mouth of the Cape Fear . . . lost the trail" and Mary's voice questioning, "Was his name Jeremiah Morse?" She could stand it no longer. With a murmured "Pardon me" she got up and went to the other side of the room. A moment later she was out the door and walking swiftly across the Green to Ann Pollock's.

Ann met her in the hall. "Oh, Ann! I've just heard the most dreadful thing! Madam Jones told Mary Warden there has been a spy here named Jeremiah . . ."

Ann clapped her hand over Angela's mouth and propelled her into the dining-room, closing the door after her. She turned to face the girl. "Have you no sense at all shrieking out names? William Warden is in the library with Cullen."

"I'm so terrified! I . . ."

"Compose yourself, Angela. This is the second time today that you have rushed in here in an emotional state. You're either angry or terrified or in tears or shouting about spies. If you don't learn discretion, I don't know what will become of you, or of Anthony for that matter. Sit down in that chair. I'll bring you a glass of Scuppernong. I'm going to talk to you. You won't like what I have to say, but I'm going to say it. You are behaving like a fool. You are old enough to have some intelligence. At least you should realize that Anthony is in danger of being discovered, and if that happens it means he will die the most degrading death possible. While you were gone there was trouble here in the village. A gang of rioters broke windows and wrecked Mr. Brinsley's place in Cheapside. He is suspected of being a Tory. Fortunately he got wind of it and got away. How or where I don't know. Clem Hull is at the bottom of it. He swears to rid Chowan County of every Tory. He has followers aplenty. Sam Johnston and Jemmy Iredell are alarmed at the feeling. You remember that once they went so far as to burn Johnston in effigy, because some rowdies accused him of being lukewarm in his allegiance."

Angela sat looking at Ann, her dark eyes enormous in her dark face. "No. They couldn't doubt Mr. Johnston."

"Well, they did. They say he comes from a titled family in England, Jemmy Iredell also. They doubted them both two years ago, but do not any more."

"Cullen?" whispered Angela.

Ann took a quick turn up and down the room. "Cullen is in real danger. I want him to go away—to the West, over the mountains . . . anywhere. Nova Scotia is out of the question, but he might get to Nassau, or join Hamilton's regiment in Georgia."

"Is Cullen still taking orders from the British?" Angela whispered.

Ann gave her a look of exasperation. She shut her lips firmly as though to control her anger, lest she should say words she would regret.

"Is he?" Angela repeated.

"Cullen is neutral," Ann said shortly. "But that will not keep these wild men from attacking him."

"Why won't he leave?" Angela asked. "Why don't you make him go?"

"Cullen won't run from danger," Ann said, a certain pride shining in her eyes. "He isn't afraid of Clem Hull and his rioters, but I am." She sat down as though her knees were giving way. "I am horribly afraid—not for myself but for him." She put her elbows on the table, her head in her hands.

Angela looked at her friend hopelessly, Ann, who was always so strong, so competent; Ann, trembling on the verge of tears. She threw her arms about her. "Why don't you come out to River Plantation—both of you? No one would disturb Cullen there. No one. We haven't any rioters in the county; we have too much sense."

Ann took her hands from her eyes. "I shouldn't have talked, Angela. But I wanted to make you realize how serious, how dangerous, this is. You, thinking only of yourself, your own emotions, come crying out about spies. Suppose someone heard you? Suppose someone other than William Warden happened to be with Cullen?"

She stopped speaking. Her face went white. "Oh, what have I said?" she murmured.

Angela looked at her, comprehension slowly growing in her eyes. "Cullen, Anthony, William Warden. Why, William Warden is on the Council!"

"Do not speak aloud." Ann grasped her arm. "It is not true. I know it is not true. I swear before God it cannot be true."

Angela thought, She doesn't know. She is not sure. That is why she is so afraid.

Ann stood looking at her, her eyes fierce. "You are in this as deep as I am. The moment Anthony placed his life in your hands, you were in it."

"No, no, I'm not a traitor." Her voice broke.

Ann shook her violently by the shoulders. "Be quiet. No one is a traitor. All you have to do is keep your mouth closed. You've never heard of Anthony Allison. Jeremiah Morse you met, a merchant from Boston. Do you understand?"

Angela drew herself to her full height. "Wild horses wouldn't drag it from me. Let them torture me. See how I can bear torture, as my ancestors bore the tortures of the Inquisition."

Ann said wearily, "No need for heroics, Angela. No one is going to torture you. The danger lies in an innocent question someone may ask. Has anyone questioned you about Morse?"

"No one—" she said emphatically—"that is, no one but Captain Huntley."

"Huntley?" Ann stood staring at her. "Huntley?"

"Yes. I told you, didn't I, that he wants to marry me? He asked my father, before he asked me."

Ann said nothing.

Angela went on: "Then the last night we were in Smithfield, we went for a walk. Captain de' Medici and my father walked ahead. It was then Captain Huntley asked me and I said, No, I would *not* marry him."

Ann's lips formed a word, but she didn't speak. Angela said hurriedly, "Wait, I'm coming to it. Huntley said, 'Are you in love with Morse?' I said, 'No, I'm not in love with Jeremiah Morse.' I could say that honestly, Ann, for there isn't any Jeremiah Morse."

"What did Huntley say?" Ann cried.

"He said, 'I'm glad to hear that. I'd be sorry to have you waste your affections on a man of his character.'"

Ann said, "Oh, Angela, I hope you didn't say anything that would give Peter Huntley information."

"No, no. I told him that I didn't need any advice from him."

Ann took a deep breath. "I'm sorry to be so rude to you, Angela, but my fears . . ."

Angela felt suddenly that she must comfort Ann, that she had more faith. "Ann, do not be alarmed. Whatever the dangerous situation is, Anthony will know how to take care of it. As for Cullen, I think you are exaggerating the danger. I haven't heard a breath against him not since he signed Parson Earle's Test. My father says that some of the leaders here were slow to take sides. They hoped some way could be found, that differences could be settled without a civil war. Why, I heard Captain Huntley say that Mr. Franklin was in communication with men in England who were working for peace."

Ann said, "I hope you are right, Angela. It may be that my fears are groundless. Come, let us go upstairs and freshen up. Mary Warden will be here soon. You must stay for supper, too."

"I hoped you'd ask me. I'm going to stay the night with Cecily Armitage, but she is going to a church meeting until nine."

They went upstairs to Ann's bedchamber. Angela thought, This time I comforted Ann. She leaned on me. The thought gave her pleasure and satisfaction.

For two weeks before Midsummer Day, the notice to freeholders of Chowan had been posted on the board beside the Courthouse door that the Flag Ceremony would take place on the twenty-fourth of June. Not only was the county invited, but similar notices had been posted on Hertford and Bertie Courthouses. Tyrrell, too, had been notified, and the eastern counties of Perquimans, Pasquotank and Camden; in truth all the district that had once been Precincts of the old Albemarle County had been asked to attend the presentation of Joseph Hewes's flag to Queen Anne's Town.

The plans had been carefully made. For some time the Whig leaders had felt that there must be some sort of rally or demonstration, to arouse the people to the ever-growing danger. The Presentation of the Flag would be a proper occasion. The counties around Albemarle Sound had responded enthusiastically. Each county would send as its representative a senator or a member of the House of Commons.

A company of General Gideon Lamb's newly recruited Continentals would be in the village on that day, on their way southward. The soldiers would add military dignity. Lamb, himself, was proud of his new rank as general.

Midsummer Day dawned bright and clear. At an early hour the countryfolk began arriving in the village—planters and their wives on horseback and in chaises; yeomen from as far north as Middle Swamp and the Sand Hill Road, Rockahock and Brownrigg Creek, Yeopim Creek and Pembroke. Yeomen came by boat, shallop, canoe,

pirogue and sloop. A carnival camped outside, at the Northern
Gate, on the Suffolk Road—a snare to catch the pennies and shillings
of the countryfolk. There was a Punch-and-Judy show for the children. A troop of play-actors from Virginia set up a tent, where a
play, *The Constant Lover*, was given twice daily; every day except
Sunday, when a miracle play was performed by the same actors who
rowdied through the bawdy weekday play. Behind the Red Lion Inn
the sheep drovers held an auction. Horse-trading went on in the
meadow beyond the soldiers' parade ground where Captain de' Medici
had camped two months before. Bunting and flags hung from every
house. Squares of coloured paper pasted in the window-panes made
gay illumination at night when the candles were lighted. Lanthorns
were set at street corners, and the ships in the harbour had extra lanthorns hanging on the masts and yard-arms, ready for the illumination
at nightfall.

Behind Horniblow's Tavern a barbecue pit had been dug, not far
from the old gaol. Three steers and half a dozen pigs were cooking
for the night and the morrow, the beef turning on spits, the pork
rolled in a plaster of clay, sunk in a pit and covered with hot coals.
The tavern-keeper, Horniblow, donated kegs of ale which had been
sent down to the water-front near the shipyard, where a second barbecue would be held for the commonalty.

The crowds wandered up and down Broad Street, overflowed into
Queen and King and Church. The Green was kept clear for the cere-
monies, but crowds of young people and children sat on the banks
of Queen Anne's Creek and the strip of land that fringed the Sound.
Fire-works, heretofore, had come only on the King's birthday.

Dusk had fallen when Major Adam Rutledge and Captain Peter
Huntley rode into Queen Anne's Town. They dismounted at Horniblow's and went into the general room. They were travel-stained,
overweary, having ridden more than sixty miles that day with small
rest at Halifax. Behind that had been the weary journey from the
western mountains, a matter of long days and ill-lodged nights.

They found the room crowded almost to overflowing. Speaking to
this one and that who called out his name in greeting, Adam made
slow progress to the small room under the stairs where the Whig
leaders met to drink, play their nightly games of chess and backgammon, and discuss political affairs behind a closed door.

At the foot of the stairs Horniblow, the host, stopped them. He shook hands with Adam, his broad dark face wreathed in smiles of welcome. He spoke regretfully. "What a pity, what a great pity, Major, that you did not send a courier in advance! We have no rooms—not a single bed." He spread his hands and indicated the crowds. "They are all here from the whole of the Albemarle."

"What is going on?" Adam glanced over his shoulder, nodding to Samuel Harvey and John Relf, of Perquimans.

"It's the flag Mr. Joseph Hewes sent to us so many months ago. There is a big celebration tonight on the water, fire-works. Tomorrow at five we will have a raising on the Green—speeches, the drums, music and the military salute." He rubbed his hands together in delight, nodding his head, his wired queue beneath its black riband bouncing up and down.

"So?" Adam said. "And there are no rooms to be had?"

"Sir, no. I regret it. I mourn the—— Wait, do me the honour to step into my office. I will send a boy to O'Malley's Ordinary, to see if by chance they may have one room left. Be seated, Major; Captain." He bustled from the small room, shouting for a slave. His voice rose high above the din of laughter and the talking of half a hundred men.

Adam followed their host from the room. He stepped to the counter and ordered two drinks of rum and lemon and brown sugar. "A pint each, and be hasty about it!" Peter heard him say to the barman.

At the door, two men in uniform bore down upon him. Peter recognized one as James Blount, colonel of the Chowan militia. The other was a stranger, a tall, impressive-looking officer of the North Carolina Continentals. A moment later Rutledge greeted him as General Lamb. He caught a few words of their conversation.

"Supposed to be at King's Town by now, but so far have only been able to recruit about half the quota. By Gad, Rutledge," the colonel exclaimed, "I can't think what's come over our people— they're deserting in the North and running, under fire, in the South! The people at home haven't a care in the world. They are lethargic, not concerned with our present danger." His words ended with a violent blow of his fist against the door-jamb. "What's wrong with us? Are we all fools?"

Adam said quietly, "They'll soon shed their lethargy."

"Ah, you know something, Rutledge. Where can we talk privately?" He glanced around the room. "Not here certainly or at my camp at the Rope Walk. Where?"

Horniblow was coming toward them. Adam said, "I'll see you after supper, Colonel."

"I've got you a fine room, Major," Horniblow announced, "a fine room with a view of the Sound, O'Malley's own bedchamber. He's moving out to accommodate you and your friend, the young captain."

"Splendid," said Adam. "Please join us at O'Malley's, General Lamb."

Blount said to Adam, "I'll come with him. I want a word with you."

The two men walked to the dining-room, which was already crowded.

Peter caught Horniblow's small shrewd eyes resting on him with some speculation. He had heard a little talk of Horniblow, a Neutral by proclamation, as much Tory as Whig, but some thought he leaned toward the King's cause even though he had taken the King's Arms sign down from his tavern at the first outbreak. An excellent situation for an informer, Peter thought. He drank his flip while Adam made arrangements for their horses to graze in the pasture behind the gaol.

"I'm obliged to charge you a pound and five shillings for stabling and pasturing, Major. A crime, an outrage!" he hastened to say before Adam could demur at the excessive charge. "It's the war. The prices of all my commodities are up to the mountain-tops. Corn is double, pork . . . Rum is almost impossible to get. I tell you, gentlemen, it is a sorry day that I turned away from my plantation to take up this hostelry."

Adam didn't answer. He took his drink from the bar-boy, lifted it. Peter followed, turning his back on Horniblow. Adam said, "Success!"

Peter touched the cup with his own. "Success!" he answered.

"We will be here three days," Adam went on, "three days for courting."

"Three days is a short time," Peter murmured.

"Much can happen in three days. I saw the senator a moment ago as he was going into the dining-room. He told me his daughter is staying with Ann Pollock for the celebration. Good fortune to you!" He hurriedly drained his glass. "I expect we had better go across to

O'Malley's with our saddle-bags or we will find ourselves without lodgings."

They made their way out through the crowd with difficulty, stopping every step or two to greet friends of Rutledge—West, of Bertie County, and young Jacocks; Brownrigg from Wingfield; Dr. Cathcart, who told them they were wanted for dinner with Sam Johnston the following day. The doctor walked across the street with them, as far as O'Malley's door, where he left them, to continue his way to the creek where a small boat was waiting to take him to Hayes.

Their host, O'Malley, was a quiet man, who minded his own affairs and took no part in politics. He greeted Adam Rutledge with evident pleasure, and himself led the way up the steep narrow stairs to a room that faced both the street and the Sound. Two beds, simple chests of pine and chairs made up the furnishings.

"I'll send a boy with hot water," O'Malley said. He opened a door that led to a small balcony overlooking the garden and a group of small buildings.

Peter stepped out to view the scene. The sun dropped below the rim of the hills on the Tyrrell shore. Two fair-sized brigantines were anchored in deep water where the creek emptied into the Sound, which at that point formed a small bay. In it were a dozen or so small boats.

Through the leafy crowns of trees Peter caught glimpses of the Green and the crowds along the shore. The long wharf was hidden but he could hear sounds that told him a ship was being unloaded. He turned to walk inside, when he caught a glimpse of a well-kept garden, and a gallery on which a group of people were moving about, half shielded by vines that grew over the gallery. He heard the murmur of voices and the sound of laughter.

Adam joined him, bending his tall body to miss the lintel of the door. " 'The lover looks longingly,' " he quoted, following the direction of Peter's glance.

"Beg pardon?"

"You are looking directly into Ann Pollock's garden."

Peter seemed embarrassed. "I didn't know," he protested, and turned hastily.

Adam smiled and laid his hand affectionately on Peter's shoulder. He had become attached to the young man in the weeks they had been together on the western journey. He had found him quick to observe and act in difficult situations, a good companion and dependable. Underneath a calm exterior, Adam thought there was a capacity for strong emotion. He wondered sometimes about Angela Ferrier, whether she was worthy of a strong loyalty. Adam knew little of her; she had blossomed from a long-legged, awkward child into an arresting young woman, during the years he had been away with the army. If she favoured her mother, it was one thing—but there was the father. A hundred rumours had circled the town concerning the Spaniard Gonsalvo. Some said he was the cadet of a noble house; others hinted that he was more likely to have been a freebooter, master of one of the Spanish frigates that preyed on the shipping around Caribbean waters.

Of these things he knew nothing, but there must be something of the mother in the girl; if so, he had no fear for his friend Peter. The lad deserved the best in a woman. Adam hoped he would find what he was seeking in Angela Ferrier. Peter had told him little, only that he had asked the father's permission to marry her.

A loud ringing of the supper bell broke the silence. Adam went inside. Peter followed, after a lingering glance toward the Pollocks' gallery.

Supper was served in a small room off the dining-room. While they were eating the simple meal of scrambled eggs and herring roe, James Blount joined them. He ordered a pint of ale and sat down at the table. He was a tall man with a narrow face and long thin nose. His reddish-brown hair was combed plain, without rolls, and his eyes had a sad, weary look. He lived at Mulberry Hill, a large plantation on the Sound, three or four miles beyond the village.

He was, he told Adam, now colonel of Home Guard, in place of Edward Vaile, who had gone with the Continental army. "This celebration has given us plenty of trouble," he told them. "First we had difficulty in getting food for the barbecue, and arranging the games to amuse the countryfolk. It's all very necessary, I know, but a heap of trouble."

Adam asked, "What about the strolling players you have engaged?"

Blount answered, "We didn't engage them. They came of their own accord. One morning we woke to find them camped on the Rope Walk. The constable ordered them off that meadow and they moved out on the Suffolk Road, just beyond the North Gate."

"I don't hold with strolling players," Adam observed. Peter looked up from his plate, surprised at the statement.

James Blount was also surprised, for a different reason. "How did you know?" he asked Adam.

"Know what?"

"That we have orders to watch carefully for spies at all fairs and gatherings, particularly unknown playing companies."

Peter laid his fork on the pewter plate and gave his whole attention.

"We've had all the players over at the sheriff's office for examination. They seem to be just what they say they are, and their papers are in order, but we found that two of them are in town much of the time. They say they are expecting costumes to come from Williamsburg, either by post or boat. They have been at the wharf half a dozen times, bedevilling the men down there, insisting on searching the warehouse."

"I don't like the look of that," Adam observed.

"Nor I. I've ordered them to keep away from the docks. We've got a heap of army material stored in Queen Anne's Town and we don't want strangers about."

"You are quite right," Adam said. He pushed back his chair from the table and lighted a pipe. He sat facing Colonel Blount, his clear-cut profile toward Peter. His blond head rested against the high back of the chair. He was quiet, absorbed in some thought; after a few moments he asked, "How is the recruiting going, Jimmie?"

"Wretchedly. Lagging beyond all comprehension. I'm as worried as General Lamb. I can't think why our people are so indifferent." He unbuttoned his uniform and took a letter from an inner pocket. "Read this. You'll see what I mean. It's from a man I sent out to receive recruits."

Madam Parsons June 2nd, 1779.

Dear Colonel:

I am very much surprised at the delay of these men that you should have sent over to me. I have been here now a whole week and not a man yet. I am much afraid you leave it to somebody else to doe. While you doe, you never will get them together, for they are a set of lazy Ras Kalls that hate to leave the fireside. You promised me you would turn out in search of them yrself for if you doe not you will never get them together. All troops on their side is marching every day, the last of them this day gone to King's Town. Consider Colonel, I am a poor young fellow and am all this time at my own expense in a tavern. I can't afford it any longer and hope you will take my case into consideration. Pray Sir, if you can't gett anney more men pray Lett me know that I may if you think proper sett off without anny.

Yr. Humbl Servt.

John Egan.

To James Blount Esq.
Col. of Militia in Chowan.

Adam finished reading. "I regret to say that's the situation all over the state. Captain Huntley and I travelled from Smithfield north to Halifax, Hillsborough, and down the Trading Path to Salisbury. We found unrest and confusion everywhere. In Salisbury it was near rebellion, so much so that troops have been sent from Hillsborough. The Tories are bolder now, since our set-backs in the North. I saw John McDowell at Salisbury. He expects serious trouble in the West."

Blount said, "I'm glad it isn't just our county. We've got our Tories, as you know, but they haven't come out into the open or made any overt act. We are watching them. By Gad, Adam, I dislike setting spies on my friends, but what am I to do?"

Adam turned his head and looked out into the hall. It was clear of people. "You mean—?" He nodded in the direction of the Pollock house.

"Yes. I've orders from the Governor. Not a long list of suspects—Lowther of Bertie, for one. Several have already left the village to join Hamilton's regiment in Georgia. I'm glad they've gone. I wish the others would go. I'd loathe like the devil to have to arrest a friend."

Adam smoked silently. Peter said nothing, but Blount's words lay heavy on his heart, for he knew the intimacy between Ann Pollock and Angela.

"There was a fellow who was here in the spring, name of Morse. Claimed to be a merchant from Boston." Peter sat up at Blount's words, his body rigid. "They say he's been in Williamsburg. They sent me word to be on the lookout." Blount got up and stood by the table. "I'm afraid that surly devil Clem Hull will get us into trouble. He swears he will chase every Tory out of the country. He's got a lot of hoodlums and ruffians bound together on oath to do his bidding."

Adam said, "You know, I've never found Hull as bad as he's painted. There must be a way to use such fierce patriotism."

Blount protested. "What can you do with a man who hates everybody?"

"I don't know," Adam admitted, "but there must be a way. Has
he any part in this celebration?"

"I've asked him to fire off the cannon when the flag goes up tomorrow."

"Good! Perhaps we can tame him."

Blount shook his head. "I'm no lion-tamer. Perhaps you can do
something, Rutledge. Maybe you can get at him through Southey
Wren."

The suggestion was not to Adam's liking. "No, I'll tackle the man
myself."

Blount nodded to Peter and left the room. Adam accompanied him
to the door, where they stood for a moment talking earnestly together.

Peter finished his ale and got up. If Senator Ferrier was in town
he would seek him out. He wanted to know what Madam Ferrier's
answer might be. Whatever it was, he wanted to know. Anything
was better than uncertainty. He was weary of the heavy feeling within
him. If Angela had the answer in her own hands he knew it would be
no. Thank God, the custom of parents choosing husbands for their
daughters prevailed here, in the Colonies as well as at home. Angela
was young. Peter felt sure that if he were patient, he could win her
love. As long as that thought remained strong in his heart, he would
not be downcast.

They walked out to the street. Herk was waiting, the reins of
Adam's mount over his arm.

"I'm riding down to the water-front. I want Clem Hull to look over
that left hind shoe," Adam told Peter. "Later, after the fire-works,
suppose we meet at Horniblow's."

Peter acquiesced. He went up to their bedchamber and dressed
carefully in his best uniform. As an afterthought, he buckled on his
sword-belt and sword. He was glad to be alone, to wander about the
village streets, push his way among the crowds that milled about the
Green and promenaded up and down Broad Street. Dark had set in.
After a time the moon would rise. Now the older people carried lanthorns, but the young folk had no need of light other than the stars.
Lads and maids walked four or six abreast down the streets, making
way, with laughter and pretended reluctance, for a horseman or a
chaise. The houses around the Green had candles in every window,
with hurricane lanthorns at the gate-posts. Every gallery was filled

with house-owners and their guests. From Horniblow's and the Court-house steps, down both sides of the Green and along the water-front, Peter had never seen the village so crowded.

The laughter was infectious. Peter found himself smiling, hum-ming a snatch of a song as he strolled along the waterside. He took up a position near the Pollock house where he could watch the doorway, perhaps glimpse Angela at a window or hear her voice. He would not attempt to see her until he had talked with the senator. He did not want to jeopardize his chances by so boorish an act. He thought of the incident of the scarf, which he had safely tucked in the breast pocket of his uniform; he did not want a recurrence of anything so *gauche*.

He waited for some time at his post. He was not rewarded, although he heard low-pitched voices; there were people walking in the gar-den.

The fire-works would be set off from a raft anchored beyond the Dram Tree, well away from the ships that lay at anchor in the bay or crowded the wharf. The crowd began to be impatient as it grew darker. A drum started a lively tattoo, followed by a fife. People be-gan to shout and press forward. Peter found himself against the Pollocks' garden fence. Very clearly Angela's voice came to him. "Let us go out on the gallery. There is no longer any privacy here at all."

Peter's heart beat violently. Even the girl's voice disturbed him with a strange poignancy. He elbowed his way through the crowd. He could not bear to play the part of a Peeping Tom. He managed, with some struggling, to get to the upper end of the Green. A gasping sound of delight rippled along the crowd as the first Catherine wheels were set off, a great mass of red and green, sparkling against the velvet of the night.

Peter made his way inside Horniblow's and ordered a drink of rum and lemon. The room was almost empty now, for the men who earlier had crowded the dining and public-rooms were on the Green, watch-ing the display. He was astonished to find that his hand was shaking when he lifted the cup. A girl's voice—and his blood turned to water. "Damnation!" he muttered. He was ashamed of such weakness. It certainly ill befitted a man to let a chit of a girl put him into such state. He was gloomily looking into the glass when Senator Ferrier, coming out of an inner room, caught sight of Peter. Hailing him, he beckoned Peter to join him.

They went into the Whig Room, which was deserted save for chess players seated in a corner, deep in their game, the board lighted by four candles.

The senator sat down at a small table under a Hogarth print of *Southwark Fair*. "I heard you were back in town, Peter. I saw Adam. He tells me you had a successful journey."

Peter said he hoped so. Affairs in the West seemed very confused to him.

"Let's see, how long were you away?"

"A matter of six weeks or so, sir." His tongue was thick against the roof of his mouth. He wanted to approach the matter nearest his heart, but he could not form the words. He sat staring at Mr. Ferrier like a yokel.

The senator was smiling a little. He reached his hand across the table and patted Peter's sleeve. "There, there, my boy! I know how you feel. I was that tongue-tied myself in like case. That was many years ago. My first wife's father was a dour Argyllshire man, and I was full of fear of him."

Peter said, "I am full of fear myself. I want my answer, sir, but . . . now I am afraid to hear it from your lips."

The hand that rested on Peter's sleeve pressed his arm firmly. "No need to fear, my son. Madam, my wife, agrees with me that you will make our girl a good husband."

The room reeled before Peter's eyes—or was it the rum he had drunk? He managed after a time to mutter, "Thank you, sir, I . . ."

Ferrier held up a warning hand. "But Angela makes objections. She says she does not know you well enough." He leaned over the table. "To speak honestly, she fancies herself in love with some officer she met on a ship, several years ago. Nonsense, I told her, but she must weep and carry on."

Peter said stiffly, "I cannot press my suit if I am so obnoxious to her."

"Nonsense! The girl doesn't know her mind. She is flighty, singing at the top of her voice or weeping her eyes out, a temperament I don't understand." The senator spoke reflectively. "To speak truthfully, Madam and I are delighted. We feel that you are just the man for Angela—though I must warn you, she needs a firm hand."

Peter sat dumb, not knowing what to say.

"You must come out to River Plantation with me for a few days. I've spoken to Rutledge. He says you are not going to New Bern before the end of the week. A few days of courtship will serve you well, my boy, so don't refuse."

Peter's smile changed his serious face. The senator looked at him for a moment. "Yes, I see. If she means so much to you, you are the man for her. We will announce the betrothal before you leave for New Bern."

"Thank you, Mr. Ferrier. You do not know what this means to me. I will ask Mr. Barker to arrange the settlements."

Ferrier's face brightened. "That is excellent. I am glad you brought up the matter. I am glad Angela will be well provided for—the more so because she is not my child and has no dower of her own. I will, of course, settle something on her."

Peter said, "Please, sir, don't think of it. I have ample. I will make arrangements for her to have her own income from the day we are married. I want her to feel secure and independent."

The senator looked serious for a moment. "You are very generous, Peter, but I must warn you that Angela will be independent whether she has money or not—take my word for it. Master her from the beginning, before it is too late."

The conversation broke up as half a dozen men came into the room calling loudly for the bar-boy. Senator Ferrier rose, shook hands with Peter. "Remember, you are going up-river with me Saturday morning." At the door he paused. Smiling, he said, "Why don't you step over to Cullen Pollock's? I think Ann would be delighted to see you."

Adam Rutledge, followed by Herk, rode along Broad Street to the outskirts of the village. He stopped at the Red Lion Inn. He tossed the reins to Herk and went inside. The room, heavy with smoke from clay pipes, was crowded. Husbandmen, artisans, drovers were there in numbers. While he waited for the proprietor he ordered a pot of beer and surveyed the room. Mostly strangers, only a few faces that he knew. He was not astonished at this, for many of the yeomen from Sand Hill Road way, Middle Swamp and Rockahock districts seldom came to the village except on high days and holidays. Often they carried their produce to Suffolk, in Virginia, a longer haul but a larger market. What did surprise him was the large number of drovers. There must be a movement of herds. He spoke to a drover who sat at a near-by table, a surly fellow who had only monosyllables, until Adam stood him for a beer. Then he said they were driving sheep and cattle to Charles Town. From Virginia they came, but would pick up other herds as they proceeded through North Carolina. A moment later the drover got up and moved to another table where a second drover sat alone. Adam noticed he was more intelligent-looking than the others. He saw Adam glancing his way. Shortly he moved so that he was half concealed by a post, one of several that supported the roof of the raftered room.

The landlord, Losch, came out then, and Adam invited him to sit at the table with him. Losch often furnished Adam with cattle and sheep, for the landlord did a bit of speculating, buying an animal or two off drovers as they went by. A sorry business. Adam supposed the profit went to the drover rather than the owner of the flock or herd.

Just now he wanted different information. He had heard in the village that the strolling players dropped into the Red Lion for a small beer or a meal. Losch was a lean man with a thin face, hard-bitten but not evil. He listened to Adam's question, shook his head. "I've not had talk, Major. They come and go quiet-like, and make no fuss about victuals or drink."

"Do all of them come here?" Adam asked.

"No. I think those of the high cast are above eating with the lowly workers. They eat at O'Malley's Victualling House, or at Horni-blow's—or did until he refused them. He doesn't hold with play-acting, Horniblow don't. He wants only the quality at his place." The man spoke without rancour, as though stating a fact, not an opinion.

"Where's Clem Hull tonight?" Adam asked casually, glancing about the room.

"I've seen naething of Hull these several nights, Colonel. Clem's all for makin' some new weapon, him and Southey Wren. I speak God's truth, Mr. Rutledge; excuse it, I mean Major. Clem's got him-self almost human since he began this work." He paused and swallowed a mouthful of ale. "All but bleating about running the Loyal-ists out of Chowan County. He's still bellowing about that." He looked over his shoulder. "I'm feared he's up to something, Mr. Rut-ledge, and he's got a heap of men behind him in it."

Adam didn't speak for a moment. He was watching a man who came in and sat down at the table with the two drovers. Realizing, after a time, that Losch expected an answer, he said, "I don't like that. The military authorities have an eye on all suspected of being Loyalists. They are the ones to take care of that situation."

"Clem says they won't, because the Loyalists are their friends— their own kind. The gentry will always look after the gentry, he says, but I don't believe that, Mr.—excuse, I mean Major Rutledge. This war is making new divisions, sir."

"You are right, Losch," Adam said absently. He was still watching the drovers' table. There was something familiar about the third man. Finally he asked the host, "Who is that man who joined the two drovers, sitting side-face to us?"

Losch looked across the room. "I don't know his name. He doesn't come here often. I think he's one of the actors, one of those who usually eat in the village."

Adam got to his feet and put his reckoning on the table.

"Sorry we've had to raise the price, Major Rutledge, but a man must live. We're paying double for everything."

Adam said, "I know. I heard yesterday that the price of a pair of army shoes at Charles Town is seven hundred dollars."

"God's mercy!" Losch exclaimed, horrified. "I hope we ain't never besieged by the British."

Adam said, "I don't suppose we ever will be. We are lucky, in this little world of ours." He bent down. "Find out that actor's name for me. I'll send Herk back later."

Losch nodded. "I'm glad to do anything for you, Mr. Rutledge. I don't forget how you helped me, and paid my taxes when the sheriff was about to sell me out from the Courthouse steps. I don't forget, Mr. Rutledge."

Adam smiled. "You're a good man, Losch. You've paid that debt— wiped it out long ago."

Losch followed Adam out the door. Before he mounted Losch said, "Them as ride in carriages is likely to be called Tories by them as don't."

Adam looked a question.

"I'm just observing," Losch said. "Not naming any names."

Adam said, "Thanks again, Losch. I'll send Herk over later, for the name of the actor."

"Yes, sir. I'll get it."

Clem Hull was working in his smithy by the light of a torch when Adam rode up and dismounted from his horse. A number of people, men and women, were seated on a bench and some hard-back chairs, watching the fire-works display. Children sat on the sand at the waters' edge, shouting their delight as each rocket split the velvet darkness. Several people spoke to Adam by name as he went by. He led his horse into the shop. Clem Hull muttered something in answer to his greeting, calling to Southey Wren to move the torch from his workbench. Adam had time to see a musket on the bench and a lever of some sort, attached to the breech.

Southey moved the light then, and he saw no more.

"I wish you'd look at the mare's nigh hind shoe, Hull," Adam said. "She cast a shoe when I was in the mountains, and I had her shod at Salisbury. I think it was a bad job."

"Damn bad work," Clem muttered, as he lifted the mare's hoof, "damn bad."

A woman walked through the shadows. "Evenin' to you, Mr. Rutledge."

Adam looked up. "Good evening, Martha. How's the lad?"

"Fine, sir. Fair fine. Grown a great big fellow. Thank you kindly, sir."

"Splendid."

She moved on through the shop and joined the others. Adam heard her say, "Always asks about my boy, 'e does. 'Twas he, being on the Vestry, that spoke up for me, and 'e fixed it so's I didn't go on the books as an evil woman. God, 'ow was I to know that the fella that spoke the marrying words 'ad no right, not being the clergy at all?"

A woman said, "It was an ill fellow that misused you, Martie. If Clem lay eyes on him 'twould be a poor day for him, I'll bet you."

"Cain't properly do that. The wretch, he went right away to the Old Country and stayed there," another said.

"That he did and 'twas best so. I don't want my man Clem to get himself into murdering no one."

The hammer came down on the hot iron with a blow that scattered sparks as the smith refashioned the shoe. Adam took a position beyond the arc of glowing sparks. "I noticed she's been favouring that leg," he said, "but I've been out of range of a farrier."

Clem held up the shoe and indicated with his hammer. "This is the way it was, causing the heel to pinch. Now you see how I've spread it and changed the curve. Wonder she hadn't gone plumb lame on you." He plunged the glowing iron into the wooden half-barrel and whirled it about in the cool water. He wiped the sweat from his forehead with the back of his hand, before he raised the mare's hind leg over his leather-covered thigh. The mare jerked nervously, but he gentled her with a quiet word or two.

Adam thought that a man who could so quickly gain the confidence of a horse must have another side to him. Aloud he said, "You're the best farrier in Carolina, Clem. I'm surprised the army hasn't taken you before now."

Clem cast a venomous look at him, which Adam did not appear to see. He thrust his crippled foot forward. "Would the army take anything like that?"

"Why not?" Adam said calmly. "You can shoe a horse, can't you?"

The two men stood looking at each other across the anvil. The glow from the charcoal fire reflected on their faces—the one clear-cut, almost classical, his smooth hair neatly clubbed; the other heavily lined, with blowing turbulent eyes and a mass of dark hair that escaped his queue and straggled upon his shoulders. For a short time their eyes met steadily. Clem Hull turned his head away. In that instant Adam knew all the tragedy that had so embittered the man before him. In a flash he knew what to say. It was better to speak frankly and not avoid mention of his lameness, as most people did.

The two were alone in the dark smithy. Outside were laughter and shouting and exclamations of pleasure as the rockets soared through the blackness like small comets, leaving their blazing trail behind them. Adam did not allow any of the sympathy he felt to creep into his voice when he spoke. "There's no reason why you can't get into the army, if you want to. Your lameness won't keep you back, if you want to go as a farrier. You'll have a wagon assigned for your forge and your anvil and iron."

"I've tried often enough," the smith said angrily. "I applied to Colonel Vaile, and only yesterday to Colonel Blount, and they turned me down."

"For infantry, certainly not. It must be a field battery or a troop of dragoons. But I think you can do a good enough job right here, looking after the planters and yeomen. The army must be fed, if it's going to fight battles."

"That's what I tell him." Southey Wren had come in. He stood in the shadows near Clem. "You're right about him being a good workman, Major Rutledge. Did you see the way he set those cannon? As good as if he'd been to Ordnance School. And that's no lie."

Clem said nothing.

"And that's not all. . . ."

Clem laid a heavy hand on Southey's shoulder. "That's enough talk, Mate."

"I thought the Major might help," Southey said.

"No. We don't need help," Clem said gruffly.

Adam took the mare's reins and slipped them over his arm. "Let me know, Hull, if you make up your mind to go into the army. I'll see what can be done." He turned to Southey. "I hear you've been doing a good job of drilling, Wren."

"Thank you, sir. You'll be seeing some of my men tomorrow, when they raise Mr. Hewes's flag. They do well enough for yeomen who's never seen a manual of arms, or heard a proper command, sir."

"Splendid! I'm afraid we're going to need all the men you have, and many more."

Clem said harshly, "It's few you'll get around here, with the place creepin' with damn Tories. I tell you we've got to get rid of every one of them."

"Now, Clem." Southey's voice was conciliatory. "Now, Clem."

"It's God's truth and you know it. Spies comin' in here and bein' housed by some of the gentry—our fine gentry. And when I report to the military, what happens? Nothing."

Adam said, "Have you proof of this, Hull?"

There was a moment's hesitation and the smith answered, "No. But mighty suspicious-acting. I'd put them in the ducking-stool at least."

"When you have proof, let me know. I'll be at O'Malley's for a few days."

Southey said, "Have a care, Major. Don't rub your uniform against the tar. Tar is hard to do away with, sir."

Adam led his mare outside and mounted. Followed by Herk, he rode to Horniblow's. For a time he had felt that he was making some progress, until Clem got off on Tories. He hadn't realized how fanatical he was. It was just as well not to get into an argument. For a moment he wondered if the smith were right . . . if there were more Tories in the Albemarle than he had realized. After all, he had been away for three years. Three years in the army is a long time—too long to feel the drag and undercurrents of home waters.

CHAPTER
17

FLAG DAY

SOUTHEY WREN had discarded his yeoman's blue smock and donned His Britannic Majesty's uniform of the Seventieth Regiment of Foot, which he had worn when he served under Major Patrick Ferguson. To this he added a blue three-cornered hat of the Continental Line, with a Whig rosette. He had his colour platoon lined up on the meadow, giving last instructions to his farm boys. They wore mixed uniforms, hastily got together, but all blue and buff.

"My lads, I want to remind you that this is not a home-town play. It's strictly military. There'll be a general observing, and a colonel of the Continental Line. I want our Rockahock lads to make as good or better showing than the other recruits.

"It's snap I want, lads. Heads up and eyes front! No casting sheep's eyes at wives or sweethearts in the crowd. Take your cadence from the guide. Remember, when the bugle sounds *Colours*, when the order comes, *Present Arms* . . . all as one man . . . precision. Stand firm as a granite block, steady on your feet. To the men who receive the flag: Have a care not to let it touch the earth. You know your routine. It's my thought that you drill better than any recruits I've had. Conduct yourselves so that you are an honour to Chowan County. That's all, men."

The first gun to start the ceremony was to be fired a half hour before sunset, by Clem Hull. To show his indifference—nay, his contempt— of the well-dressed leaders who sat on the platform, he came from the smithy wearing his leather apron, a smudge of soot across his face. Martie had washed his linen breeks and his nankeen jacket, which she had pressed until there was not a crease to be seen, but he would not change.

"Hist, woman," he said when she showed the clothes, with white hose, laid on the blue and white woollen counterpane of their pine bed. "Hist, woman. Let Southey take off the honours in his fine uniform. Me, 'tis but another chore." But he lifted her chin, with his heavy calloused fingers, and smiled into her pleading eyes.

" 'Tis nae one wha'll look at Clem Hull, when the shots roar out over the water. Nae one. They'll be shutting their eyes and putting fingers to their ears. Twa shots they've allowed me."

"But you are so fine to look at, Clem boy," she whispered, burying her cheek against his leather waistcoat. "Martie, she be fair proud of you, Clem."

He patted her cheek in unwonted tenderness. "You be a good lass, Martie, a good lass." But he went as he was to the gun firing.

The cannon stood at the wharf. Clem couldn't see Southey Wren's platoon, where they stood to haul up the flag. Two small boys, sons of Harris the joiner, had the responsibility of running from the Green to give Clem fair warning, a task they took with great seriousness. Clem could well hear the bugle that gave warning for the flag raising, and the roll of drums. But the boys begged for the honour of a part in the great day. They were poised with their bodies thrust forward, arms akimbo, one foot advanced. Unconsciously, thought Peter Huntley who watched them, they're assuming the pose of the Discobolus. Their freckled faces were serious and unsmiling.

The speakers came down the Courthouse steps, crossed the Green to their position on the platform, its new lumber hidden beneath a miniature forest of pines. The smell of pine and juniper fresh-cut was in the air.

Thomas Benbury was in charge of the speaking. This was considered proper by the committee, since he was Speaker of the House of Commons. The representatives from the counties, each a senator or member of the house, were to make short talks, William Hooper to give the long speech. Thomas Relf of Pasquotank came first; then Jasper Charlton of Bertie; for Tyrrell, Benjamin Spruill and Josiah Swain; for Gates, William Baker. Caleb Grandy spoke for Camden, although Willis Bright was present. Arthur Cotten represented Hertford, as George Wynn was ill.

General Isaac Gregory did not speak but sat on the platform, a soldierly, dignified figure. Samuel Harvey gave a stirring talk on the work Joseph Hewes had done. James Iredell and Samuel Johnston bowed when their names were mentioned, as they were the committee. Dr. Hugh Williamson spoke on the responsibility of the delegates to the Continental Congress.

"We are fortunate, in North Carolina, to be represented by a man of the high quality of Joseph Hewes. In his capacity of Chairman of the Committee of Naval Affairs he has thrown his endeavour, which is not inconsiderable, toward the building of a navy, without which we cannot gain victory. He has stood behind his protégé, John Paul Jones, in buying ships suitable for swift strikes against the foe. A small navy, it is true, but one which will grow. We have two excellent seamen in Hopkins and Jones. . . . But remember my words: When the day of victory comes, as surely it will, the navy must play a great part.

"We now have the row galley *Caswell* (which we bought from the State of Virginia) at Ocracock, to protect our commerce. Fort Johnston, on the Cape Fear, is being repaired, at Point Lookout. My friends, I say with all the earnestness that is in me: Look to the sea, for our command of the Western Ocean means victory."

Williamson's great dark eyes swept the crowd.

"The land army must fight, and fight again. Its strength must be renewed again and again. But as long as the Western Ocean lies open to the enemy, no land army, however great, can bring us victory."

There was loud applause as Dr. Williamson sat down amidst great handclapping, for he was a popular man. Men knew his worth as a broad thinker, well versed in public affairs. Had he not attended the University of Utrecht, as well as Pennsylvania? Had he not been one of a committee to observe the transit of Venus over the solar disc? They were proud that he had adopted Queen Anne's Town as his home. Now, as head of the medical staff of a draft of five thousand men, he was in a position to know what was going on. Had not Mr. Jefferson said he was of acute mind and high degree of learning? Yes, they were proud of him. Wilmington had the elegant and scholarly Dr. Eustace, but Queen Anne's Town had her Dr. Hugh Williamson.

When Adam Rutledge went onto the platform, Peter Huntley made his way toward the water, where the cannon had been set up. Halfway down, in front of the King house, he saw Senator Ferrier and Angela. The senator beckoned to him. "I'm late. I should have been on the platform before now. Peter, take care of Angela." He hurried away, mopping his face as he went.

Peter turned to Angela. "Where would you like to sit?" he asked, after he had made his manners.

She looked about her. The backless plank seats which had been placed near the stand were already filled. Many people were seated on the grass under the trees, for the sun was still high enough to be bothersome. After a moment's hesitation she indicated a spot under a wide-spreading bay tree. Peter noticed it was near the little striped marquee surrounded by small pine trees, which was designated as the actors' dressing space. The actors were sitting on the ground, for the most part dressed in their costumes of the Restoration comedy they were to play later in the evening, after the speeches and barbecue were over.

She took her place, her back against the tree trunk facing the speaker. Peter sat down beside her. She glanced toward the Pollock gallery when she sat down, but it was empty.

Peter said, "I called at Madam Pollock's this morning to see you, but found no one at home."

"We were at the Barkers', at a sherry party," she said.

He opened his mouth to say something more, but she turned her face toward the platform. William Hooper was walking toward the front of the stand, acknowledging the applause which followed Speaker Benbury's introduction.

Peter, facing Elizabeth King's house, saw the fluttering little flags, replicas of the great one, as the Tea-party Ladies rose to make their noiseless salute to William Hooper. It was a pretty sight, like a rose garden in its various colours of dimity and mull, silken sashes and wide hats. Most of the women who had signed the famous paper were there, with their families and children. Madam Barker sat in a high-backed chair under the trees, with a small blackamoor dressed in gay clothes waving a green bough from a bay tree to discourage flies. As president of the Tea-party Ladies she deserved the seat of honour, and she carried off that honour in her new sprigged muslin and tilted leghorn hat, set atop her elaborate coiffure.

Cecily Armitage slipped through the crowd and sat down between Angela and Peter, nodding silently to both, waving her little China fan. Peter frowned. It seemed symbolic to him: always someone between him and Angela. Even without speech between them, her nearness gave him a certain peace. He could think of times to come, when they would sit alone by their own hearthstone, or in a garden of roses and lilies.

William Hooper's voice, rebounding against a sounding-board, came out to them in its rich resonance, without echo. At first Peter did not listen to the orator, his mind taken over by the nearness of

Angela, but presently he was caught by Hooper's words: "For a long time I have felt that we have been making a profound mistake by not taking the people into our confidence in the progress of the war.

"We have complained in Congress, and in state meetings of our leaders, that the people were not aware of the seriousness of our situation. Our soldiers have run under fire; our soldiers have deserted by the hundreds; our men are not enlisting; not a county is up to its requirement.

"Now I have begun to ask myself why. Isn't our land as dear to us as the New Englander's land to him, as the New Yorker's land, or the New Jersey landowner's?

"I have found an answer. The fault is in our leaders. Our people have not been informed of the war.

"The heel of the conqueror has not touched our soil since the early days, when we defeated the Tories and sent the Royal Governor scudding for safety aboard his ship-of-war. The war is far away. It might be in Flanders or the Spanish Peninsula, except for the fact that now and then we hear a neighbor lad died in battle in Pennsylvania or Delaware, or in the South.

"Our fault it is, that you do not feel in your heart the alarm that your leaders feel, who know the facts.

"I have been asked by your committee to speak to you, gathered here on the old Green, before this historic Courthouse which has witnessed the procession of Lords Proprietors' Governors, through Crown Royal Governors, to a State Governor, freely elected. Queen Anne's Town is your proud name. You came into being as a village in the time of that gracious Queen, but you go back farther than Queen Anne to a grant from Charles II to Eight Peers of the Realm, the Lords Proprietors. You have come a long way, step by step in natural growth; you have by act of law received more liberties, more freedom, until now you are an independent state in a union of states, a new form of government, which advances beyond even Plato's Republic.

"Ask yourself if you are worthy of this freedom. Ask yourself what you, as an individual, have done to deserve this freedom.

"Ask yourself what you are going to do to *defend* this freedom."

Hooper paused. His sad, dark eyes looked about him over the crowded Green, and rested for a moment on the flag that fluttered from the tall mast.

"I have from now until sundown, a matter of twenty minutes, in which to tell you.

"First, let me tell you that the Whig party is torn into factions. Not Whig against Tory, but Whig against Whig.

"Let me tell you that an organized group within our own party, the party that is fighting a war, is trying to tear asunder the reputation of our great General as a leader. Let me tell you that we have a Congress that is fighting, bickering, passing silly, inconsequential bills, instead of being united in a great solid front against the tremendous power of our enemy.

"Let me tell you that we will lose the war if we so continue. In England we have many friends, the merchants, with whom our trade is their life-blood as well as ours. All the opposition to the Hanoverian King is on our side. The great Pitt speaks for us. Fox speaks for us. Wilkes, Barré, and Cornwallis lift up their voices for us. Yes, Cornwallis has opposed excessive taxation, and spoken in Parliament against the Stamp Act. There are many Englishmen who hope we will win this war. We are Englishmen fighting a group of decadent Englishmen who have sworn fealty to the House of Hanover.

"If the Stuarts were on the throne we would face extravagance and wastefulness, but do you think they would dismember the British Empire? No, I say. No."

Hooper had the audience by now quiet and attentive. Using words as an artist uses paint, he brought the war into the little village. The people who sat so quietly on the Green felt the weary years of despondency. The bitter year of Valley Forge chilled their hearts and became part of them; the desperate struggle for New York, fought by unpaid, hungry troops, with no stomach for war, whose only thought was of their starving families at home. The long years of our despair, he called them.

"The years of our desperation and despair are still upon us. In these years we have stained the earth with the blood of our dead. We have fought trained soldiers with untutored boys, with men who have had no pay to send home to their loved ones. We have lost, lost, lost, with only a few little islands of winning to keep hope alive.

"The help we have been promised from abroad has not been sufficient. We try to keep hope fanned to a flame by saying, 'The French are coming, with thousands of men and fleets of ships.'

"God above! It is not to the French we must look, but to our own people! This is our fight, Englishmen against Englishmen, as much a civil war, if you please, as the Wars of the Roses. If we gain allies, it is one more step to help us down the dark road, but our allies are not our strength. Our strength comes from our own bone and sinews, from our own indomitable hearts. If we are to be a nation, we must build stone upon stone. The French will not build us a nation. They will send help, men, a few ships, not so much to help us as to harm England, which they fight over our shoulders.

"I say to you, freeholders, our nation must arise out of our strength and purpose and unity." His voice rose until it reverberated against the sounding-board. "Let us cast off our weariness. Let us gather strength from our mountains, from our deep forests, from the fertile earth that feeds us so bountifully."

There was silence, as he paused to drink from the glass that Samuel Johnston offered him.

Then slowly, step by step, he took them through the procession of defeats that lay behind them, to the defeats that lay ahead.

"The South Carolinians did a great work when they forced Sir Henry Clinton's men back to their ships and away from their rivers. But that was in '76. It marked not the end of Southern invasion. Clinton will avenge that defeat which is chalked up against him as a general.

"You cannot expect the South Carolinians to fight your war for you. More and more British ships will come from the Indies and from the North, until their siege becomes an invasion, and Cornwallis' army marches triumphantly to our borders. What will you do then? Will you huddle in little groups in the centre of the state, or in this fertile little Eden of yours, so secure here in the Albemarle, where you are barricaded on the north by Virginia and on the east by the Banks, or will you flee over the high mountains of the west?

"No! By the living God, no! You will stand and defend your borders. Patriots, you will stand and defend.

"Let me implore you to pray on your knees to the great and living God for our leader who keeps a lonely vigil, night after night, attacked by foes without and foes within, but who returns each day with faith, who lives through his Gethsemane upheld by the faith that we must win our victory.

"Pray for George Washington, my countrymen! Pray that your leaders may keep the faith—for, without faith, we will all perish."

As the last words were spoken, the red sun went down behind the spires of pines across the Sound.

The sunset gun sounded. The militia and Southey Wren's platoon stood at attention.

There was no roar of applause from the crowd. They stood facing the flag with a new and profound reverence. William Hooper's words rang in their ears and in the beat of their hearts. "Stand and defend! Patriots, stand and defend!"

Peter, deeply moved, turned to Angela. She had gone away without his being aware. He had forgotten her as he listened to the earnest words of a man who saw beyond today, into the days to come: the long days of travail that lay ahead.

Peter saw Cecily standing near the actors' marquee. She did not see him until he was at her side. She turned her round startled eyes upon him. "Oh, Captain Huntley," she said quite loudly, "how nice! You know I never before saw anyone so engrossed in a speech as you were. Mr. Hooper was *so* nice, wasn't he? He has *such* a pleasant voice, though he's grown a little stout, don't you think? Or maybe he looked short beside Mr. Johnston. Mr. Johnston is *so* tall and handsome, don't you think?"

Peter asked, "What did you think of what Mr. Hooper had to say, Miss Armitage?"

"Say? Oh!" She looked a little bewildered. "Does one ever listen to what these politicians say, Captain Huntley?"

"I would think so."

She laughed. "I'm afraid I was looking at Madam Barker. *Such* a well-cut gown. I wondered whom she had to make it. No one here. Probably some mantuamaker in Philadelphia. I know Mr. Hewes sends her things—six pairs of shoes last week." She giggled. "Fancy having a Signer purchase such mundane things as shoes!"

"Leonardo da Vinci bought Paris hats for the Duchess of Mantua."

Cecily opened her round eyes even wider. "Did he indeed, Captain Huntley?" Peter knew his shot had missed.

"Mr. Hewes had a bracelet made for Ann Pollock out of Madam Buncombe's hair, and a locket set for Mr. Iredell. It does seem as though he had plenty of spare time from making laws and things."

Peter got the idea that Cecily was talking against time. Each time she said Captain Huntley, she raised her voice. He stepped a little to one side, the better to see the front of the marquee. Cecily thrust her hand under his arm. "Do escort me over to Madam King's house. I simply loathe to walk through such great crowds of people one doesn't know."

Peter said, "Where is Angela Ferrier?"

"Oh, Captain Huntley, I don't know. I quite lost Angela in the crowd."

"Do you think she went to the Pollocks'?"

"No, Ann Pollock is over at the Barkers'. There's no one at home there."

"Where is Mr. Pollock? Isn't he here in the village?"

"Oh, no! Cullen went to Suffolk—didn't you know? Something about some runaway slaves. He drove up in his carriage. He has such a pretty chaise—almost as elegant as Madam Barker's, but not quite. Madam Barker's is quite the nicest in Queen Anne's Town."

She chatters like a magpie, Peter thought, as they crossed the Green. He left her at the gate. He would go to Horniblow's. Perhaps Adam Rutledge would be there. On the way he met Robert Smith.

"A great speech!" the merchant said, shaking hands. "We needed just that. Hooper is right. We haven't let the people know what is going on."

Peter said, "I plan to come around in the morning, Mr. Smith. I'm told to take up the remainder of the lottery tickets, and send in the final report. What time will be convenient?"

Smith considered a moment. "Around eleven, Captain. I'll have time by then to check everything. Sorry not to be able to see you at an earlier hour, but we have a vessel coming in, in the morning. You know what that means. All the women in the village will be there to get knick-knacks."

Peter said, "You seem to be successfully running the blockade of the Banks."

"Once in a while. Once in a while we get a ship in behind Ocracoke, or over Frying-pan Shoals and up the Cape Fear. Going to the banquet at Horniblow's?"

"No, sir, I'm going to bed."

"Don't blame you, Captain. I'd like to do that myself, but I'm one of the hosts."

He went away. Peter went into the tavern. It was crowded with men and smoke and liquor fumes. It was all he could do to push his way inside. He met Ferrier near the door.

"How'd you make out?" the senator enquired.

"Didn't make out at all, sir. Miss Angela left in the middle of Mr. Hooper's talk."

"Girls are such fools," Ferrier said. He caught the eye of a barman. "Two rum and lemons," he called.

"Yes, Senator, thank you, sir," the barman shouted back over the din.

They stood near a window and drank their flip. The crowd was mellow and jovial, with vast praise for Hooper.

"Funny thing," the senator said: "a few months ago Hooper thought Caswell was a fool to be calling for troops to send to South Carolina."

"He must have had some information that changed him, sir."

"Yes. I wonder what."

Peter said nothing. That morning he had received a dispatch from the committee in Congress to finish all other business—lottery, search for spies—and be prepared to go to the western part of the states, as a liaison officer between a new general and General Washington. "But stay where you are, until orders come through," had been the last sentence of the dispatch.

The talk in the tavern was loud and boisterous as the drinks passed through the crowds. Will Hooper held court. A hundred men passed by to shake his hand, to show their appreciation. "We want waking up," Johnston said to James Iredell. "Will Hooper is the man to do it." Outside, the militia marched off smartly to their camp at the Rope Walk, followed by hundreds of cheering men and boys.

The lamplighter went his rounds and lighted the whale-oil lamps set in the corners of the Green and on either side of the Courthouse steps. The play-actors set up flares shielded by oaken barrels cut lengthwise in halves; and the children screamed and yelled as a Punch-and-Judy show began.

Peter stood, drinking his flip, gazing out the window of the tavern, while the senator talked to half a dozen friends. Peter could not help wondering what the talk was like at the Red Lion, and the tavern at the East Gate, among the drovers and husbandmen.

Nat Allen came in, his blue eyes shining with excitement. "James Blount just told me that fifty men have already enlisted in the militia. Fifty—think of that! And there is a long line waiting while Southey Wren writes down the names."

He hurried to another group, proud to be the bearer of the good news.

Here is the answer, Peter thought, as he set his glass on the table. Here is the answer to William Hooper's plea.

The senator, noticing that Peter was alone, said, "My wife gave me a message for you. She is at Dr. Armitage's, at Cupola House. She would be pleased if you would step over. She wants to talk with you."

Peter listened with a mixed feeling of doubt and fear, which showed on his countenance.

The senator smiled. "Have no worries, Peter. Madam is quite friendly toward you."

Peter thanked him and went into the street. It was dusk, and laughing crowds were making their way toward the shipyard and the barbecue pits. How hot it was! How noisy! He wished he could go to some quiet spot, instead of facing Madam Ferrier. Angela would be there, perhaps, and that little Cecily, who talked so nervously about things of no interest. Better to get it over.

He went over to O'Malley's to freshen up. As he wound a fresh stock, he wondered where Adam was. He had not seen him since noon. But one could easily be lost in the crowds. He set his hat firmly on his head and went out into the cool dusk. Something inside made him quiver like a leaf. He was angry at such weakness. It was not manly to allow himself to get into such a state. Had he no poise, no dignity? Did being in love with a woman lead to such instability?

It was not difficult after all. Madam Ferrier made it all so easy. She received him alone, in a little drawing-room upstairs, where Dr. Armitage received his guests when he was home.

She held out her hand. Peter raised it to his lips. He felt her dark eyes upon him, as though she were appraising him—Angela's eyes, only Madam's were warm and deep with wisdom.

"Peter," she said, "fetch a chair and sit near me. Not on the sofa by my side; then I cast only side-glances at you. I want to face you, Peter."

Peter brought a Chippendale chair from the opposite side of the room and placed it within easy distance.

Madam wasted no time in amenities. She read wretched uneasiness in his face and his frank greenish eyes. "My husband has told me that you have asked for my Angela. No doubt, by now, he has told you of my approval of the marriage."

Peter's mouth was dry. He tried to speak but failed. Instead he dropped on one knee and kissed her hand. "I will endeavour to make her happy," he said, so low that Madam bent her dark head to hear him.

"That I know," she said. When he got to his feet, she held his hand a moment, closing her other hand over his. "That I know. I have only to look into your eyes and see in them honesty and loyalty, Peter Huntley, and they are what I want for my child."

He sat down again, feeling more at ease as he murmured, "Thank you, Madam."

"There are things I wish to discuss," she said.

"I have already gone to Mr. Barker, Madam. He will draw up the settlement papers."

She waved her hand with a gesture, waving away the thought of money and legal papers. "That is a matter for you and the senator. My husband tells me you have been most generous. It is of Angela I wish to speak. My daughter is charming, but she is also a wilful, headstrong girl, selfish, considering only her own wishes. I wish you to understand this. She and the senator clash, being unable to understand each other. That troubles me. The senator has been the kindest, most considerate of men, to me and to Angela. If she had been his own daughter, he could have done no more than he has."

Francisca paused a moment, fanning herself with a black lace fan with such languid grace that Peter was fascinated. There was an art in the use of the fan, known only to women of Latin blood.

"It is about her father I wish to speak." She shut the fan with a snap, as though breaking through some hesitancy, some barrier of speech. "Angela has built up a father who never existed, a romantic, quixotic gentleman of Spain, who had no counterpart in Miguel Gonsalvo. I have tried to tell her he was neither a god nor even a demigod." She laughed a little, without mirth. "I have not succeeded. She conceives herself something of a duchess in disguise. I have done wrong in allowing her to live in a dream, but I am Spanish, Peter, and indolent. . . ." She left him to infer the rest.

After a time, she went on: "I agree with the senator. She needs a firm hand, firm and just. We think you have such a hand."

She regarded him with her wise dark eyes. "I do not mean that we wish to shirk our duty toward Angela, but we both feel that we should announce the betrothal at once." The inflection of her voice asked a question.

A dusky red had spread over Peter's cheeks. "Madam, nothing could pleasure me more."

Francisca smiled. Peter thought he had never seen a face so lighted by an inner radiance. "I want you to be happy, Peter. I want happiness for my daughter. I see happiness for her, through you."

"Thank you, Madam. Thank you. Believe me, I want nothing so much as Angela's happiness."

"She is so young, so unwise. It is the way of the Anglo-Saxon, this *naïveté*. In my country it is different. But I have reared my girl as her friends and companions are reared, in total ignorance of the world or its evils. You must teach her." She leaned forward and covered one of his hands with her warm fingers. "I see myself in Angela, my wayward, headstrong self. I would not listen to the wisdom of my aunts, who reared me. I married against their wishes. I had a turbulent life—wild love, and great despair. Only in these last few years have I found tranquillity."

Peter pressed her hands in his strong clasp. In those few words she had told him the secret of her wisdom, her detachment. She had lived through wild love, great despair . . . then tranquillity.

They heard voices in the hall below, footsteps running up the stairs. Cecily burst into the room, her curls flying, her skirts swirling. Angela followed, walking more slowly. She paused when she saw Peter. He thought for a moment she would turn and run away. But Madam's quiet voice held her.

"Come, Angela. Cecily, Peter has consented to dine with us. Run and tell your aunt that we have guests. I have arranged with her for the senator to bring in a friend or two." She turned to Peter, smiling at him. "As for Peter Huntley, he is *my* guest, my honoured guest."

Peter bowed from the waist, so deeply that he did not see Angela's face turn white, or her trembling fingers catch the knob of the door.

The senator came in, bringing with him Adam Rutledge and Parson Earle. Miss Hezzie, Dr. Armitage's sister, who kept house for him and watched over Cecily to the best of her ability, joined Madam, to greet the guests. Shortly afterward they went downstairs to supper. Angela and Cecily hurried down from the third floor to join the party in the dining-room. Cecily had changed to a ruffled, sprigged muslin, Angela to a cerulean blue with white fichu folded across her full bosom, and held in place with a cameo pin. Little black ribands were tied about her neck and wrists and the front of her bodice was laced with the same. Her blue-black hair was piled high, with two long curls drooping over one white shoulder. She carried her head high, and her face was expressionless.

Cecily kept glancing at her. "I declare you look as cold as a piece of marble, Angela. Whatever ails you?"

Angela caught Cecily's hands. "Your hands are cold too," Cecily exclaimed, "cold as ice! I do declare I believe you have a chill. I'll get Aunt Hezzie to get you a dose out of Father's dispensary."

Angela's grasp was tight on Cecily's thin arm. "No, don't speak of it. It is nothing. Nothing."

"And your eyes are shining and your cheek-bones have red spots."

Angela said, "I've put belladonna in my eyes to make them bright, and French rouge on my cheeks." She spoke strangely, almost hysterically. "I saw the actress do that—put drops in her eyes."

"You are fibbing, Angela. I can tell it. You want to seem very grown up, and make me out a child."

Angela paused, her foot on the last step. The others were already in the dining-room. "I am grown up. I am. Two men are in love with me."

Cecily widened her eyes. "Two?" she whispered. "Two?"

"Cecily!" Miss Hezzie's voice cut short the girl's exclamation. "Hurry, Angela, hurry," she cried.

They crossed the hall swiftly. At the door Angela paused. She let Cecily hurry to her place at table, while she moved without haste, her blue skirts sweeping the floor. She has poise and proud bearing, Peter thought, pleased with her dignity. Cecily sat at the head of the table, in place of her father.

"Will you please say grace, Mr. Earle?" Miss Hezzie said, when they were all seated.

He smiled, bowed slightly to Cecily. "Shall we allow the youngest present to ask the Lord's blessing on our food?"

A soft blush covered the girl's fair skin. She bowed her fair head.

> "Come, Lord Jesus, our Guest to be.
> Bless this food, bestowed by Thee. Amen."

The Parson spread his napkin across his stomach and tucked it under his coat. "I've always thought that a choice old custom, to allow the youngest to say grace. Young and close to God . . ."

Quick tears came to Cecily's eyes. Her aunt noticed and spoke to her. "Cecily! Miranda is waiting to serve you." Cecily blinked, and helped herself to a chicken-back, which she loathed.

The senator asked Parson Earle what he thought of Will Hooper's talk.

"Excellent. Excellent. But he didn't go far enough. We should not mince words. We should speak boldly and call a spade a spade."

"And a Tory a Tory." Adam Rutledge smiled.

"Exactly, Adam. That's what I mean. One day I may do it myself, from the altar steps." A wide smile broke across his ruddy face. "There would be precedents—driving the thieves and money-changers from the Temple."

Miss Hezzie gasped. "You never would, Mr. Earle . . . why, it would be . . ."

"Sacrilegious? No, I don't think so. The church should lead the people, not be a follower."

The senator could not restrain an exclamation of approval. "You are correct in that, Parson! I hope I'm sitting in my pew when you give that fighting sermon."

"I trust that you will be."

Miss Hezzie shook her head, then turned her mind to the service, which was slow. The sillabub was finally brought in, fluffed in a silver punch-bowl. It was eaten with relish. She was about to give the signal for the ladies to retire, when Madam Ferrier leaned forward and spoke something to her husband in a low voice.

He nodded and smiled. "Yes," he said, "yes, indeed. Very appropriate." Then, turning to the guests, he said, "With Miss Hezzie's permission, I have had some vintage wine sent in, a shipment we got from France recently, on the *Two Sisters*." He nodded to Miranda. A moment later the senator's man Jacob came into the room, carrying a bottle cradled tenderly in his arms. Miranda set delicate teardrop wine-glasses at each place. The senator poured half a glass, then set it aside; poured a second glass full and tasted it, nodding in approbation. Jacob took the bottle and carried it around the table for each gentleman to fill his own glass.

"And the ladies also," the senator said. "This is an occasion for the ladies to join us."

Angela glanced at her mother. Peter could not take his eyes from her, she was so beautiful. What was it he read in her eyes, as she met her mother's? Was it fear? He could not be sure.

The senator rose and lifted his glass. Bowing to Angela, then to Peter, he said, "Tonight my wife and I request you to drink a toast to our daughter Angela Gonsalvo and to Captain Peter Huntley, and wish them long and continued happiness in their betrothal."

Chairs scraped. Everyone rose. Glasses were raised, astonishment and congratulations voiced. . . . Cecily's reproachful voice was high and clear: "Angela, you didn't tell me!"

Angela sat looking down at her clasped hands. A slow flush went from her throat to her dark hair.

Peter got up, somehow, his knees weak. He had not known it would come this way, so soon, before he had talked to her. He said something, thanking the senator and Madam Ferrier for their kindness and confidence in trusting their beautiful daughter to him. He would keep the trust. Adam told him later that he behaved very creditably, when he went to Madam first, kissed her hand, then to Angela whose hand was cold, but who smiled as he pressed his lips to her fingers.

There were more toasts, and then the ladies left the room, the gentlemen standing until they had crossed the hall. The men sat down and the senator called for the port.

Peter managed to keep his head clear by turning down his glass after the third time the decanter went around. No one noticed his lack of conversation. The talk was of paper money, inflation, prices and Clem Hull.

The Parson said, "There is a man going wrong, who should be a strong leader. He has a fiery heart. He hates fiercely, but he could be turned into just as fiery a patriot, once he could forget his fancied wrongs."

"He hates the Pollocks," the senator said reflectively, looking at the crimson wine in his glass. "He hates most of the people of our class, but that is general hatred of a group. The Pollocks—that is different; it is a single unvarying hatred. Sometimes I think life may end tragically for Clem Hull."

"That would be a pity." The Parson tamped his pipe. "And if it should happen, we are all to blame—you and I and all of us."

"He is a dissenter, isn't he, Parson?" Ferrier inquired.

"Of course. He could never subscribe to any established order. Naetheless, I would rather put that man on the right track than save half my parish."

"Don't let the Vestry hear you," Adam admonished.

Peter thought, She will be mine, my wife. Tomorrow I will ask Madam when we may wed, perhaps soon, before I go to the western mountains. . . . She is so young; I will be very tender.

The men were pushing back their chairs. When they went up to the drawing-room, Peter made his way to the sofa where Angela sat alone. "May I sit beside you?" he asked.

"Pray do." Her voice was calm, without a tremor.

Peter sat down, not near her because her full blue skirt took three-quarters of the little sofa. He spoke a few words about the flag celebration. She answered politely. She was as far away as Cassiopeia. This would not do. He lowered his voice. "You cannot know what happiness it gives me, that your mother and father have consented to our betrothal."

"Thank you, Captain Huntley."

"I love you so deeply, Angela . . . so deeply."

Her eyes moved quickly to see if others overheard. "Thank you, Captain Huntley," she repeated, her voice almost a whisper.

Peter felt he could not pass the barrier that lay between them. He would be patient—a step at a time.

The other men were standing. Peter rose also. He kissed Angela's hand, and went to Miss Hezzie to make his manners. Last he bowed over Madam Ferrier's hand.

"Have patience, dear Peter," she said, and kissed him on the forehead.

"Thank you, Madam," he said, overcome by her graciousness.

In the hall he and Adam paused to buckle on their sword-belts. The senator went to the door with them.

"We are driving to Strawberry Hill, and spending the night there. Remember, Peter, Saturday we go to River Plantation."

"I won't forget, sir. Is Miss Angela going with you tonight?" he asked.

"No. She had promised to stay with Ann Pollock. Perhaps you will see her tomorrow, eh, Peter?" He put his hand on Peter's shoulder in a fatherly way. "It gives me delight to think that your dear father would have been pleased with this marriage, eh?"

"I am sure he would have been most happy, sir."

"Good night, all." The senator stood for a moment on the portico. Peter and Adam were halfway to the corner of Broad Street when the door closed.

Adam said, "I'm going to go over to Nat Allen's. I'll come down to O'Malley's later. Don't wait for me, Peter."

Peter crossed the Green. By now a good part of the crowd had been drawn away and were drinking beer, down at Joseph Hewes's shipyard. Each house that faced the Green and along Broad and King

Streets was illuminated and had its quota of guests. People were moving about, laughing and talking. The play was in progress at the lower end of the Green, where a stage had been rigged up with ever-green trees, pine and juniper as wings and dressings-rooms. Great pine-knot flares gave light for stage and actors, leaving the audience in shadow.

He walked down and stood at the back of the crowd that was seated on the grass. A pantomime sword-play of some sort was going on—two actors in the costumes of Court gentlemen. One of them seemed familiar to him, a tall, broad-shouldered fellow, almost as tall as Peter. He wore a small dark moustache and a minute goatee. Peter puzzled for several minutes, then dismissed the likeness as of no moment.

He left the Green to go to O'Malley's. He was walking on air, drunk, not with wine but with dreams. Halfway to Horniblow's he fell in with Samuel Johnston, Penelope Dawson and the Iredells.

Pene tucked her small hand under his arm. "I've been enquiring where you were, Peter. I take it very much amiss that you haven't called on me since your return. I don't believe you wanted to see me."

Peter pressed her hand. "Indeed I did want to see you, Madam Dawson. I told Major Rutledge I was bound to go to Eden House before I left again."

"We'll save you the journey. I'm staying at Hayes during these festivities. What did you think of them, Peter?"

"I thought everything went off well, particularly the Tea-party Ladies, and their flags. It looked very nice to see them, like a garden of roses, standing on Madam King's lawn fluttering their flags as the great flag went up to the full staff. And Mr. Hooper's speech was magnificent."

Iredell joined in. "I think it was Will Hooper at his best."

Pene said, "I thought the same. I believe, Jemmy, you could make such a charge to the Grand Jury, so it will get into the records."

"Do you think it that good, Pene?"

"I do, indeed. Particularly true when he said, 'Things of more consequence seem to hang in awful suspense. The operations of war are rather menacing than active, and prospect of peace more gloomy than could be wished for, though it is not altogether out of sight. I do not despair, however, of one day seeing peace, and on terms honourable and satisfactory.'"

"That is not my opinion," Johnston interrupted. "I don't hold with the men who think there is still hope of a negotiated peace, even though the great Franklin is one of them. I think it will be many years before we can come to peace with Great Britain. Unless the French or the Spanish send us more men, we are undone."

"We need something to stir us up, perhaps," Pene said.

"We'll be stirred considerably when our boys march away next week," Johnston answered. His voice was sharp. "I am disgusted with our people. They think of nothing but what affects them as individuals. They cannot see the Revolution as a whole, nor can they work in harmony in the Congress. Joe Hewes is desolated. He thinks we are not capable of working as a united body. We spend days in Philadelphia squabbling over inconsequential things."

"Joe is apt to be pessimistic," Iredell observed. "It is his failing health."

"Nonsense! It is his common sense that speaks. Remember how he had to struggle to get a few vessels for Captain John Paul Jones? He believed in Jones, but he had to use all his trading power to get Jones a ship."

They had crossed the hollow and come to the Iredell house. The moon was high. It cast light through the trees and made dappled, moving shadows on the lawn. The noise of the merry-making was far away. Peter placed a chair for Penelope and sat down at her feet, his long legs hanging over the side of the gallery. Madam Iredell went inside to see that all was well with the children.

Johnston continued his talk with Iredell. "Multiply the disaffection in this little village by a thousand and you will see what is happening over the country. I believe with Hooper and Hewes that the war will be won from the sea. Without vessels and a navy, we cannot possibly hope for victory." They went into the house to mix a drink.

Penelope said abruptly, "Have you seen Angela since your return, Peter?"

"Yes. I saw her tonight." He paused, doubtful whether or not to tell her of the supper at Cupola House.

She said, "I talked with the senator last night. He spoke of you. He cannot contain his pleasure. I have never seen him so jovial—if the senator can be jovial."

Peter leaned nearer. His head almost touched her knees. He started to speak, but her words came first. "Did you go to the play?" she enquired.

"No—that is, I stood at the back for a few minutes."

"I thought I saw Angela there. She goes to almost every perform-

ance of the plays." Somehow Penelope managed to put significance
into the simple sentence.

Peter thought he felt the light touch of her hand on his hair, but
he was not sure. He felt his affection for her growing. He felt warm
and expansive toward the whole world.

After a moment she said, "I want to walk down to Penelope
Barker's. Will you escort me?"

"With pleasure," he said. He slid to the ground and walked around
the steps.

They walked along the block back of the gaol. There seemed to be
a number of men in the gaol yard, shouting and cursing.

"I'm afraid Mr. Horniblow's small beer has taken effect," Peter
remarked.

Penelope's easy stride was almost as long as his own. She kept
looking up at his profile, the long straight nose and strong cleft chin,
the mouth with its indented corners, like the portraits of the early
Scots.

"Bend down your head, Peter," she said. They stood under the full-
leafed shadow of a bay tree. Even the moon did not penetrate the
shadows. As he stooped, she pressed her lips against his forehead.
"Dear Peter, I wish I could believe that you were going to get everything you deserve in life."

There was wistfulness in her voice, an immense tenderness. He put
his arm about her and raised her chin, cupped in his hand. Slowly he
bent his head until his lips met hers, a long kiss, of affection and
heart-warmth. Her lips were soft and yielding under his.

After a moment she turned her head. He released her.

"I do not know why," he said simply; "only that this is always my
feeling for you. My heart goes out to you, Penelope. There has never
been another woman for whom I felt such affection."

"But not love." Her voice was very low, scarcely audible.

Peter didn't answer. They moved on, out of the shadow. When
they arrived at Thomas Barker's, Penelope's little drawing-room was
crowded, and overflowed into the gallery and garden. A punch-bowl,
set on a table in the dining-room, was the centre of attraction. Penelope herself sat on her little satin sofa, dressed in a blue silk gown
turned back over a lace petticoat. Angela Ferrier, in a gown of some
dark material, stood in front of her, her back to Peter. Neither woman
noticed their entrance. Madam Barker's clipped words came to them
very clearly.

"No, Angela, I will not allow you to borrow Lord Craven's chaise. You know I use it only for the greatest occasions. I don't care if it is only to go to Strawberry Hill. You can't have it, Angela."

Angela said something they could not hear, but they could see the slow flush rising up her throat.

"Why don't you get Ann Pollock's chaise, or Dr. Cathcart's coach, or the one from Hayes?"

"Cullen is using theirs," Angela said. "And I have always thought of you as a good friend, closer than . . ." Her voice dwindled off.

Peter tried to see how much Penelope Dawson had heard, but she had drifted away. He didn't want to be in a position of eavesdropping, but he could not move backward into the hall, because of others coming in.

Penelope Barker spoke again. He assumed she was either angry or outraged that Angela should ask for the loan of the chaise. "It's the finest vehicle in the Albemarle. My dear James left it to me. It was ordered for him by his relative, the Earl, and I don't propose to let it out for you and some play-actor to ride in."

At her words Angela seemed to lose height. Her shoulders sagged, her body swayed. For a moment Peter thought she would fall. He came forward quickly, to catch her. She drew herself erect.

"Ah, Captain Huntley!" Madam Barker exclaimed, her voice filled with cordiality. "When did you return to our overflowing village?"

As he answered her he glanced at Angela. Her face was livid. Her hand, when he took it in his to raise to his lips, was icy-cold. Her great dark eyes held astonishment which turned to fear under his gaze.

"Take Angela out for a dish of punch, Captain. She looks as though she were going to faint."

Peter crooked his elbow. She laid her hand on his arm, light as floating milkweed. "No," she said, as he started for the dining-room, "no, I don't want punch. Let us go into the garden. It is hot, so frightfully hot in the house." She took her hand from his arm and stood leaning against a pillar. A dark figure moved in the garden. Angela turned her head. "Would you mind stepping inside to see if you can find Ann Pollock, Captain? I promised to meet her here."

"Not at all," Peter said. As he entered the hall, he turned. Angela was running down the steps. She did not go to the gate but turned to the garden where he had seen the shadow of a man half obscured by low bushes.

"I thought I could never come to you," he heard her say.

Peter stood motionless. He would not search for Ann Pollock. It was only a trick to get away from him. He was slow to anger, but once aroused his temper was high.

Penelope Dawson met him as he went up the steps of the gallery. Her beautiful eyes were filled with compassion. He didn't want compassion.

She said, "We must go back now." He stood aside as she pressed her wide skirts through the door. He noticed for the first time that she was wearing a taffeta skirt of the Johnston tartan, with a light green velvet jacket, braided in gold. A silver brooch with a large cairngorm secured a floating scarf to her shoulder.

Peter thought of another scarf which he had worn continuously in the breast pocket of his uniform. He was a fool, a silly fool, but he would not give up. Not now.

They walked through the garden. Angela and her companion were nowhere to be seen. As they passed through the little wicket in the garden, which touched Horniblow's, Penelope said, "There goes Angela Ferrier with the play-actor. Whatever has come over the girl?"

Peter saw two figures moving swiftly under the flare at the street corner. He had a fleeting glimpse, then they were lost in the crowd on the Green.

Penelope stood watching the disappearing figures. "The silly girl! If I were Senator Ferrier I'd stop that. A play-actor!" Her face and her voice showed her scorn. "A play-actor!" She was silent; then she again repeated the word "play-actor," but without conviction. Looking at Peter, her beautiful, intelligent eyes alight, she added, "Peter, Peter, did you recognize him?"

Peter shook his head. "I didn't see his face."

"But his broad shoulders, his carriage, the line of his head! Disregard the moustache. Who is it?"

Peter said nothing. A shadow in the garden had meant nothing to him.

She leaned closer. "The merchant from Boston," she whispered. "Is it not the merchant from Boston, Jeremiah Morse?"

Flag Day was over at last. The orderly citizens had trudged homeward to bed, sleeping children in arms of fathers and mothers and older brothers, others stumbling along, hanging to fathers' hands or coat-tails.

The flag, which had been hauled down by Southey Wren's platoon, lay carefully folded on a table in the Council Chamber of the Courthouse, where the women's committee, headed by Mrs. Elizabeth King, Mary Jones and Anne Haughton, had covered it with a large sheet of pure white linen. At the last the sky, dramatically red across the whole horizon, seemed to reflect the colours of the flag, with white thunderheads chasing swiftly across the blue of the upper sky to meet the crimson lower down.

Only at the barbecue pits and in the taverns did talk run high, in particular near the shipyard of that frail man who laboured in Philadelphia, Joseph Hewes, making his endeavour, far beyond his strength, to weld an unruly, selfish Congress into an instrument of statesmanship, instead of a hotbed of selfish political factions.

At the barbecue at the shipyard, where the lesser folk gathered, Clem Hull took charge. Southey Wren, well satisfied with the showing of his men before General Lamb, sat on a fish bench, drinking quietly. The more Southey drank, the more silent and morose he became. The more Clem drank, the louder-mouthed, the more belligerent he grew. The people were bound for a good time. Why not? The drinks and the food were free! And war was no more than a few men marching away now and then.

CHAPTER

18

THE GREEN

PETER could not sleep. His mind, active with plans for the future, refused to give way. He sat up in bed. The bright moonlight fell across Adam's face and yellow hair. He sleeps the sleep of a child, Peter thought. He got up and walked out on the little balcony that overlooked the kitchen-garden of the inn, and into the garden of the Pollock home.

There, under that roof turned silver by the moon, lay Angela, sleeping. Sleeping? He wondered, the deep anger gnawing at him, twisting his vitals into knots of pain. Why had she accepted him—then tricked him to run to meet another? Lights were burning in the second floor of the Pollock house. He went back into the room and held his watch to the moonlight. Half after one. He felt an impulse to go out to walk along the water in the moonlight. His thoughts returned to the woman. Was there in her any sweetness, or was he, in his determination to have her at all hazards, pushing his way toward an unhappy marriage? He had always had chivalrous views of such matters. Theory was one thing, practice another. Perhaps she had some girlish affection for a village youth, some abortive love that would never come to flower.

He buckled on his sword. There were ruffians about the quiet village. Better be armed. Adam had warned him that disaffected soldiers were straggling up from the South, or down from the North, greedy for money, even food—a pitiful condition for men who had tried to fight.

The Green was quiet, all lights put out except that from the great iron brazier in front of the Courthouse, where the watch kept a blazing fire; the wind would blow chill toward morning and false dawn. From down the street he heard the watch cry: "Two o'clock. All's well! . . . Two o'clock. All's well!"

Peter took the path that followed the shore up to Queen Anne's Creek. The lights still burned in the upper windows at Cullen Pollock's. A few couples were still out strolling among the trees, hunting the dark shadows. Once he all but stepped on a man lying on the grass, his body shielding a girl. The man cursed. The girl laughed, frightened. Peter hurried on, out of the passionate darkness into a more open path. Boats along the creek held lovers. Beyond the boathouse a body leaped into the dark water, a crescent of white silvered by the moon, and swam, splashing in the dark water of the creek.

Midsummer and madness. A night for lovers . . . and he walked alone.

In the far distance he heard a long, low cry. He stopped to listen, alert, as a soldier is alert for the unknown. He laughed to himself—a loon, or a whistling swan, or some night-bird flying low along the water. It came again, beating a certain cadence, a rhythm like the rise and fall of far-away breakers on a lonely beach.

He turned slowly, retracing his steps. He heard another sound, definable: the rattle and clank of harness and the turning of wheels, a carriage coming down King Street, to stop in front of the still lighted tavern. A figure emerged and went inside.

Peter was now on the Green in front of the Pollocks' house. The sound he had heard before was louder. It came from the water, near the shipyard. He remembered the kegs of beer he had seen down there earlier in the day. The celebration must be still going on among the commonalty. He saw the Pollocks' door open a crack, the thin streamer of light from within, then open wider. A man stepped out, followed by two muffled figures.

Peter moved on, not wanting to be caught hanging about under the fair one's balcony, like any country yokel. He stayed in the centre of the Green, walking in the heavy shadows cast by the trees. His mind seized some semblance, a familiar figure, tall, erect. He linked it with the words Penelope Dawson had said—the merchant from Boston. At the time he had brushed the idea of any resemblance aside, until Penelope had confessed it was just a flash across her mind. Now he was not so sure . . . the turn of the shoulders, the erect soldierly bearing . . .

He walked slowly toward the tavern. Several chaises were at the rack, the Negro coachmen beside them, waiting to drive befuddled masters to their plantations. Then he saw Cullen Pollock, standing as though he had just descended from his carriage. He looked toward his home. Then he put his head inside the carriage as though to speak to someone.

At that moment Peter became conscious of the noise that he had pushed aside from his mind. It forced its way to the front again, resounded against his ears: the roar of an angry mob! He had heard such a noise before, in Paris, in London. It was a sound to terrify the stoutest soul. What did it mean now?

He heard Cullen Pollock call, "Hurry! Hurry!" He was holding the door open. A cloaked figure darted up the street and ran toward the carriage.

Rage boiled up in Peter. A *merchant from Boston!* He threw his foot forward. The man sprawled on the street. His three-cornered hat went one way, his cloak open. He jumped up. In the light from the watch's brazier, Peter saw him, wig off, little moustache and goatee awry. There was no mistaking Anthony Allison. Then a voice, Angela's, terrified, crying, "Anthony! Anthony!" and Ann Pollock's, "Be quiet, I say!"

Peter had his sword out. His rage had reached the boiling point. He cried:

"Draw, my fine fellow—this time a gentleman's weapon, not the butt of a pistol!" Peter's voice was almost gay.

For a moment Allison's surprise held him. "Huntley! Damn you to hell!" he shouted, drawing his sword.

Cullen Pollock ran toward him. "Don't be a fool! Let this go! Get into the carriage, man!"

Peter cried, "Stand back, Pollock! No interference here!"

The man in the coach leaned forward. "For Christ's sake! Are you mad? I won't wait."

Allison cried, "On guard, Huntley! This time it will be a gentleman's fight. I vow I regret the butt of the pistol."

Peter smiled. From the corner of his eye he saw Angela and Ann Pollock close together, their frightened faces lighted by the glowing brazier.

Back and forth the swords flashed. Peter thought, She sees him now, with disguise awry, moustache tip-turned, goatee half gone. "Your face slips, Mr. Allison. Watch out that I don't cut the play-actor's beard from your face." Peter laughed and forgot the women.

Allison was no mean swordsman. A thrust in the nick of time.

Cullen passed back of the brazier and disappeared in the darkness. The carriage horses pranced and pawed. The coachman on the box cracked his whip.

Peter sent Allison's wig flying into the brazier, where it sizzled and went into flame.

"Goddam but he's a bra' swordsman!" cried Allison, hot for the fight. "I mistook him for a parlor-boy. I apologize, Captain." He laughed and thrust suddenly.

Peter caught the sword almost at the point, and ran his blade upward to the hilt, sending it spinning. Allison clapped his hand to his arm. He caught up the sword from the ground and sprang for the carriage with incredible speed.

"First blood for Captain Huntley," he shouted. "'Bout deferred until some future time." He leaped to the carriage. The coachman wheeled the horses.

Peter swayed as he stood. The fellow had nicked him in the shoulder before he turned the thrust. He unbuttoned his coat and thrust his hand underneath. It came out damp.

"Damnation!" he muttered. His knees gave way. He slid down, his back against a tree trunk until he sat on the ground, his legs straight out in front of him. He had no will to move. He seemed to see things through a haze . . . the smoke of the brazier. Men's voices, hot in anger, half-drunken men singing down the street to the beat of a little snare drum:

> "Said he was a Tory.
> Said I couldn't catch him.
> Now I've gone and got him
> Riding a pole to glory."

Clem Hull leading—or was it? His face was blurred. Perhaps it was two Clem Hulls—funny, he never heard there were twins—his big hammer over his brawny shoulder . . . crying for blood . . . Tory blood. . . . The women's skirts whirling in the wind—or was it a crimson scarf beneath his horse's hoofs? Angela crying, "The other carriage, quick!" She was running, running. . . . Ann Pollock dragging at her crimson cloak—or was it a crimson scarf, flying in the wind?

Angela on the box, whipping the horses: "Run! Run! Run!" Merchant from Boston: "Run! Run!" Down the street horses galloping

. . . crowds shouting, "Here it is! Here is Pollock's goddam coach!" Clem Hull's mighty figure grown to herculean size in the flames of the watchman's brazier. Black figures surrounding the coach that stayed behind.

Splintering wood following mighty blows, the clang of metal. The watch-fire leaping into great flames, licking paint from the coach doors, blistering paint.

Clem Hull's giant voice shouting, shouting, "Where's Tory Pollock? Where's the damned spy? Give me Pollock to ride on a rail! The Boston spy and his doxy—they've got away. Dinna ye see them riding in t'other carriage, you fool?"

A man's voice, Adam Rutledge's, calling, "Peter! . . . Peter Huntley, he's been hurt! Run to the tavern for Williamson."

"Adam! Adam, get your horse and ride after her."

Who was speaking? A woman's voice, far off and dimly heard. "For God's sake, Adam, ride down the Suffolk Road and take her away from Allison. Do you hear: she drove the coach with Allison and another man. I tell you, *ride*, overtake her! Ride! Ride! Ride!"

The words beat into his brain, a great aching throb that enveloped his whole body. He tried to rise. Ride, ride, he must ride down the Suffolk Road . . . ride.

He sank down. The dancing figures around the watch-fire melted into one Gargantuan figure and then began to sink down into a dark pit that had no beginning and no end.

Peter woke up cursing. A voice said, "There, there, lad, it's not that bad."

Peter swore again, lustily. "Twice!" he bellowed. "Twice, and got away with it!"

Adam's voice answered, "He's not cursing the pain, Doctor. I think 'tis wounded vanity that troubles him. This man Morse, or Allison, has twice laid him low."

"Ah, that's it. I thought 'twas the wound, which is bad enough, but not fatal, though I don't see how he stayed on his feet, bleeding like a stuck pig. A clean wound."

"Not so deep as a well, or so wide as a church-door; but 'tis enough," Peter murmured, still a little dazed.

"Ah, the lad quotes Mr. Shakespeare. But don't worry, you won't die of it, like poor Mercutio."

Peter opened his eyes wide. He was propped, held upright by a heap of pillows, stripped naked to the waist. Dr. Williamson was bending over him, winding bandages over his shoulder and under his arm.

"He didn't know it. By God, I didn't fall at his feet, the dirty bastard."

"Tut-tut. Don't let your vanity sink so deep." The doctor chuckled.

Peter looked around. Adam Rutledge was seated at the window. A gentle breeze stirred the white curtains. Birds were carolling, a thrush with wilful, beautiful song. The world was gay.

Other things came tumbling into this mind, a whirlpool of doubts and misgivings assailed him. The dim fleeting vision of Angela standing on the box, lashing the horses, her cloak flying. Angela? He groaned and looked at Adam for explanation. He shook his head, slightly, and glanced at the doctor, who was standing bending over Peter, his ear pressed against his chest.

Dr. Williamson lifted his head, returned his great turnip watch to his waistcoat and buttoned his uniform coat. "I seared the edges of the wound, Huntley, as soon as I got to you last night. It is as clean as a hound's tooth. Now if you keep away from swamps and drainage water and don't get chills and ague, you'll be good as new, as soon as the wound heals."

He sat down in the chair beside the bed and crossed his legs comfortably. "Well, I've bound up most of the wounds of last night's rioting: split heads, a broken arm or two. Reminds me of what they tell me of early days, eh, Adam? Sword-play on the Courthouse steps. That was in Burrington's time. Burrington was Governor under the Lords Proprietors, and the people rose up against him and put him out; but he was resilient, that Burrington, and a fighter. He got himself reappointed when the Crown bought out the Lords Proprietors around 1729, and came sailing back to push Sir Richard Everard out. He and Everard fought with swords on the Green and on the Courthouse steps. Roistered around, did that Burrington, banging on doors of good village folk, demanding that they come out and fight."

Williamson laughed, a deep stomach laugh that shook his whole frame. His dark eyes sparkled. "Damme if I don't like that fellow Burrington! A lusty Governor is better than a milksop. We've had both kinds in our day. The good people of Albemarle have always been quick to rise up and put out the Governors they didn't like—

always, since 'way back in 1677 when Culpepper kidnapped one
Miller and held him prisoner."

He looked at Adam. "Strange how the military disappeared last
night . . . vanished."

Adam smiled enigmatically but said nothing.

"Well, it's a good thing they threw Cullen in the gaol," the doctor
went on. "If they hadn't, no telling what might have happened. All
he lost was a comfortable chaise—and chaises are hard to come by,
these war-times. I heard Jemmy Iredell is spitting with rage."

"Mr. Iredell believes in law and order," Adam observed dryly.

"So do I. So do I. But enforcing law in times of war is another
thing. If they had asked me what to do, I'd have put the town under
martial law and clapped them all in gaol. Clem Hull first of all."

"But you said there weren't any officers in the village," Adam reminded him.

"I wonder how that spy got away," Williamson commented after a
moment. "They say he vanished." He paused. His eyes, under his
heavy brows, bored into Adam's as though to draw an answer from
him. "Something queer about this. Something damned queer."

"How long will I be here?" Peter asked.

"You can go as soon as the catgut in the stitches rots and the knots
can be pulled out. I'll leave that to Armitage." He glanced at Adam.
"You can get up any time you feel like it. I'm leaving for the Dismal,
with Gregory, this afternoon after dinner. Armitage came in this
morning for a sennight's rest. He will look after your friend here."

Adam said, "I'm going myself, day after tomorrow." He glanced
toward Peter.

"He'll be all right. Armitage can move him over to his house. Yes,
perhaps that will be best."

Peter protested. He thought he would be quite comfortable where
he was.

Adam said, "I'll leave Herk to care for him. He's as good as a doctor.
He'll make *Mankwala* over him and cure him in no time."

Peter grinned ruefully. He wasn't accustomed to having people
make plans for him.

Williamson rose and shook hands. His grip was strong enough to
make Peter wince. Adam walked down the hall with him. Peter heard
him say, "Young and strong . . . the Scots are like that . . . a trifle to
one side, and it would have been enough, like Mercutio's wound."

Peter waited impatiently for Adam's return. There were questions to be asked. Adam came into the room. He closed the door and drew up a chair.

"Angela Ferrier is at Strawberry Hill, with her people, where she belongs," he began. "I overtook them before they got to the Sand Hill Road. The coach was beside the road, Angela huddled inside weeping. Over and over she kept saying, 'He wouldn't take me with him. He wouldn't take me with him.'"

Peter groaned and covered his eyes with his arm.

Adam said, "I thought you would want to know what happened."

"I do. Certainly I do. But it doesn't make it any easier. I must see the senator. I will release her. I cannot . . ."

Adam said nothing. In their silence, the song of the thrush forced its way into the quiet room, a rich sound from a full heart.

Adam said, "It is wearisome to give advice or take it, Peter. But you have a head full of good sense, if you but exercise it. In the first place I gather from what she said that the girl has been infatuated with Allison, to give him his right name. A handsome man, ten years older, an officer—a young, impressionable girl, romantic and passionate, unhappy at home, though the good God knows why she should be—cannot you see what happens?"

"Only too well," Peter said ruefully. "Only too well!"

"Think of the first time you were in love—probably the pretty daughter of one of your father's gillies."

Peter grinned. "'Tis true. My father shipped me off to visit my grandmother for the summer."

"Your heart was broken. You were the most dejected of Highland lads, I'll be bound."

"I was fair grieved to death."

"Well, reverse that, and see how unimportant this affair of Angela's becomes. The man is a fascinating devil, handsome as a god." He paused, smiling with a certain knowledge.

"And I am—?"

Adam paid no heed to the inference. "So I advise, without being asked, to 'hold your fire.' Think it over calmly, if you can. We don't marry for love, my lad. We marry for a home and for children. Let love grow and ripen out of the familiarity of home life and the conjugal bed."

Peter had no words. Adam got up. "I've several letters to write. I suppose your dispatches yesterday gave you a hint that changes are in the air."

Peter nodded. "Gates?"

"I don't know. I think so. Certainly he is not the general to cope with the enemy."

"But he defeated Burgoyne."

Adam raised his eyebrows. "Perhaps Burgoyne defeated himself; at least that is the considered opinion of some of our other generals. At any rate we wait for orders. When will the wedding be?" he asked casually, as he brushed his hat with a small whisk.

"I don't know. I hope before I have to leave." Peter was surprised at himself for saying the words.

Adam nodded. "Splendid!" He put on his coat and wound the red sash around his trim waist. "Ferrier has been here twice to enquire about your welfare. I might add that he knows nothing about Angela's performance last night, or Morse's appearance. Damn it all, I *will* call the fellow Morse!"

Peter said, "I am glad. I would not want Madam her mother to know." He swung his legs over the side of the bed. To his astonishment, his knees did not bear the weight of his body.

"You lost a quantity of blood," Adam told him. "Better stay on the pillows."

"No," Peter said determinedly. "I'm going to get dressed." After several attempts he made his slow way across the floor to the dressing-room.

Adam opened the door and called for Herk, who was waiting outside in the hallway.

Peter, struggling to dress, was glad to lean against Herk, to have his breeks pulled on. The shirt was managed, ripped to the elbow. Shaved and with hair rolled, he felt improved.

"You may bring in the breakfast," Adam told Herk, after Peter was settled comfortably in a chair at the window.

"A fine, romantic lover," Peter grumbled, as Adam eased a pillow under his arm. "I've been trying to figure how the bastard got under my guard."

"You were facing the fire," Adam observed.

"No. That's no excuse. He's a better swordsman, I'm afraid, but next time——"

Adam laughed. "There you go—next time, next time." His face sobered. "I think the less said about Morse, the better. We must catch up with the fellow. Why did he come back here?"

"Angela?" Peter suggested.

"No. Our gallant captain has his head firm on his shoulders. He wouldn't risk his life and liberty just to catch a glimpse of a girl. I wager his heart's not too deeply involved."

Peter said nothing. Adam's words were comforting.

"The ship in which he made his escape must have been sailing north, not south to Charles Town. They probably set him ashore at the Virginia Capes. More than likely he will try to make his way south by land this time. I have a strong feeling he belongs to the Southern Army, since we know Ferguson, his old commander, is attached to Tarleton's command."

Peter said, "Had you thought that they might be watching for the lottery boxes?"

Adam nodded. "Yes, that occurred to me. It will be quite a sum of money."

"Yes. I didn't tell you, but my cases were ransacked when I was at Horniblow's and again since we have been here."

Adam sat down, tilted his chair against the wall, and contemplated the polished pine floor for some moments before he spoke. "I haven't asked you whether carrying the money was part of your assignment."

Peter shook his head. "No, but someone on the outside might think so. I do make the arrangements. Three boxes went to Paymaster-General Pierce, since I have been in North Carolina—one from Wilmington, one from New Bern, and the last when I was in Smithfield."

Adam got up and paced the floor. As he passed the pine chest between the front windows, he picked up a red scarf and laid it across Peter's lap. It had a cut in it and was stiff with blood. "I took it out from under your coat last night."

Peter made no comment. He folded it carefully and stuck it under the pillow. Angela's scarf had brought no luck to him—or did it absorb the blood and help keep the wound closed?

"No, he didn't know he'd nicked me. I'm damn glad of that."

"Still prideful?" Adam took up his hat. "I'm going across the Sound. Probably won't be back until tomorrow sometime. Herk will be in the hall if you want him. I have told him to sleep in the dressing-room tonight."

"Thank you. You don't know how I loathe this: acting like a sick cat, first at Eden House, now here. Damn his skin!"

Adam laughed at Peter's morose face. "Better forget him until your sword-arm is healed," he said, and went away.

He hadn't said so, but Peter had a feeling that Adam's trip across the Sound had something to do with Jeremiah Morse. He turned his head on the pillow and went to sleep.

Senator Ferrier came in to see Peter shortly before supper. He condoled Peter about his condition. "I'd have had all the ruffians in gaol, if I'd been on the Council. But no, they did no such thing. They took poor Cullen instead. All he said was he thought matters could be settled if half a dozen leaders on both sides were hanged. We've all made such remarks, or thought them. Said it up at Suffolk a few nights ago, at dinner. Some narrow-souled fellow from Tar River— Smith, was his name—was at the table. He went to Wells Cooper and said Pollock should be hanged himself and raised a great stir against him in Suffolk. Word went ahead and at every house where Cullen stopped, coming down, the story grew until they were made to believe his crimes were of such a nature that they were all intimidated by him. Such damned nonsense! Cullen's a fool to talk at all, but he's no knave. I think he has kept strictly to his oath of neutrality."

Peter wondered. It did not fit in with Pollock's housing the spy, Morse. But he held his tongue. Adam Rutledge said it was no good having the whole village let loose on a spy scare.

The senator was so perturbed about the Pollocks that he didn't mention Angela. Peter hesitated to bring up the question of marriage.

When he rose to leave, Ferrier said, "My wife and Angela have gone up the river. I'm to bring you up Saturday, when I return from a trip to Camden. I've talked with Williamson. He says it will do you no hurt. And my wife will take pleasure in nursing you to health. You look a bit peaked, it's true. It's a disgrace you got slashed by those rioters. A disgrace to our village."

Ferrier went away shortly after.

Peter sat staring out across the gardens to the Sound. Sailing-boats were scudding across the water, before a stiff breeze. A schooner from Cape Fear was being unloaded onto barges. He walked back and forth across the room, testing his strength. He called Herk. When the Zulu came into the room, Peter asked him to bring him a tankard of ale and a bite of cheese. After his ale he felt better and got himself undressed and into bed, without help. Tomorrow he would go out.

An idea had come to him. Perhaps he could obtain some trace of Morse if he visited the Red Lion.

He supped on egg and toast and a pot of hot French chocolate, and sent Herk away until bedtime. He tried to write a few letters but the pain in his shoulder put an end to writing, though he managed one to De' Medici, who was outside Charles Town, reciting the news of Morse and asking him to be on the look out.

It was quite dark outside. He lighted a bedside candle and took up a volume of *Tristram Shandy*, and was soon lost to the world without. When Peter laid down his book and looked at his watch it was a quarter of nine. He wound the watch absently and put it on the table. He noticed Herk had laid a second candle beside the brass candlestick. While he was debating whether he would snuff the candle and try to sleep, or further pursue the adventures of Corporal Trim, there was a light knock at the door.

He called, "Come in!" The door remained closed. Peter raised his voice. The door opened slowly. A woman's figure was silhouetted against the lighted hall.

"Captain Huntley?"

He recognized Ann Pollock's voice. "Please come in, Madam Pollock."

She closed the door behind her and advanced into the radius of the candlelight, without words.

Peter said, "Please sit down. It is good of you to come."

She said, "Thank you," and sat down in the chair near the bed. Peter wondered whether he had thrown his breeches on the chair or left them in the dressing-room.

"You must be wondering why I have come to call on you in your room, Captain Huntley. I hope you will forgive a distressed and harassed woman for behaving in a manner unbecoming to good breeding. My maid is outside the door."

She hesitated an instant, then rushed on before Peter could speak. "It is about Angela that I come. Please, please, Captain Huntley, do not take umbrage against her for her most imprudent conduct last night. I cannot think what inspired her to such recklessness. I implored her to stay with me at my house." She took a lace-edged kerchief from her little reticule, and touched her eyes. "I said I didn't know why she acted as she did. But I was not truthful. May I speak frankly?"

"Pray do, Madam Pollock. You may have the utmost confidence in my discretion."

"I am sure of that. It is that man Morse. He has charmed her, as a serpent charms a bird. She has no will but to do his bidding. Last night—oh, Peter Huntley, you cannot know what agony I suffered last night! And now, even now, my dear husband is shut up in the gaol, along with rascals and thieves and runaway slaves! Morse brought this on him. Cullen did not want to house him again—but he came, he and another one we had never seen. They came with the acting troupe. Why they are here, I do not know; I swear by the God of mercy that neither Cullen nor I know why they come. What could we do?" She paused, expecting some comment from Peter. Her distress was pitiful.

"I don't know, I'm sure I don't know, unless your husband turned them over to the military or the sheriff."

She shuddered. "I was afraid. It was Cullen's first thought to do that, but I begged him not to. You don't understand, Captain, that we have been hounded ever since the beginning of the war, because Cullen stayed loyal to his King. He took oath to have no part against the revolters, nor has he, but we are spied upon. Last night, after the rioters smashed and burned our carriage, they came to the house. It was past two in the morning. A body of men, the roughest, drunken common men, commanded by Captain Toole, came to take my husband prisoner. He refused to go. Then Toole, who is a stranger here, ordered a party of his men to seize Cullen, and he himself attempted to clutch Cullen by the collar. I fell on my knees to him. I entreated Cullen to go without force, for what could one unarmed man do against numbers? He complied with my entreaty and went, a prisoner, to the Courthouse."

She looked at Peter. In the flickering candlelight her face was that of a tragic mask. Her fine hands were clasped so tightly that the knuckles showed white.

"I waited, hoping they would bring him back. I thought surely Tom Benbury would have him released. But the longer I waited the more frightened I became. I remembered how many threats Clem Hull had made to tar and feather him. I ran down the street. I saw him standing at the Courthouse door, surrounded by a great number of armed men. I tried to enter, but they put their rough hands on my shoulders and pulled me off in such savage manner they tore the cape of my cloak. Ruffians in the street called, 'Push her down! Pull her off! Take her to the ducking-stool!' "

Tears gathered in her eyes at the thought of the indignity. "One guard, more human, gave me his arm into Horniblow's, where I was ordered searched for arms. I told them they were welcome to search me. I might be a fool but I wasn't a madwoman to carry arms to Mr. Pollock, who was so enraged I was sure he would have made use of them."

Tears overflowed and came down her cheeks. Peter felt sympathy for her and expressed it by saying that there was no dealing with a mob, for mobs are all mad, and therefore most dangerous to any cause.

"The committee, as they called themselves, wanted my husband to sign some paper. He refused. He would never sign anything under duress. So they took him to gaol. A kind friend carried me to Mr. Hardy's house, where I shall stay, afraid to go to my home. My husband lying in a filthy gaol, without friends to defend him!"

The room was silent. The noises of the street bore in on them: men talking, women's laughter, as they walked under the arch of bays along the shadowy street.

The tragedy of the woman who sat at his bedside troubled Peter. Again he saw, in this small village, the weaving of a larger pattern—thousands of injustices, in the name of patriotism. There is no middle ground in war; the Greeks' "moderation in all things" had no meaning now. He touched her hand, remembering Ferrier's words. "Do not despair. Your husband is safer where he is than in his home. Don't think you are without friends."

"Thank you," she said, her voice low. "I'm sorry to spill all my woes to you. Believe me, Captain Huntley, I had no such thought when I came here. I wanted only to speak of Angela. Let us return to her. I suppose Adam Rutledge told you how he found her, and took her home. Fortunately no one saw her or heard her, excepting Cecily Armitage, who was waiting up to let her into the house."

"Cecily!" Peter exclaimed.

"Don't worry. Cecily talks too much, but she is a loyal little creature. She would rather be drawn and quartered than betray her friend."

"I hope you are right," Peter said.

"What I want to tell you is that Angela is frightened, terrified, for fear her mother and father will find out that she is implicated in attempting to aid the escape of a spy." She spoke the word coldly, without sympathy. "I am done with this subterfuge. In my heart I have always loathed it—but I love my husband."

She got up. "Something happened last night to disillusion Angela. I know not what it was." She leaned over, laying her hand on Peter's shoulder. "Could you, in your heart, forgive her?"

"I have nothing to forgive—nothing. Last night I fought a man; the letting of blood made me dizzy, and very faint. I could see nothing."

Ann Pollock let her hand drop to her side. "I think you are a very fine gentleman," she said. Drawing her cloak about her, she walked across the room to the door and closed it softly.

Peter lay on the bed without moving. Moonlight fell upon the Courthouse roof and touched the windows of the gaol. Beyond the brick wall Cullen Pollock, Gentleman, slept, perhaps—or stood behind the bars, looking at the moonlit village street, so quiet and peaceful.

Peter was only half-awake when Herk brought him his early morning cup of yapon tea. In spite of Herk's protests he dressed himself. "Master will feel a weakness," he said. "Then come a chill and a bone-shaking."

"I'll go to Dr. Armitage," Peter said, to satisfy Herk. He intended also to make a call on Lawyer Barker. He would go ahead with the settlement papers. Adam had told him of a plantation on the Chowan River, not far from the Ferriers' estate. It consisted of eight hundred and fifty acres, mostly in timber. The original grant from the Lords Proprietors to Edward Moseley was in 1712. The second holder, Boyd, had died a few months before, and the heirs had asked for a division. If he could buy at a reasonable figure, it would make a suitable wedding gift.

Lawyer Barker sat back in his roundabout chair, his lean fingers tip to tip, and looked at Peter with his keen, observant eyes. "I must say, young man, you have been remarkably astute in handling your investments."

Peter grinned. "I had a good solicitor, you mean, sir. It was he who advised me, when I went to Paris with Mr. Franklin, to put my inheritance in bills of exchange on Boston and Paris, and take ready cash from my London bank. My land in Scotland, our home, will go to a cousin, I presume, since I chose to take up the cause of the Revolution."

Barker nodded. "Yes, certainly."

Peter sat looking at the wall, its one decoration a print of young Washington, the surveyor. His mind was on his father, seated in the gloomy hall before a roaring fire, his form wrapped in a Huntley tartan, reading.

"I regret my father's books," he said, breaking the silence. "But my cousin Andrew is a decent chap. I'm glad the place goes to him."

He watched Thomas Barker take out some pieces of legal paper, select a quill with care, and begin to write. Mr. Barker was a man of parts, he thought, elegantly dressed, fastidious in his tastes, with the niceties of a man of breeding. Seventeen years in London, as the North Carolina Agent, had kept him British in appearance. He had none of the slovenly habits of speech that Peter had noticed sometimes in America.

"This is a generous settlement, Captain Huntley, very generous. I must say that Ferrier is a lucky man to have his daughter provided for so substantially." He laid his pen aside, pushed up his spectacles until they were astride his white wig. He leaned back in his chair, his fingers together at the tips, the position which seemed to be habitual with him. He crossed his knees, showing thin shanks in white silk stockings above silver-buckled shoes. The ruffles of his plum-coloured coat were of fine lace.

Peter imagined Madam Penelope wrapping the lace stock about his thin neck and standing off to look at him, with a fine glow of pride. He was indeed an elegant figure.

"Yes, a generous settlement. I don't remember having written another of such ample amount, with the exception of Adam Rutledge's settlement on his mistress, the Arab girl, and their son David."

Peter thought he had not heard aright. "Sir!" he exclaimed.

Barker turned his eyes from his finger tips and looked at Peter. "You had not heard the story of Arab girl, Azizi? And you've been in Queen Anne's Town a month or more? Adam said nothing to you?"

"I've never heard, so perhaps it is a secret."

Barker smiled thinly. "Imagine a secret, so juicy, so exotic, that could be kept hidden! No, there's no secret. Adam bought a slave, and she turned out to be, not an African, but an Arab girl who had been captured by slave-traders at Zanzibar (the greatest slave-market of them all), taken across Africa by the Great Slave Road to Lobito

Bay, the port of the western coast of Africa slave-trade." He paused
and looked out the window. "A beautiful girl. I think few blamed
Adam, although some of the women—you know how they can cackle."

Peter felt natural curiosity but he forebore to ask questions.

"A fine boy, little David. Adam sent him out to the Illinois country—Cahokia the place is called—with his overseer and his family.
Rutledge has large holdings in the Illinois country along the Mississippi River, across from St. Louis."

Barker had something deeper than his usual smile, a certain pleasure
in a well-told tale. "I'm surprised you don't ask about the girl."

A little dashed by the lawyer's frankness, Peter said, "I didn't think
I should ask. Major Rutledge has never spoken——"

"Nonsense! It's all public property. Why shouldn't you know? I'm
damned sure I don't mind telling you. Adam sent her back to her
people. He found out who she was, in some fantastic way which slips
my mind."

He leaned forward and tapped Peter on the knee with his index
finger. "Between us, as men who have seen something of the world,
I'm not sorry Adam had a little simple and perfectly natural pleasure.
His wife Sara is a rabid Loyalist. She is now in the North, having a
pleasant time with the officers of the King's army. She was one of
those frail invalids who cling like an octopus, and destroys with her
clinging. I never liked the woman. I admire Adam Rutledge. Sometimes I wonder about young David. Not that being a natural child
will stand in his way. There isn't a man in America I admire more
than Alexander Hamilton."

"And I also," Peter said.

The lawyer returned to his papers. "Here I am gossiping and not
attending to the matters in hand. I'll have these ready in a day or
two. Bring in some witnesses and I'll finish it up. About the matter
of the plantation: that may take a little more time, but I'm sure it can
be had." He grasped Peter's hands. "We will be happy to have you in
the county. If you buy land here I'm sure you will belong to us."

"Thank you, sir." Peter went away, well pleased with Lawyer
Barker. His mind was still occupied with him when he walked into
Dr. Armitage's dispensary, a small building between Cupola House
and Nat Allen's.

He was delighted with Dr. Armitage, whom he had not met before.
He was older than Peter expected, but there was kindness and
warmth in his smile, and gentleness in his fingers.

He examined the wound through a glass and murmured, "Not a maggot," with satisfaction. He put on a clean dressing and helped Peter with his shirt and coat. "Ferrier tells me he wants to take you home with him Saturday. I see no reason why not. At any rate I'll be up at River Plantation for Sunday dinner and can have a look at you then."

Peter stood up, ready to leave, for there were people sitting on benches in the outer room waiting their turn to see the doctor.

"I understand that things transpired in my dining-room while I was away. A betrothal party, eh?" His bright eyes twinkled. "Angela is one of my favourites—but she's a handful." He stood off and surveyed Peter a moment. "I believe you'll know how to tame her."

Peter would have liked to say that he didn't want to tame Angela, wanted her as she was, high-spirited and proud. But the doctor was saying good-bye and turning to the next patient, an old Negro woman, bent almost double with a "misery" in her back. Dr. Armitage bowed her into his office as though she were a duchess, and sat down to listen to her woes, with the same interest he would show to the wife of one of the Sound-side planters. A humane man was Dr. Armitage, humane, with respect for the dignity of slave and freeman alike.

On the way back to O'Malley's, Peter met Ann Pollock hurrying across the Green. She stopped to speak to him. "You were so kind to me last night. Cullen did have friends. James Iredell and Samuel Johnston had arranged so that Cullen didn't have to sleep in that filthy gaol, but had a bedroom in the sheriff's house. This morning they got him released and he is at home again." She managed a smile but her eyes still had the hunted look. "They say Clem Hull and the rest of the rioters are boasting they aren't through with him. Please come in to see us. Cullen is so unhappy. He sits and stares at the floor, and won't speak. I'm frightfully worried." She said good-bye and hurried across the Green to their home.

Peter made his belated call at Hewes and Smith's store and finished up the matter of the lottery tickets.

Adam Rutledge came back that night after supper, his boots covered with swamp mud. He had followed a gang of drovers and their cattle, on a suggestion from the host of the Red Lion. He came upon them after they had crossed the Roanoke. They had been sullen and refused to answer his questions; but he was positive Morse had travelled with them as far as the Roanoke River ferry. He remembered passing a drove of cattle on the road, not far from where he had taken Angela from the chaise. The men had probably abandoned the chaise when they found they were being pursued, slipped in with the drovers and made their way through the village the next morning, unobtrusively. No one would challenge the drovers, who went back and forth between the two states so frequently.

"I should have thought of that the same night," Adam said, dispiritedly. "The fox had run to covert and was well away by the time I took up a cold trail."

Peter said, "I should have caught the fox myself. I had him under my hand."

Adam smiled broadly. "You were fighting a gentleman's fight, Peter. You can't do it in the sort of game you're playing. Morse knew that. He knows how to fight and when to run to earth."

"I'll get him one day," Peter said, shutting his jaw with a snap.

Adam was splashing water at a great rate, in the dressing-room, then rubbing himself down with a towel. "I saw Mr. Barker as I was coming in," he called out. "Someone had taken his wife's chaise from the rack in front of Horniblow's, where it was waiting for Will Hooper to drive out to Mulberry Hill for the night. He had it washed and put back into the carriage-house without his wife's knowledge, he told me." Adam laughed. "It seems Penelope sets great store by that chaise; he hopes she doesn't notice a few more scratches."

Peter said, "Madam Pollock called on me last night. She said Angela was terrified for fear her family would discover what had happened. I told her as far as I knew nothing happened except that I was overcome by a dizziness after getting a thrust in the shoulder and losing blood."

Adam stepped to the door. He slipped a fresh shirt over his head and stuffed the tail into his breeches and pulled up the belt. "Best for everyone," he commented briefly. "There's too much talk going round. A very sorry ending to Flag Day—very sorry indeed, and we've not had the end yet. I stopped at the smithy. Martie is worried about Clem. He hasn't been home since last night. She showed me a pot of tar and a sack of feathers in the corner of the smithy. I told her she had best burn the feathers."

He had finished dressing by that time. "I'm going across the creek," he said. "Johnston is disturbed by the performance last night. He is a moderate man and can't abide abuse."

Peter was glad to get into bed. His shoulder ached and he was very weary. He was disappointed. He disliked failure. He lighted the candle and reread the dispatch from the committee. It was then he noticed a thin sheet caught in the fold of the heavier paper. It was a line from Mr. Jay himself.

"I know you are fretting, Peter, at being kept 'doing nothing,' as you expressed it. It is wise for you to establish yourself in the eyes of everyone as being connected with the Paymaster's department on the lottery matter. It won't be forever. Rutledge understands. Be patient a week or two; then we will have something for you. The Boston merchant is not your objective, so let him go."

Peter heaved a mighty sigh. He didn't understand any of it—or like it. He had rather be back with his old regiment, fighting. It had been bad enough sitting in the Paris office, but at least there was the exhilarating presence of Mr. Franklin. Here he lost sight of the war. It was an effort not to sink into the smooth, easy-living way of the village and the plantations. It was difficult to remember the winter of Valley Forge, the cold, the long desperate marches to the north, the despair, defeat following defeat to break the soul of an army. Nothing was so devastating as to feel that one was standing alone, a small unit, without support of the people of the towns and villages and countryside. What did they know of war, here in Queen Anne's Town? Of the long toil, the weariness, the utter lonely weariness of defeated men?

Peter was awake when Adam came back from his visit with Johnston.

"I should have taken you with me, Peter. I was in ill favour with the ladies. They wanted to feed you soup and wine jellies, and nurse you—all the sisters, the Iredells, Madam Blair, the young ladies. Johnston is blessed. When his wife is away, his sisters surround him with their solicitude. Such a family, Peter! Such a tender, loving family!"

"You have a favourite?" Peter asked.

"I don't know. Sometimes I think pale, fragile Hannah Iredell. Then there was lovely Miss Isabella, Joe Hewes's betrothed. His was a fine permanent affection. I do not believe he has ever looked at a woman with desire in his heart, since she died. They say he visits the burial-ground at the plantation every time he comes to Queen Anne's Town."

Herk came in with a boot-jack and dragged off Adam's heavy boots.

"From what Will Hooper tells me, it won't be long before Joe Hewes joins his Isabella—if he doesn't have a care. He stays on in Philadelphia, doing other men's work, without thought for his health."

Peter yawned widely.

"What's keeping you awake? It's thirty after one; time that invalids were asleep."

Peter told him, "It is the war. Being off here away from the fighting. If I stay much longer I will forget that there is blood running and men leaving life, out of their time."

"No man leaves life out of his time," Adam said. For a long while he was silent. Then he said, "The Arabs have a saying, 'A star never rises or sets, save at its own time.'"

Peter, remembering the story Barker had told him, felt the significance of Adam's remark. An Arab girl, leaving her imprint and the imprint of her people.

"As for the other thing: I used to worry the same way, because I was not marching beside my own men. Now I know that the great pattern of the war has many threads of many colours in its warp and woof. Each thread has its place, to make the strength of the whole." He got into bed and licked his thumb and first finger and snuffed the candle. A few minutes later his quiet, even breathing told Peter he was sound asleep.

Peter must have slept also. He was wakened suddenly by a woman's voice crying, "Help! Help! Help! They'll murder my husband! Help!"

Soldiers both, used to alarums and quick action, Peter and Adam landed on the floor at the same time, in the dark collided at the window.

A woman, wrapped in some fluttering white cloth, was running down the street screaming enough to wake the dead. "Help! Mr. Pollock is being murdered! Help!" She was running toward Horniblow's. Peter fumbled for the flint to light the candle. Adam was already dressing in the dark, cursing. He did not wait for Peter, who was slow in getting his clothes on, but calling Herk to follow, he ran along the hall. Peter heard him running down the steep little flight of stairs that led to the street, the clatter of his sword sliding against the banister. Others were in the street; lights in the tavern. Houses around the Green were quiet and dark, but it was a dark quiet that breathed of unseen people—doors stealthily opened, window shutters moved. Stay withindoors, the silence said; this is none of your affair. Stay behind closed doors and shuttered windows.

Peter rounded the corner before he saw the rioters in front of the Pollock place. He heard Ann Pollock crying, "Mercereau and Hull are breaking into the cellar. We haven't any liquor; I swore it. Give them money! Tell them to go away, go away!" Her voice rose to a shriek and she broke into hysterical laughter.

Horniblow's heavy voice called: "Bring her in. The woman is fainting. Bring her inside."

The lower Green was thronged—a roistering, drunken mob, much more powerful and unwieldy than the night before. Adam was ahead of Peter. He heard Adam shout, "Clem Hull! Where are you, Clem Hull? Southey, can't you stop him?" Men were running down the street from all directions. Flares brightened the darkness. Some men, militiamen in uniform, ran silently toward the warehouse. An officer shouted commands, without men to carry them out.

The unruly mob surrounded the house, trampled over Ann's lovely garden with clumsy, heavy feet. With axes and crow-bars they prized open cellar doors and windows.

Cullen Pollock came out on the gallery. He tried to make himself heard.

Saner men were gathering in numbers. James Iredell was calling for the law. The law was reluctant to move, and the military had no authority unless the law called for them. Presently Peter heard Southey Wren barking commands, over and over. A drum started to beat. A bugle-call came from the military camp, the quick staccato alarum and call to arms.

Adam reached the gallery beside Cullen Pollock. Herk, carrying a flare he had snatched from a drunken rioter, stood below him as Adam shouted, "There is no liquor here, men. Disperse and go to your homes, before the militia come."

A shout went up: "They won't come; they're afraid." Almost in answer, the bugle sounded again, closer now.

"Disperse, you men!" Adam shouted. "It's the militia. Southey, make haste. We want no rioting here tonight."

"He's Tory, he is," a drunken voice shouted.

Adam said, "I'll vouch for him. Hull, you have sense. Take your men home."

Hull answered, "Take your men home! No liquor here. Carriage burned ... Take yourself off, goddam you! Take yourself home!" His drunken voice rose in anger.

Adam breathed deeply.

When the military company marched around the corner, there was nothing to detain them—no noisy demonstration, no rioters, only a few flares burning on the Green and a few shadows moving silently along the water-front.

Far into the night, until the first cock-crow, Ann Pollock sat writing in the common-room at Horniblow's. Page after page fell from the writing-table to the floor. She was registering her protest to her old friend who sat in the high place in the Congress. As the first rays of the sun tipped the pines back of the tavern, she wrote the last paragraph:

Oh, Mr. Hewes, I am sure those feelings of humanity so paramount in your breast must be shocked. Do consider, and use that power vested in you, toward the security of a civil peace. Let not a respectable member of society be made the victim of a barbarous few. I am sure you never thought soldiers necessary in this part of Carolina, nor could you have thought they were paid to ruin individuals, or disturb the peace of society. To you I look for Justice. Surely you will not suffer authority to be thus trampled under foot. None are safe. All are as guilty as Mr. Pollock. May the Almighty direct your counsels for the happiness and peace of America, is the sincere wish of, sir,

Your sincere friend,

A. Pollock.

These persons I mention to you are accused by good evidence. I beg you will keep the list I enclose.

I fear this is scarcely legible but when you reflect on the agitation of my mind, on a retrospective view of my sufferings you will excuse all.

The sun rose and flooded the quiet Green with its golden light. The people of the village slept quietly. A boat put out from the plantation across the creek. Before the early risers were in the streets, Ann Pollock was laid on a litter carried by four slaves, and taken to the wharf, where she was placed in the bottom of the long canoe. Cullen, her husband, followed, almost too weak to stand alone. The strong-armed rowers took them across the bay to the Johnston landing.

Hospitable doors opened wide. Gentle hands lifted the unconscious woman and carried her inside.

Peter and Adam Rutledge turned back to the boat. Peter did not speak. He was thinking, The pattern of war is here in this quiet village—the crushing, devastating pattern of war.

CHAPTER

19

PETER MAKES A VISIT

TORMENTED by the rapidly changing events of the past few days, Angela Ferrier was glad to return to River Plantation. Familiar surroundings, her own room and the routine of family life, had a quieting effect upon her turbulent spirit. Her mother's soft, tranquil voice, the treble of the children, brought a measure of peace. The night before, she had dropped asleep to the singing of slaves in the quarters line, singing after the field work was over.

She got out of bed and pulled aside the muslin curtains. The sun was high. The Negroes were in the fields, their chopping-hoes busy. The rain had wetted down the sandy soil and brought new growth to the corn, but the rain had brought also a new crop of weeds and grass that must be chopped out and the rows cleaned. Her eyes rested on the river, as they had rested day after day in all the years she had lived on the plantation since she was a small girl no older than her little brother Philip was now. The river too was quiet. She heard a faint whispering. She knew they were there, each seated on a little stool outside her door, Philip and little Bella waiting for her to awake. Angela opened the door a crack. Then she ran across the room in order to jump into the great tester bed, her long legs carrying her barely a foot ahead of Philip. It was an old game, often played, which one would reach the bed first. The children came shrieking and yelling. Philip overtook her. Bella's short little legs pumped close behind. Slipping and sliding, the girl made it, up into the high bed. She threw herself on her sister's breast, wound her little arms around Angela's white neck, pressed a damp kiss on Angela's chin.

"Why did you go away, 'Gela? You missed Philip's party. He had a cake, a big cake with seven candles."

Angela hugged Philip. "I'm sorry. We'll have Tulli make another, so I can eat it."

317

"No." Philip sat on the edge of her bed. He was much too old to snuggle any more. Seven. "No. My name-day is past. I won't have another cake for another year. Then it will be an eight one. Tulli told me."

"Well, I'll have a birthday, with nineteen candles."

Bella sat up, busily winding Angela's long dark braids around her arm. "How many candles is nineteen?" Angela, her back against the pillow, demonstrated with her fingers.

Philip said, "I know. I can count. Mr. Earle showed us how to say our numbers."

"But you are seven," Bella pouted. "Seven is old. I am five." She nestled back against Angela's shoulder. "Five is a little girl."

"Sugar and spice and everything nice," Philip sang. "Spice—cinnamon and ginger, just like a spice-cake."

"I like spice-cake." Bella turned her round dark eyes on him. "And you do too, Philip."

Philip got up. "Father gave me a pony, a little black pony. It came from the Banks. He gave me a slave, too. Mulu is his name; he's just as old as me—as I am," he corrected quickly.

A little tap at the door, and Madam Ferrier came in. She was dressed in a white muslin sprigged in yellow and she wore a large leghorn hat, tied with a yellow riband.

"I'm going to the dispensary," she said, after she had kissed Angela's cheek.

The children sprang from the bed. Bella squealed, "Let me go! Let me go! I want to give out the pills."

Philip said nothing. He went to the door and opened it, waiting for his mother to pass through.

"You can't go this morning, *carita*," Francisca said, patting the little girl's cheek. "I have a little task for you. You may run and ring the bell for Tulli to send up your sister's breakfast." The child ran out of the room, delighted at the task. Francisca turned to Philip. "You need not wait, my dear. I saw your little pony tied to the rack."

Philip lost his dignity and good manners in an instant. With a whoop he darted down the hall. Francisca inclined her head to listen. "He is sliding down the banister again. So many times have I admonished him." She spread her hands, hopelessly.

"Your children are worrisome," Angela said, slowly, her sombre eyes turned to her mother. "Your eldest child the greatest worry of all."

Francisca came over and sat on the bed. "I said my Hail Mary's this morning with a thankful heart that I had a daughter who would come to me to confess her waywardness. My Angela, I pray that the Virgin watches over you and gives you guidance. Pray that your mother may have enough of divine wisdom to advise you."

She sat quietly beside Angela, not touching her, looking at her yet not seeing her. "We have no priest to serve as father confessor, Angela. We must find strength in ourselves to act with wisdom."

"Oh, Mother, Mother, pray for me! I am so bewildered!" Angela's dark head pressed against her mother's shoulder.

Francisca arose. A slow smile came to her lips, illuminating her face. She touched her lips to Angela's forehead. As she moved slowly across the room, she put her hand into the pocket of her voluminous skirt. Angela heard the click of her beads as she walked away down the long hall.

Angela covered her eyes with her hands. How could she have been so selfish, so cruel, wanting only her own way? Anthony, that night, had been a different Anthony from the one she had known. There had been something hard and cruel in his face. Even when he smiled. How strange he had acted! He did not want her. She was ashamed, ashamed.

Promisy came in with a tray. Her smile was broad and warm. "Tulli she say she send you little pullet egg, fresh off the nes', jes' fo' you, missy. De rose, Jacob he fotched from the ol' gyarden. Ain't he pretty? So sof' and red, jes' lak dress you' mamma she wear when company come."

Angela lifted the rose to her face. "It is like red velvet," she said, "but its perfume is its own."

"Yes, missy, dat what I say to Tulli: a lilac he smell lak a lilac, and yaller jasmint he smell lak heself, not honesuckley. Flowers jes' natu'lly is smellin' lak theyself."

The girl stood by the bedside waiting anxiously for Angela to begin eating. "Tulli she mighty proud if you is *hongry* this mawnin'. She say when she cook the egg, 'Miss Angela she surely enjoy a fresh egg.'"

A little smile came across Angela's mouth. She sat up and took up a knife. Giving the egg a sharp crack she cut off the small end. "Perfect," she said. "Tell Tulli the breakfast is perfect."

The dusky girl grinned broadly, bobbed and hurried back to the kitchen to give the news. "She eat jes' lak sheself. Whyfor you say she cry and cry las' night, when she mamma sit a-talkin' so late? She eat fine, jes' lak she *hongry*."

Being young, once she had touched food Angela found a healthy appetite asserting itself. After all, one can't stop eating forever. The tears dried on her cheeks, forgotten.

The senator and Peter sailed up the river and landed at the wharf. The sun was two hours above the horizon, but ahead the long slivers of sunlight slanted down through the tall pines, made a golden carpet on the young green grass. Saddle-horses were waiting, pawing the pine-needle carpet under a primeval tree. Peter looked about him. Instead of the high banks covered with heavy bushes and vines and great hardwood trees, here was a small flat sandy beach of three acres or more, rimmed with clean yellow sands. Giant sycamores, mammoth pines and large bay trees made an entrancing grove. Along the river at the north side was an old fish-house. A dozen nets were drying, hung from broken underboughs of the pine trees, long nets, apparently hundreds of yards of nets. Two old Negroes were working on repairing breaks. A third lay on the beach, a fishing-pole stuck in the sand.

The senator spoke to him. "Any luck, Ancient?"

The man scrambled to his feet. "No, sar. No, sar. Not yet I ain't. Mayhap come sundown."

They started up the long slope that led to the flat land above. "The fishing was good this year," the senator observed. "I have enough herring salted down to last the winter." He rode ahead up the path. At the top of the hill Peter saw a small boy racing a pony down the wide roadway bordered with conical-shaped juniper trees. The child was shouting and slapping the pony's flanks with the long bridle-reins to make it go faster. A pickaninny was also astride the pony, clinging to the boy's waist for dear life, his eyes rolling in fright.

The senator pulled up his horse and waited.

"She's fast, Father—fast as your Black Bess, Father."

The senator smiled. Peter saw the sternness fade from his eyes, and a look of admiration temper his austerity. "My son Philip," he said. "Speak to Captain Huntley, son."

The child bowed gravely. "Good day, Captain Huntley." Then he laughed aloud. "Mulu is scared he will tumble off. He did once, right among the prickly pears."

"You should not laugh at that, my son. Never laugh at anyone in trouble."

They turned in, in front of a long, rambling house. Like many of the early houses, it was built with a broad front and double galleries, set to command the prevailing summer breeze. Wings had been added from time to time. Sprawling out from it around a rectangular grass plot the farm buildings were set. Rose vines climbed over the galleries, a few bright crimson blooms showing. A black boy took the horses and led them down a lane to the barns.

They went up the brick walk to the gallery. The door opened and a little girl, with huge black eyes like Angela's and her mother's, came flying down the path to meet them. Ferrier caught the child up in his arms. "This is Isabella, Captain Huntley."

Without any self-consciousness, the child held out her hand. Peter bowed gallantly, kissed her chubby fingers.

"Bella is a little coquette. I warn you," the senator said.

Peter thought how different from his austere self the senator was here; how warm, how proud of his beautiful little children.

They found Madam, dressed in white, seated in a large cool room, the jalousies slightly opened to let in light. She greeted Peter cordially, pressing his hand with both of hers. "Angela will be back shortly. I sent her on an errand to Martinique, to take Mrs. Parker some strawberries. Ours have come in early, this year." She spoke to a manservant who came to the door. "Show Captain Huntley to the north room in the old wing. Where are his boxes?"

"They will be up in a few minutes. I sent a cart down to the landing."

Madam said, "I've put Peter as far away from the children as possible. You have a river view, Peter. I always want our guests to see the river when they first wake in the morning."

Peter followed the man down a hall, across a gallery to a wing which was also double-galleried. They ascended an outside stairway to a room with windows on three sides. On the north was a door opening on an upper gallery. Peter stepped out. He stood silent, looking at the crimson path which the sun cut across the river. Two miles to the opposite shore, the senator had told him when they came up in the boat; beyond the opposite shore, great hardwood forests for miles and miles, a fertile land; the river teemed with fish. Tomorrow, after morning service in the little chapel on the plantation, they would ride over to the Boyd place. Peter did not tell Mr. Ferrier that he had asked Lawyer Barker to purchase that land if it were possible to do so.

The house-boy came out from the bedchamber. "The Captain's bath, he laid."

Peter thanked him and had turned to follow the boy when he caught sight of Angela. She was galloping down the lane, mounted on a black hunter. She dismounted quickly near the side entrance. She was wearing a linen-coloured habit. A red scarf bound about her head completely covered her hair.

The children ran out to greet her, hanging onto her hands, skipping and dancing by her side. Their high childish voices rose above her deep tones. She was laughing, her head thrown back.

She was different, younger, almost a child. She said something to Philip, and started to run, racing him to the front door. Peter couldn't believe this was Angela. He had much to learn, perhaps too much.

He whistled a familiar tune as he splashed in the tin tub the boy had brought. He felt happier than he had for months. He almost forgot he had a wound until he raised his arm too quickly when he stepped from the bath. He felt a deep, biting pain run from his shoulder to his back. It made him sink into a chair suddenly, leaving a pool of water on the floor. The boy, who was waiting to help him dress, mopped it up quickly with a towel.

"You surely scratch you'self bad, sar," he said, wringing out the towel into the tub of water, his eyes fixed on the bandages. "Want I should get Tulli to wrop you a fresh little cloth? She wrop them jes' fine."

"No, thank you. The doctor is coming tomorrow. He will fix the bandage. How long before supper?" Peter asked.

"First bell, then fifteen minutes, then second, then time for going to great room."

Peter stepped onto the gallery to go below. He paused. The colours on the water were sharp-drawn; the trees merged into broad shadows. He heard a quail calling, calling. It made him think of home, hunting for eggs in the heather, under bushes, the frightened call of the mother pheasant. This was a good land, good and plenteous. Nature was kind almost to overflowing.

Angela was alone when Peter entered the great room. She was standing near a window that overlooked the rose garden. She wore a thin gown of pale yellow, with many ruffles under the looped pelisse. A band of yellow bound her dark hair and she had placed a yellow rose behind her ear among the curls that fell over her shoulder. Peter stood at the door looking at her for some seconds before she was aware of his presence.

Then she turned and saw him. There was an almost imperceptible pause before she said, "Good evening, Captain Huntley." Peter crossed the room quickly and kissed her hand. "Will you be seated?" she said politely. She sat down near the window, in an elbow chair of French satinwood.

Peter crossed to the fire-place, where a small fire burned. "You have cool evenings even in June," he said, equally polite.

"Yes, that is true. Sometimes in the middle of July we have a little rain and a cool spell."

This is infernal, Peter thought uneasily. Why doesn't someone come?

"Did you have a pleasant trip up-river?"

Peter could answer the question with enthusiasm, and did. "It was a beautiful trip, just enough wind." He said he had been interested in what Senator Ferrier told him about the estates, and the great pocosins that ended at the river, where the giant cypress trees grew far out into the water: a magnificent sight. He was interested, also, in the story that Sir Richard Grenville had sailed so far up the Chowan River from his base on Roanoke Island. "Great men, the Elizabethans, great men of imagination and daring. Theirs were the greatest days England has ever known," he remarked.

Angela pays only slight attention, Peter thought. Of course she is Spanish. What a silly ass I was to mention so enthusiastically the men who fought against Spain! What a stupid, boorish fool I was!

He welcomed the advent of the senator and Madam, who came in as the second bell rang. The children were nowhere visible.

He offered his arm to Angela and they fell into step, following the senator and Francisca into the dining-hall. Angela was tall, taller than he had realized. He was happy that he was taller than she— much taller.

They sat down to eat, a small group at one end of the long table. After the senator had said grace, there was a bounteous meal served by several house-slaves. "All the food is from the plantation," the senator boasted, "all excepting the rice. We bring that up from the Cape Fear River. Rice is scarce since the British have interfered with its culture in South Carolina."

Francisca spoke occasionally, about the affairs of the plantation, and their neighbors. Peter was made familiar with new plantation

names and their owners: Martinique, the Evans plantation, across the
Sand Hill Road; Brownrigg of Wingfield; the creek and the mill; old
Saram Creek; Cheshire Ferry; the Elliotts, Privotts, Boyds and the
Welsh Evanses. Besides the larger plantations he learned that there
were many smaller farms of the English yeomen who cultivated their
fields successfully. Here was a country life like that in Scotland and
England.

Angela spoke a word occasionally. She blushed when the senator
made some comment about the select little family group; blushed and
did not raise her eyes from her plate until her mother drew her into
the conversation. Once Peter looked up and caught her gazing at
him—a strange contemplative look, as though she had never seen him
before. He wondered if she were comparing him with Allison. He
would not stand up against Allison in looks, though he was as tall and
his shoulders were as broad. He thought of his hair, in colour like a
ginger cat, and his green-grey eyes, not beautiful but keen. He could
see a long distance, he thought, trying to laugh at himself. When he
caught her looking at him, her eyes did not turn away immediately,
but slowly, when she had finished her scrutiny. Now there was
nothing disdainful in her eyes, as there had been earlier in their
acquaintance, more a look of enquiry.

He was aware that Madam Ferrier had made a small gesture to
Angela, and they both rose to leave the table. Peter sprang to his
feet to escort them to the great room. When he re-entered the dining-
room, the senator had poured his port. He pushed the decanter
toward Peter. "To the dear ladies!" he toasted.

Peter said, "To Madam Ferrier and Miss Angela!"

He sipped his wine slowly. He had no idea of keeping up with the
senator, glass for glass. He hadn't the head for it. The senator was
a big man. Even sitting, he looked broad and bulky, large-boned, a
true Scot. He must weigh sixteen stone, Peter thought. He was, himself, fifteen stone in weight.

Angela was playing the harp when they joined the ladies, singing a
gay Spanish song, her mother humming accompaniment in her rich,
deep voice. The senator stood leaning against the mantel.

Francisca noticed that a little impatience showed in the restless
movement of his fingers on the long stem of his pipe. When the song
ended she turned to Peter. "Perhaps you will sing one of your Scottish songs? My husband loves Laments."

Peter hesitated. "I haven't my pipes. I cannot sing without the pipes."

The senator said, "Nonsense, Peter! Sing something strong and stirring. I can't abide these sentimental languishings. Sing something. Let Angela follow on the harp. 'Tis time she learned to accompany you," he added slyly.

Peter went over to Angela, leaned over and plucked a chord to set the key. He remained standing beside her, his hands clasped behind his back. His voice was resonant and strong and it filled the room.

"The king sits in Dumferling toune,
  Drinking the blude-red wine:
O whar will I get a guid sailòr,
  To sail this ship of mine?

"Up and spake an eldern knicht,
  Sat at the king's richt knee:
Sir Patrick Spence is the best sailòr,
  That sails upon the sea."

Peter stopped. The harp strings muted as Angela laid her slim hands across the wires.

"Go on, lad! Go on! Don't stop!" the senator called. He was smiling, keeping time with his pipe. "'Tis a fair good ballad, that." Peter sang another verse:

"Late late yestreen I saw the new moone,
  Wi' the auld moone in her arme;
And I feir, I feir, my deir mastèr,
  That we will come to harme."

The sound of crickets came from the garden, the boom of swamp frogs from the swamp, as Peter ended the Lament:

"Half owre, half owre to Aberdour,
  It's fiftie fadom deip:
And thair lies guid Sir Patrick Spence,
  Wi' the Scots lords at his feet."

Ferrier turned to Francisca. "There is a song! Something to stir a man! Canna ye see the fight they made against the sea? Peter lad, I wish you had sung every verse of it." He waved his pipe back and forth.

> "O lang, lang, may the ladies stand
> Wi' thair gold kems in thair hair,
> Waiting for thair ain deir lords . . ."

He paused, lost. Peter finished for him:

> "For they'll see thame na mair."

Francisca said, "I think it is *very* sad, and bleak, but you have a voice of some excellence, Peter. You must learn duets." She looked at Angela. Her eyes had that curious inward composure Peter had noticed before.

To his deep amazement Angela said, "Yes, Captain Huntley, I think we should learn some two-voice ballads, yes." Her voice was low and very gentle. Peter's heart melted. She was sweet, so very sweet.

That night before Angela went to sleep, she opened the breviary her mother had laid on her night-table. Her mother had written something on the fly-leaf. She held the book close to the candle flame.

SAINT TERESA
Lines written in her Breviary

> Let nothing disturb thee,
> Nothing afright thee.
> All things are passing.
>
> God never changeth.
> Patient endurance
> Attaineth all things.
>
> Whom God possesseth
> In nothing is wanting;
> Alone God sufficeth.

Angela sat looking at the lines in her mother's elegant, angular writing. She laid the page against her cheek. After a long time she fell asleep, comforted.

Parson Earle, instead of his lay reader, Mr. Pettigrew, rode horse-back from the village. He arrived in time to hold morning service at the small log chapel Alexander Ferrier had built a few years before in the woods on the river-bank. Churchmen and women from the neighbourhood arrived on horseback, or walked a mile or two through the fields.

The Parson was in fine form. He would hold service, then go down to his place on Brownrigg Creek where he had his fishery and a small house in which he lived in the summer. He loved his house, and the stream lined with bay trees, and the woods that surrounded the field. Only under protest had he consented to live in the winter at Straw-berry Hill, near the village. He liked and respected his son-in-law, and loved his daughter, but a man's roof-tree was his roof-tree.

Peter walked to the chapel with the family and took his place in the family pew, sitting down beside Angela. Although there had been no formal betrothal, the countryside knew. White and black alike were curious to see the young gentleman.

The house-slaves sat in the back seats. The children played outside under the care of young Negro girls. In the midst of a prayer there was a yapping and moaning of hounds. For a moment the Parson's gaze wandered from his prayer-book to the window, as the scratch pack, owned by some unregenerate dissenter, came down the lane and crossed the field. "Out of season" said the look in the Parson's eyes, but his voice went on with monotonous exactitude.

Peter held the hymn-book for Angela when they stood up to sing, moving closer to her so that their arms touched. He heard whispering behind them, a woman's comment: "At least he's a head taller than she is."

The sermon over, they all stopped at the entrance. Introductions were made, enquiries about absent ones. The Parson was surrounded and carried off for dinner at one of the neighbouring plantations. Peter walked back with his host, the women walking ahead, Philip and Bella at their mother's side.

When they reached the lane that turned to the house, one of the white overlookers, named Giles, spoke to Mr. Ferrier. "The man you sent for to cut shingles came in late last night, sir."

"Good!" the senator said. "Good! Tell him I'll see him tomor-row."

The overlooker hesitated a moment. "He's bound to see you now, sir. He's got his girl with him."

"His girl?"

"Yes, sir. His daughter."

"Where are they?" Ferrier asked. "Where have you housed them?"

"I put them in that house next to mine. Was that right, sir? He seemed a superior person, and his daughter . . ." He left the sentence unfinished.

"I'll walk home with you, Giles." He turned to Peter. "Will you tell my wife I'm going to walk down the grove? I'll be back to the house in time for dinner."

Peter delivered his message. Francisca said, "My husband is like that. One is ready to sit at table, and he disappears—gone to the lot, or the river, or the east field. It's always the same. I hope, Peter, you are a punctual man."

The little lines at the corners of his greenish eyes indicated laughter. "I'm afraid——" he started to say.

Angela's low-voiced "Mother!" made him pause. She was looking at Francisca, a sad, quiet protest in her eyes.

Francisca laughed. "Why not know the habits of the man you are going to marry?" she said, with her charming frankness. "I assure you it is very much better to know than to be ignorant. A little while, a few short weeks, and you will be wed. It is time, Angela, to throw off those little modesties of maidenhood and look at the man you are to marry, not as a stranger."

Angela said nothing. Colour rising in her face told Peter that she was painfully embarrassed. He went to her and took her hand. "Perhaps Madam your mother is right. Let us sit down and talk about our likes and dislikes." He smiled engagingly at her as he led her over to a sofa. She did not resist. He thought there was a faint ironic smile deep in her eyes.

Francisca nodded and smiled and took a seat in the far end of the room, as a proper duenna should. The children came in, quite sedate in their Sabbath clothes. Their mother motioned to them to sit on stools and look at the Bible picture-book. They did as they were bidden, but their round eyes more often rested on flesh-and-blood Peter and Angela than on the picture of Ruth the Gleaner.

Peter's voice spoke more frequently than Angela's. After a little some of her reserve melted and she began to talk naturally. Once she laughed aloud.

Philip looked up. "Promisy said it's best not to laugh on the Lord's Day."

Francisca opened her mouth to speak, but she heard her husband's voice in the hall. He came into the room, and stood for a second looking at his wife. "Gil Roi came to the plantation last night."

"Gil Roi!" she exclaimed, not trying to hide her astonishment. "Gil Roi! Why is he here? I thought you . . ." She glanced at the children.

"I asked him to come. He has taken a contract to cut juniper shingles at Middle Swamp. I need shingles."

"You didn't tell me," she said quietly.

"Didn't I? I expect it slipped my mind. But this is the complication: he has fetched his daughter along. He has some strange idea that I will take her for a bondwoman, so she will learn what she needs to know about household duties. I thought . . ." He looked at his wife helplessly.

Peter was conscious that Angela was listening, her body taut, her eyes watchful.

"What shall I do?" Francisca said. "Where can I use her? Wait, she might be trained for a maid for Angela. I will have to see the girl first. Of course, you can't take her as a bondwoman."

"No, certainly. I told him that."

"Or a sempstress, perhaps, being French. What is her appearance?"

Ferrier hesitated. Then he said, "I don't believe she will take kindly to instruction. She seems to me to be morose, wilful."

"What are her looks? Is she neat and cleanly?"

Again he hesitated. "I told Roi to bring her to you in the morning. I knew you would want to see him."

"Certainly I do. Are they well housed, comfortable?"

"Yes. Giles has them at his place for eating. They are in that vacant cottage at the entrance of the grove."

"Yes. It is better that I talk with him to find out what is on his mind. I will see him directly after dinner."

"Tomorrow will do, my dear."

"No, Alexander. This afternoon." She sat quietly for a moment, then she said, implying a question, "When she was a small child she promised to be very beautiful?"

"Yes," said the senator absently, "yes."

The butler came to the door. "Dr. Armitage and Miss Cecily jes' ride to the block, and Mr. Rutledge he tie he hoss to the rack."

Ferrier went out of the room. Angela rose. "Pardon me, Captain Huntley." She followed her father out onto the gallery.

Francisca turned to Peter. "Gil Roi is a Frenchman," she said. "He lives in a great swamp near the mouth of the Cape Fear River. It was Gil Roi who swam out into the great waves, and brought me and my child safe to shore."

She sat looking ahead of her, her eyes blank and staring, her face set. Peter had seen that look in Scotswomen who had second sight. She shivered and covered her face with her hands. She recovered herself after a brief time. "I have grave forebodings, Peter. I must do what is given me to do, but I am full of fear."

She held out her hand. Gently he assisted her to arise from her chair. He said nothing of having seen Gil Roi before, or the girl. Madam had not given him the opportunity. She was too absorbed in her own thoughts.

When the guests entered the room, she walked toward them in easy dignity, a smile of welcome on her lips.

Adam drew Peter aside. "A dispatch-rider came this morning. I brought your letters with me." Peter thanked him. There was no time for further discussion, as dinner was announced at once.

It was not until the long dinner was over, and the doctor had changed the bandage on Peter's wound, that he had an opportunity to glance at the dispatch Adam had given him. It was a brief order to come to Philadelphia to appear before the committee, to receive instructions. He and Adam were standing on the gallery off Peter's room while he read the letter. When he finished, he handed it to Adam.

"Yes, I got my orders also," Adam said. "I'm riding north Tuesday morning."

"I'll ride with you."

"Then meet me at the cross-road at nine. I'll have a travelling chaise and pair; we can go more quickly," Adam said. "What about your wound? Dr. Armitage may have something to say about your travelling plans."

"I shan't tell him," Peter said.

Adam laughed. "You won't have to worry about inaction any longer. From now on there will be plenty ahead of you, or I miss my guess."

"Thank God for that!" Peter said, piously. "No good can come from this waiting. If I stayed here any longer, in this lovely Eden, I would forget that there was any work to be done."

Adam turned toward the door to go inside. "Another Ulysses, eh?"

he said over his shoulder. "Circe has woven a spell. A tragedy if there
is a faithful one waiting."

"God forbid!" Then Peter glanced at Adam. His face was very
grave. "Let's go in. I think I hear feminine voices. The little siesta
is over."

Gil Roi came up to the gallery where the senator and Francisca
were seated. Francisca greeted him cordially. He pulled off his woven
palmetto hat. His brown face was wreathed in smiles. In spite of her
invitation he refused to step up on the gallery and take a chair.

"It is a pleasure to see madame in such good health. A pleasure."
His white teeth flashed. He stood firmly on the balls of his feet, set
well apart, the stocky, strong figure of French peasantry. Some of
their native shrewdness shone from his black eyes that missed nothing.
A forest man, alert, ready, poised, prepared. The unexpected, his daily
companion. Danger always at his back, waiting to overtake him. A
man who knew his place, yet a bold man—one who would endure no
liberties.

"If Madame has a moment, I would like to consult her about my
girl."

Francisca smiled. "Tell me about her, Roi. Let me see, her name
was Michèle."

His smile broadened. His teeth flashed white in his dark face. His
curly black hair and beard would make him look almost piratical, if
he had golden loops in his ears, thought Francisca.

"Yes, it is my daughter that disturbs me. She is a woman now,
going on eighteen, Madame, and she lives the life of a wild creature. I
have ask' the senator please to take her as a bondwoman, so that she
may learn how to live with some decency. I am without a woman to
guide her. Sometimes I am away in the forest, a fortnight, maybe
more. She is alone, with only her dogs. That is not good." He looked
at Francisca, waiting.

"No, that is not good."

"Then, when I prepare to come here, the thought comes to me
quick, so!" He snapped his thumb and finger together. "I will take
her with me. I will ask Madame to let her serve her, let her learn
gentle ways. I do not want she should grow up a wild thing, without
some little graces." He laughed, his body shaking. "The gun—yes,
she shoot as straight as a man. The fishing-rod—yes, she catch the
biggest fish in the ocean, I think. All day she follow the trail of a

panther, and shoot him, just to make a rug for in front of the fire. She cook, yes, French-fashion; make the delicate sauces with herbs of her own garden. But—" his face darkened—"I do not want Michèle to be alone. She is a woman, almost. Men, they cast sheep eyes at her. No, she must not be alone."

Again he looked at Madame Ferrier for understanding.

"You are right, Roi; quite right. But we must have no talk of bond-woman. I will set her to work with my sempstress or in the weaving-room, until we decide."

The man's eyes brightened. "Good! That is very good. She like the little needles. Strange, those strong fingers of hers that caress the gun so amiably can make those little needles fly."

"When the children's governess comes home next month, she can teach her a little."

Gil Roi shook his head. "Not too much out of the book, madame, if you please. My Michèle must not get the notion to look above her station. Let her be well taught in the arts of the household—if you please, madame." He spoke to Francisca, but he looked at the senator.

"Gil is right. Not too much out of books."

Roi nodded his head solemnly. "What she need is restraint. She run free too long."

As they spoke, the girl Michèle came up the path from the grove and stood behind her father. She, too, stood firmly in her wooden shoes. She was not so tall as Angela, but more of a woman, with her full breasts and curved hips that swelled below her narrow waist. Her dress was made of some French woollen stuff of blue, turned over a petticoat of crimson. She wore a Spanish hat of black beaver tilted over one eye. Under the wide hat her dark hair was bound with a crimson scarf. Her eyes looked out steadily from under her straight black brows, with a challenge, a look of wariness, like some wild thing of the forest.

Francisca's heart sank. The dress, so flamboyant, as flamboyant as the girl herself! Here was a problem to be met. Holy Virgin, help me! she prayed within her heart. "Come here, Michèle." Francisca spoke gently. "Sit down on the steps."

Her father turned and saw her. "Michèle," he said rapidly in his own tongue, "I told you not to come."

"I know. But I want to see this woman you pulled from the sea, and the girl—is she prettier than I am?"

Francisca gave no sign that she understood what the girl was saying, or her father's sharp "Be silent!"

They went off soon. Michèle would come in the morning for instructions.

Francisca watched her walking away. "She has the grace of a panther," she said slowly, "—and the claws. Oh, Alexander, I think it is a task we have, to tame that one!"

The senator put his hand on her shoulder. "Do not worry, my dear. You will find a way."

Peter stepped out onto the gallery in time to see the Frenchman and his daughter walking down the path. Cecily and Angela came out immediately afterward.

Angela said, "I heard you talking to Gil Roi, Mother. Did I do wrong to listen?"

Francisca shook her head. "I don't think so, this time."

Angela did not hear; she was halfway across the gallery. "I'm going to speak to her, Mother, and to Gil Roi." She ran lightly down the path calling, "Gil Roi! Gil Roi! Wait!"

Francisca glanced at Peter. "She is very impulsive."

Peter answered vaguely. In his heart he was pleased. There was kindness back of the impulse.

Cecily said, "Oh, Madam, it would be so wonderful if Angela had a companion! A girl of her own age."

"I'm afraid Michèle Roi will not prove an ideal companion—but we shall see."

The doctor and Adam joined them. The senator called Zeb to bring drinks. Peter sat beside Ferrier. He told him he was leaving Tuesday morning. He was glad he had not been on the gallery when Roi and his daughter were there. That would have called for explanations. He didn't want Ferrier or anyone else to know of his trip down the Cape Fear in search of Jeremiah Morse.

After a little time Angela returned, walking slowly. "She is very pretty," she said to her mother. "I think she does not like us."

"Your imagination runs away with you, daughter," the senator said. Peter noticed that Francisca kept her own counsel.

The talk became general. Peter and the two girls walked in the garden. Guests arrived on horseback and there was the usual hustle of coming and going, of bringing horses from the stables, of servants carrying drinks and food—a form of life that belonged only to plantations. Hospitality was not so lavish here as at Eden House, nor were there so many political figures among the visitors. The talk was more the talk of planters—the crops, the weather, the hopes of a good harvest.

The children came in with their nurse, on their way to the nursery. They made their manners, charmingly, to each guest. When Bella came to Peter, she threw her arms about his neck and kissed him, clinging to him, refusing to leave. "I want to stay with Peter." There was an alternative. "I want Peter to put me to bed." Nor would she be denied. Peter picked her up and carried her pick-a-back, and the child shrieked with delight.

Francisca looked at her husband. "The children already love him."

Adam Rutledge grinned. "Have the hounds and horses expressed an opinion yet?"

Francisca tapped his knee with her fan. "Adam, you are teasing. You like Peter, don't you?"

Adam sobered at once. "I do more than that; I admire him. Peter has integrity."

Angela sat quietly by, her face expressionless.

Shortly after a hasty cup of hot chocolate, Peter was in the saddle, following the senator on his daily round of the plantation. "Every day that I am here," the senator said, "I look into the work my slaves are doing. They work fairly well for a good overlooker, but we have an old saying in this country that the sound of the master's footstep is worth a load of manure."

Peter laughed aloud. "At that, I suppose it does take real supervision."

"Yes. You'll find that out when you become a slave-owner."

"I'm not sure I want to own slaves."

The senator looked at him keenly for a moment. "You can't plant in this country unless you own slaves," he said without emphasis. "Look at that," he added, with a chuckle. Peter turned. A young Negro man was driving two oxen hitched to a harrow, cultivating the rows. He had tied a reed basket to the yoke of the oxen. In the swinging basket a Negro child lay asleep. "You will find the Negro the most ingenious creature on the face of the globe when it comes to arranging comfort for himself," Ferrier commented.

They had finished the inspection of the fields where the corn was knee-high. The senator suggested that they ride across a strip of woods to the Boyd place. Halfway through, they came on an opening

in the heart of the woods. An old chimney, listing a little, showed
where a house had once stood; near by were two giant oaks, covered
with Spanish moss falling almost to the ground.

"Those are the most beautiful trees I have ever seen," Peter remarked.

"They are on old Boyd property," the senator told him. "This is
Angela's favourite ride. Ah, there they are now!"

Angela and Cecily were coming from the opposite direction. "We've
been for a bathe in the creek," Angela told them. "It's wonderful
this morning." Peter said something about the beauty of the trees. "I
come here every day," she said. "See! One of the slaves made a seat
for me, long years ago."

The girls rode off, declining to return to the creek. It was a lovely
spot, the water dark, almost black. "Sweet water, we call it here," said
the senator. "Above here, a few·miles, is a mill-pond and a mill where
we have our corn ground."

Peter was tempted to tell Mr. Ferrier that he was negotiating for
the property. But he had the Scot's caution. He wanted to be sure.
He was delighted with the land—the small open field; the tall pines
and hardwood; holly, oak and maple; a giant tupelo; birds everywhere.
He sat on his horse, dreaming, a house by the meandering stream, a
long driveway through the woods . . .

The senator's voice broke into his dream. "I declare we must make
haste. It's close to dinner-time."

On the way back, they talked of a possible date for the marriage.

"If it could be arranged, I would like so much to have the wedding
as soon as I return from Philadelphia."

"We will see. We will see. In this we must consult my wife, Peter."

The carriage moved along swiftly over the road. Adam, with his
eyes closed, nodded in his corner. Herk was driving; a second man on
the box. Peter was glad of the quiet. He would have more time to
think of Angela—Angela racing with the children; Angela playing the
harp; galloping her horse down the lane; Angela visiting the slave
cabins, playing with the little Negro children; Angela sitting close to
her mother, looking at her adoringly; Angela watching him with eyes
that held an aloof awareness, but not in anger or disdain—something
more detached.

He found his mind wandering away from Angela. What was the
next step for him? In this pattern of war would it be New Bern, or

the Sand Hills along the Peedee, where the North Carolina troops were ordered, or would it be the back-country, near the great Blue Ridge Mountains? He turned it over in his mind until all thought of the peaceful life of the village and the tranquillity of the plantation grew dim. Ahead of him the great pattern of the war was unfolding. In it he must play his part. To that he looked forward with quickening heart.

After a time his eyes closed and he, too, slept.

CHAPTER
20

PHILADELPHIA

ADAM RUTLEDGE and Peter arrived in Philadelphia in a pouring rain and drove at once to Joseph Hewes's lodgings in Second Street. It was supper-time when they arrived. The long journey had been dull. The last day, to escape boredom, they had made wagers on the time of arrival, whether they could secure lodgings, and whether Mr. Hewes was still in Philadelphia.

The trim maid dressed in grey, with a crisp muslin fichu, who answered the door, told them Mr. Hewes was in, confined to his room by a severe cold.

She held onto the shining brass knob, keeping the door open only enough for a quick appraisal with her shoe-button black eyes. Satisfied, she widened the crack until the door stood open. She invited them into a wide hall, from which opened a series of panelled doors painted white, all closed. Two Suffolk benches were placed along the side-wall which was papered in grey and blue and gold, commemorating Independence Day.

"Step upstairs, gentlemen, the second door on the left."

Peter turned when they reached the landing. The girl was standing where they had left her, watching them. She smiled briefly, then walked down the hall, and disappeared under the turn of the stairs.

They found Hewes sitting in bed, propped up by pillows, a scarf wrapped around his shoulders, his stocking night-cap on his head. The bed was piled with papers and pamphlets, a mountain of them, until the man himself seemed shrunken into nothing but a long thin nose and deep mournful eyes, set in a sallow face.

He smiled with pleasure when he saw Adam, and held out a thin hand. "Adam! What a pleasant surprise! I had no idea you were coming to Philadelphia. I thought you were in the far West by now."

"That comes later. I have to be instructed further, it seems. I am sorry to find you ill."

"Yes. The old story, freeze to death one moment, burn up the next. This one was a bone-rattler, with a touch of blackwater."

Adam looked serious. "Blackwater?"

"Yes, but thank God the doctor got the best of that phase before it got me. But who is this young gentleman?"

"Sorry," Adam said with a laugh. "I was so interested in you that I quite forgot Peter—Captain Huntley—who has been in Queen Anne's Town for a month or more."

Joseph Hewes held out his hand to Peter. "I have met Captain Huntley. Indeed, I sent Johnston a letter by him. My most indefatigable correspondent, Penelope Dawson, writes often mentioning you. But be seated, gentlemen."

Peter said, "Queen Anne's Town was all you told me, and more. Your friends speak of you so often, Mr. Hewes, that I really felt, sometimes, that I saw you walking from your shop to your shipyard, or sitting on Mr. Allen's porch."

Hewes's sallow face wrinkled into a smile. "Queen Anne's Town is loyal to its sons and daughters. Did you enjoy your stay there? Let me see—didn't my partner, Robert Smith, write that you were checking up on the lottery?"

"Yes, sir. For General Pierce."

"Peter was in Paris with Mr. Franklin, for some time," Adam volunteered. "He is up now to get a new assignment from the Committee on Foreign Affairs."

"Yes. Yes, Mr. Lovell, chairman."

"I report to Mr. Jay, sir."

Hewes took off his spectacles and laid them on the night-table. "They wanted me on that committee, but I preferred to work on the Committee for Maritime Affairs. The navy is nearer my heart."

Adam rose. "I had almost forgotten. I think I had better talk with the landlady and enquire about rooms."

Hewes touched a bell. Immediately his Negro man came in. He smiled broadly when he saw Adam. "I 'clare I is proud to set eyes on you, Mr. Rutledge. We need to see some of our folks, sir. Livin' up here with foreigners not so good for us. No, it ain't."

Hewes interrupted: "Cato, run down and ask Mrs. Srunk whether she has lodgings for my friends, Major Rutledge and Captain Huntley."

"Yes, sar." The man left the room quickly.

"I don't know what I'd have done without Cato, since I had this spell. Luckily, I wasn't busy in Congress, just the work on the Maritime Committee."

Peter asked, "Have the new North Carolina representatives taken their seats?"

"Yes. Burke, Penn and Sharpe are here," Hewes replied.

"What are they doing in Congress?" Adam asked.

"They are engaged in a long debate over conditions of pacification, the right of fishing, particularly as to the Mississippi and its fishers, and whether or not to recall Arthur Lee from Paris."

Peter pricked up his ears but he did not ask about Lee, as Hewes went on: "It's a disgrace, gentlemen, that with General Washington calling for money and troops and leave to work out a campaign, our Congress is split a dozen ways, wrangling over things of no moment."

"And your committee?"

Hewes fingered a sheet of paper. "I have a letter from Mr. Jay, putting the case squarely. He thinks that while the maritime affairs of the continent continue under a committee, they will be exposed to all the consequences of want of systematic attention and knowledge. I agree with him. We have a delegate from each state. They fluctuate; new members are constantly coming in and old ones going out. Only three or four have been in from the beginning. Most of the men don't even understand the state of our naval affairs, or have inclination to attend meetings. There is as much intrigue in the State House as in the Vatican, but as little secrecy as in a boarding-school."

The men laughed. Hewes hastened to disclaim credit. "John Jay's words," he exclaimed, "in a letter he wrote General Washington. The General was amused and repeated it to his officers. It is amusing but it is tragic." He tapped a pile of letters. "There is a letter here from General Washington to John Jay. He says, 'To me it appears that our affairs are in a very delicate situation; and what is not the least to be lamented, is that many people think they are in a very flourishing way, and seem in a great measure to be insensible to the danger with which we are threatened. If Britain should be able to make a vigorous campaign this summer, in the present depreciation of our money, the scantiness of supplies, want of virtue and want of exertion, 'tis hard to say what may be the consequence.' This was written last month from Middlebrooke. Things are even worse now."

There was a knock at the door; the little serving-maid who had let them in entered the room. "Madam Srunk says the gentlemen may have Mr. McKean's room, while he is away."

"Thank you, Betsy. Will you kindly show these gentlemen the room?"

The girl bobbed. "This way, please."

Herk soon unpacked the boxes, and managed to get hot water for shaving and a bath. Before the second dinner bell rang, Adam and Peter were ready to go downstairs.

"Don't you think Mr. Hewes is very frail?" Peter asked as they were descending the stairs.

"I was shocked when I saw him," Adam replied. "I hope I didn't show what I felt. If anything happens to him, we have indeed lost a fortress."

A tall woman, with clear chiselled features and excellent bearing, met them in the hall. "Major Rutledge? Captain Huntley? I am Madam Srunk. I hope your room is comfortable and that you have everything you need."

Adam bent over her hand. "Thank you, yes. You are so kind to find space for Captain Huntley and me. We are indeed fortunate."

"Philadelphia is crowded, with Congress in session, but I am glad to accommodate friends of Mr. Hewes."

"He looks bad." Adam lowered his voice. "I was shocked when I saw him."

"You should have been here a month ago. He was really ill then. Now he talks of going home, soon, back to Queen Anne's Town." She smiled slightly. "It must be delightful there. I feel that I know the village and all the people, from Mr. Hewes."

Two men came down the stairs. One was thin and cadaverous-looking, the other nearly as tall but stocky, almost burly. Madam introduced one guest to another in the manner of a hostess in her home: "Mr. Peabody of New Hampshire, and Mr. Gary of Massachusetts." They paused for a moment, spoke a few words and went on into the dining-hall.

Madam Srunk asked them to accompany her. The dining-room was large. There was a long table down the centre of the room, a drop leaf with separate ends, that accommodated twenty. Several men were seated. They stood up when Madam Srunk entered the room and took her place at the head of the table. She mentioned their names: Mr. Marchant of Rhode Island; Mr. Duane of New York; Mr. Drayton of South Carolina. Adam shook hands with Mr. Drayton, an old friend, and asked for Mr. Laurens, who, Mr. Drayton said, was in a committee meeting.

Peter and Adam took their places. Madam Srunk said, "There must be several committee meetings, or is there a night session?"

"Not tonight, madam," Mr. Marchant replied. "But I think there will be tomorrow."

She glanced down the table. "Mr. Jenifer of Maryland; Mr. Fleming of Virginia." She reminded Peter of the Clerk of Congress calling off the members' names. She was well content to have so many distinguished gentlemen at her table—"sometimes called the Little Congress," Mr. Hewes told him later.

Peter thought that Philadelphia with Congress in session was much the same as Smithfield when the State Legislature was in session, excepting that the affairs discussed by these gentlemen were broader in scope: world affairs instead of local affairs. Mr. Drayton was telling the men at his end of the table that Mr. Burke, of North Carolina, had made the proposal, seconded by Mr. Drayton, that "if Great Britain will acknowledge and ratify the liberty, sovereignty, and independence, absolute and unlimited, as well in matters of commerce, of these United States, and agree to the other articles in the ultimatum resolved upon by Congress, the present war shall not be continued, notwithstanding Great Britain shall decline to make an express and particular acknowledgement of the rights specified."

There was some discussion of this, Mr. Marchant saying he was opposed to all offers of negotiated peace; he was opposed to Mr. Franklin's negotiations with Mr. Hartley to endeavour to reach the Opposition in England, to induce them to make a peace. "What we want is a clear-cut victory. Once and for all, let us settle this problem."

"Have we the strength necessary to gain a victory?" someone asked.

"We fight against bitter odds, without and within," was Mr. Drayton's enigmatic remark as the men rose from the table.

Mr. Drayton asked Adam to stop by his room and have a brandy. He turned to Peter. "Will you join us, Captain?" Peter accepted. He liked Mr. Drayton. He was a gentleman of fine behaviour and manners. He had intelligence as well as tolerance.

Drayton swept papers and clothes off a sofa, and complained about his man. "He's surely spoiled since I brought him north. He's not worth a damn. I've a notion to sell him or send him back home. I told him to keep wood in the fire-place. Strange that in the last of June one would think of a fire, but this dampness gets to the bones."

He went to the door and shouted several times, "Nate! Nate! . . . The rascally fellow's gone. I suspect he's got some wench, down by the river."

Peter laid a few sticks and lighted them with his flint. The wood was dry. In a few minutes a merry blaze was going. Peter put in a lump of coal from a brass scuttle.

"Thank you, Captain, thank you. If I were young and had a flat stomach, I wouldn't mind bending over either." Drayton went to a secretary and took out a decanter and glasses. He poured the brandy, pulled a chair up near the fire and sat down. "Wretched little fireplaces. On the plantation we use six-foot logs; then you really get a fire." Peter and Adam pulled up their chairs and made a little semicircle around the blaze.

Drayton at once launched into the situation in South Carolina. "Your North Carolina men must get the idea firmly in their minds that they will be invaded, sooner or later. The more soldiers you send us, the farther off is the day of invasion. We get reports. We've a good Intelligence in England and in Paris. You'd be surprised how many of Howe's plans we know." He spread his hand across his stomach, nodding his white-wigged head.

"I hope you don't depend on Arthur Lee's reports," Adam remarked dryly.

Drayton glanced at him, a keen interrogating look. "You are suspicious of Lee? Of Izard also?"

"I don't know about Mr. Izard. I profoundly distrust Mr. Lee's judgement in selecting his staff."

Peter did not enter the conversation. He had the feeling that Rutledge was trying out Mr. Drayton.

"You are a Franklin man, Major Rutledge?"

"Yes—without qualification."

Drayton nodded, and changed the subject. "We are told that General Lincoln has had an advantage over Prevost in an open field fight, where the militia behaved to admiration, on the twentieth of June. That is encouraging. We haven't had much confidence in the militia. They run too readily."

"You can't expect men to stand up to the Line, when they haven't guns all around, and only half enough powder and ball," Adam said with bitterness. "I've seen them mowed down, the poor devils."

The steady beat of rain on the small-paned windows, the warmth of the fire, the long day's travel, caused Peter's eyes to close. Words came to him endlessly, without connection: "Caswell . . . we must be prepared for a violent attack." He opened his eyes. Adam was on his feet, smiling at him.

"I am sorry, sir," Peter said to Mr. Drayton. "It must be the fire." Both men laughed. Peter glanced at the fire; it was black and dead, without embers.

"It is past midnight. You've been sleeping for an hour."

Peter was embarrassed. "What must you think of me, sir? I am truly ashamed."

Drayton clapped a hand on his shoulder. "It's youth, my boy, youth. Oldsters are the ones who sit propped up in bed hour on hour, wooing Morpheus."

By nine in the morning Peter was at the door of the hall. He was at once ushered into Mr. Jay's office. The President's secretary, Huff, who knew Peter, said Mr. Jay would see him in a few minutes.

The interview was not long. John Jay was not one to spend time on non-essentials. He shook hands with Peter, told him to be seated, and himself sat down in a tall-backed chair, beside an escritoire. They went over the Morse incident at some length.

"We have come to certain conclusions which we will go into some time later. The affair is of no importance at the moment." He sat, swinging his long silk-clad leg over his knee, his hands resting on the arms of the chair. "Mr. Franklin would like to have you in Paris, Peter."

Peter was surprised. "Mr. Franklin? Paris? I thought I was to go into the mountain country. I don't quite understand," he said. "Do I have a choice, sir?"

"You have the choice."

"I love Mr. Franklin, sir, but Paris is too far from the fighting. I would like to go to the mountains."

Jay lifted his head and laughed aloud. "I told Lovell you would say that."

Peter was troubled. "I feel a very mean person not to go if Mr. Franklin wants me, but I must be frank. I have been quite unhappy in this last assignment. It was too easy, too removed from the things that count. I've wanted to get back to my regiment."

"I'm afraid you won't have your wish for some time. We've only a few young officers with your training or your knowledge of languages. I'm going to turn you over to Mr. Lovell. He will give you

letters and papers to read. I want you to be well up on the co
tions in Paris, as well as here in the army. Now, if you will excuse
it is time to attend the session. Huff will take you to Mr. Lov

Mr. Jay rose and shook hands again. Peter found Mr. Lovell
small, darkish room at the back of the great hall.

Mr. Lovell was a quiet-spoken but shrewd man, noted for a sl
and caustic tongue on occasion. He had none of the grace of Mr.
or the warmth of manner. He was quick; he was abrupt, as thougl
had a thousand things on his mind, weighing him down as the Cl
man of the Secret Committee of Foreign Affairs. His tasks \
weighty and onerous. With the Embassy in Paris rent asunder \
arguments, prejudices and hatreds, and inadequate representative
other countries, he had worriment enough for two men. There
trouble about the flour from Wilmington, which caused the Fre
Ambassador at Philadelphia to write polite but caustic notes to C
gress, asking why civil authority should interfere with flour being :
to His Majesty's fleet.

Right now, he was composing a conciliatory letter to M. Gérard,
French Ambassador, but the flour was gone, no one knew where.

He pressed into Peter's hands two great bundles of papers tied \
red tape. "Sit down at that desk by the window. Read Mr. Fr;
lin's correspondence, and the letters from the General, also. And
is of first importance, Captain: read every word of Mr. John Ada
report to the President of Congress, dated August 4, 1779. Mr.
is emphatic on this. By the way, where are you going—Paris or the
West?"

"The West, sir."

Lovell glared at him. "Jay said you would. Now I must find anot
interpreter for Mr. Franklin, and that, sir, is no easy task. You kr
Mr. Franklin." He paused. As Peter made no comment, he
sharply, "Well, there's the desk and your work is in your hand."

Peter walked across the room. Lovell turned to his desk, took
the quill, and began a letter to Arthur Lee in Paris:

There is really no Committee of Foreign Affairs existing. N
secretary or clerk further than I presume to be one and the othe
The Books and Papers of the distinguished body lay yet on th
table of Congress, or rather locked up in the Secretary's privat
box. There was a motion to choose a new committee, then a
indifference took place as to filling up the old one. You, M
Lee, have no enemies on the Committee; it is impossible. Th

status of Mr. Deane is the opposite. Do not think of me as "an innuendo man."

The news of Wayne's conduct and the success of Count d'Estaing ought to serve us greatly in Europe.

Peter glanced through the bundle. Being orderly, he first made a notation of the title content, before he started in to read:

A. Lee—to Comm. FA., Nantes, Mar. 8. Franklin to Vergennes, Passy, Mar. 9, 1779. Franklin's Circular respecting Capt. Cook, Passy, Mar. 10. Franklin to Arthur Lee, Passy, Mar. 13. W. Lee to Pres. of Congress, Mar. 16. Franklin to LaFayette, Passy, Mar. 22. Deane to Congress, Mar. 29. Abstract of several letters dated Martinique.

This last paper had a peculiar double line on it, which meant secret and confidential. He untied the red tape. The first was dated February twenty-fifth.

The King's vessels *Robuste*, of seventy-four guns, commanded by the Count de Grasse, Commander of Squadron; *Magnifique*, seventy-four, by M. de Branche; *Dauphin Royal*, seventy, by M. de Millan; *Venegeut*, sixty-four, having sailed from Brest 14 of January, arrived at Fort Royal on 20 this month. They had on board the second field regiment; eight hundred and fifty recruits and a company of miners.

Mar. 6. We learn that Admiral Byron has, on his part, received reinforcements. He has not yet undertaken any operations. He has only twice sailed out with some ships, but returned the day after. It is true that he has not troops enough to make conquests and preserve them. Sickness continues to make great ravege upon those that are at St. Lucia.

Mar. 9. The convoy from France, so much wished for, has just arrived. The Islands of St. Martin and St. Bartholomew, which the English took, have just been retaken.

M. de Kersu took two prizes last week: one merchant Store Ship, the *Eliza*, twenty-eight twelve-pounders, one hundred and forty one-pounders. The other a privateer, coming from Halifax loaded with fish and foods.

Martinique Mar. 14. Portuguese vessels returning from India report English have commenced hostilities against the French in month of April.

Baltimore. Captain of sloop, just arrived twenty-two days from Martinique, reports sickness made dreadful ravage in English army and fleet at St. Lucia. French frigates constantly at sea often engaging English. French seem satisfied with situation, unconcerned with regard to success of the operations Admiral Byron intends to undertake.

Peter read the notes through and laid them aside. He wondered why they were given to him when they were marked secret. His eyes fell on a large map of the eastern coast and the Caribbean. For a long time he studied it without finding the key.

Lovell spoke to him. "You enjoy reading maps, Captain?"

"If I can read them properly, sir."

Lovell strolled across the room. His quick sharp eyes fell on the folded paper. He reached for it, then withdrew his hand. Peter gave no evidence of having noted the gesture, but he made up his mind to lock up the papers that night. Perhaps Lovell had read them all. Perhaps they were just as they were sent by Mr. Jay. He was aware that Lovell was watching him warily.

"I thought you would choose to go to Paris," Lovell said after a silence. "Why didn't you?"

"I want to be in the fighting, Mr. Lovell."

"There's no fighting in the western mountains, unless the Cherokees erupt."

Peter said, "There might be." Lovell went back to his desk. Peter picked up a single sheet of paper that fell from a larger bundle. He recognized Mr. Franklin's writing. It was addressed to John Williams and written from Passy on February fifth.

"Dear Cousin:" it began. Peter skipped the first lines of greeting, came to an item that made him smile:

William Green, Esqre., Governor of the State of Rhode Island, has sent me some bills of exchange, amounting to 1,080 livers, which he desires to be laid out in following articles; one piece dark calico, one piece bed tick, best silk handkerchief, linen ditto, Hollands, cambrics, muslins, sewing silk, one box of window glass, seven inches by nine. I send you the commission.

He read another short letter in Mr. Franklin's hand. It was dated February 24, 1779. It was to Paul Jones.

Dear Captain:

Mr. Alexander called this morning to deliver a little message to be communicated to you from Lord Selkirk. The purport was that his Lordship had written an answer to your letter, which had been detained in the Post Office and sent back to him. That as to the proposition of returning the plate, if it was made by an order of Congress or any public Body, he would accept it, and endeavour to make suitable return for the favour. But if, by a private person's generosity, the Captain's for instance, he would by no means receive it.

You will judge whether it is worth while to give yourself any further trouble about that matter.

I am, with great regard, dear Sir, B.F.

Peter could not help but chuckle over this, as well as he would have chuckled over the audacity of the raid Captain Jones had made on the British coast.

He returned to the first letter. He remembered vividly how many letters of the same character had come to the Minister for America. "A piece of dark calico," when men's minds were weary with the impasse of peace negotiations, or the dismal reports of troops that were hungry! John Paul Jones crying for ships and more ships! Franklin's own words, "The extraordinary indifference of some of our people, to all our distress, when the difficulties are so great to pay for our arms and ammunition, so necessary for our defence. I am astonished . . ."

"A piece of bed tick," and a negotiation in the morning that would mould the fate of many ships and their crews! He slapped the bundle on the table with a bang. Lovell watched him take up his hat. "I'm going over to the tavern," Peter said.

"I'll go with you," Lovell said. "It's eleven. There will be a dozen men from the Congress slipping over for a refresher. Find the papers interesting, Captain?"

"I'm out of touch with the progress of the war," Peter said evasively.

"There *is* no progress." Lovell's voice was edged with cynicism. "No progress anywhere, only confusion."

Peter had worked more than a month on the papers, checking, filing and making himself familiar with the events of the past six months. Then one morning in late August the Paymaster Department sent for him. Lovell gave him the message reluctantly. "I never get a man in my department who shows any ability but some ranking official sends for him." He looked glumly at Peter. "What does Pierce want of you, anyway?"

"I suppose it is about lottery tickets," Peter answered, secretly amused at the left-handed compliment. In the weeks he had been there Lovell had been civil, but no more. "You know I had charge of one of the Southern districts."

"I didn't know that. I hear they have taken in so much money that they intend to run a second series."

"I hadn't heard." Peter put his three-cornered hat under his arm and left the office.

Congress was in session. As he neared the Hall, he heard someone speaking. The words came clearly through the open door. Peter paused to listen.

"Mr. John Adams' report says in part, 'France deserves the first place among those powers with which our connections will be most intimate . . . I . . . assure Congress that . . . I have the strongest reasons to believe that their august ally, his ministers and nation, are possessed of the fullest persuasion of the justice of our cause.'" There was a scattered clapping of hands, then the voice went on. Peter recognized it now; it was that of Mr. Jay, the President of Congress. "'The peace of Germany, signed at Teschen the thirteenth of last May, has not equally satisfied the belligerent powers, who were on the one part the Emperor, and on the other the King of Prussia and the Elector of Saxony, his ally. . . . The King of Prussia, to whose interest this augmentation of power would have been dangerous, has crowned an illustrious reign by displaying all the resources of military genius and profound policy in opposition to it. . . . The Palatine House of Bavaria, the Duke of Deux Ponts, and particularly the Elector of Saxony, have obtained all they could reasonably demand. . . . The King of Prussia has covered himself with glory, to which he put the finishing stroke by not demanding any compensation for the expenses of war.'"

Mr. Jay paused, but no hand-clapping followed. He continued: "'In the opinion of some, the power with which we shall one day have a relation the most immediate, next to that of France, is Great Britain.'"

Mr. Jay was interrupted here by a loud burst of applause. Peter, who had stepped inside the hall, was amazed at the spontaneity. We are still British, he thought, as he studied the faces of the delegates nearest to him. "We cannot forget the Mother Country," one of them whispered. "We will soon be at peace."

Mr. Jay held up his hand and went on with the Adams report. " 'But it ought to be considered that this power loses every day her consideration, and runs toward her ruin. Her riches, in which her power consisted, she has lost with us, and can never regain. With us she has lost her Mediterranean trade, her African trade, her German and Holland trade, her ally, Portugal, her ally, Russia, and her natural ally, the House of Austria; at least, as being unable to protect these as she once did, she can obtain no succor from them. In short, one branch of commerce has been lopped off after another, and one political interest sacrificed after another. She resembles the melancholy spectacle of a great wide-spreading tree that has been girdled at the root. . . .

" 'Between the Hollanders and us . . . Too many motives of fear or interest place the Hollanders in a dependence on England, to suffer them to connect themselves openly with us at present. Nevertheless, if the King of Prussia could be induced to take us by the hand, his great influence in the United Provinces might contribute greatly to conciliate their friendship for us. . . .

" 'Portugal, under the administration of the Marquis de Pombal, broke some of the shackles by which she was held to England. . . . It would be endless to consider the infinite number of little sovereignties into which Germany is divided, and develop all their political interests. . . . The State of Germany, with which we may have commerce of an honourable kind, is the House of Austria, one of the most powerful in Europe. . . . England may possibly make a new treaty with Austria. . . . The port of Trieste enjoys liberty without limits; and the Court of Vienna is anxious to make its commerce flourish. Situated as it is at the bottom of the Gulf of Trieste, the remotest part of the Gulf of Venice, tedious and difficult as navigation of those seas is, we could make little use of it at any time, and none at all while this war continues. . . .

" 'The jealousy between the Emperor and the King of Prussia, and that between the Houses of Bourbon and Austria, are a natural tie between France and Prussia. The rivalry between France and Great Britain is another motive. . . .

" 'Poland, depopulated by the war and a vicious government, reduced by a shameful treaty to two thirds of her ancient dominion . . . has no occasion for the productions of America. . . . There is, therefore, little probability of commerce, and less of any political connection between that nation and us. . . .

" 'It is not probable that the Courts of Petersburg, Stockholm, and Copenhagen have viewed with indifference the present revolution . . . yet the motive of humbling the pride of the English, who have endeavoured to exercise their domination even over the northern seas, and to render the Danish and Swedish flag dependent on theirs, has prevailed over all others, and they are considered in Europe as having given their testimony against the English in this war.

" 'Italy, a country which declines every day from its ancient prosperity, offers few objects to our speculations. The privilege of the port of Leghorn, nevertheless, may render it useful to our ships when our independence shall be acknowledged by Great Britain, if, as we once flattered ourselves, the Court of Vienna might receive an American minister. We were equally in error respecting the Court of the Grand Duchy of Tuscany, where an Austrian prince reigns, who receives all his directions from Vienna. . . . The King of the Two Sicilies is in the same dependence on the Court of Madrid. . . .

" 'The Court of Rome, attached to ancient customs, would be one of the last to acknowledge our independence, if we were to solicit for it. But Congress will probably never send a minister to his Holiness. . . .

" 'The States of the King of Sardinia are poor, and their commerce is very small. . . . The Republic of Genoa is scarcely known at this day in Europe but by those powers who borrow money. . . . Venice, hitherto so powerful, is reduced to a very inconsiderable commerce, and is in an entire state of decay. . . . Switzerland is another lender of money. . . .

" 'Whether there is any thing in these remarks worth the trouble of reading, I shall submit to the wisdom of Congress, and subscribe myself, with the highest consideration, Your most obedient and humble servant, John Adams.' "

Peter slipped out of the hall, as the soberly dressed, bewigged gentlemen of the Congress clapped loudly in their approval of Mr. Adams' summary of the situation abroad. He recognized it at once as the same report Mr. Jay had advised him to read.

He wondered that Mr. Adams had made no mention of his association with Mr. Franklin, for he knew much of the material for the report came from the files in Mr. Franklin's office. Bad feeling in the Paris Ministry remained, no doubt, jealousy and hatred.

He hurried into the gloomy old building, once a warehouse, that housed the Paymaster-General's office.

General Pierce came in shortly. He greeted Peter cordially, and announced at once that the last lottery box had come in from Queen Anne's Town, sent by Mr. Robert Smith. Everything was in good order.

Peter said, "I am glad of that. You know some of the merchants take the lottery very lightly. Tickets are sent out, not listed or checked."

Pierce, who was an elderly man, rotund and well upholstered, smiled ruefully. "Don't I know! I've had much correspondence with Governor Caswell on the subject. However, it goes well, Captain. Very well indeed." He pushed a box of receipts toward Peter. "Look at these, Huntley, while I speak to one of my clerks. I think I have an appointment."

Peter shuffled through the papers; two letters caught his attention.

MorrisTown, June first.

Sir:

By conveyance you will receive my monthly account, for May. The balance on hand will be used by his Excellency's direction, for discharged men.

The Two Hundred Thousand Dollars you mention, will be sent. It will be well not to have it known to any person when it comes, as it will not answer in any measure for the payment of troops and his Excellency will apply it to some particular purpose.

John Pierce.

To Col. Palfrey.

So that was the amount of the lottery prize money. And at the General's order it would be used to pay discharged soldiers. After these months of drearily checking tickets, it was interesting to know something about the result. The next paper also concerned lottery tickets.

Lottery Office.
Philadelphia, June 26.

Sir:

We are particularly called upon by the Treasury for a state of the Lottery, in order to learn the cash lodged in different Loan offices.

We request you will furnish us, as soon as possible, with a complete state of your account, for all three classes, enclosing us vouchers for tickets delivered to the Governor and President and cash paid to the Loan offices, which will enable us immediately to reply with the above requisition of the Treasury.

The prize list will be furnished us in a few days, when we shall, without loss of time, forward them with the necessary directions for completing the fourth class, which we expect daily from Congress.

Joseph Bullock.
Sharp Delancy. Managers

John Pierce, Esq.

General Pierce came in as Peter finished reading. "By now, you know what I want with you, Huntley." He grinned engagingly.

Peter let out a groan. "I can imagine."

"Don't suffer so, Peter. The lottery is really a pleasant task. What if you had to turn down requests for money to pay hungry troops, day after day? Then you would think the lottery was a gala affair." He pushed the iron box toward Peter with his pudgy fingers.

"If you want any information, call one of my clerks. I'm off to explain to a choleric general why I can't procure nine thousand dollars in bills of exchange on Spain, and deliver to him, at present rate of exchange, a ten-day sight draft for three hundred and sixty thousand dollars." He went out, banging the door after him until the shot in the little glass ink-wells rattled and rolled over on the desk.

Peter took off his coat and hung it carefully on a peg. He had been sitting so much since he came to Philadelphia that the seat of his breeks had grown shiny, but he could not find time to go to a tailor to order another pair. He pulled a stool up to the slanting desk and began to work.

At six o'clock a clerk stuck his head in the door. "Everyone's gone. Want I should get candles for you, sir?"

Peter looked up. "Yes, yes, some candles." He leaned back, stretching his arms above his head. "I think I'll keep on working."

Suddenly he realized he was hungry. "Is there an eating-house near by?"

The clerk, a young, almost beardless boy with a mop of unruly red hair, looked doubtful. "The food around here is direful, they say. I don't be eating it myself. I bring my lunch in a paper poke, but the ale is good."

"Splendid! Bring ale and cold cuts and a hunk of cheese."

"No bread, sir?"

"Bread? Yes, of course, bread." Peter put his hand in his pocket and drew out some coins. "Have them send it over on a tray, will you?" he said, dropping the money in the boy's hand.

The clerk looked dubious. " 'Tain't that kind of a tavern, sir. I'll bring it over myself."

"Good fellow," Peter muttered, already back at the figures. "God in heaven, I must have done some dirty, evil deeds in my last existence, to take such bitter punishment now!" He shut his lips firmly and thrust his long jaw forward and went at the column of figures.

The clerk came back with a black lacquered tray covered with a white cloth. Peter asked him to sit down and eat with him. He hesitated. "Come, sit down. I don't enjoy eating alone," Peter told him. "If the food is bad, I need someone to complain to; if it's good, someone to hear me smack my lips in enjoyment."

The boy laughed and sat down. "The landlord insisted on sending hot onion soup, sir. He said they made it proper good."

He lifted the napkin from the tray. The food was appetizing. "I'll get glasses from my office." The boy went to the outside room and returned with two heavy tumblers. "I heern that if you lay a spoon in a glass it won't crack when you pour hot liquid into it," he volunteered.

"Well, let's test it." Peter poured the hot onion soup into the tumbler, which remained intact. "What's your name?" he asked, as he poured the ale.

"Gurley, Willie Gurley. I lived up Morris Town way, until Mr. Pierce brought me here."

"Like the work?"

"Well enough. I know I like the pay. I've got my ma and a little brother. Pop's with General Lincoln, in South Carolina. They don't pay them anything in South Carolina."

They ate the food to the last crumb. Gurley offered to return the tray to the tavern, which was on his way to his boarding-house.

Refreshed, Peter settled down to work. It was near midnight when he finished totting up the last column of figures.

The Managers of the United States Lottery,
In account with John Pierce.

To 346 tickets unsold and delivered at their lottery,
    March 20, 1780 . . . . Dollars 10,380
To cash received for sale of tickets   42,542
To 1 ticket, No. 4248, which drew 500 dollars in
    2d class, taken in tickets in 3d class . . .   500
To 12 tickets, which drew 30 dollars each in 2d
    class, renewed in 3d class   360
To ½ per cent. for sale of 1454 tickets   218
                                       ————

                                     Dollars 54,000

Credit.
By 1800 tickets of the 3d class, received for sale at 30 dollars 54,000
    I am, gentlemen, with respect, your obedient servant,
Managers U. S. Lottery.

All was finished except the signature of John Pierce, to be written in his own hand.

Peter slid off the stool and stretched a few times to relieve his aching back. He put on his coat and took his hat from the peg. He picked up a candle to light his way through the cavernous warehouse, snuffed it and gave it to the watchman at the door.

Outside, a stiff wind was blowing off the river, but the three days' rain had stopped. A few stars struggled through the swift moving clouds, lined in silver by the unseen moon. Peter settled his hat more firmly on his head, and walked briskly in the direction of Madam Srunk's boarding-house. He kept well to the middle of the street. At the corner he met the watchman with a lanthorn, going his way. He felt better, for his sword-arm was still not much use to him, and Philadelphia abounded with rogues and cutthroats.

He fell to thinking of Angela as he walked behind the watchman with the lanthorn. Other late stragglers fell in with them, until there was a little queue, which peeled off, one by one, as the men came to their corners. They came at last to Madam Srunk's house. The hall was lighted by a hanging lamp halfway up the stairs. Peter opened the door to his room quietly. By a little blaze among the coals in the fire-box, he saw that Rutledge was in bed and asleep. He undressed in the dark. The ewer clattered against the wash-basin, when he attempted to pour water to wash his grimy hands. He cursed softly, turned back the covers on his bed and crawled in. A few minutes later he was sound asleep.

CHAPTER

21

INTERVAL

ADAM came back at the end of the week from a visit to Northern headquarters, where he had conferred with the General. Peter poured out his discouragement. He was chained to a desk, and no end to the work Mr. Jay was piling up.

"I might as well have gone to Paris," he declared. "I'm engaged every day in tabulating the European communications to Congress, Mr. Franklin's letters, the trouble over the French and American ships, and John Paul Jones's complaints."

Adam said, "You don't know when you're well off, my lad. You should hear General Washington's officers. There's nothing so dangerous as inaction. But we've plans, my young Peter, plans."

"I've heard nothing but plans and plans and a Southern campaign for months."

Adam said, "You won't have to wait much longer. Before another year is past you will have all you want of action."

"A year!" groaned Peter. "A month is what I'm dreaming of, a day. If tomorrow morning I had orders to leave my desk, I'd go down to Christ Church and say a prayer and let all my good Presbyterian forbears turn in their graves."

Adam stripped off his clothes, preparing for bed. Peter lingered at the window, looking at the moon through a chestnut tree.

"Even the moon is confined to a narrow space," he complained. "At the River Plantation it was a free, fine moon moving majestically. Here it skips from tree to tree, from house-top to house-top, no space, no swinging motion across the great dome of the heavens."

"Missing the lady?" Adam asked, tossing his boots across the room.

Peter did not answer but continued to gaze out the window. Adam watched him, amused. Peter was not always so composed as one would imagine him to be.

356

"Better get your sleep," Adam said. "We're making an early start."

Peter turned quickly. "We? Making an early start? Where?"

Adam said casually, "Your orders are on the chest there."

Peter took the distance in two long strides and lifted the paper to the candle. After a long silence he said, "We are going tomorrow. Thank God for that. I think I would have lost my mind if I'd had to stay cooped up any longer. When do we start?"

"Around seven."

"But Mr. Jay! Mr. Lovell! I must see them before I go. I can't just step out without saying by your leave, go to hell, or something."

"It's all arranged. I saw Jay this afternoon; he will explain to Lovell. You are released from all that type of work. From now on, you belong to General Washington."

Peter stood looking quietly at Adam. Then he said, "I am in the army once more. Thank the good God for his mercies."

Before he slept Peter had discovered, by judicious questioning, that they were to go to Salisbury, then to the mountains at a rendezvous where Enos Dye would be waiting for them. The names of the men they would seek were Campbell, Sevier, the two McDowells, Shelby and Cleveland. "Each of them has a hundred or two men trained to Indian fighting, who can be brought together on call," Rutledge commented. "It won't make an army, as you know an army, Peter, but every man is an army in himself. Now go to sleep and don't ask any more questions."

The next morning they were on their way south. "We are to meet with Governor Caswell at New Bern, before we go west." Adam grinned. "I didn't tell you last night for fear you wouldn't sleep a wink, but River Plantation is definitely an overnight stop on our route."

Peter did not talk as the chaise sped along over the dusty roads. The morning was beautiful. Birds were singing and a gentle wind was blowing as they followed the river. What more could a young fellow want than be riding along on an August morning? Along the roads were signs of plentiful harvest—people in the fields with scythe and sickle, carts loaded with corn and fodder, wheat being threshed in the fields, hay on the ricks. The world was singing an autumn song, and Peter's heart was gay.

They arrived at River Plantation the eighth day, having been delayed once by a broken wheel, and once to buy a horse to replace one that had gone lame.

They crossed Brownrigg Creek at the mill-pond at sunset; the long shadows lay among the trees and slithered into the water. The mill-wheel was silent, the mill closed for the day. Peter said, "three miles more," with a sort of suppressed impatience. At last they turned into the entrance of the long grove, its great oaks with long streamers of Spanish moss. Pickaninnies were playing in the sand in the gate-house yard.

"They're all gone away, Master, all gone away."

Adam said, "What's that?"

"Master ride away in he coach, this morning."

Peter said, "The ladies?"

The Negro children ran to the chaise, eager to impart news, good or bad.

"They go too. Every one of them go riding away."

Adam said, "We'll drive on up to the house to make sure."

They found the front door closed. Tulli, the old cook, was sitting in the shade of the kitchen, the gardener Jake beside her. Jake got up quickly and came to the carriage-block, Tulli waddling along after him. Both talked at once. The senator and Madam and Miss Angela had gone away to the place where the Governor lived, to meet a number of men, all captain bosses, Jake explained.

"What time did they leave?" Adam asked.

" 'Zern o' dawn," Tulli answered.

Peter looked enquiring. "Cock-crow," Adam explained.

Jake said, "Yes, sar. When the cock crows he 'zerns the dawn."

Adam spoke to Herk. "Are the horses too weary to go on to Queen Anne's Town?"

"They are fresh after they get a fair drink."

Jake shouted for boys to bring buckets of water. Adam glanced at Peter. "Don't be so glum. Eventually we will arrive at New Bern."

"Two days more," Peter said.

Tulli regarded them, her hands on her ample hips. "They take dat new white girl along for a maid. Promisy she cry lak anything. But Madam she says to Promisy, 'Dat white girl she sew such fine seams, so she mak' dos' nice white clo'es for a bride.' "

Peter could not help smiling. He tossed a coin to the woman, who caught it deftly, bit it to test its worth and tucked it in a fold of her headkerchief.

Twelve miles to go. Dark overtook them near Bennett's Mill, where they took the wrong turn and made a half circle back. When they got to the village Horniblow's was crowded, but O'Malley's was hospitable. It took some time to get their room ready. Adam told Peter he thought their host had ousted some traveller to make room for them. They supped on hominy and bacon and onion gravy and drank copiously of scuppernong wine, which was, according to Adam, too sweet for anything but a liqueur, and exchanged talk with other guests until their room was ready.

After supper they strolled over to Penelope Barker's. The soft warm night brought fragrance of roses and honeysuckle and spice pinks. Voices came out of the darkness. Villagers were sitting on the galleries, talking over the day's happenings. They found the Barkers at home, and were welcomed warmly. Nat Allen and Robert Smith were sitting on the steps. Adam launched into an animated description of the Philadelphia scene. Peter sat next to Thomas Barker; during a lull in the questioning Thomas turned toward Peter.

"I have the plantation for you, Captain, and the papers ready for your signature. Stop in my office in the morning."

"It will be early," Peter replied.

"Good enough. I am an early riser myself. I like to work in the cool of the morning and take my quiet in the heat of the day. God never intended us to work all day long in hot weather. I'm sure of that."

Peter laughed. "I'm very grateful to you, Mr. Barker. Is the deed of gift drawn up, too?"

"You are determined to give it outright to the girl?"

"Yes, sir, I am, as a wedding present."

"Very well, if you want it that way. It's a nice piece of land. You ought to keep it in your own name. I think there is a little fortune in fishing up that river."

"Splendid! We will fish and cut timber and raise a few crops."

Barker nodded. "Land will tie you down, but no more than marriage. Enjoy your freedom, young lad. Enjoy it while it's young." He got up and went inside to see about drinks.

Penelope Barker called Peter to her side. "I haven't seen you since your betrothal to Angela was announced. I've already congratulated her and I wish you happiness, Captain Huntley."

Peter smiled. "I thought the groom was the one to receive congratulations."

Penelope's chair scraped the floor as she moved. He could not see her face in the dark. After an interval she repeated, "I've congratulated Angela."

A slave came out with a tray of tall glasses. The talk became general. The Pollocks had gone north after their horrid experience. Had Adam and Peter heard that Clem Hull, the smith, had won a second-class prize at the lottery? Thirty hard dollars, some said. Everyone was surprised when he didn't get drunk.

"How did you leave Mr. Hewes?" Penelope asked.

Adam said, "I just told Nathaniel I think he is a very sick man. I tried to get him to come home, but he feels it his duty to remain. There was no budging him."

"That good man!" Penelope said. "That good man and faithful lover! I think his country has become the wife he lost and the child he never had."

Nathaniel Allen's voice answered, "I believe you are right, Penelope, though I would never put it that way."

"Is Madam Dawson in the village or up the river?"

"She is at Eden House. Will you be riding that way?"

"Yes, I think so. I want to stop at Rutledge Riding."

Nat said, "The corn harvested well this year, better than for the past three years."

Adam laughed. "Peter said I was farming all the way down through Virginia. It was a pretty sight to see a full harvest."

"Everyone has gone to New Bern," Penelope said. "A big meeting of the Committee of Correspondence or Safety or something. I've heard the Governor and Madam intend to give a garden-party to take the place of the Inaugural Ball. People say the Palace looks forlorn—only about half enough furniture to go around."

Robert Smith interposed: "Didn't Caswell get some of the furniture that came in that French ship? We heard every stick was sold in Wilmington and New Bern. We didn't get any here, I know."

Penelope addressed Adam: "The Ferriers drove in early this morning. I think they must be at the Hermitage, with Madam Johnston, by tonight."

Adam said, "I think we will be going to O'Malley's. We want to make a very early start."

"At the 'zern of dawn," Peter said.

"Ah! You are progressing, when you know how to use our colloquialisms." Thomas Barker patted Peter's shoulder. "That is good,

good. I'll be at my office in time to watch the lamplighter put out the lights on the Courthouse Green."

After the men had strolled off into the velvet darkness, Penelope turned to her husband. "Why are you going to be at your office so early?"

"To have some papers signed, my dear."

"What has that to do with Captain Huntley, Thomas?"

"He's buying some land. Now don't ask questions, my sweet pet, for I'm not going to answer."

Penelope laughed indulgently. "You're so obvious, Thomas. Peter is making a marriage settlement."

After a short silence Thomas said, "How did you know that?"

She made no answer in words, only in laughter. Then she said gravely, "I hope the girl is worth it. I like that Peter Huntley."

"Older women do. They see his worth, but I doubt if young women would. They dream of a more romantic figure, like De' Medici, or those young Frenchmen who were here."

"De' Medici was delightful. Where is he, do you know?"

"I heard his dragoons had been absorbed in Sumner's regiment, and the lot of them camped somewhere along the Peedee River."

"Too bad. Really too bad." Madam reflected. "Cosmo should be in a court in Europe, not sitting in the sand hills with a crowd of country yokels."

"Cosmo and the yokels have the same idea in the back of their minds, my sweet Penelope."

"What is that, pray?"

"The desire to live in a land that is free."

"You are tedious, Thomas. I don't like to think of those things. I don't want to think of the war."

"Unfortunately there are a hundred thousand in like case, my dear," Thomas said dryly. "A hundred thousand ostriches, with their heads buried in the sand."

The ferry chains clanked; the shore-rope stretched in the winch. Adam dropped the fee in Augustine Dishon's hand and guided his horse off the apron of the ferry. Peter followed.

At the crest of the bank Adam drew rein. "Suppose you ride on to Eden House, Peter. I'll be over after I've seen my overlooker at the North Plantation."

"How long will that take you?"

Adam reflected. "I can't tell. Perhaps we may decide to stay at Eden House overnight—that is, if we're offered the hospitality," he added.

Peter grinned. "Perhaps we will have good fortune."

Adam and Herk rode on. Peter turned his horse to the right, into the road that led toward Eden House. He found himself singing as he rode briskly along the cool forest road. His disappointment in not seeing Angela had passed away. He looked forward to meeting Penelope Dawson with a certain quickening of the pulse. A wonderful person, Penelope Dawson, with beauty and poise and great understanding. He could not understand why some people spoke of her caustic tongue. He had never seen that side of her. He had heard that she was scornful of mediocrity, but he remembered how patient and gentle she was with the slaves on the plantation.

He turned into the long drive that led to the house. The panorama of the river, the long low house and the blossoming garden swept into view. He reined his horse. Penelope was riding toward him. She wore a linen habit and a wide straw hat tied with a scarf to keep it in place. She was riding slowly, her eyes on the field beyond. He waited until she came close, before he spoke. She turned her head, startled, one gauntleted hand going to her heart. A look of pleasure came quickly and she spoke his name.

"Peter! How very nice!"

He dismounted and went to her side. He stripped her gauntlet from her hand and kissed her fingers.

"Where did you come from?" she asked.

"Philadelphia. And Queen Anne's Town."

"In all these months you didn't write me one letter."

"I had none from you."

"Gentlemen write first."

"I'm sorry. But I thought of you very often."

"Were you very gay in Philadelphia?" They were riding slowly along, side by side. "I've heard that Lady Washington holds a court and the gay Madam Arnold is only slightly less regal."

"I confess to dullness. I went nowhere. I only worked, and made stupid reports about lottery tickets."

"Poor Peter!" She laughed. "You must have been born on a Saturday. 'Saturday's child must work for a living.' But don't try to keep up that subterfuge of the lottery. I know it wouldn't take you three months to add up those figures."

Peter smiled. "I admit there were a few other papers to be looked at and shuffled around. By the way, Adam Rutledge will be over later. He stopped at his plantation, and when he comes, he will ask you if two weary travellers may have lodging for the night."

"You know how welcome you both are." There was no smile on her lips or in her eyes. "Mary Warden is staying with me," she added quietly.

Governorcharleseden was at the block when they rode up. He was pleased to see the captain, he told Peter; it had been a long time. Like the gentleman he was, the old Negro made no reference to Peter's humiliating experience when Jeremiah Morse bashed his head with the butt of his pistol. But Peter thought of it as he bathed and got a fresh shirt from his saddle-bags. Governorcharleseden had carried away the shirt he had discarded. Selina would wash it, so the captain would have a fresh shirt to journey in.

Mary Warden was in the library when Peter went downstairs. He kissed her hand, thinking how very thin she was. He wondered what caused the worried expression in her frank eyes. She was pleased to see him, and Peter had the feeling of home-coming.

The dinner was gay and full of nonsensical talk, a release for Peter, who had been working so long without let-up. After dinner the ladies excused themselves. The afternoon rest period was rather a pleasant thought. He took a book from the library shelves and put it under his arm and went upstairs.

He stood for a moment looking out the window. The slaves, who had been picking beans earlier in the day, were resting. They sought the shady side of the cabins and lay on the porches and stretched out full length, faces buried in their folded arms.

He took off his coat and boots. He picked up the volume he had brought, glanced through the pages and smiled ruefully. It was a copy of Pindar's odes in Greek. What little Greek he had learned in school he had long since forgotten. He was about to lay the book on the night-table when a leaf of paper fell out. He saw that it had writing on it, lines of Greek with several synonymous English words under the Greek text, then two lines which had evidently satisfied the translator:

> The long Toil of the Brave
> Is not lost in darkness . . .

Underneath the verse was scribbled, "Translation by Gabriel Johnston." It was dated April 14, 1753. He repeated it slowly, "The long Toil of the Brave." The words rang rhythmically in his ears. The cadence was sheer music. The meaning of the words forced its way into his mind. For a moment he glimpsed the past: the long view of history seemed to unroll before his eyes. In the great struggle of the present, they did not stand alone. There had been others who had not counted the cost, nor had their toil been lost in darkness.

A strange exhilaration came over him. The oppression and discouragement which had surrounded him during the past few months fell away.

The sunlight fell softly through the green jalousies. He knew he could sleep now, without dreaming.

The sun was low on the river when he woke. He bathed and dressed and went downstairs into the cool hall. Madam Dawson called him from the library where she was seated at the little Queen Anne tea-table.

"This is an occasion, so I have brought out my Bahia tea." She poured a cup and added sugar from a silver box, and a splash of milk. "Adam and Mary are in the garden watching the sunset," she remarked.

Peter looked through the window. He saw Adam's tall figure. He was wearing his new uniform of the Continental Line, and he looked a very erect and soldierly figure. He was bending slightly toward the small-statured Mary. "Do you think he is in love with her?"

Pene gave him a swift glance. "I think so, but he is not aware of it."

"How can that be?" Peter was genuinely surprised at her answer.

The corners of her full red lips and the corners of her grey eyes twinkled, as a smile spread over her face. "Men are not as aware of emotion as women are, Peter; their minds are filled with other things. Adam Rutledge thinks very little of himself. But I've noticed how much he counts on Mary. He brings her his worries and his deep problems, as well as his joys. Perhaps it is as well that he isn't aware," she said thoughtfully. "It is an impossible situation, for neither one of them would stoop to anything cheap or tawdry."

Peter wanted to ask a question, but he hesitated. Almost as though she had read his mind, Penelope said, "I suppose someone has told you that at one time he was infatuated with an Arab slave girl."

Peter nodded an affirmative.

"Azizi was a beautiful, exotic creature. I was really very fond of the girl."

"I should think everyone would have been shocked."

"You *are* Calvinistic, Peter." She pushed back her chair and walked about the room, touching a book and straightening a bowl of flowers. A remote, dispassionate expression made her eyes unreadable. After a time she said, "We women of the South close our eyes to many things that go on between some of our men and the slave women. It is wiser to know nothing; we are obliged to be blind. I don't mean that all our best men allow their lust to overcome them, but many do. We ignore it, just as we ignore the fact that Nat Allen keeps a mistress a few doors down the street from his own house."

Peter whistled softly. "I suppose I am rather a Scot, at that. We don't allow these little indiscretions to penetrate into our living or come to the attention of our womenfolk."

Penelope considered a moment. "That is more civilized, more of the great world, but we are a small community." She poured a second cup of tea for him.

He thought of the translation from Pindar, took the sheet of paper from his pocket and handed it to her. "This afternoon I found this in a volume of Pindar's odes."

She took it from him and read it through. An expression of sadness and longing came over her lovely face. "It is my father's writing," she said. "He used often to translate bits from his favourite Latin and Greek writers."

It was then that she noticed the date. "The day before he died," she murmured, brokenly. "It is a message from my beloved father. Do you see what he says to me? 'The long Toil of the Brave is not lost in darkness.' Thank God, it can never be! Those long, weary years he spent trying to bring order and law to this chaotic country!" Her lips trembled. "To think that after so many years he has sent me this message! Tonight, out of nothing, he has reached out his hand to comfort me. I am glad that it was you who brought it to me, Peter."

Peter thought, The words have a personal message to her. She does not see the other, larger meaning. "Dear Pene," he said softly. He gave her his handkerchief. "Now dry your eyes, for I see Adam and Mary Warden coming for their dish of tea."

"You are sweet, Peter," she said, drying her eyes with his handkerchief. "I think you're far too good for Angela. Did you know that that wretched man came through here again? My slaves saw him on the road, riding along with the cattle drovers."

He could not keep pace with the quick change in her. "What man?" he asked.

"Morse!" she said quickly. "Angela's Morse. Oh, Peter, I am sorry; but I'm fond of you, so very fond that I want you to be happy."

"I think I will be happy." There was some hesitancy in his tone which she caught at once.

"Don't walk into unhappiness with your eyes open," she said earnestly, almost as though she spoke out of her own experience.

He looked into her serene grey eyes. How deep and unreadable they were. A quickened pulse warned him that to look too longingly into her eyes meant danger. He realized a startling truth at that moment. It would be easy to allow his emotions to get out of hand. Between them was some intangible attraction, deeper than his love for Angela. Between them there was little need of words. The question he had asked a moment before, might have applied to themselves, 'Nothing tawdry, nothing cheap.' It was well that they were going on, or he would have difficulty in remaining constant to vows to Angela. He must stand firm in that, for he had given his word, and a man's word is his honour.

"You look so intent Peter. What are you thinking?"

"Of a man's conception of honour." He spoke slowly, thoughtfully. "A vow given must be kept if a man is to live with himself." He was thinking of his own situation, and that of Adam Rutledge.

She moved a little and changed position, so that he did not look into her eyes.

"I made a vow once. A vow that I would never marry again." His eyes were on her clear-cut profile. "Did you love your husband so much?" His voice was low.

"I thought I did. Now I am not so sure. I was very young." She turned and met his eyes. "Do you think I was too young to know what love is?"

He pondered the question. "I don't know."

She went on. She might have been unaware of his words. "I think not. Infatuation perhaps, not a deep and lasting love."

He leaned forward. "Do you regret?" He waited. It seemed to him that her answer had great importance to him.

"No. I do not regret." She spoke slowly. "My marriage with John was happy and gay. It did not last long enough to be tested by sorrow or tragedy. It was young love, no more, but when I give it thought I know that my vow not to marry comes from something else. When

I was a child, I was often teased by other children, because my grandmother had married so often. She had four husbands. My mother also had more than one husband. Adults laughed. I heard one say, 'Pene will doubtless marry half a dozen times, if she follows her grandmother's and her mother's example.' I was old enough to feel shame and humiliation.

"Now that I know more of the world, and people, I believe that those idle words, the laughter of thoughtless people, made an indelible impression on me. Am I being absurd?"

"No. Certainly not," Peter hastened to say. "I think I can understand. Childish impressions go very deep. Too deep." He answered her question quickly enough, but his thoughts went back to his own problem. "I know little of marriage."

Through the window Peter saw that Adam and Mary Warden were at the foot of the steps leading to the gallery. In a few moments they would be in the room. He lowered his voice. "The men in our family have never married for love alone. We marry for a wife who will keep the honour of our name and bear our children. To such a woman we give loyalty—sometimes with love, sometimes without, but always loyalty."

Mary came into the room, followed by Adam. Her eyes were sparkling. She held out her hand for her tea-cup. Peter thought, Every woman in love is beautiful.

Adam made himself comfortable in a big, leather-covered chair. "I must tell you that we almost lost Peter. Mr. Franklin's long arm reached across the sea and all but snatched him from our shores. He would have been across the Western Ocean by now, if it had not been that the General had first call on him."

"The General? Do you mean General Washington?" Mary asked.

"My dear Mary, 'the General' can mean only one person."

Penelope smiled at Peter. "How does it feel to be sought by our greatest Ambassador and our greatest General?"

"Now, really!" he exclaimed.

"Is it the thing to ask why General Washington wants Peter?" Mary questioned.

"You may ask, but you won't have an answer," Adam teased.

Peter thought, He has dropped *years* from his shoulders since yesterday. What is happening?

A gong sounded in the hall. "Dressing-bell," Penelope said, rising. "We've been late with our tea. Half an hour until supper."

They were drinking their Madeira in the library after supper when Dr. Cathcart and his young daughter Peggy drove in. They, too, begged lodging, as they were too late for the ferry which was tied up for the night on the opposite shore of the Chowan.

The doctor was in excellent spirits; he had been visiting his daughter Frances, Samuel Johnston's wife, at the Hermitage, and they were now on their way to the village. The doctor had been over to Salisbury.

"The mountain country is alive with active Tories. I declare I like them better than the men who pretend to be Whigs, but who are Tories at heart. At least one knows where they stand. Moore was within an ace of winning, if the Governor hadn't taken prompt action and sent the troops from Hillsborough. A mess of rowdies and gaol-breakers and counterfeiters in that wild back country. It's as much as a man's life is worth to travel through some of those counties without an escort."

Adam smiled at that. "I've been all through the mountains to the other side. I've followed Boone's Yadkin and gone in through Cumberland Gap. I've had no trouble; I don't understand this talk of danger."

"I've heard the contrary from every traveller I've met, unless you go up through the Moravian country and get one of the Moravians to guide you."

"Enos Dye is a good enough guide for me," Adam said significantly. Peter remembered the man vividly from Smithfield. So that was the plan which was being discussed at Smithfield when Dye came over from the mountains at the Governor's request.

The doctor retired early. Peter walked in the garden with the others. The harvest moon rose round and red; it made a golden-red path on the river.

There was a little desultory talk. The Pollocks' place was closed. Much better that they should stay away from the village until the thing blew over, Penelope remarked. "In the North and in the South we are getting more conscious of divisions in thought than at any time since the war began. Ill-advised, I think. It is the same here, in this country. Several families have been all but ostracized—the Lowthers, for instance. They may have leanings toward the Crown but they certainly would never take any untoward action."

De' Medici's name came up. "He is in New Bern, I believe, importuning the Governor for funds to keep his men from starvation. Curiously enough, they don't desert as they do from other companies."

"He is an excellent officer, one who thinks first of his men, and they know it," Peter said. "I hope we will see him there."

He and Penelope moved on to the river-bank. She laid her hand on his arm. "Peter, I am sorry I spoke as I did this afternoon. I can't think why I did. Angela is a beautiful girl, and when you think of her mother, you know she *has* to be a fine woman."

"She has a father also, whom we don't know."

Penelope looked at Peter curiously when he spoke. "I think I am a little jealous." She laughed lightly to cover her seriousness. "A little. You know you are something special to me, Peter. I think it is because I see my father in you—not that you resemble him in looks, but in your fundamental honesty, your quiet way of weighing things, your dispassionate viewpoint. Yes, I am jealous."

Peter said, "I can't understand my feeling for Angela, quite. When I was in Philadelphia, working hard, I scarcely gave a thought to her, but when I see her my veins turn to water."

"Did you ever think of me when you were in Philadelphia?"

"Often, Penelope, often. We talked of you—Mr. Hewes, Adam and I. You have strong friends in them both."

Penelope caught her breath. Peter knew she was touched and pleased. "I love them both. I make as much effort to retain friends as most women do to retain lovers. I have found that friends last longer."

"I cannot tell you how much I value your friendship." Peter's voice was low. "It means a great deal to me."

She did not speak for a long time. A bird stirred in the pine overhead. The gentle call of a quail sounded. Fire-flies' lanterns glowed through the garden. It was a night for soft voices and dark confidences, for lovers' sighs and soft laughter. Peter stirred restlessly and sought her arm in the darkness. "You must give me your friendship—something that will last as long as we both live."

"When you marry, there will be no place for friendship with another woman, Peter."

"That is not true. If I were married a dozen times, I would still be your friend."

Her laughter was light. "Turk, talking of a dozen wives!"

"You haven't answered!" he protested.

"Peter, you are so intense. Such importuning! You sound like a lover wooing his lady."

"Perhaps I too am a better friend than a lover," he admitted, but he did not smile. "Right now, standing beside you in your lovely garden, it seems more desirable to have you as my friend than to gain another woman's love."

"My dear, you know I am your friend. My heart goes out to you."

He was close, so close that he heard the sweet intake of her breath; smelled the perfume of her hair. He stooped toward her, but she drew back. "Even in a rare friendship there is a line we may not cross," she whispered.

He lifted her hands and kissed the palms, one and then the other. In her heart she was saying, What a lover you would be, my dear!

Her face was a white blur in the darkness. Her voice was calm, when they joined the others.

Peggy was begging Adam to go rowing on the river. "I want to catch up with the moon path and row and row, straight into the moon herself."

Peter felt Pene's arm tremble under his hand. "It is cold in the moon, my dear," she said, "deadly cold and remote."

When they went inside, Peggy got out the loo-table. They played a game of loo and Peggy won, to her extravagant delight. She was sixteen and well developed, thinking of balls and beaux. "I implored my father to take me to New Bern. It is so gay there, with all the young officers, and next week the garden-party at the Palace." She sighed, a Lydia Languish sigh of regret.

Penelope said, "I was of a mind to go down myself, but I do not like to be away from the plantation at harvest. Something is bound to come up."

Adam agreed. "I know how you feel, but to my astonishment they get on quite well without me. My overlooker tells me they have a bumper crop of corn which he's already contracted to Smith, who in turn is selling it to the army."

"I've wondered about that," Penelope said. "But I've decided to store my crop. It may bring more later."

"If the British don't come sweeping through Virginia and carry it all away," Mary remarked. She was laying out a game of patience on a small table.

"I like these Whig cards," Peggy said. "They are sweet. I want so much to wear a Whig patch on my cheek, but my father says no, not yet. Isn't it annoying to be young?" she complained.

Mary smiled at the girl's *moue*. "Most women envy you, my dear." She turned over a jack and slapped it on the black queen.

"I'm as tall as Cecily. I'd like to have a beau, even if he has to die in the war, like Jaspie."

"Peggy, don't talk that way. The Lord will punish you," Penelope said sharply.

Adam glanced at Mary. "Didn't you know? Jaspie Charlton was killed at Briar Creek. We are all disturbed about Cecily, she is grieving so."

"Cecily told me she wasn't really betrothed to Jaspie, but she loved him. She knew they would be married when he came back from the wars, but, you see, he didn't come back. So now her heart is broken." Peggy's voice rose in excitement. "Really broken."

"I think it is time for you to retire, Peggy."

"Oh, Madam Dawson, it's not late."

"Run along. That's a good child." The girl, reluctant but obedient, presented a cool round cheek for a good-night kiss, made her curtsy to the gentlemen. "You are to sleep in Mary's room, Peggy."

"Thank you. Good night."

Penelope said, "I hope you don't mind the same room with Peter, Adam. I had to put Dr. Cathcart in yours."

"Indeed not, we are accustomed to doubling up. Sometimes in Philadelphia it's four to a room."

"How shocking! Philadelphia must be a dreary place."

Adam walked about the room. "Jaspie's death must have been a shock to the Charltons."

"Tragic, truly tragic. They had such plans for him. He was a nice lad." Pene sighed.

Adam said, "Our Carolina men made an excellent showing at Stony Point."

"I am glad," Mary said. "The reports we heard from the South were not too good. It breaks one's heart to think of such defeats, one after another. Is there no end?"

"I'm afraid we'll have to steel ourselves against even greater losses."

"That's what William says. He thinks the British are preparing for a great campaign next spring."

Adam changed the subject abruptly. "What's this about Cecily?"

Mary and Pene exchanged glances. "She is really grieving for Jaspie," Mary said slowly. "I can't be certain how deep it is. You know the child is so imaginative, and she thinks of herself so dramatically. If she were my child I would be worried, but neither Miss Hezzie nor the doctor is worried."

"She came to Eden House last week-end. I was shocked at her appearance. All she would do was to walk to the summer-house and sit, looking at the water in a sort of daze," Pene observed.

"She is young; youth is resilient," said Adam. "She will come out all right. I think she only fancied herself in love."

Mary said, "I hope you are right, Adam."

Pene glanced at the clock. "We must not keep you up. I know you will want to start early. Be sure and allow time for breakfast. Governorcharleseden has his orders."

They all walked into the hall. Peter lighted the bed candles.

Mary said, "Good night. I won't say good-bye. You will be back soon, we hope."

"Not before next year," Adam said.

Mary's eyes widened. The hand that held the candle trembled. "Next year?" she said.

"At least not until after Christmas. Peter and I are going to the mountains."

Mary went up first. She could not trust herself to speak. Somehow she had hoped Adam would not go away again.

Pene stepped into their room and looked around. "Towels, hot water . . ." she explained. "One never knows whether the slaves remember to do the little things. The last guest we had slept without pillows, because he was too polite to ask for one. Next year is a long time," she said slowly, looking at Adam Rutledge. "Much can happen. I think I will kiss you both—not farewell but a little remembrance among friends."

She kissed Adam first. He put his arms about her and held her a moment. "God keep you, Pene! Promise me you will look after Mary." She turned her large, intelligent eyes on him questioningly. He nodded almost imperceptibly.

Peter did not understand, but he noticed that Adam had given no hint of their real destination when he spoke to Mary. He remembered the lists he had seen in Philadelphia, the black check and question-mark after William Warden's name.

Pene came to him. She lifted her face. "Go with God, my friend!" He held her a moment, her lips warm against his. She broke away and walked swiftly from the room.

In the early morning they started for New Bern, two days away.

CHAPTER

22

MOTHER AND DAUGHTER

SEPTEMBER in New Bern was almost as gay as when the Assembly was in session. The judges were already there, making ready for autumn court. Some brought their wives and young daughters. Then there were the young French officers arriving in increasing numbers, importuning Governor Caswell for leave to recruit companies and regiments. Soldiers were bivouacked at the edge of the town, on their way to join the Southern Army.

Ships from France lay in the river, filled with merchandise, for France was eager to pick up the rich trade that England had lost since the beginning of the war. Ships from Portugal and Spain sometimes got through the loose line of the blockade, which His Majesty's Navy was endeavouring to maintain along the coast line from the West Indies to New York Harbour.

Every night there was some ball or supper-party. Groups of young officers sat in taverns until all hours, playing cards or casting dice, drinking Madeira or wines from France.

Peter and Adam went at once to the Queen's Arms Tavern, where a room had been reserved by Adam's factor. It was not far from the Palace and there was a view as far as the confluence of the Neuse and Trent Rivers.

Peter took time to wash and don fresh linen, then went out to seek the Ferriers, who were stopping with their friends the Cornells, in River Street.

It was not the fashionable hour for a call, but Peter was oblivious to everything but his desire to see Angela.

The senator was at the Palace, the butler told him, but Madam was in, and the young miss. He was ushered into a little morning room. He was too impatient to sit down. He paced back and forth, avoiding chairs. He didn't like cluttered rooms; when he had a home it would

373

have space, and not too much furniture. A man needed space to walk about. He looked up, as he heard a small sound, like a stifled laugh.

Madam Ferrier was in the doorway smiling at him. She was wearing a short loose muslin jacket with lace ruffles around the front and bottom over a very full skirt of changeable taffeta.

"Peter, you make this room look the size of a doll's house," she said, giving him her hand. He brushed it with his lips and led her to a chair by the window.

"I know. I seem to take up a lot of space," he said apologetically. He looked toward the door.

"Sit down, Peter. Compose yourself. Angela will be here any moment."

His face cleared. "I thought she might be out. I had no time to send word to you, to ask if I might call."

"Young girls need more time to primp than we old women."

"Madam!" Peter's tone was horrified. "How can you speak of yourself in such terms? You are as young as—at least to be her sister."

Francisca smiled. "I think you are delightful, Peter, so natural. I like it even better than the excessive flattery of our gallant French officers."

Peter's face fell. "Ah, they are here! I suppose Miss Angela . . ." He paused, looking at Madame Ferrier. "I mean they are very fine gentlemen."

"Yes, indeed. And also they are very unhappy gentlemen. They left France with great hopes of fighting for a noble cause, drawing their swords for freedom. But instead they spend their time sitting on the Governor's doorstep, begging him to allow them to fight. It is all so sad. I do not understand."

Peter had no time to explain. There was a rustling of silken skirts and Angela came into the room. She paused inside the door and made a little curtsy. As she had not extended her hand, Peter bowed deeply.

She was lovely, more lovely than he had remembered her. She, like her mother, had on some soft, bewilderingly attractive little lace-trimmed jacket over a rose silk skirt. Her hair was in curls, bound by a rose-coloured riband. She was smiling slightly.

A servant appeared. "Madam Cornell's compliments. Will the ladies and Captain Huntley join her in the breakfast-room for a cup of chocolate?"

"We will be delighted." Francisca rose. Peter stood aside as mother and daughter swept through the door. He glanced at the little white marble clock on the mantel. It was only eleven.

Two ladies were seated at a small breakfast-table drawn up by the fire. Madam Ferrier presented Peter to her hostess, Madam Cornell, and her daughter Betsy. Peter seated the ladies. He placed a chair for himself, between Madam Ferrier and Angela.

Betsy was an attractive young girl with blond hair and hazel eyes. As he drank his chocolate and ate his hot buttered scone, he was aware that she was looking at him curiously.

It gave him pleasure. It meant, perhaps, that Angela had been talking to her friend about him.

Madam Cornell said, "You come at a good time, Captain. To-morrow the Governor and his lady are giving a garden-party at the Palace, and then afterward we are having a picnic across the river. It will give us pleasure if you will accept both invitations."

Peter said, "I would be delighted, Madam Cornell—" he hesitated a moment—"unless Major Rutledge has made an appointment for me at that hour."

Madam Ferrier said, "You can send madam word after you have seen Adam. Of course we expect him also."

"Thank you. I will deliver the message." He turned to Angela. "We stopped at River Plantation on our way down from Philadelphia. We were disappointed that you had already started for New Bern."

Angela asked whether he had seen the children. He said he had not.

Betsy leaned forward. "Have you been in Philadelphia? How wonderful! We hear it is vastly gay up there. Tell us, what do they dance at the balls? Only minuets, or do they hop a reel?"

"I am sorry, I went to only one ball while I was there. They danced minuets and contra-dances, for the most part."

"Where was the ball, at Lady Washington's?"

"No. Madam Washington was not in Philadelphia. She was at Mount Vernon. She does not give balls while the General is away." He ended the sentence lamely. What was on the tip of his tongue to say was that she would not think of having a ball when the General was away fighting battles. "The ball was at Madam Arnold's," he added.

Madam Cornell said, "Ah, yes, Peggy Shippen. She is a very attractive woman and very gay."

He made some reply and rose. He had already been at the table fifteen minutes, the length of a proper courtesy call.

"We will expect you and Adam at four, unless you send us a message to the contrary, Peter."

"Thank you so much for the invitation, Madam Cornell. I feel sure we will be able to accept."

He made his bow and left the room. He heard Betsy's high, clear voice saying, "Angela, I think he is wonderful!" The door swung to and he heard no more.

He walked up the street to the inn. He found Adam in the public-room, seated at a small table with William Hooper. Adam beckoned to Peter to join them.

Mr. Hooper greeted Peter warmly. "I've just been hearing the Philadelphia news. I am very much disturbed about Hewes's health. You know how it is with a willing horse—they will work him to death. Why doesn't he let Harnett and Penn bear the brunt in the interim? He really has no official capacity, excepting his naval committee."

Adam said, "I do not know any one person so deeply selfless in the cause of liberty, with the exception of General Washington, as Joseph Hewes."

"In that I concur with all my heart. Let us hope that someone up there will realize and take some of the burden from him. I'll write to Penn myself."

Hooper left shortly after. Adam took a letter from his pocket and gave it to Peter. "No need to open it here. It's your marching orders."

"When do we leave?" Peter asked, fingering the paper. It would be just his evil luck if he were obliged to leave before he saw Angela again.

"Don't look so gloomy," Adam said, smiling at him. "You have until Wednesday morning to do your courting."

"Two days!" Peter exclaimed. "Only two days!"

Adam pushed aside his glass. "His Excellency is well pleased that you are undertaking this journey. He is even more pleased that the committee is turning its attention to our state. He told me that, to date, you are the only soldier that Congress has seen fit to send into the state. Always it has been the other way—our men have gone out. So you have a unique distinction."

Peter grinned. "A strong army of one, I am. But I have not asked you your own mission."

Adam said, "It is all arranged. I will go with you to the mountain country. Then from there each of us goes on alone. I follow the Yadkin, you go south among the western mountains." He dropped his voice. "People at the next table seem interested. We have a room; let us go up. I'll show you the maps so you will be conversant with the country before you start."

On the stairs they met Cosmo. When he saw Peter he made a series of exclamations of delight and embraced him with enthusiasm, to Peter's embarrassment. Cosmo turned around and went back with them to Adam's room.

He had been with General Lincoln, he told them, at Purysburg, near Savannah, on the northern shore of the river. The general had poor material, raw recruits and some few of the Continental troops that had met too many defeats. The British Campbell had captured Savannah and was rallying Loyalists to join his army. Many of the patriots were in prison ships; he, Cosmo, had had a hairbreadth escape from such a fate, thank the good God!

"Last month, August, Campbell had two thousand men to risk, and marched them up the Georgia side of the Savannah River. That helped the Tories and opened communication with the Creek Indians, in the West. The Tories had devastated some of the country along the South Carolina border. Our men, under Colonel Pickens, rallied, and defeated them on Kettle Creek, killed seventy Tories, and hanged Boyd, the commander, on the charge of treason."

De' Medici got up and demonstrated the battle lines on the counter-pane of Peter's bed. "Ah, but I have a splendid position. I and some men with me, very special picked men. We joined Colonel Marion, the Swamp Fox, and we live in swamps; we rush out in the night, we attack and rush back. It is a filthy life we live, but full of movement."

Cosmo's eyes shone with excitement. "Now, other things are transpiring. I came here to get a little money, a few men, so I can be once more in the thick."

Adam asked, "Where is General Moultrie?"

"He joined General Lincoln last April. He was with General Lincoln when he made the march to Savannah, but the British Prevost had twenty-five hundred men. What could General Moultrie do but retreat? But it was a good retreat. He burned bridges, but the troops disliked swamps and they deserted." He spread his hands in a characteristic gesture. "The situation there is critical, very critical.

After that, Prevost pushes into South Carolina. He is determined to take Charles Town. But the city, she is prepared, and Prevost got himself a fright and he withdrew."

Adam said, "We heard that. What is the situation now?"

"It is said that there is a movement on foot to retake Savannah in September, this month. But we must wait for Count D'Estaing, who returns from the West Indies. He must come up and close the river with his ships. They say he has twenty-two sail of the line, and six thousand troops; but one never knows. I doubt if he has so many ships or so many men. I doubt if Savannah will be taken."

They talked a little more. Peter enquired about the situation on the border between North and South Carolina.

"We have a few troops in the Sand Hill country, waiting, but not enough. I hear your Colonel Lamb led his detachment to Camden, and the Salisbury troops have joined him."

"Were you at Stono Ferry?" Peter asked.

De' Medici said, "No. That was Butler's militia and Sumner's Continentals." He laughed. "Your jovial Colonel Hamilton, from Halifax, was there with his regiment of Loyalist Carolinians, but it did not stand up." He said to Adam: "That was where Lieutenant Charlton was killed, and Major Dixon wounded. A Major Davis also. He was quite a hero, leading his cavalry with great bravery. They were all North Carolinians, I believe."

He looked at his watch. "Ah, as always when among my friends, I talk too much and stay too long. I must depart, and plead once more with his Excellency for money. Pray for me, my friends." He went away quickly and clattered down the stairs, his sword beating a tattoo on the banister rail.

Adam was thoughtful. "The pattern begins to be clear. The General has been perplexed this year about the policy of the British. He thought they would concentrate in the South, on account of the supposed strength of the monarchist partisans, but I don't believe the Tory strength is here. I think the British will have to bring in thousands of troops and ships from the North, before they subdue our South. This year and the next will tell the future, and you and I, Peter, will play a little part, because we are among the few to go before and prepare the way—an honour, as I see it."

"I would like to fight with my sword, not with my wits. I trust my sword-arm more than I trust my wits," Peter complained.

"Necessity sharpens the wits," Adam said.

Angela came into her mother's room and closed the door. Francisca glanced up from her crewel-work, and smiled. Her daughter, with the air of a tragic muse, stood back to the door, waiting for her to speak.

"What is it, Angela? You wear the air of Madam Siddons. What ails you?"

"Mother, do I have to marry Captain Huntley?"

Francisca thought, I must have a care what I say. She is tense and at the edge of hysteria. "Is Peter so obnoxious?"

The girl hesitated, brushed her long fingers across her forehead. "No." She spoke slowly, as though considering. "No, not obnoxious, not that. Betsy thinks he is delightful, and very handsome, in an ugly way."

Francisca started to laugh, then thought better of it.

"Do you think he is handsome, Mother?"

"My child, handsome is something intangible. A man may be called handsome by one person and not another. Peter has a strong face. His features are not clear-cut, as Major Rutledge's, for instance, but they have strength. His eyes look at you honestly. I think Peter never told a lie knowingly. He might withhold the truth, but he wouldn't lie."

"You like him, don't you?"

"Yes, Angela, I like him very much. More than that, I think he is a man to whom I would trust my very dear child."

"Betsy says marriage is either very good or very bad. It can be fun, she says, if you are in love, but very dull if you are not. I would not like a very dull marriage. I'd rather stay unmarried. Some spinsters lead a pleasant life."

"Sit down, Angela. I see that there are some things that should be said. It is the destiny of a woman to marry and bear children. No matter what her life may be, gay or sad, unless she has loved and married and borne children, her life is incomplete. She may fill it up with other things, other interests, but there is a gap."

"Why should I get married to have children? Miss Cleo, down on King Street, has two children and she is a spinster."

Francisca looked at her daughter. Mother of God! she thought, have I brought up my child in such ignorance? "Children born without the sanction of Holy Matrimony are natural children, not legal. But this has nothing to do with you, Angela. Your father and I have selected Captain Huntley for your husband. You must have confidence that he is in every way suitable for you."

"I have confidence in you, Mother, but not in Mr. Ferrier. He wants to get rid of me. When I am there under his eyes, he is reminded that you had another husband, whom you loved madly; a gallant, handsome husband."

Francisca said sharply, "Angela, you know that is not true. Mr. Ferrier has done everything for you from the time he helped us off the sinking ship. It was he who made our rescue possible. We owe to him our lives and all our pleasant living."

"I do not owe my life to him. I owe my life to my own father, Señor Miguel Gonsalvo, and no one else, nor do I want to. I am strong, like my father. I can stand quite alone." She got up and walked back and forth, her face set as a mask, without expression. Only her dark eyes burned with some deep emotion.

Francisca looked out the window, the pleasant vista of trees and river before her eyes, but she did not see them. She must make up her mind whether to speak or not. It was hard to decide. To tear down the image of her father which the child had built up was cruel, too cruel. No, there must be some other way.

She said, "Try to think of marriage as a natural thing, dear child. Think of it as something built on friendship and respect. Those are firm beginnings. Do not think only of love. Let love grow naturally out of friendship and respect. What you think of as love may be infatuation. Infatuation is passing and it destroys as it passes."

"No, Mother. No!" There was so much anguish in the girl's voice that her mother turned to her. There was something behind that emotion. She must move cautiously. She waited, hoping Angela would speak. After a moment the girl continued: "I do know what love is, Mother. I love Anthony."

"Anthony?" Francisca tried to keep the alarm out of her voice. "Anthony? I do not know anyone named Anthony."

"Yes. Yes. I told you. I met him on the ship when I was coming from England with the Pollocks."

"Yes, I remember now, but that was three years ago. It is childish to think that you are in *love* with a man you haven't seen in three years."

"But I have seen him, Mother."

Francisca did not move, nor did the expression on her face change, but a fear clutched her. "Where have you seen this man, Angela?" There was cold disapproval in her voice.

"At Ann's. I met him there once, twice. He was at Balgray when

I went there last spring. He went away after a few days, but he came back. He came back with the actors."

Francisca sat up straight in her chair. Her usually placid, tranquil expression gave way to sternness. "Angela, I cannot think what has come over you to deceive me in such manner. To steal away to Ann Pollock's house to meet this——" She paused for a word.

Angela said, "Don't blame Ann, Mother. She did not know he was coming. He just came and said he must stay with them." She could not meet her mother's questioning eyes. "I did not mean to be so in love—" her voice was very low, almost inaudible—"but when he takes me in his arms to kiss me, I want nothing in the world but to be with him." She hesitated, then went on with a rush: "That is not infatuation!"

Go gently, very gently, Francisca warned herself. "I am hurt in my heart, Angela," she said slowly, "that you should set out to deceive me; hurt deeply in my heart."

"I did not set out to deceive you, Mother. It happened. He is so strong, so powerful that one cannot withstand him."

"Angela!"

"It is true. He loves me." She faltered. "I thought he loved me, but when I implored him to take me away with him, he would not."

Her mother rose majestically. Her eyes had flecks of angry light in them. Anger and something more, something like disdain, showed in her face. "To think a child of mine, Castilian-born, should so demean herself as to importune a man to take her away from her mother, from her home!"

Angela put her hands over her face. "I don't know why I did it. I was mad! Mad! But no one knows but Major Rutledge and Captain Huntley."

"Mother of God! No one but Adam and Peter!"

"And Ann Pollock," Angela rushed on, "but they don't know his real name. He's Jeremiah Morse now."

Francisca looked at her daughter, her mind active and alert. "You are incredible! Didn't it occur to you that this man might be a spy?"

"Yes, certainly. I knew it the first day I saw him, at Ann's. But he told me not to mention the word spy. So I did not. I put it in the back of my mind and tried not to think of it. After all, we are Spaniards, Mother, and spying on the English did not seem so terrible to me."

"You say Adam Rutledge and Peter knew of this—this behaviour of yours?"

"Yes. Captain Huntley fought a duel with Anthony. People were after him, so I drove him away in a coach. I helped him to escape. It was the night the mob went after Cullen."

"Sit down!" Angela had never heard her mother speak with such harshness. "Tell me what happened." Francisca listened, her face cold and without sympathy, as though all the warmth and affection had been drained away. When Angela finished, she sat immobile, looking at the floor.

After a time she rose from her chair. "I shall speak of this to your father."

"No! No!"

"Then I shall speak to Peter Huntley."

Angela caught her hand. "Mother, please, please don't." Tears ran down her cheeks. "I told you, you only. I came to you because I was perplexed. Can't you see how contrite I am?"

"The man is not worthy. Can't you see? He comes secretly, talking love to a young, innocent girl. Does he come to your father, to your mother, to ask permission to pay his addresses to you? No, he comes secretly, beguiling you with love words, without respect. He thinks no more of you than the common yokel who takes a kitchen-maid to walk in the lane at night, and forces her to the ground behind a hedgerow; or a slave who takes his pleasure with a wench in a cotton row. He has no respect for you, or for me, your mother."

Angela was crying convulsively now. She had never seen her mother like this before; the tie between them had always been so close, so strong in love.

"Mother, don't. I can't bear it. I will never see him again. I promise you."

Francisca gathered up her wool and her patterns and put them in a work bag. "You had better go to your room and compose yourself. Madam Cornell will be coming home soon. I shouldn't care to have them see you as you look now."

Angela looked at her mother imploringly, but there was no yielding in her face. Angela turned and went out. She climbed the stairs slowly to her room on the second floor, which she shared with Betsy. She sat down by the window that overlooked the street. For a long time she sat motionless, staring at the corner of the Palace parade.

Words her mother had said bore down on her. "He has no respect for you!" That was true. If he had, he would not have sought her secretly; he would have gone to the senator.

She got up and bathed her eyes, then rang for Michèle. The girl came after a little delay. Angela asked her to arrange her hair and get out her puce silk with the cherry piping. The girl was deft with her fingers, but a sullen piece, with little to say.

Now she combed Angela's blue-black hair into place, with two long curls over her shoulders. A little hat with cherries, a wisp of tulle over her eyes and a short warm cape completed the costume. Angela studied her face in the mirror for some time, and rubbed colour into her cheeks with a towel.

"Mademoiselle goes to meet a lover?"

Angela glanced at Michèle's face reflected in the mirror. The question wasn't impudent; it wasn't even a question, more a statement.

"What do you know about lovers?" Angela asked, impulsively.

"Enough. Always there have been boys and men running after me, like dogs after a bitch in heat, but I know how to keep them off. I have my knife and my fingernails." She laughed without mirth. "I've left the marks of my fingers on more than one swamp lad."

"Why?" Angela asked. "Why?"

"Why, Mademoiselle? Because they want nothing but to sleep in my bed. They didn't want to take me home and carry me across the threshold as a bride. They wanted to lie with me, because I am beautiful and I have firm breasts and my thighs are strong. But marry with Gil Roi's daughter? *Non*."

A queer sensation crept through Angela's veins. Something strange was here. Something she did not understand, but that drew her.

"Why not, Michèle? You are, as you say, beautiful. You have a fine eyes and a lovely face."

"Little a man thinks on that. What he likes is something different."

"Firm breasts and strong thighs?"

The girl's eyes widened. A look of knowledge lay in them that baffled Angela. "Yes, that is what a man thinks of—not a pretty face." She leaned over Angela's shoulder, looking into her mirrored eyes, "Has Mam'selle never kissed a man until she was aflame with love, until she would do his bidding if it were to jump into a fire and burn to ashes? *Non*? Then Mam'selle has not touched life."

She drew back and began picking up Angela's discarded garments.

You . . . Angela wanted to ask the question, but the words stuck in her throat.

Michèle didn't notice her embarrassment. Once she had spoken, the words flowed from her. "I have known such a man. He came to me tired and hungry, for comfort. He found release in my body. He does not love me; he seeks warmth. He doesn't have a great desire, only weariness. But I have love, and I seek him. I will seek him day after day until I find him." She spoke with savage fierceness. "Then he shall seek me, not for weariness but for desire. Pardon me, Mam'selle," she said suddenly. "I should not speak so of myself."

Angela said, "It is quite all right, Michèle. I understand." But she did not understand. The girl's fierceness, the expression on her face and in her eyes was beyond her comprehension. Not even Anthony's kisses had aroused such thoughts in her. For a moment she forgot her own sadness, but when Michèle left the room, it returned. For a long time she stood at the window. The girl's words had opened her eyes. Anthony had been like the man she talked about. He didn't want to marry her. Suddenly her vague childishness dropped from her. She put her hands before her shamed eyes—but only for a moment. Then she rose and walked to the door. She would see Captain Huntley at the Queen's Arms Inn. She would tell him that she would marry him before he went away to the back country.

CHAPTER

23

ANGELA MAKES A DECISION

PETER ran down the steps, the note that the Negro tavern-boy had brought him held open in his hand. He was in a state of amazement. He found Angela sitting in a far corner of the gallery, her maid Michèle standing behind her chair. Men hurrying up and down the steps to the open door of the tavern stared at them. He saw one fine-looking young officer sweep his hat from his head and bow elaborately. Angela turned her face away and sank deeper into the chair, but the girl Michèle stared back with bold insolence.

Peter was of a mind to slap the man's face, but instead he hurried to Angela, his broad frame a shield between her and passers-by.

Angela, when she saw him, rose hastily and came toward him. Her dark eyes looked enormous in her ivory-white face, and her mouth and chin were firmly set. Peter's spirits flagged. It was some disagreeable errand that brought her to him.

She spoke hurriedly, even apologetically. Her usual poise, her haughty arrogance had disappeared. She looked frightened. "Captain Huntley, is there somewhere to go where we can talk without being heard? I didn't know it would be like this, with all these staring strangers."

Peter hesitated. "We might walk across the Public Parade, or to the Palace garden—" he glanced at the small cape that covered her low-cut frock—"unless it is too cold. The wind from the river blows chill. Or shall we walk toward Madam Cornell's?"

"No. No. The Palace garden would be better." She turned to Michèle. The girl nodded and dropped back far enough to be out of earshot. In silence Peter guided Angela across the street, where the walking was smoother. They passed the church and went straight down the street to the Palace grounds. The sentry in the box saluted. Peter returned the salute and asked permission to walk in the garden.

The sentry opened the gate. "The flowers are mostly bloomed out," he said, "but there are some of Madam Tryon's late roses down by the wall."

Peter thanked him and they walked on. Michèle lingered behind. There were several of the guard lolling on benches behind the sentry-house, who sat up to stare boldly at the buxom girl.

Angela did not speak until they were well away from listeners, half hidden by shrubbery. Then she turned and faced him, her gloved hands tightly clasped.

"Captain Huntley, I know this is unseemly in me. But I have been thinking hard. I have come to a decision. Since you have done me the honour to ask my mother and my stepfather, Mr. Ferrier, for my hand, I think it would be best if we were married immediately, now, before you go away to the back country."

Peter let his arms drop to his side. He stared back at her, not believing he had heard aright. "You want to be married at once?" he said stupidly. "I don't understand."

For an instant a flash of the old arrogance came over her; she drew herself erect. "Is it necessary to understand?" she said coldly. "Perhaps you have changed your mind."

"No. No, indeed, Miss Angela. I have not changed my mind. Come, let us sit down." He led her to a little ornamental iron bench set at the end of a brick walk. Then he said gently, "Tell me what is in your mind, Angela."

Now she found it hard to speak. The thing that seemed so clear to her an hour ago was vague and indistinct—the thing that had determined her to ask Peter Huntley to marry her at once. She thought by it she would assuage her mother's anger. She would comply with their wishes. Her mother would love her again, even with the old sweet affection. Suddenly she knew that was not the reason. It was something different. It was because she was angered herself, angry because Anthony Allison had not asked her to marry him. Something the girl Michèle had said brought a wave of anger and humiliation over her. The way those men had treated the French girl ... They did not want to marry, only to ... The red blood flamed to her face. Anthony . . . That was the reason she had turned to Peter Huntley. She wanted her deep wound made well. She wanted to feel herself honoured. But he must not know; never must he know.

"Don't speak if it is painful to you," Peter said, his eyes very kind, his voice quiet.

"Yes, I want to speak. My mother has talked with me. She thinks we should marry."

"Your mother is my dear friend. For that I am thankful. Angela, this morning I talked with Senator Ferrier. I explained to him what I must do, and my duty as a soldier. I asked him if we might wed when I came back in December."

"No! I want to marry right now—today. Today!" Her voice broke. "Take me away—to Wilmington—anywhere! Take me away! We can find someone to marry us."

He leaned over and took her hand. She started to draw it away, then, remembering, let it lie in his.

Peter's mind went back to his childhood. One day on the moor he had captured a young grouse. It lay in his hand, palpitating in fear, but not moving. Angela was like that. She was trembling with some deep emotion which he did not understand.

He said, "Angela, do you love me?"

Her eyes met his frankly. "No, I don't think so, Captain Huntley, but I respect you. We could be friends at first, then . . ."

"You think love would come?"

She dropped her eyes. Her long lashes swept her cheek. She nodded wordlessly.

Peter's hand tightened on hers. "You give me happiness by your words," he said. "But I am going to say something to you, which I do not want you to misunderstand."

She looked up quickly, alarmed at the tone of his voice.

"A little while ago I would have taken you in any circumstances, but I know that would have been wrong. When I marry I want a chance for success. If you forced yourself to marry me now, for some reason which is obscure to me, you would not be happy, and I would be wretched in your unhappiness." He reached over and took her other hand. "When we marry, Angela, we will be married for all the world to see. Your family, your friends, your people around you. It will be a marriage for you to remember all your life. Between us there must be no slipping around corners, no Gretna Green."

She stared at him. Her eyes frightened him, they were so deep in misery. She was remembering her mother's words about Anthony, yokels and maids among hedgerows, Michèle's bitter denunciation. That was Anthony. This man wanted to stand before the world as her husband. She drew her hands away and covered her face.

He read her thoughts. "Don't think I resent another man, my dear.

That I understand. It is only that I want you for all the years of our life. I don't want you to think back, regretting. You must know how deeply I love you—so deeply I cannot let you do anything to hurt yourself or your dear mother." When he spoke the words they brought enlightenment to him. His love for Angela was a protective love. He wanted to keep her remote from sorrow, from trouble. He could not endure her tears. He spoke quietly as one would speak to a child.

Tears ran down her cheeks. "Oh, what have I done! What have I done!"

"Nothing to trouble you, my dearest." He wanted to take her in his arms and comfort her, but he could not take advantage of her humility. He took his linen handkerchief from his pocket and put it in her hand. "Dry your eyes, like a good child, and I'll take you home."

She dabbed at her eyes with her handkerchief. "Thank you, Peter," she said. "You are so kind."

Peter's heart sang. She had called him Peter. She had leaned on him for comfort, if only for a moment. He realized, more than he had before, that she was very young. He must wait. He must be patient.

Michèle looked at her mistress curiously, but fell in behind them without comment.

When they arrived at the Cornell home, Betsy came running to meet them. "Where have you been? Have you forgotten the picnic? Hurry and change! We are going out to the race track. Half the people have gone already—the servants and the food." Betsy was so excited that she did not notice Angela's eyes.

Angela escaped up the stairs. At the landing she met her mother. Peter saw her throw her arms around Madam Ferrier. "Oh, Mother, you are so wise!"

Madam laughed aloud. Over Angela's shoulder her eyes fell on Peter standing at the foot of the stairs. He was smiling broadly. She nodded slightly.

Peter walked into the room where the family and some of the neighbours were gathered to have a drink before they braved the dangers of the race track. One young officer had his betting-book out. He was riding in the chase and he wanted odds against himself. Peter felt light of heart. He had successfully passed a crisis. But deep in him there was a modicum of regret. If only he could have married her now, today, even as she wanted! The long waiting was hard to contemplate.

The race track was across the town, in the open country on the Neuse River. The forest surrounded the course, and low bushes grew in the oval.

Games had been arranged—fencing among the officers, horseshoe-pitching; and someone had set up pall-mall stakes and wickets. A pleasant game of archery for the ladies. Angela was expert at archery. Peter thought she looked quite like Diana, as she stood in position, drawing the bow.

Cosmo de' Medici was the favourite. His skill in fencing commanded the respect of the gentlemen. He played battledore and shuttlecock with the children, and challenged Madam Ferrier to a game of pall-mall.

The races came after the supper. Negro cooks made fires and set up spits. Brunswick stew, in a great iron kettle, swinging from a crane, bubbled and sent off pleasantly appetizing odours.

Peter had little speech with Angela, until the races began and he sat between her and Madam Ferrier. The senator came over late, as did several men of the Council.

The races were exciting. Cosmo borrowed a hunter from Billie Cornell, and won the sweepstakes. He was a superb rider. He rode with skill and gaiety, as a centaur must have ridden in the days when the great gods roamed the earth. Peter thought he looked at least as one of the lesser gods must have looked, with his black curling hair, his dark skin and gleaming white teeth. Half the women were swooning with love for Cosmo. He smiled at them all! All! He loved the whole world, Cosmo cried with a sweeping gesture of his hands. That day he had got money! Money for his men! New shoes they would have and warm uniforms before the snow flew.

After the race he flung himself on the ground at Betsy Cornell's feet and made frank love to her before everyone. The women all smiled and thought him extravagantly handsome.

Peter thought, He is the only man who can make love openly to every woman he sees. No other man would be allowed to flirt so extravagantly with a young girl in front of mother, aunts and friends. It was an amazing spectacle.

Once Cosmo caught Peter's eyes on him. He said, "I relax. I relax from the horror and the deadly monotony of war. It is pure bliss, I assure you, Peter, pure bliss." He kissed Betsy's hand, then Angela's. They both laughed in delight at his flattering phrases. Nor did he neglect the older women. He wooed them with little courtesies. He filled their wine-glasses and plates. He waited on each one as though his every thought was for her comfort.

"What a husband he would make!" sighed Madam Cornell, with a glance at her stout, money-making spouse who had little thought beyond his ships and his counting-house.

Cosmo heard her words. "No, Madam, no. It is a very poor husband I would make. It would bore me to remember only one and forget all the other charming women. No, a lover of all is best for Cosmo."

They laughed.

Angela turned to Peter. "I think he is the most delightful man I ever met. I am glad he is your friend." She blushed then. It was as though she had said, "When we are married he will be our friend."

"He is one man in a thousand, Angela. He has innumerable worries, and he carries the burdens of his men on his shoulders, but still he can laugh."

"And play the fool, also." Cosmo looked up at Peter. "Hi, my friend Pietro is more serious. In his country the people do not laugh so easily as in our sunny Italy. But he is a firm rock to lean upon. If I am at war, in a battle, or in trouble, it is Peter that I want to stand beside me. I know he will stand there, firm and steady." His eyes turned to Angela, but he did not address her directly. "There is no retreat in Peter. It is a word he does not know."

Peter glanced at Angela. Two little tears glistened on her downcast lashes.

The sun went down and the women searched for their long capes before the carriages were brought up to carry them back to the town. Cosmo helped Betsy to her feet. "You must wrap yourself well, my little friend. It would be sad if you caught a throat and went croaking to his Excellency's garden-party tomorrow."

"Will you be there, Captain de' Medici?"

"Indeed, yes. It is my last joy. The following day I ride south again to the army and my brave lads."

Betsy said, "I heard that his Excellency is having a canvas spread on the parade-ground, so there will be dancing."

"I shall ask your mamma for the honour of dancing a minuet with you, my little friend."

Betsy's cheeks glowed. She dropped a little curtsy. "Thank you, sir. I am sure my mamma will be pleased."

"And you?"

"I shall be most happy, Captain," Betsy said primly, suddenly remembering her dancing-master's lessons in deportment, "most happy."

Cosmo turned and offered his gold-and-enamelled snuff-box to Senator Ferrier. He was at once serious and deferential, as to an elder statesman. "I wish so much to thank you for speaking today for me to his Excellency. I think it was your calm, wise words, rather than my impetuous pleading, that convinced the Governor of the needs of my men."

The senator took a pinch of snuff, placed it on the back of his hand and inhaled, then sneezed into a large silk handkerchief. "I am always on the side of an officer who thinks first of all of his men, Captain. I can see you are such a man. We all are proud to have you here in America. I hope, after the war is over, you will remain with us."

Cosmo looked serious. "That I want to do, if I am permitted." He smiled then. "You know I have those one thousand acres of land I bought some time back. I do not know whether it grows anything or not, but it is beautiful red earth, beautiful."

Someone broke in then to say that the senator's carriage was waiting. Cosmo and Peter mounted their horses and rode alongside. It was a gay cavalcade that came into the town of New Bern that night—gay, with no thought of war.

The next day was warm for mid-September, and sultry. Michèle, when she was dressing Angela's hair, said she smelled a storm.

Angela laughed. "I have never heard that expression before, 'smell a storm.'"

Michèle was quite serious. "I can do that. I can smell weather. Tonight I think she blows a storm."

"Oh, I hope not. It would spoil the Governor's garden-party."

"You would run into the house, Mam'selle. But the poor people who eat their barbecue on the river beach, and dance in the street— they will not be so happy."

Angela had no reply for a moment. Then she said, "Of course they have a place. They can dance in one of the big warehouses."

"With tar and pitch on the floor, and great bales and boxes and rope coils to stumble over. No, Mam'selle, it will not be good dancing."

All New Bern and the countryside from Bath to Wilmington rode into the capital city for the garden-party. The town was gay in bunting and flags. The taverns were filled with cheerful voices, the fumes of wine and beer and heavy smoke. Along the water-front, the ordinaries too were crowded, for the feasting was not only for the quality, but for the common folk as well. Fishermen and warehousemen were busy preparing a great fish muddle, with plenty of ale, a present from the merchants of the town, to drink. There was dancing in the streets. Fire-works from a barge, anchored out in the middle of the Trent River, could be seen from the Palace and the wharves as well. For the common people there were wrestling, games and jumping and single-sticks; with country dances and reels for the women and girls and active men.

The fishermen lifted their fingers and tested the wind, squinting at the sky. They hoped the storm that lay off the coast would blow straight north and not swoop in, following the river from the sea.

It would be gay tonight, but not so gay, the oldsters said, as during the time of the King's Governor Tryon.

He was a proper man for feasts, was Tryon, gay-like, proud perhaps, but he loved his drink and his dancing and he liked to see the people gay and happy.

Caswell was well enough, but he was too busy with war and the militia to think much of the people. He thought of their money, 'twas true, and taxes, but he did not go among them, as the Royal Governor had gone in his elegant uniform, riding a fine horse, tossing a coin to the children, chucking a pretty girl under the chin. A proper fine man, Governor Tryon was.

The youngsters didn't remember Tryon; they remembered Martin, the scared cat who ran away. He had fled by the tunnel in the Palace that led to the river, where he kept a boat waiting night and day. Even now he was down the Cape Fear, on H.M.S. *Cruizer*, sending out proclamations to his loyal subjects, calling himself Governor still. He was for laughter, that Martin, they said.

Peter, dressed in his best uniform, was putting on his ruffles and cravat of lace-edged linen, while Cosmo sat on the edge of the narrow bed watching him. Cosmo was a bird of Paradise. Tonight, instead of wearing the sombre blue and buff, he wore the uniform of his own land, grey-blue, laced with gold and scarlet, with a scarlet-lined cape and a gold-laced jacket slung from his shoulder.

They were preparing to leave when Adam Rutledge came in, with Herk behind him. His boots were caked with swamp mud. He had ridden up from Wilmington and he was dog-weary. Herk pulled off his boots and took his coat. Adam threw himself on the bed.

"I'll be over later," he said briefly, turned his face to the wall and was asleep before they left the room.

"You must have had a difficult trip," Peter said to Herk, who had picked up the boots. "We expected you yesterday."

"Yes, sar. That *was* a trip. We made ourselves lost in Holly Shelter. The horses bog down. We have to get them out with poles under they bellies." He went down the hall carrying the boots to be cleaned and varnished.

They arrived at the Palace in time. It would not have been proper to come late, after the Governor had led his lady out on the floor to dance the first minuet. They entered the wide hall and were shown at once to the gentlemen's room. A servant in livery took their capes and hats. On the bulletin board was written the order of dances: March, Minuet, Minuet, Contra-dance, Minuet and Reel. Each of them received a card with the name of the young woman he was to lead in the march, which would follow the official opening dance of the Governor. The same young lady would be his supper-partner.

Peter's card bore the name of Mistress Angela Ferrier; Cosmo's, Mistress Elizabeth Cornell. Cosmo made a little face. "A sweet child, but young, very young," he said. The fact did not spoil his pleasure. There were older and more worldly belles with whom to dance other minuets and sit in little secluded corners, or walk on the roof in the starlight.

They stepped into the hall. The Governor and his lady were receiving on the stair-landing. Madam Caswell was quiet-mannered, with a pleasant smile. The Governor looked tired; there were lines at the corners of his mouth, and his large eyes, with their drooping lids, were weary. But his smile was natural and his welcome generous.

He put his hand on Cosmo's arm and detained him a moment. "Captain, if I could have you intercede for me at the Congress as well as you interceded for your men, I would drop my worries to the ground." To Peter he said, "He gets money from me when I have no money to give."

Others were behind him, coming up the stairs, and the two young men moved on upstairs.

The Palace had had rough usage since the first glorious days when it was the most beautiful house in America. At least the New Bernians made the claim. Perhaps it was, but time had gone hard with it. The vacancy after Martin's flight had not helped. Caswell stayed here only on occasions, for he preferred to live quietly at his own home at King's Town.

There was little furniture, only enough to furnish the Palace scantily. Tonight in the upstairs rooms were arranged card-tables and sitting-rooms and a powder-room for the ladies.

In the wide upstairs hall Peter and Cosmo met Madam Ferrier and the two girls, and then accompanied them down the second stair-case, so that they would not interfere with the guests coming up.

The downstairs rooms were cleared for dancing, with the exception of the dining-room. Already many guests strolled in the garden and on the parade-ground, where a band made up of soldiers was playing. Peter walked beside Angela to the garden, happy to be near her. Behind them, Betsy and Cosmo talked animatedly. The sun was setting. It threw long rays on the water and the parade-ground, lighting up the western windows with squares of fiery light.

Angela spoke first. "You were kind yesterday. I cannot think why I behaved in such an outrageous way. I think another man would have misunderstood me, and not have been so kind."

"It would have been very easy to agree with you, to take you at your word and carry you away. All last night I was thinking it might have been our bridal night, and I was sick at heart. But I know we chose the right way. I have said to myself, a hundred times, that it will not be long until Christmas."

She moved a little closer to him. The yellow silk of her swaying skirts brushed against him, and her little furred cape nestled against his arm as they strolled down the brick garden path.

"I have not told my mother," she said after a time. "I think that I have hurt her enough."

"No, there is no need to speak of it again. It was an impulse, nothing more."

"Best forgotten," she agreed; "much better forgotten."

The sun went down behind the rim of pine trees. A cool breeze from the river touched Angela's ruffled skirts. Peter saw Adam Rutledge walking slowly down the path, his eyes on the ground. His face was set in sad, almost stern lines, and he passed people without seeing them. Angela and Betsy went into the house, Cosmo with them. Peter would join them in time for the march.

He turned to follow Adam, whom he found seated in a quiet corner of the garden, on the little white iron bench where he and Angela had sat.

Adam glanced up. "Sit down, Peter, sit down."

"Perhaps I am intruding on your thoughts."

"No. No. It is true I had slipped back into the past. I was thinking of a night when Governor Tryon gave a great ball, and there was a riot. People were protesting the expense of a Palace like this when many farmers up the rivers and creeks were starving. It had been a year of drought, and many families were living on a little corn or maize. I cannot forget that year."

"You were at the ball?"

"Yes, and many of our friends. Mary Warden was here. I remember we helped get Lady Caroline away when the mob was after her." He was silent, absently twisting a button on his waistcoat. "Mary was always resourceful and without fear." His tone was one of affectionate admiration. "There was a fire in the kitchen wing, too, and disgruntled farmers in boats on the river ready to take drastic measures. Only quick action saved the night from being one of horrible bloodshed that would have been a blot on the name of the Province."

He rose, shifting his broad shoulders as though to cast off the old memories. "Listen. There is a bugle. The Governor and his lady will take their places in the *salon*, and the march will begin."

They went to the house quickly. Peter found Angela at once. He crooked his arm for her slim white hand and they took their place in the line that would march around the room, each couple making its obeisance to the Governor as they passed by, the ladies a small curtsy, informal, far removed from the dignified performance that prefaced a grand ball in the days when William Tryon ruled North Carolina.

Down on the river shore the ale was flowing, spirits were high, and voices raised in song and shouting. Dancing was in full swing, a country dance in groups of twenty couples. Three fiddles and a French horn furnished the music. An old man in a white wig beat time and called the figures:

> "S'lute you' pardner. Let her go.
> Balance all and do-se-do.
> Swing you' gals and run away.
> Right and left and all sashay.
> Gents to the right and swing or cheat.
> On to the next gal and repeat."

Michèle, whose partner was one of the sentries she had spoken to yesterday, danced and swayed, her sober grey skirts swirling about her well-turned calves. She was smiling and humming along with the caller.

> "Balance next and don't be shy.
> Swing you' pardner and swing her high."

Michèle's bright red garters showed for a moment, and the bare skin above her rounded knees.

> "Bunch the gals and circle round.
> Whack you' feet until they bound."

The soldiers stamped and balanced and swung their partners.

> "Form a basket. Break away.
> Swing and kiss and all get gay."

The invitation was given twice. The soldier grabbed the French girl, holding her close, his body bent over her, kissing her mouth long and hard. "Tonight," he said, "tonight will you walk to the lime-kiln with me?" She held her head back, her eyes slanting, her lips parted.

> "Swing you' opposite. Swing again.
> Kiss the same gal if you can."

Again his lips lay on hers, hotly, his hand hovering over her bodice. "Now. Now. The dark will be here soon," the soldier whispered.

> "All join hands and off you go.
> Gents, salute you' little sweets.
> Hitch and promenade to seats."

The soldier hurried Michèle to the shelter of bushes beside the stream. This time he had no words; his mouth came against her half-closed lips. His strong body was seeking. "Come, let us go," he whispered, half dragging her to a boat. "Ten minutes and we will be far up-stream."

She spoke no word. She sat with her legs stretched flat in the bottom of the boat, her back braced against his spread knees, as he rowed strongly. The man, too, was silent, his mind on one thing only. Presently she twisted her head about and lifted her face to him. He could see her white teeth gleam in the dark.

"By the Saints, you are a proper fine lass!" he said, and laid his lips upon her throat. He spoke huskily, as he pointed the boat ashore. "Come, lass, come," he said. He half pulled and half lifted her from the boat. Taking her hand he made his way up the bank, into the velvet blackness of the pine woods.

The storm was on them with a roar. The dancers on the parade fled to the Palace; the dancers by the dock to the cavernous warehouse. For two hours the wind was beating against them, breaking out the crowns of trees, hurling boxes and garden-chairs and benches. Servants ran to windows, to close and lock them. Others stood by to relight candles as they flickered out. Once all the candles in the drawing-room chandeliers were out. Angela gasped, terrified. She was afraid of the lightning, the roar of the thunder. She clung to Peter's arm, hiding her face against his shoulder. It was blissful to him to stand close, protecting her with his arm, his lips close to her perfumed hair.

Someone was speaking in a loud voice, intended to quiet the fears of the frightened women, as the rain dashed against the windows and the cannonading of thunder beat upon them. "Not a bad storm," the man called out, "nothing like the hurricane of '69, ten years ago. Why, a third of all the houses in the city went down then. But this Palace stood firm as Gibraltar. This house is built for eternity, I tell you, eternity."

A slave came into the room, carrying a hurricane lanthorn. It sent a slender beam across the room. Angela moved away. Peter bent over her. "This is farewell, my dear. We are leaving in the morning at cock-crow, Adam and I."

She touched his hand for a moment. "Go with God!" she whispered.

In the early morning, making their way over fallen trees and debris, Peter and Adam Rutledge mounted their horses and started on the long journey. Herk rode with them. When they turned into the Cape Fear Road, which led to the Moravian settlement at Salem, they overtook James Iredell. He was travelling by chaise to Salisbury. And so they made a little cavalcade, and a pleasant journey.

Cosmo de' Medici, with two dragoons, rode a way with them, then turned south. The parting had a little sadness in it. They all knew it would be months before they would meet again. Months, with some battles of great import to the Revolution.

Unknown to them, another traveller was journeying toward the army in the South, Michèle Roi. She lay, sleeping heavily in a waggon designated for camp-followers. Twice, when the column halted, a red-faced soldier looked into the waggon. A blowzy-looking girl, who sat cross-legged on the floor of the waggon, looked up. "She sleeps like the dead," she volunteered. "She must have had a skinful."

The soldier grinned, showing a broken tooth. "Yes, she had a skinful."

The bugle sounded. The column began its march south, through the Sand Hills.

CHAPTER
24

TOWARD THE SETTING SUN

The road from the Cape Fear to Salem was near to four hundred miles, a weary road of storm and rain, of heat and red dust. Day after day they rode, stopping at an inn or a wayside ordinary, sometimes at the home of some friend; but more frequently Peter and Adam slept on the ground, with saddles as their pillows, while the judge slept sitting upright, his head resting against the padded upholstery of his carriage.

They took the road that followed the Neuse River to Cross Creek, and stayed overnight at Colonel Rutherford's. Shortly above Campbell Town the road converged with the Cape Fear Road to Salem and Bethabara, the Moravian towns. Near the Caraway Mountains, just west of Husband's Mill, they intersected the Western Trading Path, which ran westward and later became the main Trading Path to Salisbury. This was Judge Iredell's destination, and a stopping-place for Peter.

There were swollen streams to cross. They soon passed through the fever-ridden swamps of the coastal plains and reached the softly rolling hills, which grew ever higher and more rolling as they drew closer to the high mountains.

Adam Rutledge and Herk left them when the Trading Path crossed the Cape Fear Road. The night before he left, Adam told Peter something of his task. He would cross the Great Smoky Mountains, riding a path that followed the Yadkin River. Over the high mountains he would visit the North Carolina and Virginia men who had gone westward to pioneer in the fertile valleys as far north as the Ohio River. It was in the mountains and the valleys that he would come to the frontier plantations of the men whose names were already well known to Peter, the men who captained from two to three hundred pioneers of the back country, trained to woodcraft and Indian fighting.

Like the clan leaders of the mountains and glens of Scotland, they would go out on signal from their leaders. Sometimes pyramid fires on the high peaks would be the signal; sometimes a runner would go from small farm to small mountain cabin giving the warning. Sevier, the two McDowells, Shelby and Cleveland must be made acquainted with the plan for the coming year, with orders to stand ready. From there Adam would go down the Ohio by flat-boat to the Mississippi. There was work to be done in the West and it was of importance.

From Salisbury, Peter would follow a more southerly route to the Blue Ridge Mountains, where there were other leaders. He would follow the Catawba through high mountains to the Quaker Meadows, then drop south to the southern border of the state.

They separated where the Trading Path crossed the Yadkin River. Adam planned to spend a day at Bethabara, outfitting for the long journey toward the setting sun. Peter Huntley sat on his horse, watching his friends vanish through the trees that bordered the road.

The judge's carriage had vanished westward. Peter felt very much alone. He realized how much he had leaned on Adam Rutledge's superior judgement and his knowledge of the country. From now on, he was on his own. He stiffened his sagging back and urged his horse on. Perhaps it was as well. He would learn to rely on his own judgement, make his own mistakes, perhaps, and get out of difficulties by his own wit. He crossed a little ford at Abbot's Creek; it made him think of the rivers of Ayrshire, his mother's country. He began to sing an old song:

> "Th' Ilissus, Tiber, Thames and Seine
> Glide sweet in mony a tunefu' line;
> But Willie, set your fit to mine,
> And cock your crest,
> We'll gar our streams and burnies shine
> Up wi' the best."

From that time on, he matched a Scots song with each stream he crossed.

> "Lord Gregory, mind'st thou not the grove
> By bonie Irwine side. . . ."

Then there was the "Song of Kilmarnock Water." When he crossed the broad sweep of the Yadkin he sang a song of the Doon at the top of his voice and made a noise that was not inconsiderable.

The momentary sadness of parting from a friend gave way to antici-
pation. He would sleep on a bed that night. That was a good thought.

"A sword red wi' bluid, lassie, the bluid of kith and kin,
   Is waving o'er puir Scotland for her rebellious sin."

That was too solemn, but it was the way of Scots to let gaiety be
bordered in solemn thoughts.

It occurred to Peter that he had seen no one on the road for some
time. He wondered whether he had missed the turning. He got
down to look for tracks, to see whether the judge's chaise had passed
that way. The dust was red and deep and no tracks were visible. He
walked for a time before he saw where the chaise had turned out.

It was then that he saw a side path following a small stream. The
ground was beaten down by the tramping of cattle hoofs. The rem-
nants of a small fire showed where the drovers had camped. It was
not an old fire—a day or two old, no more. It put Peter in mind of
his enemy Morse—for he *was* his enemy. He hoped above all things
to find the rascal and give him a proper trouncing. He would like to
beat him with bare fists, not as gentlemen would fight, with swords,
but as two enemies standing up to each other in strength, or as in the
old times, contending with long knives, each with an arm tied behind
him.

Presently he met travellers on the road. A farmer coming back
from market in Salisbury drove his big-wheeled cart to the edge of
the path in order to pass the time of day with the stranger. He had
seen many strangers in Salisbury, he told Peter. His weather-beaten
face showed his pleasure. A lone man he was, and it was good to see
others at times. They talked for a moment, then he drove on.

Peter stopped at a little stream to let his horse drink and to rest an
hour. He lay on the green bank of the stream, thinking of Angela.
She had been sweet, so sweet and gentle, so different. He was not
sure he liked her too demure; he loved her flashing eyes and the
spirited toss of her head.

That night he slept in the house of Michael Braun near Salisbury,
a strong, sturdy house of field-stone, in the style of the Pennsylvania
houses, built a decade before. He slept heavily, from sheer bodily
fatigue. It was the end of one phase, the carefree phase, of the journey.

Michael Braun would be back from Charlotte Town in the morning. Peter had orders to speak to him. If he gave the proper answer,
Peter was to go a step farther and seek information.

In the morning a bright-eyed girl, with red cheeks and a nice smile, served his simple breakfast of grits and eggs, with a rasher of bacon. Mr. Braun was in his little counting-room behind the stairs, where he worked at his farm books, she told him.

Peter finished his breakfast and drank the fresh milk she brought. When he opened the door to the counting-room he found several men seated there with Michael Braun. Braun was a stocky man with very broad shoulders and heavy brow.

Peter gave his greeting and his name. He then said that he was on a journey westward, looking for cattle for the army. There followed a silence of some moments, while Peter bore the scrutiny of shrewd black eyes under overhanging brows.

After a time Peter said, "I am told that you have a map which shows the passes that cross the high mountains."

There was another silence. Then Braun spoke with some hesitancy. "I have a map. It was drawn by John Collet."

Peter smiled. "Is it the drawing of 1770, dedicated to the King of Great Britain?"

"The same." The tension in Braun's voice lessened. He nodded to the men. They got up and filed out of the room. Peter noticed that they wore moccasins such as Indians used, and that their tunics were made of leather.

Braun took a roll from a shelf and spread it on the table. He was still watchful. Peter looked at it. He spoke as to himself: "Salisbury, Oliphant's Mill, then follow the Catawba to Quaker Meadows. Am I right?"

"Right," said Michael Braun. His smile came slowly. "I must have a care. Last month a man came asking questions, some the same as you asked, but he left out one thing. He forgot to ask me the year, or mention the King of Great Britain."

"Perhaps he never knew," Peter answered. He also was smiling.

"I had no information for him," Braun said grimly, "and he went his way—he and his drovers and his cattle. More than one man has come here, with some of the words, but not all of them, until you came today, Captain Huntley." Braun took up a long clay pipe and filled it.

"I must be cautious," Peter remarked.

"Yes, cautious. This is a country of violence, Captain. The Tories are strong. They flaunt their scorn, or did until Moore was caught. Now Mr. Iredell comes to prosecute, but it will come to naught. A few weeks in gaol will be all the punishment that will be given." He puffed thoughtfully, taking long draughts of tobacco into his lungs and expelling with vigour.

Peter said, "I expected to meet Enos Dye here, but I have not seen him."

"Ah! Enos Dye." He went to the door and called out something. Peter did not understand the words. A few seconds later, three woodsmen filed in. "Captain Huntley expects to meet Enos Dye here in Salisbury."

One of the men stepped forward. "We have a message, sir. Enos, he is kept close at Quaker Meadows; wants we shall guide you over. We live in that direction. Sallee is my name. These be Blasingame and Matthew Ord."

"When are you leaving?" Peter asked.

"Tomorrow, as the sun comes up."

"Good! My mare can have a day's rest."

The men went after a few minutes' discussion about an extra mule to be bought, to carry the food they must take with them. Peter was leaving the room when a Negro boy came to the hall door, enquiring for him. He had a note from James Iredell, asking him to dine that afternoon with Madam Steele, a good friend of the cause.

Peter scribbled a note of acceptance and prepared to ride into Salisbury.

Braun came outside while he was waiting for his horse. "I've taken the precaution of telling one of my men to get a woodsman's suit for you for your journey. You may leave your clothes here until your return." He smiled slightly. "You would be too conspicuous dressed as you are."

Peter thanked him. "That was one of my reasons for visiting town today—that, and arrangements for the food."

Braun watched the stable-boy bring up a fine black horse. "This is my saddle-horse, Captain. I had my boys put your mare out to pasture. A day's rest will not be amiss."

"That is splendid, Mr. Braun. I've asked Sallee to get a second horse for me in town."

Braun nodded. "Yes, you have long, stiff climbing ahead of you, sir." After Peter mounted he came close, seemingly busy with a buckle on the bridle. "Major Avery, the liaison officer between General Washington and General Lincoln, will be here tonight on his way north. I had word by express early this morning."

Peter was pleased. He knew of Avery but had not had the pleasure of meeting him.

"A good man. A very good man," Braun said. "He knows every inch of the road from here to Savannah and Charles Town. A valuable man for you to know, if I may be so bold, sir."

The Steele home was a little beyond the village. Peter rode with James Iredell in his travelling chaise. Iredell said, "You will meet a charming, intelligent woman in Madam Elizabeth Steele, Captain, and a fiery patriot. I think her boys are away. Bob Gillespie, a son by a former marriage, is in the Northern Army. I don't know where John is."

It was at the dinner-table that Peter Huntley picked up the cold trail of Jeremiah Morse. Madam Steele and Judge Iredell had been talking of the war. Madam Steele was discussing a periodical her brother-in-law had sent to her. It was called *The Crisis*, published by an itinerant soldier named Thomas Paine. "It has value," she said. "I think his opinions will last us through the war. I think of them every day, and they comfort me. 'These are the times that try men's souls.' That sentence served to brace my mind, long relaxed by the inactivity of the army through the winter season."

The judge had two numbers of the periodical: the first, which had come at the opening of the Revolution; the second in January of '77. Peter had not read them.

Madam Steele had other information of interest. The assault of Savannah would be launched soon, she had heard from passing officers. And the alliance of Spain with France, against England, last April, would be of great help to us, she thought. Although the treaty did not include America, it did provide for recognition of America's independence.

"You are a knowledgeable woman," James Iredell remarked. "You seem to be the centre of information, instead of on the outskirts."

Madam Steele's large intelligent eyes dwelt on Peter a moment. "You know, Captain, we *are* in the centre. One of the roads from Pennsylvania and Virginia goes through our village to the southern border, and thence to Charles Town. You would be surprised at the number of officers we entertain here. Only last month we had a very delightful young Boston merchant, a most charming visitor from the North. As a rule I am dubious about New Englanders. Perhaps it is because they are shrewd, and they are apt to get the best of one in a horse trade. This gentleman was buying horses and cattle."

Peter stopped eating and laid down his fork. Somehow, before she mentioned the buyer's name, he knew she was going to say Jeremiah Morse. She did, a moment later. "Mr. Morse did not haggle on price, nor did I, seeing that he was buying for the army."

She turned to speak to the slave who had just brought in a second platter of fried chicken and journey bread. "Pass the dish to our guest." She took up the conversation where she had left off. "Mr. Morse brought us much news from the Northern Army. He was not too hopeful about General Washington's situation, even though Anthony Wayne had won a first-rate victory for him at Stony Point."

Peter looked at Mr. Iredell. He was helping himself to chicken, as though he had nothing on his mind but the excellent food in front of him. Madam Steele's mention of Jeremiah Morse meant nothing to him. Peter remembered that besides Samuel Johnston and Adam, Penelope Dawson was the only one who knew there was suspicion about Morse. He doubted if Angela had questioned him. She had listened to what he had told her, without question. He thought, This is important, very important. I must be adroit, not arouse suspicion in anyone.

"Is this a good cattle country, Madam Steele, good pasture?"

"Only fairly good. The native grass dries up if we do not have our normal rainfall. Then the herdsmen drive their cattle into the mountain meadows, where there are more streams. I think Mr. Morse was sending his cattle to Quaker Meadows. He told me he could buy corn from some of the little farms, and the pasturage was better."

"Quaker Meadows!" Peter could not help the name pass his lips.

Madam took the exclamation for a question. "A great meadow in the mountains. It lies beyond Little River Three, which runs into the Catawba near its source."

They left the table and shortly afterward made their adieux. Peter left Mr. Iredell at his lodging-house. He would retire early, he said. The trials began tomorrow. He would have a troublesome time convicting the Tory prisoners. There were too many of their kind in the region. "Upward of eighty Tories have been indicted, mostly for capital crimes, the greatest number for high treason." He sighed a little, harassed and worried by the work ahead of him. "Notwithstanding my utmost diligence, no more than ten can be tried, but every one of them must be convicted, and condemned, if we are to maintain order and uphold the majesty of the law."

Peter endeavoured to express his sympathy for the overworked man.

"That is not all, Captain. I must be in Hillsborough by October first for court, Halifax by the fifteenth of October. I suppose you heard that Colonel Walker, of Virginia, has been arraigned for passing counterfeit money. I want to interest important men of the Assembly and convince them that we must have a law against counterfeit money. So I must get my rest, Peter. Good fortune to you!" They shook hands cordially and Iredell went into the house.

Peter mounted his horse and rode out to Braun's. It was a night of brilliant moonshine. The rim of the high mountains with their jagged outline rose high against the night sky. He felt a certain sense of jubilation. He was on the trail of Morse. He would find him, certainly. His doubts had been dispelled since he had picked up the man's footsteps again. Morse is walking heavily, Peter thought, not bothering to conceal the marks of his feet. He has no notion that he is suspect in the western country. He has lost all sense of caution. His guard is down.

When he reached Braun's place he saw several horses tied to the rack. Braun was in his office talking with a lean man of twenty-six or eight, with a tanned, weathered face and eyes that looked through one.

Braun said, "Major Avery, this is Captain Huntley."

The two officers shook hands, each scrutinizing the other. There was some desultory conversation. Then Braun said, "I will retire, gentlemen. I am sure you will have things to talk about."

Peter detained him. "Mr. Braun, I wonder whether by any chance you have recently had a guest, a merchant from Boston, by the name of Jeremiah Morse?"

"That I had, sir. That I had. You will remember what I told you this morning—several had come who pronounced some of the key words, but not all. Morse was one of those. I let him pass on without the information he asked for."

"Was he buying cattle?"

"Yes, he was, Captain. He said he was on his way to the mountains, to Quaker Meadows, but I suspected he was straight from Savannah and the British lines."

"I wonder," Peter said thoughtfully. "I wonder."

Major Avery entered the conversation. "There was a suspected man who passed through about a month ago. I had advices about him, a British dragoon officer by the name of Anthony Allison."

"One and the same!" Peter exclaimed. "Do you know what he is up to?"

Avery smiled. "I hoped you would enlighten me. His name remains on my list, with a question-mark following it."

Braun said, "There are Allisons in Mecklenburg County. I wonder whether he could be kin."

"I don't think so. This man is from England. He was in the North with Major Ferguson's dragoons."

"Yes," Avery added. "I wonder where Ferguson is. He's an officer we must watch for when the British send another contingent south— Major Patrick Ferguson, the finest rifleman and pistol shot in the British army."

"So?" Peter queried.

"Yes. There is a story that he had his rifle sight on General Washington once, and withheld fire."

"I have not heard that story!" Peter exclaimed.

Braun sat down and lighted his pipe. "I can't vouch for the truth but 'tis told that Major Ferguson and some of his riflemen were lying in a skirt of a wood when two officers rode into the clearing, within a hundred yards. One was in hussar dress and the other in dark green and blue, with a high cocked hat. He was mounted on a bay horse, while the other was on a grey.

"The officer on the bay drew rein and sat brooding, looking at the ground. One of Ferguson's men asked permission to shoot him, but Ferguson refused. A sergeant offered to hit the horse and not injure the rider. Still Ferguson refused. He did not tell his men that he was sure the rider was General Washington. Later it was ascertained that shortly after the Battle of the Brandywine Washington rode off without any of his staff save Count Pulaski."

"A nice story, indicating a sporting officer," Peter commented.

"Yes, so I think. I forgot to say that Ferguson was injured in his arm, but he afterward recovered. It is told that after his recovery he at once set to work to practise the sword and pistol with his left hand and became just as proficient."

Braun said to Peter, "Captain, Major Avery can give you the names of all Tories hereabouts and in the mountain country."

Peter rose. "In that case let us go to my room. We will not be disturbed."

They sat at a table. Peter wrote. Avery smoked. After a time

Avery said, "We may as well begin with the Moores and Bryan. Moore, as you know, was defeated at Ransom's Mill in June, and many of his people driven from that country, while others await trial in Salisbury."

"Yes, I know. I came from New Bern with the Attorney-General."

"Colonel Innes is in command of a Tory force somewhere on the North Fork of the Tyger," Avery went on. "He has with him Major Dunlap, Colonel Ambrose Mills and around seventy dragoons. They have been followed and attacked on the head waters of the Saluda by Whig soldiers under Elijah Clark and John Jones, who have now formed a junction with our Colonel McDowell's forces near Earl's Ford on the north Pacolet. This is all near the South Carolina line."

"I've understood that General Wade Hampton is either with or near McDowell," Peter said.

Avery nodded. "Yes, I believe that is true. Now here is something that may give you an idea. Several Whig woodsmen, making out to be Loyalist, have penetrated into the western country. A crippled lad named Kerr has brought in valuable information—he and a woodsman from near King's Mountain named Blasingame."

"Blasingame!" Peter exclaimed. "Why, he is one of the men who is going to guide me to Quaker Meadows."

Avery nodded several times, showing his satisfaction. "When you reach Quaker Meadows you will not be very far north of McDowell's force. Remember that if you get in a tight spot."

For half an hour he gave names and drew maps. Finally he yawned. "I'm dead for sleep and I'm off with the dawn. I'd best bid you good night, Captain. If your report is ready I will take it." A knock interrupted his words. Braun appeared at the door with decanter and glasses.

"Well thought!" exclaimed Avery. "We can toss a night-cap to Captain Huntley and the High Mountains."

Peter lifted his glass. "To Major Avery and the Army of the South!"

Both together tossed off a second, "To Michael Braun, our good host and firm patriot!"

Dressed in his newly acquired woodsman clothes, Peter followed the three guides. They jogged quietly along the road that led to Oliphant's Mill. The autumn morning air was sharp. The foliage was turning, the sourwood trees a bright crimson among the pines; sycamore leaves quivered like molten gold, and the gums were crimson and gold. The Blue Ridge lay concealed in haze. Tryon Mountain stood out boldly among the lower hills.

Peter thought of Adam Rutledge, wondered how far into the mountains he had penetrated. His companions were silent men. They rode as they walked, single-file, although the path to the mill was wide enough for an ox wagon. Squirrels skipped among the lower branches of the pines, and a mourning dove sounded its melancholy call.

Men were on the march, not only the men who fought battles, trudging with heavy foot-sore steps, but pioneers moving westward. These mountain men were the vanguard. Tomorrow others would follow. It seemed to Peter that there was something in the glorious clean air, some stirring beat at the very heart of the earth, that set the tempo of the march.

Why did these men leave the more settled places? What did they seek? Danger? Or the right to live as they wanted to live?

Halfway to the mill they overtook a man on horseback, a stout yeoman from Sussex in England. He was riding a long-legged mule. He hastened to tell Peter that he was a Whig. He had been in this country, in Pennsylvania, for ten years. But he had sons growing. He wanted more land. He was a jolly, red-faced man, broad and short. His name was Huskinson. He wanted to talk about land. Land was so abundant, miles on miles to be cultivated. He wanted land. Land was stable. It was the true basis of wealth. But no husbandry worthy of the name was practised; not a fit flock of sheep had he seen. Why was that?

Blasingame ventured a word. "Sheep get lost in the hills. It's next to impossible to keep them close. Mountain cats, 'painters,' wolves and foxes ravage the flocks."

"I've seen many herds of cattle moving this way. Why is that? Do they winter in the mountains?"

There was silence. The men had dismounted to eat their noonday meal.

"Some does," Blasingame said after a time. "Some seeks mountain meadows."

Ord handed him a rasher of bacon skewered on a small pointed stick. "Best eat while it's hot," he said.

They left Huskinson at Oliphant's Mill and pushed on. They had a long journey ahead of them. Up and up they climbed, through a path cut in the forest. Higher, the frost was sharper, the foliage more brilliant and clear-cut red and gold; the pines were taller. Sometimes they followed the stream banks; sometimes they rode over a crest and along a ridge.

On the second day they camped by a small stream. Peter went into the woods with a musket, to see if he could bring down a deer. He followed a spoor, but it was cold. On the way back to camp he was overtaken by a rangy woodsman sitting astride a bare-backed horse. He stopped to exchange comments on the weather, which was hot, and on the country. The man, Smithers by name, had been two years in the valley. He asked Peter to come home with him, a short distance up the creek. "My missus will cook you a proper meal," he said, with shy pride. "She says there ain't nothin' fit to eat 'twixt here and Philadelphy."

"The missus" was young, with red cheeks and merry blue eyes. She was working in the strip of ploughed ground back of the house, where she had her kitchen-garden and some hens. She washed her hands at a wooden pump and invited Peter into the house. The cabin was spotlessly clean, the earth floor swept and pounded firm. A few treasures from another world made the large room homelike—a brass fender and andirons at the fire-place; brass candlesticks; a woven counterpane of blue and white over the bed; two mahogany chairs and a large chest on which stood a pewter tea-set; in the centre of the room, a large table with drop leaves, on which were a basket of sewing and a Bible.

The woman busied herself at the brick oven outside the door, while the men talked of the problems of the settlers. The meal was soon ready—deer cutlets breaded, broiled ham, eggs, gooseberry pie, butter, cheese and coffee; at the end, waffles with honey. The woman was proud of her ability to make waffles, which she had learned from a German neighbour.

The country was already overrun with people, the settler told Peter. He was thinking of selling and moving on over the Blue Ridge, where a man had room to stretch himself and breathe. He'd have gone before but for the war.

On they went, each day to see the sun set over a new ridge, a new horizon rising above them. Speech grew less and less among them. These were silent men to whom the silence of the forest was not new.

Presently the quiet communicated itself to Peter. The silent curtain of the forest dropped down, and cut off the outside world.

At River Plantation, Madam Ferrier was standing on the east gallery, speaking with Gil Roi. The Frenchman was brown, almost the colour of a mulatto, from his weeks in the swamp, cutting cypress shingles for the senator.

Madam's face was set to sadness, her voice full of sympathy, as she told the sorrowing father of the disappearance of his daughter. "We had no knowledge that she even knew a soldier," she said. "In fact the senator could not ascertain his name. Only at the very end of our visit to New Bern did the senator discover that Michèle had been seen dancing with this man. Later it was found that there were two waggons in the column for—" she hesitated before she said the word— "camp-followers."

Roi did not speak. He stood looking at the ground, his eyes dull and uncomprehending. Suddenly he threw back his head. "She has gone," he said. "Dem, I could keel, keel, such a man."

Madam turned white; there was such violence in his voice, such rage in his distorted face. "Perhaps she is married," she faltered.

"Bah! Pardon, madame, but I know heem, the soldier. I have been one in my youth. In one country or another, they are the same. Some good men, some bad, very bad."

He shifted his foot and loosened his firm hold on the gallery rail. "Madame, I am sorry to make this trouble for you, who have been so kind. But I speak true when I say my girl she have not been same since one man he come as refugee to our roof. I think something happen. Maybe he sleep with her, maybe not. Maybe jus' she love heem. But she is changed from that time."

"But this couldn't be the same man?"

"I do not know, madame, maybe. I think I go now, madame. I thank you and the mees for being kind."

"We liked Michèle. My daughter was attached to her. She cried half the night when we found she had gone."

"Not worthy of tears, madame."

Madam Ferrier looked long at the Frenchman, wondering what words of hers might give comfort. In the end she said impulsively, "Don't think hardly against Michèle. Do not cast her from your thoughts. Perhaps we will find out the truth one day. I cannot believe that Michèle is a bad girl."

"Thank you for kindness. Michèle's mother she ran away with a bad man and left her, a babe for me to help grow to womanhood. I have do what I can, madame. I have pray' often, oh, so often, to the Holy Virgin for help." He twisted his cap in his brown knotted hands. "I think I keel heem if I find heem."

"Oh, Gil, don't, don't! Have faith that she is safe and unhurt."

"Thank you, madame, for your kindness." His voice was without hope.

Francisca watched him walk away, not with that lithe, even tread of a forest creature which had characterized him, but heavily, as a man who bears a burden. She turned and went into the house, her mother's heart heavy within her.

CHAPTER

25

LORD CRAVEN'S COACH

MIDDLE November had come, and with it the crisp chill of frost in the air. The scarlet and gold of the forest had turned to russet. Hay was in the ricks and corn piled in shocks, ready for shelling and winter storage. The early morning quiet in the village on Queen Anne's Creek was shattered by the hunter's horn and the baying of hounds. The Albemarle Hunt was having its last run. By sun-up three foxes had been lost and a fourth led the hounds along the west side of the creek, where it went to earth in the pocosin just outside the East Gate of the village.

The hunters rode gaily into the village for a hunt breakfast at Horniblow's, fifteen or twenty of them. Mary Warden acted as Master of the Hounds, with a scratch pack made up of couples or fours from various plantations. There were many green riders from the militia and Home Guard. It was not like the old days, when Parson Earle blessed the hunt at St. Paul's, and Adam Rutledge was Master of the Hounds, but there was some sport to be had, even in war-time, to relieve the monotony.

The hunters were led up and down by grooms in the lot back of the tavern before being hitched to the racks, while the masters and mistresses ate breakfast with the hearty appetites of riders who have been abroad since the early hours, stimulated by the fresh frosty air; stimulated also by great slices of smoked ham or roast joints, washed down with ale.

It was near noon when the riders came out of the long dining-room to find the inn filled with men from near-by towns and Sound-side plantations.

At noon, promptly, seven blocks of timber along the Chowan were to be sold from the Courthouse steps for back taxes. A second auction block was to be held at the side of the inn, where furniture and house-

413

hold goods were to go to the highest bidder. High tester beds, sans canopies, were set up. Chests, highboys and chairs sat side by side with iron fire-dogs and brass fenders, huge iron pots on swinging cranes, blackened by smoke of ages, and copper cook kettles. There were kegs of square-cut iron nails, hand bellows, a heterogenous mess of garden tools and chopping-hoes.

Back of these things were high-wheeled carts, ox yokes, mule harness, a few gentlemen's riding saddles and one chaise. Crowds had gathered, two to three hundred, half the village number. They came in most part for the excitement, but many came as bidders. Women's wide, swaying skirts brushed the yeomen's, husbandmen's and herders' smocks. The elegant town ladies elbowed Negro slaves and upcountrymen.

The auctioneer, a hale fellow of sturdy build and narrow mouth, surveyed the crowd out of steel-grey eyes, shrewd and watchful. Higgins was his name and he came from Hertford Courthouse, miles away on the Perquimans River.

He spoke to his assistant, Flynn, out of the corner of his mouth, without moving his lips. "We've got the quality out today, me lad. The bidding will run high."

Flynn spat a wad of tobacco from his mouth and wiped the spittle with the back of his sleeve. "Mostly they come to look, and not to bid."

"Not today. I smell bidders. 'Tis my Lord Craven's chaise that brings them. Look, there's Mr. Samuel Johnston. Twice I've seen him walking around, looking and looking at the chaise, opening doors and peering underneath at the springs, tapping wheels."

" 'E's got a coach, be'n't he? Whyfor he want another?"

"These rich fellers they want only the best. He's lookin' to see if Lord Craven's vehicle is better than the one reposing in his own carriage-house."

"Hope you make 'im wait," Flynn said.

Higgins smiled slyly. "Every object in its turn, that's my motto. Mayhap I won't get around to putting up yon coach till the sun gets low."

Flynn grinned. "Don't overstretch yourself. These quality, they're like to get tired and make their way home. Then where'd you be?"

They were interrupted by the voice of the Land Agent standing on the Courthouse steps. Some of the crowd, men for the most part, surged toward the steps, leaving the women to hover over the furni-

ture. One woman opened the chaise door and endeavoured to get in
to try the comfort of the cushions. Her farthingale caught on the door
latch and her skirts tilted. She could move neither in nor out and
stood teetering on the little step until Flynn untangled her, to the
delight of small boys and a few leering men. Flynn tied the door shut
with a twist of rope. "That'll keep them out," he muttered as he
walked away to hear the rival auctioneer push up the bid on uncut
timberland to four shillings an acre.

Mary Warden and Sarah Blount came out of the ladies' entrance
of Horniblow's, and walked over to inspect the chaise. They were
joined by Penelope Dawson and Angela Ferrier. All were in riding
habits, Angela and Sarah in bottle-green, Mary Warden in blue. Only
Penelope Dawson wore a red coat, against all custom.

They examined the chaise. While Angela stood a little way off,
Penelope said, "I wouldn't mind having it myself. It's in perfect condition. Only one scratch on it, there on the side, under the crest."

Angela heard. Her face grew crimson. She felt as though every
one of them knew how the scratch came on the fine blue paint—from
Anthony's unsheathed sword, as he leaped into the moving vehicle.
The old restlessness returned then, and the longing. She thought she
had laid all feeling for him aside. She had tried, keeping her thoughts
on Peter, on all his excellent qualities, which her mother so often
reaffirmed. But it had been many weeks since Peter went away. Only
once had she had word from him. That was when Mr. Iredell returned from the far West. Peter had written a short note saying he
was about to start on the long journey, a very small note that might
have been written to a stranger, with the exception of one line, "I
think of you constantly, Angela."

That was not a letter from an ardent lover, yet, when she thought
it over, neither had Anthony ever written the word love. Perhaps it
was a word to be spoken, not set down upon paper.

Someone had untied the rope and opened the door of the coach—
Sarah Blount probably, for she had as much curiosity as a little white
kitten. Penelope was sitting inside, leaning back.

"It is delightful," she said. "I have a very good notion to have it
bid in."

Sarah said, "You will have to go high. It is said Sam Johnston's
father has written for him to get it."

Pene beckoned to Angela. "Come get in, Angela. It is really most
comfortable."

Angela held back. She had a curious feeling at the pit of her stomach. The whole scene returned to her: Ann Pollock pleading with her not to go; Anthony with his devil-may-care, sardonic look; the impatient horses; the muffled figure of Anthony's unknown companion. Her extraordinary behaviour rushed in on her consciousness, overwhelming her. Slowly the face of Anthony Allison rose out of the blackness that had surrounded him. She heard the sound of his voice, felt again the strength of his arms and the slow, hot pressure of his lips on hers. This was intolerable. She must push him away, but she could not. She could not bring herself to think of the scene in this coach, to hear her own pleading voice, crying, "Anthony, Anthony, take me with you!"

What had he said? It was so vague now that the words had lost their sting, their cruelty. "I say no. Go to your home and forget me!"

The stranger had come back as he said this, and a drover. "We will leave the coach here," the stranger had said. "We've no time to waste, Allison."

"But the girl! We can't leave her here in the road." Anthony's voice had risen in feeble protest.

"Bah! We've no time for camp-followers."

Anthony had torn her clinging hands from his arm. She had fallen back against the cushion, where she was sitting now. There she had stayed, drowned in tears, until Adam Rutledge came and carried her back to Cupola House.

She was recalled to the present by Sarah Blount crying, "What's wrong, Angela? Look, her face is white as chalk."

"Nothing is wrong," Angela protested, "nothing."

Penelope said, "We will go over to the Barkers'. You could do with a glass of port, Angela. I'm afraid the hunt was too much for you."

"I tell you I'm quite all right, Pene. It's hot in the coach. I'm all right."

But she wasn't all right. After months of not being able to see Anthony's face in her mind, he was before her, as dear to her as he had been before.

They walked through the little gate that led to the Barkers' garden. "Perhaps we shouldn't go in," Mary Warden said, a little frown of anxiety on her smooth white brow. "You know how extraordinarily fond Madam Barker is of her chaise. It must be agonizing for her to part with it."

Pene said, "Come along. If Angela doesn't have a stimulant, she will faint on our hands."

Sarah linked her arm into Angela's. "I know what's wrong with Angela. She is whipped down, listening to Horniblow's speech about what great friends he is with General Arnold. He's always boasting about it. I will wager that General Arnold doesn't even remember him. Just another innkeeper."

None of the women paid any attention. They let Sarah prattle on. The auctioneer's powerful voice broke the silence. "Here is an iron pot, big enough to hold a family wash. I'll start it at five shillings. What am I offered? Six. Seven. Eight. What? No one offer me nine?" A moment's silence followed by the sharp sound of the hammer on the block. "Gone at nine, and many a fine wash-day to you, madam!"

They found Madam Barker seated in her little parlour, a fire blazing briskly. She sat on one side of the fire-place. Thomas sat on the other, his foot swathed in bandages on a small stool. "A touch of the wretched gout," he told Pene Dawson, who dragged a chair to sit beside him. "Was it a good hunt?" he enquired, taking his church-warden pipe from his lips.

"Good for Monsieur Reynard." Pene smiled. "But we had the fun of the chase and that's all that matters. Only the hounds came off without pleasure. Then we had an excellent breakfast at Horniblow's."

"But he talked and talked about Benedict Arnold, his good friend!" Sarah exclaimed.

Thomas smiled his little crooked smile. "To know the great, to sit in the refulgent glow of greatness, is bliss to some."

"You must know hundreds of great men, Mr. Barker," the girl went on, "with all the seventeen years you lived in London. Did you see the King often?"

"Often enough, my child."

"Was he nice?"

"An overfed Hanoverian, with all the elegances of a fat swine."

"Ah!" Sarah was disappointed.

Pene dropped her voice. "Is Madam grieved to sell her coach?"

Thomas gave her a knowing look. "I don't think so, not now. She has finally visioned the idea of selling it for the sake of her country."

"You mean she is——" Penelope broke off suddenly.

"Yes. She is going to give the money to a war fund, to be put directly into General Washington's hands."

Pene said, "The darling!" She rose quickly and went to Madam's side. Bending down, she pressed her red lips to Madam's cheek. Madam Barker looked up enquiringly. "Mr. Barker told me. I think you are a very wonderful woman."

"Ah, Thomas, you swore you wouldn't tell!"

"No, my dearest wife, I did not swear. You told me to swear, but I had no such intention. I am a man who wants his friends to know that he has a wife of extraordinary patriotism and self-denial."

A smile came over Madam's face, a rare sweet smile. For a long moment the two looked at each other, husband and wife, an understanding look that was built up of companionship and affection.

"Thomas, you always get the better of me. How can I scold you when you say such disarming things?"

Angela sipped her wine as she watched them. This is what my mother means, she thought. They enjoy each other even though they are old.

Pene said, "I've a mind to bid. I think I should be going back."

Madam said, "No, don't go yet. Higgins is to let us know when Lord Craven's chaise is put up. No one need to stand out there with that crowd." She turned to Angela. "Go lie down on my bed, my dear. You look beat. I think you have been running about too much—New Bern, Wilmington, Halifax. What is happening?" She looked at the girl shrewdly. "Are you trying to run away from yourself?"

"No. No, indeed."

"Because you will find you can't run away from yourself, however much you try, my child."

Others came in, among them William Warden, searching for Mary. He stopped to drink a glass of Madeira and talk with Thomas, to inform him that Robert Smith, who was with him, had a ship laden with salt. Wells Cowper had broken the salt blockade more than once.

"That is good news indeed!" Thomas Barker exclaimed.

The little parlour was soon filled. Some came with sober looks ready to commiserate or condole, but Madam's bright smile changed that. They were wondering, not understanding. After all, her chaise had been the very heart of her possessions.

"She has pride," one woman whispered to another, "a vast pride that wouldn't allow her to show her feelings."

Pene looked at Madam Barker. She knew Madam was not concealing any hurt vanity. She was speaking to William Warden of poor little Cecily Armitage's untimely death. "They found her early in the morning. She lay on the dark bosom of the creek, her hair floating on the water; like the maid of Astolat in Sir Thomas Malory."

Her husband said, "I don't think Sir Thomas had the fair maid drown, but there is a similarity."

"Why did she do it?" Sarah asked, quick tears in her eyes. "Cecily wasn't really engaged to Jaspie. At least she never told me she was."

"Cecily lived in a dream all the time," Madam said. "I hear Dr. Armitage intends to put a stone on the grave, just as she requested: 'She died of a broken heart.' Isn't it pitiful?"

Pene nodded. "I think we all could have done more for Cecily than we did. I mean all excepting you, Penelope. You were so good to her."

"Not good enough, it seems. Parson Earle says it was her destiny and no one should take blame."

"She was so delicate, and so very young," Sarah said sympathetically, touching her eyes with her handkerchief. "She was always creating stories in which she had a part."

"Cecily would never have faced life," Thomas Barker said. "I think I have convinced Penelope that no one is to blame, no one."

Robert Smith changed the subject abruptly. "There hasn't been an auction like this since Francis Corbin's furniture was sold. I hope prices are high."

"Fair, I think, fair."

A small boy ran across the garden and spoke to Thomas Barker's body-servant. "Mr. Higgins he say he bound to put up the chaise at four o'clock prompt." His voice was so loud that everyone heard. With one accord they all looked at the clock on the mantelpiece. It was a quarter of four.

Madam said, "I will have some chairs taken down. We will sit on this side of the garden fence, so we do not have to brush against so many ill-washed people." Her maid brought in a fur-lined cape with a hood. Madam offered wraps, but Pene said that padded habits were quite warm.

The chaise had been wheeled out to a position near the block. Crowds were standing in a semicircle, closing the street, and had overflowed to the Courthouse Green.

Higgins was in fine form. It was not often that he had a chance to auction an article as fine as the chaise, or have so many prominent men of the Albemarle as bidders. There were strangers in the crowd, men of good deportment, well dressed and bewigged, or with hair carefully queued and rolled. It was almost as though the Assembly were in session, or some judge, such as McLaine or Iredell, about to read the charge to the Grand Jury, an occasion which always brought out the freeholders of the county attired in their best.

Madam Barker seated herself in an elbow-chair near a holly bush which acted as a screen. The others took stools or stood behind her chair. Thomas, of course, was relegated to the fire-place, and William Warden, looking like a death's-head, so thin and drawn, stayed behind to keep him company.

Pene asked Ormond, the lawyer, to bid for her. He asked her limit. "Not more than two hundred pounds," she told him.

"You won't get it for that." He shook his head gloomily. "You won't get it for that. There are too many bidders who mean to have it," he said and went away, to stand near the block where he could watch the bidders.

Horniblow had set a table on the gallery, where bidders could walk up and get a drink, and a bite of cheese to spread on bread fresh-baked in the kitchen oven. It was a merry crowd, set for a pleasant time. Albemarle people were like that. They made a party of a birth, a wedding or a death wake, a market or a feast-day. The feast of St. Michael's, when the county folk came in to pay their quit-rents, was a great party day.

War was no deterrent to good humour. In truth, there had been little heard of war, of late, save some desultory fighting between Tory and Whig along the border. General Sullivan's overrunning of the valley of Wyoming meant little to them.

Five campaigns had proved that the Colonies were not easy to subdue, but the villagers did not think of that, nor did they see that the Burgoyne defeat and the expedition of George Rogers Clark through the valley of Virginia into the country of the Illinois had any bearing on their situation. They could not know that the capture of Kaskaskia in the Illinois country or the surprise attack on the garrison at Vincennes meant anything to them. But these things had increasing importance. Wherever the redcoats had been defeated, one more toe-hold on the continent was loosened. Adam Rutledge knew this, for he was far across the land, along the Wabash. He saw soldiers up to their armpits in icy water slog through lowlands, through forests; a heart-breaking, weary journey for a small victory. Yet even that small victory was part of the pattern.

The bidding on the chaise started at one hundred pounds. A gasp went up. Many bidders were eliminated before their mouths opened.

"Hard money! No Provincial Notes accepted! Cash in hard money!" Higgins shouted. "Cash in gold or hard money! Golden joes accepted! Even golden guineas! We're not so tempestuous against the Mother Country that we won't take her gold away from her, when and where we can. Bills of Exchange, on Baltimore or New York, will serve, but none of that baled paper printed by the Assembly at New Bern."

That caused a laugh in the crowd. A little bitterness still remained in the village that once was the seat of government, in whose Court-house Royal Governors had sat in the Council Chamber.

"One hundred pounds as a spring-board. Like the text of a sermon, we will never return."

"One hundred twenty-five," a voice called. A stranger made the bid.

"That gentleman yonder, in the fine brown coat and chamois waist-coat. One twenty-five. Do I hear two hundred?"

"One seventy-five!"

"One eighty!"

"Two hundred!" Ormond got in his bid, but it was topped at once by the stranger in the brown coat. Ormond moved over to the fence. Pene shook her head. That was her limit and no more.

Samuel Johnston's voice rose above the chatter. "Two hundred and seventy-five!"

Higgins picked it up. "Two hundred and seventy-five from Mr. Samuel Johnston. Think, gentlemen, an honour to top that bid, a great honour to go higher than the owner of Hayes Plantation." This caused another laugh, for Johnston stood head and shoulders above his near neighbours.

"Two hundred and seventy-five! Do I hear three hundred?"

A woman came to the edge of the crowd, forced her way forward. "Seventy-five? I bid eighty."

"The lady bids two hundred and eighty pounds."

A shriek arose from the woman. "Good lawks!" she cried out, her voice shrill. "I thought it was seventy-five pounds. I bid eighty. What shall I do? What shall I do?"

"Withdraw your bid, madam," said Higgins, with a courtly bow. The crowd was in an uproar of laughter. The woman tried to get away, but they closed about her with high good humour.

Higgins rapped his gavel for order. "Enough, gentlemen and ladies! Do I hear a bid of two eighty? A legitimate bid?"

The man in brown bid two eighty. Flynn eased his wiry body through the crowd until he reached the block. He signalled to Higgins, who bent down to listen to what his assistant had to say. The auctioneer smiled and straightened up, rapped for quiet.

"Two hundred and ninety pounds has been bid by the gentleman from Halifax." The crowd screwed their necks. "The gentleman from Halifax, who represents the Honourable Wylie Jones."

"Damn!" said the brown-coated man. "Damn!"

Higgins turned the bit of news to his advantage. "Gentlemen, would you see this beautiful chaise leave the Albemarle and be driven up the Roanoke River to Halifax?"

"No! No!" the crowd shouted.

Higgins waved his hand. "This beautiful coach, that once drew Lord Craven to a meeting of the Lords Proprietors at St. James's Palace? Examine the coach-work, the upholstery, the fine silver-mounted harness! A more elegant coach never drew a fair lady to a levee at the Palace, or drove along Pall Mall, or clattered down Birdcage Walk. Who will bid three hundred?"

"Three hundred," said Samuel Johnston, shutting his lips tight. Pene thought, That is his limit.

A bid or two followed. Relf of Pasquotank said three twenty-five. Higgins tried hard, but got no other bid.

"Going! Going at three twenty-five, the most elegant, the most beautiful coach ever to be seen in Carolina, Lord Craven's coach! Going . . ."

A clear, sharp voice interrupted the auctioneer. "Three hundred and fifty pounds!"

"It's Dr. Cathcart." Mary leaned over to Pene. "Dr. Cathcart—I see him over back of Wylie Jones's agent."

Higgins glanced at Relf, at Johnston, and at the strange bidder. Each shook his head in turn.

"Gone! Sold to Dr. Cathcart, of Bertie County, for three hundred and fifty pounds cash, in hard money!"

The crowd surged and pushed back onto the Green. A few gathered about the chaise.

Madam Barker rose and moved majestically through the garden toward the house, followed by her guests. Her face glowed with pleasure. Three hundred and fifty pounds, less the auctioneer's commission, to be sent to General Washington!

They had come to the steps and were talking, when they saw a courier on a foam-flecked horse gallop down Broad Street and stop in front of Hewes and Smith's store. He spoke to a man who answered, waving his arm in the direction of the Barker residence.

The rider wheeled his horse and rode up the street to the little picketgate. They saw he was travel-stained and very weary, with heavy lines on his tired young face.

"Mr. Robert Smith?" he asked. Smith strode forward to the gate.

The boy dismounted. They heard him say, "Philadelphia . . . the tenth . . . Dr. Burke . . ."

Smith stood staring at the courier, his lips moving, his eyes not seeing the letter the man held out to him. The courier put it in his hand, mounted and rode away down the street.

Smith turned and walked slowly up to the group at the steps. They were silent, waiting for the news. His face was as white as a piece of paper, and the lines at the corners of his lips deepened. He moved his head slowly, looking from one to another. For a moment no words came, then he found his voice. "Joe Hewes is dead," he said.

No one moved, shocked into silence. William Warden came to the door, followed by Thomas Barker, supported by a gold-headed cane.

"What's that? What's that?" Barker asked urgently.

Madam said, "Joseph Hewes has passed away."

"God! God!" William Warden's white face went even whiter, if that were possible.

Pene said," Where is Nat Allen?"

Everyone looked at Robert Smith. "He is in Wilmington. He went down to Masonborough Sound last week."

Barker asked, "What does the letter say? Who is it from?"

Smith opened it again. "Dr. Burke. Only an announcement that Joe Hewes is dead and will be buried at Christ Church in Philadelphia. The whole Congress will attend the burial."

William Warden spoke. "Don't you think it would be wise to go over to the Green and make the announcement? The people love Joe. It is their right to know."

Thomas Barker agreed. William Warden and Smith went out through the garden.

Madam Barker wiped a tear from her eye. "I am ashamed of tears," she said. "We all know it is a blessed relief to our friend that his tired body has found rest."

Pene said, "I hope they bring him home, so that his body may lie beside Isabella. They have been separated too long."

Little Sarah was weeping. Angela, dry-eyed but visibly shaken, said, "He was our friend. All of us loved him. He never treated us as children. Why, just last month, he sent me some satin shoes. He never forgot us, even there in Philadelphia, with all the work he was doing for our country."

Thomas Barker interrupted. "Listen!" The wind was from the east; it carried Samuel Johnston's voice back to them. He made the simple announcement, then read the letter. "Joseph Hewes was my brother in spirit," he said, "and he was my good friend, as he was a friend to every one of you. So we will mourn for him, but our country has lost one of the pillars that upheld the arch."

There was a long silence. In the dying rays of the low sun the people went silently to their homes with saddened hearts. They had indeed lost a friend.

The little group on the steps went inside. In a short time Samuel Johnston joined them with Robert Smith.

Hannah Iredell ran over from her home, a cape thrown about her shoulders. "I just heard," she said. "I cannot believe it, although Jemmy told me he had been ailing so long." She turned to Samuel Johnston. "I do not know whether I should speak of it now, Sam, but Jemmy said if anything should happen while he was away, to tell you that Joe's will is in the strong-box at the office. He said you would know what to do."

Samuel put his hand on his sister's shoulder. "Thank you, Hannah. I will attend to everything."

She leaned against him, crying softly. "I want them to bring him home to Bella," she said. "They have been apart so long."

Mary Warden rose. "I think we had better start for Queen's Gift, Pene. William is driving us. I've had the horses sent out. 'Twill be night before we get home."

Pene also rose. She stood for a moment at the window, looking out on the quiet water of the Sound, turned red by the sunset. "I am glad it came to us this way, at the Ave Maria hour. It is a quiet hour. Joe loved it. I remember how often he used to stand on our bank watching the sunset on the river."

They said good-bye soberly, as people who have had a deep sorrow thrust upon them. Madam Barker was greatly moved. "We shall miss him. He always stopped in for a few words with us every day he was in the village. We shall miss him."

She went with her guests to the door. They heard the reverberation of a drum. It came from a distance, down by the shipyard, a slow beat of a dirge. "The Negroes have heard," Madam said. "They know they have lost a good friend."

In the morning the Pollocks' old retainer, dressed in his funeral suit, with old Squire Pollock's full-bottomed wig on his head, went around the town, knocking at each door in turn. In his outstretched hand he had the roll of parchment, with the words inscribed in heavy black ink that their beloved townsman, Joseph Hewes, the Signer, had passed out of earthly life and gone to his reward.

Angela, at Pene's earnest request, went to Eden House with her the following day. They sailed up in Pene's shallop, and stopped at Balgray for a little visit and to inform the Pollocks of Joseph Hewes's death.

Ann was particularly distressed. "I've lost a friend, I've lost a friend," she said, over and over. "Don't you remember," she asked Cullen, "how kind he was to us, what a fine letter he wrote to me after we had the trouble with the mob?" She turned to Pene. "He knew what to say to soothe our troubled spirits. He gave Cullen advice which he has followed." She paused a moment and glanced swiftly, almost furtively, at her husband. "That is, always if it was in his power. Sometimes things happen outside ourselves, over which we have no control." She spoke cryptically, not in the least like Ann Pollock, who was overly straight forward.

"A curious thing happened the other day," she continued. "A man came here whom we had never seen before, and demanded, I say demanded, hospitality."

Cullen turned his sombre eyes on his wife. "Ann!" His voice held a warning.

"I know what I'm doing, Cullen. These are our friends. We owe it to ourselves to let them learn it from us, not from outside."

He let his hands fall listlessly, as though he were at the end of his tether.

"So we put him outside in one of the vacant houses we used for our overlooker. Since that time we have been living in constant terror. We never know when some stranger will come during the night, to sleep and move on. What can we do?"

"Report them to the Committee of Safety," Pene said promptly.

Ann hesitated a moment, then said, "We did that. We reported to William Warden."

"What did he say?"

"He said it was evident that Balgray was a relay stop. There was nothing to do unless some untoward incident happened."

"I think the presence of a spy on your land is an untoward incident," Pene said acidly. She rose to go. Angela, who had taken no part in the conversation, rose silently. She kept glancing at Ann, alarm in her eyes. Cullen sat staring at the floor, immobile.

Ann put a restraining hand on Pene's arm. "It all came from having Anthony Allison. . . ." she said.

Pene said, "Anthony Allison?" Cullen uttered an exclamation.

Ann gazed blankly at Pene Dawson. Pene looked at her steadily. Not for worlds would she betray Peter's confidence. Perhaps Ann was trying to find out what she knew, playing her with a long line. One never could tell, these days. Out of the corner of her eye she caught a glimpse of Angela's terrified face. The girl will betray herself in a moment, Pene thought. She did not want that. She wanted things as they had been. Ann's confidences must be checked.

"I really must go, Ann. The wind is just right for sailing. It will drop by sundown."

Ann did not release her arm. "Let me tell you this. We have spies watching us all the time, day and night. They wait on the creek and in the swamp."

"Nonsense! You are letting your fears conquer your good sense, Ann. Why don't you get word to these people that they aren't welcome?"

Cullen spoke without looking up. "Don't think we haven't tried. I could kill myself for getting Ann into this mess."

Ann rushed to him and flung her arms about his neck. "No, no! Don't say that, Cullen! Don't ever say that!"

Pene turned her eyes away; she could not look upon the tragedy of her friends.

Ann stood beside Cullen, her hand on his shoulder, a protecting gesture, unconscious of its implication. "It's Clem Hull that's behind it—he and his rioters. Once I saw him."

"Why should Clem Hull spy on you?" Pene was surprised.

"Because he hopes to trap spies here. He has constituted himself a Committee of Safety. He would like to implicate Cullen. He's been wild, I tell you, wild, ever since the authorities refused to keep Cullen in gaol and dismissed the accusation."

Pene looked at her friend thoughtfully. She is not telling everything, she judged, just enough to create a semblance of truth. "I should think you would talk to the authorities and tell them the situation. Nothing can be lost by a frank review of the case before the proper people."

Ann shrugged her shoulders hopelessly. "I can't make you understand, Pene. You have shut yourself off from the war, as the other Queen Anne's women have. You say to yourself that it doesn't exist. I can't do that, when night after night I wake up trembling, with perspiration pouring off my face, for fear that some spy is hiding here at Balgray. You don't know how many there are, or how often they come, or in what disguise."

Angela opened her mouth to speak, but Pene was before her. "I'm sorry, Ann, very sorry, but I'm afraid I can't help you in this."

"We've made our bed," Ann said bitterly. "This one thing I want you to remember, Penelope. Cullen has never made an overt act against this government. Never. He has kept the oath he took to maintain strict neutrality. These people come without his knowledge. I hoped you would be understanding."

"Perhaps I am, Ann."

They went away without any betraying words from Angela. For that Pene was devoutly thankful.

At Balgray the next day, after dinner, Cullen and Ann took their afternoon rest. They were awakened by the arrival of men on horseback. A knock at the door followed. Cullen got up and put on his shoes and coat and went downstairs. "Stay were you are, Ann," he cautioned. "The less you know, the better." For a wonder she agreed and lay down on the bed, fighting the inclination to go to the window to watch for the visitors when they left. She heard voices and the sound of footsteps on the piazza, the creak of saddle-leather as the men mounted. She heard Cullen say, "I'll get there as soon as you do. I'll take the short cut."

Her heart sank. She felt the horrible weight of fear strike her vitals. Another spy! Was there no end? She had asked Cullen that question before they went to sleep.

"We are on a main road between the North and Charles Town," he had said. "We must expect this."

"Let us go away!" she had begged. "Cullen, let us hide!"

"Where?"

"Where indeed?"

It was dark when he returned. He was dishevelled and infinitely weary. "They are sheltered," he said; "I hope safely."

"Where?"

He shook his head. "No need for you to know. They think they are followed."

"But why?"

"Ann, don't repeat those words again. I am at the place where I can't endure much more."

She got up and left the room. Presently she returned, followed by a slave with a tray of hot food, which he set upon a small table.

Cullen dismissed the man. "You may go. I won't need you any more tonight." The slave left the room.

Ann said, "Do you expect these people to come to the house?"

"I don't know."

"Have you ever seen them before?"

"Yes. Will you stop asking questions, Ann? Can't you see I'm spent?"

Ann did not move. She sat watching him while he ate. After he finished, he took up a book. Ann was not fooled: he was waiting, waiting. She took the tray to the dining-room and set it on the polished mahogany table. She went back to the little sitting-room. Cullen had not moved, but he was not reading. He had his eyes on the door that led to the piazza.

Ann took a paper spill, touched it to the blazing log and started to light the candles in the candelabra.

"No. We have enough light," Cullen cried. "Sit down."

She sat down in a chair opposite to him. For a long time they sat without moving, without speaking. The clock chimed nine, then ten. A little time later, the door from the piazza opened and a muffled figure entered the room, illuminated only by firelight. Another figure followed.

A voice said, "I do not like this stealthy entrance, but one must be wise."

Ann sat up, her back stiff and straight. She had recognized Anthony Allison's voice.

Angela was in a fever for confession. Pene held her off in one way or another until after supper, when they sat in Gabriel Johnston's book-room.

"Why do you keep me from talking, Pene?" Angela appealed to her hostess.

"Because I have enough cares and worries with my plantations and my slaves. I don't want Ann Pollock's worries, nor Cullen's. They should have been warned by the reception they had in Queen Anne's Town and Suffolk. By the way, Wells Cowper, who opposed them in that town, has run the blockade again, and brought in another salt ship for our army."

"I don't want to talk about Ann's and Cullen's troubles. I don't care if Wells Cowper did bring in a salt ship. I want to talk about myself—me—and I don't know where to turn except to you."

Pene spread her dark crimson wool skirt about her to cover her feet and adjusted the lace fichu so that it hid part of her rounded breasts. Scipio had mended the fire and set the irons in the fire. All that was needed was to thrust the hot irons into the rum mixture, when they were ready for their night-cap.

Just before he left the room, Pene said, "Don't go down to the quarters, Scipio. I want you and Governorcharleseden to sleep in the room over the kitchen tonight."

"Aye, Mistress." He did not ask questions. He knew that for some obscure reason they were to be on call.

Angela said nothing at the time. When the slave left she made her request, which she repeated.

Pene sat back, "I am now resigned to listen."

Angela was not disturbed by her hostess' reluctance to hear her troubles. She plunged right on in her impetuous way. "You know how hard I have tried to forget Anthony, ever since my mother arranged a marriage between Captain Huntley and me. I was determined to forget him. I succeeded." She corrected herself: "I almost succeeded, until I could not even remember how he looked, or bring his features before my mind, until yesterday.

"Yesterday when I sat in the coach, everything came back to me with a rush. I remembered him only too vividly, his face, his eyes, the feel of his lips against mine. I am afraid, Pene. I am afraid that I still love him. What am I to do?"

Pene looked at the girl. Angela sat erect in the high-back chair, her mustard-coloured frock enhancing the blackness of her hair and eyes, the ivory of her skin. "What am I to do?" she repeated help-lessly.

Penelope Dawson picked up the painted candle-screen and moved it to shield her eyes. It also shielded her face from Angela. "If you forgot this man Allison as you say you did for these months, you can forget him again." She spoke coldly, without emotion, yet she felt anger rising within her.

"I didn't say 'forget him.' I said I could not remember how he looked."

"That amounts to the same thing. My advice is to wash him out again, obliterate him, bury him, cover his memory with ballast stones."

Angela looked at her, in surprise at the vehemence in her voice.

Pene pushed the screen aside. "Look at me if you will. When I think of a chit like you, with no more integrity than a green water beetle, playing fast and loose with Peter Huntley, it makes my blood rise. He is worth a dozen of you . . . a hundred, yet you say—" she mimicked Angela's voice—" 'What must I do? What must I do?' "

Angela started to rise. Her mouth fell open. She stared at Penelope in complete astonishment.

"Sit down!" Penelope said. She rose and stood, tall and straight, by the fire. "You asked for my advice. You make a play for my sympathy. You get no sympathy. Peter is my friend, my dear and trusted friend. You gain nothing by running to me with your sickly, sentimental cries about Anthony Allison, or Jeremiah Morse, or what-ever his real name is. You deserved what you got from him."

Angela started to speak. "Be quiet, until I have finished. No one ever talks to you the way you should be talked to. Your treatment of that fine man, Mr. Ferrier, is a disgrace. Why, he has given you the sanctuary of his home, fed and clothed you! And you speak arrogantly of your stepfather, you silly child!"

She took a turn about the room. "It was in my power to keep Peter from you," she said, facing Angela. "I could have stopped it in the beginning. It would have been simple. You think, because I have been a widow these years, that I have lost interest in men. That is because you are a simple, provincial girl, without knowledge of men or of the world. I'm not anxious to marry again but I am experienced and attractive enough so that I could have turned him away from you *to save him*. I didn't take him, because of your mother. There *must* be something of your fine mother in you. So far I don't see it, but it must be there, deep within you. When your wretched father ceases to dominate you and your mother comes to the surface, then you will be worthy to speak of Peter Huntley, and not before."

Angela opened and closed her mouth. She wanted to speak, but dared not. Penelope's eyes were flashing in anger. Before her Angela was afraid. She put her hands over her face. Her body shook.

Penelope did not soften. Let her work it out herself, she thought. I am being harsh, but there is a chance that she will come to her senses.

Presently Angela's hands slid down and rested on her knees. She lifted her tear-stained face. "I'm all you say, Pene. Help me to find myself."

Inside, Pene's generous heart softened. Outwardly she remained aloof. "I will see how you conduct yourself, then . . ." A loud knock, followed immediately by a second, interrupted her words. Someone on the side gallery. Penelope took up the candle and started for the door.

Angela cried, "Don't go, Pene! You don't know who it is!"

"I'll soon find out." Pene walked into the hall, Angela close behind.

Pene opened the door, shielding the candle against the rush of wind. "Who is it?" she asked. Clem Hull stepped out of the shadows. Pene saw there were others standing below the porch.

Clem lifted his cap from his head. "I'm sorry, Ma'am, to disturb you this late, but we are seeking a spy."

"There is no sanctuary for enemies at Eden House," Pene said firmly.

"That we know, ma'am." Southey Wren stepped out from behind a pillar. "That we know, ma'am. We chased two men from Balgray, but we lost them. That is the truth. We flushed them at Pollock's place, but they got away. I always said he be Tory."

" 'Tis a man named Allison, an officer in the King's army."

Pene shook her head. "I've seen no such man, but you are at liberty to search. Ring the great bell—three short rings, then a long one. I don't want my people to think it is a fire, Hull. My men will help. They want no spies on this plantation."

Clem went off swinging his lanthorn. Southey lingered. "I recognized the man, Madam Dawson. Often I've seen him in the Old Country, when I was with Major Ferguson. He was a lieutenant then, and a good one."

Pene asked, "What is he doing here?"

Southey spat his wad over the rail into the flower bed. "I don't rightly know, ma'am. 'Pears like they are right many of them about. From Virginia they come. This one he buys cattle, seemingly. Calls himself Morse, Jeremiah Morse. If we get him, we'll put him on a strong limb, that we will."

Angela gasped. Pene dug her fingers into the girl's arm. The plantation bell began to sound. A moment later voices were heard. Scipio came running down the outside stairway that led to the kitchen loft.

Pene held the door wide. "Come in, Southey. Take a man and go through the house. Scipio will guide you. Go everywhere. Look everywhere—under beds, in closets."

Southey was embarrassed. His thin face reddened. "Ma'am, I do not rightly like the task."

"I understand. But it must be done, for my protection, as well as yours. Best to start on the upper floor, I think."

Scipio led the way and the two searchers followed. Penelope went back to the book-room, Angela close behind her. She sat down and looked at the clock. Almost ten. Angela went to the window. Lights were bobbing up and down in the garden, going toward the stables.

Pene sat in silence. Angela moved restlessly about the room. After a time she seated herself on a stool near Pene and laid her head on the older woman's knee. Her shoulders were shaking, her whole body trembled. Pene's eyes were without expression. After a time Angela regained her composure and lifted her head. She got up from the stool and sat on a chair, letting her head rest against the wing. No word was spoken. No recriminations came from Penelope.

After a seemingly interminable time, the men went away. Southey came up to the gallery to tell Madam Dawson they had found no one, nor any trace. "We must wait until morning, Clem says."

"My men will fix beds for you," Penelope said.

"Thank you, ma'am. We have a spot where we can rest. 'Tis fair onto midnight now. Good night, ma'am."

"Good night, Southey. Tell Hull to come back in the morning. I want to be sure there is no one here."

She walked slowly down the hall to the library, where she had left Angela. The girl was still seated, but she was very white. She tried to keep her hands from shaking by clasping them firmly about her knee. Her eyes had a strange haunted look.

Penelope said, "What is wrong with you, Angela? You look as though you had seen a ghost."

"Nothing. Nothing," the girl murmured. "Shall I heat the posset?"

"Yes, pray do. It is midnight and time for us to retire. I'm sure I'm ready to seek my bed."

Angela took a knitted holder from the hearth, lifted the irons from the fire, and plunged them into the posset mixture. Penelope lay back in her chair, her eyes closed. Suddenly brought from a half sleep by the clatter of the heating iron on the brick hearth, she opened her eyes. She felt a draught of air.

The door that led to Governor Eden's escape tunnel stood open. A man wrapped in a black coat held a lanthorn that cast a moving circle on the dark polished floor. Behind him was another figure.

The first man advanced. Pene recognized him before she heard Angela's "Anthony!"

Anthony tossed cape and hat onto a chair. The second man stepped in.

"Close the door, John," Anthony said; "the Governor's tunnel is dark and cold as a tomb."

Penelope Dawson remained seated. "To what do I owe the honour of your visit, sir?" Her voice was clipped and cold.

Anthony made a sweeping bow. "I am regretful, madam, that we enter in this manner, through a secret passage, rather than by your front door as befits gentlemen."

Penelope said nothing. Angela sat looking at Anthony Allison as though she could never take her eyes from his face. The girl is distracted, Penelope thought. She is so vulnerable, so very vulnerable. I could weep for her predicament. She was ashamed to have the villain see Angela's look of adoration.

"Angela!" she said brusquely. "Ring the bell!"

Allison stepped forward, placing a hand on Angela's arm. "No, my dear, sit as you were when I came in. You are very lovely. Let me feast these eyes on you."

"Captain Allison—" Penelope's voice was stern—"you forget yourself!"

"Ah, you know my name. Has this pretty one been tattling?" There was no playfulness in his tone to match the playful words. His eyes were as hard as obsidian.

"No. A man was here a short time ago—a number of men, to be exact. They were looking for you. One among them knew you in England, a man of your own regiment. He called you by your real name. It seems you are not Mr. Jeremiah Morse of Boston, but a

British spy." She reached over quickly and gave the bell cord a jerk.

Allison strode toward Penelope and caught her arm. She pulled away. "You will keep your filthy hands off my arm, sir!"

He took a step back. A slow, painful red crept over his face. "Madam, I make my apologies. In war a man must do things that are not of his nature to do."

"Such as make war on defenceless women!"

"Such as keeping women's mouths shut," he said, angered by her contempt.

There were footsteps in the hall. Both men drew pistols, and faced the door.

"Watch the women, John," Allison said. "I'll take the slave."

"You will not touch my man." Penelope moved quickly across the room, her hand on the door.

"I would loathe to shoot a beautiful woman, but, by God, I may have to! Step aside, madam."

Scipio opened the door. He had a tray with some cheese and biscuits. "Thought you'd lak a little food with your toddy, Miss Pene."

"That we would." Scipio looked up. He came near dropping the tray, but Allison caught it. " 'Fore God, 'tis that spy-man!" He turned and started for the door.

"Come back, you black rascal!"

Scipio moved reluctantly into the room, his eyes on his mistress.

"Come here, Scipio," Penelope said. "Stand on this side of me."

Allison's eyes were on the food. "Manna from heaven, John. Food and a hot drink." He ladled out the hot posset into a silver goblet and handed it to his companion.

"With madam's permission," the stranger said courteously.

Pene nodded but did not speak.

" 'Tis some time since we dined," Allison said. He lifted his glass, drank the liquor quickly and poured a second. "A bit of cheese and a biscuit, John." He passed the tray. The stranger hesitated a moment, then took the food, but declined a second drink.

Each time Allison reached for a posset he allowed his hand to brush Angela's shoulder. Once he leaned across in front of her. Pene saw him lay his hand on the girl's breast.

"Angela, come here!" she commanded. Angela moved to a chair near her as though she were in a daze.

Allison was on his third goblet. "Madam is a fine protector, but it is not necessary. The girl is quite able to look after herself. Did

you hear how she made a rescue under Captain Huntley's very eyes?"
No one spoke. Allison looked from one to the other. He leaned
toward Penelope. "The girl is mad to sleep in my bed." He rose suddenly, caught Angela's arm. "Come on, my pretty, there is time.
There is always time for a pretty woman."

The stranger was on his feet instantly, but Penelope Dawson moved
first. She raised her hand and slapped Allison hard on the mouth.
Her rings cut his lips and blood began to come into his mouth. He
stood looking at her, dazed and glassy-eyed.

The stranger strode forward. "Enough of that, Captain! Get into
the passage!" He turned to Penelope. "I am very sorry, madam, that
my companion has forgotten himself in this manner. If you will
pardon us . . ." He bowed and disappeared into the passage.

Angela did not stir. She sat white-lipped and silent.

Scipio started for the door. "I'll ring the bell, Mistress."

Penelope held up her hand. "Wait. Wait a moment, Scipio. Let
me think." She was trying to remember something her father had
told her about the desert law of the Arabs. After a moment it came
to her: Even the bitterest enemy must have two hours without pursuit, after he has tasted coffee under a man's tent. Let it stand in that
way. Two hours, and she would ring the plantation bell. "Go to bed,
Scipio. I will call you later." She crossed the room and slid the bolt
on the door that led to the Governor's tunnel.

"I'll sleep outside you' door."

"Very well. Angela, I think it is time for you to retire."

Angela got up from her chair. Like a sleep-walker she moved out
of the room, Scipio lighting the way.

Penelope sat down in her father's red leather chair, and leaned her
face against the cool surface of the wing. Two hours and she would
walk out into the garden and pull the rope of the great bell.

They would be gone by that time, with a long start. Perhaps it was
best that way. As for Angela, she could only hope that the infatuated girl had had her eyes opened. She wondered whether she had
done the right thing. She yawned. She drew her hand across her
weary eyes. When she woke it was broad daylight, and the bell had
not been rung.

Joseph Hewes's flag was flown at half-staff on the Green. The village folk by twos and threes walked to St. Paul's, where the memorial
services were to be held.

William Hooper, who, not so many months before, had made the presentation of the flag, today would give the final tribute to his friend and fellow Signer.

The church would not hold the crowds, and the Vestry had granted permission for the oration to be given in the old churchyard. The people congregated and stood beneath bare-limbed trees, or sat on flat tombstones of men and women dead these many years. It was a solemn moment when Hooper came out of the church and stood on the worn step in front of the wide door. He spoke briefly. The whole service lasted no more than ten minutes.

"I must strike upon a melancholy string," he began. "It is eternally strongest in me. The death of Joseph Hewes still preys on my feelings. He was my very intimate friend. I had probed the secret recesses of his soul, and found it devoid of guilt and replete with benignity. I loved him. I believe that I was very dear to him. A long series of sicknesses had prepared his mind for the fatal stroke. His body, shattered with repeated violence, could not, I was well assured, long brave the periodical attacks. The news of his dangerous illness was, to me, the harbinger of the worst. I anticipated it, yet, when the shock came, I was unprepared for it. How happy are they who view the changes of human life as necessarily growing out of the eternal system of things! Not to be lamented are they. Once he said to me, 'We die daily.' I think that was true of him. Every day during these past years of stress, a little of him died.

"The news has come to us now of the burial of our neighbour and friend in alien ground. Here is where he belongs, among the friends of his great heart. They tell us that his funeral in Christ Church was attended by the Congress in a body, by the Minister for France, by the authorities of the state of Pennsylvania, and a great assemblage of the people of Philadelphia. They tell us also that every member of Congress will wear a crape band on his arm for one month, as a symbol of mourning—a great honour to a man who worked on the Declaration, our Charter of Independence and Freedom, and was one of the Signers; a great honour indeed, given to but few, and to none more deserved.

"I look into the faces of the citizenry of Queen Anne's Town. I see men high in the councils of the state, his friends and co-workers. But I see also labourers, men from the shipyard, clerks from the stores, doctors and lawyers and artisans of the village. I see freeholders of the county, farriers and herdsmen. I see Negro slaves and free Negroes whom he has helped to their freedom.

"I say to you all, standing before me, you do him the greater honour. You do not wear the symbol of mourning on your arms. You mourn him as the people of this village must always honour and mourn him—in your hearts."

William Hooper stood for a moment looking silently at the upturned faces before him. He saw tears streaming down the cheeks of some, a mist that for a moment obscured the vision of others. He bowed. The doors of the church were open and he went inside.

The crowd lingered a few moments among the old tombs, satisfied now that they had paid the final tribute to their friend.

CHAPTER
26

STORM CLOUDS GATHER

By THE end of November the storm clouds hanging along the coast line of the southern states began to move inward. By December they had come almost to hurricane strength. The defeat of American and French arms at Savannah weighed heavily upon the hard-pressed leaders and men. The six South Carolina regiments were so depleted that they had to be bolstered up with local militia. General Lincoln gathered up his forces to meet the attack he knew would come, but he was ill prepared and Charles Town's fortifications were inadequate.

In January word came through to Charles Town that Sir Henry Clinton, accompanied by Lord Cornwallis, had set sail for the South the day after Christmas.

The strength of his army was given as seventy-five hundred men. Besides General Arbuthnot's fleet, one British troop of marines and a ship-load of paid mercenaries from Hesse were a part of this vast army. They were to meet at the entrance of the Savannah River, reinforced by troops now in Georgia, which included British troops and Hamilton's regiment of Carolina Loyalists.

Besides the soldiers of the fleet, General Sir Henry Clinton would now have a force of more than ninety-five hundred men, all trained and seasoned with the exception of the Loyalist regiment.

This was the news that Peter Huntley carried to General Lincoln when he rode into Charles Town one morning early in January, his first trip as liaison officer between General Washington and General Lincoln.

The autumn months during which Peter had been in the western mountains had been filled with interest and some danger. Twice he had been sniped at; once a ball had passed through the sleeve of his buckskin shirt—a token from some Tory on the outlook for any stranger; the kind of man who would rather shoot and kill than try to find out who the stranger was.

438

Enos Dye had been with him at the time. He sent an answering shot into the bushes as a precaution. They heard a yell, saw the bushes disturbed, as though someone were thrashing around. When they crossed the stream they found no one. Enos circled the spot, detected traces of a camp-fire. Widening the circle, he found a blood trail that led them to the rocks high up the mountain. There they lost it.

"Some of Patrick Moore's men," Enos said grimly. "I've heern that he was at it again."

Peter said, "I thought he was captured after Ramsour's Mill, Enos."

Enos spat disgustedly, "Gad, no, he and his brother John got away. Some say they're here in these mountains. Some say they're in South Carolina, near Camden. Haven't you heard that old Colonel Sam Martin caught up with him by the old ironworks on the Pacolet? The colonel captured him all right, but some British troops got him off. Mayhap Moore's in command at Thicketty Fort now. 'Tis a great place for the Tories to gather. From there they branch out and plunder the Whig farms, even take clothes off'n women and children."

"Perhaps we should go down to Thicketty Fort, Enos."

Enos' mouth changed to a slow, narrow grin. "Not me! I'm set for mountain work." He laid the sticks he had gathered on the small fire and squatted down to cook their supper. They had been travelling all day south from the Meadows.

"Speaking of women, there's some fine women in these mountains and down by the border—yes, and below the border where King's Mountain rises out of the low hills." He skewered a strip of bacon and held it over the blaze. Peter stretched himself out on the ground near the fire; the mountain nights were chill.

"Ever hear of Miss Nancy Jackson, her that kicked a Tory man down the stairs when the fellow plundered their house? That was down by Fair Forest. Then there was Major McJunkin's sister. She delayed Patrick Moore and his men. They came to the McJunkins' house and demanded shelter. When they was goin' away in the morning, they took all the family's clothes and the bed quilts too. Bill Haynesworth, him a Tory, he put a quilt right over his horse like a blanket. That made Miss Jane see sparks. She snached it off, and they was both hanging on, strugglin' like a tug of war, with the soldiers sickin' them on. One cried, 'Well done, woman'; another 'Sick 'em, Bill.' They had a laugh on Bill, all right, for his feet struck some slime in the yard and flew up, and he fell flat on his back.

"Miss Jane she run over and put her foot on his chest. Bill he snuck off. I bet he hears about it to this day." Enos laughed silently. Peter sat up and took the tin plate he held out—bacon, potatoes; that was a meal for a king when the appetite was high.

Enos went into the high mountains on some unknown mission early in December, and Peter returned to Salisbury, his work finished.

He went to Michael Braun's home and found a hearty welcome.

"You're in time, just in time," Braun said. "Major Avery will be back tonight. He was looking for you last week, when he went south."

Peter went to his room, bathed and dressed in his uniform, then called for his horse. "I'm going to hunt for a barber," he said.

Braun laughed. "You look mighty seedy with that beard," he said. "No one would ever recognize you, and that's God's truth."

After Peter was shaved and had his hair rolled and queued, he called on Madam Steele. She greeted him with great cordiality. She had news for him—mostly speculation and rumour—of the spring campaign. Then she mentioned Joseph Hewes's death. "A great loss to the state," she said. "I can't think what we would have done without him. And John Paul Jones, who is now making fame for our navy—what would he have done without Joseph Hewes to encourage him and help him?"

"What, indeed!" Peter said. He was saddened by the news. He thought of the sick man he had seen while he was in Philadelphia, so ill, yet sitting in his bed surrounded by papers, working deep into the night until he fell asleep from exhaustion.

When Peter returned to Braun's, he enquired about Major Avery, but he had not arrived. He went to his room to write his report. It was a long one. It covered all his findings, route maps and possible camp-sites, and what he thought would be the line of the British army advance into North Carolina, provided they decided on a siege of Charles Town. He had arrived at his theory by a roundabout method, based on the number of cattle he had discovered scattered over a large territory, hidden in the mountain valleys, parcelled out on the farms of known Tory sympathizers. Peter had not seen the pattern at first, nor could he find the answer to Jeremiah Morse's actions, until he had made the long journey from Quaker Meadows south to the South Carolina line.

He had made careful notes of where the cattle were held, but not until he sat down with a map and placed the known cattle depots in their proper place did he see the design. The British had already figured their route of invasion. The cattle were there, ready for the invading army. Other food was ready, corn and pork.

This was his own finding. No one had suggested to him that the activity in cattle-buying by Morse and his agents was more than buying for the army at Savannah.

It took him until midnight to finish the report. When he wrote the last line, he read it over carefully. He felt a sense of pride in the achievement. It was clear and logical and easy to read.

He melted a stick of wax over the candle and sealed it with his own ring.

Now he would write to Senator Ferrier that he would be in Queen Anne's Town by Christmas-time, and the wedding day could be set. After that he would write a letter to Angela. This time it would be a letter a man would write to the woman he loved, who would soon be his wife.

He put his hands over his head to stretch his back, and yawned widely. He was not sleepy or tired. He was too exhilarated by his accomplishment to sleep. For the first time since he had left his regiment, he felt as though he had something that was useful. He had uncovered information of value to the General.

He sat smoking, reviewing the months of incessant moving through the mountains and valleys of the Blue Ridge. He had grown hard and brown. His face was as thin as Enos Dye's, and his legs as strong from climbing. He had gone to the camp of Colonel McDowell below Quaker Meadows. Together they had drawn up the plan for reaching the back-countrymen, in case of invasion through the Broad River route. He had visited Old Fort, and gone deep into the mountains into Tennessee country, over Gillespie Pass. He had walked along the head waters of the Tyger from Prince's Fort to where it emptied into Broad River.

He knew the country now.

He finished his pipe and drew the paper toward him. Dipping his quill into the ink, he began the letter: "My dear Senator Ferrier." He got no farther. There was a knock at the door, the quick, sharp double knock used by Major Avery.

Peter jumped to his feet and flung the door open. Avery came in. He was smiling, although the deep lines in his face showed his weariness. He shook Peter's hand with a firm, hard grasp. "Peter, you don't look the mountaineer. I'm disappointed."

Peter grinned. "Wait until you see me in my Enos Dye suit. I'll wager you'd never pick me out among a group of back-countrymen."

"Good! Good!" Avery flung himself into a chair, his long legs sprawled out in front of him.

Peter poured him a drink. "Mountain still," he said, raising his eyebrows.

"Again, good! I can drink anything, and a lot of it." Avery tipped his head, tossed the fiery white liquor far back in his throat, and followed it with half a glass of water.

"You know the way to drink it," Peter observed. "The first time I tried it I came near choking to death."

Avery glanced at the table and the sealed letter. He nodded. "Got your report ready? Want me to take it in my case? I'm leaving for Philadelphia before sun-up."

"I hoped you would. I have two other letters to write. Can you drop them at Richmond, for the Charles Town courier to carry as far as Queen Anne's Town?" He hesitated an instant. "They are rather important to me. They have to do with my wedding."

"Wedding?" Avery lifted his brows. "Do you plan to get married soon?"

"Directly after Christmas," Peter replied.

Avery shook his head. "I'm afraid you can't carry that idea through. From now on, you are my southern half of the route. I come this far; you ride dispatch to General Lincoln at Charles Town."

Peter stared. Avery said, "Don't you remember? You are a liaison officer between General Washington and General Lincoln."

"Yes. Yes, of course. I remember, but I thought that was after the British were reinforced in the South."

"They are going to be reinforced all right. Our Intelligence has plenty of information on their spring campaign."

He again glanced at Peter's report. "Find anything of interest in the mountains? Get a line on the number of likely fighting men?"

"Yes, I got all that, and something else." He leaned forward and abstracted a map from the litter of papers on the table. "Look. I want to show you. I want your opinion on my deduction. I want to know whether I've stumbled on something, or whether I'm just mad."

Avery hitched his chair to the table. The sandy head and the dark head were close together. For a long time Peter talked, quill pointing to the map, putting down the numbers of cattle-pens and pasturage, figuring and testing. Avery listened, smoking his pipe, sometimes furiously puffing out smoke until they both choked, again letting it go out completely.

When Peter finished, the major clapped his great hand on the younger man's shoulder. "Peter, you've got it! By God, you've got it! It's as simple as how-do-ye-do, and we haven't got it figured at headquarters."

Peter was pleased, but he said nothing.

"Got two copies?"

"Yes. I made a copy."

"Good! I'm going to meet one of our men at Bethabara. I'll take both copies that far, then give one to him. We go by separate routes—Wells up the valley of Virginia, through Pennsylvania; I through Richmond, back of their lines. Two couriers are better than one in this instance." He leaned back, looking at the ceiling. After a time, he said, "This will interfere with a wedding, I'm afraid. Your time is the General's from now on until God knows when."

Peter said nothing. That thought had already occurred to him.

"Write your letters, my lad. Tell your young woman that war is war and you are being sent on a long journey. Let all think you are going out beyond the mountains to the Mississippi—anywhere. Don't let anyone know what your duties are." He glanced at Peter's well-fitted, well-pressed uniform. "Put it away again. Get out your Enos Dye buckskin with fringed pants and coonskin cap. That will be your uniform for some time to come."

He stretched his long arms and yawned mightily. "I've got your route here. Learn it. Learn your stops, the names of our Whig friends. Learn it by rote and burn it on your candle by morning. If you get lost in Tory country after you cross the border into South Carolina you may have the devil's own time. I can't instruct you. You will have to use your own wits." He grasped Peter's hand. "Good fortune to you, Peter! Remember we are on the General's mission. No torture, no threats, no matter how severe, can make us talk."

He took a small lead tube from his pocket. "This is for General Lincoln. If the enemy catches you, take out the contents and destroy the papers." He grinned. "I've swallowed the damn things more than once." That was the nearest Major Avery came to saying it was a dangerous mission.

"I don't need to go into the dramatic," he said as he was at the door. "I don't want to say that the fate of armies rests on your timely arrival at Lincoln's camp at Charles Town, but I will say that it is an important message—one from the General himself. Read it. Memorize it." He went away then, leaving Peter standing quite still, looking at the closed door.

Peter thought of these things as he sat outside Lincoln's temporary headquarters outside Charles Town, where he had time for some reconsidering, on his own accord. The trip had not been too difficult; on the other hand, it had not been too easy to swim a stream with snipers on the bank splashing bullets within a few feet of his head, or to sneak a bateau through the swamp, or pleasant to have one horse shot from under him. He had felt terribly alone at those times, alone with the weight of the whole army resting on his shoulders. But he was here, in one piece, with General Washington's message in the palm of his hand.

A smile came to his lips. An aide standing on the other side of the tent looked at him curiously. Peter was thinking of the day a Tory had caught him asleep and searched him at the point of a musket. He had been lucky that time, for he had taken the precaution to tie the little lead tube in among the fringe on the front of his worn hunting-shirt, where it was quite invisible among dangling beads, bear and panther claws. They had released him finally, forced to believe that he was on his way to Savannah, to join Colonel Hamilton's North Carolina Loyalists.

Another aide lifted the fly and beckoned to Peter. "The general will see you now, Mr. Huntley."

Peter stepped inside. General Lincoln, a harried and worried man, sat on a camp-stool. Peter saluted smartly.

The general looked at him. "I was not told you were an officer, Huntley. What is your rank?"

"Captain, Headquarters Staff, special assignment, sir."

"Sit down, Captain. You have something for me? An oral message, perhaps?"

Peter extended his hand and laid the lead capsule on the table.

General Lincoln unscrewed the top and took out the roll of paper. "I need a glass for this," he said after a moment's scrutiny. He ruffled through his papers. "I never can find anything I want. There should be a magnifying glass."

Peter offered the burning-glass he carried on a rawhide thong about his neck. Lincoln took it and held it close to the paper. After a time he let it fall to the table. The expression on his face was one of utter weariness. Peter thought, I have seen the same expression on the faces of men and officers since I came into this area.

He had an opportunity to observe General Lincoln. The bones of his frame were buried under layers of fat. He moved heavily. His expression was pleasant and agreeable, but Peter was afraid it was indolence, and not good humour.

This man had been at Saratoga and other battles, but somehow he did not inspire confidence. Perhaps it was his tired, lack-lustre eyes. Perhaps it was that his heavy chin was without strength.

"Do you know the contents of this dispatch?" the general asked, after a time.

"Yes, sir," Peter replied. "I had orders from Major Avery to memorize it, in case anything happened."

"Then you know this is bad news for me, very bad news." He seemed to forget Peter as he swung the glass to and fro on the leather thong. "Come back in the morning, Captain. I'll send a message with you." He lifted his voice, calling, "Captain Miles! Captain Miles!"

A young officer with fiery red hair put his head inside the tent, followed by a long lean body. He saluted.

"We are returning to Charles Town, at once," the general said. "Give the necessary orders to break camp. Wait. Can you take Mr. Huntley into your quarters for the night?"

"Yes, sir."

Captain Miles was turning to leave. "Wait. One thing more. Send an orderly to Governor Rutledge, with the general's compliments. Will he be so kind as to come to the general's quarters this evening at eight? The general would wait on him but for the fact that headquarters maps and papers will be necessary at the conference." He looked at the officer, who was writing the order on a pad of paper. "Read it back, please."

Captain Miles read the message.

"Good! Now ask Colonel Laurens if he will be so good as to step over to my tent."

Peter left with the captain, with orders from the general to be at his headquarters at a quarter to eight. He rode into Charles Town, a matter of eight miles, with the aide. It was raining, a cold rain that in a more northerly clime would have been a wet snow. Now it dripped drearily from the long grey moss that festooned the trees.

Peter's buckskin tunic turned the water as readily as the captain's long riding cape.

The young captain kept glancing at him from time to time, curious, no doubt, about a man who looked like a back-countryman, yet had the general's immediate attention. But the general was queer at times. He was a Northerner and did not see eye to eye with some of the Southern officers or the merchants of the town. Captain Miles asked no questions nor did Peter volunteer anything. So they rode in silence.

Captain Miles left him when they entered the town. His orderly rode with Peter to show him the way to his quarters. There was time for a hot bath and a shave before his host returned. They walked over to the officers' mess for supper.

They had no more than entered the door when a man seated at one of the long tables jumped to his feet. "Peter! My friend!" he exclaimed. In his haste to reach Huntley's side, he overturned a glass of water on the table.

"De' Medici!" Peter grasped his hand. "This is good fortune."

Cosmo turned to the table. "Gentlemen, this is my good, good friend . . ." Something in Peter's expression warned him and he hesitated.

Peter said, "Huntley is my name."

"Of course, Huntley. I say it so seldom because it becomes a mouthful for me. I say Peter, or Pietro, which comes much more readily."

The officers rose and bowed.

"How are all the people . . ." Cosmo began.

"Of the mountains? They are in excellent health, and the deer-shooting is good this year. You should come back and take another try for a four-pronged buck."

"Yes, of course. I had such ill luck the last time, but I will return to the mountains one day. I've had my fill of the Sand Hills."

Good fellow, Peter said to himself, good fellow.

Captain Miles said, "Since you have found a friend, Huntley, I will turn you over to him." Peter thought he was relieved. He was young and had pride. He did not relish being escort to a mountain man, even though he was a scout who had the ear of the general.

This was good, very good, Peter thought with satisfaction. I really appear to be a back-countryman to these officers. That was as he hoped it would be.

"You will stay with me, Peter. I have an extra cot in my quarters. Where is your gear?"

"At Captain Miles's."

"I will send my orderly for it directly after supper." Cosmo dismissed the subject as settled and the talk became general—the situation in Charles Town, Augusta and Savannah. Rumours were free, and speculation was the core of conversation of an inactive, restless army.

"How do you happen to be here?" Peter asked; he spoke with a slow, woodsman's drawl, without lapses in grammar, but using a colloquialism now and then, in order to arouse no suspicions. It was important that no one, even among the officers of the army, know what his mission was. He would explain enough to satisfy Cosmo, but Cosmo was a soldier; he would recognize the necessity of secrecy.

"I'm attached to Colonel Harrington's North Carolinians, thank the good God," Cosmo said. "I stay no longer in the sand country. Here we have a little touch of the sea, and I get my strength back."

"Have you had a sickness?"

"No, no—save nostalgia, which is, in truth, a sickness." He dropped his voice. "We hear so many rumours; it is incredible how many. But I think we shall see action before too long, Peter."

Peter nodded, neither denying nor affirming.

After supper they went at once to Cosmo's quarters, a long, barracklike building near the entrenchments. "My men and I are stationed here, not far behind the guns. I cease to be a dragoon, Peter. They have taken our horses to drag tree trunks and earth to bolster the emplacements. We man guns now. But my men do well. I am proud, very proud. They would do better if they had more powder, to make trials, but we have none for practice." He shrugged his shoulders.

The orderly, a big, heavy-shouldered fellow with high colour, came in with Peter's saddle-bags. He set out a bottle of brandy and some glasses.

Cosmo said, "I have to speak to you, Cooke. My colonel make complaint that your girl she fights with the camp-followers. You must reason with her."

"Saving your pardon, sir, she is one that is not to be reasoned with. She will fight and scratch and claw."

"Better send her home, Cooke."

The man shook his head. "Captain, sir, she will not go. She has something in her head about the army. I do not know what. Sometimes I think she seeks someone."

Cosmo waved his hand. "Do your best, Cooke. The ways of women are strange, but you are a big brawny fellow."

A grin came across the orderly's face for an instant. "Sir, I once tried that, but . . ." He turned his head. There was a red scar along his neck behind his ear. "She is a wildcat, sir."

Cosmo laughed. The orderly left the room.

Peter said, "I am not sure I like the idea of these camp-followers."

Cosmo shrugged indifferently. "Better than finding relief some other way," he said, and dismissed the subject. He poured a drink. Lifting his glass, he said, "To Queen Anne's Town and our friends!"

Peter lifted his glass. "I do not ask questions, but I at once sense that for the moment you are not Captain Huntley, but Huntley a scout. Am I right?"

"Yes. I'm sorry, Cosmo, that I cannot talk—not that I would not trust you, but you understand. We think there are some very famous British spies in Charles Town at this moment. I would lose my value if I were known to them."

"Yes, yes, I know these military secrets. But you, my Pietro, why do you not praise me for the quickness of my tongue, back there at the mess? 'A four-pronged buck.' Am I not fast to think? Do I not play my part excellently well?"

Peter grinned. "You do indeed. For a moment I thought you would call me captain, or speak of Queen Anne's Town. But you were swift to see."

"Ah, yes, indeed, swift. But wait. If you have been long in the mountains, I may have news for you. Have you heard of the death of your friend Mr. Hewes?"

"Yes, I heard that before I left the mountains."

"Well, there are other things." He rummaged in his bag. "Ah, here it is, a letter from our good friend Madam Dawson."

Peter felt a surge of blood, a quickening of the pulse. Strange. Penelope's face rose before his eyes, the deep quality of her low voice saying, 'We are friends, Peter, always friends.'

Cosmo thrust the letter into his hand, and lighted a second candle. Peter scanned the letter: Joseph Hewes's death, the memorial service at St. Paul's; Mary Warden had had a letter from Adam Rutledge, who had gone to the far West; the auction; Lord Craven's coach—

Sam Johnston had wanted it, but his father-in-law, Dr. Cathcart, had bid it in; some people fancied he would give it to his daughter, so that it would repose at Hayes eventually. Everyone was fussing about a new rule of paying two and one-half per cent to the state every time one bought at an auction, a measure set up by Timothy Bloodgood, the Wilmington Assemblyman; it would be hard on the poor, who must buy almost all of their cooking utensils and farm implements at auction.

Then paragraphs stood out:

That wretched Morse was here again. He entered my house one night by Governor Eden's tunnel, frightening us almost to death. He is a vile wretch. He spoke to Angela in a way no gentleman would speak. I am sorry to say that I slapped him across his face—no feeble slap either. He was drunk, I suppose, but 'tis said a gentleman remains a gentleman, drunk or sober.

Poor Angela! She looked stricken. She went into a high fever that night, a return of the chill and ague, I presume. We could not move her home for a month. Madam Ferrier came here to nurse her. What a wonderful person she is! I hope Angela grows to be like her. I wonder, sometimes. She is so vacillating. She appears not to know her own mind.

Madam Barker had a letter from General Washington. She is proud. Did you know that she gave all the money she received for the coach to a war fund? That was wonderful of her, was it not?

There was one line more: "We miss you, Cosmo, and we miss Peter Huntley and Adam Rutledge. If only this war would cease!"

Peter folded the letter back into its creases and laid it on the table.

"A wonderful woman," Cosmo said, nursing his brandy glass in his two hands. "Wonderful! I am at a loss to know why she does not marry. She is young and beautiful. I cannot see how she escapes the marriage-bed again."

Peter did not reply; he remembered the long talks they had had at Eden House. He drained his glass. Somehow he resented Cosmo's words. He looked at his time piece; it was seven-thirty. He put his glass on the table. "I've a meeting to attend," he told Cosmo. "I don't know what time I'll be in."

"No matter, the latch-string is out." Cosmo grinned. "You see?

Now I get your language, I say those little things that make it rich and enjoyable. Wake me when you come in. I will think of many questions to ask you about our dear friends in Queen Anne's Town."

"I think Madam Dawson told you as much or more than I know." Peter thought of Angela lying ill. He remembered a time when he had stood at her bedside at Eden House. He had not had a line from her or from anyone in the village, and he had been gone close to six months. Someone must have written to him, Madam or the senator.

He took up his cap and put it on. Cosmo leaned back in his camp-chair, overcome with laughter. "It is the *kepi!* It is so strange, so American, to wear fur animals on your head."

Peter retorted, "No stranger than a coq feather streaming over your shoulder."

Cosmo stopped laughing. His eyes opened wide. He slapped his knee smartly. "You are right, Peter. You are right. I see it now. It is only the strange that is amusing to us."

Peter was the first to arrive. Captain Miles came a moment later. "Are you settled with your friend De' Medici?" Miles asked.

"Yes, thank you."

"He is an amusing cuss."

"Amusing?" Peter looked blank. "He is a good shot and he has a strong sword-arm. That's all a woodsman asks of a man."

Miles was embarrassed. "Yes, certainly," he said hurriedly.

An officer came in, a lieutenant-colonel by his insignia. Miles snapped to his feet. The officer greeted him casually. "Sit down, Miles." He glanced at Peter. Peter gave him a level look that missed nothing. A remarkably handsome man, with large dark eyes and classical features.

"Thank you, Colonel Laurens," Miles said. He sat fidgeting, evidently not knowing what to do about Peter.

Laurens crossed the room and put out his hand. "You are Huntley," he said. "The general told me you were here." He nodded to Miles, who left the room, a bewildered look on his face. Peter knew of Laurens, knew he was now in command of a battalion of light infantry. Laurens drew up a chair. "Sit down, Huntley," he said. "I am eager to know what message you brought. But I will curb my impatience until General Lincoln arrives."

Peter asked, "Do you know who will be here, Colonel?"

"Governor Rutledge, and a committee of merchants—the Secret

Council, I believe they are called. Colonel Pinckney may be here."

Peter nodded. All these names he knew. Laurens made some remark about the necessity of planning for beef for the army, in case the British arrived in force. He thought it could be had in sufficient quantity from Lempriere's Point, if they remained on that side of the Cooper River. By his conversation Peter realized Colonel Laurens did not have knowledge that the British had already sailed and were more than three weeks at sea.

General Lincoln and the Governor came in. They were in earnest conversation. Peter had a moment to view the eagle profile of the chief executive. He was a tall man. He, too, wore the same weary look of long and continuous toil and anxiety.

Lincoln saw Laurens and Peter and motioned them forward. "Governor, this is Captain Huntley. He is our liaison with General Washington."

The Governor was gracious. "I understand that you are teaming with Major Avery. Did you have trouble getting through the Tory country?"

Peter hesitated a second. "Nothing to speak of, your Excellency."

Lincoln smiled. "Captain Huntley is skilled in woodcraft." He turned to Peter. "It is necessary that these gentlemen, whom you are to meet tonight, be acquainted with your rank and your mission, Captain. I assure you it will go no farther. I have been told that you have found a friend here, Captain de' Medici."

"He knows nothing of my work. He is too thorough a soldier to ask any questions."

"Good!" General Lincoln and the Governor crossed the room to a long table covered with maps and papers. Shortly Lincoln said, "The others are waiting to come in. Shall I send for them, your Excellency?"

"Please do."

Half a dozen men came into the room, some in uniform, some in sober civilian clothes—"The merchant committee," Laurens said to Peter.

After his Excellency the Governor had taken his place at the end of the table, the general waved the others to their seats. "Anywhere, gentlemen. Captain, perhaps you will sit near me, in case there are questions." Peter took a place between Colonel Laurens and General Lincoln.

The meeting was informal. Governor Rutledge rapped on the table with a bronze letter-opener. "Gentlemen, General Lincoln has received a communication of great importance to us. With your permission, I will ask him to tell you the details. After he has finished, there will be discussion."

The general took the lead tube from his waistcoat pocket, and his reading-glass. "The dispatch is from General Washington," he said. "Captain Huntley brought it to my camp outside the city a few hours ago. After it has been read, if you wish, Captain Huntley, I am sure, will answer any question in his power. Captain Huntley, gentlemen, is liaison officer between General Washington's headquarters and the Southern Army. He was for some years connected with Mr. Franklin's office in Paris. He has represented the Committee on Foreign Affairs on confidential work and was with the Headquarters Staff during the winter of Valley Forge. I mention this because you have the right to know who it is that brings you this vital information.

"One thing I must ask of you is that you will preserve his real identity, since he will come to us from time to time as he is now, a woodsman and scout from the high mountain country."

Colonel Laurens put two candles so that the light was right for the reading-glass.

Lincoln read slowly. Each word fell clear and distinct upon the listening ears like words of a doom.

"Having enjoyed the Christmas holiday in New York Harbour, General Sir Henry Clinton, accompanied by Lord Cornwallis, sailed from Sandy Hook the next day with the fleet under General Arbuthnot, transporting an army of seven thousand five hundred men, including some Hessian troops. They will, according to our Intelligence, join with the British Southern Army near Savannah. This will be a formidable army for the general to use against Charles Town."

A postscript had been added, but not initialed.

"The situation here is such that I cannot hazard the Maryland troops, as proposed by Congress, in such a venture. I would suggest Fabian tactics and warfare, if the situation proves untenable."

There was a heavy silence following the reading of the dispatch. More than one man turned his eyes from Lincoln to Peter, wondering, no doubt, if he had more information than was contained in it. But they waited for Governor Rutledge to speak.

"That is the situation, gentlemen. It is serious, very serious, but not different from what we have been anticipating throughout the late summer and autumn."

"But seventy-five hundred troops! Does that include sea troops?" A merchant asked the question, a quick-spoken, nervous man who fidgeted in his chair and rattled the seals on his fob.

General Lincoln looked at Peter.

"No, sir. It does not include the sea soldiers."

"How many?" snapped the merchant.

Peter answered quietly, "Major Avery said around two thousand."

The merchant barked, "Plus the soldiers in Georgia." He looked at Lincoln. Peter had a momentary glimpse of the enmity between the townsfolk and the military.

Governor Rutledge's calm voice interrupted. "Do you know of other troops at the command of General Clinton, Captain Huntley?"

"There is intelligence that Lord Rawdon's brigade has been ordered to ships. But that force may be designed for the Chesapeake or Virginia waters. We do not yet know."

"Thank you, Captain."

The merchants began to talk. "What does he mean, Fabian tactics?" one said to Lincoln. "Explain, please. We do not understand military terms."

"In broad lines, it means 'fight and retreat; fight and retreat.' "

A fist came down on the table. A second merchant rose to his feet. "We'll have no retreat from Charles Town, General. Charles Town will be defended."

The general looked anxiously at Governor Rutledge.

"Our defences are inadequate. Food is scarce—certainly not enough to feed a city of fifteen thousand," he said. "We may as well face it."

Colonel Laurens said, "We have gone over that before. We know that beef is to be had."

"If the British do not cross the Cooper," Lincoln said, not raising his voice. Peter thought he showed remarkable restraint. The argument was an old one evidently, fanned into new flame.

Peter leaned over and spoke to General Lincoln. "May I be excused, General? I have no further information and I am leaving early."

Lincoln looked at the Governor, who nodded assent. "Thank

you, Captain Huntley. We trust you will be the bearer of better news on your next journey south."

Peter bowed and went out of the room. The merchants did not notice; they were busy arguing with the military.

On the eleventh of February the British forces landed on St. John's Island, within thirty miles of Charles Town. They built fortifications on James Island. Officers reported they saw General Cornwallis standing near a redoubt. Continental officers agreed on their inability to guard the town. The engineer, DuPortail, reported to Washington that the defences of Charles Town were untenable.

But the merchants were still adamant. The city must be defended. The siege of Charles Town lengthened. Defeat was inevitable, and there were long and anxious days ahead.

By this time Peter was back in Salisbury for a second meeting with Major Avery, at the stone home of Michael Braun.

CHAPTER

27

"WHAT OF THE NIGHT?"

APATHY, deadly and devastating, hung over the village on Queen Anne's Creek. Militia companies which had camped from time to time, out beyond the Rope Walk, had marched away, allowing the land to return to cow pasture. No gay young French officers came to flutter the women's hearts or give elegant balls in the Council Chamber. It was a wet winter: rain day after day, dismal and dark skies. In the North the most severe winter in years held campaigns in check, and the morale of the army was at its lowest ebb.

The chains that bound the village with the Congress snapped with the death of Joseph Hewes. Samuel Johnston was in New Bern, Dr. Williamson gone with the army; Adam Rutledge had not been heard from for half a year.

The women sewed a little, scraped lint, and tried to comfort themselves that they were helping some vague and far-off army. The town sank into the backwash of a war that had never been real, other than during a few brief moments when news of the death of some soldier or officer came back to them, months after the tragedy had occurred. Even the couriers who used to pass, riding to New Bern or Charles Town, seemed to come less frequently.

The new governor, Nash, was involved with routine work, while the Assembly made the dull and routine laws that belong to the beginning of a state.

Parson Earle stopped at Eden House one day. He had been to Bath, to hold service. He held service, now that people had dropped the idea that he was a Tory at heart. He sat talking to Penelope Dawson, while the rain beat against the window.

"Five days in a row," he said, watching the bare-limbed trees whip in the wind, "five days I waited at Bath. Swollen streams. Ferries tied on the banks."

455

"I'm glad you came this far," Penelope said. "I'm growing very tired of myself. I was in despair until Mary Warden came in this morning, during that two-hour pause between downpours."

The Parson poured himself a glass of Madeira. Mary came in a few minutes later. She shook hands with the rector, drew her chair close to the light, and took out her knitting.

"Four o'clock and candles lighted," complained Penelope. "I'm glad you came in, Parson. We can have an exciting game of loo after supper. I declare I'm desperately weary of patience; weary of myself as well."

The Parson shook his head. "It is unthinkable for you to be in the doldrums, Penelope. We must think of some way out of that." He lifted his glass to the light. "Marvellous! Marvellous! I've never tasted better Madeira."

"Sam got it for me before the war began. I will send you a little keg next week—if it stops raining."

The rector smiled. "I was not hinting, only enjoying; but nevertheless, I will not refuse." He turned to Mary. "Has anyone had a communication from Adam?"

Mary shook her head.

"Or from that nice Peter Huntley?"

Penelope sparkled then. "Yes, I had a letter from him. He's been in the high mountains."

The Parson twirled his glass and looked thoughtful. "I hoped I would have the pleasure of reading the marriage banns in December, but the senator told me that Captain Huntley had been sent away on some mission. I believe he was quite disappointed that there was no wedding at Christmas."

Penelope said, "I wonder if Angela is sufficiently recovered to be married. You visited her last week, Mary. What do you think?"

Mary laid her knitting on the table and drew her chair closer to the fire. "She was not herself when I saw her. She was listless, almost apathetic."

"Apathetic!" The Parson almost shouted the word. "Apathetic! That is what we all are. I am so distressed about our collective state of mind that I sometimes wish the British would send a ship-of-war up the Sound and give us a salvo." His lips broke into a smile. "A *very* small shelling, very small, that would do no hurt, save tear away some of those old buildings on the water-front."

"Why, Parson!" Mary exclaimed.

"I mean it. We need to be shaken out of our complacency. Sometimes I think I could preach a sermon that would bring people to their senses. I could if I were a shouting Dissenter."

Penelope leaned forward. "Do that, Parson! Do that! Wake us up to the fact that the war is our war, not South Carolina's war, or Georgia's war, but ours!"

The Parson was silent for a moment. "I've been thinking of it. Perhaps I will."

"Don't wait too long. We need it now. Right now."

The subject was dropped when supper was announced.

"Where is William?" the Parson asked Mary when they were seated at the table. "I haven't seen him for some days."

"He is in Charlotte Town. He wants me to come over next month. He thinks I should spend a month at Catawba Springs, to drink the water."

Penelope asked, "Are you ailing again, Mary?"

"No, but listless.'" Mary smiled at the rector. "Perhaps it is a case of this prevailing apathy."

Parson Earle sobered. "I am quite serious, my dear woman, quite serious. We must do something or we will lose our immortal souls."

He insisted on leaving after supper. "I promised Pearson I would stay the night. If you will lend me a slave and a lanthorn I will be moving on."

Penelope said, "Certainly. But we hoped for your company and a game."

"Thank you, but I must slog along." He took up his cape, which Scipio had dried by the fire, and threw it across his shoulders. "Good night! Good night!"

Penelope said, "Inform me in time to get over to St. Paul's. I want to hear you rouse the people from their apathy."

"Would to God that I had the power!" He went off in the rain, waving a cheerful good-bye to Penelope, who stood in the door to see him out of sight down the turn of the road.

Mary was turning the heel of a sock when Penelope came back into the room. She looked up and nodded, the extra needle held between her white teeth. Penelope walked restlessly about the room. When the proper stitches had been taken, Mary put the sock on the table. "My fortieth pair," she said with satisfaction.

"I don't see how you do it. I would be as crazy as old Tim, if I knitted as you do."

"Knitting can be very quieting," Mary observed. "I think you should go over to the Springs next month when we go."

Penelope shook her head. "No, I can't leave. We are too busy here; we are behind in our spring planting. It's too wet to get a plough in the fields."

"I'm not going until early May."

"Can't. I may go over for two weeks, the last of August, or the first of September. I will have to go to Charlotte Town, then, to put little Pene in school at the Queen's Museum. I may run up to the Springs. But I can't go before. You must remember that I am a planter."

Mary smiled. "So am I, but I leave more to the overlooker than you do."

"You wouldn't if you had the fellow I've got. Now, there's no one to be had; every man of any integrity has gone off with the militia."

"I understand Governor Nash is going to let the farmers come home to set their crops, and again at harvest-time."

Penelope picked up a book, laid it down, and continued her pacing about the room. "That overlooker of mine is one of the worst characters I ever had on the plantation. He's a good man in the field, but he's chasing the black girls all the time. I think he has one in his bed every night." She sat down opposite Mary. "I'm ashamed to tell you this, but I am really so hard-pressed for help that I have to keep him. So I pretend I don't know what goes on. He thinks there is no one who will tell me about his behaviour."

"Pene, you ought not have the man on the plantation. You ought to get rid of him at once," Mary said.

Pene laughed. "There's no danger of that—what you mean. He keeps himself well supplied. Sam is trying to get me someone trustworthy, but so far he hasn't been successful." She sighed. "Sometimes I wish I could get myself into the notion of marrying again." She laughed. "Remember the story about old Squire Pollock's second wife, Hester? She married again, directly after one of her husbands died. When she was chided about the short period of mourning, she said she couldn't afford to buy another feather-bed. It was easier to take on a husband."

Mary glanced at her companion, "I've sometimes wondered whether you would marry again, Pene."

Penelope hesitated before she answered. "I've asked myself that question, Mary. When I considered, I always come to the same conclusion. I prefer being John Dawson's widow, to being the wife of any other man."

Mary said, "Perhaps the right man had not appeared, when you came to this decision."

Penelope looked at her steadily. "You are thinking of Peter Huntley?"

"Yes, of Peter Huntley."

"Peter is in love with Angela."

Mary took up her knitting, "I wonder," she murmured, "I wonder." Penelope apparently did not hear her low spoken words. "Mary, yesterday morning I rode from here to Mt. Galland, the day before to Scot's Hall, over land that has belonged to my people for several generations. I love it inordinately. I could never expect any man I might marry to have the same feeling I have for my acres."

Mary knitted around the cuff of the sock before she answered. "I think I understand that. All of the people of the Albemarle have the same deep-rooted love of our land."

Penelope interrupted. "My father, in his will, made a request that I cultivate and improve my plantations. I have not failed him, save in one thing, the raising of silk. I tried, but I failed in that. He also said he wanted me to be brought up in sobriety and moderation—not aspiring 'after gaiety, splendour or extravagances.' I cannot tell you how I have struggled to be the woman my father saw in me, a little child. His words to my stepmother were 'to bring her up in the fear of God, and under a deep sense of her being always in His presence.' She leaned forward a little; her grey eyes were steady and clear. "Do not think me strange, Mary, if I say I feel His presence most deeply when I am here at Eden House, on my own land, on the soil where my people are buried."

Mary had no words to answer. She realized how stirred her companion was. It gave her deep insight into Penelope's complex character, which called further admiration.

Penelope got up and went to the window, making any answer unnecessary.

"The rain has stopped. Let's ride over to Pollocks'," she said.

"But it's pitch-dark!"

"What matter? Scipio will light the way for us."

"The wind is rising."

"What matter? I love the wind. I love a storm."

Mary got up. "You are restless, Pene."

"No, not restless. It is only this interminable waiting. Waiting for what? I don't know. I feel as though the whole world were standing still, waiting for some cataclysm. It is like waiting for a hurricane to strike. One knows not where it will come. Some great doom is suspended in the air, waiting. . . ."

"Come, we'll ride over to Ann Pollock's," Mary said.

The water dripped from the branches of the trees onto their faces. Penelope rode without a hat. Her hair and face were splashed as she ducked her head to ride under the pines that crowded the narrow path across the pocosin.

They found the Pollocks sitting in the small room that faced Salmon Creek. Cullen laid down a book when they came into the room. Ann got up from a table where she had put out the patience cards, and greeted them warmly as though glad of company.

They stayed an hour or more. Penelope tried to remove the atmosphere of restraint that seemed always near when she was with the Pollocks. Only once was war mentioned.

Cullen said, "Have you seen any of the militia troops that have been passing today?"

Penelope said no, they had seen none along their road.

"They will be coming. If I were you, I would send the horses to Black Rock or Mount Galland."

Penelope thanked him. He insisted on riding with them through the swamp. "We have Scipio as protector." Penelope laughed. "Anyway, no one will be camped along the swamp." But Cullen insisted, and escorted them to the Governor's Road.

Before he left, he reiterated his warning. "Do send your horses away and keep off the roads, Penelope. I heard in the village when I was there today that the ferry will be transporting men and horses all tomorrow. Cannon too. Robert Smith has told me that Clem Hull is taking two cannon down to New Bern by order of the Governor."

Penelope said, "So Clem is going to war at last."

Cullen's voice was cold. "Yes. Some of Adam Rutledge's doing. He is the one that got the fellow interested in repairing ordnance. But do take care, Pene. Soldiers are soldiers. Even our own are not to be trusted. Keep your women out of sight, mind you."

When they got home, Penelope did not wait to take off her damp habit. She sent Scipio to call Governorcharleseden. "I want to plan for tomorrow," she told Mary.

"Tomorrow?" Mary asked. "Oh, you mean to send your horses to Mount Galland?"

"No. No, indeed. All my stock that I didn't sell to the army is right here in use on the plantation."

Governor came into the room. "Scipio says you want something, ma'am."

Penelope nodded. "Mr. Pollock said there would be many soldiers marching along the road to New Bern, beginning tomorrow. I want to set up a little food-station where our lane crosses the main road. We are going to feed them milk and hot corn-cakes and maybe some bacon. How many cows are we milking?"

"The feeder said twenty head, Miss Pene."

"Splendid! Plenty of fresh milk. You and Scipio will take charge. Have some young boys wait at the ferry to let you know when they are coming. Have you a couple of men who can cook?"

"Yes, ma'am. More than that, ma'am."

"Have them take down an iron oven, then. . . . Fix it as we do for a picnic."

Governorcharleseden looked dubious. "Most of we be afraid of soldiers. They might like to carry us away."

"No fear. I will be right there to protect you."

The old slave chuckled. "Yes'm. I reckon you like you' papa. He wa'n't afeered of man or debbil."

"Tell the boys that these are *our* soldiers, going to fight for us."

"Yes'm. Yes'm."

Mary listened, an expression of admiration on her face. "I thought you wouldn't hide, Pene."

Penelope tossed her cloak over the banister rail. "No, I never intended to. Poor Cullen! He has had such a bitter experience that he is timid. He never used to be that way." They walked into the library. "Let's have a posset before we go to bed, Mary, for I want to be up with the dawn."

"I'll be right with you. I think we should take bandages and ointment for blistered feet. You know how it is when they first begin to march, and are wearing those wretched boots they issue to the soldiers."

"Yes. Yes, of course you would think of something useful. I'm afraid I didn't go any farther than to get something for their stomachs."

They sat down. Scipio came with the hot drink. Mary said, "I can't tell you how I felt when I saw those two sitting there. They seemed so alone. I'm glad you suggested going over. Ann couldn't keep gratitude out of her eyes."

Penelope said, "I drop in every day or so. I don't want them to feel that the whole world is against them."

"Most of the village is." Mary's voice was sad.

"I am determined not to lose my faith in human beings, even though we *are* at war. Think of our friends in England. They haven't changed, I am sure. They couldn't change their characters in a few years. By what strange circumstance do we come into war, Mary? I've spent many hours thinking, thinking, but I find no answer."

"Nor I, Penelope. It is all so horrible. These glorious young men——" Her voice broke a little. She picked up the sock from the table and began to knit.

By daybreak the message came that the first ferry-load was crossing the river. Penelope had her horse brought around and rode down to the station Scipio had established at the road, leaving word for Mary to follow. The rain had ceased. The east was streaked with red. Birds were singing, flying from tree to tree, searching for a nesting-place. She hoped the mockers would find their old nest in the tall pine near her window. She loved to wake to their morning song, or to sink into deep sleep to their lovely moonlight serenade.

The floor of the forest was blanketed with delicate spring flowers. Where the ditches had been burned, early in February, the azaleas had sprung up and were now a lovely pink. She felt a glow of satisfaction. Now at last there was something for her hands to do for the marching men.

The fires were going. A couple of long planks had been placed between two stumps. The shining copper kettles were filled with milk. Gourd dippers for ladling were ready. Half a dozen of her people stood watching a very black man cook corn-meal cakes in the ashes. The slaves brightened when they saw her riding down the lane. A boy ran up to take her horse when she dismounted, and led it into hiding behind a thicket of pines.

Penelope said, "No. Tie her right here. I am not going to show any distrust of our soldiers."

They had not waited long when the first of the militia company came into sight. As they came near, Penelope saw that they were young men, very young. They were marching easily, but they had no laughter in their eyes.

"Will you breakfast with us?" she asked, as the officer drew abreast.

"Why, this is a fine thought, miss. My men got off before the break of day." He gave an order: "At ease! Break ranks!"

Mary Warden rode down the lane as the men were drinking the milk, eating corn-cakes that had a strip of bacon in the middle, with relish and words of praise. She got off her horse and slung her saddle-bags over her arm. She went up to a boy who sat on the ditch-side, his shoe off, trying to ease his sock over a blistered foot. A moment later she was surrounded by boys wanting ointment or a strip of bandage about a heel or a toe. They ate and drank, pulled on boots, and marched on.

"Others are coming," the officer told her. "A pontoon loaded before we did. Bless you for your good thoughts, madam." He saluted and the little band moved down the road.

Four times the ferry crossed, each time bringing its quota of men. Each group had its fill of food, and its blisters dressed.

"One more ferry, but that carries the cannon, madam; only a few battery men. Then no more until tomorrow."

Mary straightened her tired back. She and Penelope sat on a log, and drank milk which Scipio brought them. "It is a good feeling, to do something useful," Mary said. "I've talked more than once to Dr. Armitage about being a nurse. I even worked in his office, learning about bandages and splints; to hand him the right instrument when he asked. But I've had no call so far—" she laughed a little—"only this bandaging of blistered feet."

"I'm sure those boys were grateful for that, Mary. I watched you. You are so skilful with your hands. . . . What's that?" She was looking down the road. One of her farm hands was galloping toward them, urgency in every lash of the whip with which he was belabouring the mule he was riding.

"Man's killed!" he shouted. "At the ferry! They want help."

Mary and Penelope mounted their horses. Two men got on the mule.

"Who is hurt?" Penelope called as she passed the messenger.

"Mr. Cullen and another—I don't rightly know his name. It was when the cannon slipped."

When they reached the ferry landing, they saw a crowd of men pulling a cannon carriage up the bank. A group were standing at the top of the bank.

Cullen Pollock, white and shaken, was bending over a man stretched out on the ground. He looked up when she stopped. "It's too late, it's too late," he said brokenly.

"What happened?" Penelope asked. She slid off her horse and approached Cullen.

"Clem Hull," he said. "He saved me." He couldn't say more.

"Is there something we can do? Mary has bandages."

Southey Wren rose from the ground and came to the two women. He was as white as Cullen. "It's too late, ma'am. He's gone, he is." The man's voice broke. "He's gone."

"He saved me," Cullen kept repeating, dazedly. "Me. He didn't know it was me."

Southey turned. His bright eyes blazed. "He did too know. Didn't ye hear him shout 'Squire Pollock! Squire Pollock!' before he threw himself for'ard and cast you out of the way of the cannon wheels?"

Cullen stared at Southey. For a moment he did not comprehend. "Squire Pollock." He whispered the words. "Then he did know. Oh, my God!"

Mary went over to the little group on the bank. They made way for her as she bent down and placed her fingers on Clem Hull's wrist. There was no pulse beat under her fingers.

"He's gone," Southey said, "with never a word to any of us, his good friends."

Mary looked at the crushed chest and maimed and broken body. "Thank God he was not held for suffering," she said gently.

Cullen gathered himself together. "Make a litter, men. Carry him to the road and I'll send my cart for him. At Balgray he was born; at Balgray let him be buried."

Southey made no protest. He turned to Penelope Dawson. "A woman can speak better to a woman. There's Martie to be told."

"I will go over at once." Penelope turned to Mary. "Will you ride back to Eden House and tell them, after these men are fed?"

The gun-carriage was at the crest of the bank now. A moment later the heavy ropes, guided by brawny men, pulled it onto the road. An officer rode over to where Southey Wren was standing. "Do you want to stay? You can join us at New Bern."

Southey saluted. "No, sir. I'll go on. There is nothing I can do now for Clem Hull."

Two days later, half of Queen Anne's Town came across the Sound to see Clem Hull's body lowered into the fertile earth of Balgray. Martie, dry-eyed and sad-faced, stood beside Ann and Cullen Pollock while the last rites were being said in the burial-ground in the field.

" 'Tis a pretty spot where he lies," she said to Ann when they walked to the house, "a fair beautiful spot. I would be proud to stay here in the little house, like you said, but if I did, who would do fine washing for the gentlemen of the village? Thank you just the same, ma'am. It was the drink that made him speak mean. I never held aught against him. Clem would understand. He was a fair understandin' man, was my Clem. For all his brash talk, he had a good heart in him, ma'am."

Martie went back on the boat with her friends, and the village was proud of her, and proud of Clem Hull.

That night at the Red Lion his old cronies met and spoke little. They raised their glasses in silence. They were inarticulate folk, but in their hearts they sorrowed for big, brawny Clem, with his loud voice and his denunciations. He was a fine, bold man, was Clem, and he died in a fine, bold way, without fear, like a soldier in battle. It was Southey who said those words, a long time afterward, when the war was over: "Clem died in battle, the same like he'd been killed by a cannon ball." And so it was that Clem Hull became a hero, and many a silent toast was raised to his memory at the Red Lion Inn.

Mr. Pettigrew was ready for the processional when Parson Earle came in the Vestry door at St. Paul's. With a nod the rector drew off his tailed coat, buttoned his long cassock, and set his wig straight. His boots were splashed from riding on the muddy roads and fording the creek. He gave no thought to his boots and motioned Mr. Pettigrew to precede him up the aisle.

The church was crowded. The rumour that the Parson would preach that morning had reached not only the town but the countryside.

There had been a Vestry meeting in which some of the members threatened to leave if he walked to the altar. But they were cried down. "Let him say the Church stands above warring nations. Damned if I don't think he is right!" cried one member.

"We've had enough intolerance," said another. The more timid said nothing, but when the secret ballots were counted, there was only one vote against, so Parson Earle was to preach.

The church was crowded right up to and including the slave gallery. Mary Warden sat in the choir with the two Blount girls and a stranger from a detachment of militia camped for the night at the Rope Walk. He had a splendid ringing voice.

Mr. Pettigrew conducted the first part of the service. As he sat in the tall side chair, Daniel Earle glanced down and saw his muddy boots below his cassock. A suspicion of a smile crossed his lips. He recalled another time when he had worn his hunting-boots, and the indignation of some of the church-goers. His mind went back without effort. He had blessed the hunt that morning, fully forty riders and Adam Rutledge's fine hounds. It was the morning they had run down Harmon Husbands, who later came into unpleasant notice at the time of the Tryon Rebellion. Blessing the hunt, a pretty custom. Next week he would make a little ceremony of blessing the plough. No need to let these little old country customs die just because of war. It wouldn't last forever.

Mr. Pettigrew's voice, without accent or change, went on. A hymn, the Creed, the first lesson. Daniel Earle, out of long habit, answered at the right time, knelt in prayer, rose again and responded. What was he to say to all these people? This was the day he was going to speak words tinged with fire, to rouse them from complacency, from complete apathy.

God give him help! He had worked at a sermon until the early morning hours. It lay now on the lectern where a little choir-boy had placed it. The sermon that had seemed good last night would not do. He realized it now. One got nowhere by lecturing people. It only stiffened their backs.

"God help me!" His lips moved. Then, like a revelation, he knew. It would not be a sermon. It was the word of God that would speak. The page came before his mind . . . the Prophet Isaiah. Let his voice thunder as it had thundered down the ages!

Pettigrew was looking at him. The rector rose and moved to the pulpit. The Bible was open to the reading, but he did not look at it. He spoke quietly.

"Today I shall take the prophecy of Isaiah." He stood quietly, his hands folded. He closed his eyes and spoke.

"The burden of the desert of the sea. As whirlwinds in the south pass through; so it cometh from the desert, from a terrible land.

"A grievous vision is declared unto me; the treacherous dealer dealeth treacherously, and the spoiler spoileth. Go up, O Elam: besiege, O Media; all the sighing thereof have I made to cease.

"Therefore are my loins filled with pain: pangs have taken hold upon me, as the pangs of a woman that travaileth: I was bowed down at the hearing of it; I was dismayed at the seeing of it. . . .

Prepare the table, watch in the watchtower, eat, drink: arise, ye princes, and anoint the shield.

For thus hath the Lord said unto me, Go, set a watchman, let him declare what he seeth."

The church was quiet as the rector spoke. His words spoken, not read, took on the spirit of prophecy. They felt the old voice of Isaiah speaking to them.

"He calleth to me out of Seir, Watchman, what of the night? Watchman, what of the night?

"The watchman said, The morning cometh, and also the night: if ye will enquire, enquire ye: return, come."

An altar-boy came to the speaker and laid a sheet of paper before him on the lectern, and slipped away.

"For thus hath the Lord said unto me, Within a year, according to the years of an hireling, and all the glory of Kedar shall fail:

"And the residue of the number of archers, the mighty men of the children of Kedar, shall be diminished: for the Lord God of Israel hath spoken it."

He spoke more quickly now, his powerful voice reaching the slave galleries with rising power. Negroes turned one to another. The Spirit was upon him. The black men recognized the voice of the Spirit.

"The land shall be utterly emptied, and utterly spoiled: for the Lord hath spoken this word.

"The earth mourneth and fadeth away, the world languisheth and fadeth away, the haughty people of the earth do languish.

"The earth also is defiled . . . Therefore hath the curse devoured the earth, and they that dwell therein are desolate. . . .

"The new wine mourneth, the vine languisheth, all the merry-hearted do sigh.

"The mirth of tabrets ceaseth . . . the joy of the harp ceaseth.

"*The city of confusion is broken down: every house is shut up, that no man may come in.*

"*There is a crying for wine in the streets; all joy is darkened, the mirth of the land is gone.*

"*In the city is left desolaton, and the gate is smitten with destruction. . . .*

"*The earth is utterly broken down, the earth is clean dissolved, the earth is moved exceedingly.*

"*The earth shall reel to and fro like a drunkard . . . and the transgression thereof shall be heavy upon it; and it shall fall, and not rise again. . . .*

"*Then the moon shall be confounded, and the sun ashamed, when the Lord of Hosts shall reign in mount Zion, and in Jerusalem, and before His ancients gloriously.*"

The rector paused a moment, then repeated the words, "*Watchman, what of the night?*" He opened his eyes, and he saw the paper the altar-boy had placed before him. He glanced at it, then leaned over, lifting the paper close. He stepped forward, his eyes sweeping the congregation. There was almost no break from the words of prophecy to the words that followed:

"All soldiers and militiamen in the church proceed at once to their camps. . . . Charles Town has fallen."

A gasp went up like a great sigh. Soldiers in uniform rose quietly and left their places. Both doors were thrown open to allow them to pass out into the churchyard.

The congregation started to rise, but Daniel Earle's uplifted hand held them. Many sank to their knees and bowed their heads.

The rector abandoned the hymn on the calendar. He lifted his powerful voice:

> "Rise, crown'd with light,
> Imperial Salem, rise!
> Exalt thy tow'ring head
> And lift thine eyes!"

Mary Warden's voice rose clear and sure, others falling in while two verses were sung, until the exalting hymn became a triumphant battle song.

> "But fixed His word,
>   His saving power remains;
> Thy realms shall last,
>   Thy own Messiah reigns."

With a word to Mr. Pettigrew to complete the service, Parson Earle strode down the aisle. Still clad in his vestments, he crossed the churchyard rapidly and called to his driver. He lifted his cassock above his knees, and jumped into his driving gig. No soldier would leave camp that day without his blessing.

As his horse trotted swiftly down the street, he thought once more of his sermon. There was no need of words of his to wake the people to the reality of war. He had looked into their faces. Four words were all that were needed: "Charles Town has fallen."

All the way home Penelope Dawson thought of the events of the morning. The Sound was almost blue. The freshet waters of the Roanoke had not yet roiled it with the mud of her tawny red banks. The rector had had the Spirit, and the Spirit had answered. It was a symbol that everyone could read.

That afternoon she took her writing-pad and went down to the bank. She sat down on Governor Eden's tomb to write a letter to Peter Huntley. She told him first of Clem Hull and his death. Cullen had been so different, almost as though he had been released from some overheavy burden. More than once he had said to her, "He called me by name, 'Squire Pollock.' He knew he was saving me. . . ."

She told Peter other things—of the food-station at Eden House; Mary's bandages; the movement of troops; the awakening of Queen Anne's Town; the rector's Vision of Isaiah.

At the end of the letter she returned to Clem Hull.

> And so we have two patriots now, two men we have taken to
> our bosoms, Joseph Hewes and a more lowly man. But, Peter, I
> am sure that the good Lord, who sees into our hearts, will put the
> brightest crown on the dishevelled dark head of Clem Hull.

Captain Anthony Allison joined Major Ferguson's corps at Savannah on March fifth. He was happy, so happy that his fellow officers thought he was drunk. He bathed, dressed himself in a fresh uniform and, having wrapped Jeremiah Morse's Boston suit around a piece of iron, he tossed it into the Savannah River. Free forever of spying work!

The next morning he marched with his new company, the American Volunteers, Major Patrick Ferguson commanding.

He was glad to be back under Ferguson once more, a soldier if ever there was one. He hummed a tune as his charger danced along. Even the horses were eager, with Charles Town ahead.

Other troops were marching: Major Graham's Light Artillery; the New York Volunteers, Lieutenant-Colonel Turnbull; Hamilton's North Carolina Loyalists; Colonel Innes' South Carolina Loyalists; Major Cochrane's dismounted Legion; Georgia Dragoons; and the first battalion of the Seventy-First Regiment, Major McArthur—in all, near fifteen hundred men. That was the fifth of March. Allison wished that there might have been more British soldiers, but the Tories seemed eager. He knew Ferguson would whip his men into shape, for he was as famous for drilling men as he was as a marksman. Anthony felt good. The column had welcomed him with open arms.

They moved into a little village garrisoned by British, where the inhabitants were High Dutch. It was raining and the march heavy. There they remained for two days, because many of the men were taken ill with pain and swelling extremities, from a weed, people said, that poisoned where it touched the naked skin while the dew was still on it.

By the fourteenth they took ground at Coosahatchie Bridge, where the Americans had been defeated the previous May.

Anthony called his orderly and they rode up-stream to the edge of a swamp. Here they had the good luck to discover a quantity of Continental stores and ammunition, which had been hidden there by John Stafford, the rebel commissary. Most of the powder was useless.

The next few days there were several skirmishes. Major Ferguson was wounded in the arm by a rebel bayonet, painfully but not seriously.

They made good headway. On the twenty-second, Colonel Tarleton joined them at Beaufort with his dragoons. He had ridden ahead of the contingent to get horses, for his had been on a ship that was lost coming from New York.

Anthony had never met the famous officer and he was curious to see the man who swore that he would rape more women than any other man in the army. He was handsome in a sullen, petulant way, a rake known throughout the British Isles, but an excellent officer. One could see that his dare-devils would follow him anywhere.

The next morning the army was late getting into motion. They went through a village of fifty or sixty good houses on the Pon Pon, a rice market for Charles Town, and they came on some stores of rice, but every damned rebel had run away, save a bedridden old man and a doctor.

Colonel Tarleton crossed the river at Governor Bee's plantation, killed ten, took four prisoners. Bee had been a governor under His Majesty's government, but turned traitor and was now a member of the rebel Congress.

They were all anxious to push on to Charles Town. The soldiers were wild to be in on the kill.

Major Ferguson got rear-guard duty, to do his King and country justice by protecting friends and widows, and collecting live stock. The army collected horses, cattle, sheep, hogs and mules, and took the slaves to drive them.

Rain. Rain. Rain.

Colonel Hamilton, of the North Carolina Loyalists, went in front of the army, with Dr. Smith of the hospital, and proceeded to Governor Rutledge's house. Here they were surprised by three hundred of the Continental Light Horse, and taken prisoners.

Anthony rode in the rear, a position he did not like. Too long had he been collecting cattle. He longed to ride with Banastre Tarleton's Legion. That reckless, swashbuckling officer interested him.

Charles Town drew him also. He had been there during his spying days, and stayed at Edward Shrewsbury's house. It was there he had met Major John André. André, dressed as a country bumpkin, was in worse case than he was as a Boston merchant.

It was the same day he had met the French girl, Michèle Roi, again. Someone spoke his name quietly, with caution, as he was walking near the fish market. He did not recognize her at first. He had always made it a rule not to speak to girls he had slept with. But she was beautiful. He remembered how she had rested his tired body when he was escaping down the Cape Fear River.

He stopped and went to her room with her, to threaten her to secrecy, or buy her if necessary. He found he had to do neither. He solaced her to secrecy with his body, for that was what she yearned for.

She had been seeking him for months. How she lived, why she was in Charles Town, he did not ask. He fancied she had come with some soldier. She volunteered nothing, and asked nothing. When he left her, she told him she would wait for him.

"You will come as certainly as night follows day," she had said. Then she had given him valuable information which she must have learned following an army.

Time had been when he would have been squeamish about sharing her with someone else, but here in America one could not pick and choose.

As the army neared the city, he thought of her more frequently, and with desire. She had strong thighs and warm, soft breasts.

They had passed Drayton's Hall and marched to Middleton Plantation. From here they heard the constant cannonade from the rebels in the British works on the Neck, returned by the batteries at Wapoo Cut.

Rain. Rain. Rain.

In the night, the rebels were reinforced by General Scott. Nineteen hundred, at least, the Intelligence informed Colonel Tarleton. The rebels went wild and fired a *feu de joie*.

Short-lived was their joy, for in the afternoon following the fleet hove in sight. The ships came beautifully, under full sail, under a fine strong breeze from the southwest.

They passed Fort Moultrie, a fine impregnable fort of the rebels on Sullivan's Island. It was beautiful. A cutter lay across the fort, in full line with their guns, to point the channel. One ship lost a mast, and they could not see what other damage had been inflicted. But they were inside, and Admiral Arbuthnot was ashore.

Late that night Major Patrick Ferguson returned from a visit to headquarters. He told his officers that they had lost seven men killed and fifteen wounded, and the town had been summoned to surrender to His Britannic Majesty, only to receive a defiance from General Lincoln that he would defend the town to the last extremity.

CHAPTER

28

THE SHUTTLE

THE patterns of war were taking colour and form. The swiftly moving shuttle set strong patterns, little islands of colour under the heavy grey of the background, patterns dyed crimson with blood on this side and on that.

The Patriots struck and ran. After Lincoln surrendered, the heart went out of them. It took time to rally men and horses, food and clothing.

Lord Cornwallis took command of the British. Day after day his officers reported a sortie: the rebels ran, or so many rebels were taken prisoners. Lempriere's Point, with its beef cattle, had long been in the British hands, a sand-bank where the wind rioted, casting sand into eyes and ears and mouth. Mount Pleasant was silenced. Communication with Sullivan's Island was cut off. The Patriots ran after firing a dozen shots.

Major Ferguson moved in and relieved the navy at Fort Moultrie. This suited Anthony well. He could go to Charles Town now. A little later in the month they crossed into Charles Town. He found Michèle with very little trouble. She had managed to stay where he had left her. Like the little cat she was, she had made her place gay and comfortable. Anthony took his pleasure of her that night, and made arrangements for her to follow his army when they marched.

"I can sew for you, mend your clothes and cook you a good meal."

"I don't keep you near me for those purposes." Anthony laughed. She made him laugh. She was gay and blithe, except when he looked at another woman. She saw him one day walking with Lady Colleton and a saucy young maiden who was her guest.

That night Michèle bit and scratched, and Anthony laughed when he subdued her.

She never spoke of love, but her eyes worshipped him.

One day he got in a rage with her. It was when Michèle, who had gone to the market to purchase a fish, told him she had set eyes on Colonel Tarleton. "He was with my Lord Cornwallis and Lord Rawdon," she said. "They were all very fine gentlemen, but I liked Colonel Tarleton best. He has a bold, roving eye."

Allison gave her a cuff that knocked her from the chair to the floor. "Keep yourself out of Tarleton's sight," he said gruffly.

When she picked herself up from the floor, she smiled a little secret smile, as she dusted her skirts. Allison gloomed the rest of the evening, until they went to bed, when he forgot Tarleton and his sudden anger.

Michèle didn't forget. She hugged the thought to her heart. She was his woman now. She was necessary to him. She would move with him as the army moved. She would not lose him again.

She bought pieces of cloth and silk with the money he threw casually on the table from time to time. Her skilful needle fashioned a gown or two, not the gay colours she had revelled in before, but more sober and elegant like the ladies she saw in church, officers' wives for the most part.

Anthony noticed and expressed his approval. "By the living Jehoshaphat, girl, you can hold your own with the best of them! I've a notion to take you out on the Battery Parade one day."

Then he scowled. No, Tarleton might be in the city and cast his eyes upon her. Lord Cornwallis was safe. He was in love with an American widow in New York, the beauteous Madam Powell. He was too absorbed in war and making war, and in his feud with his commander, Sir Henry Clinton. Major Ferguson had his own tastes, of a more mousy type. But Michèle would brighten Tarleton's eye and cause his perpendicular lower lip to droop.

"Stay in your house and keep off the Battery," he told her when he left.

They got orders, moved at two o'clock in the morning, and marched to Colonel Thomas' plantation. The fields were beautiful with mimosa and passion-flower. As soon as they camped he sent a messenger for Michèle to join the waggon-train. He saw her there briefly. When they lay at Congaree stores and went to the Saluda Ferry, he knew they were marching for the North Carolina border.

Peter Huntley learned of the disaster of Charles Town ten days after the surrender. Sallee, the scout, met him on the road one evening near King's Mountain, just below the North Carolina line. Peter had been north into Virginia to get his dispatches, which were now useless. Sallee had the whole story. How he got the information, Peter did not know, but he assumed that Sallee had methods which he kept secret.

His story began on the eighth of May. Early that morning Sir Henry Clinton demanded the surrender of Charles Town. The American general asked for a cessation of hostilities from eight until twelve. Lincoln did not show proper respect, the British general declared after he had received what he called a very insolent request. He doubted if Lincoln intended to give up the town. At eight o'clock the British began a tremendous cannonade, enough to split the eardrums.

"So you were there!" Peter cried.

The scout grinned sheepishly. "Yes, I was there. No harm you knowing that now, I reckon. Anyway, shells fell all night and musketry too. Then the town was set on fire, first a small group of houses. General Lincoln sent another flag. Sir Henry was supposed to cease firing and he and the Admiral held another meeting."

"Ah! So you were on the British side of the river."

"Who said I ben't? Said I was there, didn't I?"

"Good fellow, Sallee! I only wish I had been with you."

"On the twelfth the gates were thrown open and General Leslie marched in with the British Grenadiers, Seventh, Sixty-third and Sixty-fourth Regiments. They levelled the American flag to the dust, God damn them to hell!"

Peter had never seen Sallee angered before. It lasted only a few minutes, then he dropped back to his slow woodsman's drawl. "The British standard was hoisted and there was a hellish amount of noise and rejoicing, till a magazine blew up and scairt a lot of people. The British thought some American spies lingered in the city." He chewed his wad of tobacco in silence for a time, then spat it far out on the ground. "Shouldn' be surprised."

Peter raised his eyebrows, but Sallee's face was blank. "Hessians moved in, and Major Ferguson's Americans. God damn them, fighting agin' their own people! New Yorkers, but some Carolinians." He got up from the stump. "They say he's a proper fine officer, that Major Ferguson, treats prisoners all right—no lopping off ears or anything."

Peter was thinking about supper and a bed. He asked Sallee where he was staying.

"Over near King's place below the mountain, about half mile down the road. That's where my family lives."

"I didn't know you had a family," Peter said, surprised.

"A sister and two brothers, youngsters mostly. They stay in a house on King's farm." He hesitated. "We ain't got much, but you're mighty welcome, Captain."

Peter thanked him. "I am grateful," he said, as he followed his guide. He walked, leading his horse.

The King house was at the foot of the flat-topped table mountain, which rose to three or four hundred feet out of the floor of the valley, a well-shaped mountain, with open top, one end lower than the other, as though a bit of the rock had slipped off in some past age. It was well timbered, with dense growth up the sides.

"A fair mountain for a look out," Sallee said, catching Peter's eye. "It's all flat on top, like a long racquet. The handle points this way," he continued, pointing southwest.

"Excellent for a signal fire."

"Aye, I've thought of that. It won't be long now, Captain, I'm a-thinkin'."

"Everything is in readiness?" Peter asked.

"Aye. I saw Enos Dye. He says his men know just where to go when the signals are given."

"Good! Good!"

They came to a clearing. A long low house stood in it with two porches, front and rear, made from an extension of the roof. Smoke was rising from the chimney. It was neat and well cared for, surrounded by a rail fence, with flowers growing inside. A house for chickens was behind a low barn and the well-house stood at one side. The road to the mountain passed the door.

When they came in sight of the door, Sallee lifted his voice in a call like a "painter's" wail.

Two young boys, between ten and fourteen, rushed out on the porch and ran down the dusty road, letting out whoops of delight. A slim young girl, wearing a blue frock with a snowy white fichu, came to the door. Her blond hair hung in two long braids over her shoulders. She shaded her eyes with the palm of her hand as she looked in their direction. She waved vigorously and went inside.

"She'll stir up a mess of corn-cakes," Sallee said with an engaging grin.

The boys stopped when they saw a stranger and progressed more sedately, but their freckled faces shone with delight. They, too, were tow-heads. They caught Sallee's hands and bowed a little when he mentioned Peter's name.

"This is William and this is Perry," Sallee said. "How are you fellows and how is Virginia?"

"We're fine. Perry has sixty chickens, Jamie, and I have a duck and a drake. And our sow had six the last litter. I raised all but one."

"Perry is our farmer," Sallee explained.

"Perry?"

Sallee explained. "My mother called him Pierre, but none of us can twist our tongues, so we call him Perry."

The girl came out of the house. She spoke to Peter pleasantly, with a quiet, self-contained air. She was like Sallee in that.

"I've brought a guest for the night. Have you a bed for him?" Sallee asked.

"Yes, certainly," Virginia said. "I must have sensed we were going to have guests for supper. I jugged a chicken today, a nice fat hen."

They went inside the cabin. It was one large room, with a bed in one corner, a table set for supper in another. A ladder led to the loft. The kitchen was a lean-to, attached to the large room. Everything was spotlessly clean.

Sallee, whose name Jamie Peter had heard for the first time from the boys, led him to the well to wash up for supper. Virginia had supplied them with towels.

They sat down at the table. Jamie said grace.

"The mountain has been clouded all week," Virginia told Jamie, "crying, perhaps, and hiding her head. But this morning the mists cleared away and she smiled, and I knew that meant good fortune." She smiled happily at her brother.

The food was good. After dishes were cleared away, the girl put fresh sheets on the bed, and pulled a screen made of criss-cross latticework in front of it. It was the guest's bed, the boys told him. They slept upstairs always. They had two rooms with little side-windows.

Peter slept like the dead. The sun was well up when he woke. He smelled bacon cooking and he was hungry. He heard Virginia and Jamie talking in the kitchen.

Jamie said, "I would not trust anyone of that family, Virginia. They're Tories, and you know it."

"Henry isn't. He's a Whig. His brothers treat him mean because he went Whig."

"Well, be careful, won't you, Virgie? Bad times are coming and I don't trust anyone. Don't tell folks around here about me coming and going. Nor about Captain Huntley, neither."

"He's a pretty man. Is he Whig?"

Peter heard James Sallee laugh. "Wouldn't have thought of calling Captain pretty now, and him so brown and hard."

"I don't mean that. I mean pretty-mannered, like a gentleman."

The dishes rattled, pans banged. Peter dressed behind his screen and went out the front door to the pump.

They left after breakfast. Peter returned to Salisbury, hoping to connect with Major Avery for further orders. Sallee went along the border to do "a spell o' lookin'."

Major Avery came into Michael Braun's the second day after Peter. He had little news from Charles Town, not so much as Sallee had told Peter.

"A pity, a great pity that General Lincoln stayed to defend the city," Avery said. "He would have been more useful following Marion than in the hands of the British."

"Who is going to block Cornwallis' passage to North Carolina?" Peter asked.

"God knows. General Gates is coming, or is somewhere in the state. But I've no faith in him. He's a boastful boor, with no great military knowledge."

"He defeated Burgoyne."

"Yes. We've heard that often enough. I'm on the side of the officers who believe that Burgoyne defeated Burgoyne. But let us have supper and go over these maps again. The General is very well pleased with your report on those cattle depots. We are counting on the British following the route you indicated. Since you no longer report to General Lincoln, you will roam about the border counties, and meet me here at stated intervals. You are to watch border Tories and have eyes peeled for Ferguson's American Legion."

July passed, hot, dusty and waterless. August was the same. Corn shrivelled in the heat, streams dried up, gardens and fields were parched.

The Tories grew bolder, the closer Cornwallis' forerunners approached. Patrick Ferguson's Legion lay in a field at Ninety-six the last of June. A few soldiers went out and encountered the Whigs on the South Fork of the Catawba. They escaped by swimming the mill-pond. Major Ferguson sent out forty of his Loyalists. They marched seventy miles and returned to Ninety-six.

Sallee reported to Peter, when he met him at Colonel McDowell's camp, "They're setting in camp at Ninety-six. They parade and drill and drill. Those Tories ain't up to much parading though they can shoot. They fight with the Britishers, who look down on them as military men. I lay in the attic of a house, one night, near the Saluda Run. Two of Ferguson's officers came for shelter. There was a woman there, and one of the scoundrels made advances, but she held him off with her quick tongue. One was a doctor named Johnson; he was a gaunt fellow. The other's name was Captain Allison."

Peter's exclamation of astonishment caused Sallee to pause.

"Know anything about him, Captain?"

"Nothing good. He is a scoundrel. He is Jeremiah Morse."

"Ah! So that's it. That is why he knows this country."

Peter did not say anything about his own personal quarrel with Allison. "When did you see him, Sallee?"

Sallee calculated. "Must have been a month back, round the ninth or tenth of July, if I got my head-calendar working."

"What was he doing?"

"Scouting about the country, out from Ninety-six encampment. He's close to Ferguson, they tell me, mighty close. I'll get more about him next trip. I think Ferguson's going to be disappointed; likewise my Lord Cornwallis. They think this country will give them thousands of Tory followers. Well, they won't get more'n a few hundred, and mighty puny specimens they be."

Sallee went on. Peter had a conference with Colonel McDowell that night. McDowell told him he had heard that Major Ferguson and forty or fifty of his volunteers and a hundred militiamen were marching up through the mountains to the head of Cane Creek with the idea of surprising him. When his Intelligence informed him of the sortie, McDowell had moved his men. However, they had engaged a part of the divided company, taken fourteen prisoners, wounded a few Tories and killed one.

"Ferguson swears to smoke us out," McDowell said, his dark eyes glinting with amusement. "They are poor mountaineers, these British. They fight better in ranks."

"Where are they now, sir?" Peter asked.

"They returned. The last news we had was that they were still at Walker's plantation."

Peter asked McDowell's advice. "How long will it take to get those Indian fighters into your camp?"

"We must allow three weeks at least. Some of them must walk many a weary mile before they reach camp."

At midnight they came to the conclusion that the time had come to put the signal fires on the mountains and send out the messengers. Two days later, those fires would be lighted on Tryon Mountain, Mount Wright, Table Mountain, New River Head, Meadow, and King's Mountain.

The signal of fire by night and a smoke column by day would send messengers to the back-countrymen to rendezvous at McDowell's camp near Quaker Meadows.

Peter Huntley set out for King's Mountain. He was to light the signal fire, if Sallee was not there. Enos Dye would be at Tryon Mountain, other selected men at the other mountain stations. Some men of the far mountains would need a month to get to their rendezvous with Colonels Shelby, Sevier and the McDowells. Indian fighters all, they could all be relied upon, Peter had been assured by the General.

It was late evening when he rode inside the rail fence that surrounded Sallee's place. For the last third of a mile the hounds had been barking. When Peter dismounted he found Sallee waiting for him. He was alone. In answer to Peter's question, he said that his family had gone to King's place for a day or two. He gave no reason and seemed disquieted.

"We will go up the mountain tomorrow night and light the fire," Peter said.

Sallee thought they might better go in the afternoon, so that they could see to the timber for the fire. "Even in September it is cold on the mountain," he said.

The climb was not difficult. They were at the top before two. Peter looked about him. He was surprised at the extent of the open space.

"Room enough for an army to camp. An excellent spot. One can see in every direction. An enemy would have difficulty approaching."

Sallee looked at Peter for a moment. "I had forgotten you were trained to mass fighting, Captain. Look. See all that scrub? That heavily forested side? That precipitous rocky stretch? It would be impossible to defend."

Peter shook his head. "I see what you mean, but I still think it could be defended for days, even weeks, if there were food and water."

Sallee said nothing more. He set out with his axe to cut fire-wood.

Peter helped until they had a pile large enough to run them through the night. They watched the sun go down, a great ball of fire, behind the mountains.

When night fell they sat down and ate the cold corn-dodgers and bacon Sallee had brought from the house. The heavens turned slowly from blue to velvet blackness, and the stars came out. The evening star, bright as a lanthorn, shone above the horizon. Red Mars and Jupiter and the other planets swung in their circles. Peter lay on the blanket he had carried up on his shoulder, and gazed at the sky. The stars were close to him, their brightness stronger than at low levels. Perhaps it was only imagination. Perhaps it was that at low levels there were obstructions to clear vision. He looked into the valley; little pin-points of light showed where the few scattered houses lay. It was the dark of the moon. They had chosen this time so that the fires could be seen more readily.

Peter waited until the trees across the mountain-top were no longer trees but a mass of shadow. He found himself waiting with a strange sense of suspense, as one waits for the first shot in a battle. Perhaps that was what this signal fire would become—the first shot in a long series of battles.

He said to Sallee, who sat a little apart, "I think it is time now."

"Yes, Captain."

"Will you light the fire?"

Sallee hesitated. "I think the honour should be the Captain's." There was a stiff formality in his voice and in his words, as if his thoughts paralleled Peter's own.

Peter laughed slightly. "Let us light it together. You take the north, I will take the south."

"Danger will come from the south," Sallee said. He struck flint. Peter's missed fire. He tried again, holding a little bundle of dried leaves and twigs close. It caught and blazed a little and he pushed it against the dry wood. Sallee's side of the fire leaped into flame. The north was blazing high. That was symbolic, Peter thought, as he fanned his small flame with his cap. If danger comes from the south, it is to the north we look for our defence, to the north and to the west.

"I'll stand the first watch, Sallee. I have no wish to sleep."

Sallee lay on the ground in his blanket. In a few minutes he was asleep, breathing evenly.

Peter sat by the fire, his arms about his knees. It was so quiet—

only an occasional flutter of wings as some night-bird flew across the mountain-top. Far below in the floor of the valley a dog barked sharply. Then silence came, the great profound silence that belongs to high places. Peter thought of the eagle he had seen planing in the sky. Only eagles were above him, between him and the stars. He fell to dreaming of the events that had passed so swiftly these last troublous days. He thought of Queen Anne's Town, of Angela, and the little letter he had safe in his pocket at that moment. It was only a few lines written, he felt sure, at the suggestion of her mother, and curiously childlike, like the letter of a very immature girl. She had been quite ill, but she was improving. Her mother was in good health. Mr. Ferrier was away on matters that had to do with the war. The children asked for him, and she was his very sincere friend, Angela. Peter sighed. It seemed all so far away. He got up and pushed a long log farther into the fire. The flame shot high again.

He fell to thinking what this flame meant. It would be seen for a long distance, far enough for another watcher to light his beacon, and from that on to another, until light had reached the northern boundary. He thought of the woodsmen in the forest who waited to see the beacon. They would move out across the mountains, following paths known only to their kind. The word would go out, "Danger from the south! Danger from the south!" Then from little farms and clearings woodsmen would hack their way westward through the great forests. They would turn from the plough, lay down the axe and, shouldering their long rifles, would strike out, each to his own rendezvous, under his own leader, Sevier, Shelby, the McDowells, Cleveland. Those would be names to remember.

Where would the battle be fought? He wondered. There might be many battles, or only one. No one could tell. But there must be a turning-point. Cornwallis' men sweeping through South Carolina, Tarleton ravaging, raping, killing . . . it *must* come to an end.

A feeling of helplessness, of utter discouragement, swept over him. Men were fighting and dying. Weary, disheartened men hid in the slime of fetid swamps, ill and wet and filled with the horrid fear of the weary. And he sat here quietly, giving nothing, nothing, to the great drama of the war! He got up and kicked viciously at a log. The charred edge snapped and broke and he was enveloped in smoke. The wind changed. He moved about and stood staring into the blackness of the valley. How far away were they? Not more than two hundred miles. When would the thin column of redcoats wind up the river valleys. He wondered how many people were raising their eyes to the mountain-top. Tory or Whig, it didn't matter. They would wonder only for a moment.

Emerald eyes looked at him from the black shadow, two feet or more above the ground—a timber wolf, a red fox, or perhaps a panther, though he had heard no blood-chilling cries.

He threw a piece of wood in the direction of the emerald sparks and they disappeared. He stood looking to the west. He thought he saw a light that flickered, far off in the mountains. He watched for a time, turned his head away and looked again. It was brighter now. His pulses leaped. It was a signal fire answering their fire. God be thanked, the light was moving on! The depressing thoughts fell away from his unhappy soul. It was the beginning, not the end. The light was moving on and on, the signal fire of war. He threw more logs on the fire. He was reckless with fuel. He wanted the lonely watchers on high mountain-tops to know that they were not alone. They were a part of a great company of men who were marching to defend their own. Words formed on his lips: "Let us look to the mountains." He spoke aloud, not knowing. "I will lift up mine eyes unto the hills whence cometh my strength."

Sallee stirred and sat up. Peter caught his arm and whirled him about until he stood facing the western signal. It was rising higher now, in answer to his. For a long time the two of them stood silent, each thinking his own thoughts, and beyond, in the high places of the forest, men kept watch with them.

Peter Huntley's days and nights were spent on the march. Again, an army of one, he roamed the mountains and the rolling hills of the sand country.

It was deep in September before he heard that North Carolinians had met North Carolinians on the battle-field, Tory against Whig neighbour. Davie's five hundred had joined up with Sumter's three hundred and made a combined attack on a British outpost at Hanging Rock. Here on the fifth of August, branded forever as "the unnatural fifth," neighbour fought neighbour, brother met brother in battle, for Bryan's Loyalists and Hamilton's regiment of Tories were at the British garrison. The Whigs surprised and took the garrison, but while they plundered, the British rallied, and the Whigs were forced to retreat minus horses and men.

Peter had the story of the battle when he came into Salisbury after weeks in the field. He heard then that Gates had come to Carolina and experienced a major disaster at Camden, a defeat so devastating that it almost wrecked the spirit of resistance in the South.

Gates, against advice, set about intercepting a British convoy in a country deserted ever since the defeat of Buford. The Tories held this country. There was no food for man or horse from day to day, but Gates was stubborn. He was new to the country, underestimated Lord Rawdon's force, and in every way laid the ground for his own defeat. Not only had he been defeated, but he had forced General Smallwood's Marylanders, Caswell's North Carolinians, a Continental regiment from Delaware, and Stevens' Virginians to take the brunt. DeKalb, a good military man, was ordered to cover the right, while General Gates placed himself in a safe and comfortable position behind the front lines and well protected by the rear-guard.

Cornwallis' right wing, with Colonel Webster, made a furious surprise assault. Stevens' men fired a few rounds, then threw down their arms and ran. Caswell's militia, threatened front and flank, followed. Stevens and Caswell, with their officers, tried repeatedly to rally their men, but there was no cavalry to charge and give them support.

The shameful panic became a rout. General Rutherford, of the North Carolinians, was wounded. General Gregory threw his men into position, but the line gave. Baron DeKalb made the last stand for victory, but he fell, his body pierced by a dozen wounds. Dr. Williamson, Surgeon-General with Caswell, set up a station for prisoners and his own men, but the confusion was so great that little could be done. More than a third of the Continentals lay killed or wounded on the field.

Gates did not wait to learn the outcome of the battle. Some said he did not draw rein until he reached Hillsborough, two hundred and thirty miles away, which he reached in seventy-five hours. Near Charlotte Town he met Major Davie and some of his troopers. Gates shouted the story of the disaster.

Davie answered, "Who will bury the dead?"

"Let the dead bury the dead," shouted the general, whom some members of Congress wanted to supplant Washington. "Let the dead bury the dead," he repeated, and galloped away toward his camp at Hillsborough. Even as their general galloped down the Trading Path to a safe haven, some soldiers still stood firm, but all the raw troops had fled, and the bright banner of the Southern Army lay in the dust.

From then on there was no stopping the redcoats. From short

sorties into the Whig country, from cattle and fodder raids to the larger engagements, the British were on the march.

Davie's cavalry lay at Charlotte Town. By day and by night they had but one object, to annoy the enemy. With two hundred men they could do no more than that.

Lord Cornwallis' army moved slowly and inexorably forward, with Tarleton's dragoons riding ahead to cut the path and terrorize the people. On the twenty-fourth of September Cornwallis' army crossed the North Carolina line and the second invasion of the state had begun.

Salisbury was in the midst of alarums from the day the fleeing general rode through the streets without pausing. Soldiers passed one another on the narrow roads. Some were marching to the border, others were fleeing. Talk was loud and boastful, or quiet and fearful. "Sumner and Davidson have two thousand men in Mecklenburg County, but the British have thousands of trained men, who stand their ground." There was fear in their hearts, fear that they might be in the path of the marching army.

Peter heard these rumours, and more. He tried to sift the truth from the terror-lies, but he could not. Of Ferguson he heard nothing further than that Lord Cornwallis had detached him on the first of the month and sent him to the west side of the mountains. Colonel Williams and his little band of South Carolinians had followed, harassing sentries, cutting out waggon-trains, ambushing, plundering.

Peter waited a day for Major Avery, and then, after leaving a message with Braun, departed to go toward Gilbert Town, supposedly Ferguson's objective. He began to lose sight of the war as a whole. He began to wonder whether all the work he and the guides had been doing for the past months would go for naught. In the morning he would leave, riding the new horse Michael had bought for him.

In the morning he found Salisbury streets crowded from house to house with dishevelled, dusty soldiers, half asleep, riding on jaded, weary horses—Davie's cavalry.

Cornwallis was at Charlotte Town, in possession of the Hornet's Nest.

The street took up the cry. The town rang with the words, repeated over and over, from mouth to mouth, until it became a great roar of warning, "Cornwallis is coming! Cornwallis is coming!"

It was a battle-cry, not a cry to rally men to arms but to disperse men in flight to the mountains.

CHAPTER
29

THE LONG MARCH

WITHOUT orders of any sort, Peter rode southward. The feeling was strong in him that he must go to King's Mountain and try to find Sallee.

All day he was passing soldiers on the march, militia, Continentals. They were not fleeing from Cornwallis now, but marching out of range of the British advance. Peter had two alternatives, to go to Quaker Meadows Camp or to strike farther south, after he had tried to reach Sallee. He questioned a dozen soldiers. No one had heard of Major Ferguson's corps, or been in contact with Colonel McDowell.

One weary Continental fell out by the roadside to accept a twist of tobacco. "You'd better turn around and make back north. Don't go out seeking the British. Believe me, they are soldiers and they fight." He spat his wad, staining the dust on the road. "We got a runnin' general. By God, I bet he can run faster than any man in the army! Now, ye looks a proper smart woodsman—what do ye think of a general who quit the field before the Continentals broke and hadn't planned a rendezvous in case of retreat?"

"Not much," Peter commented. He remembered Gates unpleasantly because of the Conway Cabal.

The man shouldered his gun. "Well, I'll be moving, son. It's a far piece to Salisbury and farther still to Hillsborough." He slapped his thigh. "God a'mighty! I bet Gates is up in Philadelphy by now, tellin' Congress what bad soldiers they gave him." He moved off, along with other weary marchers.

Near sundown Peter turned from the Trading Path and took a side-road. He had no desire to run into a British advance-guard. Toward evening, from a little knoll he saw a file of horsemen riding toward him. They were half a mile away. He didn't like the look of their coats. They were riding briskly. He started for cover, but they had seen him and their horses broke into a gallop. Best to brazen it out. His well-worn mountain clothes, his scrubby beard and shaggy hair might be disguise enough to fool them; at least he had no dispatches and nothing to conceal. He pulled up his horse and waited.

Two officers and three men. They pulled up. One of the officers rode forward. He was young.

Peter thought there was bewilderment behind his arrogance. "What are you doing on this path?" he demanded.

Peter shifted the wad of tobacco which he had hurriedly placed in his mouth when they drew near, and spat it out. "Goin' home," he said shortly.

"Where's your home?"

"Over there." Peter waved in a westerly direction.

"Be more explicit," snapped the officer. Peter thought, He's frightened about something.

"Let me question him." A second officer rode up. He spoke naturally. "Do you know this country?"

"Wel-l-l, can't say no," drawled Peter.

The man took a little map from his pocket. "Show us where we stand." Peter grinned inwardly; they were lost. He took the paper and studied it, taking in more than he was supposed to see. After a short wait he put his finger on a spot. "We stand here. That's Buffalo Creek yonder." He pointed east. "Caudle Creek's there. Down below, a spell, is Rocky River."

The two officers bent their heads over the map. The first speaker said, "Shall we ask him, Doctor?" His voice was low but Peter's ears were sharp.

"Why not?" said the doctor. "I don't relish wandering about this country after dark."

"Are you a Whig?" the second officer snapped.

Peter looked at him vacantly.

"Are you on the side of the Whigs or the Tories?"

Peter shook his head. "I be mountain man."

"Are you King's man?"

Peter's face brightened. "Aye."

The first officer said, "I don't trust him."

The doctor responded, "No need to trust him, but I'll take a venture." He turned to Peter. "Which direction is Colonel Alexander's?"

Peter managed a blank stare. He was enjoying this.

"A mill. Alexander's Mill."

A silly smile came over Peter's countenance. " 'Tis Xander's Mill ye want. Yes, sir. Shall I show ye the way? 'Tis nae so far from the path we be on. I be goin' part way."

"Go ahead," the first officer said. He's still suspicious, Peter thought. He wanted to allay their suspicions so that he might overhear some conversation of interest. But they spoke little and in such low tones he could not make out the words. The only thing he made out was that they were an advance foraging party. He must think of some way to warn Colonel Alexander. Nothing occurred to him until they came to the spot where the Trading Path crossed Buffalo Creek. Here he reined his horse. He pointed eastward toward Fiffer's place.

"Over yon is the mill," he said, "straight by that path. My way lies over there."

The officers hesitated. The doctor said, "Shall we keep him, Fletcher? Take him to Major Ferguson?"

"We won't see the major for a day, maybe two. I see no reason to be burdened. He's just a stupid mountain man." He turned to Peter. "How far is it to the mill?"

"A short spell. It's a good mill," Peter volunteered, "and he's got black cattle, he has."

That settled them, as Peter intended it should, and they rode away. Peter watched them for a time, then went on at the same jog-trot he had employed before, until he was out of sight over a little hill. He raised his horse to a gallop. He hoped there would be time for Colonel Alexander's men to drive the stock toward the hills before the party got to Fiffer's and found that they had been tricked. But maybe they wouldn't find out. Fiffer's was deserted, with only a Negro or two and a few scrawny cattle left. Perhaps they would camp the night. He urged his horse on.

He found an overlooker at Colonel Alexander's and told his story. At once the place broke into feverish activity. Horses from the barns, cattle from the lot, began their drive toward the hills, the overseer and some of the men following with a farm drag to obliterate the hoof-prints and droppings. Peter went with them as far as the creek, a small branch of Rocky River. Here the herders drove the stock into the stream. The animals waded into the water and headed up-stream. When they were all in, the drag came into use. Nothing was left save old cattle traces.

Peter left then. It would not do to be around, if the British foragers found out they had been tricked. Nor would it do to go south that night—he might run into other parties. He, too, set his horse into the water and followed the stream for some time. Then he turned north, doubling back. He lay that night among the graves at Poplar Tent Churchyard. He hoped that it was too late in the season for snakes, but ticks bit him and he slept little. By daybreak he was on the way south again, this time by a path that led through the Catawba Indian Town. He had been that way before; he could go through the forest until he reached Broad River.

He rode swiftly. The feeling that he must get to Sallee was strong and impelling. Sallee would know where Ferguson's troops were. He was sure now that they were moving with some definite plan, fanning out from Charlotte Town, searching for McDowell's little army. Peter hoped that Colonel Shelby had found him by now, and that the Indian fighters had come down from the Yadkin and the back-country. Sallee would know; he would have been scouting from McDowell's camp these three weeks past. He rode on his lonely way, trying to forget the faces of the weary, toiling men he had seen marching along the Trading Path. He would find Sallee at King's Mountain. He must keep moving so that he would not miss him.

Ferguson's dragoons were on the march. He had a score to settle with one of Ferguson's dragoons, a long overdue score. The leather boot of his long rifle scraped against his leg.

Settle a score? Without a sword? He cursed softly.

Major Ferguson, having had intelligence of the movement of the over-mountain men, had decided to move his troops to a more protected camp than the one at Gilbert Town.

"Never two nights in succession in one place," Anthony Allison complained to Dr. Johnson, who shared his tent with him.

"Little you care where you lie, so long as it is with a woman," Johnson retorted.

Anthony laughed good-humouredly. "These mountain roads are rough. The waggon sways too much for comfort."

"You're a fool, Allison, a complete fool about that wench. She'll bring you bad luck. She's a witch."

"A pretty witch, you must admit, and a very homey little body. Look how she keeps my shirts and stock and my uniform pressed."

"You are as great a dandy as Banastre Tarleton," the doctor said with disgust, and walked away. Tempers were wearing thin from long marching.

Anthony rode back to the waggon-train. He opened the back flap of a waggon and looked in. Michèle lay sleeping, wrapped in an army blanket. He poked her in the ribs with his musket. "Wake up, my pet. It's time to be on the march again."

Michèle turned and opened her eyes, heavy and dark with sleep. She saw Anthony. Throwing the blanket back, she got to her knees, her hands on the tail gate of the waggon. "Anthony," she whispered.

He put his horse close and leaned over. Glancing about, he made sure there was no one near by to listen. "Have Ben drive off ahead of the other waggons, when we start for the next camp. When you come to a small farmhouse at the foot of a mountain, have him pull in and wait until I come up. I have a map to give directions. Show it to no one. Do you understand?"

"I understand. What is the name of the farmer?"

"Sallee. It is on the farm of a man named King."

"Where is the map?"

He said, "Come close." He put his hand inside the waggon flap and pushed a folded paper into the bosom of her gown, fondling her warm breasts for a moment. Eagerly she covered his hand with both of hers.

"You're a devil," he said, "a very devil."

She showed her even white teeth. "But you like devils, is it not so, M'sieu? To match the devil in you, yes?"

A trumpet sounded. There was the sound of voices, men calling out. He withdrew his hand quickly. "Remember, no one is to see the map. I want you to have a good camp, for we may rest several days, even a week." He wheeled his horse and rode away. Michèle sat back on her haunches, watching him. A fine strong figure of a man was her Anthony, but demanding, very demanding. She had been comfortable, these past weeks, ever since she got rid of the woman who rode with her. She didn't like a companion, a woman companion, so she made it unpleasant until the wench was glad to take up her abode in another waggon. Now they would move on again. It was wearisome, moving constantly. She looked forward to days in the same spot, when she could get out and wander through the woods and bathe in some cool stream.

She heard the jangle of harness, and Ben, the waggoner, came up, riding sidewise on one of the grey mules.

Michèle spoke to him, giving him the captain's message. Ben was a rosy-cheeked Sussex man with a profound loyalty to Captain Allison.

He nodded. He would hasten to hook up and manoeuvre his waggon into first place.

"The captain always looks ahead, so we can have a good camp," he said with satisfaction. By the time he had backed the mules and hooked them up to the wagon, the second bugle sounded the swift staccato call, "Forward march!" Waggon wheels creaked and began to roll. Michèle made herself comfortable, half lying, half sitting on the bedding spread on the floor of the waggon. From her position she could see the blue sky showing above the pine trees. Life was very good, she thought. Then she quickly made horns with her fingers. One must never speak of good fortune, lest Fortune wrap her draperies over her head and turn her face away.

Major Ferguson cared well for his men and protected them when he could. He suffered now for lack of trained soldiers. He was saddled with Loyalists who came into his camp from heaven knew where, undisciplined, untaught. They were a menace. But the mountain men constituted a heavier menace. Ever since he had marched from Ninety-six, in skirmishes and at camp on the Pacolet, at Thicketty Fort, at Wofford's and Musgrove's Mill, and on the western waters of the Watauga, they had crept up and shot his sentries. They had stampeded his cattle and run down his forage detachment.

By a Whig prisoner named Phillips, taken at Musgrove's and released, he sent word to McDowell's camp that if they did not desist from their opposition to British arms, he would march his army over the mountains, hang the leaders and lay the country waste with fire and sword.

The messenger went direct to Shelby. "Come and be damned to them!" was the immediate answer.

Shelby rode post-haste to a horse-race, forty miles away, and found Colonel Sevier.

The signal fires had been seen. Men were poised and ready for the last signal.

Between placing bets and watching final heats of the races, last plans were made.

Andrew Hampton's men, who had retired before Ferguson on the Upper Catawba, were camped on the Watauga.

Colonel William Campbell, of Washington County, Virginia, just above the line, was notified. "Rendezvous at Sycamore Flats on the Watauga!" was the rallying cry.

Enos Dye brought in the word that Cornwallis planned to march from Charlotte Town to Salisbury for a junction with Ferguson's corps, incite the southern Indians, invade Holston and Watauga settlements, and go on into Virginia, squeezing North Carolina in a giant trap.

The mountain people had little money and few horses, but they were roused to swift action. Men came through the forests by twos and threes, by small detachments, by companies. They marched silently through the dim aisles of the sheltering forests. Down old forgotten paths along river and creek and dry run, they came, each with his long Deckard rifle slung over his shoulder, each with his blanket and his cup and his little poke of dried corn. They moved silently, as men long trained to the forest hunt. They were brown, lean men, hardened by the hills and the sun and the wind. They slept on the ground by day, and moved swiftly down the known trails by night. Theirs was a holy cause, a holy war, for they were coming back to defend "Old North," and in his heart each silent, inarticulate mountain man loved "Old North."

The leaders sat in council on the night of the twenty-fifth of September. Young Campbell acted as secretary and counted the men from Washington County, Virginia, under Colonel William Campbell, 400; from Sullivan County, North Carolina, Colonel Isaac Shelby, 240; from Washington County, North Carolina, under Colonel John Sevier, 240; from Burke and Rutherford, under Colonel Charles McDowell, 160; from Wilkes and Surry Counties, under Colonel Benjamin Cleveland and Major Joseph Winston, 350.

That gave them thirteen hundred and ninety men, with others trickling in over the mountains, and Colonel Williams, whom they were to meet at the Cowpens, marching up from South Carolina.

Then some difficulty arose. All the leaders were of equal rank and there was no general officer to take command. After a spirited argument, it was decided to send Colonel Charles McDowell to headquarters to invite General Sumner or General Davidson to lead them. The colonel would leave his men under Major James McDowell.

Some said it was a trumped-up plan to get Colonel McDowell out of the way. Shelby said he was too indecisive for such a mission. There was some dissatisfaction also with the way he marched and countermarched the men without getting any nearer the enemy.

Meanwhile Colonel William Campbell of Virginia was put in command of the "Colonels' Army," because he had come the longest distance and had the most men. This decision anguished many Carolinians. They did not want a Virginian to lead them anywhere, at any time, particularly into battle.

They broke camp to march over mountain paths clogged with snow, to push their way through deep forests and to ford icy streams.

A service was said as the sun rose. Samuel Doak, rangy and hard from long years of pioneer preaching in mountain settlements, held service. He reached his long arms heavenward and asked the Heavenly Father to bless each soldier who that day moved out to meet the enemy. *"The Sword of the Lord and of Gideon!"* he cried.

"The Sword of the Lord and of our Gideons!" cried the sturdy mountaineers.

They followed Bright's Trace, ascending the mountains through a gap between Yellow and Roan Mountains. The higher hills were snow-covered, and shoe-mouth-deep. Crab Orchard lay far below them, lovely and verdant. On they went into the rare air of the high hills. That night they camped at a summit, the Bald of the Yellow, a table-land large enough for men to drill on.

Two men slipped away here. This desertion caused deep anxiety among the colonels. Some blamed Sevier, whose men they were. "We are betrayed!" they cried. "They will go direct to Ferguson." After a consultation that lasted far into the night, they changed their route and went through a northerly depression, instead of the gap. They would outwit the deserters and any spies Ferguson might send looking for them.

On they marched, to meet other men marching down from the north. That great mountain of a man Cleveland—who like to boast that he descended from a natural son of Oliver Cromwell and a beauty of the court of the first Charles named Elizabeth Cleveland—brought his people down along a ridge to a junction with McDowell's men.

Colonel Williams and the South Carolinians waited at Flint Hill. He had recruited on the slogan, "A call to arms! Beef, bread and potatoes!" Some said he promised also the privilege of plundering Tories—all the Negroes and horses they could take. It was a tall tale, not verified.

The night they camped in the gap of South Mountain, Colonel Cleveland stood before the troops and asked them to seat themselves in a circle. The other commanders stood by to listen, Campbell, Shelby, Sevier, McDowell and Winston.

Cleveland, who had a way with him, took off his hat and, looking from one to the other of the men seated on the ground, said: "My brave fellows, I have come to tell you the news. The enemy is at hand, and we must up and at them. Now is the time for every man of you to do his country a priceless service—such as shall lead your children to exult in the fact that their fathers were the conquerors of Ferguson. When the pinch comes, I shall be with you. But if any of you shrink from sharing in the battle and the glory, you can now have the opportunity of backing out, and leaving; and you shall have a few minutes for considering the matter."

Major McDowell strode forward. "My men, what kind of story will you who back out have to relate when you get home, leaving your braver comrades to fight the battle and gain the victory?"

Shelby had his moment. "You who desire to decline will, when the word is given, march three steps to the rear."

The word was given. No man moved. A cheer went up from the militiamen. Every man was proud of his neighbour. Those men from the back-country had no intention of slipping away. They knew only one command—to go forward.

Colonel Shelby stood easily before them, a little smile on his austere face. "I am heartily glad to see you to a man resolve to fight your country's foes. When we encounter the enemy, don't wait for the word of command. Let each one of you be your own officer, availing himself of every advantage. If in the woods, shelter yourselves, and give them Indian play; advance from tree to tree, pressing the enemy, killing and disabling all you can. Your officers will shrink from no danger—they will be constantly with you. Be on the alert."

He looked at the mountain men as he made his charge, and they answered him with a cheer. "From tree to tree . . . fire and kill"—they knew that kind of fighting of old.

Colonel Cleveland and Major McDowell brought out the liquor. "Men on the march must have their treat," Cleveland said with his great laugh.

This was the night of October the fourth. Early next morning they were on the road again.

On the third of October Ferguson's men lay in camp on the Second Broad, on Sandy Run. It was there that Peter stumbled onto their camp. It was dusk when the sentry detached himself from the shadows and challenged him.

Peter Huntley's heart rose and pressed against his throat. His tongue clung to the roof of his mouth. The sentry challenged a second time.

Trusting to the dark and the trees to obscure him, Peter made no move. A shot whizzed by and missed him by inches. The sentry made no further move. After a time Peter extricated himself from his hiding-place in the low bushes and began a slow retreat. He was glad that he and Sallee had approached the British camp on foot.

He wondered what had become of Sallee. He was not sure that he liked the woodsman's plan to walk boldly into camp as a Tory who had come to join up with Ferguson's corps.

He could get inside the camp readily enough, but to get out again was another matter. Peter moved with more caution now. Very slowly he skirted the fringe of small trees. It was an orderly camp, well set up in soldierly fashion, but why was Ferguson lingering here at Tate's plantation for two days, when the Whigs were pursuing him? Peter could not figure this out.

He became bolder and pressed toward the waggons which were pulled up in close formation. By the fire-light he saw men lying on the ground, their arms beside them. This meant they expected an attack. He let himself down on the ground at the edge of the fire-light, his face hidden in his folded arms. He had no fear of detection now. Back-country Tories moved in and out of Ferguson's camp. If he were questioned, he would be an over-mountain Tory, like Sallee.

As he lay there he heard a commotion and men scrambled to their feet. An officer's "At ease, men!" broke the silence. Peter did not move. He lay inert, like an exhausted man asleep, but his pulses were racing. It was a voice he knew well—Jeremiah Morse's voice. He peered out between his arms. No doubt of it. The man's face was clear in the fire-light. In his uniform he was a fine figure, erect and soldierly. He spoke to the men, asking a few questions regarding their comfort, and went on toward the waggons.

There was silence while he was in earshot. Then one man quite close to Peter said, "Officers have the luck. He'll crawl in with that French broad and get him a good night's rest."

Another growled, "I'd laugh fit to kill if a battle caught up with us, and him out of his fine uniform."

"No fear. That man walks with luck hanging over him. I've seen him in many a battle, and he always comes out scatheless."

"Who's the woman?" someone asked. "I ain't seen her. He keeps her hid in that waggon."

"Don't know. Ain't seen her closely, but she looks a fine strong figger from a distance."

"She's a Frenchy. They say Frenchies is good at it. Got some rare funny name like Mitchel."

Peter moved a little. "Mitchel." Of course, Michèle, the girl who had run away with a soldier at New Bern, Angela's maid. He remembered her well, the scowling, dark-faced beauty with the wide passionate mouth. But how had she come to be Jeremiah Morse's woman? A camp-follower with the American army, now with the British? He could not fathom it. He must see the girl, to find out if this were true. He remembered something else. Was there any connection? When he was leaving Salisbury, he had drawn up by the roadside to allow some militia to march by. He saw a familiar face in the column and recognized the Frenchman Roi, whom he had seen at River Plantation. There was no mistake. It was the man who had rescued Madam Ferrier and Angela. He had not glanced in Peter's direction. His face was set in a tragic mask.

What did these things mean? Was some obscure pattern moving into place? A chill feeling ran over Peter, a fear that he was near some tremendous force that was sweeping them forward. To what purpose? He stirred a little so that the waggon was in his line of vision. Damn it to hell! He hadn't come into this camp at the risk of his life, just to keep check on Jeremiah's Morse's liaison with a camp-follower.

As Peter lay on the ground, his eyes fixed on the waggon, Sallee waited in front of Major Ferguson's tent as he wrote a letter to his commander:

My Lord:

A doubt does not remain with regard to the intelligence I sent your Lordship. They are since joined by Clarke and Sumter—of course are become an object of some consequence. Happily their leaders are obliged to feed their followers with such hopes, and flatter them with such accounts of our weakness and fear, that, if necessary, I should hope for success against them myself; but numbers compared, that must be but doubtful.

I am on my march towards you, by a road leading from Cherokee Ford, north of King's Mountain. Three or four hundred good soldiers, part dragoons, would finish the business. Something must be done soon. This is their last push in this quarter. I am, etc.,

Patrick Ferguson.

Sallee went inside the tent when Major Ferguson called for the scout. Major Ferguson sat holding the letter in his hand. His fine, pleasant countenance was solemn, as though he knew he was in a position so dangerous that he had little hope unless help came. He had allowed many of his Tory soldiers to go home on leave at the beginning of the march, not aware that the "backwater men," as he termed them, were closing in on him. His Intelligence had failed him more than once. What he hoped for was that Tarleton's dragoons would be sent to his aid. He looked at Sallee with piercing blue-grey eyes, the marksman's eyes that had won fame for him in the old days.

"I have been told by my officers that as a scout you are without peer, Sallee, and that you know this country like the palm of your hand."

Sallee bowed slightly. His blue eyes met Ferguson's steadily. "That is true."

Ferguson tapped the paper against the palm of his hand, still studying the scout. "I wish I could look into your mind and heart to see if you are as loyal as I would wish a man to be who holds my life and the lives of my men in his hands."

Sallee drew back a step and made a slight gesture of denial. "Don't give me the letter, sir, if you don't fully trust me. Send it by someone you do trust."

Ferguson spoke sadly. "Alas, I have no such scout. My Intelligence has broken down completely. I get no answer to dispatches I send out, no information of the enemy movement. I must send you."

"Send a second messenger, sir." Sallee spoke quickly, his face working a little. "I do not want to think that an army rests on me. I might not get through."

"It's a chance I must take." Ferguson handed him the letter. "It's curious that the fate of whole armies hangs on some small thing, some little fault in planning." His voice was very tired.

Sallee could have said, Already you have risked your army by remaining in camp for two days, instead of pushing on.

Ferguson rose. "I must get some sleep before we march again. Wait, scout. If you should be questioned by Lord Cornwallis or Lord Rawdon, tell him for God's sake to send Colonel Tarleton and his dragoons."

Sallee backed out of the tent. The letter burned his fingers. Never before, since the war began, had he felt sorrow that he must betray a hard-pressed man, a soldier of excellent quality and a fair enemy.

He rolled the paper and put it in his powder-horn. He made his way among the sleeping soldiers. He wondered what Captain Huntley's luck had been, but he could not pause to find out. He must ride post-haste to the Whig camp, but first he must take the road for Charlotte Town, in case Ferguson sent a man to cover his movements. Somehow he didn't think he would, but he must be cautious.

"The fate of an army rests on your loyalty." The words burned into his soul. "Judas Iscariot," he murmured aloud.

He passed the sleepy sentry. A horse was waiting. With a word to the young hostler, he mounted and rode off. The first red fingers of dawn were glowing in the eastern sky.

Peter fought sleep, but at last his tired eyelids closed and he fell into the deep slumber of complete exhaustion.

He did not wake until someone called and poked him in the ribs. "You sleep like the dead!" a voice exclaimed. He rolled over and sat up, rubbing his eyes. A second passed before he could remember where he was. He sprang to his feet. The soldier who had prodded his ribs with the toe of a heavy boot laughed, but his expression changed when he looked at Peter. "I thought you was Sawyer, but you ain't. You're a new man." Peter thought his small sharp eyes were suspicious.

"Got to camp late last night," Peter said. "Walked myself to sleep." He laughed shamefacedly.

The man's face cleared. "I thought you was a new one when I saw your musket."

Peter did not glance at his gun. "Took it off a dead Whig at Cane Creek," he said carelessly. "When do we eat?"

The soldier grinned. "We're all askin'. Cook disappeared. Say, can you cook?"

Peter hesitated. This might be a good opportunity. "Cook for my own self," he acknowledged. "Corn-bread and bacon."

The soldier lifted his voice. "Say, I've got a cook here."

A sergeant came to where they were standing. "Are you a cook?"

Peter cast a baleful glance at the soldier. "He got no call to say that, sir. I said I could cook for my own self."

"Well, you can cook for the rest of us. Get going! Over there is the mess tent."

"Don't know how to cook for all these." He waved his hand around vaguely. "Liken enough they won't want my kind of eatin'."

"Our cook's got lost, and there'll be hell to pay if we don't get something into their stummicks. They'll take what we give them," the sergeant growled. "You don't have to cook for more'n twenty. This is a staff mess, it is." His eyes fell on the rifle. "Say, what's this?"

Peter picked up his gun as though he feared for its safety. "It's mine. Honest, it's mine. I took it off a Whig over at Cane Springs."

"It's one of those long guns, ain't it? Say, after breakfast I want you to show me how it shoots." He winked at the soldier. "Can you load fast?"

"Faster than some."

"Want to bet four shillin' you can put four bullets in a target faster than me?"

"Wouldn't mind, but ain't got four shillin' in my poke." Peter knew it was a fix. He'd heard some of these men had the rifle Ferguson had invented, a wheel that would fire four balls, but he had not seen one close up.

The sergeant said, "All right. After you cook breakfast. Make tracks."

Peter walked over to the mess tent. He passed close to the waggon he'd been watching the night before. The flap was down and there was no sound from within. He felt better when he found the mess tent stood close to the waggon where he could watch it. Women from the other camp waggons were out and standing by their cooking-fires.

The breakfast was no ordeal. The second cook had everything at hand.

"Why don't *he* cook the meal?" Peter asked the sergeant. "I ain't no way walked a hundred miles to cook breakfast food for nobody. I come to fight."

The sergeant soothed him with promises, a tot of rum and some Indian tea, "same as the major himself uses." The second cook had tried, but he didn't please the officers.

Peter set about the task. He was thankful that during the year he had spent in the mountains and among the mountain men, he had learned to make a good pan-bread and fry bacon to a proper crisp brown. The sergeant stood by, satisfaction growing on his face, while the helper arranged the dishes. The major did himself well, with silver serving-dishes set in a fine leathern case marked with his crest.

Peter lolled against a tree, smoking a pipe made of a section of cob, well worn, burned to a golden brown. He saw the fly of the waggon open up, and a head covered with a mass of blue-black hair came to view. The girl called out and the waggoner came up.

"Is the fire ready?" she said in a strong, clear voice.

"All ready, ma'am. Want I should cook the breakfast?"

"No, thank you. That I will do myself. Has the captain returned?"

"No, ma'am. The major sent for him."

"I'll get out now." The waggoner brought wooden steps and set them against the tail-gate of the waggon.

The girl got down, with a generous display of trim ankle and leg. It was Michèle Roi, without a doubt. She said to the waggoner, "Did you find any chickens?"

The young fellow grinned. "Yes, ma'am. There's a farm girl here with some chickens. She came early this morning. Fine little broilers, ma'am."

"Good! You know how much the captain relishes a tender broiler, yes?"

Peter moved so he was not in vision. He didn't think the girl would recognize him, dressed as he was, his face covered with hair, but she was sharp and he must be wary. He sat quietly smoking, planning how he would get away without causing suspicion. He saw the sergeant's rifle lying on a bench. He walked over and picked it up. A damned ingenious weapon, with its revolving magazine. He'd like to try it. He was still looking at it when the mess sergeant returned, followed by the helper.

"So that's how you aim to win a wager," Peter said swiftly, to cover any chance of anger in the sergeant because of his handling of the rifle.

The sergeant grinned. His humour was excellent; the officers had complimented him highly on the breakfast. "I'll let you shoot it at target. Like enough the major will issue you one, if you keep on cooking good meals."

Peter put the rifle down. "Damned if I'm any man's bloody cook!" he retorted, scowling heavily.

"Now, now, feller, don't get so roiled!" The sergeant followed him as he stalked off. "It's good pay you'll get, and no gettin' out in front around the firin' if they give battle."

Peter spun around. "Who says I don't want to get out in front?

I'm a fightin' man and I don't want this cookin'." His voice fell. He saw two officers walking across the parade. One was Allison. The other was the doctor he had sent off on the wrong road. He didn't relish seeing either of them at close quarters. "I'm going to walk out. Maybe I'll be back in time for dinner-cookin'."

"I'll keep your long rifle," the sergeant said with a sly grin. "I'll keep good care of it, mister."

"See that you do," grumbled Peter. The sergeant flared up. Insubordinate, was he? But he calmed at once. He had heard mountain men were like that, touchy, and he needed a cook.

Peter sat down under a tree and watched some men dicing. They invited him in. He had a feeling to try his luck. He cast and won. In a little time he had ten of the King's shillings in his poke.

He got up then. "Like to play another round but I got cookin' to do." He sauntered away amid howls of protest. The men were hot to win back their money but he kept on walking. He turned the corner of a tent and all but ran into Captain Allison. Peter mumbled something and moved on, his face enveloped in smoke from his ill-smelling pipe. He thought that Allison watched him walk away. He was not afraid he would be recognized by his walk. He had adopted the woodsman's moccasin-footed gait for so long it was second nature to him.

"Who is that man?" he heard Allison ask.

"Don't rightly know, sir," a soldier replied. "I think he cooks for officers."

Peter had a struggle to keep walking at an even, unhurried gait, but he managed. Damn the fellow! He would have given something to cross swords with him that very instant. He grinned. He had neither gun nor pistol nor sword, only a hunter's long knife worn on a strap inside his hunting-shirt, under his armpit. It felt comforting to the pressure of his arm.

Not long after, an orderly came to ask the cook to step to Major Ferguson's tent. Peter cursed. "No time to take a man from his cookin'," he grumbled to the mess sergeant. He cautioned the helper, "Keep turnin' the spit, and don't let the drippin's burn in the pan. I aim to make a good rich gravy with that grease from the fowl." He washed his hands and took his time tidying himself. He eyed his rifle. It was in a crotch of a tree, but there was no chance to get it.

The sergeant was plainly excited. "What do they want of you now?" he complained. "Dinner will be spoiled and hell will be blocked up again."

Peter walked leisurely. No need to lose his wits. He would need them. He had no illusions. Even if he *were* only a liaison officer and not in combat, he would be termed a spy, and treated as such. He measured the distance between himself and Ferguson's tent and the sentry. He couldn't make it. He would have to wait. There might be a chance to get to the little cabin down the road, where he had left his horse with an old Negro.

He need not have worried. Major Ferguson was concerned not with a spy, but with his dinner. He asked Peter a few questions and was satisfied when Peter said he was a mountaineer, a hunter and trapper. He usually came down from the hills when the leaves turned, and spent some time in the settlements. A man got lonely, listening every night to wolf howls.

Major Ferguson nodded absently. "If you will cook . . ." Peter uttered a word of protest. "Yes, yes, I know, my mess sergeant said you have come to fight. I could order you to cook, but that's not my way. I want my men satisfied." He smiled a slow, rather sad smile. "At least, I make my endeavour, but it's an old adage that an army marches on its stomach."

Peter said nothing. He must keep in character.

"We've had beeves slaughtered, so there will be meat. You will cook for my staff only—Captain DePeyster, Captain Allison, Dr. Johnson, Lieutenant Fletcher and me. The duty will not be onerous."

" 'Tis not that, sir, but I'm no gentlemen's cook. I don't properly know how to feed them, or what wines goes with what. I've heard gentlemen is particular."

Major Ferguson laughed. "We've only one kind of wine. We've moved too fast to have variety. What do you say, woodsman?"

"I'll do my best, sir."

"Good! Now you may return to the mess tent. Wait! What's this?"

There was a stir outside, and harsh voices, one high and hysterical. "I've got to see the major. I tell you I've been prisoner of those barbarians. That's it, a prisoner. Tortured me, they did, the rebel buggers."

Major Ferguson called out, "Captain DePeyster, what is this racket?"

A young officer with a thin face and long nose put his head inside, saluted. "It is your cook, sir. Says he was captured by Whigs. He says he has a letter for you."

"Tell him to step in." Peter started to leave. "No! Stay where you are. It will do me no end of good to have two cooks under my eyes at one time."

The distressed cook came in. He was dishevelled, his clothes stained and torn. He was barefoot and his white feet were bleeding. He was too hysterical to observe rank. "They stole my shoes and my good breeks and shirt, and gave me this."

Major Ferguson looked him over. "Did I hear you say they tortured you?"

"Yes, sir. They did, sir. They made me walk—me, who hasn't ever walked since I joined the British army. They are barbarians, sir, pure barbarians. They don't even know that a cook always rides in a waggon, along with the utensils."

Ferguson's face reddened. The Scot in him, Peter thought, slow to anger, but——

"Get out!" he said sharply. "Take him away."

"But the letter. I've got the letter that the Whig general sent." The cook laid a soiled paper on the little folding-table in front of Major Ferguson.

The major looked at it with distaste. "Please read it, DePeyster." Peter noticed two other officers stepping inside headquarters tent. He dared not turn his head.

DePeyster took up the paper.

"Sir:
"We are returning to your camp one of your men. We could have kept him prisoner but we did not wish to deprive you of such an important personage. We trust that you will treat him well and return him to his butlership."

The letter was not signed. Ferguson observed that it was the work of some inferior and dismissed the fellow. "You may rest until supper," he said. The man left, still cursing the rebels.

Peter turned, hoping for permission to leave, but Ferguson did not give the word. Much to his distress he heard Dr. Johnson's low-spoken words, "Major Ferguson, I've seen this man before. He's the one that put us on the wrong road."

Peter knew he must act quickly. He glanced up at the doctor. A slow smile spread over his mouth. "Howdy, sir. Did you and your friend get your meal that day?"

Johnson said angrily, "You put us on the wrong road."

Peter looked pained. He turned to Ferguson. "Sir, I met this gent'man and another on the road. They be lookin' at their little map. They be lost, and they ask me to read it to them 'cause they didn't know rightly where they stood."

Ferguson glanced at the doctor. Peter moved closer. "I pointed it out for them, the spot on the map. If I remember he asked about a grist-mill. There be two grist-mills thereabouts. I showed him the near one. I didn't know whether they would find it or not, since they have so much trouble with that little map they had." He looked guilelessly at Ferguson—he hoped not too guilelessly.

Johnson said nothing. The major said, "I'm afraid you and Fletcher will have to study your maps more diligently. Don't you agree, Captain Allison?"

Peter quaked in his moccasins.

Allison's lazy voice came, "It's always well to know the terrain when one makes a sortie."

Ferguson dismissed the doctor. He turned to Allison. "I don't like these suspicions. I wish to God I didn't have to depend on untried men, Allison, and I like this fellow's cooking. Suppose you question him. You know this country."

Allison stepped forward and glanced at Peter. There was no sign of recognition in his eyes. He said, "How far is it from here to Pinnacle Peak?"

"Twenty mile, sir, excusin' two."

"And King's Mountain?"

"Close by, this way, six mile, maybe five." Peter kept to the mountaineers' way of not giving either definite mileage or a definite answer.

"If you were going to King's Mountain, what road would you take?"

"As crow flies or as man walks or as an army moves?"

Ferguson concealed a smile.

"As an army moves," Allison said.

"'Tis by the old Cherokee Ferry Road I'd go, sir. I'd then be between the Buffalo and King's Creek. Then along the old quarry road to King's Creek." Peter gave the correct route. Out of the corner of his eye he saw Major Ferguson was following on the map.

Allison turned to his commanding officer. "That's correct, sir."

Then he spoke a question sharply. "Do you know Sallee's farm?"

Peter opened his eyes wide. "Everyone knows Sallee lives on Mr. King's farm, close to the shadow of the mountain."

"Can we make it in one day?"

"Readily, sir, if you march sharp, starting at sun-up."

"Mountain! I don't like the idea," Ferguson said to Allison.

Peter volunteered, as though pleased to give information, " 'Tain't rightly a mountain, sir, more a hill, a little hill with a flat top, some six hundred yards, maybe, of bare top." He was thinking of the signal fire that had flared up one dark night.

Ferguson turned to his officers. "What do you think?"

DePeyster, who had taken no part in the talk, said, "It was an excellent breakfast."

Ferguson laughed. He had a pleasant laugh and his face lost some of its worry lines.

Allison was watching Peter. He knows, Peter thought. He is not fooled. Allison said, "Suppose you turn the fellow over to me. I'll put a watch on him so he does nothing but cook." There was a laugh in his eyes and in his voice that enraged Peter.

"Suppose he is a Whig. Suppose he puts poison in my food," said Ferguson lightly.

Peter stepped forward. "Pleasing your presence, sir, the major could have his captain taste all the food before you eat."

"*Touché!*" said Allison, his voice low.

"What's that?" Ferguson asked.

"Nothing, sir," Allison said.

"Am I a prisoner, sir?" Peter persisted. "I call it ill that a man who wants to stand to fight must stand to cook."

Ferguson picked up some papers. "Wait until the fight comes. You are under Captain Allison's orders for now."

"Come along, Sandy," Allison said. There was a laugh in his voice.

DePeyster raised his handsome brows. "So you know his name?"

"Not I. I call him Sandy for that fine heavy beard. I wonder what I'd find if I had it cut?"

"You'd find a Scot," answered Peter tartly. He was raging inside, but Allison had him hamstrung and hog-tied.

They went outside. Allison dropped his voice. "Make no mistake, Huntley: I'll put a watch on you who won't have any compunction about shooting."

"Who?" Peter said swiftly. "Who? Your woman in the waggon?"

No bright *"Touché"* followed. Peter knew he had flicked the fellow on the raw.

"Damn your evil tongue!" Allison muttered. He turned on his heel and walked away.

In a little while a soldier took up a station near the cooking-fire, a rifle over his knees. Peter paid him no mind. The chickens were browned to a turn. He himself removed them from the spit and arranged them on the major's silver dish. He placed the potatoes in a circle around, and made the fine rich gravy. If he had to cook he was going to make a damned good job of it.

"I'll carry it to the major myself," he told the mess sergeant.

He walked across the space between the mess and headquarters, the heavy-browed soldier with his rifle following close. He passed Allison walking toward the waggon. Peter paused. "I think, sir, from the smells that are arising from behind your waggon, you're going to have a mess of hog and cabbage for dinner, sir."

The sun was still high when the trumpet sounded the call. A sergeant-major's great voice boomed out the order: "Break camp!" In record time they were on the march. Peter took his place in the cook waggon, his guard immediately behind him. In front of them was the waggon that carried Michèle Roi. The waggons waited by the roadside as the troops swung into column. Peter estimated there were near to fifteen hundred. The quick movement portended that something had happened since he carried the dinner to the commander's tent. That something must mean the back-mountain men were drawing near.

CHAPTER
30

KING'S MOUNTAIN

THEY marched slowly, hampered by heavy clinging earth. The rain beat down, long streamers of rain that chilled them to the marrow.

Peter, snug in the waggon, watched the toiling men. Blanket packs, waterlogged, weighed heavily upon them. They tried to shelter muskets, wrapped them in bits of cloth or an old shirt or a length of hay from a stack, bound into place with vines. Powder-horns bulged out from under their coats, front or back, or in the seat of their breeks. They slogged along wearily. A piper blew a marching tune, until the rain stopped him and he cradled his pipes under his coat, leaving his body exposed to the cold wind. As they moved higher into the hills it grew colder and the rain increased, a deadly drizzle, more discouraging than a tempest or a sharp strong wind.

The monotony of grey rain beat against men's spirits, bogging them down.

Peter knew his own army marched even more wretchedly, more tiredly. The men who had travelled the long paths over the mountains, how were they faring? In a slow driving rain or a swift downpour, or was the road dry and hard for swift movement?

He had watched for a chance to break and run, but there was no chance. Beside him was the waggoner with a rifle at hand hanging in a boot. Behind him in the bed of the waggon were two guards, one sleeping, one on watch.

Allison was wary. He had asked Peter for his word not to attempt escape. Peter would not give it. Allison had said, "I have no intention of allowing you to escape. I did not discover you to the major because I intend to turn you over to Lord Cornwallis myself. I want the credit of capturing you. So I must put you under strong guard."

Peter had not replied, and Allison strode off and mounted his horse. More than once he rode up to see that the prisoner was still on the waggon seat. Peter did not speak. Inwardly he raged and planned, and planned and raged, to no avail.

When it came light, he recognized the country. In the distance, touched by the rising sun, the jagged outline of the Pinnacle was in view. Presently King's Mountain, with its long, flat top, came out of the black mass of shadow and stood above the forest of pines.

They would pass the mountain to the south, the column breaking, one part going by the Quarry Road. His eyes closed. There was no longer any hope of getting away under cover of darkness.

The waggon slid into a ditch and stuck firmly in the heavy earth. The waggoner lashed the mules with his whip, and cursed a mule-skinner's curse, but there was no releasing the clinging earth. The foot soldiers behind marched around them.

"Seems as though the very ground fixin' to hold us back," the waggoner muttered. He climbed down and went behind the waggon to see how far the back wheels were in the ditch. Another waggon tried to pass. It, too, struck the slime and skidded.

Waggoners shouted. Soldiers, covered with the spurt of slimy mud, growled and cursed. Chains rattled. Wheels creaked.

Peter found himself looking into the other waggon and into the great black eyes of Michèle Roi. The girl gazed at him. A puzzled frown crossed her white brow. The expression gave way to incredulity. "Captain Huntley!" she exclaimed.

Peter said, "Eh?" He must have managed to put her off, for she shook her head doubtfully. He said, "Lonesome, miss? There's room aplenty in this waggon."

Her eyes blazed and she dropped the curtain. He was sure that she was confused and uncertain. Not that it made much matter, but it did show one thing: Allison had told her nothing. He glanced over his shoulder to see if the guard had heard the girl's exclamation, but he was watching the men struggling to get the wheels out of the mud by laying poles across the rut.

The guard jumped over the seat and took the reins. If it had been dark Peter would have made a try then, but it was too light. After the first streaks of colour, the grey skies had closed in, and it began to rain again.

Instead of veering northeast for Charlotte Town, they were heading for the mountain. A halt was called in sight of the Sallee house. The cook, who had been riding in another vehicle, came to get his pots and pans. Peter got out. The guard shouted for him to stop.

"I'm going to make breakfast," he said, and followed the cook. His eyes were on the Sallee house, but there was no sign of occupancy. He said to the cook, "I'll look in the house. Mayhap I'll find provender."

The guard looked from one to the other. Satisfied that his prisoner had no intention of running off, he sat down on the porch.

Peter went through the house. A half-eaten meal showed that they had fled. He took a long hunting knife from over the fire-place and put it inside his shirt. A slight noise made him look up. He thought the trap-door moved a little. "Perry?" he said cautiously. "William? Virginia?" The door moved. Perry's face showed in a crack. Peter strode quickly until he stood directly underneath.

"My brother's gone."

Peter put his finger to his lips. "There's a guard outside. Tell your brother that I'm a prisoner. Do you know where he is?"

"He will come back. He told us to stay here. Virginia's gone."

The guard called, "What did you find?"

Peter motioned to Perry to close the door. "They've run away," Peter said; "left nothin' but a piece of cold bacon on a plate." He went outside and over to the cooking-fire and began to cut bacon.

"Look!" someone cried. "They're a-ridin' up the mountain. 'Fore God, are we goin' to camp there?"

Peter raised his head. A small column of red-coated horsemen was making its way up King's Mountain. He turned toward the road; messengers were galloping back and forth. At the fork, a platoon blocked the main road, turning the marching men toward the hills.

Before God, they *were* going to camp on King's Mountain!

The sergeant, whom he had not seen since they started on the march two days before, came up. He shouted to the waggoner to move on. "You're blocking the road!" He cursed the cook for building a breakfast fire before a halt was ordered.

The men about the fire grabbed bacon from the pans and gulped the scalding tea Peter had poured into their cups. The second cook tossed pots and pans into the waggon.

Peter said to his guard, "We'll walk now." The soldier hesitated but, being well disciplined, he accepted the command and they started for the hill.

The rain had stopped, and mist or a low cloud drifted across the top of the mountain. Peter thought the army could be wholly concealed, if the rain obliterated the marks of wheels and tracks. But for all it seemed a country barren of people, he knew better. He was sure that even now swift horsemen were riding toward the American army, wherever it was, loyal Whigs who risked their necks to go through lines and carry intelligence.

After a time they gained the mountain-top. It ran from south by west to north by east. At the turn, the waggons moved ahead, so that camp could be set up on high ground at the northeastern end of the little plateau, which was like the head of a racquet, as Sallee had said. Peter could not but admire the speed and military precision with which the British soldiers raised tents, arranged waggons and made camp.

The waggons were placed on the left of this northeastern end, and the headquarters tents were raised on the right. Together they covered the widest part of the summit, overlooking the floor of the valley.

DePeyster and his American volunteers camped close to the waggons. The regulars took up ground outside, spread around in a thin circle. Peter realized how few regulars Major Ferguson had—not more than seventy or eighty.

After breakfast he lay down on the ground. When one was on the go from four o'clock each morning, it was easy to drop into heavy sleep.

He was awakened by the assistant cook pulling at his foot. "God, prisoner, waken! Waken! The major's crying aloud for your cookin'."

Peter sat up. "What time is it, Cooky?"

"Ten o'clock, sir, an' 'e wants chicken for dinner."

"Have you got the chicken?" Peter asked. He went to a bucket to dash water on his face. He could have slept until nightfall.

"The major he's in a proper stew," the man replied. "Five men have come in and told him sumpin he don't like."

Peter appeared indifferent. "Where's the chicken?" he asked.

"The girl that brings chickens is over there by the tree."

Peter walked through the bushes toward the tree some yards away. His guard, now that Peter was at the cooking, didn't bother to follow him; he sat against a tree, his eyes shut, his mouth open, his rifle at his side. Peter thought, If it were only night, I would make a break for it and get down the mountain.

He came out from the bushes and saw a woman on horseback, with a sack of chickens strung over the cantle of her saddle. He put his hand to his mouth to conceal his surprise. Virginia Sallee sat on her roan horse looking down at him.

He made some remark and went up closer to examine the chickens. She bent over to open the sack. She spoke hurriedly, for the second cook was following. "My brother asks if you are tied up at night?"

"No. I sleep on the ground, near the cooking-fire."

"He will try tonight."

"No. Don't let him risk it. If he were caught and taken before the major, it would be the end."

"Near to two thousand men are on the march," she breathed, and held up a fine, fat hen for his inspection. A look of understanding passed between them.

"I'll take them," Peter said in a loud voice, "the lot. The mess-sergeant will give you your money, madam." His tone lowered. "Better get away from here. Twelve to fifteen hundred is my count, well armed."

The girl said, "Thank you kindly, sir," and turned her horse toward the commissary tent.

Peter felt better. At least he had sent out a modicum of intelligence, and Sallee knew where he was. He wished he might have lingered long enough to ask where their own troops were. As he sat on his haunches watching the chicken turn on the spit, he tried to visualize their march.

The Tory soldiers, under Captain DePeyster, lay on the ground. The men were dead beat. The waggoners did not look to their jaded horses until the sergeant-major made his rounds, driving them to watering and feeding. The foot soldiers lay without stirring.

After allowing a short rest, Ferguson posted the men: the drilled Loyalists at the crest of the mountain, a line that extended almost all the way around it: DePeyster's New York regiment, the New Jersey volunteers and the Queen's Rangers. The untrained men were broken up into groups and distributed among the trained.

After Ferguson had placed his men, he called his officers. His eyes were dark-circled, as though he had not slept for days, and his voice was tired. "Set your sentries down the mountain, some at the road-way, others scattered through the forest on an uneven line, until the whole hill is covered. You can exclude the rocky wall if you see fit. I doubt if it can be scaled. Let the men be well fed and get a day's rest." He hesitated, drumming the little camp-table with his fingers. "They will need all the strength they have."

Allison lifted his eyes from the ground. He had been watching a beetle which was lying on its back try to regain its feet. "We will wait and give battle here?" he said quickly.

"That is my thought." Ferguson spoke slowly, looking at each officer in turn.

DePeyster was quick with his reply. "It is impregnable, sir. Impregnable."

Ferguson looked around at the faces of the others. "Fletcher, what do you say? Johnson?"

Each one answered, "I agree." Allison alone did not speak.

Ferguson waited. Finally he said, "Captain Allison, do you consider this good ground?"

Allison weighed his words carefully. "If we were fighting troops of our own kind, I would agree heartily. With backwater men, I'd not be so sure."

"Why? Captain Allison, why?"

"Because they don't know civilized plans of warfare, Major, and so they don't follow them. They fight like savages." A slow smile came over his well-formed lips. "They know no rules; therefore they observe no rules. They would not know this is an impregnable position; therefore they are quite likely to storm it, and take it—that is, sir, if our enemy are the back-countrymen."

Ferguson took up a paper from the table. "My Intelligence brought this report of the enemy force since we came on the mountain: Colonel Campbell from Holston and Watauga, Colonel Sevier, Colonel McDowell, Colonel Winston, Colonel Hambright, Colonel Lacey, Colonel Williams, Colonel Cleveland and Colonel Shelby, each with his own selected fighters—near two thousand in all."

Allison exclaimed, "My God, there can't be nine colonels! One major against nine colonels! It becomes ridiculous, sir."

A faint smile came to Ferguson's lips. "I'm afraid it won't end ridiculously, Captain."

"Holston and Watauga men, Scotch Presbyterians, as puritanical as Oliver Cromwell himself. Merciful heavens!"

Ferguson glanced at the paper again. Suddenly he ceased to be morose and became himself. "For good or evil, King's Mountain is the battle-ground. Captain DePeyster, I must impress on you to send out your best scouts. Let them fan out about the mountain, studying terrain and roads. Fletcher, place picket-guard in strategic spots."

"I have already done that, sir."

"Double the number. Let it be known that we are under battle orders. A sentry asleep means a sentry shot. Tell all men to keep a sharp outlook over every road and report anything strange at once. The rest of you officers study every possible ascent, by path or road or trace. Report to me in one hour's time. Captain Allison, I want you to remain for further orders."

The officers saluted and went about their duties. Ferguson got to his feet, paced the length of the tent and back. "We are in a grave position, Anthony," he said. He fingered the silver whistle, which he wore on a braided cord around his neck, and looped on his shoulder like an aiguillette. "You are the only one who saw it. But we have no alternative. Look at those men. They are exhausted. They have no fight in them, unless they have time to rest. We are bound to remain a day. If the rebels overtake us, we . . ." He did not complete the sentence.

"Have you had any return from your dispatches?"

"Not one word. I'm beginning to feel that none of the dispatch-riders was loyal. No word from General Cornwallis or Lord Rawdon or that devil Tarleton."

"He's the one I'd like to see riding along that Quarry Road," Allison observed.

"With four hundred dragoons. That is what I asked for."

Allison looked surprised. He had not known Ferguson had sent for help.

"Yes, I asked, I begged, for help. By God, it's the first time I ever cried for help! And no help comes." The man's face was tragic. "I can't think why Lord Cornwallis has not given me support. He knows the fighting quality of these backwater men."

Allison said, "Perhaps Tarleton will come today." He spoke hopefully, but he felt no hope, so his voice carried no conviction. After a little silence he added, "How many men do we have that we can depend on, sir?"

Ferguson laughed shortly. "A foolish question. You know as well as I that we have seventy trained British regulars." He took a turn about the tent, his chin sunk on his chest. "Seventy men—pitifully few, Allison, to act as a bulwark between me and the backwater men. Pitifully few." He shrugged his shoulders. "By God, I won't give ground! Let every man think that we will win. That is your task—to put courage into the white-livered Tories. You've plenty yourself, Allison. Give them something to whip them into battle spirit."

Allison was touched by his commander's plight. "I will, sir. I will. By God, we'll hold King's Mountain against the devil himself!"

Anthony Allison left headquarters and walked toward the spot where his men lay. The ground was wet. They were too exhausted to notice that, but too tired to sleep soundly.

He saw Peter Huntley sitting by the cooking-fire, watching a man place a roast hen on the major's silver platter. Taken by impulse, he stepped to the fire. "No need carrying on this farce, Huntley," he said. "Go over to the waggon with the other prisoners."

Peter glanced up, his grey eyes unreadable. "Thank you, sir, but I don't call a fine hen like that a farce. It's an achievement, a notable achievement, sir."

An odd look of admiration crossed Allison's face, "Why, in God's name, are you with the rebels, Huntley? We should be fighting this war side by side."

Peter's expression did not change. "A fine roast hen for the major. Good to have something in the stomach when there's a battle to be fought."

Allison swore and turned on his heel. Peter watched him walk away, his handsome, erect body stiff with anger.

Mayhap I was wrong to annoy him further, Peter said to himself. He knew there would be no softening in his heart until he had vanquished Allison, fairly, with swords.

The guard came over. "Captain says you are to go to the waggon with the other prisoners."

The waggons were circled. Inside the circle were six or seven prisoners, yeomen for the most part. One mountaineer sat on the ground, carving a face in a hickory nut. He glanced up but said nothing. Peter sat down on the ground, his back against a tree. Battle or no battle, he must have sleep.

He lay quiet in the circle of waggons not far from the ammunition train. He slept spasmodically. Near dawn he was awakened suddenly by the startled cry of a wild turkey, repeated twice. Then silence again. He knew it was Sallee's call—Sallee somewhere, waiting. He could not answer and he heard it no more. As the morning advanced, he began to think he had dreamed it. But he made his plan—the long knife, the guard and the guard's rifle. That was his plan.

The British commander had used skill and conventional military science in placing his men. His Provincial troops and few trained

Loyalists were a thin line along the crest, but they extended almost from one end of the mountain to the other, from headquarters tent at the broad, higher ground of the northeast end to the long pan-handle on the southwest (the lower end of the sloping table-top). They followed the southeastern side. The southwest side was more sparsely posted.

Ferguson knew he had no reserves, and he had given up hope that Cornwallis would send reinforcements.

The terrain, which might have been a strategic defence against reg-ular troops, was the opposite for the British against backwoodsmen. On the mountain-sides was a dense growth of pine trees and under-brush, which afforded protection for Indian fighters and mountain men. The camp lay to the northeast of the summit and would be exposed to rifle fire from every direction, once the enemy surmounted the crest. The situation was one that did not offer any chance of re-treat to better or safer ground.

The Patriots left their horses at the foot of the mountain and took their positions. Campbell was to the right at the narrow southern point, Shelby on the left. On the right of Campbell's troops came Sevier's and McDowell's along the southeast side. Lining the curve around the northeast end, from east to west, were Winston, Ham-bright and Cleveland. Lacey and Williams took the long northwest-ern slope, which put Williams on Shelby's left flank. It was a com-plete encirclement, with no loop-holes.

Ferguson had posted his sentries down the mountain slopes and surrounding the crest. All night his soldiers had waited, tense, resting on their arms. But nothing had happened to disturb the quiet. A mist had lain heavy and dank through the cold night, a night to chill a man to the marrow. It was little better in the morning. A slow steady drizzle created a grey fog which only the tops of the pine trees pierced.

The enemy appeared out of the mist suddenly. The British, re-laxed from the tension of the night before, were unprepared—at the beginning they could not discern the shape of men from tree-tops, for the attackers had put twigs of pine in their hats and caps.

The attack came as a surprise, a thunderbolt from the sky, no sen-try call, no warning until the sharp Beat to Arms and the thrilling sound of the commander's silver whistle. Major Ferguson did not know that one by one, the sentries on whom he relied had been picked

off, knifed and made eternally silent. One, as he leaned over a spring
to drink, fell with his face in the icy water, reddening the stream with
bright blood.

The Beat to Arms sounded out, repeated over and over with rising
tempo, as the enemy swarmed up over the crest, after the first volley
was fired by Campbell's men. The camp broke into cries and shouts.
The drums beat a mad tattoo. Officers shouted orders. Men dropped
cups and plates and grabbed for rifles.

Suddenly the air was split by Indian war-whoops. A great voice rose
from the trees on the mountain-side. "Shout like hell and fight like
the devil! Forward, brave boys. . . ." A volley cut off the voice.

Peter sprang to his feet and made for the opening. Three guards
leaped forward. Evidently acting on orders, they forced the prisoners
back to the waggons with the butts of their rifles, while two others
tied each prisoner to a waggon wheel, his hands behind him.

Peter turned and twisted. In spite of his great strength they had
him trussed like a fowl, standing firm against a great wheel. Each
time he pulled or turned, the leather thongs cut deeper into ankles
and wrists. A soldier ran in, carrying a bucket of water, and doused
it against his arms and legs.

"You devils!" shouted Peter. "You goddam devils!" The leather
would shrink and cut deeper.

Pandemonium was all about him. Shots and flashes from muskets.
Men screamed and cursed and tried to reach the rocks for safety, but
there was no safety. He heard DePeyster's voice, high and shrill:
"Here are the dam' yelling boys again!"

That mighty voice arose once more from beyond the waggons:
"My brave fellows, advance!" It was Campbell, an Argyl claymore
in his hand, leading his Virginians against the southern end of the
mountain.

Peter turned his head. There came McDowell and Sevier men up
the east side. He knew half of them.

Ferguson, mounted on his horse, dashed from one threatened point
to another, giving orders with shrill blasts on his silver whistle. He
ordered forward his regulars who were placed on the lower plateau.
The advance pushed Campbell's men halfway down the mountain-
side. But reinforcements came to the Americans—Colonel Williams
and his South Carolinians. Lacey and Shelby were now on the northeast crest. Peter did not see Allison anywhere. Men fell screaming.
Redcoats lay on the damp earth over bodies in woodsmen's brown.

Peter felt a movement—someone working on his bonds, cutting through the tough leather. He glanced down. It was the girl Michèle. The bonds gave and his feet were free. She hacked at his wrists. "Don't move! Don't move! I may cut you." She repeated the words over and over. At last his wrists too were loosened. The girl caught his arm. "Tell her. Tell Mam'selle, I take one of her men; I give her one in return. Go quick, quick."

Peter caught her shoulder and pressed it. The girl's face was working strangely—not in fear, some other deep emotion. She was very beautiful. "Tell her. Tell her mama."

Peter said, "Your father is with Sevier's men. I saw him."

She stood, white-faced, not moving. She was holding to a spoke of the wheel, her whole body trembling, her lips moving without sound. He left her there and ran out into the open. He saw Ferguson and Allison, both mounted. They were down at the end of the spur with the regulars. He ran on, stumbled over a fallen officer. He heard the whistle of a bullet as it went by his head and hit the rocks beyond. He fell to his knees, reached out to the body, which was lying crumpled against a tent. He took the officer's sword from his hand, glanced into his fast-glazing eyes.

Then he leaped to his feet and ran, crouching, toward the rock shelter on the low, narrow flat. Bullets were flying. The mountain was covered with flame and smoke and thunderous noise. Smoke rose above the trees. He could look over the crest from where he lay, but the foliage was thick and he could see little. He made out that the redcoats were still charging with fixed bayonets against Campbell's men who had retreated part way down the mountain.

Shelby's men were at the southwestern end. They too were retreating, but slowly. Shelby was calling to them over and over the same cry, "Reload rifles! Advance! Reload rifles! Advance!" They were almost at the bottom of the hill now. "Advance!" he cried. "Advance! Give them a hell of fire!"

When Campbell's men attempted to come over the crest, they were met by the British with fixed bayonets and were forced to retreat. They went down the hill, rallied and came up again. This time Shelby pressed the British from the rear, but the British turned on them and charged, and they too retreated again down the hill.

The right and left wings of the American Whigs came in after Shelby and Campbell were engaged in hot battle. Campbell's men had rallied and come up the mountain. Red-haired Campbell was fighting at their head, "his blue eyes glittering with lurid flame," as one of them said later. Hand-to-hand fighting began as Shelby's and Campbell's wings swung together and closed the lower end of the handle.

The other Americans were crawling over the crest. Peter dared not move lest he be caught. He did not see how the Americans could escape their own cross-fire. Words that Major Avery had spoken to him at Salisbury flashed across his mind: "The General says you are at no time to engage in combat." In his present position he did not see how he could escape from one side or the other. He crouched in the rocks, the sword in his hand. There was one man he would engage, Captain Anthony Allison. He had the feeling that the time was drawing very near.

The back-countrymen were moving slowly behind rock and tree, dodging, advancing and again giving ground, but gaining a little with each volley.

Every man for himself. Indian warfare—against the ranks of the British platoon, drawn up the old way used by armies from time immemorial. Fire, drop behind, load, advance, fire. Redcoats, even in the grey of the mountain mist and smoke, make excellent targets.

A sharpshooter in a tree was picking off British with sickening precision, until a branch was broken by a shot and exposed his hiding-place. A moment later he was dangling, head down, his long rifle and his coonskin cap falling to the ground.

Major Chronicle, who had taken the place of Colonel Graham when he had been called home by his wife's desperate illness, led the South Fork boys. His men, with Cleveland's and Hambright's, had the most difficult position, at the far northeastern end of the mountain.

Ferguson dashed across the length of the plateau. Already two horses had been shot from under him. He stood within a few yards of Peter, looking one way and another for a horse. Allison came into view. His sword was out. He had lost his cap. There was blood on his forehead. He saw Major Ferguson's plight, wheeled and leaped from his horse. He stripped off the white hunting-shirt he wore over his uniform, pressed it on Ferguson. "Every damn' rebel knows your uniform and your horse, sir." Over his bright coat, decorated with medals, Ferguson put on the buckskin jacket and mounted Anthony's horse.

Peter heard Ferguson's voice saying, "DePeyster is urging a white flag. But I swear to stand my ground today, live or die." He was off, riding to the northern end of the mountain, where the fighting was now heavy. Cleveland was there on the west side, with Winston coming up on the east. Ferguson commanded a grand rally. His men were fighting desperately, but making little impression on the encircling force of the Whigs. The mountain men everywhere were recovering their ground, pushing up the hill, closing the circle. Ferguson relied on his regular troops, skilled in bayonet-fighting; there lay his strength. But there were not enough of them. Even the rocks which he had thought impregnable were scaled, and the breastwork of waggons afforded little protection.

After ten minutes' fighting the wings came around; after half an hour of galling struggle the circle began to close in.

Major Ferguson, on Allison's horse, rode to the position of the Rangers, withdrew some men with bayonets to withstand a heavier force at the north end.

Captain DePeyster, with reinforcements, a full company, marched at double quick. When he got to the station he had only twenty men left, so deadly was the rifle fire.

Ferguson, his face white and despairing, rode from post to post, endeavouring to keep up the courage of his troops. He did everything a man of bravery could do, but his impregnable position proved of advantage to his enemy. His soldiers, now drawn into battle-line along the ridge on the bare summit, were easy marks for the mountain men safely protected behind the cover of trees.

Several charges, brilliantly executed, drove back Shelby's line. Wheeling, Ferguson led a charge against Cleveland, who had got into boggy ground and was the last to arrive at the line. Cleveland's great massive figure mounted on Roebuck, his grey horse, came into the fight bellowing and roaring. In his heart he was Cromwell, leading his Roundheads to battle. Colonel Sevier supported Shelby and Campbell and gained ground. The North Carolinians were fighting like demons.

Three strong charges were made before the steady pressure from every side began to squeeze the British soldiers into the upper end of the racquet-head near the waggon-trains. With the movement forward, Peter Huntley was able to get out of his confined position and follow Campbell's men, protected by a rock which jutted out some distance from the encampment. He was carefully, cautiously reconnoitring when he saw Allison on a heavy bay horse riding down on him. He leaped back and gained a foothold high enough to strike.

"Defend yourself!" he cried, giving his foe warning. Allison wheeled and struck at the same time.

The clash of metal vibrated in the heavy air. Peter's sword cut one of the leather bridle-reins and pinked the horse. It reared and plunged. With only one rein, Anthony guided the animal by knee and heel.

"Get off your horse and fight like a gentleman!" Peter shouted. "Off, I say!"

Anthony had no choice. The horse, frightened and wild-eyed, plunged, and he slid to the ground. Peter stood by, waiting for him to pick himself up. Anthony got to his feet, swaying. Peter waited until he steadied himself.

It was a quiet spot behind a great boulder on the lower flat that Shelby's men had held. It was protected from the shots of the battle. The ground was flat, the footing excellent, and there was no sun to reflect bright steel. Presently Anthony found himself, whipped his sword through the air, cried, "On guard!"

Thus they fought the long-delayed duel amid the sound of gunfire, the groans of the wounded, the shouts of battle-maddened men.

They were evenly matched. They stood at almost equal height, although Peter had a little the advantage. Steel upon steel, with precision and matchless rhythm they fought on, wordless and intent, fought quietly, deliberately. One fought to satisfy a grudge, the other fought for his life.

Peter exclaimed, "By Gad, sir, you can fight!" Anthony's blade had slipped perilously near his shoulder. He turned it at the last moment.

"A compliment I can well return," Anthony said politely. He was breathing hard. The dissipation of the past months was telling. Drinking aplenty and lying in bed with an avid woman do not make for strength.

Peter was hard, trained to muscular thinness. He breathed evenly, as he had learned in a year of living, climbing, walking, in the high thin air of mountains.

He saw the end was near. So did Anthony. Anthony's lips, which had held a half smile, stiffened and hardened; his eyes became more wary. He was no longer the easy, careless swordsman. He was fighting, fighting, but he hadn't the wind or the clear, quick eye. In the end Peter caught him without guard, ran the point of his sword along his opponent's limber wrist.

Anthony's sword dropped to the ground at Peter's feet, while he clasped his wrist with his free hand. He said sharply, "You have my sword. I am your prisoner by the rules of war."

Peter picked up the sword and handed it back. "No. We fought to settle a question that 'roubled me."

Anthony said glumly, "It is your victory, Huntley. But I'm damned if I relish taking favours from you, even if it keeps me out of prisoners' camp."

"Go, before the rifleman behind me picks you off."

Sallee, who had been hiding in the rocks for some time, came forward, his long rifle pointed at the British officer. "Want I should shoot?" he asked Peter.

"No. Let him go. I want no prisoners."

Anthony went quickly, moving along the chain of rocks until he came to his company.

Sallee said, "I've had him on a bead this long time." ·

"I saw someone from the tail of my eye," Peter said. After a moment he added, "It was an old quarrel."

"So I thought. You let him go to kill some good Whig."

"Not with a sword or pistol," Peter answered, starting for higher ground. "He won't use his wrist."

Sallee followed Peter. "Come this way. No need exposing yourself. You do no good, being a dead man."

They had come to ground where they had a clear view. The fight was in the last stage, the ground littered with dead and wounded. Peter caught up a rifle from the ground, and a dead man's powderhorn.

The fight was in the northeast about the waggons and headquarters tents. Peter crouched and ran, taking cover behind trees, following Sallee's tactics.

When they reached the higher ground they saw the great mass of men struggling hand to hand with rifle or bayonet, and horsemen slashing with heavy swords.

"Ferguson's killed! Ferguson's killed!" Peter heard the cry ring out with hysterical joy. "See, he's fallen from his horse! Over by the tents!"

Peter turned sick at the pit of his stomach. He closed his eyes to the bloody scene.

A few minutes later he saw DePeyster run forward waving a white flag. In his heart he despised the man.

"A truce! A truce! A truce!" Voices were loud, high above the roar and the screams. "A truce! A truce! A truce!"

The Whigs shouted, "Cease fire! For God's sake, cease fire!"

The confusion that followed was worse than the confusion of battle but for one thing: there was no gunfire except, now and then down the mountain-side, scattered shots from men who had not yet heard the triumphant cry.

"Cease fire! The British have surrendered!" Less than one hour had passed, and a great and far-reaching victory had been won.

The mists came down and brought chill that sank unto the very veins. Men went about in small details to care for the wounded. Peter carried water, lifted the dying and closed the eyes of the dead. Far down the mountain-side and in the little ravines, they lay. When he struggled back up the hill, cooking-fires had been lighted. Victorious soldiers lay prostrate, the living close by the still bodies of the dead.

Peter moved about quietly, bending low to listen to heart-beats, to feel pulses beating faintly. It was almost dusk when he came to a heap of bodies along the outer ridge, near the trees that rimmed the summit.

Once he found a breathing man lying under corpses. He worked feverishly to extricate him. Then he placed the bodies in a decent row to wait for the burial detail. So he came upon Michèle. She was lying with one arm thrown over the shoulder of an officer whose face was hidden in the earth. She had been shot in the back. Her face was unmarred, and curiously tranquil in death.

The hand that clasped the officer's arm was already stiff. Peter could not disengage it. He laid them carefully and tenderly on the earth. Before he turned over the officer's body and looked at the face, he knew it was Ferguson. He wore the white hunting-jacket Allison had given him to conceal his fine red coat and his medals of honour.

He knelt beside the body, working the earth from the face, which wore the calmness that death brings. He counted eight bullets that had gone into Ferguson's body. Someone had snatched the silver whistle with such force that the cord had burned a thin red ring about Ferguson's neck above his tunic collar.

By what destiny had this man died today, while others who fought beside him still lived? What strange and sinister fate had coupled him in dying with this girl? The answer to that was clear to Peter.

In her desperate, agonized search for her lover, Michèle had found death in a white jacket, and a jacket had tricked her as life had tricked her.

He covered the bodies with an officer's cloak and went away. An intense weariness had come over him, so intense that he could scarcely make his way to the fire. He would rest for a moment on the wet earth—just a moment. Then he would report to Colonel Campbell where the gallant Ferguson lay.

He woke with a start. Sallee was calling him by name. "Captain Huntley! Captain Huntley!" He got to his feet. He felt stiff and his muscles ached. He answered. Sallee came through the shadows, his long lean body silhouetted by the light of a camp-fire.

"What time is it?" Peter asked.

"Past midnight, Captain."

"I must see Colonel Campbell," Peter said. "I must tell him I found the body of Major Ferguson. It is over there, near that tree." They walked quickly to the spot. It was bare of bodies.

"It was here. I tell you they were right here—Ferguson and the girl Michèle."

"Burial detail has gone through. Buried most of the bodies."

"Where?"

Sallee shrugged. "No one knows who is in what grave."

"I must see the diggers. You can't have a defeated commander thrown into any grave, like carrion."

"Dead is dead," Sallee said grimly. "Colonel Campbell is calling for you. He wants you to ride to Salisbury to headquarters, with reports for General Davidson."

Peter was too weary to ask why he must ride to Salisbury. Why didn't Campbell send one of his own men? He couldn't get Ferguson and Michèle out of his mind. He did not know that they lay deep in the earth in an unmarked grave, the gallant soldier and the passionate girl ironically together.

"Did you see Captain Allison, Sallee?"

"Yes. I seed him. He was lookin' on the battle-field for that woman of his'n. But they marched him off with the other prisoners. There's aplenty of them, so they say, and they left some two hundred and fifty dead behind them. But they ain't regularly counted yet."

They gave him a sturdy horse and a dispatch-case. Campbell walked out of the tent with Peter. Cleveland lifted his huge bulk out of a groaning camp-chair and followed.

"Ride like hell, Huntley!" Cleveland said. "Ride as fast as Captain Jack did when he carried the Mecklenberg Resolves to Philadelphia." He waddled back into Major Ferguson's headquarters tent, where Shelby and Sevier, Winston and Hambright sat in council.

Williams had been mortally wounded on the field, and Major Chronicle and many a back-mountain man would ride no more in the lofty blue hills.

Peter mounted his horse. Colonel Campbell shook his hand and said quietly, with deep feeling, "God has given us victory today. I pray we shall prove worthy."

Peter and Sallee rode down the hill. A small crescent of the fading moon hung low over the western hills. It gave a luminous, unearthly light. It touched the floor of the battle-field gently, obliterating the redcoats and the russet, covering them all with its silver oblivion.

Peter rode slouched in the saddle, letting his body sway to the even gait of the mare. He was weary, with an ancient weariness from which there was no escape. It came to him that men had felt as he felt now down the ages from the very beginning of battles. This was an inevitable reaction.

He turned and looked back at the mountain. He remembered it alight with signal fires, the flames that kindled other and greater fires. He had experienced exultation then, and high hopes. Tonight, the culmination, brought no high peak. Instead he was weighed down by emptiness and futility.

They had told him he was riding tonight with victory riding beside him. He felt no exultation, for even in victory there were defeat and death.

Little flares dotted the mountain-top, shining bravely in the dark, the camp-fires of weary men. Tomorrow they would march at sunrise. Tomorrow night the mountain-top would be given over to the hungry cries of timber wolves.

Peter Huntley, once more in uniform, stood waiting for the commander of the Southern Army to finish writing a dispatch, which he had ordered Peter to carry to Governor Jefferson of Virginia.

General Gates had lost some flesh, but none of his pompous arrogance. He dictated slowly, pursing his lips, grunting, making much of the simple chore.

Hillsborough.
October 12, 1780.

Sir:

This instant I have received the great and glorious news contained in the enclosed letter of Brig. Gen. Davidson to Gen. Sumner, who directly dispatched it to me by express. The moment the supplies for the troops arrive from Taylor's Ferry, I shall proceed with the whole to the Yadkin. . . . I desire your Excellency will dispatch copies of all the letters I now send to the President of Congress.

Peter saluted, took the letter and put it carefully in his dispatch-case. He prepared to leave.

General Gates detained him. "Wait! Wait, Captain Huntley. I want you to read the letter of thanks I have just composed for the King's Mountain victory." He handed the paper to Peter, and sat back, his fingers tip to tip across his paunch.

Hillsborough
October 12, 1780.

To the Officers Commanding
in the late defeat of Maj. Ferguson:

Sirs:

I received, this morning early, the very agreeable account of your victory over Maj. Ferguson. It gave me, and every friend of Liberty, and the United States, infinite satisfaction.

I thank you, gentlemen, and the brave officers and soldiers under your command, for your and their glorious behavior in that action. The records of war will transmit your names and theirs to posterity, with the highest honor and applause. . . . I have this morning, by special messenger, transmitted intelligence to Congress.

I am now only anxious about the disposal of the prisoners, as they must be ready to use in exchange for our valuable citizens in the enemy's hands. Send them under proper guards to Fincastle Courthouse, Virginia. I will desire the Colonel of that County to have a strong palisade, eighteen feet high out of the ground, instantly set up, within which log huts may be built to cover them. The guard must be without, and the loop-holes eight feet from the ground. Provisions, etc., will be ordered for them.

Gates, Commanding
Southern Armies.

Peter finished reading.

Gates said, "Well? Well?"

Peter saw that he wanted praise. Words of praise for General Gates stuck in his throat, but he managed to keep the distaste from his voice as he murmured a commonplace. After that, the general dismissed him.

He walked out into the clean, crisp air, breathing deeply. He mounted his horse and rode down the main street of the town. It was crowded with visitors, for the Assembly was about to meet. He could visualize the excitement among these men, who had worn defeat like a banner, at last to have victory.

A sergeant was standing near the sentry stationed at the outpost of the town. He saluted when Peter stopped to show his paper. "God be thanked for the fine news you brought us, sir! The ignominy of Camden has been wiped out by our brave men."

Peter rode briskly on the Trading Path that led to Suffolk, Richmond and Governor Jefferson.

Then for Queen Anne's Town! As he rode swiftly through the deep forest, he wondered whether Anthony Allison would be one of the prisoners to languish behind Gates's eighteen-foot stockade.

CHAPTER

31

HUNTERS' MOON

THE news of the Battle of King's Mountain did not reach Queen Anne's Town until the middle of October. It came in a letter from Judge Iredell to his wife Hannah, written from New Bern. She read it aloud to Penelope Dawson, who was staying with her for a few days. Penelope had come down the river from Eden House to bring a load of corn to warehouse for the army.

"The action happened," Hannah read, "on the afternoon of the seventh, at a place called King's Mountain, in what county I do not know. The parties in pursuit of Ferguson all joined. One thousand horse were selected out of the whole to come upon him.

"They overtook him with about fourteen hundred men, five hundred of whom were British; engaged, defeated the whole band, killing one hundred fifty (among whom was Ferguson himself), took eight hundred prisoners and one hundred fifty wounded, and fifteen hundred stand of arms. Our loss is said to be only twenty killed (among whom was a very brave officer, Colonel Williams), the number of wounded uncertain.

"This intelligence comes from the very best authority. I thank God things again wear a reviving aspect. There is a spirit rising that cannot easily be quelled. So your fears may be quieted, as well as the hopes of any who had rather see redcoats than blue ones."

When Hannah had finished reading, Penelope rose quickly from her chair to look at the letter with her own eyes. "This is important, Hannah! Have you done anything about it?"

Hannah Iredell lifted her round, childlike eyes to Penelope. "Done anything about it? I don't understand. What could I do about it?"

Penelope repressed her impatience. "Listen, my dear. Jemmy has sent you news of a great battle, of extreme importance to us. This news must be made public. Come, get your bonnet and wrap and we will take it to Sam. He is in his office today, getting ready to go to Philadelphia."

Hannah protested feebly, but she could not stand up against the enterprising vigour of her cousin.

"Don't you see, dear? It must be posted on the board at the Courthouse."

Hannah, bonnetted and cloaked, sat down. "No," she said firmly, "I will not let the riffraff of the village read my Jemmy's letter."

"You dear little fool! No one will read your letter but Sam. He will have his clerk make a fair copy in large print on heavy paper. No one will see your Jemmy's letter, or his writing, just what he says about the battle. Now come."

They walked down a narrow lane that led to King Street. The wind was cold and penetrating, blowing strongly off the Sound. It caught Penelope's crimson cape and whipped it about her tall, graceful body. Her eyes were bright, her clear-cut features were alight from some inner fire.

"You are like a man, Penelope, taking such interest in battles and men's affairs, and you walk so fast."

Penelope slowed down. Dear Hannah, she is a homebody, with little interest beyond her children and her house and her Jemmy, Penelope thought. How can she be a Johnston and have so little interest in the world we live in? This horrible, heart-breaking world! She looked down on the lovely, delicate face. So fragile, so timid a person was Hannah. Penelope loved her fondly. Her impatience died in her and she suited her long free stride to Hannah's short one.

Samuel Johnston stopped in the middle of sorting his papers. He was leaving in a few days for Philadelphia as senator, to take the seat of Wylie Jones, who was coming home.

"What is it?" he asked, looking at Penelope's glowing face.

"We've won a battle," she replied, thrusting the letter into his hand.

Johnston displayed even more excitement than Penelope. He opened the door and shouted for his clerk. "Copy this, please. You know the size for the bulletin board. How long will it take you?"

"Give me fifteen minutes, sir."

"Good! Now start writing. Jack! Jack!" he shouted. "Where is that rascal Jack?"

A moment later his Negro body-servant ran into the room. "Yes, sar. Yes, sar."

"Jack, run down to Mr. Smith's store. Ask Mr. Smith please to be so good as to come directly to my office. Then call Mr. Allen and tell him the same. I will slip across to Mr. Barker's myself."

"Thank you, Hannah," he said, patting his sister's shoulder. "You did just right to come to me with this magnificent news. King's Mountain . . . Ferguson's corps destroyed . . . good, good for our back-country boys!"

Hannah opened her mouth to say that it wasn't her idea, but Penelope spoke first. "Back-country boys? What do you mean, Sam?"

"Hadn't you heard that our back-countrymen were gathering to defeat Ferguson?"

He hurried away, his great strong body moving with unusual swiftness. Hannah turned her wondering eyes to Penelope. "Well, I never saw Sam so excited."

Penelope scarcely heard Hannah's voice. She was thinking of Peter. Peter had been in the back-country these many months. There had been no news of him since Jemmy returned from Salisbury and said Peter had gone over the mountains. He hadn't written to her. The Ferriers had gone to New Bern, so she couldn't enquire if Angela had had a letter. She felt anxiety. What if he had engaged in battle? Her vivid imagination saw him fighting, wounded, lying on the ground . . . still in death.

"Pene, what is wrong? Are you going to faint? Sit here. I'll get some water." Hannah ran out of the office.

Penelope loosened her grasp on the back of the chair and drew herself erect. When Hannah came in with a cup of water, she was herself. "Thank you. It is nothing," she said.

"I never saw anyone turn so white, or look so terrible. You frightened me. You must call on the doctor."

"It is nothing," Penelope repeated. "Nothing but a passing pain— in my heart," she added below her breath.

A drummer stood on the Green and beat a sharp tattoo. A bugle sounded. Samuel Johnston stood on the Courthouse steps. The great flag with thirteen stars, which Joseph Hewes had presented to the village, had been placed in front of the doors, the staff held erect in a bronze base.

The drumming brought men from their offices in King Street, shops in Broad Street, and warehouses on the water-front. Men came running out of Horniblow's.

The doors of the houses on the Green opened and women poured out, shawls hastily thrown over shoulders. Children pattered down the street. Street after street, house after house was emptied of people, who hurried to find out what the news might be.

A bell began to ring, swiftly, joyously. Could the news really be good? Could a people, braced and conditioned by constant defeat, be on the verge of hearing joyful tidings?

Presently the Green was crowded. Even sailors left their ships, anchored in the stream. More than one man came wigless, his stocking-cap covering his pate. Some men carried rifles, others swords. Women came with their hair concealed under mob-caps, some in bright scarlet dresses, and some in sober blue, puce and grey. Children came half dressed. Still the crowd gathered from every corner, as the news fanned out. Red Lion patrons mingled with the gentry from Horniblow's, militiamen from the Rope Walk, and freed Negroes.

Johnston waited. A giant of a man, he stood firm and stately, as a figure cut in stone. Men looking at his strong, firm countenance, his penetrating eyes and powerful body, felt a thrill of pride in their leader. A proper senator we have to stand for us in the halls of Congress, was in many minds, while they waited for the roll of the drum to cease.

Then Johnston read the letter. His deep powerful voice carried to the crowd the story of the first victory for long months. The people were quiet until he had finished the last word. Then they went wild, shouting and yelling. They crowded to look at the proclamation which the clerk had posted on the board by the Courthouse door.

Horniblow came out and announced free ale in the court-yard at the back of the tavern. Heavy work shoes and jack-boots made their way swiftly to the bricked yard. Buckled shoes moved more sedately, as the women clustered in groups in the houses about the Green.

A fife-and-drum corps marched up and down the middle of the streets, followed by shouting crowds. Ships' bells jangled.

The stage-coach from Suffolk and northern points drove slowly down the crowded streets, the startled passengers looking out the windows.

Penelope and Hannah were standing in front of Madam Barker's, watching the jubilation of the crowd, when the coach came to a full stop. Penelope glanced up to see Peter Huntley looking at her from the high seat. He waved his hand and, with a word to the driver, climbed down to the street. He pushed his way through the crowd and came up to them.

"What is this?" he asked, holding Penelope's hand in both of his.

"It is the victory," she said. She hoped he did not know how her blood was racing, how fast her heart was beating.

"Victory? What victory?"

"The Battle of King's Mountain. Didn't you know?"

The light went out of Peter's eyes. "Yes, I know," he said abruptly. "I know."

He turned to Hannah, who was watching the crowd. "I hope you and all of your children and your husband keep excellent health."

Penelope did not understand why he spoke so abruptly, nor did she understand the look of weariness, almost despair, that came over his face.

Peter talked to the Whig leaders assembled in Samuel Johnston's office. He related the battle, the situation as it appeared.

"Cornwallis is withdrawing to Winnsboro, but only for a time. We believe he intends to send three columns north—one from Augusta, one from Camden, and one from Ninety-six. He has the soldiers, and more arriving by sea."

Johnston said, "We know that. For days, in New Bern, we thought the French fleet was arriving. When ships came off the coast, they were another British fleet on the way to Charles Town."

Outside the windows people were still milling about, not wanting to go home, although it was near to sunset. The Courthouse steps were never free of a group of men reading the bulletin. They wanted to see with their own eyes. Some eyes were bleary by now, but voices were loud and triumphant.

"Poor devils, let them have joy while they can. They've been devoid of it for a long time," Robert Smith observed.

Peter went on with his narrative. "Virginia is to send four thousand troops, so Colonel Morgan tells me—eighteen-months men. Governor Rutledge was in Hillsborough, he says. South Carolina is struggling to get an army in shape before spring. In Salisbury there are eight hundred men from Maryland and two companies of Continentals, and Colonel Washington has one hundred horse."

"That is encouraging," remarked Allen, lighting a pipe. "Perhaps we are awake at last."

Peter said, "I think so. A Virginian, Colonel Preston, said he and other gentlemen of Montgomery County have raised a thousand men. Two hundred and fifty are horse, the others are riflemen, nearly all equipped. They were to rendezvous at the Moravian town of Betha-bara on the fifteenth."

Johnston said, "I heard through Iredell that Colonel Clark marched one hundred riflemen through the back-country of South Carolina, and picked up seven hundred more on the way. Then he marched into Augusta and brought away a vast amount of stores that had been intended to equip Indians to fight against us. He didn't have strength to attack the city, but he did what damage he could."

Peter nodded. "Like Colonel Marion. He has three hundred men at White Marsh in Bladen County. Colonel Harrington has four hundred and fifty, and others coming in, at Cross Creek. I have this on best intelligence—official letters to General Gates and the Board of War."

Peter did not say that he himself had gathered the intelligence.

Robert Smith said, "New Bern is really benefiting by this war. The town is filled with all kinds of goods from Europe, particularly France. They are supplying all the Southern states, and even the state of New York. There is so much money there that everything is rocket-high." He sighed. "Our shelves are empty. We have no ships getting through the Inlet."

Peter had a few other items for these men living so far away from the present lines of communication. "The British elections are over," he told them. "The Ministry has carried all before it. Our friends are left out, Mr. Fox, Mr. Wilkes, Mr. Burke. So that means there is an end to peace talk."

Mr. Barker, who had said nothing, spoke now. "That is excellent. Excellent! We will cease talking negotiated peace and prepare to fin-ish the war with our own power and to our own advantage."

"Pray God we do!" said Johnston.

The men left the office. Johnston asked Peter to remain. He had many enquiries to make. Peter, knowing Johnston was in the confi-dence of the committee, gave him the information as he knew it.

Mr. Dana was to be appointed to the court of St. Petersburg. Colonel Laurens was to go to France on a special mission. The enemy had possession of some of the ports of Virginia. Four thousand troops under command of General Knyphausen had left New York for an un-known destination. And the last and best piece of news was that Gen-eral Gates would shortly be relieved, and General Nathanael Greene, the General's "Right Arm," would take over command of the Armies of the South.

"That is indeed good news!" Johnston exclaimed. "It means a spring campaign in strength."

As he was leaving, Peter said, "Do you remember the Boston merchant, Jeremiah Morse, who was in this vicinity last year?"

Johnston smiled. "Very well indeed. Did you discover that he was a spy of the first water?"

"Yes, I did, sir." He told Johnston of the cattle reserves. "It worked out well enough—for us. Now we have the cattle waiting when our armies are on the march. But about Morse—he turned out to be Captain Anthony Allison, aide to Major Ferguson."

Johnston raised his eyebrows. "So?"

"Yes, and a gallant officer at that. He was at King's Mountain, and taken prisoner."

"Splendid! Very splendid!"

Peter grinned ruefully. "I'm sorry to say he is no longer a prisoner. He escaped from the captive group when they camped at Bethabara, en route to Fincastle Courthouse—he and his boon companion, a Dr. Johnson—thank God, no relation to you, sir!"

"Were they overtaken?"

"No, sir. It is thought they made their way to Cornwallis' headquarters. It could have been done readily. He knew all the Tory houses on the escape route."

"Too bad."

"Yes. I wish I had the opportunity to go after him."

"But you haven't?"

"No, sir. I thought I would have a fortnight's leave. But four days is what I got. Major Avery has cut my leave. I am to go to Hillsborough. I am—" he hesitated, then said—"I am sure you will be informed as soon as you get to Philadelphia. I have been appointed liaison officer between General Greene and the General, to begin my duties in a week's time. I will ride between the General's headquarters and General Greene, who will be at Salisbury shortly."

"Splendid, Peter! Splendid! It is too bad that you will not see Miss Angela this trip."

Peter looked startled. "Why, I intend to ride to River Plantation tonight."

"The senator and all the family went to New Bern last sennight. I think they will be gone for another two weeks at least."

Peter's heart sank. With only two days remaining, there was no time to go to New Bern.

Sensing his companion's distress, Johnston laid his hand on Peter's shoulder. "The fortune of war, Peter. It is too bad. I know what it means to you, for I myself must leave my dear wife and my little family behind me when I start for Philadelphia tomorrow."

Peter said, "I am sorry I have not had the manners to congratulate you on being sent to Congress."

"Don't congratulate me. Commiserate with me. But we must accept our responsibility. Thank you, Peter Huntley. You have brought us much news. Now that our little village is alive to the dangers of war, we are hungry for news."

"I wish it all might have been as good as the battle on the mountain."

"A most important victory," Johnston said thoughtfully.

"An hour of fighting," Peter said. "How can it be so important?"

Johnston got up and moved restlessly about the room. "A battle is not the fighting alone, Peter. King's Mountain Battle began the moment you and your woodsman Sallee lighted the first signal fire. I again say, a most important, perhaps a crucial battle."

"Mr. Jefferson exclaimed, 'The joyful turning of the tide!' when I brought the dispatches from General Gates. And a man with him, whose name I didn't hear, said, 'The victory is like the rising at Concord in its effect on the spirit and, like the success at Bennington, you will find that it changes the aspect of the war.'"

Johnston was thoughtful. "Yes, I can see that."

Peter said, "It is difficult to keep in mind these wider aspects. I can only remember the long marches, the weariness of our men, and their men, their haggard faces . . . and the dead, the dying."

Johnston looked at him silently for a few moments. "Why don't you sail up-river tonight with Penelope? She has a houseful of young people, and Madam Blair, but I know she will be happy to put you up for the time you are here."

The gloom left Peter's face, "That would be delightful," he said. "If Madam Dawson will allow me, I would love to go."

A dusky steersman sat at the tiller-bar. Two others set the sails. It was easy sailing with the wind behind them, and the course direct across the Sound to the point where the Pearsons' land jutted into the water and the Chowan River flowed into the Sound.

It was a sparkling night, the air cold and dry. Peter Huntley and Penelope sat on the after-thwart, their faces turned to the moon, a great red globe rising over the Sound, its circle cut by spires of pine trees silhouetted against it. Penelope was wrapped in a plaid to keep off the wind. The hood of her crimson cape covered her red-brown hair, and her grey eyes were almost black in the shadow.

"You know, Peter, your year in the mountains has done something for you. You seem stronger and more assured."

"That is true. I have led a woodsman's life—" Peter grinned— "seeking out merchants from Boston. Yes, and that reminds me. I found the merchant from Boston on King's Mountain. Only his name was Captain Anthony Allison, of Ferguson's corps, and a very fine soldier he was in his red coat and gold-laced hat, very handsome, and an excellent swordsman."

"Ah! You met him at last."

"Yes. I met him."

"Now, Peter, pray tell me what happened. You are not to be so Scotch and non-committal."

"By chance, I pinked his sword-arm—wrist, I should say. Just by chance. It was touch and go for some time. I had the advantage too. The battle was all about us and he knew they were losing."

"So Captain Anthony Allison became your prisoner."

"No, by Gad, I would not take his sword!"

Penelope touched his hand. "You are a generous foe, Peter."

"I had respect for him as an officer, none for him as a spy. But when I come to analyse it, I was being something like that myself. A patriot or a spy—it depends on which side you fight."

"I know. It is all so horrible."

"Besides, I was his prisoner for a time, and he didn't treat me too badly."

"Peter! Tell me about it this instant."

Peter told her about cooking the chickens for Major Ferguson. Her laughter rang out over the quiet water. The boatmen turned to look at their mistress. They, too, smiled, showing their strong white teeth.

Little by little the story came out. Peter hesitated before he spoke of Michèle Roi and Anthony. It was sordid, yet part of war in its ugliness. He said as much.

Penelope's comment startled him. "She must have loved him very much."

Peter thought about that. "I suppose so," he said, but he did not sound convinced.

"Can't you see? From first to last the girl was seeking him. There were other men, yes, yet in her heart there was only one. Nothing she did was wrong, to her, because it was means to an end. She found him and died in the finding."

"And lies buried on King's Mountain, in the grave with Major Patrick Ferguson."

"A strange fate."

"There is something else that goes with this story. Whether it fits in or not, I don't know. I saw her father Gil Roi—Gilroy, the soldiers called him—when I came down the mountain. He was sitting by the roadside, staring into vacancy. The men in his company said he had acted thus ever since the battle. He'd keep repeating that he had found his daughter, and then he would repeat something like 'It is the end.'"

"What do you make of it, Peter?"

"I don't know. One thing is plain, she was killed after the cease-fire order, and Sallee found out from one of the burial squad that she was shot in the back as she bent over Ferguson's body. You could tell her position by the course of the bullet. Her hand was grasping the officer's arm, and they could not loosen it. So they put them in the same grave. What matter? They were not enemies."

Penelope did not speak for a long time. Then she said, "Her beauty marked her for tragedy, poor lost girl."

"Allison was made a prisoner, but I heard that he escaped when they camped at one of the Moravian towns. He and one other got away."

"Are you sorry for that, Peter?"

"No. I don't think I am. Strange, but I have no further animosity toward him—not since we fought it out with swords."

Penelope shifted her position a little. The moon was up above the tree line now, and the red fire was paling.

"No animosity even if you knew that when he was here, Angela helped him hide and get away?"

"Why do you ask?"

"Perhaps I should not have mentioned this. But we are friends, Peter. I think you should know. Angela told me herself. She was quite hysterical—frightened, very frightened."

Still Peter did not speak. He wondered how Angela had happened to tell Penelope.

"Don't take it so hard, Peter."

"I'm not. I was just thinking. The man has such damnable fascination. Perhaps it is because he holds women so lightly."

"Perhaps, but I don't think so. He has no fascination for me; a fascination only for girls without experience, a surface fascination which will quickly die."

"I don't know. Perhaps he will remain a martyred hero. Anyway, all this was more than a year ago, the night on the Green, when his sword pinked my shoulder."

The wind lessened. The boat made little headway. He was conscious of her shoulder touching his, of her nearness. The irritation he had felt died out.

"Are you one of those men who think women should tell everything, every experience, every infatuation, to the men they marry?" Penelope asked.

"Good Lord, no! No more than I would be expected to tell my own experiences."

"Then you must forget Anthony Allison and let Angela forget him. She will probably tell you her reasons for never mentioning it, whatever they are, when you see her."

"I shall not be seeing Angela this trip." Penelope turned to look at him. "I haven't time to go to New Bern. I am on my way back to Salisbury, then to Philadelphia.

"Ah, I didn't know."

"From now on, I'll be in Philadelphia quite often. I learned a few days ago that De' Medici will be my opposite. You understand, we carry the same message, but travel by different routes as a measure of safety. This pleases me very much, although I will see him only at the end of each journey."

"You are doing wonderful things, Peter. I am proud of you, so very proud that I think I will kiss you on your brow."

Peter put his arm about her under the plaid and drew her closer to him. "Not on the brow, my dear," he murmured. "Lips are for kissing."

He had not meant it to be like that. On the long marches he had thought often of the two women. He had not drawn comparisons. He had tried to see clearly, but he could not. The confusion of war and the confusion of his own life mingled and became one. But something stronger than his will came over him. He kissed strongly, out of desperate need.

She drew away slowly, her hands against his body, to keep him from crushing her. "Peter! Peter, my dear, we must not!"

He said thickly, "Your lips are so sweet, so sweet." His face was close to hers. "Penelope, must you deny me?" His voice was rough, oppressive. He felt her body move in his arms."

"Peter," she whispered. Her tone carried a warning. He allowed her to slip from his arms and move away, but not far.

He was troubled, his body shaken. He had not known that any woman could so disturb him. The response of her lips had made him forget everything except her nearness, her soft, fragrant nearness. He sat silent, struggling for command of himself.

Penelope spoke first. "Peter, we must not. It is too dangerous."

He could not answer her, he was still too profoundly moved.

The man at the tiller shouted, and the sail swung.

"We will be at our landing in a few moments," she whispered.

The boat came along the dock. One of the slaves sprang ashore, wrapped the rope around a pile, and made it secure.

They walked up the steps, up the high bank to the garden. The moon was in its splendour, flooding the barren garden.

Peter held her arm close to his side. When she started for the house, he guided her down along the path to the edge of the garden, where it led into the deep woods. The little garden-house on the bank was in deep shadow. There was something inexorable in the night. The luminous light of the moon lay on her upturned face. The very silence held them.

He leaned against the closed door of the garden-house and drew her to him, his arm low on her back. He bent over her, seeking her lips. He felt their warm response. He felt her body trembling against his. The silence lay heavy about them, the rich, seeking silence that belongs eternally to lovers.

After a moment she drew herself from his arms. Only her voice betrayed her emotion. "Let us go into the house, Peter. My friends will be eager to see you and learn of the battle of King's Mountain from your lips."

Peter went away early next morning, riding a horse from Penelope's stables. She rode with him part way. The silence between them was the silence of understanding. They came to an opening in the forest. Beyond were fields and a glimpse of the river.

She reined her horse. "I must leave you here, Peter."

He dismounted and went to her side. "Walk with me a little longer, Penelope."

She hesitated. "It will only make parting harder. You must understand." She looked at him with her steady grey eyes. "You are young and your mind has turned to a home and a family. You are lost in the horrible maelstrom of war. You told me last night that you were terrified lest you be killed by some sniper's bullet before you had known marriage and had your first-born son laid in your arms. I understand. You seek security in this seething confusion and unrest."

"Perhaps," Peter answered, not knowing what she was thinking.

She turned to him, her eyes bright with tears. "I will never bear another child," she said. "When little Pene was born, they told me. I was very sad then. I do not weep now, only in my heart, for lost happiness."

"I have never known a woman of such understanding, Penelope. I told you last night my life was in your hands."

She put her hands on his shoulders. "We are not weak people, you and I, Peter. I could not live with myself if I stood in the way of your happiness. For we could not be happy. The time would come when you would regret, and I could not bear that."

After a little she went on: "Last night, after I left you, I could not sleep. I could think of only one thing. Tomorrow you would be gone. It seemed as though I reviewed my whole life, as does a person who is drowning. I was drowning in misery and despair."

"You are torturing yourself, dear. We are not saying farewell."

"Let us not dissemble, Peter. For us this is the end."

He made a gesture with his open hands. She slipped from the saddle into his arms. He held her for only a moment, then released her. All about them was the quiet of the forest. They walked slowly along a bright carpet of gold and crimson leaves. The pungent fragrance of pine followed their steps. The road ahead was a long tunnel canopied with the dark green of pine and juniper. It narrowed to a point in the distance.

He turned and faced her. He did not take her hands or touch her. "Need it be the end for us, Penelope?" he asked.

She did not turn her head to meet his questioning eyes. "It is the end," she repeated. "I faced that last night. You also are bound, Peter."

"I know." There was despair in his voice.

At the last she clung to him. "Carry me in your heart, Peter, your deep and secret heart." Her lips sought his, heavy with love and renunciation.

He held his clasped hands for her to mount, and stood for a moment with his face against her knee.

She bent over him, her cool fingers caressing his cheek. "You must go, my dear. When we meet again, when the war is over, we will find a way to be friends, dear and understanding friends. You have a life ahead of you. You must build toward your home and your family." Her voice was low. "We have felt deep emotion together, you and I, Peter. That can never die." She leaned over and touched his cheek with her lips. "Go with God, dear friend!"

"Go with God, my sweet Penelope!"

Penelope watched him ride down the forest path, dappled with sunlight, farther and farther, until he was a part of the deep shadow. She had sent him away, knowing the cost. Now she waited motionless, hoping he would look back. But he did not turn his head.

Peter rode swiftly down the road cut through the forest. The wind was cold, the swamp cypress limbs were bare of leaves. As he drew nearer to Hillsborough, the marching men, who had been present all along the way, grew in numbers. They were already weary, with feet wrapped in sacks, or barefoot, leaving blood behind them at each step. How could these men who marched so wearily give battle and win?

Penelope, proud, generous and wise! Her words were in his heart as he rode: "Love grows deeper with renunciation, Peter." He did not know. He could only accept her wisdom.

General Nathanael Greene rode south. With him were Light Horse Harry Lee and his dragoons to the number of three hundred. They arrived at Charlotte Town on the second of December. Cornwallis had withdrawn from the "Hornets' Nest," leaving a ravaged country behind him, a country so bare that Peter's first task was to carry a dispatch to the Board of War requesting them not to send more soldiers until food could be found.

The men were starving. Many were living without tents, without shoes, without suitable garments. Some wore pieces of ragged cloth, pinned together with thorns from the locust trees. "Thousands are so naked that they cannot be called for duty except under the direst necessity," General Greene wrote in a dispatch Peter carried.

For weeks he travelled, mile upon mile, dodging enemy camps, making detours, always in haste, haste, wearing out horse after horse, until his eyes became a blur of passing woods and tired marching men . . . always tired, tired and weary men, with sunken eyes and hopeless faces.

Weeks passed.

It was late December before Peter Huntley found opportunity to go to Queen Anne's Town. Arrangements for his marriage to Angela had been made when he met Senator and Madam Ferrier at Hillsborough, where the senator attended a meeting of the Assembly and Board of War men. The day was set for the ninth of January, at the end of the Christmas festivities.

For a time Peter did not think he could get a furlough, but at last things came his way, and General Greene gave him a fortnight. "But be back on the twelfth without fail, Captain Huntley," the general said, handing him his papers.

Greene's kindly face now wore a look of perpetual worry. His large frame was stooped more than it had been the first time Peter saw him. But he always gave the appearance of confidence. And his men believed in him, would believe in him even during the days of the great retreat.

The holiday season brought fair weather. The rains stopped. Frost crystals and thin ice covered the little creeks and brooks. Two days before Christmas Peter Huntley rode through the gates and trotted up the long drive of River Plantation.

The children, Bella and young Philip, ran to the upping-block to meet him, each trying to outdo the other in welcome. Shouting and laughing, they caught Peter's hand and dragged him up the brick walk to the portico, crying, "Angela! Angela! He's here! Peter's here!"

Philip said, "She's been sitting at her dressing-table for an hour. Twice she boxed Promisy's ears because her hair didn't suit. Promisy just laughed. 'He'll think you prettier than a lily, no matter how you' hair fix'.'"

"You shouldn't tell on Angela," Bella said indignantly. "Our mother says we shouldn't tell what people say."

"I'm not telling what Angela said, just what she did, goosey."

They ran away to continue their private argument, when Madam came out to greet their guest. "My dear! Did you have a tiresome journey? You look in excellent health."

"I am," Peter answered, kissing her hand. "The journey was long and tedious because I wanted to be here."

"You must rest." To a servant she said, "Take the captain to his room."

Peter said, "I'm not weary. I came in on the late coach and rested the night at Horniblow's."

They walked into the house. Peter exclaimed as he looked around. It smelled of fresh-cut pine and cedar. Garlands hung over windows and doors. Great sprays of shining green holly with bright red berries lay on mantels and over doors.

Philip and Bella followed them. They lured Peter under a great round ball of mistletoe that hung in the arch of the T-shaped hall. "Bella wants her forfeit. Bella wants a kiss." Peter bent down. The little girl threw her arms around his neck and kissed his cheek.

Madam watched them, smiling. "Now run up to Promisy, Bella, and don't kiss Peter any more."

Bella's dark eyes sparkled. "I know. Peter must save kisses for Angela." She darted out of the room.

"You must pardon their exuberance, Peter. 'Tis the holiday season. Lessons are over. Their tutor has gone home for a respite. They are running wild, quite wild. Come, let us go into the senator's study. He will be home soon. He rode over to Wingfield on some planta-tion business with Madam Brownrigg."

She took her accustomed chair beside the fire, pulled her tapestry-frame to her and began to work. "Angela will be down soon," she said, selecting a coloured yarn and threading a needle. She looked at Peter with her unfathomable eyes. "You will find Angela much changed. Her long illness, perhaps . . . A year can bring great changes."

Peter's throat constricted. Is she trying to tell me that Angela will not marry me? His face must have expressed his thought, for Fran-cisca smiled at him and said, "There is nothing to worry about, Peter. The plans are the same. The wedding is set for Twelfth-night."

Peter said, "That makes me very happy, Madam Ferrier. I live in such uncertainty that it seems as though there were no security left in the world—that is, until I see you and feel the great tranquillity of your presence."

"You are a dear boy, Peter. Come, let me kiss you for your very nice thoughts." Peter bent over her, and she kissed him on the fore-head.

"The senator saw Captain de' Medici at New Bern," she told Peter, as she matched her wools. "He said he would be here the day before the wedding."

"That is splendid news. I wrote him from Williamsburg, but I was not sure he would be able to come."

"He is a fine person, so joyous," Madam said. "We will all be better for seeing him."

"Now if only Adam Rutledge were here!"

Madam shook her head. "I'm afraid Adam is too far away, much too far to be here for the wedding. I have heard that he has gone as far as the Mississippi. That I do not know, except by rumour."

Angela came in then. She had on a scarlet coat with three little capes, and a small scarlet turband wound around her black hair. Her lips were scarlet and her eyes looked very black.

Peter jumped to his feet and watched her cross the room. She moved with grace, a fine, free movement of her long limbs and body. When he saw her walking toward him all the old doubts fled. He knew she was the right woman to be his wife, the right woman to be the mother of his children.

She extended her hand with a shy smile. "Welcome, Peter," she said.

Peter kissed her fingers. Francisca observed, "I think it would be fitting if you kissed her, Peter."

Angela coloured and raised her chin slightly. Peter embarrassed, touched his lips to her cheek.

Angela turned to her mother. "I promised the children I would go down to our great oak, to get that big ball of mistletoe and the yule-log. Will you come with us," she said to Peter, "or do you wish to rest or to chat with my mother?"

"I will come with you, if I may."

They walked through the woods. The frost of the night before had left bright crystal drops on the trees, which had turned to ice. The long grey moss was like crystal streamers, so delicate and fragile that the woods were an unbelievable fairyland. They walked among the sparkling trees, the children, in their gaiety, skipping ahead of them. Slaves with axes and a cart drawn by an ox followed.

Little Bella came running back now and then, to tell them she had seen a quail or a hare, and Philip thought he heard a wild turkey call, and perhaps a deer crash through the brush on its way to drink in the creek.

He drew a great breath. Angela turned. "You gave such a strange, long sigh, Peter. Are you sad?"

"No, no. On the contrary, I am extremely happy. If I sighed, it is because everything is so quiet and so beautiful, and because you are near me."

She turned her fine eyes to him. "I think I understand. It is the war."

"Yes, Angela, it is the war. It does strange things to men."

"Then do not think of it—not while you are here. Can you forget for a little time?"

"Will you help me forget, my dear?"

She put her hand on his arm lightly, a slight touch like the passing of a leaf blown by a small river breeze. "I will try, Peter."

It touched his heart to see her so gentle, looking at him so seriously. He wanted to see laughter in her eyes, see her red lips parted over her white teeth and hear her laugh as he had once heard it when she played with the children, carefree and happy. Laughter would heal the wounds made from looking on battle-fields and long straggling columns of weary men, bent under the loads they carried.

They came to the great oak. Peter stopped short. Never had he seen anything so beautiful—the great spreading crown of the tree, the long streamers of moss that touched the frosted earth, a mass of frost and crystal. The sun slanting through the trees turned it into thousands of little rainbows moving gently in the wind. He felt her intent gaze, but he did not look away from the tree.

"Peter Huntley, I'm sure I am going to like you." Angela's voice had a lilt in it and her eyes sparkled. "The tree—I can see it in your face—you love it too."

"I never saw a more beautiful sight," he said.

The children came running to them. They had stuck sprigs of holly in their caps. "Did he like it?" they cried. "Did he like it, Gela?"

Philip explained: "Angela said if you liked our tree, she would certainly like you."

Angela, horrified, cried, "Philip!"

Peter said gravely, "I'm glad I stood the test."

The cart came up and the hunt for the yule-log began. Running through the aisles of trees in the forest, the children called, "Here's one! No, it has a gnarled place; it won't do. Well, here, isn't this one perfect?"

Finally a tree was selected and the chopping began. The slaves' axes rang against the wood and presently the tree crashed to the ground. It had still to be cut into logs. Philip had a bit of string in his pocket and measured the length for the fire-place.

Peter and Angela wandered off down a narrow path toward the creek. They came to a boundary tree. Peter stepped across a little ditch that marked an old field. He held out his hand, but she followed lightly and they walked on down to where the creek flowed into the river.

Peter recognized the spot. He knew that he stood on his land. It was a good feeling. It seemed to him that the earth gave back to him something that he had lost. He took Angela's hand. She didn't draw back. He told her that he had bought the land, the place would be their home, close to her family, yet something that was their own. She listened silently. When he looked at her, bright tears were in her eyes.

"You did this for me," she whispered. "You thought of this months ago? . . ."

"I've thought of you for a long time, my dear, always with love." He put his hand into his pocket and drew out the crimson scarf. "I have worn it there, over my heart, since that first day. I think it has brought me good fortune." He tied it around her neck. Angela lifted the end of the scarf. The blood-stain showed brown and ugly against the pure colour. She turned enquiring eyes on Peter.

"Is it blood?" she asked.

Peter reddened. "Yes, it is blood. I'm sorry. I forgot it was there."

For a few minutes she remained silent. She began to untie the scarf.

Peter put his hand over hers. "Do not shrink from blood," he said. "Please wear the scarf. I like to see it about your throat. It makes your eyes so warm, dark and unfathomable."

"Whose blood is it?" she asked him, still busy with the knot. "How did it come to be there in the silk?"

Peter could not say, "Anthony Allison's sword drew blood, one night on the Courthouse Green," nor could he escape an explanation. He said, "My blood, Angela. The scarf, folded against my heart, saved my life."

She made a small exclamation, and her hands dropped to her side. "Saved your life? The scarf saved your life?"

"Yes," he smiled down at her. "You see why I am really devoted to it."

For some time she looked back at him, her face very grave, her eyes brooding, unreadable.

"Peter——" she began.

"Yes, Angela?"

"Peter, there is something I want to tell you. I must confess something."

"My dear, don't say the word confess. I don't want you to tell me anything that is painful to you." He must keep her from revealing herself or talking of Anthony. He didn't want her to have to bear the humiliation of confessing.

"But I must," she said impatiently, with her old quick emphasis. "I will tell you. I must. You have said you loved me the moment you saw me that day on the Green. But I saw you before that and I was angry at what I saw."

"I don't understand."

She did not heed his interruption. "The dragoons were riding down the River Road, on your way to Queen Anne's Town. I went with the children to see them pass. I saw you then."

Peter tried to remember, but could not.

"You were talking to a poor daft girl, getting milk. You kissed her." Her face became as crimson as the bit of silk about her neck. "Then you . . ."

"Then I what?"

"You put your hand down the girl's bodice. I hated you, an officer, a gentleman, for taking advantage of the poor daft creature. I was so angry that for a moment the thought came to me to ride you down, let my horse trample you. A child, with no wits . . . to make love to her!"

Peter's eyes did not leave her face. His expression was one of wonder. Then as the incident returned to him, he took her hand.

"My dear, it was not as you think. The girl would not take pay, so I tried to press a coin into her hand. She caught my hand and the coin slipped down her bodice. Surely you cannot think that I would——" He paused, distressed.

"And when I saw you in the village, and your eyes admired me, I was angered the more. You were the kind of man that turned to any woman."

"So that is what you were thinking!"

She interrupted: "Soldiers are different. At times I thought you were like some of the others, that you made no distinction in class or degree."

Peter did not speak. Spurred by his silence, Angela went on. "I should have known differently, but there on the Green I could not control my anger and hurt. You see, that scarf was one that Anthony had bought for me, at Madeira, when the boatmen came to the ship with merchandise. And you came and trampled it into the ground."

He took her hand. "Now that I understand, I am more sorry than ever."

"Oh, Peter, forgive me for the wrong I have done you in my thoughts."

He put his arms about her. "Never the word forgive between us, Angela."

"It was my pride," she whispered, her face against him, "my horrible, fearful pride. I thought, He woos a daft girl one day, and the next he turns his eyes to me."

"Kiss me, Angela."

She lifted her face. After a moment she said, "Cosmo told me I loved you, because I hated you so. He said hatred was close to love, but I didn't believe him, then. My mind was too full of——"

He put his lips to hers. He did not want to hear the name of Anthony Allison again.

Slowly he kissed her, no passing momentary kiss, but long and deep with love. Her lips were warm and soft, and parted to his desire.

When he released her, her body was trembling, but she looked at him with a little smile. "The mistletoe!" she said. Over their heads hung a ball of green, covered with waxen white berries. "Our own mistletoe, on our own land!" she whispered. "Oh, Peter!"

He broke a little sprig. "In our country mistletoe has always been the emblem of worship," he said, as he tucked it into the folds of her scarlet turband.

"Come! The children are calling. It is time to drag in the yule-log."

They walked up the path. When they came to the little ditch that divided the fields, he held her close for a moment. "A tribute!" he said, as he kissed her. "A boon, before you leave your own soil to set foot on the land of another!"

She broke suddenly into gay, spontaneous laughter.

THE END

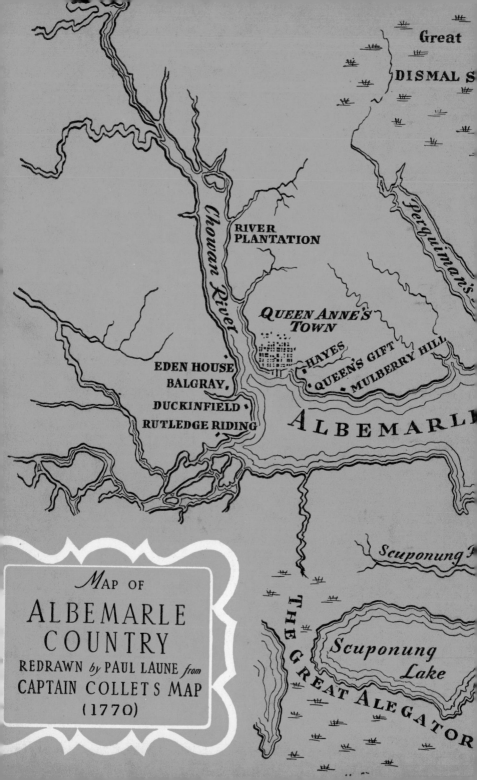